"A masterpiece—a new American classic of th
first lines to the catch-your-breath desperat
tale's grimmest moments, Tananarive Due insists on
power of simple kindness. You have to read this book."
—**JOE HILL**, **#1 *New York Times* bestselling author of *The Fireman***

"One of the best novels published in 2023. A superb mix of literary fiction, horror, and historical fiction."
—**GABINO IGLESIAS**, ***NPR Books***

"*Moby-Dick* might have flipped America on its back to show the rotting underbelly, but *The Reformatory*'s looking just as closely at our bad history, and somehow finding the heart beating underneath it all. This is the novel I've been waiting for. It breaks your heart, but it also holds it together."
—**STEPHEN GRAHAM JONES**, **bestselling author of *The Only Good Indians* and *My Heart Is a Chainsaw***

★"The writing here is spectacular; the pacing, engrossing; the setting, heartbreaking but honest; and the characters are given a nuance and depth rarely seen. . . . A masterpiece of fiction."
—***LIBRARY JOURNAL***, **starred review**

★"With fully realized characters and well-placed twists, Due ratchets up the tension until the final, extraordinary showdown."
—***BOOKLIST***, **starred review**

★"A vividly realized page-turner that is at once an ingenious ghost story, a white-knuckle adventure, and an illuminating if infuriating look back at a shameful period in American jurisprudence."
—***KIRKUS REVIEWS***, **starred review**

★"This masterful work of historical horror . . . is sure to stick in readers' minds."
—***PUBLISHERS WEEKLY***, **starred review**

"ONE OF THOSE BOOKS YOU CAN'T PUT DOWN." —STEPHEN KING

PRAISE FOR

THE REFORMATORY

"*Moby-Dick* might have flipped America on its back to show the rotting underbelly, but *The Reformatory*'s looking just as closely at our bad history, and somehow finding the heart beating underneath it all. This is the novel I've been waiting for. It breaks your heart, but it also holds it together."

—Stephen Graham Jones, bestselling author of *The Only Good Indians* and *My Heart Is a Chainsaw*

"Beautiful and expertly executed, *The Reformatory* is a horror masterpiece that derives its power from both the magical and the mundane."

—*Bookpage* (starred review)

"Her fiction is always powerful, and *The Reformatory* promises to be her most moving—and horrifying—tale yet."

—*Vulture*

"One of the greatest living horror writers. . . . Sure to be as powerful as it is haunting."

—*CrimeReads*

"Due knocks it out of the park every damn time."

—*Book Riot*

"A riveting masterpiece that manages to be both heartwarming and chilling. . . . Literally impossible to stop reading."

—*Locus Magazine*

THE REFORMATORY

A NOVEL

TANANARIVE DUE

LONDON AMSTERDAM/ANTWERP NEW YORK SYDNEY TORONTO NEW DELHI

1230 AVENUE OF THE AMERICAS, NEW YORK, NEW YORK 10020

First Saga Press trade paperback edition January 2025

SAGA PRESS and colophon are registered trademarks of Simon & Schuster, LLC

For information about special discounts for bulk purchases, please contact Simon & Schuster Special Sales at 1-866-506-1949 or business@simonandschuster.com.

The Simon & Schuster Speakers Bureau can bring authors to your live event. For more information or to book an event, contact the Simon & Schuster Speakers Bureau at 1-866-248-3049 or visit our website at www.simonspeakers.com.

Interior design and frontispiece photograph by Esther Paradelo

Manufactured in the United States of America

1 3 5 7 9 10 8 6 4 2

Library of Congress Cataloging-in-Publication Data is available.

ISBN 978-1-9821-8834-4
ISBN 978-1-9821-8835-1 (pbk)
ISBN 978-1-9821-8836-8 (ebook)

For Robert Stephens
My great-uncle who died
at the Dozier School for Boys
in Marianna, Florida, in 1937
He was fifteen years old.

Patricia Gloria Stephens Due
1939–2012
I miss you, Mom.

John Dorsey Due, Jr.
Freedom Lawyer
Thank you for collaborating with me, Dad.

I

McCORMACK ROAD

1

June 1950
Gracetown, Florida

Robert Stephens held his breath and counted to three, hoping to see Mama.

Some mornings his nose tickled with a trace of talcum powder or Madam C. J. Walker's Glossine hair grease, and he felt . . . *something* hovering over him, watching him sleep. His groggy brain would think . . . *Mama?* If he gasped or sat up too quickly, or even wiped the sleep from his eyes, it was gone like a dream. But sometimes, when the June daylight charged early through the thin curtain and broke the darkness, movement glided across the red glow of his closed eyelids like someone walking past his bed. He felt no gentle kisses or fingertips brushing his forehead. No whispers of assurances and motherly love. Nothing like what people said ghosts were supposed to be, much less your dead mama. That morning he was patient, counting the way he'd practiced—*one one thousand, two one thousand, three one thousand*—and slitted his eyes open.

A woman's shadow passed outside of the window above him, features appearing in the gaps between the sheets of tinfoil taped across the glass. In a white dress, maybe. *Maybe.* Moving fast, in a hurry.

"Mama?"

The shadow didn't stop, or turn around, or step inside the room through the wall to show her face. His hope that she would say something to him died before it was fully awake. That's how fast she was gone. Always.

Robert jumped from his mattress to peek through a gap in the foil, but of course she wasn't there. Nothing was visible except the old chicken coop, long empty. And it was an ordinary day again, with Mama in heaven and Papa in Chicago—starting out wrong already. Robert had given up trying to convince his older sister, Gloria, that Mama was visiting him, unless she was just jealous that he still had a piece of her that she didn't. But it was such a small piece, not even enough to touch or hold.

Since Robert and Gloria lived downwind of the McCormacks' turpentine camp, the sweet scent of cooking breakfast ham filled the cabin like a shout. Robert's violent hunger overpowered any happiness he'd won from the quick-moving shadow that could have been Mama's ghost, but probably wasn't. That day started the same as the rest: the vaguest shadow and the smell of meat. Robert's empty heart whimpered and his empty stomach roared.

Later on, when the bad thing would happen and the judge would ask him, "Why'd you do a fool thing like that?"—and in the days to come he would cry himself to sleep in secret with the same question—the answer rested squarely with the frying ham at the turpentine camp. The camp was down the path from the two-room, ninety-year-old oak-and-brick cabin their grandfather built on the patch of land Master Powell had given him to die on when he was no longer useful—and luckily Papa had just fixed the leaky roof before he was chased off to Chicago. The money Papa sent the first week of the month never lasted long enough to keep the pantry stocked, so he and Gloria couldn't afford regular meat anymore except on Sundays. After church, Gloria might surprise him with a squirrel or rabbit she'd trapped, or she'd chop up a handful of smoked pork from Miss Anne in her greens so he could remember the taste of something other than cornmeal and soup. And the camp was no more than a quick run from their cabin—close enough to smell the food, but as far away as the moon.

When he and Gloria opened the door that morning, the box from Chicago was waiting, dropped off overnight by Uncle June,

Miz Lottie's grand-nephew, who carried Papa's packages from the post office. Papa never dared address his mail to his children directly for fear of reprisals or tampering by spiteful postal employees. This box was larger than usual, wrapped in brown paper, crisscrossed with twine and tape, slightly crushed in one corner during its trip from Chicago, or else in Miz Lottie's old truck.

"Told you they'd come," Gloria said.

The boots! Robert had been waiting on new boots since his soles had started falling apart in May. When Robert saw the box, he swooned with excitement, his hunger forgotten.

He ripped away twine, brown paper, tape. And stared.

The brown boots with bright white laces were large, crammed in the box from end to end.

Not for a child at all. His stomach curled in a knot with disappointment. "These are like Papa's boots—they won't hold my feet, Gloria!"

"Course not. You think Papa has money to send you boots special—all the way from Illinois—from a catalog every two weeks, racing to keep up with how your feet grow?"

Gloria's long sentences were dizzying. His school friends said his sister sounded whiter than white folks on the radio shows. His favorite programs were *Dragnet*, *Dimension X*, and *Suspense*, and Gloria sure enough sounded just like the hysterical ladies seeing an alien or staring down a gun barrel, the way she talked so fast.

Robert slipped his bare feet into the boots. His toes rattled inside. He flopped around the porch in the giant boots. "I can't even wear 'em!"

"We'll wrap your feet," Gloria said.

"I can't run in 'em like that!"

"Why do you need to run in your boots?"

"'Cause Papa says don't run barefoot."

"Then don't run," she said.

She might as well have said *Don't breathe. Don't let your heart beat*. All pleasure was gone lately. No Mama. No Papa. No sweets. No meat, most days. And now he couldn't run?

Robert's salty tears broke free. Gloria was forever telling him not to run—*It's just like Mama always told you*—but the Mama in his memory was a smiling face, birdsong voice, gentle touch. Gloria was forever talking about a scolding and rule-setting Mama he did not remember.

Gloria rubbed his chin. "By winter," she said, "your feet will fit."

Later, when Gloria would feel especially tender toward him because of his terrible ordeal, she would confess that she'd asked Papa to send boots two sizes too big. But that day she scolded him for his selfishness when so many children had no shoes at all. Made him promise to write a thank-you letter to Papa.

Robert was unhappy in two pairs of hot woolen socks and too-big boots as he and Gloria let themselves out of the chicken mesh fence they still kept latched tight even though the chickens were long gone. With a grumbling stomach and sweating feet, Robert was in a bad mood as they set out on the uphill climb through woods to the clay dust farm-to-market road that passed within shouting distance from their door. Rusty barbed wire from a long-ago hog pen was still strung along the path.

"Why we gotta wear shoes at school?" Robert said, but he stopped short of complaining about school. Luckily, it was the last week of school before summer break. Half his class was already gone to start picking in Quincy, although Gloria said Robert could never go to any white man's cotton field no matter how little money they had. That was what Papa wanted. Gloria had been forced to quit school after Papa left, and he often caught her wiping away a tear before she left for Miss Anne Powell's to clean. Gloria treated school like it was holier than church. Robert liked to kick off his shoes under his desk, but Gloria had told Mr. Harris to rap his knuckles with a ruler if he ever saw him barefoot in the classroom. Papa had written in one of his letters that no one in Chicago would be caught dead barefoot, and Gloria hoped to beat Robert's country habits out of him so they would be ready for city life.

They *would* join Papa in Chicago one day. Gloria had promised him.

The dirt path let out on State Route 166, or McCormack Road, which stretched from one end of the county to the other, mostly through timber farms. He and Gloria lived just outside the Gracetown limits, with a three-mile walk to Frederick Douglass colored school on Lower Spruce, so they needed an hour to get there on time. In winter, the sun was still hidden when they began their walk to the school. If Robert was tardy, Mr. Harris gave him a paddling in front of the class. Robert had been late only once, and once was enough to last his whole life; the surprisingly sharp pain from the paddle hadn't smarted nearly as much as the eyes of his classmates on him, and the titter through the room: Robert Stephens's son being paddled! He could almost hear them planning how they would tell their parents. Like Papa said, everyone knowing your name wasn't always a blessing.

As they passed the McCormacks' fence, Robert heard the snorting of six-week-old piglets rooting near the roadside. Four of them, already fat enough to eat. The sight of the piglets made Robert's stomach growl again. He wished he could reach through the McCormacks' log slats to swipe one of the piglets. It would hardly be like stealing, with all the money the McCormacks had from slavery days. No one but the piglet's mama might ever know he was gone. But Robert walked past, his belly complaining as he recited his commandments under his breath: *"Thou shalt not steal. Thou. Shalt. Not. Steal."*

He'd promised Mama he would keep God in his life. She'd said God was the only thing she had to give him. She'd given Robert plenty more than that—almost gave him Miss Anne's old piano once, if she'd been able to find someone to haul it into the woods for them, and if it could have fit inside their cabin. But when Mama had played for him during his lessons, Robert heard Mama sing how much she loved him even if she couldn't give him the piano to keep.

Robert remembered Mama's hollow-jawed cheeks and wide-open dead eyes before Mr. Kendrick had come to fetch her in his hearse to take her to the colored graveyard. Whenever Gloria said "Mama" or someone mentioned her name, Robert saw her dead face instead of the smiling one he'd known. He was thinking of Mama's dead face when the voice called out from the thin Florida pines.

"Hey there, Robbie!"

Two years had roughened Lyle McCormack's voice, but Robert still knew it well enough to stop and turn to him with a smile. Papa had taught him that if a McCormack addressed you—any white man, really, but especially a McCormack—you smiled like he was family you thought you'd lost in Normandy. You smiled like he was Christmas morning itself.

"How come y'all don't come to the swimmin' hole no more?" Lyle said.

At fourteen, Lyle McCormack had been another boy splashing with him and his cousins at the swimming hole near the swamp just beyond the McCormack fence. Two years later, at sixteen, Lyle McCormack was nearly six feet tall, broad-chested, with a patchy beard trying to grow over his ruddy cheeks. Robert had never considered Lyle McCormack a friend, but Lyle could not be a playmate now that he was becoming a man. Why was Lyle even asking?

"Don't know," Robert said. He shrugged in the way his sister hated. He felt her nudge his back, a silent correction.

Robert didn't mention he'd been busy with school. Six months before, he'd been walking in town with a primer under his arm when a white man he'd never seen knocked it free and kicked it into the street. "Strong-lookin' boy like you don't need to think about anything except tobacco," he said. Robert had been too shocked to smile. He'd stood gape-jawed while the stranger examined him. Asked him how old he was. Got angry when Robert said he was only twelve. Insisted he was tall enough to be fourteen. The tears in Robert's eyes seemed to convince the stranger of his age, and he finally walked on, leaving Robert with shaking knees.

Later, Gloria said he was probably one of the growers' agents looking for pickers, and he probably worked for the McCormacks. Men who didn't hire themselves out for picking got thrown in jail for vagrancy and sent into the woods or fields by the sheriff. Since then, Robert never walked with his primer in town unless he hid it in a sack. Tried not to walk in town, period. Anyone knew it was best for Negroes to stay clear of Main Street, not to venture beyond the railroad tracks that separated Upper Spruce from Lower Spruce. None of that fear had touched Robert on McCormack Road—until now. Lyle McCormack was asking about swimming, but Lyle didn't give a snot about Robert, so he must have another meaning. Guessing at a white man's meaning was a dangerous game.

"We don't got time for swimming now," Robert said.

Robert expected Lyle to say, *Condolences on the passing of your mama, and I know you must miss your papa now that he's gone,* but he didn't. He was staring at Gloria.

Gloria had brought Robert and his cousins to the swimming hole each night after supper until the end of summer two years ago, wading alongside the young McCormack twins under Lyle's watch. White and Negro, they all raced under the water to try to catch the flat, shiny stones Lyle McCormack threw in; they all pulled strands of moss from their hair that floated like snakes on the water. They had thrown their clothes on the riverbank and complained about mud stains. White and Negro, they had lain in the soft soil with their fingers locked behind their heads as pillows, staring up at moss strung from the old oak's branches, speculating on whether or not haints lived in the rotting wood and dropped moss into the water to try to tangle and drown them. Those swimming days had been the last good days, with sunset so late in the summer, Mama still alive and breathing, Papa coming home each night.

"You oughta come by like before." Lyle McCormack ambled closer to them, leaning on his fence bordering the woods. Closer to Gloria. "You too, Glo. We could swim, you and me."

Gloria hated being called Glo, but Robert knew she wouldn't sass at Lyle McCormack. All at once, Robbie understood that Glo was the real reason Lyle had stopped them. His sweaty feet made him squirm.

"Robbie's right," Gloria said. "No time to play these days, Lyle."

Instinct made Robert glad for the fence that separated them, but Lyle suddenly hopped over the rails to sidle closer, breathing as if he'd come running across the field.

"Everyone's got some time to play," he said. "How 'bout on Sunday?"

"She says she don't want to," Robert said. His mouth moved before he could think.

His muscles felt tense all over, coiled like a rattlesnake. He said it like Papa would.

Gloria's head whipped around. Emotions paraded in her eyes, one by one: Shock. Delight. Anger.

"I can speak for myself, Robbie," Gloria said, schoolmarm proper. She gave his arm a sharp yank for emphasis. "*Hush.*"

"Yeah, hush," Lyle McCormack said. "Nobody's talkin' to you."

"Sure you was," Robert said. Hadn't Lyle called him over first? But Robert decided to keep the rest silent when the angry blaze in Gloria's eyes burned at him.

Lyle squinted at Robert, a challenge. "What you say?"

"He ain't said nothing, Lyle," Gloria said. "He's a stupid kid."

The hunger in the pit of Robert's stomach twisted, making him feel sick. Gloria had stripped the schoolmarm out of her voice, replacing it with country sweetness, like lemonade with too much sugar. She took a halting step closer to Lyle, showing him her full face, her lips upturned as if she were really smiling.

Lyle's eyes drifted back to Gloria. "So come swim on Sunday, then. After church. Close to dark. The sun sets pretty on the water."

"Bet it's pretty, all right," Gloria said. "But I'm goin' on to work. I'm Miss Anne's girl now, you know. Good mornin', Lyle McCormack."

She took a step farther down the path and Robert quickly followed, glad to be away from a moment pricked sharp, even if he wasn't sure why. Something to do with the swimming hole, and Lyle asking Gloria to go swimming as if they were courting. But no McCormack would court a Negro girl—no white man, period, would—so why was he bothering Gloria?

Lyle McCormack flipped a tuft of flat golden hair from his face as he matched Gloria's pace. He took her arm to stop her walking and lowered his face close to hers. For an amazed instant, Robert thought he meant to kiss her—but instead, he whispered in a voice just loud enough for Robert to hear, "You look nicer'n those gals at Pixie's."

Gloria stared at him with a moon-eyed face Robert had never seen on his sister, so childlike it frightened him.

Lyle McCormack grinned. "You can do more'n scrub floors, Glo. I know you can."

Then he winked at her. As Lyle McCormack's eyelid slid shut above his grin, locking into a leer, Robert understood one of the last things his father had told him before he fled to Chicago: he was never, ever to wink his eye at a white girl or white woman. Foolishness like that can get you killed, Papa had said.

And here was Lyle McCormack winking at his sister in broad daylight, standing in the middle of the road where any passerby or farmhand could see. A hundred years could have passed since their twilight swimming days. The bright morning sun, his stomach's knotted hunger, and Mama's death face stirred Robert into a rage. He didn't want Lyle McCormack's hand and eyes on his sister a breath longer. He squeezed himself between Lyle and Gloria.

"Leave her be!" Robert said.

Lyle's eyes dropped down to him. "What's got into you?"

Gloria backed up a step behind Robert, but Robert remained fixed, a wall.

"Move, Robbie," Lyle said, and shoved him aside, so much power in the blunt motion that Robert stumbled two steps. His upper arm smarted from the heel of Lyle's hand.

"Stop it!" Gloria said to Robert. "Mind your business."

But Robert ran toward Lyle McCormack, swinging his foot at the bigger boy's left knee, and his new boot's bulk sank into the side of Lyle's kneecap with a thunk of bone. It wasn't like he'd done it: he *watched* himself do it.

Lyle McCormack yelled in pain. "You little *shit*," he said. He hopped on one leg.

"You pushed me first," Robert said, his voice and eyes low. The kick had taken all the fight out of him. Instead, he was realizing what he had done.

"He didn't mean it, Lyle," Gloria said. "He's stupid! It's just me looking after him since Mama died. He don't have his daddy now either." Gloria was talking fast, as if Lyle McCormack were holding a shotgun to his head.

Lyle McCormack was red-faced, so tall above Robert that he blocked the sunlight. Lyle pursed his lips, eyes staring death at Robert. "I oughta brain you, Robbie."

"Walk on it, Lyle," Gloria said gently. "Your knee's all right. Ain't it?"

After a last glare at Robert, Lyle hobbled in a circle, testing his knee. "Dammit!"

"But you're fine," Gloria said, a feeble plea in her voice. "Ain't you?"

Robert knew better than to lay hands on a McCormack. Any Negro knew better than to lay hands on any white man, but especially a McCormack. At best, Robert calculated he was about to get the thrashing of his life. The worst was too big to form a picture.

"You do that again, I'm gonna knock your teeth out," Lyle said, his finger pressing the tip of Robert's nose. "You hear me?"

"Yessir. I'm sure sorry," Robert said, more grateful than scared. Amazed it was over. But it wasn't.

"Lyyyyle!" a man's voice called across the field, from beyond the fence.

Their heads snapped like owls toward the fence. Robert hoped the voice didn't belong to Lyle McCormack's father, who everyone called Mister Red because of his bright orange hair, but his hope died as his hair charged through the pine grove.

Gloria took Robert's hand, squeezing it. They both wanted to run.

"Did this little nigger just kick you?" Red McCormack said. He ducked the fence rail. The closer he walked, the more Robert felt the earth parting around him, a hole swallowing his feet. *Mister Red is gonna kill me*, Robert thought, the most certain thought he'd ever had.

Lyle's eyes went to Gloria in an apology meant only for her to see. Then he went to his father, hiding his limp.

"Yeah, he kicked me, Pa," Lyle said. "Wasn't nothin', though—"

Red McCormack boxed Robert's right ear so hard that he and his sister screamed.

2

Robbie kicked Lyle McCormack. And Red McCormack saw.

Gloria's thoughts wouldn't let her sleep. Memories slapped at her as she lay in the bed her parents had shared, already an uneasy place to rest: Lyle McCormack's sour breath on her neck. Robbie's kick to Lyle's knee. (His knee! And he wanted to play football for Florida State!) Red McCormack storming over so quickly that he might have meant to snap Robbie's neck. And blue flames in Red McCormack's eyes as he boxed Robbie's ear, daring her to move or speak.

What would Mama have done?

Mama had kept most of her childhood stories locked in her eyes. Mama's stories were unsuited for the ears of children—stories of evil without consequence and pain without cease—the unholy things that happen when God blinks. Or maybe sleeps. Surely God sleeps sometimes, Gloria thought; the evidence of slumber was all around. Secretly, since Mama's passing, Gloria wrestled with her father's unshakable belief in God, but sometimes she made peace with the notion that Mama's cancer had come while God's eyes were shut. Mostly God's eyes are open, but God blinks, there's a hurricane, or, blink, there's an orphan. Reverend Miles had never put it so plainly, but to Gloria it was a truth as bright as summer sun.

At least Mama's terrible crying and sweating had a swift end. Mama's dying had a measurement: it began, it flashed with bright pain, it ended. Emptiness so big it made her feel blind. Painful enough to make any good in the world a lie. But it ended.

Papa in Chicago was a different thing entirely. They needed

him now. Papa had fled to Chicago and she did not know when, or if, he would send for her and Robbie. He said he would try to bring them to Chicago by fall, but it wasn't certain . . . and fall was months away. She couldn't hear his laugh or feel him nearby when she heard night noises outside her window. He hadn't called her at Miz Lottie's at his usual time on Sunday, so her father might already be dead and they were the last to hear. And if that were true, God help them—

She couldn't form new thoughts beyond it, though she knew she had to. She needed a plan. Mama and Papa both were planners: Mama had run her six sewing and laundry girls like a sea captain, and Papa knew how to move men to singing and unionizing.

Gracetown had a long history of beloved Negro singers, but the history of union-talking Negroes was bleak. Everyone knew that—Papa especially. But still he'd called a meeting and spoken before twenty-five colored mill workers—at least!—and said enough with his voice raised to be chased out of Gracetown that same night. She could have told him that you can only trust explosive secrets or plans with three people at most. Maybe four. Beyond that, loyalties tended to buckle beneath the thrill of the telling.

So of course at least half a dozen men had gone running to the bosses before Papa even warmed up or said the word *strike*. What happened next had been a Negro "riot," or, by eyewitness accounts, a mauling of Negroes by twice the number of white men with clubs, tire irons, and shotgun butts. Clyde Frazier—the barber who worked from his back porch near the railroad tracks on Lower Spruce—lost an eye. But at least no one died like when Papa was a boy and had to hide out in the woods with his parents, grandparents, and cousins during the Marianna riots. Or like the Rosewood survivors a dozen years prior, like Mama. And the way Papa's grandmother had hidden under her bed in 1909, when three Negro boys went missing on McCormack land—and when their papa fired a warning shot demanding news of his sons, a mob of angry whites killed him and rounded up a score of other Negro fathers, brothers, and sons who were never seen again.

On Florida soil, sometimes killing broke out for its own reasons. *Florida's soil is soaked with so much blood, it's a wonder the droplets don't seep between your toes with every step,* Mama used to say. Sometimes, when Gloria walked along McCormack Road, she thought she heard whimpers beneath her footsteps. She wondered if blood turned the muddy clay roads in Gracetown the stubborn red-orange color that stained the folded cuffs of her dungarees.

This time Papa had been the one they wanted to hang. They wanted to swing him up like Claude Neal in Marianna when Papa was a boy; Papa had seen the body swinging in front of the courthouse, and on that day he decided he could not let white people scare him or he'd be scared all his life. Most of Papa's lessons were about the ways of white people, which made it all the more unthinkable that he had not heeded his own warnings.

While the mobs had been looking for Papa, trying to scare the shotgun house dwellers at the far end of Lower Spruce, someone invented a story that Papa tried to rape a white lady behind Pixie's. Anyone who knew Papa knew that was a lie, since he'd had eyes for no other girl but Mama since they were both in third grade. And he didn't drink, gamble, or frequent juke joints. But that hadn't stopped somebody from pointing a finger toward the house Papa was building out on the other side of McCormack's land. This had not surprised Gloria either—she knew from school that not everyone was happy Papa had scraped together savings to build a house "out near the lake," as her once-friend Rose had put it, as if lake water and comfort were a betrayal. By the time the Klan burned down their unfinished house, Papa had hopped a train and asked Miz Lottie to keep an eye on Gloria and his namesake, little Robbie. And Miz Lottie, a spinster with a glass eye at eighty-three, couldn't watch her own self, much less a boy of twelve and a girl of sixteen. Gloria had felt less safe at night knowing she had to keep Miz Lottie's oyster knife sharp under her pillow to protect not just her and Robbie but maybe the old woman too. After three weeks, she and Robbie had gone back to their own house to live. She'd promised Miz Lottie she was grown enough to care for her brother—and she'd believed that until they ran into Lyle on McCormack Road.

Their cabin felt like a dead space now. Empty chicken coops and a chicken wire yard of dusty grass patches. Soured memories in every corner, especially the formerly happiest, the wooden table for four where they had shared so many meals. It was a hostile space too: so many dripping places when it rained, flies and mosquitoes wheeling freely inside the walls, so much stagnant heat and darkness, not enough windows, and Reynolds Wrap instead of curtains. Her great-grandfather had not built big windows like Miss Anne's and the houses in town.

Even before Mama got sick, they had begun to talk about the cabin as their old place, a relic from Papa's slave-born grandfather, a parcel doled out to a dying servant. ("White folks can love their property like a hunter loves his hound," Papa had said.) Papa and his friends had built the new house from sturdy Florida pine, board by board—*three* bedrooms. An indoor bathroom and plumbing he'd hired workers for, not an outhouse. A picture window in the living room looking out on the lake.

All of it burned now. A black circle seared in the soil. That burned-up house had been Mama's dream for them before she died. Now all of their dreams were dead. Every photo carefully posed in Mama's ornate frames felt like a lie, even the photos of her and Robbie. They looked too young. The photo taking had stopped when Mama got sick.

Robbie kicked Lyle McCormack. And Red McCormack saw.

Should she take Robert on a train to Papa and try to make it to Chicago to find him? She had no money for train fare, so she imagined getting arrested or thrown off the train, stranded somewhere trying to find work with Robbie in tow. And what "work" was waiting for a girl who knew more about Langston Hughes and Zora Neale Hurston than the laundering, sewing, and cleaning Mama had tried to teach her?

Robbie kicked Lyle McCormack. And Red McCormack saw.

Gloria turned on the dim lamp on the night table beside her mattress. The cabin had only one bedroom, and no door separated her from Robbie's sleeping form on the trundle bed on the other side of the old cabin's coal stove and dining table. She heard his calm, steady breathing and longed to be in his place—untroubled, all fears forgotten with sleep.

Gloria hunted down a pen and lined paper in the night table drawer: Papa had forever been writing his thoughts and plans, sometimes late into the night. She found a blank page and addressed it in neat lines the way Mama had taught her before Gloria even started school:

Mr. William Jones
101 47th Street, Apartment 16A
Chicago, Illinois

It was not his actual name or address, Papa had explained, but that was where he'd arranged to pick up his mail from a friend. She stripped her report to the bare facts: Robbie had kicked Lyle McCormack and his father Red had witnessed it and boxed his ear bloody. She added that Red McCormack had sworn to make Robert's life a misery, so *I can hardly think of all the sorrow that will rain on us if we stay here.*

Papa had complained for years about how petty the McCormacks were, how tightly they held their grudges. Papa's family had once been owned by the McCormacks, and both sides of the McCormack fence held long memories. With their cabin so close by, half the things Papa said were rules to keep away from McCormacks. Two years ago, Papa had announced that he and Gloria weren't allowed to swim there anymore, even if they were invited.

Too late, she now fully understood why. If she'd known how casually catastrophe might strike, she and Robert could have stayed closer to the tree line and far on the other side of the road to keep away from that McCormack fence each day. Robert was sleeping as if he thought the kick on the road was forgotten, that his bloodied ear had squared him with the McCormacks. But Gloria knew better. Knew in her heart.

Gloria Patricia Stephens did not sleep that night.

She wasn't surprised at dawn when the sheriff's deputy came to the door.

3

The deputy looked angry to be on an errand so early. None of Gloria's rehearsed apologies or excuses swayed the gruff boy in his too-big deputy's uniform, barely older than she. His black-and-white sheriff's car sat parked outside their chicken wire, a sight she knew well: sheriff's cars often had parked in that spot in the months before Papa left—usually at dinnertime, when Papa had stood at the window while she and Mama and Robbie sat with their forks frozen above their plates, waiting for flames or gunshots. Had this boy deputy come to the house before? If you asked the operator to call Sheriff Posey's office, the Klan klavern would pick up on the other end.

The deputy's clothes were rumpled. Handcuffs gleamed in his hands.

"Where's Robert Stephens Junior? The judge is waiting on him at the courthouse."

His voice sounded muffled, as if Gloria had cotton in her ears. Why, oh, why hadn't she run away with Robbie when she'd had the chance?

"You're here for me?" Robbie scurried to the deputy when he should have been climbing out of his window and jumping the wire. He sounded more confused than scared. He had slept in Papa's old blue mill shirt. Robbie hopped on one leg to pull on his pants as the deputy stepped toward him.

"He's under arrest?" Gloria said.

"What you think?" the deputy said, fixing the metal cuffs around Robert's wrists. The *click-click* was as loud as a gunshot.

Gloria had seen gangster pictures where outlaws were arrested by the police, and she had expected more ceremony. But she'd overheard Papa and the pickers complaining about how the sheriff broke down their doors and dragged them to jail on vagrancy charges when they got tired of picking. The sheriff in Gracetown wasn't like police in pictures or on the radio.

Robert didn't cry or fight the deputy, but his head hung like it was boneless. He didn't look Gloria's way. Family couldn't do anything for you when the sheriff came, just like family was helpless against sickness—except through prayer, Mama would say. And the judge was involved. The son of Robert Stephens would not go unnoticed.

Gloria had hidden her unmailed letter in her dress, but what good was the letter now? Letters took days to arrive in Chicago! Instead of writing a silly letter, she should have packed their clothes in Mama's powder-blue suitcase and fled, even on foot. They should have run, just like Papa had.

"He's twelve years old. What's going to happen to him?" Gloria said.

"Ask the judge," the deputy said.

"They wouldn't send a young boy to a work gang, would they?"

"Just shut up and come on, if you're comin'."

"Can you wait and let me get dressed proper?" Gloria didn't have any clothes better than the faded gingham dress she wore, tattered at the hem, but she was frantic to stop the motion of the day. The deputy was quick about his business, like Robert was a calf he had tied with a rope. He tugged on Robbie's arm to pull him to his car.

"Catch up," the deputy said.

Gloria had to run to keep pace with him, but she climbed into the back seat beside Robert before the deputy slammed the door. Robert lay against her while she rode with him the way he had when he was small. With the mesh separating them from the deputy, they might both already be in a cage.

"What's he being charged with?" Gloria said. "Lyle McCormack pushed him first."

"Shut up or I'll arrest you too," the deputy said. "I'll lock you up for obstructing justice. He twitches a muscle, he's resisting arrest. You talk too damn much. I better not hear a peep."

Gloria sat with Robert and stroked his wrist where his shackles met his skin.

Gloria had never been inside the Gracetown Courthouse, a monument with a golden bell tower at the center of Main Street. She lost sight of Robert on the steps because the deputy said Negroes went in from the rear, so he was gone before she could hug Robert or say she could fix everything, even if it might not be true.

Papa had been to the courthouse many times on behalf of friends and family, but he had never brought her or Robert. Why would he? The only Negroes in the courthouse were the accused and their families, with whispers up and down Lower Spruce when so-and-so was arrested or about to go on trial. Golden arrows pointed out windows on property taxes and probate (the latter a word she did not know), but no one would believe a visit to the courthouse was about anything except shame. If anyone who knew Miss Anne saw her at the courthouse, Miss Anne would ask Gloria terse questions about why she had been there. Would Miss Anne fire her because Robbie had been arrested? Gloria sorely needed the fifteen dollars a week Miss Anne paid her for cooking and cleaning.

"You lost, little missy?"

A Negro uniformed custodian with a long-handled broom was the only person who noticed her. He was about ten years older than Papa, in his forties, with white hairs sprayed throughout his curly black crown. His eyes were big behind thick glasses.

"Yessir," she said. "I'm trying to find my brother."

"He in trouble?"

"The deputy said he was going to see the judge."

As the man listened, his lips curled up slightly in a hidden smile. Gloria knew he was struck, perhaps bemused, by the crisp way she spoke. But his eyes were sympathetic.

"Only judge on the bench this time of mo'nin' is Judge Morris. Courtroom's up ahead."

Finally—information! Gloria said a hurried "Thank you" and ran in the direction of the double doors the man had pointed out at the end of the hall.

"Don't you go in them doors!" the custodian called. "Colored door's to the side."

Gloria stopped three strides short of the wooden doors and their burnished gold-colored handles. Sure enough, the COLORED sign was posted to the right, with an arrow pointing down a narrow corridor. A smaller door met her there, propped slightly open with a wad of cardboard. Inside, narrow wooden stairs rose in a dimly lighted stairway.

Gloria at last found her way to the courtroom balcony, in the gallery set aside for colored observers. The benches were empty. The walls smelled of sweat, chewing tobacco, and waiting. Gloria moved past the spittoon near the door to the first row of benches to peer down at the courtroom, so far below. Only four anxious spectators sat in the neat rows of white seating. The plump, thick-shouldered judge occupied his bench like Saint Peter in the clouds, but in a black robe instead of white.

A thin white man in an ill-fitting suit was standing before the judge.

"Billy, you promised me you'd give up corn whiskey," the judge said, leaning forward, elbows propped. He hocked a wad of tobacco into his own spittoon.

"I know it, Your Honor." The man's voice was all trembling misery.

"Well, this time you've left me no choice." The judge rapped his gavel, a sound so harsh that Gloria jumped. "Spend a year at Raiford, that'll sober you up. Go on, now. You're lucky nobody got hurt worse."

"I sure do know it, Your Honor," the man said, his head low. He was nearly in tears. The spectators all rose and went to him. One tearful older woman in Sunday dress, probably his mother, hugged him.

"I'm sorry, Doris, but the law has my hands tied," the judge said.

"It's not your fault, Judge Morris," the older woman said. "We warned him 'til we was red in the face." The grown man sobbed on the woman's shoulder before a deputy led him away.

This private scene felt like the worst kind of omen. As the miserable man exited by a rear door with a deputy Gloria did not recognize, Robert appeared, hands still chained behind him.

The same deputy who had come to their cabin followed Robert, guiding him to the bench by his arm. Gloria suppressed a cry at how small Robert seemed, swallowed inside the massive courtroom. He looked for her, but he did not notice the gallery. She waved to get Robert's attention, and he saw her but did not smile. He moved slowly, nearly too frightened to walk.

"Robert Stephens Junior?" the judge said.

Papa's name rang in the courthouse, an indictment in his absence. The room seemed to quake with Gloria's racing heart.

Far below her, Robbie mumbled. *Speak clearly!* Gloria's thoughts screamed.

"Speak up." The judge already sounded impatient.

"Yessir." Hearing him speak, Gloria breathed.

The judge studied a page in front of him. "Did you kick Lyle McCormack?" Gloria's shoulders hunched when she heard it aloud. And with none of the facts to explain it.

Robert hung his head again. "Yessir."

"Why'd you do a fool thing like that?"

Say it! In Robert's long silence, Gloria thought of her shock and anger at how Lyle McCormack had taken hold of her arm, comparing her to the colored whores who worked in cars behind the juke joint. And proposing they meet on a Sunday! Had Robert understood? Was that what had riled him senseless? Gloria wanted to rise to her feet and tell his story, but didn't dare.

"Don't know, sir. He . . ."

He pushed me. Say it! Gloria's thoughts screamed. But Robert said nothing more. "Well, son, you'd be in a world of trouble if you'd run off from Red McCormack. Might be dogs after you right now. He said you stood there and took your whupping. Is that true?"

"Yessir," Robert said. He was deathly afraid of the McCormacks' dogs.

"Boxed your ear pretty good?"

"Yessir."

Gloria's heart surged. The judge's questions had taken a turn away from confession to consequences paid: that could only be a good sign! Had she heard grandfatherly kindness in the judge's voice? Maybe Robert would endure a stern lecture and be sent back home. Robert would still have time to go to school, and she'd make up an excuse to Miss Anne about why she was late. Their true day was about to begin as normal, with Robert sitting at his school desk and her wringing undergarments in the sink in Miss Anne's laundry room.

"You know you'd be lynched in some counties for foolishness like that?" Gloria nearly gasped aloud. How could the judge speak that word?

Robert's lip shook. "No, sir," he said. His voice sounded smaller.

"Your mama and daddy both dead?"

"No, sir. My daddy's in Chicago."

Blood stalled in Gloria's veins. How could Robert have forgotten *never* to say where their father was?

"What's his address in Chicago?"

Robert shrugged—*shrugged!* Mama had forever told him never to shrug at an adult; it was disrespectful, she'd said, a flaunting of indifference. Had the judge seen it? Of course he had, staring down at Robert from his perch of gleaming wood.

"You don't know your own father's address?"

Don't say anything else! As if he'd heard her, Robert's head jerked as if to look back at her, but he fought the impulse to turn. Robert had always been a baby, quick to cry: she'd never seen him more restrained in his fear. He *had* listened to Mama's stories. He *had* heeded Papa.

Now, if only he would remember—

"No, sir," Robert said. "I don't know the street or nothin'."

"Well, that's a hell of a thing: a man goes to Chicago and leaves his son to go wild."

Robert looked up, facing the judge's eyes. "No, sir. My sister's 'bout grown."

Gloria rose to her feet, as if she'd been called. She purposely brushed back against the bench to make the wooden leg squeal against the floor. The shiny bald patch on the judge's head winked as he looked up at her.

"I'm Gloria Stephens, Your Honor," she said loudly, as she had rehearsed in her head all morning. "We're both in the care of Miss Lottie Mae Powell, who is a deaconess at Holy Redeemer Baptist Church. I promise you, Robert is not 'running wild.' "

Gloria's fear left her as she spoke. She was ready to enunciate clearly when she answered his questions. She would quiver her voice when she told him all about Mama's terrible cancer and how she was raising Robert to know the Lord. She would say nothing about her father.

The judge looked away from her. He closed a sheath of papers and pushed it aside. "You'll go to the Gracetown School for Boys for six months," the judge said to Robert. "A nigger who won't learn respect and a trade won't live to see thirteen. I see you in front of me again, you'll go on a work crew to Raiford like a grown man. Hear me?"

And he rang that terrible gavel again.

The Reformatory! Six months? Even *nigger,* which she'd heard her whole life, cut deeper from a judge's lips in this church-like chamber. If she had known those words were coming, she would have screamed and begged all this time instead of sitting in her good-girl silence. But even wishing to object with every part of herself, she couldn't make a sound.

His sermon finished, the judge beamed at Robert as if he expected to be thanked. After all, it wasn't a year at Raiford or a work gang in the tobacco fields, turpentine farms, or phosphate mines. The Reformatory was called a *school*.

But for the first time since the deputy had come, Robert wailed with childish tears. By the time Gloria rushed back down the flight of narrow stairs in hopes of talking to Robert, hugging him, she could only peek through the forbidden double doors to see a flash of his shirt as the deputy led him through a doorway on the opposite end of the courtroom, across a vast wooden floor her feet were not permitted to touch. Gloria let out a pained rush of air when the door shut closed. The empty courtroom had stolen her brother.

In the hall outside, Gloria's worry for Robert twisted her stomach, but her mouth would not obey to make demands. Her feet would not move toward the window boxes without COLORED signs. She was dizzy and ill with it: How could a court of law have no provisions for a child to be given comfort by family? Had Robbie been formally charged and convicted? If so, why had there been no jury? Why had *she* been punished with such faceless formality—wrested from her only family, given no chance even to say goodbye?

And what, oh, what would she say to Papa?

The idea of Papa's anguish jolted Gloria from her stupor. She would have no time to learn the ways of the courthouse, which was the biggest building on Main Street, full of warrens and long hallways.

Instead, she must find her way to the Reformatory.

Gloria ran mostly uphill from Main Street to Miz Lottie's seawater-colored house at the end of 14620 Fillmore Street on Lower Spruce, just past the railroad tracks and wooden trestle at the border of Negro Town. She ran so fast and hard that she could only spit up her empty stomach by the time she waded through the untended crabgrass to Miz Lottie's front porch. Her body shook with sobs as she bent beside the porch railing over a patch of mud by Miz Lottie's cabbage and collards. Miz Lottie opened her screen door to see who was there, and Gloria wasted precious seconds with a clogged throat. Finally, she heaved out her story.

"Robbie's been arrested!" she began, and told all the rest.

Miz Lottie held her in a way no one had since Mama died. Her bosom smelled like her steaming kitchen. "I'd like to give one o' them McCormacks a swift kick myself," Miz Lottie said, and Gloria's laugh came as a tiny sob instead. Miz Lottie rested her hand on Gloria's head, heavy and earth-sweet from her gardening glove. "I know, pumpkin. I know. But you dry those tears. We gotta get Ole Suzy warmed up. Might be we can get there ahead of 'em."

Ole Suzy was Miz Lottie's red 1939 Ford truck at the end of the driveway, and Gloria trembled with the promise of it: What if she could be there waiting for Robert? The happy prospect burned so brightly that Gloria swallowed her tears.

"You've got enough gas to go and back?" Gloria said. The drive was at least ten miles, at the far west side of the county, near the peanut mill. Papa had driven her out that way once to collect money he was owed, and he'd pointed out the Reformatory as they passed the sprawling, regal green lawn behind mighty spiked fences.

Gloria remembered, as if for the first time, exactly what Papa had said as they passed the grounds: "That's the *first* place they start killing us." And for the first time she had noticed the barbed wire. The memory clapped her with such force that it carried the scent of her father's pipe. *This* was where her brother was being sent. A killing place. Papa had said so.

"Grab that gas can out the carport," Miz Lottie said. "We got enough."

Until that moment, Gloria had only seen Miz Lottie's deficiencies: her weak joints and bad eyesight, her inability to stand Robert's constant motion, her too-meager meals she could barely afford to share. Gloria saw no weakness in Miz Lottie now. Her good eye was clear and alert. She moved slowly but with purpose as she retrieved her cane from the side of the porch steps. She gathered the oversized pocketbook she always carried when she left her house, as big as a carpetbag. While Gloria fumbled with the heavy, rusted red gas can, spilling a few drops when she stumbled over a box in the carport, she caught Miz Lottie glancing at herself in her compact mirror, vain even now.

And Miz Lottie had called her *pumpkin*. Only Mama called her pumpkin. Gloria could barely see through her tears as she tried to fit the can's nozzle into the rusted gas tank of Miz Lottie's truck. A gasoline droplet on her hand stung her right eye like fire when she rubbed it.

"Chile, gimme that 'fore you spill all my gas," Miz Lottie said, so Gloria stood aside for the old woman, who angled the gas can with a practiced hand. "Eighteen cents a gallon—you better treat this here like gold."

On Miz Lottie's street of houses with small yards, her neighbors were behaving as if it were a regular day. Someone's gas lawn mower burred, and Ivory Joe Hunter's "I Almost Lost My Mind" played through an open window with a flapping curtain. Miz Lottie's neighbor, Clyde Frazier, was plucking ripe mangoes from his tree, not noticing her—maybe on purpose. Minding his business.

Gloria wanted to scream her story to them. Papa would have rushed out in the middle of the night to help any of them.

"Come on," Miz Lottie said. "We'll get there faster if we cut through the woods."

4

For thirty minutes, Robert stood under the midday sun with his arms chained to the hot iron banister by the rear courthouse door. The deputy watched him from the shade under the awning, out of the sun's glare. Robert's knees shook the way Mama had trembled with fever. He counted every minute on the courthouse clock tower between a V of live oak branches above. At eleven o'clock, he counted thirteen strikes of the bell—a bad sign for sure.

Where was Gloria? All the time he'd waited, he'd expected her to round the corner with the good news that she'd phoned Papa somehow. It couldn't be that he was about to be sent to live somewhere without Gloria or the Philco radio Papa had bought him or his last Easter snapshot with Mama, their white clothes matching. Or anything at all.

A green Ford Woodie approached the driveway behind the courthouse, low undercarriage scraping against a dip in the road. The deputy ground out his cigarette with his heel. "'Bout damn time," he muttered.

Robert had not cried since he'd left the courtroom, but he wanted to cry now. The station wagon was so long, it looked like Mr. Kendrick's hearse. "For me?" he asked the deputy.

"Ain't a milk truck."

The station wagon stopped a few feet from him, and the curly-haired white man driving opened his car door and fixed on his hat to block the sun. His shoes shone like a starry night. He stood, his legs unfolding until he was as tall and thin as a pine tree. He made the deputy look like a little boy beside him. But no gun.

Whenever the deputy was near him, all Robert noticed was his holstered blue-black gun.

"Transport isn't exactly my purview," the tall man said. He had a flat, dull accent Robert had only heard on the radio. He sounded like private detective Johnny Dollar. Papa loved that program.

"Wouldn't know about all that," the deputy said. "Sheriff Posey said to wait on you, so . . ." He shrugged. Gloria was right: shrugging *was* an ugly gesture, especially when it was meant for you. Your situation. Your life.

For the first time, the tall man looked down at Robert from eyes a mile high. Irritation deepened creases across the man's forehead and jawline. Robert had never spent so much time with white men. The man's linen suit smelled like womanly soap. His fingernails were like a woman's too, clipped and smooth and clean. His teacher Mr. Harris was fussy, but even Mr. Harris's hands weren't so smooth and unblemished. Robert wondered how shabby he must look to this giant white man.

"Where's his admit form?" the tall man said.

"Judge Morris just said carry him over to Haddock."

The name Haddock soured the tall man's face. "No paperwork. Guess that's how you know you're in Gracetown municipal. Get those cuffs off, would you? This boy's not gonna give me trouble. Are you?" He tapped Robert's shoulder lightly.

Robert shook his head. "No, suh." Gloria had told him it was best to sound dumb when talking to white men. If he was dumb and young enough, a white man might leave him be the way he might walk past a dog. He'd tried to sound dumb to the judge but not dumb enough to make him mad. Robbie cast his eyes down, staring at his too-big boots from Papa.

"What's your name?"

"Robert Stephens Junior."

"Look me in my eye when you speak. I'm Mr. Loehmann."

The tall man outstretched his smooth hand, expecting a handshake. Robert tried, but he could not meet his eyes, his head too heavy to move.

The deputy sucked his teeth, but he reached to his belt for his keys and unsnapped the handcuffs. Only then did Robert realize how tight the hot metal had been, grinding against the lower bone of his thumb anytime he moved.

His hands free, Robert reached to shake Mr. Loehmann's hand. He first reached with his left hand but quickly corrected himself. Mr. Loehmann gripped tightly, not letting Robert pull away as quickly as he tried to. The tall man leaned down to stare in Robert's eyes. Dark brown eyes matched his own.

"We'll have no trouble on the ride to the Reformatory. Is that understood?"

Robert nodded. "No trouble," he said. "I swear on my mama."

A miracle: Mr. Loehmann smiled! He gestured toward his open car door. "Slide in. Passenger side's yours."

If anyone had told Robert that he would have a reason to feel glad on this horrible day, he'd never have believed it. But as he gazed at the wide-open car door and the expanse of the clean, pale leather seat, he felt his mouth upturning, his teeth poking out. He'd never had a ride in a new car, only old cars. Mr. Loehmann's car smelled fresh. And no more handcuffs!

"See him grinning?" the deputy said. "You see that?"

"Same way any kid smiles when you say they can ride up front," Mr. Loehmann said. "Since there's no form, tell me: What's Robert's crime? Ran away from home? Orphan?"

"He kicked Lyle McCormack. Assault's a crime."

"Lyle McCormack, huh?" Mr. Loehmann said, eyebrows raised when he looked back in Robert's direction. Robert was ready to blurt an apology and explanation—How could he have forgotten to tell the judge that Lyle pushed him first?—but Mr. Loehmann gestured again for him to get into the car. "Well, that explains it."

The front seat was so smooth that Robert glided from one end to the other. He wished he could have lingered at the dashboard, shiny with silver, and its knobs, meters, and numbers. He couldn't resist a tug at the two-toned steering wheel as he passed, but it didn't budge.

"I been meaning to ask you, Mr. Loehmann . . . ," the deputy said, with an odd emphasis on his name, drawing out *LOW-mannnn*. "Where you from? Miami, I bet?"

"I'm from New York. Lower East Side."

"New York, huh?" the deputy said. "Well, that explains it."

"Explains what, Deputy?"

"I'm surprised your car ain't painted pink. Or red."

Robert watched through the windshield as the men stood locked in a moment he didn't understand. The deputy smirked as if he'd gotten away with an insult. Pink was a terrible choice, but red wouldn't be such an ugly color for a car, would it? Why had Loehmann's face gone pale?

"Remind your boss that we have procedures and a state juvenile board," Mr. Loehmann said. "I'm pretty sure rules apply even in Gracetown."

"Tell him yourself."

"Oh, I intend to."

"You drive safe out there, Mr. Loehmann." Again the deputy said it like an insult. Then he pretended to sneeze, saying *A Jew* where his sneeze should be.

When Mr. Loehmann climbed into the car, he slammed his door. His face reminded Robert of Papa's for an instant, tight with ugly knowledge. So, when white men argued, they did not say the thing they were arguing about, not like with Papa and his friends shouting over each other on the porch. These white men hid their arguments behind polite words and sneezes.

But that was the white men's business, not his. He bounced in his seat, his grin breaking free. As Mr. Loehmann turned his key and the engine whispered to life without choking or gurgling, the radio played Nat King Cole's "Mona Lisa" so crisply that Nat and his orchestra might have been hiding under the hood. Nat King

Cole was a Negro, Mama's favorite. Suddenly, Mama was in the car with him, singing in his ear. *Mona Lisaaaaaa.* Cool air blew from the vents like a fall breeze. And a car like this probably could drive fast! He'd only had a quick glance at the speedometer, but it went up to a hundred miles an hour at least.

A clanging across his window startled Robert and made his sore ear throb. The deputy had tapped the glass with his handcuffs. "You won't be smilin' long, boy," the deputy said.

Mr. Loehmann reversed his car so fast that the deputy jumped back. Robert turned in his seat to watch the deputy through the rear window and saw that he was laughing.

After they passed the last tack and feed at the far end of Main Street, the road was bordered by woods. Cars and a few horses had crowded Main Street, but the county road was empty except for trees and farms. Robert peeked to see how fast Mr. Loehmann was driving: only fifty, the speedometer said. Still, the ride seemed fast and free. Papa always drove slowly, like an old man. *So no one has an excuse to pull me over,* he always said.

Robert pressed his own foot against an imaginary gas pedal, urging him to drive faster.

Sure enough, the car lurched ahead. Like magic.

"You act like you've never been in a car," Mr. Loehmann said.

"Not like this one."

Mr. Loehmann slumped lower in his seat, relaxing. He stretched out his arm. "Always wanted a Woodie, but the canvas roof wouldn't have survived New York winters. Then I moved down here. And they came out with this tin roof last year. I like her pretty well myself."

"Why'd . . ." Robert started to ask why he'd left New York to move to Gracetown, which felt like going about life backward. He had seen the grand city in picture shows and heard it sung in songs. But he had no business asking a grown-up, a white man, to explain himself.

"Sometimes life throws you a curveball, Robert, and you end up in places you never expected. My mother was reared in Tallahassee. When my father died in the war in '42—he enlisted as a surgeon—she moved to Gracetown to be near her family. Now she's sick, so I moved to be closer to her. But I'll tell you what: I never thought I'd live down here. Never in a million years."

It was an answer that opened more questions, but Robert did not ask how the man's father had died and if his mother had cancer like Mama.

"My mama was sick," Robert said. "Then she died."

Telling never made Robert feel better, but he couldn't help it. Her dying always sat at the tip of his tongue. Mr. Loehmann glanced at him with sadness that shocked Robert so much that it pricked his eyes.

"Sorry to hear it, Robert," he said. "You're young to lose your mother. Your father too?"

"No, sir. My papa's not dead. He's . . ." Robert remembered what his nervousness had made him forget in the courtroom: Papa being in Chicago was a secret. The sheriff in Gracetown might hate Papa enough to try to track him down. Now he'd gone and announced it in a courtroom where anyone might have heard—a judge! "He's somewhere else."

Mr. Loehmann asked his own questions with his eyes. Robert fidgeted and turned to his window. During the drive, woods had turned to cow pastures. Robert rarely traveled farther than walking distance, so he tried to memorize everything he saw: the hulking old tobacco barn, the skeletal oak burned dead at the roadside, the aging albino nag pulling a hay wagon under a farmer's watch. He filled his eyes to forget where he was going.

"Let your window down if you want," Mr. Loehmann said. "I like the air-conditioning, but my kids and our dog like the wind in their hair."

Despite the thrill of the cool air massaging him from the car's vents, Robert was glad to crank his window down. The wind was hot, like the car was taking off in space, breaking through the atmosphere with a *chunk-chunk-chunk* sound of the air thrashing inside the car.

Robert's stomach growled. Loudly.

"When's the last time you ate?" Loehmann said.

"Dinner. Last night." It seemed so long ago, Robert could barely remember the scrawny chicken wings he and Gloria had shared—scraps from Miss Anne's table, where wings were not anyone's favorite. And at least two days old to boot, judging by the toughness of the meat. Even the bones had been dry, with no good moist marrow to suck out. Gloria had sounded so proud when she brought the food home, he hadn't had the heart to complain. And with the pain in his ear pounding so bad, he'd barely noticed he was still hungry. And he'd been hungry when the deputy came. And hungry while he waited in the sun. He was so often hungry, sometimes he didn't notice it, the way he was getting used to the throbbing deep inside his ear. The drumbeat of pain had kept him awake much of the night, so he hadn't thought about being hungry.

"Nobody's fed you today?"

"No, sir."

Mr. Loehmann cursed then: "Damn hicks."

His anger frightened Robert. The car swerved slightly off the road, spitting gravel as Mr. Loehmann reached behind him to grab a Woolworth's sack from the back seat. Robert clung to his seat, bracing to feel the car roll into the parallel ditch. His favorite teacher, Mrs. Cherry, had died this way on a stormy night, her car running headlong into the earth.

Sack in his lap, Mr. Loehmann righted the car as if it had never strayed. "Take this. I was saving a sandwich for later."

Robert's mouth flooded. He grabbed the sack and rifled through, past napkins and paper straws. The sandwich was at the bottom, wrapped in paper. The soggy, toasted bread hugged lettuce and a yellow core he did not recognize right away.

"Egg salad," Mr. Loehmann said.

Robert could not remember ever eating egg salad. Mama had never made it, or Nana. Maybe Miz Lottie had made it for church picnics, but he'd never tried it. "I'll like it fine, sir." Robert hesitated, shy about saying grace before a stranger. His stomach rumbled again. Acid scalded his belly.

"Thought you were hungry," Mr. Loehmann said. "Like I tell mine, if you're hungry enough, you'll eat what's put in front of you. Go on, now."

Robert had forgotten that everyone didn't say grace. Or expect you to. Before now, he'd never seen it with his own eyes. His chin nestled his chest. *Thank you, dear Lord, for this bounty*—a silent, abbreviated version of Papa's dinnertime blessing. He took his first bite of the food, and it tasted more than fine, like the gift from God it was. A mash of boiled eggs and celery and mustard and pepper filled his cheeks, soft down his throat. Oh yes, but it was good. He'd hardly blinked before the first half of the sandwich was gone.

"Go on, eat the rest," Mr. Loehmann said. "I'll grab a bite somewhere else."

His stomach screamed for more, so Robert ate the second half, but more slowly this time, remembering that he might not eat for a long time again. What kind of food would he eat at the Reformatory? Nothing but porridge and gruel, like in Mama's storybooks? For the first time since he'd climbed into the grand car, Robert let himself think of the place. Let himself wonder.

"Better?" Mr. Loehmann said.

Robert forced a nod. He felt worse somehow. As if the food had awakened him. "Lyle McCormack started it," Robert said. "He pushed me first."

"Wondered when we'd get around to all that." Loehmann didn't sound interested. "You tell your side to the judge?"

Robert stared at his boots, which looked all the bigger now. He shook his head. "No, sir."

"Might've been a good idea, don't you think?"

"The deputy, he said keep my mouth shut."

Loehmann lit a cigarette with his car lighter. Then he cranked his window down a bit.

The swooshing wind in the car evened out, making it easier to hear through his sore ear's buzzing. "How long did the judge send you there for?"

"Six months!" Robert said, emotion cracking his voice. He'd counted on his fingers, and six months meant he wouldn't get out until January. He'd never spent Christmas away from home. "And Lyle started it. We weren't doin' nothin' but walkin' down the road. He started the whole thing."

"Well, I can note that in your file. *If* there's a file," Loehmann said. "And I can mention it to the judge when I see him next."

Robert's eyes widened. Mention it to the judge! In the hot sun all morning, he'd cursed himself for not telling the facts. He'd expected Gloria to explain, but the judge hadn't given her time. Could it all be set right now? Was it as simple as two white men passing in a hallway?

"But don't get your hopes up it'll change anything," Loehmann said. "I take it you know who the McCormacks are. Red McCormack owns half the county land, and no one wants to be on his wrong side when it's time to ask for favors. Whole town goes to church together, their children go to prom. Judge Morris was lenient, at least in his own mind."

Robert couldn't gather sense from what he'd just been told. What did any of that have to do with Lyle McCormack shoving him and looking at his sister that way? Touching her arm?

"You know what the word 'indefinite' means, Robert?" Loehmann said. Robert shook his head.

"'Indefinite' means for an undefined period of time—like forever. I've seen files for two or three runaways, white boys, who were sent to the Reformatory for an 'indefinite' sentence. That means there's no intention of setting them loose until they're twenty-one. So six months may seem like a long while to you . . . but the judge tried to go easy. You're too young to play football. Just be grateful for that."

The more Mr. Loehmann spoke, the more he confused Robert. What did he care about an election and proms and football? What did any of that have to do with him? He'd never heard the Reformatory was for boys as old as twenty-one. That did not fit the picture in his head of young Negro boys at desks.

And Loehmann had mentioned nothing about the thing that worried Robert most, aside from being away from Gloria so long. But Robert was shy about bringing the words to his lips.

"Are the stories true?" Robert said, inching up to it.

Loehmann took his eyes from the road again. He stared, not blinking. Funeral serious. "Which stories?"

"The . . ." Robert struggled with the word. "The . . . haints."

Loehmann looked relieved, his attention back on his driving. "Gracetown and its ghost stories. I've never seen a more superstitious place. All summer long with the kids I've seen, nothing but talk of strange noises in the house."

"Only children can see or hear," Robert said. "That's why."

He'd been foolish to think Mr. Loehmann would believe tales of haints. All grown-ups lost their patience for haints after a time, even Gracetown grown-ups—even if they'd seen the haints' mischief, or worse than mischief. In summer, sometimes babies died in their sleep, petrified by ghosts. Or kitchen dishes or farming equipment were broken overnight, the blame laid on the children. His friend Sammy had told him he'd seen a buck naked white woman standing in his bedroom door in the moonlight, and he'd peed his bed out of fear she might be real—because although Sammy was only twelve too, if anyone heard tales he'd been within six steps of a naked white woman, he'd be lynched for sure.

Loehmann chuckled. "Well, I'll tell you the same thing I tell the rest: there's no such thing as ghosts. That's an absolute fact. And even if there were, ghosts would be the last worry on my mind if

I were on my way to the Reformatory." He looked at Robert again when he said the last part, his eyes serious.

Ahead, four milking cows with bloated udders had wandered into the road, two in each lane. They only looked up when Loehmann beeped his horn. But aside from swishing their tails, they didn't move. The car came to a stop.

They sat and waited. Papa would have inched forward to nudge at the cows, but Mr. Loehmann didn't and Robert didn't dare tell him to. Maybe Loehmann was afraid of scratching his pretty new car—or maybe he knew even cows might try to ram you if they got mad. Still, anything that delayed his arrival to the Reformatory was fine with Robert Stephens.

A memory peeked out that Robert had tried to hide from: Sammy's brother Luke had died at the Reformatory. Three years ago, Luke and his friends had stolen a car parked behind the clothing store on Main Street, so he'd gotten a long sentence—and Sammy's family had been allowed to visit him only once. Sammy said he barely recognized Luke when he saw him: so thin, his eyes wild like a cat's, his face an old man's. His fingers shook. When Sammy asked him what had happened to him, Luke said the Reformatory was full of haints who kept him awake at night. Who sometimes dragged him from his bed. He said no one could sleep for the screams or the fear they might be next. And when Sammy asked Luke what the haints did after they dragged you away, he only shook his head in his old-man way with tears in his eyes. And Luke *never* cried, not even when he'd fallen from the big oak outside Sammy's house and broken his arm in two places. Sammy had nightmares after he visited Luke at the Reformatory, so his parents had never taken him back.

A year later, Sammy's family got a letter that Luke was dead. The warden said he'd died from heatstroke trying to run away, but no one believed that, least of all Sammy. Luke had been buried at the Reformatory without a proper funeral, so no one in his family had even been allowed to say goodbye. Sammy had told him at the fishing hole just two weeks before, "Your mama died from cancer, but my mama's been dead on her feet since Luke never came home."

Those ugly thoughts of Sammy had come only once his stomach was full, his hunger gone. He was sorting out the day in pieces.

"You seem to me like a smart boy, Robert."

"Yessir," Robert said, so as not to contradict him. His teacher sure didn't think so.

Mr. Loehmann stared at the cows, dangling his cigarette out of the window. "If you're smart, you'll learn enough to get out and stay out. That place pays the county a good sum for every boy sent there, so you've just been sold. Never forget that. They don't want to send you home. They want any excuse to keep you. Any special problems, any special talents, will mean trouble for you. Try to be invisible."

They were the scariest words anyone had ever spoken to Robert, aside from when Gloria said *Mama's dying*. The words punched Robert in the stomach, stealing the air from his lungs. He'd imagined going to classes and maybe doing some sweeping or picking.

"Did you hear me?"

"Yessir." A whisper.

"I don't mean to scare you, but I want you to have a chance to go home while you've still got some childhood left. So you can get back to a real school and make a life for yourself."

"It's not a school?"

"Oh, there are classrooms, but it's a prison for sure. I think you know that already."

The remnants of the sandwich he'd eaten tasted rotten in Robert's mouth. He wondered if he might spit up his lunch. Why hadn't he thought the word *prison* before? Robert was not tough like his father, who had once been a boxer. Only the toughest boys would be waiting in prison.

Just as Robert was sure he would pee himself the way Sammy had the night he saw the white-lady haint in his doorway, colors captured him through his window: the most beautiful peacock he'd ever seen strutted by the pond ahead, its tail fanned. He'd never imagined such colors. Joseph's coat in the Bible could have been spun from those feathers. Mama's smiling face came to mind, as if it lived in those colors.

"Some days, you'd see a dozen or more peacocks out here," Mr. Loehmann said.

"Can I get out and touch it?" Robert said.

"Sorry. He would run—or *you* would." Mr. Loehmann's voice turned hard on the last words, and they both knew it was true: Robert wanted to run. Robert's hand twitched toward the door handle, almost against his will.

With a stony jaw, Loehmann inched his car toward a gap in the cows and slowly gained speed as the cows obliged him, lazily clearing a path.

Robert stared over his shoulder at the peacock, trying to count the colors of its tail, which looked like a giant green fan with purple and blue eyes staring back at him. Green like the fishing hole. Dark blue like the stove's flames, another blue as pale as the June sky. Purple as deep as night. When the bird and its display became a pinprick down the road, and then only a memory, Robert's tears came again, setting his eyes afire. He would not cry, he told himself. He *would not.* He could not be a crybaby at the Reformatory. Tough kids would never let a crybaby alone.

Neither of them spoke a word the rest of the drive.

5

At first glance, Gloria could almost overlook the barbed wire at the top of the gate.

GRACETOWN BOYS' REFORMATORY—EST. 1901, the painted sign on the gate read in script worthy of a palace. On the other side of the driveway, a blue-and-yellow football banner flapped, tied to two-pointed iron gateposts: GRACETOWN BULLDOGS, 1A CHAMPIONS 1949 1947 1946.

The grounds were as beautiful as Gloria remembered, like a small college nestled between a pine tree farm on the west side, a cornfield to the east, and then just all wild woods. Even now, she could not unsee the loveliness of redbrick buildings and neat pathways cutting across an endless, neatly mown lawn. Was it two hundred acres? Much more, counting its farms. She hoped to go to Spelman College like Mama wanted her to one day—Papa had promised to do his best to help her fulfill Mama's dream for her—and the Reformatory did not look so different from the way she'd imagined that magical Atlanta campus. The gate stood wide open to the gravel path leading to the closest brick building, two stories high and woven with ivy.

But Gloria knew that evil isn't plain to the eye. She felt the gooseflesh of premonition across her arms: ugly was just beneath the surface of this place. She hadn't had a worried feeling so strong since the day she woke and saw Mama standing over the sink and knew she was a remnant of a bygone time, soon before the doctor said she had cancer. Why hadn't the premonition come when she'd been walking Robert to school? Why had it only come too late?

Here, doggie doggie.

The future memory in Gloria's head was so loud that she wondered if Miz Lottie had heard the mocking voice too. Or felt an age-old hanging tree somewhere in the woods, calling like a mournful bird just below her hearing. So much silent screaming. Or was it only crows? Although she was older now and the feelings weren't as strong, sometimes Gloria still had trouble telling what was real, what was only imagination.

Miz Lottie pulled her truck off to the side of the road just outside the gate, and they sat idling. Waiting to think of a plan. The truck's engine sputtered and complained as it idled. After a moment, Miz Lottie turned off the engine to save her gas. Gloria hoped they would be able to get Ole Suzy started up again for the drive home.

"Well, chile, if he's already here, they likely won't let you see him. Not 'til visiting days and whatnot." Miz Lottie's shoulders were hunched. She had shriveled to a knot in her seat. She was afraid of the place too.

"Shouldn't we drive in and ask to see the warden?"

Miz Lottie studied the gate entrance, uncertain. Her hands tightened on her steering wheel, then fell away. "With the trouble with your daddy . . . I don't b'lieve so, pumpkin."

"Why not? I haven't done anything wrong."

"Got nothin' to do with right and wrong," Miz Lottie said. "It might be worse on Robbie if we raise too much fuss. Like we think we're better'n other colored. We can wait awhile to see if he comes. If we're too late, we'll go back and call by phone and see when it's visiting day."

"That's not what Papa would do. He'd be in there right now."

"Uh-huh. Sho' he would," Miz Lottie agreed. "That's why your daddy got run off to Chicago. That's why he ain't here to raise and protect his chirren. You right about *that*. There's good men laying dead in the ground, early to meet their maker, 'cause o' the fuss he raised, gettin' those white folks so riled. Don't tell me nothin' 'bout what *he* would do." For the first time, Miz Lottie sounded upset, lapsing into country talk she avoided around Gloria, who had far surpassed Miz Lottie's third-grade schooling. Miz Lottie's parents had been slaves, and she had picked tobacco alongside them as sharecroppers until they died. She had fled a burning house as a child, and she'd lost kin in Rosewood. Gloria saw Rosewood in Miz Lottie's fearful eyes.

So Gloria couldn't call Miz Lottie stupid, weak, or a liar. Gloria had overheard many of her parents' late-night conversations, and Mama had warned Papa to count the cost of trying to organize the mill workers and register colored voters. This silver-haired woman with years etched in her face might smell like she soiled herself at times, but her mind was sharp and quick like Papa's. Miz Lottie and Papa were more alike than either of them would admit.

But, oh, did it sting. Gloria had never expected to park and wait by the gate like outlaws.

And what if they *weren't* too late and saw the deputy's car? That might be no better. "They'll drive right past us, Miz Lottie."

"But you can wave. You can let him see you. You can smile—he'll need a smile." Gloria doubted she would be able to smile. The idea of it brought back her tears. "Stop fretting," Miz Lottie said. "Just makes it worse."

A motor rumbled from the parallel road. A truck was coming, maybe two. Gloria's door squealed from rust when she opened it to hop to the ground.

"Don't go runnin' in the road!"

"I want him to see me."

"Well, don't you get locked up too!"

But the approaching vehicles weren't sheriff's cars: they were heavier, kicking up a veil of dust as they crawled past the stand of pines. The first vehicle lumbered out: a tractor hauling a trailer crowded with so many white boys with their legs hanging off the sides that it looked like a giant caterpillar as it drove past. Their swinging legs fell still when they saw her, and at least ten sets of eyes craned to see her. On Main Street, this passing truck would have subjected her to noisy taunts and come-ons, or nails and pencils thrown like missiles, but these boys stared as if she were a curious apparition. She stared back at faces weary at midday, gray work clothes grimy with soil.

The second tractor came at a steady pace behind it, identical except that the boys were Negro. And there were twice as many of them, at least twenty. Gloria's heart raced as she looked for Robert in their noses, chins, eyes, brows, craning to see any faces hidden on the far side. She took a few running steps after the tractor, and some of the boys grew anxious, half rising to see if she were a loved one. Some were teenagers, some as young as Robert, sweaty brown skin glistening. But she did not see Robert, so her running halted as the second truck followed the first through the reformatory gate.

Gloria's disappointment at not seeing Robert warred with her relief. He was not yet among those tired-eyed, overworked boys.

"Guess they send 'em out to work in the mornings," Miz Lottie said.

"Send them where?"

"I don't know, chile. The Reformatory's got all manner of farms. They grow enough corn for the whole county. They work these boys out here. Or lease 'em out."

Papa's greatest hope was that Robert would not be tied to any white man's field or grove, and Robert was already bound for that fate at twelve. He should be at school, not at a work camp! This *had* to be a bad dream, and she would wake again with no deputy at their door.

Then a green station wagon with wood panels appeared from the main road, a white man at the wheel. The car slowed—and Gloria saw Robert. He was bouncing up and down in the passenger seat, and she heard him through the open window: "It's her! That's my sister, Gloria!"

The car had hardly rocked to a stop before Robert jumped out and ran to her with so much fervor that he nearly tripped over his feet. He did not look harmed, and his face was alive with joy that was contagious. She heard herself laughing as she clung so tightly to Robert that their hearts raced side by side.

"You all right? Nobody hurt you?" Gloria said.

"Naw—he gave me a sandwich."

For the first time, Gloria took in the tall young white man in a gray linen suit climbing out of his car. She expected him to be angry, but instead he only looked resigned and harried, wiping his brow with a handkerchief. He casually angled himself between Gloria and the truck, an obstacle if she tried to run with Robert. He looked furtively toward the Reformatory grounds. "Haddock's a stickler for rules, so hurry and say your goodbyes," he said. "Visiting hours are Sundays. I think it's twelve to two."

Gloria knew right away that the man wasn't from Florida, or anywhere in the South. That was plain in his northern accent, his casual manner among Negroes. Gloria's heart jumped.

"Can you help us, sir?" she said. "This is all a misunderstanding. Robert's a good boy; he doesn't belong in a place like this. The judge just didn't give us time to explain."

"Yeah, he seems like a good kid," the man said, but without hopefulness. "Like I told him, I'll try to have a word with the judge. Still, six months—that's not too bad. He does what he's told, he'll be all right."

"But, sir . . ." Gloria's mind raced as she tried to think of a way to make more of an impression on him, to let him know that Robert Stephens was not a sack of feed to be disposed of for an entire half a year. "My name is Gloria Stephens. That lady in the truck, she's Lottie Mae Powell, Robert's godmother." Miz Lottie gave him a wave.

He smiled a friendly smile, tipping his hat to Miz Lottie. He raised his voice to address Miz Lottie as well. "David Loehmann. I'm a social worker based out of Tallahassee. I was in Gracetown on other business, so I was asked to give Robert a ride. What happens now is, ma'am, I'll take him to the superintendent, Mr. Haddock, to process him in. He'll get clothes, shoes, meals, anything he needs. The boys sleep in dorms. He'll be on the colored side."

"But they'll put him to work?" Gloria asked. The tractor trucks were still visible, shrinking as they drove deeper into the campus. "What about school?"

"All the boys work a bit. But don't you worry: he'll also get his schooling here. I know the teachers, and they're quite fine. They're paid well, so it's a plum job for them."

The girl's eyes sopped up every word David Loehmann spoke. She was a pretty girl, with bright, almond-shaped eyes. A smart girl. She and the boy too. Loehmann poured cheer into his voice, perhaps too much, but he couldn't make himself bring bad news to Gloria Stephens and her eyes. Or that old woman in the truck, who looked ready to faint in the heat.

So, *these* were Robert Stephens's people. He'd heard complaints about Robert Stephens's unionizing efforts almost from the time he and his family got off the train, and it had struck him how courageous it was to try to organize Negroes in the heart of the land of lynching. He had noticed that no Negroes dared venture to town after dark in Gracetown.

"The nigger Stephens" fueled conversation at lunch counters and diners as far as Tallahassee, so he hadn't been surprised by the allegation of rape. David Loehmann didn't know what had or hadn't happened outside of Pixie's that night, but he'd heard a rumor at the courthouse that the girl, Lorraine, hadn't even been there when the attack supposedly took place, that it was her married boyfriend on the town council who'd beaten her bloody. Heard another rumor that Robert Stephens didn't frequent Pixie's, a segregated roadhouse just outside the Gracetown border, either. Which would explain why Sheriff Posey hadn't scoured the ends of the earth to try to bring Robert Stephens back to Gracetown to face justice. How hard would it be to find him, with his children still living locally?

But they'd found a way to get to Robert Stephens, all right: through his boy. Sentencing the younger Robert Stephens to the Reformatory might be a way to lure the elder Robert Stephens back home. Or a petty retribution like his father had faced organizing workers in the AFL in New York before the war. As bad as that had been, he'd witnessed how much worse circumstances were for Negroes in the South, or even the poor crackers down here whose sole comfort was knowing they were better off than Negroes.

But he'd promised Sarah. The boys were already getting teased over their curly dark hair, accused of being "part nigger" in addition to being Jews. Writing checks in New York was one thing, but raising his head in Florida would be a good way to get their house burned down. As soon as he'd heard the names Robert Stephens and Lyle McCormack, he'd known this case could be none of his business. Hell, he'd halfway expected that pimple-faced deputy to tail him to the Reformatory just to try to intimidate him. He worked long days and nights to try to improve conditions for white and Negro children alike through his job, giving them equal attention and care. Sometimes the only justice was a hot meal and a bed to sleep in.

". . . so there's not much more you can do," he heard himself saying. He didn't want to be seen talking to Robert Stephens's family. A white gardener by the gate was already edging closer, maybe trying to listen. "But like I said, don't you worry. It'll all turn out all right."

The old woman, the girl, and the boy all stared, not believing him. Their eyes reminded him that his distant cousins might have had similar conversations with bureaucrats in Munich before they were sent to the train cars.

"Sir, my brother didn't have a lawyer," Gloria said. "Wasn't he supposed to?"

Loehmann sighed. This girl was too smart for her own good. "Well, that all depends. Not so much with a juvenile case, since there was no jury trial. That meeting with Judge Morris was more an informal thing."

"But shouldn't there have been?" Gloria said. "A jury trial? If he committed a crime?" Robert clung to his sister, swaying with anticipation as if any coming word might free him. He trusted her with his life. "So we could tell our side?"

"Again, not with a juvenile case, a minor offense. You'd see a jury trial with bigger crimes. This was left to the judge's discretion."

Gloria blinked. The tears she was hiding appeared like a slap across his face. "Did Robert tell you how Lyle McCormack grabbed my arm on the road? Said improper things to me? That Robert was just defending me from Lyle McCormack's advances?"

Loehmann's mouth went dry. "No, miss, he didn't. I'm terribly sorry."

The girl waited for everything he wished he could give her. He wasn't from Gracetown, so she expected something different from him. The old woman's eyes had nearly popped out of her head when he called her *ma'am*. He'd tried to shake the habit, but politeness was a lesson as old as brushing his teeth. He couldn't understand calling silver-haired Negro men and women *gal* or *auntie* or *boy* or *uncle*. He had yet to learn the language in Florida.

"Is there a way I can reach you?" Gloria said in a tight voice. "Do you have a card?"

Loehmann made a show of patting his pockets, as if he didn't have at least a dozen cards tucked into his billfold if he looked for them. "Out of cards, but I'm with state children's services. L-O-E-H-M-A-N-N. Just look me up if you need me."

An image came to Loehmann unbidden: the bedraggled white mother who'd stopped him in the hallway with a story that her son had been beaten like a mule by Superintendent Haddock himself. And her insistence that she knew another mother afraid to step forward whose son had never made it home after he tried to run away, and they were sure he'd been killed.

With a flare of conscience, Loehmann almost reached to give Gloria Stephens his card after all, since his home telephone number was printed there, but he thought of his sons and couldn't. He'd been in Florida less than a year. He couldn't afford idealistic mistakes when he was still learning the customs where some townspeople scorned "nigger lovers" worse than Negroes. Mikey and Josh were still crying themselves to sleep at night after the umpteenth playground skirmish. Next year, God willing, he would send them to private school. Maybe he could risk crossing Haddock then.

And Gloria saw it all in his face. He would not help her further.

"Well, this cannot happen to my brother, Mr. Loehmann," she said. "I'm getting Robert out of here. No matter what it takes."

"Then he's in the best of hands," he said cheerfully. But his eyes winced.

Far-off machinery whirred in the sad and silent afternoon. Gloria hugged Robert, resting her chin on top of his springy hair, damp from perspiration. How tall would he be when he finally came home again? He shuddered against her with a sob, and she stroked his back.

"You hear me, Robert?" she whispered. "I'll get you out as soon as I can." Robert nodded against her. His hot tears seeped through her dress.

"At least I got to see you, right, little peanut?"

He nodded again. Not seeing Gloria today would have been unimaginable. The sight of Gloria and Miz Lottie waiting by the gate had proven that God *was* watching over him after all, just like Mama had said.

"You be extra good, do your lessons, and stay away from troublemakers," Gloria said.

"I'll send you a sweet potato pie!" Miz Lottie called, and Robert smiled. She never let him forget the time, at six, he'd swiped half of a pie all to himself from her table. "Come here, boy. Give me some sugar."

Robert ran to the truck's driver's-side window and stood on the sideboard to reach her.

Her kiss was hurried against his cheek. She nestled his good ear to whisper. "Don't let nobody in here, white or colored, know how smart you is. Hear? And don't never talk about yo' daddy."

"Yes'm," Robert said.

"Invisible, Robert," Mr. Loehmann said from the road. "Stay clear of the superintendent." Mr. Loehmann's voice broke the spell of comfort. Robert remembered the things Loehmann had said in the car that he had not repeated to Gloria and Miz Lottie. And that was best, or Gloria would be crying too.

Robert wiped his tears. He had to get used to having no one to hug or go crying to. With Mama and Papa gone, he was mostly used to it already.

"Maybe there's a piano here," Robert said.

"Oh, that there is!" Loehmann said. "There's a Negro marching band too. They march in the Christmas parade. I'll tell the staff you like music."

They all pretended to smile. Gloria grabbed Robert for a last squeeze packed with sadness, but again Robert pulled away.

"I'm not a baby," he said. "I'm not scared."

She cupped his cheek. "Bullshit," she whispered, and they both smirked. Robert had never heard Gloria cuss like a man. He almost laughed, then realized that was why she'd done it.

Robert ran back toward his open car door. He still had a ride in the car before they reached the buildings, a long path ahead. Until he was inside the place, the worst hadn't started.

"See you on Sunday, Robert!" Gloria called after him.

"Like I said, I think visiting hours are twelve to two, but check on that," Loehmann said. "You need to get your name on the list before you come, or they'll turn you away. You can call to schedule your visit anytime between nine and five—regular business hours. It's best to call early in the week, though. Slots fill up fast."

"Thanks for your help, sir." Gloria barely kept the sarcasm from her voice. Two slamming car doors and the car's whisper on the road ended the visit. From the woods, all of them noticed the rough, low sound of barking.

II

THE REFORMATORY

6

Just past the gate, the smell of smoke was so strong that Robert cranked up his window. He looked for signs of fire in the woods and outbuildings but saw none. Still, he nearly gagged on the smell. The taste of sour eggs played on his tongue.

"Where's that smoke at?" Robert said.

Mr. Loehmann gave him a blank glance. The closer they came to the paved circular driveway in front of the nearest brick building—and they were upon it in no time—the more Loehmann's face hardened into a mask more like the deputy's. The invisible smoke fed the sick feeling in Robert's stomach: no longer hunger, but far worse.

"You know how to cook?" Loehmann said.

"I can boil rice and scramble eggs." Gloria had taught him since Papa left. She complained it wasn't fair she had to spend half her day cooking and then cook for him too.

"Then be sure to say so. Kitchen's not a bad job, and Negro boys work the kitchen. That way, you won't be out in the sun."

Could that be where the smoke was from? The kitchen? But, no—it smelled like *burning*, not cooking. Like the woods were ablaze all around them. Or the school itself. But Robert did not ask Loehmann again. How could Loehmann *not* smell it?

Maybe he was only smelling smoke because it was summer, when things that weren't real had a smell, or a taste. Or made strange sounds. Usually, children's summer sights and smells went away if you ignored them. That was how Gloria said it was for her, before she got too old to notice them as much. Summertime was when the haints came out. Did some haints smell like smoke?

They rolled up to a circular driveway, and the Reformatory's main building appeared as if the windshield were a picture show screen. The building was two stories high, with tall windows and a coat of green vines almost covering the brick walls. The vines looked like a beard beneath two windows on the top floor that stared like hollow eyes.

Robert had never seen a building that looked so alive—*waiting* for him, even. This was a bad place, and this building was the heart of the badness.

Robert expected Loehmann to race away from the driveway to protect him, but instead the car stopped and Loehmann turned off his radio. He reached into his jacket pocket and pulled out a billfold. He slipped out a small white card and gave it to Robert. "Should've given this to your sister, but that's my number. You need me, call me."

"But—" *You can't leave me here by myself,* he wanted to say, but he didn't have time before Loehmann was out of the car and gesturing for Robert to slide out after him, one last scoot across the sweat-damp leather. Robert touched the shiny steering wheel and tapped his boot on the gas pedal, wishing the engine were still running. Then he was standing outside, the adventure over. The rest was coming.

Robert's pants didn't have pockets, and he was sure he wouldn't be allowed to wear Papa's mill shirt. He saw a few white boys laying bricks on the side of the building, their rhythm quick and sure, and their shirts were identical gray. Robert gave the card the barest glance—*David R. Loehmann, State of Florida Children's Services*—and slipped it into his boot, snug in his sock. Maybe it would be safe there. Maybe he could keep hold of one thing.

Six wide brick steps led inside the Gracetown School for Boys. The front room was large, like a museum. A portrait of Florida governor Fuller Warren stood high on the wall, a face he knew from an identical portrait in his school hallway. Mr. Harris had told his class the governor had made a speech against the Klan.

("If that ain't the pot callin' the kettle black," Papa had said.) In his portrait, at least, he had kind eyes. Beside the portrait, a large glass case showed off photographs of smiling white boys, trophies, and football pennants.

Below the trophy case was a sofa long enough to stretch across half his house end to end.

Beside the sofa was the biggest radio Robert had ever seen, with a wooden cabinet at least twenty years old, standing on four legs like furniture. The radio was silent, but Robert imagined he would hear it all the way back to the gate.

Robert stared at the radio so long that he almost didn't notice the white woman at her desk near a closed door. The woman had brown-red hair piled atop her head and wore matching eyeglasses. Loehmann went to her and tipped his hat.

"Mornin', Doris. This is the boy from Judge Morris," he said. "Robert Stephens."

She waved a sheet of paper. "Don't bother with section B."

Loehmann leaned over and began scribbling. "Can't do much with A either."

"That won't matter none," she said. "Superintendent Haddock will take care of it. This the one who kicked Lyle McCormack?" She craned to look at Robert, whose heart throbbed when he heard Lyle's name. Did everyone know?

Seeing him, her eyebrows jumped with surprise. She grinned. "This scrawny little nigger? Red's called over here twice already, and you should hear him wailing about Lyle and football camp. Like Lyle just boxed a round with Joe Louis himself."

"I expect Robert's got the worst of it," Loehmann said, still writing. Robert had noticed his hand pause when the woman said *nigger*, but he'd started up writing again.

The woman wagged her fountain pen at Robert, her grin gone. "What was in your thick head? I guess the apple don't fall far from the tree."

She was talking about Papa! Robert's rage from McCormack

Road returned. "Lyle McCormack pushed me first," he said, the way he wished he had in front of the judge—though maybe not as loudly. "Ma'am."

The woman looked startled, then her face pinched with anger. She glanced back at Loehmann. "They'll teach him how to behave here. That's one thing certain."

Loehmann handed the form back to her. "Oh—he cooks."

The woman punched a button and leaned over a speaker on her desk. "He's here, Superintendent Haddock. The one you've been waiting for. Robert Stephens."

Loehmann didn't meet Robert's eyes. Instead, he patted Robert's back—once, twice, three times—and was gone.

The smoky smell grew stronger when Robert opened the warden's door.

Tremors raced up and down Robert's legs as he walked into Fenton J. Haddock's office, making him cling to the doorknob to stay upright. The tall window behind his desk gave the office so much raw sunlight that Haddock was a silhouette before him, as if he had no face. He felt as big as the cigarette-choked room, the tallest man Robert had ever seen.

"Go'n—close it behind you," Haddock said, his low voice scraping the floor.

Robert was so quick to comply that the door slammed. Robert's bladder pulsed in a way it had not since he was younger. He prayed he wouldn't pee, tightening his legs to prevent it.

Haddock pointed toward a rug beside his bookshelf. "Lemme get a look at you."

Robert prayed that he could walk without stumbling or peeing as he shuffled to the green-and-brown braided rug, keeping his eyes so low he could barely see in front of him. The rug's pattern looked like railroad tracks. His heart shook his ribs.

"Candy?" Haddock said.

Robert was confused until he looked up and saw a crystal candy jar at the edge of the desk, brimming with wrapped red-and-white mints like the ones Miz Lottie brought to church to keep him from squirming with boredom.

"Go on. Take one," Haddock said, more a command than an offer, so Robert took a mint and held it in his palm, squeezing tight. It didn't occur to him to open the wrapper or try to slip it into his mouth. He couldn't help believing the kindness was a kind of trick, and he didn't think he could produce enough moisture in his mouth to suck on the candy anyway.

Haddock sat atop his desk with his knee hiked high, smoking his cigarette a long while. His face was narrow and hollowed at the cheeks when he took a draw. Robert looked away from him so he wouldn't be accused of staring. A small family portrait on the bookshelf looked a hundred years old, in an oval frame like the ones Mama liked to hang: a white family in old-fashioned dress crowded on a sofa in a sitting room—a man, a woman, and a reedy young boy with an infant girl in a dressing gown in his lap. The baby girl faced forward, but her eyes were closed; she was sleeping against the boy's chest. The photo was cheerless. For a reason Robert couldn't name, the faces made him so uneasy that he snatched his eyes away.

"I oughta give you twenty lashes—I promised Red I would—but I've got a headache and I don't need the hollerin'," Haddock said. For the first time, Robert noticed the thick leather strap hanging on the wall behind Haddock's desk, big enough to drive a mule. Maybe he had seen it from the start, but he hadn't *let* himself see it before.

Robert tried to say *Yessir* but he couldn't push air to his throat. Papa said if he stumbled across a panther or injured wild hog in the woods, sometimes the only thing to do was stand frozen. That was how he felt, facing off against a creature that could maul him.

"Doris, she don't care for the hollerin'. Says she can't hear herself think. Sometimes she'll get up and go out to the church or take a walk and won't come back for an hour just to be sure the beating's done." Haddock smiled. "Sure enough, sometimes it ain't. Not by a ways." He took a long drag on his cigarette.

Was it a game to Haddock, trying to make him cry? Would the strap come off the wall if he did? *Don't cry. Don't pee. Don't look. Don't move. Don't breathe.*

Haddock sat quietly a moment while his office clock ticked tiny explosions. "You see that sign above the door? Can you read?"

"Yessir." Robert looked for the words seared into a glossy board of wood. He had trouble making out the letters.

"Read that sign to me."

Was it possible to forget letters of the alphabet? As Robert tried to read the words, the shapes looked like nonsense. The script was odd, with strange flourishes. Icy sweat sprang across his face and chest. His legs quaked. "H-he that . . ."

"Speak up."

Robert tried to huff air past his shrinking throat. "'He that spareth . . .'" It was a Bible passage, from Proverbs! He knew it from Sunday school. The rest tumbled out nearly from memory: "'. . . his rod hateth his son: but he that loveth him chasteneth him betimes.'"

"Well, how 'bout that?" Haddock said. "You read pretty."

"I l-learnt it in church, sir." Too late, Robert remembered Miz Lottie's warning not to let anyone know how smart he was. "I c-could barely see them words up there."

"Here's what that sign really says in plain English: as an officer of the state, I will beat you bloody and sleep like a babe at night because it will make you a better man. God himself says so. Do you understand?"

"Y-yessir."

Haddock stood up and walked a step closer to Robert with each growling sentence that spilled from his lips. "This reformatory is my domain. And in my domain, there is no swearing, no sassing, no unruly or disrespectful behavior of any kind. Every man is 'sir' and every woman is 'ma'am.' You do what you're told when you're told to do it, or your back will be full of stripes. And if you try to run away . . ." He paused, rage passing across his face and lips. His eyes stared through Robert to a faraway place Robert never wanted to follow him to. His voice went quiet, like a pastor's during prayer. ". . . not only will I keep you here until you're twenty-one, but you will be beset by dogs, clubs, or bullets. You will surely wish you'd never been born."

Robert blinked furiously to try to stop his tears, but one slipped free down his cheek. He lost his battle with his bladder and felt hot urine wash his thighs. He thanked the Lord his shirt was so long; maybe Haddock wouldn't see. *Please don't let it drip down to the floor. Please don't let it muss his rug.* Could Haddock hear his heart thrashing? Haddock breathed smoky breath down on him.

"You hear me?"

"Yessir." A whisper was all Robert could manage.

"I'm your last chance, boy," Haddock said. "A Negro child who'll kick a white man will grow up to poison society and his own race. *If* he grows up. Getting sent here is the luckiest thing could have happened to you."

"Yessir."

Haddock gave Robert a long look. Then he walked to a shelf in the rear of his office and pulled down a gray shirt, a tie, and dungarees. While Haddock's back was turned, Robert desperately checked himself to see if any pee had dripped down to the floor. He felt moisture down to his socks. But not on the rug. Not the rug, thank God.

"You get one set of clothes and one set only. You lose or muss these clothes, you get a whupping. You'll get your Sunday shirt in your dorm. You wear the tie to church. You lose the tie, you get a whupping. Understand?"

"Yessir."

The long pause confused Robert while Haddock waited. "Well, go'n, then. Strip down."

Robert had never undressed in front of anyone who wasn't

family except the doc when he had chicken pox blisters all over his body. He fumbled to untie his boots first. Next he unbuttoned his pants, relieved that Haddock was still behind him and would not see any stains. Better to strip buck naked than to let the warden see the mess he'd made. He quickly pulled down his pants, wiping down dampness as he went; he hadn't had time to find his drawers before the deputy came, so he wasn't wearing any. He balled the pants on the floor, beyond the rug's border. Papa's shirt still nestled him, but Robert saw with horror that urine had carved bright brown trails down his ashy legs. Could Haddock smell it?

"I said *strip down*. Everything except your socks."

The buttons of his shirt nearly broke as Robert tugged at them. He dropped his shirt atop his pants on the floor. The cold gooseflesh across Robert's skin had nothing to do with the hot room. Every part of him was shaking now, not just his legs.

"Bend over. Spread your cheeks. Hurry up, now."

Robert started to bend right away, blood rushing to his head, but the words *spread your cheeks* had no meaning. His hands felt ready to shake loose. "S-sir, what . . . ?"

"Your *ass* cheeks, boy. Gimme a look-see. Make sure you're not hiding nothin'."

Robert trembled like he might have if he were naked in the snow. He hoped the lady at the desk outside would not come inside and no one would see him through the windows. While he struggled to grip his skin with slippery fingers, holding himself in this unnatural way, he remembered the card in his sock and wondered if Haddock would find it. Should he say something now? Would Haddock beat him if he didn't? Or if he did?

"All right, turn around," Haddock said.

Robert turned slowly, his hands falling to hide himself, his heartbeat a flurry. "You're not big enough to be worth a damn to me," Haddock said, half to himself.

"I . . . I c-cook, s-sir." All he could remember was Loehmann's last words: *He cooks.*

Anything to take this man's attention away from his bare skin.

For the first time, Haddock looked pleased. "That right?"

"Yessir. A little."

Haddock stared at Robert a long while. What was he looking for now?

Haddock suddenly tossed the pile of clothes to him, and Robert caught everything except the tie, which fell to the side. When his genitals were exposed, Haddock's stare deepened and the air in the room grew nearly too heavy to breathe. Papa would not like this one bit. Or Gloria.

Robert thought of Papa's stories of slaves being carried from Africa, sold at market like hogs. "There's a pair o' drawers inside the dungarees," Haddock said, still studying him.

"Yessir."

Robert found thin blue boxer shorts, like Papa wore, and slipped them on so fast he nearly lost his balance. He could breathe more easily once the boxers were on. They were a little big too, like the dungarees and shirt, but not as big as his boots. After he'd slipped his boots back on his feet—his socks were a little damp, but not too bad—he carefully picked up the tie and folded it the way he'd seen Papa fold his on Sundays, laying it across his arm. He grabbed the bundle of soiled clothes with his other arm and held them against his hip, hoping the pee wouldn't smell or stain his new, fresh-smelling clothes. Every motion held his hope that Haddock would not be displeased or find a reason to grab his strap.

"I'm gonna call over to one of your dorm masters to take you to class. School's in session for another hour. Then you'll go straight to the kitchen. But don't lose that tie."

"No, sir. I won't."

Haddock rubbed his temples. "This headache's got the upper hand now, but I'll give you your twenty lashes. You just won't know when, day or night."

Robert didn't answer. His tears tried to return. How could he sleep knowing that Haddock might come to beat him at any time?

Haddock walked toward his door. He stopped before the bookshelf with the framed family photo Robert had noticed. "You were lookin' at this?"

"I . . ." A lie tried to sprout—*What if he wasn't supposed to?*—but Robert told the truth. "Yessir. I saw it."

"This here's my family. That boy is me when I was just six years old. Holding my sister." His voice grew gentle. "June of 1900, so it's fifty years ago now, almost to the day. But it could've been last week, as well as I remember it. Mama wanted to hold her, but she wasn't up to it. They hired a photographer from town, made a big to-do. That was the tradition back then, or no one would remember your face. I was the only one strong enough. The only one." Haddock looked over his shoulder at Robert with the same storm in his face Robert had seen when he warned him against running away. "Truth was, I never wanted a baby sister."

An icy sting shot across Robert's skin. The smell of smoke choked him again—not cigarette smoke, but the terrible charred smell that had met him at the gate. Robert squeezed the peppermint in his fist more tightly, waiting for something terrible he could not name.

Haddock went to his door and opened it to call out. "Doris, tell Boone to come fetch him. And bring me some Bayer's. Cancel my one o'clock call, hear?"

"Yessir, Superintendent Haddock," he heard the woman say, chipper.

Robert dared one last look at the photograph, at the infant in the dressing gown, eyes closed tight. Yes, something was terribly wrong with the photo, every piece of it. The mother's eyes were wild with grief. The father's face looked whittled to the bone. Only young Fenton Haddock wore the barest trace of a smile. Robert finally understood what he had almost seen at first glance: the limp baby sister Haddock hugged to his chest was dead.

7

Robert was glad when the man who came to fetch him at the rear door was a Negro. But this Negro laid cold eyes into him, roughly grabbing Robert's arm to pull him outside through a rear door, already cussing: "If you think a ashy li'l damn coon like you's *ever* gonna get the best of Boone, you can lay down an' die right now. 'Cuz there ain't been one yet, and won't never *be* one." He squeezed Robert's arm hard enough to pinch bone. "You hear me?"

"Y-yessir." Robert noticed how thick-chested Boone was, his arms swollen with muscle. Like Papa, but not as tall. Boone wasn't even six inches taller, but big in the ways that mattered.

"I don't give a damn about you—'til you mess up. Then you gonna be *all* I care about."

"Yessir."

"When Warden Haddock say, 'Boone, who's ready to go home?' if Boone don't call yo' name loud and clear, you gonna stay here 'til you don't remember nothin' else. You gotta git past Boone."

"Yessi—"

"If Boone say, 'Lights out,' you better be the first one 'sleep. If Boone say jump over the barn, you best learn how to fly."

Boone was walking so fast that Robert stumbled to keep pace to reduce the pinch to his arm, his boots ready to slip off. Even concentrating on his feet and stones hidden in the grass that might trip him, he noticed Boone's odd habit of calling his own name—Papa said only conceited or crazy people did that—and how his words rushed out in a fountain, his voice not changing as if he were reading from a schoolbook. *He just wants to scare me,* Robert thought, and his nervous heart slowed. *Him and the warden both. They just want to put on a show.*

So Robert made his first promise to himself as the newest resident of the Gracetown School for Boys: he would please the adults by acting scared, but he would never *be* scared from that moment. He would never again wet his pants. Maybe the warden's threat to give him twenty lashes was just like a church school skit for every new boy. Robert let himself forget, for the moment, the terror that had crawled in his belly with his last glance at the photograph of Haddock holding his dead sister. Mama and God would protect him from evil, he decided. So he would put on his own show with a sad, scared face.

Boone stopped his march and stared Robert down again. "What I just said?"

It was like Mr. Harris's hourly quizzes to him at school, since Robert sometimes forgot to hide how far his attention had wandered. Not listening was a sure way to get a paddling, so Robert had trained himself to recall words even when he did not remember hearing them.

"'And if you give that schoolteacher a lick of trouble, you'll deal with Boone,'" Robert recited. For his life, Robert would not have remembered the sentence before, but his partial recall satisfied Boone, who yanked him forward again.

"You damn right you will."

At that instant, in the middle of the bare field between the warden's office and the colored schoolhouse, the first unusual incident happened to Robert Stephens at the Reformatory: his skin began to burn. He cried out and swatted at the arm Boone held as if it were swarmed with bees. If not for Boone's stare, Robert might have tried to pull away.

"S-somethin' bit me, sir," Robert said, a lie. An insect's bite did not feel like fire. He had touched flames somehow.

And the heat! The June sun in Gracetown from noon until dusk was almost as legendary as the sun in July or August, but the wall of heat he passed through with Boone was packed more tightly, a baking oven. The air was too hot to breathe, stinging his nostrils and throat. But Boone just kept walking and talking, his voice lost in a deafening whooshing sound plugging Robert's ears. His sore eardrum pounded him. His skin felt like it was sizzling grease in a pan. The sky above him went black as he waded into thick smoke.

Then came the worst: the screams. Mama had whimpered and screamed in her sickness, but Robert had never heard human screams so wretched they were like animals. The sound was solid enough to touch, all around him. Boys. A room of screaming boys. Burning in a fire.

In a flash of knowing as thin as a spider's web, Robert *saw* the writhing boys, faces twisted with pain and terror, half hidden in the smoke clouds, some already charred black. They pounded with frantic arms against a wall, thunder.

Begging and screaming. Dying.

Boone gave him a hard yank again, and Robert was plucked from the smoke and the burning room, only in the empty field strewn with pine needles and cones again. He expected to see the soil charred black behind him, but nothing remained of his vision except a watery dance like the air above a campfire.

Robert panted at the coolness, trying to soothe his lungs. Had Boone felt it too?

Boone leered back at him as if they were sharing a joke children shouldn't hear. "You like that?" Boone said.

Mute, Robert shook his head.

Strange excitement played in Boone's eyes—or *behind* them. "Ev'rybody don't go home," Boone said. "You best 'member that every damn day."

Robert nodded, his eyes so wide, they hurt from the effort of holding back tears.

Boone leaned closer. His breath smelled like rotten teeth. "Don't listen to them haints," he said. "Or you'll be a haint too."

And Boone pulled Robert up the steps to the schoolhouse.

Still shaken from the phantom fire, Robert summoned all his will to show no tears as he stood before the classroom. He was wrapped in screams, trembling from flames. He'd hoped the teacher would continue her lesson, but the hand of the young Negro woman fell still on the chalkboard and every eye turned to him.

With Boone's shadow in the doorway, at least thirty colored boys sat with backs high in their desks, hands folded, at attention. Strangers, all of them. Not a single face from church or school. Their curiosity was deep enough to cut his skin. Robert saw noise in their faces—questions, taunts, threats. From their scowls and curled lips, three or four of the bigger boys in the back row had decided they already didn't like him—that it would be their job, not Boone's, to teach him about life at the Reformatory. In the front row, smaller boys looked at him with sad eyes that seemed to say, *Can you smell the fire too?*

"Tell the class your name and then have a seat in the second row." The teacher spoke carefully like Mama, but her face might never have smiled once.

"Yes'm," Robert said. When he reached for an imaginary cap on his head, almost everyone smiled, though no one laughed aloud. "I'm . . . Robert Stephens."

"I'm Mrs. Pournelle. Take your seat. Thank you, Boone." Boone half bowed to the teacher before he turned to leave.

"Paper and pencil are in the desk. You get one pencil only—and we count pencils at the end of class. Boone's run through the rest of the rules. Find an empty cubby to put your things."

She pointed vaguely, and Robert struggled to see past the wrenched faces and scrabbling arms that still seemed to reach for him, the *BOOM* of so many hands pounding the wall. He finally saw past his memories to a row of bland, open shelves. Most were empty, so Robert shoved his soiled clothes on a lower shelf and hoped no one would smell the pee.

The teacher began her lesson again, but Robert felt the boys' eyes watching him, judging and assessing. He looked at no one as he made his way to the nearest empty desk in the second row, closer to the door than the window. No window seats were free. Far across the room, through the window, he saw thick rows of corn in the sun, too short to be ready for harvest. He sat a moment staring at the corn but only hearing screams, seeing only fire. His breathing sped until he had to curl his fingers hard around the edge of his desk to slow it.

The boy next to him roughly nudged Robert's foot—Robert must have crossed an invisible line, an insult—so Robert moved his feet closer together. He did not look at the boy to challenge him. He was still trying to unsee the burning boys.

The fire is gone, he told himself. *Those boys aren't real.*

But they had been real, once upon a time. Those boys were ghosts now. Anyone who'd been reared in Gracetown knew ghosts were real, especially to children, but some people were lucky enough to rarely, or never, cross the ghosts of strangers. Was there a marker on that spot in the empty field? He must never walk there again. *Never.*

Robert felt a sinking panic that he would never break free of the fire's spell. Then he remembered the paper and pencil promised in his desk. He lifted the lid and found a fresh notebook with lined paper and one fat pencil, hardly sharp. He had not used such a fat pencil since he was in the second grade, and he was in the sixth grade now.

But Robert began writing, hardly aware of the teacher's words. He had forgotten her name, and her voice sounded as if she bored herself, but he clung to each word and wrote everything she said to clear his head, trying to escape his horrible passage. Slowly, the classroom felt more real than the fire and his fingers stopped trembling against his pencil. He saw the room around him: the large cards with cursive uppercase and lowercase letters of the alphabet lined up above the chalkboard just like Mr. Harris's, but Mr. Harris had a portrait of W. E. B. Du Bois pinned to the board instead of President Truman. The classroom was also bigger than his class at Douglass, the desks newer—the way he'd imagined a white school.

Mrs. (Pournelle?) was tall enough to wrestle any of the boys. She was speaking in an end-of-the-day drone, like when his real teacher Mr. Harris's temper was short and he checked the clock as often as Robert. Finally, Robert heard the name Becky and understood she was talking about *The Adventures of Tom Sawyer*, which Mama had read to him when he was small. He'd been scribbling without thinking, catching words when he could. Now he had something to hold on to. He liked that story. The more he thought about the book, the less he remembered the fire.

Mrs. Pournelle felt his interest catch; she looked his way. "What happened to Tom and Becky in the cave?" she said. She might have been asking anyone, but Robert was so sure she wanted him to answer that he raised his hand.

"They got lost from their class," Robert said. "For days and days. Becky was real scared. They didn't have no food except some cake. An' they almost got caught by Injun Joe."

Mrs. Pournelle nodded. She made a coaxing motion. "So they really had no business wandering in that cave, did they? What should Tom have done instead? Should he have followed his whim, or should he have stayed where he ought to?" She scanned the room, settling on the rear row. "Cleo? What was the lesson of the cave?"

Robert glanced back and saw a boy with wavy hair shrug. No one else raised a hand, so Robert's went up again. He didn't know what *whim* meant, but she'd laid the answer in plain view. "He should've stayed where he ought to?"

Light broke across Mrs. Pournelle's face. She *could* smile after all. "Yes. He should have stayed where he ought to. He should have followed the rules. That isn't so hard, is it, Cleo?"

Robert felt Cleo's eyes glaring behind him. Again he remembered Miz Lottie's warning not to let anyone know he was smart. In Mr. Harris's class, nobody liked Franklin Reese hogging up the answers and staying after class to ask Mr. Harris if he could wash his chalkboard or straighten his papers. Robert had once put a giant bullfrog in Franklin's lunch pail, and the whole class had laughed when he yelled in the schoolyard.

"I guess," Robert added, too late, trying to seem less sure.

He didn't speak a word or raise his hand for the last forty minutes of class, but he'd already rubbed his classmates wrong. When Mrs. Pournelle excused them and they stood in a line to file out, no one looked at Robert, as if he had turned invisible. Once he was outside, he realized he'd taken too long to gather his soiled clothes, because the other boys weren't in sight.

He took it all in: the schoolhouse behind him, the lush cornfields behind razor wire twenty yards to the side, the distant outbuildings beyond the school. Last, he peeked back at the long stretch of field toward the warden's office where the burning ghosts died forever. He didn't see the strange shimmering, but the presence of the place rang strong and sour.

I could just run—

The thought had hardly appeared when the boys were upon him and he tasted his blood. A flurry of fists and kicks made Robert cover his head. Four of them. His class had turned the corner of the schoolhouse, out of sight, and four bigger boys were waiting. He knew from radio boxing matches he'd listened to with Papa that he shouldn't be pinned to the wall. As he moved, a kick to his rear sprawled him face-first to the ground. After that, he could only curl up. With only one or two boys, he would have gotten his own licks in, but he was helpless in an ambush. His nose was bleeding and his lip was split. A hard kick to his stomach took his breath, and someone's boot pummeled his hand when he tried to protect his privates. These boys fought like grown men, with no sport in it except to hurt him. Pain burst everywhere.

A sharp warning whistle ended the thrashing, and the boys fell away. "And you better not say nothin' or I'll cut you," Cleo hissed over him.

Since the other boys were scrambling to form a line, Robert swayed to his feet too. His vision doubled, but he saw his clothes strewn near the wall and hugged them close before he took his place at the end of a line winding around the corner of the schoolhouse. He wiped his bloody nose against Papa's work shirt and curled his lip to hide it. Coppery blood seeped into his mouth.

"Ya'll up to some foolishness?" Boone's voice came. He rounded the corner, studying their faces. His gaze stopped on Robert, who was biting his bloody lip at the end of the line. *If he asks, I won't tattle,* Robert thought. But Boone didn't ask him anything. Instead, he snatched the clothes from Robert's hands. "I'ma burn these. You don't need 'em now."

Losing Papa's work shirt brought a stone to Robert's throat. The name STEPHENS was embroidered across the pocket. When the warden let him keep the shirt, he thought that was the end of it. Still, Robert did not cry. He held his sore chin high.

"Yessir," he said. "I don't need 'em."

Boone pointed, and Robert saw his blue tie hiding in the grass like a corn snake. "Get yo' damn tie 'fore I take you to the Funhouse."

Robert didn't know what the Funhouse was, but the dead silence from even the mean boys ahead of him in line told him he didn't ever want to learn.

8

"Gloria Stephens, I'll be—"

Miss Anne was so flustered when she met Gloria at the rear screen door that her cheeks splotched with red pinpricks. "Do you know what time it is, missy? Yesterday you're twenty minutes late, today it's lunchtime—"

Gloria's eyes alone hushed Miss Anne mid-complaint. She was only five years older than Gloria, and sometimes she knew when to give Gloria room for a breath here and there, not just treating her like hired help. Gloria had known Miss Anne since she was little—Miz Lottie used to bring her and Robbie to the white Powells' when she was their cook, and Mama often had played their piano to lead Christmas carols—but they were mostly strangers even though Gloria had cleaned and cooked for her almost a year. Miss Anne kept the habit of asking after a missing silver salt shaker or a favorite hand mirror, and then just as casually tell her a day or two later, *Don't worry, I found it in the drawer,* as if it didn't matter that she had just called Gloria a thief. Gloria prided herself on honesty, but she remembered how Miss Anne was ready to accuse her of wrongdoing at the first opportunity. Gloria lowered her eyes to hide their boiling sadness. And shame—an emotion she had just discovered. She'd never felt shame after the lies on Papa.

"I'm sorry, Miss Anne. Robbie got locked up at the Reformatory today."

Gloria hadn't planned to tell her, but Miss Anne would have heard from someone. "My goodness, what—"

Gloria politely squeezed past Miss Anne toward the hall. "'Scuse me, Miss Anne, but how many for lunch?" Gloria would choke on the words if she tried to tell the story now—with her last hug with Robert so freshly stolen.

"Nell and Fred will both be here. And Ma-Ma upstairs. Maybe do something with the leftover beef stew in the refrigerator? I don't want it to spoil." Miss Anne waited to see if Gloria would tell more about Robbie.

Gloria didn't, and Miss Anne did not follow her past the laundry room to the kitchen.

Good. The electric washing machine's basin was splashing. Miss Anne must have been desperate; Gloria had never seen Miss Anne wash her own clothes except to rinse out a stain, and she seemed afraid of the machine, especially the wringer. Gloria did not know any Negro families with a washing machine, and Miss Anne's washer was still so novel that neighborhood children hid in the gardenia bushes and peeked in at it through the screen door. Gloria wondered how she would get used to washing her own clothes in a washtub again if she wasn't working at Miss Anne's. There was no colored Laundromat in Gracetown, and how would she afford it? That thought calmed her anger. Miss Anne wasn't the one who'd touched her on McCormack Road.

Giving her anger somewhere else to go helped Gloria start planning. She would have to see the McCormacks. As soon as she finished at work. This idea gnawed at Gloria as she stirred the thick beef stew heating on the stove, cleaned the coffee grinds out of the coffeemaker's bin, wiped the counter, swept the floor, and scrubbed the breakfast dishes Miss Anne had left for her in the sink. What was Robbie doing at that exact moment? Was he cleaning too? *He's getting the beating of his life,* her own voice whispered to her. *And it won't be his last one, not even his last one today.* Gloria knew that voice, the one that had told her that day Mama was at the sink: *Look at her cheek and how the bone jumps out. She's sick and doesn't even know it.* That voice brought only bad news; her future self who already knew the worst.

Miss Anne peeked in on her, and Gloria turned her face away. When her brother, Fred, got caught brawling after a football game six months before, the deputy had brought him home with a warning. His only punishment, as far as Gloria could tell, was an earful from Miss Anne, mostly about their father's legacy and how he must not ruin his good name with low behavior. She'd been shut behind a door with him, but Gloria had heard her say he was "acting just like a nigger." It was the only time she'd heard Miss Anne use the word, but Gloria didn't have to wonder what she would think of Robbie's troubles.

"So you're just going to stand there and say nothing about it?" Miss Anne said.

"I'll fix it, Miss Anne. The trouble's mine."

"Well—the Reformatory! That's very serious, Gloria. It's one step away from prison."

"That wire looks like prison to me."

"You're only making my point."

"What do you expect me to do, Miss Anne?" She held off from pointing out that *her* papa had never been a town councilman who went hunting with the now-retired sheriff. And she, unlike Miss Anne, did not have a fat insurance check from her dead father's car crash sitting at the First Bank of Gracetown she might use to hire a lawyer. Unkind words stewed in Gloria's thoughts, making her mouth burn. *Girl, you're gonna get yourself fired today for sure.* Gloria tried to breathe the bricks out of her chest. *Inhale. Exhale.*

"Learn from Fred, Gloria. Once they start getting in trouble, they can hardly keep out. I was only twenty-one when I had to finish rearing Fred. But you! We both know Auntie Lottie has no business raising children and no business behind the wheel of that truck. She almost ran down my mailbox when she dropped you here."

With that slap of truth, Miss Anne left the doorway. Gloria had hoped Miss Anne hadn't seen the truck bump against the mailbox, but Miss Anne must have been waiting at the window.

Nothing was worse than a scolding that couldn't be argued

with. Gloria's anger bubbled until a thought screamed at her: this is Papa's fault. He should be here.

The judge had said it. Miz Lottie had said it. Miss Anne had said it, in an indirect way. Even Mama had said it, back in the days she had the strength for arguing with Papa, when she said, "Count the cost." Now Robbie was the cost. If Papa could have stayed quiet and done his work without complaining, he would still be in Gracetown. Robbie's temper had quickened since Papa was gone. Lyle shouldn't have pushed Robbie, but the old Robbie would never have kicked him.

Gloria felt herself floating toward a great open space where her anger at Papa could free her. But she would not, could not, take another step toward that void. Papa was a good man—an *important* man, Reverend Jenkins and the rest of the back-porch men said—and all important people made sacrifices. The Bible had taught her that, even if too many of the stories sounded like fairy tales. Freedom was Papa's calling, the same as God to a preacher. Hadn't Abraham been willing to sacrifice Isaac on God's word? And then God had saved Isaac in the end? No, it wasn't Papa's fault. She should have seen Lyle McCormack from a mile away. She should have taken Robert by the arm and walked as fast as she could. Papa was breaking his back in Chicago to send for them. *Wasn't he?*

Lunchtime came before Gloria had figured out how to smile, so she suffered through inquiries and remarks from Fred ("Dang, gal, that frown's ugly as a possum's ass"); his wife, Nell, voice low ("I'd be frowning too if I had to spend all morning cooped up with Anne and the old lady"); and Old Lady Powell, Miss Anne's great-grandmother, who rarely left her room upstairs ("You think I don't know an evil eye when I see one?"). Old Lady Powell was nearly ninety and old enough to remember slavery, said she'd known Miz Lottie when she was a "li'l nigger gal" who used to warm her mother's feet at the edge of her bed on cold nights, although Miz Lottie insisted she remembered no such thing and said she'd slap Gloria silly if she kept telling that foolish story.

"You used to warm my mama's feet," Old Lady Powell said again as Gloria set down her bowl of stew and tea at her bedside table. The mattress smelled of urine no matter how often Gloria washed the sheets and helped her walk to the bathroom down the hall. No one had yet opened Old Lady Powell's curtains in the dim little room, so Gloria yanked open the heavy felt curtains and hoisted the window up to let fresh air in.

"That wasn't me, Missus Powell," Gloria said. "It was Miz Lottie. And she says that never happened."

"She says . . ." The old woman's raisin face puckered. "Well, that's—that's—"

Old Lady Powell couldn't stand when Gloria contradicted her. Most often, Gloria kept her objections silent. After all, this was just an old lady losing her memory, or making up memories. The true rumor on Lower Spruce was that Old Lady Powell and Miz Lottie had the same white granddaddy, Gracetown Civil War hero Arthur Powell, but Gloria knew better than to say so. Gloria doubted it herself, since Miz Lottie was mostly brown-skinned, although her hair *was* thin and fine like an Indian's.

"Well, she's a lying little pickaninny then, because that's *exactly* what happened. She'd lay right down at the end of Mama's bed across her feet."

"I guess if that's what your mama told you."

"Didn't I say not to give me that evil eye? I want Daisy to get you *out* of this house." Daisy was Old Lady Powell's daughter who had died of flu during the Depression.

"Yes, ma'am" was all Gloria said.

Old Lady Powell's glare softened as she studied Gloria, trying to place her. She often had that faraway look, lost in time. The sadness and confusion made Gloria feel sorry for her despite the awful things she said. The weaker Old Lady Powell got, the meaner she got. Gloria had learned to tolerate the meanness by reminding herself that the old woman's tiring body must be in pain. Even breathing was a labor. Even eating. Gloria had strained the beef out of her stew, and all but the softest potatoes and carrots.

"Let me spoon your stew, ma'am," Gloria said.

Old Lady Powell snatched the spoon away. "I'll spoon my own damn stew. All that evil in your face, you'd prob'ly choke me."

Gloria was on the verge of leaving the old woman to spill broth all over herself, but instead she waited for Old Lady Powell to change her mind. "All right, then. But I'm watching you. You better not choke me or slip me poison."

I'll try, Gloria thought. *God help me, I'll try.* Was this all life was? A series of experiences and then someone feeding you as if none of it had ever happened? As if you'd never left any impression on the world? Each day Gloria worked at the Powells' house instead of going to school the way she and Mama had planned, she felt an unlived version of her life sailing away, out of grasp. She'd never felt so trapped, wishing to be anywhere else to help Robbie.

An upright black phone gleamed from Old Lady Powell's telephone table in the corner. The Powells had their own home telephone line, a luxury; most people in Gracetown had a party line. At least no one outside of the house could spy on her. Gloria picked up the phone.

"Who you think you're calling, Lottie?"

Gloria had forgotten Old Lady Powell was with her. Her heart jumped. "I have to call to the pharmacy for your medicine." Gloria was learning she could lie easily, with no trouble from her conscience. Not when it was for Robbie.

"Anne takes care of all that," Old Lady Powell said. Oh, her mind was sharp when she wanted to thwart you.

"She asked me to. Pay me no mind, ma'am." The nightstand clock gave Gloria inspiration when she saw it was 1:45. "It's time for *The Guiding Light*, Missus Powell."

Delight smoothed wrinkles in the old woman's face. Gloria flipped on Old Lady Powell's bedside radio, and the Duz detergent ad was still playing with cheerful music and voices that sounded nothing like washing clothes.

"Turn that up," Old Lady Powell said.

With the dull chatter from the radio on, Gloria had the freedom to sit at the telephone table and dial the operator to ask for Children's Services in Tallahassee. She was relieved when the operator said, "One moment, please," and a line burred. Gloria looked furtively up at the closed door, hoping Miss Anne would not choose that moment to hover. She *would* tell Miss Anne she'd made the call, but she did not want it interrupted. If a call to Tallahassee carried extra charges, she'd pay out of her salary.

L-O-E-H-M-A-N-N. Gloria had memorized the spelling of the man's name.

It took the entire fifteen minutes of the radio program before Gloria's call was transferred to an office where someone had heard of a social worker named Loehmann. While she waited for him to come to the line, Gloria imagined a spirited conversation with him, a plan of action.

"He's not in. May I take a message, miss?" a secretary finally said.

If Gloria had visited his office in person, she might have been sent to a separate colored area, much less would anyone call her "miss." The telephone line hid her race and won her courtesy. She added another drop of primness to her voice, like playing dress-up.

"Tell him this is Gloria Stephens—S-T-E-P-H-E-N-S. He took my brother, Robert, to the Reformatory this morning. I wanted to find out if he'd had a chance to talk to Judge Morris yet."

A moment of silence during routine note-taking. "All right, miss. Is that all?"

"Yes, that's all."

"Where can he call you back?"

"Uhm . . . he can call over to Anne Powell's. The late Councilman Powell's daughter." And she gave Miss Anne's telephone number. "Tell him it's very urgent, please."

Gloria felt empty when she hung up. The grand plan she'd imagined had resulted in nothing but a phone message he might never see or would ignore outright. The organ music at the end of *The Guiding Light* sounded like a funeral march to match her mood.

Gloria was surprised to see Old Lady Powell staring at her with strangely lucid eyes. "The Reformatory," the old woman said in a soft voice. "That's a terrible place. Terrible. I hope Fred doesn't end up there."

Gloria turned down the radio until the announcers' voices were too low to hear. She didn't mention that Fred was a grown man now and too old to go. "You've heard bad things?"

"It was the boogeyman for my boys: 'Don't mess up or you'll go straight to the Reformatory.' Kept them in line. But not Fred. Nothing keeps Fred in line. He *blasphemes*." She sounded heartbroken. "You remember that fire in 1920, Lottie—don't you?"

Gloria shook her head. She decided there was no use in correcting her.

The old woman sighed. "All those boys dead. Just a scandal. They ought to have shut it down back then. But they didn't." She pointed a craggy finger toward the radio. "Turn that back up. I want to hear."

"But can you tell me—"

"Hurry up and do what I say! Why is everything a negotiation with niggers nowadays?" Old Lady Powell's voice trembled, her face red. To Old Lady Powell, Gloria's "insolence" was more evidence of the world that had left her behind. The old-timey days gave Miz Lottie nightmares, but memories were Old Lady Powell's only comfort.

"Sorry, ma'am," Gloria said.

She turned up the radio, gathered the old woman's dishes, and slipped through the door. Miss Anne was waiting on the other side.

"I just don't understand you, Gloria. You'll sneak phone calls all the way to *Tallahassee*—"

"All the way to goddamn Tallahassee?" Fred mocked Anne from where he lay on the couch as Gloria and Anne passed him from the staircase. "Seventy whole miles away! She's tryin' to bankrupt us."

Nell laughed beside him, stroking his hair. Since his summer break from Florida State started, Fred often napped downstairs with a *Gracetown Herald* across his face, claiming he was looking for summer work. He loved teasing Anne, and Nell loved laughing at his jokes. As far as Gloria could tell, that was the basis of their marriage. They'd only wed because Nell was with child, but when she miscarried after three months Fred could hardly hide his relief. Miss Anne thought Fred was running around on Nell during her waitressing shifts at the diner. Gloria knew more about them all than she wanted to.

"Miss Anne, that call will come out of my pay," Gloria said.

"But you won't tell me what's going on with Robbie? As long as I've known you and your family?" Hurt shined in Miss Anne's blue eyes. "Come with me, young lady."

While Fred and Nell snickered behind them, Miss Anne walked Gloria down the hall to the room at the far end that she kept as her father's shrine: Mr. Powell's office. This was the same room where she had lectured Fred after the deputy came, as if its history gave her authority beyond her own. Miss Anne flipped on the overhead light, but this room too was dark from the drawn shades. Everything was brown: mahogany desk, paneled walls, wooden filing cabinets.

Please don't let her fire me, she thought. Not today.

"Miss Anne, I quit," Gloria blurted before Miss Anne could fully close the door.

"Quit?" Miss Anne repeated, whirling to face her. "What for?"

"Aren't you fixing to fire me?"

Again hurt glowed in Miss Anne's face. "Do I seem that petty to you?"

In truth, she did. "No."

"I wanted us to have privacy so Fred and Nell don't blab your business all over Gracetown. You know they will, don't you?"

"Yes, Miss Anne."

Miss Anne walked closer to her—closer than Gloria was used to anyone standing near her. Close enough for Gloria to smell the washing detergent on her hands. Miss Anne seemed so soft now that Gloria almost wished she could hug her the way she'd hugged Miz Lottie.

"Now tell me. All of it."

So, Gloria did: starting with Lyle McCormack on the road the day before, she ran through the horrible series of events. Miss Anne listened with pursed lips, a shake of her head, a sigh, and widening eyes. Afterward, Miss Anne paced the room in thought. Tears streamed Gloria's face again.

"Six months is ridiculous," Miss Anne said. "He's so young! Fred did worse than that every weekend of high school and never got sent to that awful place. It's always Negroes. Or poor white boys."

"I know it, Miss Anne," Gloria whispered.

For a moment they both stewed in the unfairness of it.

Miss Anne spoke in nearly a whisper. "All right, then. We'll just have to bail him out. How much money will it take?"

While Gloria stared, dumbfounded, Miss Anne reached into her skirt pocket for her key ring and unlocked a drawer on her father's old rolltop desk. She pulled out a book of checks. Gloria was so surprised, her eyes stung. She doubted that even Fred knew where his sister hid her checks. She doubted Miss Anne would trust Fred enough to show him.

"I think it's too late now, Miss Anne. He's sentenced."

Miss Anne looked startled. She hadn't thought of that. "Oh. That's right."

But the money had been offered. Gloria tried to think of other ways to spend it. "Maybe you could hire him a lawyer. Just to . . . ask him questions. Get some advice?"

Miss Anne considered it, frowned. "I can't think of a lawyer in Gracetown who'd want to take up for . . ." She stopped, blushed. "I'm sorry, but it's true. Not your kin. Not now."

Gloria and Miss Anne rarely mentioned the charge against her father, and Gloria wanted to press past it quickly. "Could you write a letter to Judge Morris and ask to set him free? Or give him less time? Being as you're Councilman Powell's daughter?"

Miss Anne nodded, but not before Gloria saw her hesitation. Miss Anne sat down in the plush rolling chair at her father's desk, something Gloria had never seen her do. The chair hissed beneath her weight. "Daddy retired eight years before he passed. His name . . . doesn't have the same weight now. Not like Red McCormack. I'm nobody to them but a woman with an opinion, and that won't go far."

"But you can try."

Miss Anne nodded again, but in a way Gloria thought still meant no. If Gloria were white, she thought, she'd try to walk on air just to see if she could. What was the point of white skin if you couldn't do whatever you put your mind to?

"What about that letter you wrote your father?" Miss Anne said.

"I mailed it before I got here." Miz Lottie kept stamps in her pocketbook, so Gloria had dropped her wrinkled letter in the mailbox downtown before coming to Miss Anne's. "But . . . I don't know what he can do from Chicago. He may not even get it."

"Look at us, Gloria: two sad gals missing their daddies."

They sat a moment in silence. Miss Anne never said a word about Papa's troubles, except one time she'd reminded Gloria how lucky she was she'd hired her despite her Stephens name.

She'd never seemed to judge Papa, and Gloria was grateful. Miz Lottie said most whites in Gracetown couldn't choose what to loathe about Papa more—that he'd been accused of rape or that he'd been trying to unionize Negroes at the mill and had nearly caused a strike.

"I'm gonna talk to Mister Red," Gloria said finally.

"That's foolish, Gloria. You stay far away from all those McCormacks. The way Lyle McCormack behaved was disgraceful. He had no right."

Gloria didn't answer, a part of her agreeing. She didn't want to see the McCormacks either, but what choice did she have?

"I have a friend," Miss Anne said finally. "My very good friend. She's a woman law student, Channing Holt. She doesn't let anything stop her. She'll have ideas about what to do. She may have an idea for a lawyer to hire—someone who doesn't care about the charges against your daddy and isn't scared of the McCormacks."

Gloria smiled, excited. She had never heard of a woman lawyer or law student. "Yes, ma'am. I would appreciate that so much."

"She's fishing with her parents out on their boat today. But I'll talk to her tomorrow." That simple promise gave Gloria her most hope since the deputy came.

9

Gracetown School for Boys

The giant metal steaming pots and stovepipes in the kitchen looked the way Robert pictured the engine room of a spaceship, or the galley of a warship in the Pacific like in the old World War II newsreels. This kitchen looked like machinery. It even spoke in its own language: a clanging of pot lids on boiling water, chopping knives, whirring electric blenders. Everything sharp leered like grinning teeth. The kitchen's only air was steam.

"Every meal comes through this kitchen," Boone said. "Workin' the kitchen is a *priv'lege*. Don't everybody git to work in here." Boone walked quickly through the maze of metal counters, so Robert kept pace so he wouldn't get lost.

Four Negro staff members were standing guard, but watchers didn't see everything.

Robert sensed that boys had been stabbed in this kitchen, perhaps killed. More than one, maybe. The smell of death was still fresh to his senses from the fire, and that sour smell followed him to the kitchen too. Sometimes guards had taken bets over which boys would die. They were old deaths—not yesterday or even a year ago, but Robert felt the boys' dying: sharp pricks to his abdomen, neck, throat. Then his back. He tried to rub away the stinging, swatting his skin like he was covered in bees. If not for the fire before, he would have been more frightened. Now he knew that, in time, the flickers of pain would go away.

So he listened to Boone's instructions even while he felt the stinging. He kept his eyes free of tears. Instead, he stared at the tall, odd chef caps the oldest boys wore. Younger boys wore smaller paper hats like at a burger stand.

Boone's thick neck bulged from raising his voice over the noise. "You do your job right, you stay in the kitchen—and nobody in the kitchen goes hungry. You mess up, you're out of the kitchen an' in the fields. Sun's hot an' hours is long out there, so yo' belly's gonna growl at night. That's why you want to stay in the kitchen. But you steal food, you go to the Funhouse."

"What's the—"

Two boys' eyes flurried to Robert, then quickly away. *Don't ask,* the boys' eyes seemed to say. From their eyes, the Funhouse carried the promise of bad news.

As Boone pointed out the hook with Robert's apron and paper hat, Robert couldn't help glancing at the two boys, who were about his age: they were two of the boys who had watched him with such bright eyes when he first walked into the classroom. One was openly staring at him, but the taller one was careful not to look his way, head low over the sink where he stood washing plates, but Robert saw his eyes tracking him too. The tall boy was high-toned, with reddish hair, and the other was darker and shorter than Robert, his head shaved nearly bald. He had midnight skin and white, white teeth.

Robert had pledged not to look foolish trying to make friends, but he longed to talk to them so badly that his throat stung. Boys swarmed everywhere at this place, but there were no smiles. Robert hadn't realized how lucky he'd been before today, since Gloria never failed to smile at him in the mornings even when she was tired and unhappy. Trying to be Mama. These two boys did not smile, or even close to it—but they *saw* him. They seemed kind, even worried for him. They wanted to be *his* friend. Knowing that he might look forward to something besides beatings made it easier to soothe the fire in his throat, his ache for Mama.

"Git your apron and hat—you wear them at *all times* in the kitchen—and go to the sink. Ev'rybody starts at the sink."

When Robert saw Boone pointing toward the two boys at the sink, he had to catch himself so he wouldn't show how glad he was.

"Watch out," the taller boy said when Robert joined them. "Water's hot."

"*Real* hot," the smaller boy said.

They both lifted their dripping fingers out of the sink, wrinkled as if they were old men. "Useta have gloves," the tall boy said.

"Yeah, rubber gloves," said the other.

"But somebody took them."

The smaller boy's big eyes hinted toward the right, and for the first time Robert noticed Cleo in the rear, stirring a large, steaming metal vat in the corner with a spoon so big that it looked like a broom handle. Robert looked away fast so Cleo wouldn't see him. His nose and cheeks still smarted from his beating, and he'd cut his gum with a tooth.

"Takes what he wants," the tall boy shrugged.

"Better stop making him look dumb," the small boy said, looking up mournfully at Robert. He had an accent Robert had never heard, sharp *g*'s and *t*'s. He was younger, maybe ten. "He's going to keep whupping you 'til you fight back or he gets bored."

"But don't fight back *too* much," the tall boy whispered. "Just show heart. If you hurt him, or bloody his nose . . ." He rolled his eyes and whistled softly. "Whooo-*eeeee*."

"Naw, you don't want to do *that*. He's crazy."

The boys fell silent, palms slapping back into the water, suddenly busy. By instinct, Robert lowered his hands into his sink too, and the heat grasped him in a tight palm. But he didn't snatch his hands out because he heard footsteps on the shiny white floor, and a thin Negro man in a white shirt and black satin vest strolled past, watching them. Rings shone on his fingers.

"Better not find spots or food on those dishes, gentlemen," the man said. He dipped his finger in the tall boy's sink and moved on, satisfied. As soon as he was out of earshot—

"That's Mr. Crutcher," the tall boy said. "He useta be real nice."

"Sure was."

"But not no mo'. If the water ain't hot enough, he'll put your head down in that sink." Robert stared after the man, trying to picture it. He didn't seem as mean as Boone.

"Nobody stays nice," the younger boy said. "Not unless they're like us."

"What you mean?" Robert said.

The boys looked at him as if his question were silly. The younger boy giggled. "Children, dummy," he said.

"Shut up," the taller boy snapped. "How's he gonna know?"

The smaller boy still shook his head, chuckling to himself. The boys talked too fast—and so softly that Robert had to crane his ears to hear them. His bad ear rang.

"How long you gonna be here?" the small boy said.

"Six months." It stung to say it.

"Six months, that ain't too bad," the tall boy said.

They exchanged names. The tall boy's nickname was Redbone, or just Bone. The smaller boy said he was called Blue because he was blue-black, and he surely was. Robert said his nickname was Robbie, but he wanted to be called Robert. He did not want to be Robbie here. "We'll get you a better nickname," Blue promised him.

Redbone and Blue finally got around to instructing Robert on his duties: one sink for plates, one for cups, one for forks and spoons. There were only two rules to live by, they said. One—don't break the dishes. Two—don't leave grime or spots. Boys who made it past washing dishes could start cooking or mopping the floor. Boys who failed at washing dishes got sent out to the fields. Blue had never been to the fields, but Redbone said he'd worked on a thresher and never wanted to see corn on the cob again. Blue's family had sent him to Miami from the Bahamas when he was eight, but he'd been brought to the Reformatory after his grandmother died. He was waiting on an aunt to come get him from Bimini, but she kept getting delayed.

Redbone gave Robert a knowing look, as if to say, *That ain't true.*

Redbone, who was from St. Augustine, had taken his neighbor's car joyriding when he was ten, and he'd been sentenced to two years. His sentence would be up in December, a month before Robert's. He might go home then or he might get leased out to the peanut mill or one of the farms. He wasn't sure. The warden would decide, based on his behavior record. Both boys looked grim at the mention of Haddock. Robert didn't want to talk about him either.

Robert listened to their stories between bouts of thoughtful scrubbing, so he could be sure no grains of rice or dried food was stuck between the tines. The water scalded his palms bright red. Washing forks was the worst job, the boys had said. Forks trapped food out of reach.

"You gonna need to wash faster'n that," Redbone said.

"A hundred years faster," Blue said.

That was when Robert looked up and saw him.

Across the kitchen, Cleo was gone. Instead, a white boy in a chef's hat and a long white apron stood in his place. He stared dead at Robert as if he'd been waiting to be noticed. His hair was cut short like Blue's, the color of pale sand. He was thin and barefoot, maybe twelve or thirteen. Robert looked away fast. When trouble started with white boys, colored boys lost out.

"I thought it was only colored boys in the kitchen," Robert said.

Redbone and Blue shrugged.

"Well, how come they let *him* in here? Like he's spyin' on us?"

Redbone and Blue stared blankly, so Robert gestured toward the vat with his chin.

The white boy was still there, still staring. "What white boy?" Redbone said.

Robert thought they were teasing him, but their faces said different. They didn't see the boy. They looked straight past him.

"He's right there," Robert said.

"You say so," Redbone said, and went back to washing.

Robert squeezed his eyes shut tightly, opened them, and looked again. The boy stared on.

Robert could see his cool blue eyes from across the room. He had never seen eyes so blue.

A tiny *clink* rang as Redbone lifted a dripping plate he'd rinsed. "Just tell him he ain't real and he'll leave you be," he said. "Most times."

Not *real*? The boy was as real as he was, casting a shadow against the large metal vat. Robert could see his freckles.

Blue spoke, hushed. "I've seen that white boy. The one with the knife?"

Heart speeding, Robert checked to see if the boy held a knife. He was relieved to see the boy's hands empty, hanging limply at his sides.

"He ain't got a knife," Robert said.

"Must be another one, then," Blue said. He checked the plates he'd stacked for chips. "White boys must've worked in the kitchen before."

"They keep coming back," Redbone said. "I bet haints get hungry, huh, Blue?"

Haints. Robert's heartbeat was thunder, but he couldn't look away. What did he see in this boy's face? He didn't seem angry. He didn't quite seem sad. His eyes reminded Robert of Mama's when she used to cling to his arm to keep him from pulling away when it was too hard to look at her dying.

Redbone went on talking to Blue, unbothered. "They must be hungry. They're punching open the rice and flour bags at night—an' then *we* get blamed. That ain't right."

"If you're dead, *stay* dead," Blue said. They could be talking about rats or roaches.

"You're not real," Robert whispered toward the boy, a test.

As if Robert had shouted, the white boy turned to walk away, although he had nowhere to go except the back wall. A butcher's knife was buried in his back, the hilt lodged between his shoulders, blade shining in the light. The circle of blood was thick and black near the knife, soaking red down his back, leaving smudged footprints as he walked toward the wall. One stride and he was gone, through the whitewashed bricks. Robert gasped.

"He . . . he . . . he . . ." Robert clung to the counter to stay upright. His words withered.

"Yep," he heard Blue say, a tiny voice on the other end of a long tunnel. "Told you, Bone. Must be the one with the knife."

Robert's wooziness passed as soon as his knees buckled, so he snapped himself back to alertness and stood straight before anyone saw, even Redbone and Blue. He asked for water, and Blue scurried to get it, dodging Boone and Crutcher and the other watchers in a stealthy zigzag across the room. It wasn't a long distance, but Robert could not have made it without attention. The tepid glass of water helped clear Robert's head.

"It ain't nothin'," Redbone said. "You get used to it."

"Just pray at night," Blue said. "They'll let you alone."

"There's worse things to worry about than haints."

"*Way* worse," Blue said.

That didn't make Robert feel better about the boy and the blood and the knife—or the fire in the field—but was enough to get him back to work. The urgency of too-hot water and forks to clean helped him convince himself that nothing he'd seen could hurt him the way Cleo and those bigger boys had. Or the way Haddock would.

The dishes had no end. Dishes waited before dinner, and a steady flow of dishes came back to them on carts after the two dinner shifts began. Robert couldn't see the dining hall from his sink station, so the din sounded the same to him for both shifts: a furious, steady hum of conversation. Even some laughter, although it was careful, not too loud. Everyone was happy to be eating. Maybe they looked forward to eating dinner all day. Any angry shouts were quieted by angrier shouts from adults and a thick silence before the talking started again.

But all of those dramas were far from the dishwashing station, past the wall and thick glass of the long picture window. To soothe his hunger, Robert snuck finger wipes from plates before he shook scraps into the garbage: buttery mashed potatoes, gravy, beef. A sweet apple dessert. Not as good as Mama's or Miz Lottie's, but good enough to make him eager to fix his plate. That was the hardest part of the job: feeding others before he could eat.

The kitchen crew ate last, Redbone and Blue had told him, but they could eat as much as they wanted so the food wouldn't go to waste. They could have seconds or even thirds sometimes, although it was nearly impossible to have more than one dessert, and dessert was often gone before their turn. No one skipped dessert. They would have to spend time cleaning up afterward, but like Boone said, they would never go to bed hungry.

"Here," Blue said, and snuck a small apple pastry in Robert's wet hand. It was mostly intact except for a split along the seam. And it was hot. Maybe hotter than the dishwater. "Eat it, dummy. Hurry up. Won't be none left."

After a furtive glance for Boone or another guard's eyes, Robert stuffed the pastry into his mouth whole. It was so hot that it flared against his sore gum and numbed his tongue. Plus he could taste dish soap from the sink. But *so* good. Yes, the kitchen was all right, ghosts or no ghosts. The three of them stood in a row at the sinks, scrubbing hard, trying to chew softly and hide their full cheeks.

Finally, it was their turn for dinner. With most of the other boys gone, the last wooden chairs squealing away from the tables, Robert could sit at last and gnaw at a thick slice of meat loaf drowned in gravy. The meat had no flavor, but it was filling. He felt no worries about Cleo and the older boys because they were huddled at the tables at the far end, speaking in low voices, their laughter far away. The older boys had seated themselves first, and Robert noticed that Redbone and Blue wanted to sit nowhere near them, choosing the table farthest away.

Two other boys were close to their age: Troy and Eddie, who had graduated to sweeping, mopping, and wiping counters, and who sat mostly watching and listening at their end of Robert's table, shy and quiet. Redbone told funny stories about when he stole that car, and how he could barely reach the gas pedal or see up through the windshield, and how he nearly drove himself into the Atlantic. Although half the stories sounded made-up—how could Blue claim that *six* patrol cars had chased Redbone when he hadn't been there to see it?—it took all of Robert's concentration to try not to choke on his food or laugh too loudly. Once he noticed Cleo staring over at him and his food grew heavy in his stomach, his smile fading, but the next time Robert looked up, Cleo's stare was gone.

Now Robert could see a kind of way through it: he would go to school, work in the kitchen, be with his new friends, go to bed, go to school, work in the kitchen. Six months was a horribly long time, but if he stayed clear of Cleo and didn't make anyone mad . . . he could do it.

Except for the one thing still bothering him most. He would never sleep unless he knew. "Does Warden Haddock do everything he says he will?" Robert said while everyone's mouths worked on their meals.

Their chewing slowed. Troy and Eddie looked at their plates.

"Depends," Redbone said. "What he say?"

Robert spoke softly. "Said he was gonna give me twenty lashes." No one answered, but Robert saw his future in their faces. "He said I won't know when. I thought . . . he was tryin' to scare me."

Blue shrugged. "Oh, he means it."

Redbone gave Blue a sharp look. "It's called the Funhouse," he said after a while. "That's where they whup you. Mostly Warden Haddock and that other one, Mr. Ames. Boone sometimes. Twenty's a lot."

"Thirty's worse," Blue said, shrugging.

No one spoke for a while. Robert wanted to ask if any of them had been to the Funhouse, but he didn't, since no one brought it up. He had changed everyone's mood. His stomach was bloated, and he hoped he wouldn't get sick. Without the laughter, all he remembered was the screaming in the field and the bloody knife in the boy's back.

"Helps to holler and cry," Redbone said. "Some fools try to act like it don't hurt. Warden Haddock don't like that. He'll just whup you harder 'til you do."

The other boys nodded as if they had all been beaten. Robert wanted to confess he'd never had a beating except one school paddling and a few smacks across his palm with Papa's belt, but they might call him a sissy. Besides, he hadn't made a sound when Cleo and those boys licked him, and crying might have made it worse. Being scared of Papa's belt had been worse than the belt.

"Twenty's nothin'," Robert said. "I won't holler."

Redbone shrugged.

"I ain't scared of the Funhouse," the one called Troy said.

Blue made a sound like half a laugh, but he smothered it with his dinner roll. "He's scared of his shadow," he murmured toward Robert's ear. "Always jumping."

Robert checked the older boys again, saw no one looking in their direction. The guards were mostly in the back, with only Crutcher eating alone at a table out of hearing range. Robert's heart pounded.

"Does anybody ever run away?" Robert said.

He said it more loudly than he'd intended, so everyone at his table seemed startled. The one called Eddie dropped his fork.

"Don't talk about that," Redbone said.

Robert whispered. "But do they?"

"Some try it," Blue said. "Sneak out right before dark, break into the mill, try to hide in the peanuts. That's only a couple miles down the road, so that's where they go—"

"*Hush,*" Redbone said.

"—but it don't work. All these cracker farmers round here, they get fifty dollars if they snitch. *Fifty*. This place is full of snitches too. Plus they catch you, you get fifty lashes. Or you end up at Boot Hill."

"What's Boot Hill?"

"The graveyard," Blue said. "That's where they bury you."

The rest of the room had lost all of its sound; no laughter, talking, silverware clanking. Troy and Eddie, sensing trouble, rose to clear their plates back in the kitchen. Robert glanced over at Crutcher again; his head was bent over his food as he sopped gravy with his roll.

But Cleo was watching. *Really* watching. Had he heard all the way across the room? Redbone kicked Blue under the table. "Shut up," he said from behind his teeth.

Blue shrugged. "Nobody else heard."

But he was wrong. Robert knew it, and so did Redbone. Robert pushed his plate away. He didn't know which was worse: that Cleo might have overheard them, or that boys from the Reformatory got buried in a graveyard with its own name. He'd rather be sitting at dinner with the ghost with a knife in his back. Robert felt dizzy again.

Blue rose from the table, making a loud clatter as he jostled Redbone's plate and fork, as if to bring attention to them on purpose. He sneered at Redbone over his shoulder as he followed the other boys to the kitchen.

Cleo's eyes, thankfully, had returned to his friends.

Robert wanted to stop asking questions, but he couldn't. "You ever . . . know anybody who got buried at Boot Hill?"

"Sure did," Redbone said. He shoved mashed potatoes into his mouth. "Fat kid named Garrick. What business a fat kid got trying to run? We all helped pitch dirt to bury him."

Cleaning up after dinner was a race. No talking, just scrubbing and closing jars and putting away food wrapped in foil in the massive refrigerator in case the staff got hungry later. Curfew at the dorm was seven thirty, and no one wanted to be late. Robert noticed that Crutcher and the other guards were gone, and noticing it worried him—both because Cleo might come and jump him again and because he did not want to be tempted to run. So soon after hearing about Boot Hill, it scared him to be wondering how long he would be left without adults watching him in the kitchen each night.

It would be dark outside soon. Could he find his way to the peanut mill like Blue had said? Could he get past the tall fences, or would he get lost in pockets of fires and screaming? His thoughts felt too loud, as if Blue and Redbone could hear.

"I'm going back," Blue said, and the unwanted part of Robert's mind took note that Blue would walk to the dorm on his own. No one guarding him. "I wanna hear the radio show."

"He got a clock in his head," Redbone whispered to Robert.

"Be late if you want," Blue said, and left through a rear door only strides from where Robert had seen the ghost pass through the wall. The gleaming metallic vat winked.

"We're gonna be late?" Robert said.

Redbone waved his hand. "Nah. We got time. Wanna see what nobody else sees?"

Troy lingered close, eager, wiping his hands on a tattered dishrag. "In the back?"

"Yeah, let's just show 'im real quick," Redbone said.

Robert hesitated. He liked Redbone fine, but he didn't know anything about Troy. And he didn't like the easy way Redbone had talked about burying a kid, like he hadn't felt sorry. He'd have sounded sadder about burying a dog, probably. *No one stays nice,* Blue had said.

"You not gon' b'lieve yo' eyes," Troy said. And Robert was following him, curious despite his better sense. Redbone and Troy jostled for the lead while they led Robert through stacks of boxes and swollen burlap bags in the long, wide pantry behind the kitchen. The temperature was cooler by at least ten degrees. In a few strides, they had walked from summer to fall. At the rear of the pantry, they came to a metallic door twice the width of a normal door, with a long iron arm barring it shut.

"What's that?" Robert said. "The fridge?"

"Better," Redbone said.

Redbone tugged at the bar on the door, lifting it high. Troy helped him pull the door open. The door fought as if someone were trying to keep it shut from the other side. Once it was open, fog flew out in a thick cloud. Cold air washed over Robert's face and bare arms.

"What is it?" Robert said.

"The freezer," Redbone said. "They put it in a year back. *Zero* degrees."

Again Robert thought of a spaceship as he saw the foggy interior. He had never imagined a freezer so big, yawning open to nothing except slowly swirling fog.

"I'm not goin' in there," Robert said. His heart was awake again, thumping.

"We'll go first," Troy said. "Chicken."

"Just don't touch *nothin'*," Redbone said. "Come on."

After Redbone took a few steps inside the freezer, he was wrapped in fog. Troy was huskier, just past Redbone's shoulder, both of them already less visible. Without wanting to, Robert wondered if he could beat either one of them in a fight, much less both together. He stood in the doorway wanting to turn around and run away. The fog shrouded the shelves inside from view, and Redbone and Troy had vanished within it.

"Keep the door open some," Redbone called back, but Robert had thought of that: he'd left the freezer door wide open so he could back out fast. And so someone could hear him if he yelled. He watched and waited to see if the door would fall closed by itself on a hinge, but it was fixed in place. Firm to his touch.

The fog was clearing as it seeped out of the open doorway. He could make out crates on shelves now. Robert wasn't as nervous once he could see more than five feet through the misty gray. He took tentative steps behind Redbone and Troy, then sped to catch up.

The freezer was crammed with packed shelves, but Robert looked up and saw a giant hook. A row of them.

"Come on—faster," Redbone said.

Robert's feet kept their pace against his will. His eyes were grabbing what they could see in the thinning fog. A row of hooks on either side, spaced apart. Robert noticed how cold he was: his earlobes stinging, the air too cold to breathe. Yes, it *was* like a trip on a spaceship, and they had landed in a frigid new world.

Redbone and Troy were laughing. Robert turned to know what they had seen.

A grown man, large and dark, was swinging back and forth between them on the hook in the fog as they took turns hurtling themselves against him with all their strength. The hook squealed under its burden with every swing, but the man was frozen solid. Robert thought of Papa's stories about Claude Neal swinging from a tree.

Robert's breath was trapped in his throat. He nearly vomited up his supper. "You see this?" Redbone said, grinning.

The fog stopped its tricks against his eyes, and Robert saw that the two boys were playing with a frozen side of beef, that was all. Another identical one hung on the hook behind them. The carcass was long, probably a hundred pounds or more; it would be taller than him even set on the floor—stubby, gristled legs pinned together to the hook. The slab of meat spun lazily between Redbone and Troy, smooth and white with fat on one side, thick curved ribs red and raw on the other. A snake of exposed bones stretched from its severed neck to its flank.

"You said . . . you said . . . not to touch nothin'," Robert said. Redbone had seemed so sensible before, at least compared to Blue, but the danger in the freezer pulsed like a snake that might strike. Robert didn't like the door being out of his sight. The cold was terrible, chewing at his skin. And what if the meat fell from its hook? How could they lift it back up?

"Naw . . . you right," Redbone said, hugging the beef closer to stop its swinging. "We just wanted to show you. You might never see all this meat again yo' whole life."

"Sometimes they got more," Troy said. "Hangin' all up and down here."

The meat looked only dead to Robert, like it should be buried at Boot Hill. The cold was making his heart thump louder. Robert rubbed his arms, which prickled to his touch. "We got curfew, right?"

Redbone shrugged. "We got plenty of time 'til—"

Then, a *WHUMP* sound. The air felt sucked out of the room. Robert's hurting ear ached with the pop. Redbone and Troy were yelling and running toward the door before Robert heard the lock click into place with a final scrape and snap.

"Quit playin'!" Redbone pounded against the metal. "*Open this goddamn door!*" Troy was crying, banging the door with his fist beside Redbone.

Robert watched them, unable to move, thinking maybe the day *was* only a bad dream. He'd had that feeling since Mama died, always expecting to wake up and discover she was still alive, and maybe this was a part of the same nightmare—starting with the courthouse, ending in this frozen death house.

"Is there another door?" Robert said, hoping. His voice was so soft that no one heard. His teeth were clicking together. "Is . . . th-there . . ."

The cold was another kind of fire. His skin was burning.

"*You open this goddamn door or I'll break your head open!*" Redbone yelled.

Troy jumped up and down as he cried, "Who is it? Who locked it?"

But there was no window in the door, so they could only see their muddy reflections. "Blue, that better not be you!" Redbone said.

Robert finally went closer to the door to listen. "Blue?" All they heard was the freezer's hum.

"What if it's Cleo?" Robert said.

The bubble of hope—Robert's growing *certainty* that it was Blue—burst. Redbone gave Robert a look that seemed to wish he'd never let him sit at his table or acted like his friend.

Robert's breath puffed out of his mouth in panicked clouds. His lungs were bound tight by cold and a thought worse than Cleo: What if the ghost of the boy stabbed with the knife was on the other side of the door, unseen, ready to walk in and make himself known? Maybe a ghost could yank down the bar to lock the door. And maybe the ghost hadn't liked what Blue had said: *If you're dead*, stay *dead*. Maybe the ghost was still mad he'd gotten stabbed.

"It wasn't me who stabbed you," Robert whispered loudly enough for a haint to hear.

Redbone and Troy started pounding again, and this time Robert joined them, thumping against metal so cold that it snatched at his skin. But Robert didn't feel it; his fists were as numb as the rest of him. He tasted the terror of the boys in the fire, their voices clear in his mind again. *Is that smoke? Who locked the door?*

"Leave me alone," Robert whispered. "It wasn't me."

"We know it wasn't y-you," Redbone said. "The door l-locks from the outside."

Robert pounded until perspiration sprang and froze on his brow. He was winded; his lungs hated the cold. He stopped, bent over, propping himself at his knees with his palms that were ringing and raw with pain. His heartbeat shook his body.

No one was answering. No one was coming. Would they survive an hour? Thirty minutes? He scanned the shelves for blankets or clothing, but of course there were none. Not even a burlap bag in sight, and there were plenty on the other side of the door.

"We gotta keep moving," Robert said. "To warm up."

Troy let out an animal wail of despair. "I don't wanna die in here!"

Redbone ignored Robert. Tired of using his fist, he kicked the door with the sole of his shoe. "Open this damn door! *I mean it!*"

The laughing sounded so soft, so far away, that Robert thought he'd imagined it. Was it the ghost taunting them? Redbone stopped kicking; he'd heard it too.

"Blue?" Redbone said. He said his friend's name like a prayer. The laughter again, more loudly.

" 'I don't wanna die in here!' " Blue teased, muffled on the other side of the door. He laughed again. Robert's body sagged with relief.

Troy was senseless, talking in a circle, still crying. "Please, please, please, please."

"Just open it, Blue." Redbone's voice was calm as a sunny sky. He stroked the door.

"You promise you won't lick me?" Blue said.

Redbone smacked the door with his palm. "I promise I won't do nothin'—just open it 'fore we all miss curfew! I oughta choke you."

"*You ain't right doin' that!*" Troy screamed. "You ain't s'posed to be here!"

"And Troy won't lick me either?" Blue said.

"Troy won't touch you," Redbone promised. But Troy's fists were clenched. Blue was satisfied. He fumbled with the latch, struggling.

"Ain't so easy the other way, huh, shrimp?" Redbone said. "Hurry up!"

Just when Robert started to think maybe Blue wouldn't get the latch open without help from an adult—and whatever new heartache *that* might bring—the bar scraped against the metal like a fingernail on a chalkboard. With all of them pushing, the door opened right away.

Robert ran far from the freezer to the pantry doorway leading back to the kitchen. He would have gone farther into the kitchen, but he didn't like how the kitchen was so dark now, full of shadows. Troy's arms pinwheeled as he tried to lunge at Blue, but he was off-balance and missed by a mile. Blue darted behind Redbone, giggling. Redbone pinned Troy to hold him still. Troy was shaking with rage.

Blue was so small that Robert probably could whup him on his own, but he didn't have a taste for it. He was just grateful to be out of the terrible cold so he wouldn't learn what it felt like to freeze to death. He still couldn't feel his ears. He wriggled his fingers and swatted at his earlobes to try to bring back the stinging.

The pantry clock said it was only seven twenty-one, not seven thirty yet. They hadn't missed curfew. Mama and God must be looking out for him for sure.

"None of y'all can take a joke?" Blue said. "I would've let you out!"

"Do it again and see what happens," Redbone said.

"Yeah, see what happens!" Troy was still trapped by Redbone's grip. He swung so wild, his fists were nowhere near Blue. "We're not scared of you! You don't scare me none!"

Troy finally settled down, so they rushed through hanging up their hats and aprons and turning off the pantry lights. Robert felt lucky when he remembered the tie he'd left hanging on the peg; he'd been promised a beating if he lost it. Why had he let himself get distracted? He'd known better than to go into the freezer—he'd *known* it. He would never ignore his own good sense again. And now they might be late! And even if they weren't late, how could he sleep wondering if Warden Haddock might come?

Robert wished he were nowhere and no one. His hands were trembling, and not from the cold. As Robert left the kitchen through the rear door with the other boys and met the humid air outside, he looked over his shoulder to make sure the ghost from the kitchen wasn't standing behind him.

10

Miz Lottie kept every piece of her life she'd ever touched. Miz Lottie's house had three bedrooms and was twice as big as Gloria's, but every inch was filled with clutter, with pathways carved through the mess. Yellowing *Pittsburgh Courier* newspapers about Jackie Robinson, Jesse Owens, Lena Horne, and Joe Louis lined the hall. Even her bathroom was a home to old *Ebony* magazines and junk, filling the bathtub: such a waste of indoor plumbing! Miz Lottie bathed standing at her sink. The clutter was another reason Gloria had moved out with Robbie, since he was forever knocking things over. To Gloria, the mess looked like trash, but Miz Lottie had a fit when anyone moved her things. Uncle June and Waymon were almost too big to walk through the maze. Miz Lottie's house smelled like dust and time.

Only the kitchen looked the way a kitchen should, except for a stack of papers on one corner of the kitchen table, and a collection of milk bottles behind the rear door. Miz Lottie moved less now, spending more and more of her days sitting at the table.

Gloria buttered the rolls while Miz Lottie carved the chicken she'd roasted. Gloria's stomach growled for the first time all day. She'd had a bite of the stew at Miss Anne's, but her appetite had died since Robbie was taken away.

Telling the story of her day exhausted Gloria, but she told it.

"A law student, huh?" Miz Lottie said. "Guess that's almost good as a lawyer."

"It's a girl law student. Chandler somebody. Miss Anne says it's her 'very good friend.'"

Miz Lottie glanced at Gloria over her shoulder, then went back to carving. She started to say something but didn't. Gloria felt unspoken words floating near them—about how Miss Anne never had a boyfriend and said she would never marry. Miz Lottie herself had never married but as a younger woman had photographed herself often with a woman she always called her *dear, dear friend Sadie*, who had passed years ago.

"Well, womens is doing so many things they never did before" was all Miz Lottie said. "Too bad she ain't Negro."

"A Negro *lawyer*?" Gloria said, smiling.

"Girl, hush. You ain't never heard of Thurgood Marshall at the NAACP? He's fighting those lynching cases. He's arguin' in front of the Supreme Court! The world ain't just what you see. That's just what these crackers want you to think. I'm surprised your daddy ain't told you."

Miz Lottie did not read well because her schooling had not gone far, but she sounded out every word in her newspapers and magazines if the article was about a Negro. Sometimes, when her good eye was tired, she asked Gloria to read to her. Gloria *had* learned about Thurgood Marshall and other Negro lawyers arguing faraway cases, but it was hard to imagine a Negro lawyer in Gracetown. Would the judge call him a nigger too?

"You think Mr. Marshall would help me with Robbie?"

"I don't know, but the first thing is to write letters. So write one to him too. You need to send one or two letters every day. And put Zora Neale Hurston on that list."

"The *author*?" Mama had read *Their Eyes Were Watching God* until the cover frayed.

"What other Zora you know? She wrote a story I saw in the *Negro Digest*. You git a news story, that shames 'em. No one will help at that Gracetown fish wrapper—someone at the *Courier* or *Ebony* magazine. A big name. Then just watch these folks scurry to act right."

Gloria tried three different pens from the crammed mug of pens and pencils on the table before she found one that would write. Since Miz Lottie's back was turned and she couldn't complain, Gloria tossed a handful of dried-out pens into the trash can. Then she wrote *Thurgood Marshall* and *Zora Neale Hurston* on an old envelope on the table, a bill from the Gracetown Electric Company. The postmark was a year old.

"Where can I get all these addresses?" Gloria said. "Those newspapers?"

"Ain't a paper worth reading you can't find in my hallway. They always got the address right inside where you can find it." She brought a plate of chicken to the table with a victorious smile. "See? Never know what you'll need. And you always tellin' me to throw my papers out."

"Miz Lottie, if there was ever a fire—"

And she stopped mid-sentence. Gloria felt a jolt of electricity when she said the word *fire*, with Miz Lottie's good eye staring hard. All her life, especially when she was younger, Gloria had felt an odd, special bond with Miz Lottie, as if sometimes they knew each other's thoughts. Usually it was a private joke about something Mama or Papa had said, but not tonight.

"Was there a fire at the Reformatory?" Gloria said. She'd tried to hold the thought to herself, but she blurted it out.

Miz Lottie lowered the plate, face morose. She sank into her chair. She'd refused Gloria's offer to help her serve the food, but she seemed more tired than usual for seven thirty. Her head dangled low on her shoulders. When she reached for Gloria's hand, the wrinkled folds of her forearm jiggled, muscles long gone. Miz Lottie clasped Gloria's hand and closed her eyes.

"Dear Lord . . . make us truly thankful for the food we are about to receive, for the nourishment of our bodies . . ." Her voice trailed off. Miz Lottie was never one to linger over the blessing, but this time she sighed and shook her head slowly from side to side. "We need your help, Lord," she said in the scared, humble voice she'd used in her prayers at Mama's bedside. "We need you tonight. Our Robbie's in trouble, at the mercy of that place."

Gloria peeked at her face: raw pain so powerful it snaked around Gloria's chest.

"Lord, we know you look after the wide world, but please keep Robbie cradled in your arms. Please help his mama's spirit find him to guide him and keep him. Lord, let no one harm him from this realm or another. Spare him, Lord. Spare him. Amen."

From this realm or another. "Amen," Gloria whispered. Her heart pounded a storm.

Miz Lottie slowly fixed her plate: a chicken thigh, rice, greens. Gloria remembered the spare little meals she'd been fixing for Robbie without Miz Lottie and wished, yet again, they had never left the shelter of her home.

"Who told you 'bout a fire?" Miz Lottie said at last. "Did Robbie say something?"

"How would Robbie know?" Gloria said. Miz Lottie only pursed her lips, not answering, so Gloria went on. "No, it was Old Lady Powell. She said it happened in 1920."

Miz Lottie nodded. "She can talk sense when she wants to."

"How would Robbie know, Miz Lottie?"

"You go'n' and eat too."

Reluctantly, Gloria spooned food onto her own plate. She took a bite and chewed, but could taste nothing except her waiting.

"Robbie's still a chile more'n a man," Miz Lottie said once she was satisfied Gloria was eating. "Chirren always know. It's a sin to send the little ones to that place. They feel it most."

"Feel what?"

"We got a sickness here in Gracetown, Gloria. Maybe at the Reformatory worst of all."

"What kind of sickness?"

"A blood sickness. Too much killing and dying. Too many restless spirits. Angry spirits. You think ghosts walk in the summer in ev'ry town? You think creatures steal children in the swamp down in Miami, or Palm Beach? Or leeches nest inside babies over in Tallahassee? Maybe it's a curse on us—a town named for Grace that don't act like no godly place."

Abruptly, Gloria rose to her feet. Miz Lottie looked at her, surprised. Gloria's heart was turning flips in her chest, crowding her lungs, so maybe she'd stood up so she could breathe.

"Sit down, girl. You need to hear it, 'specially now."

Of course Gloria had heard stories. In elementary school, everyone had a story about bumps from the floor, or flickering lights, or hand towels that moved from one place to another, or faucets that turned themselves on and off, Gloria's own experience every summer. Even Robbie insisted he could see Mama's ghost. But Mama had always explained Gloria's stories away, and then Robbie's after hers. Vivid imagination. Faulty memories. Bad plumbing.

Gloria shook her head. "Mama said—"

"Lemme tell you somethin' 'bout yo' mama, Gloria, rest her soul. Now, you know I loved her like my own, but that woman was contrary and a wee bit seditty. She thought book learnin' could take the place of stories from right under her nose. She didn't *want* to see it. So whatever she told you, it ain't what's so. Ev'ry child in Gracetown, colored or white, feels it. Some worse than others. You used to feel it too. You used to wake up cryin' at night. Said you heard hollerin'. I used to say to your mama, 'Well, tell her the truth and she won't be scared.'"

Gloria didn't remember waking up crying at night or hearing any noises. Besides the tricky sink faucet, she remembered *feelings* most—a stronger version of the ones she sometimes felt now. Her intuition had always been strongest in summer. Sometimes Mama used to ask her how long the rain shower would last, or if an item she'd ordered from the Sears catalog would come, or if a sick neighbor would get better. *Hadn't she?* The scariest thing Gloria remembered was seeing Mama washing dishes in the sink, and knowing . . .

"Sit back down," Miz Lottie said.

Only then did Gloria realize why she'd stood: she didn't want to hear more. Her mind wanted to know, but her body wanted to flee Miz Lottie's house and go on not knowing.

But she sat. Robbie needed her to listen.

"I don't b'lieve in 'evil' in most ways," Miz Lottie said. "I believe in the devil, all right, but man don't need no help from Satan to do what folks call 'evil.' Man do evil ev'ry day and call it doin' their job. Slave drivers was 'doin' their job,' beatin' the skin off folks. Slave catchers settin' dogs to rip out eyes and limbs. Don't nobody know to this day how many Negro men and boys got kilt on McCormack's land when Isaiah Timmons faced McCormack with a shotgun looking for his missing sons. Back in '09, that was. I guess the sheriff was jus' 'doin' his job' when he rounded up men that had *nothin'* to do with Timmons and his gun—and nobody saw 'em again. 'Cuz, see, colored folks fighting for what's theirs is like a virus to white folks—and they kill a virus so it don't spread. That killing is the work of man, not the devil. And if there's any such thing as evil on this earth, Gloria, it's here in Gracetown. In the soil, hear? Gracetown soil remembers. It's like a mirror that shines yo' ugly back at you."

"And . . . the fire?"

Miz Lottie sighed. "I can't hardly think of no evil worse than that '20 fire." Miz Lottie's hand shook when she tried to pour herself cold water from the mason jar she always chilled in her icebox, so Gloria helped her. After a few unsteady sips, Miz Lottie went on.

"Best to start with that Reformatory. That place. Right after the war, Junior got offered good work cleaning there. Most of the work for Negroes there is janitors, in the kitchen, a few dorm masters and the like. They save the best jobs for white folks. So Junior was tickled to death when he got that job. Best salary he'd ever made. But he worked there six months 'fore he had to quit—'fore we *made* him quit."

"Why'd he quit?" Uncle June was quiet, especially compared to

Waymon. It was easy to imagine him sweeping all day and minding his business. He was big, and stern at times, but he didn't rile easily or raise his voice.

"It was either quit or lose his soul," Miz Lottie said. "Junior told me so himself, cryin' like a baby in my arms. An' I told him he better quit the very next day—so he did. That place changed him, Gloria. *Worse* than the war. Day by day, he wasn't the sweet boy who'd gone to work there. Day by day, you could see somethin' growin' behind his eyes that wasn't him anymore. Nothing like the Christian-raised boy I knowed. He told me about things he saw. Things he did."

"What did he do?"

"Worst thing was, one night the alarm sounded. Some boys had run. Wasn't quite dark yet, and he could see three or four boys runnin' toward the woods. His boss put a rifle in his hand an' told him to shoot anything that moved—and, God help him, that's what he did. He fired."

"He shot at *boys*?"

Miz Lottie nodded. "Little Negro boys. Like it was wartime again."

"Did he . . . ?"

"Junior swears he thinks he missed, he didn't hit nobody. But he was *tryin'* to hit one. He said he didn't give it a thought when he pulled that trigger three times—not 'til later, when he couldn't sleep. That was the worst thing. But wasn't the first. He didn't tell me ev'rything, but you could see it in his eyes. All those secrets. An' he said the others working there, it didn't hardly bother them none. They'd say, 'You gotta teach 'em a lesson,' and 'You gotta show 'em who's boss,' and all the while boys are hollerin'. Carried off in the night. Or disappearing, never seen again, with a note home to their families with a made-up reason.

"Now, Junior wasn't there way back in 1920—he'd barely been born—but that's how I imagine it was then too. Ev'rybody doin' they job, showin' the boys who's boss. Way I hear it, there was a mess o' boys in trouble that day, white and Negro. I don't know what they did or why it was so bad, but they got locked up together—maybe that was punishment to the white boys, since white and colored don't mix. Twelve, thirteen boys, maybe more, locked together in a shed behind the warden's office all night long. What folks *say* is, the workers was drinkin' and carryin' on while the warden was away, so they decided to go to look for beer. Gracetown's a dry county, see. Say they planned on comin' right back to keep watch on the boys. And somehow—*somehow*—a fire started while they was gone. And since those boys was trapped, locked from the *outside*, not a single one of 'em could get free. Folks say they was screamin' to raise the dead. But it was too late 'fore help came. They all died. Every single one."

Did that explain her feeling when they'd driven to the Reformatory? It *had* felt as if screams were fresh in the air. So many boys dead at once! Gloria held her cramped stomach.

Was Miz Lottie right? Did Robbie feel it? "Miz Lottie . . . was the fire an accident?"

"Like I say, that's how folks tell it. But after Junior quit there, he told me it wouldn't s'prise him a teeny bit if somebody set that fire on purpose. To show 'em who's boss. 'Cuz when you start working there, Junior said, it turns you into somebody else. Brings out all the worst, buried parts of you. Any wrong you ever wished you could do—that place sets you free."

Miz Lottie had told her not to walk home after dark—*"Ev'rybody knows who yo' daddy is"*—but Gloria had left Miz Lottie's as fast as she could, promising she had made the walk dozens of times and would be fine. She'd heard all she could stand.

Miz Lottie's terrible stories rang in Gloria's head the whole while she walked past the settling homes and shuttered businesses on Lower Spruce. Only Pop's General Store stayed open until nine because Pop sold bolita tickets and whiskey in brown bags at his back door. She walked past the watchful eyes of old and young men gathered by Pop's window. During the day, she might hear, *Good afternoon, Miss Stephens*, or, from someone bold, *You growed up nice, Gloria*, but from the shadows, these men spoke to her with their eyes. Gloria couldn't get used to men she'd known since she was young looking at her like a stranger. Maybe it was only Miz Lottie's stories, but their silence quickened her pace.

"You be careful out on Tobacco Road," Pop called to her from his window. Many people in town called the road Tobacco Road, or "Out by the farms," but Gloria's family used the name from slave times because her family had known the name a hundred years: McCormack Road.

"I will," Gloria promised him, trying to sound cheerful. She wanted to ask Pop to send his oldest son, Mikey, with her to escort her, but no Negro man could help her with what she needed tonight. Asking would be the same as sending them to jail, or worse.

On darkened, unpaved McCormack Road, Miz Lottie's stories rang fresh in Gloria's ears.

Every sound was amplified: the chorus of crickets and cicadas, the rustling of raccoons and rabbits in the brush, the swamp water along the road that growled and splashed with snakes and gators. The noises seemed to follow her. *Was* there an unseen world in Gracetown, hidden beneath the angry soil? Even the full moon, her torch and beacon on dark nights, filled her with suspicion: it was too bloated, colored a deep golden orange so fiery. It looked unnatural.

She was small and alone: on the road, near the woods, in the world. Her smallness threatened to smother Gloria—until she saw the lights.

McCormack's farm was the only property with lights this far from town, with a lamp at the gate and several at the house set back a couple of acres from the roadside fence. Whenever she reached the McCormack lights at night, she knew her walk was two-thirds done, only another half a mile to home. When she was little, she'd thought of McCormack Farm and its swimming hole as a *piece* of her home—until Papa made her swear to stay away. Gloria could hear Papa's warnings in her head, fresh. And Miz Lottie's story about the Negro men who had died after Isaiah Timmons stormed to this place with a shotgun, looking for his missing boys. Those boys had never been seen again, just like Isaiah Timmons and the Negro men the sheriff rounded up. This land hid bones that had not been properly spoken for.

Gloria wanted to keep walking past the McCormack gate, but how could she? This place was the root of Robbie's troubles. She couldn't stand the thought of Robbie spending a single night at that Reformatory, and only one call from Red McCormack to Judge Morris might get Robbie sent home. She couldn't sleep if she left Robbie to fend for himself against haints and lost souls.

The property proclaimed itself McCormack on an iron archway trellis painted bright white over the private driveway that wound to the house. The driveway gate was closed, but the latch was only to keep animals from straying out—no lock. A simple nudge, and the latch raised to let her in. The ranch-style gate yawned open. The red clay driveway waited.

Gloria's heart pounded as she closed the gate behind her. The colonial house ahead was large, more a mansion than Miss Anne's modest house in town. This was the Big House in Miz Lottie's stories from slave times, the house where Ma Ma had grown up, before the McCormacks' and Powells' lines had diverged. This was where the cakewalks and Christmas dance had been held, where Miz Lottie's mother had felt privileged to cook and polish silverware even though her child had been expected to warm the mistress's feet. The slave cabins were long gone, but Gloria could imagine where they had stood in sullen rows across the field.

At the house, most lights were still on downstairs, one light on upstairs. It was eight o'clock and already dark, but it was after suppertime and before bedtime. McCormack would be surprised by her visit, but the hour wasn't late enough to doom her effort. Not if he was reasonable. *It's now or never. Just walk.*

Gloria had walked only half a dozen steps toward the house when she heard barking. The dogs! Two dogs, maybe three. And swishing in the grass moving toward her from the trees at a running pace. She looked toward the sound and saw a blur of pale fur in the dark.

Gloria was a quick thinker and a fast runner, but her body would not move. She became as fixed as a tree herself, a part of her hoping the dogs might run past her. Her only movement was twitching skin all over from the cascade of adrenaline and her heart's thrumming race.

The light-colored dog ahead of her growled, a partial blur in the dark. From behind, two paws landed against her back and broke her uneasy balance, sending her to the dirt in a heap.

Gloria screamed as a muzzle lunged for her face. She webbed her hands across her face and neck. Slobbering drool from a dog's tongue washed her cheeks, her forehead, her mouth.

Drool and a tongue, but not teeth. No pain.

Gloria opened her eyes—and saw a German shepherd's coat, mostly dark with a beige muzzle and belly. A bright red collar. A *wagging* tail?

"Duke!" she choked out, remembering his name, and the dog's tail wagged harder.

Lyle's German shepherd Duke, named after actor John Wayne, had been less than a year old when she and Robbie used to visit the swimming hole, and sometimes he'd splash in the water with them. He was bigger now, fully grown, but he still knew her scent. She'd often brought Duke jerky as a treat when she saw him at the fence, and now she was glad. Dear Lord, the dog *knew* her!

Two other dogs she didn't know circled, one still growling, but Duke nipped at the lighter-colored hound that tried to come closer. Duke was bigger, and Duke was boss. The third dog was a smaller German shepherd, a female, who barked from a cautious distance.

"Hey, Duke," Gloria said, rubbing the dog's neck with an unsteady hand. "Hey there, my good boy. That's right—it's Glo." Her voice was happier than she felt. Tears fell from her eyes. She'd been certain she was about to die—a deep, clear perception of life's ultimate lie—and now that she wasn't being torn apart by dogs, life felt so good that it stung.

Once Gloria was back on her feet, wiping dust from her knees, she saw a flashlight beam swinging as someone came running from the house. She thought she saw a shotgun too. All her fear had been spent by the approach of the dogs, so she wrapped her arm around Duke at her side and hoped no one would take a shot at her with a beloved dog so close.

Gloria made out only one person behind the bright beam before it blinded her. "It's Gloria Stephens!" she called out.

"Glo?"

Lyle McCormack's voice. Gloria hadn't expected to be relieved to see Lyle, but she was.

At least he wouldn't shoot her, and he was her best chance for an audience with Mister Red.

"Sorry to rile your dogs." She quickly checked her dress for rips, conscious of Lyle being so close. She straightened her dress so it hung well past her scuffed knees. "Duke was a little too happy to see me."

Lyle gave a sharp whistle, and Duke grew sober, dutifully trotting to his master. The two other dogs followed, all of them lining up away from her.

"You coulda got your head blown off, Glo," Lyle said. "I thought they were after a snapping turtle."

Yes, her plan to show up at the McCormacks' unannounced after dark had been reckless. Waiting until morning would have been much less dangerous. But here she was.

"Did you hear Robbie got sent to the Reformatory?" Gloria said. "For six months, Lyle. You know that's not right."

"Why're you puttin' that on me? Nobody told him to kick me."

"And you wouldn't have done the exact same thing if it had

been you? After somebody pushed you? Ain't that just self-defense? And you so much bigger than him?"

Lyle was silent. Gloria realized she was taking the wrong approach, giving Lyle no room to have a change of heart on his own. Papa used to complain that when Mama went after him with her "machine-gun tongue," he got so mad he couldn't listen. Gloria stepped closer to Lyle to make better use of the tears on her face, hoping the droplets were shining in the moonlight.

"Lyle . . . he's just a little kid," Gloria said. "He's so scared. You know he's sorry he kicked you. Wasn't it bad enough how your daddy boxed his ear? Did you see the blood?" She gave her voice more softness. No blaming, just gentle begging.

"You heard me tell Daddy to let it alone, didn't you?" Lyle said. "I tried to tell him."

"I know. You need to try again. Both of us. He's the only one who can tell the judge 'Never mind.' I bet he can raise the judge or the sheriff any time he wants."

"He's gonna raise a *stick*, that's what he's gonna do," Lyle said. "He'll prob'ly cuss a blue streak and whup us both."

"Please, Lyle? This is Robbie's only chance."

Gloria waited an eternity while the dogs sniffed the grass for more excitement. The smaller German shepherd whined while Lyle seemed to think it over.

"I wouldn't do this for nobody else, Glo," Lyle said. "You better know that. And I can tell you right now it won't go the way you want. But . . . you'll have to see for yourself."

Red McCormack was in his workshop behind the house.

A table saw whirred from inside. Through thin slats in the wood, a flurry of white-orange sparks made her imagine the Reformatory fire.

"You wait here." Lyle rested his gun against the shed wall and went in. The saw gnawed on, uninterrupted.

Gnats and moths drawn to the light from the shed swatted

Gloria's face. The dogs waited with her. Duke licked the chicken grease from her hands, but the other two dogs weren't sure of her and kept their distance. Just as well: dogs could smell fear, and Gloria was plenty afraid.

As Gloria stared at that shotgun standing within reach, she swore she knew what must have been in Isaiah Timmons's heart all those years ago, his boys stolen from him, wanting them home safe. She could see herself picking up the gun, storming in the shed, and telling Mister Red: *You call that judge right now and tell him to set Robbie free.* She could see his shocked face, and Lyle's, when they would hear her jack a shell into the chamber the way Papa had taught her. Her heart pounded in terror of herself, so she looked away from the gun. Even in her imagination, the idea felt dangerous enough to get her killed, and Robbie too. She would be buried here next.

Lyle called out to his father over the saw noise, and Mister Red answered, already irate.

He was as big as a barn and seemed to have grown since she'd seen him last. He had a reedy voice that didn't suit a man so large, but he used words like choppy hatchet blows. He had always set Gloria on edge, long before Papa's warnings. Lyle and his father spoke back and forth over the saw, with Lyle more childlike and his father getting madder.

The saw went off with an angry whine, and Mister Red's voice filled the silence. "What the hell'd you bring her here for?"

Gloria took a step away from the looming shed.

"I didn't bring her; she came on her own. Walked up the driveway."

"And you brought her to *me*?"

"Yessir," Lyle said. "So she can say her piece. I started the ruckus yesterday, so it's my responsibility. You always say to stand up for—"

"Shut your damn trap, jackass." And the unmistakable sound of a hand slapping flesh.

Gloria held her breath and didn't move even to swat gnats from her nose. She felt sorry for Lyle, stuck with Mister Red for a father, but she felt sorrier for herself.

As Gloria realized this man would never grant her wish, she heard Mister Red say, "Well, bring her in. We don't want to keep the Stephens Negress waiting, do we?"

And the shed door opened. Lyle was in the doorway, sweating like he'd been swimming. His father's handprint was painted across his cheek in bright red. Lyle didn't speak, but he gave Gloria a long stare and a nod, so she walked in. She was glad when Lyle didn't shut the door behind her. Even the dogs had sense enough not to follow.

This was Mister Red's hobby shed, full of wooden furniture he built himself: tables, chairs, a baby's crib. The shed glistened with expensive machinery and stank of chemicals. He had two dark planks laid across the table where he'd been sawing. Like Lyle, he was sweating. His hair really was bright red.

He pointed his cigar at her. "Let me tell you somethin', nigger—you are not welcome on this property, day or night. I catch you here again, I'll send the sheriff after you too."

Gloria nodded. "Yessir, Mr. McCormack." She'd almost called him Mister Red, which was what Papa called him. She was sure it would sound too familiar.

Mister Red came from around his table, pulling off his gloves. He threw them down one by one before he folded his arms. Even the tiny hairs on his arms were red. He was stout like Lou Costello from Abbott and Costello in overalls. He pulled on a billed cap as he studied her. He smelled like wood pulp and cigar tobacco.

"You're here now," he said. "You came trespassing. Go ahead and talk."

"Yessir," Gloria said, and she began. She recited everything she'd planned to say in the courtroom, speaking slowly and clearly, the entire map of the situation—except she said Robbie "misunderstood" Lyle's advance at the fence. Even so, Mister Red's eyes shot over to Lyle and she felt him squirming behind her.

"So you see, Mister Red, justice has already been served and Robbie should be sent home right away," Gloria finished. "He'll never do anything like it again. I promise you that, sir."

"Just like your goddamn daddy," he said, and Gloria's heart withered. Coming from Red McCormack, that couldn't be a compliment. "I don't have to ask where you got the nerve to march here and give me a damn speech." He glanced over at Lyle again, who stood in the doorway at his own safe distance. "What she's sayin' is true?"

"Yessir," Lyle mumbled. "I told you the kick was nothin'."

"Well, what's done is done. There's a system to things, and six months won't hurt him none. I still say any colored boy who'd kick my son is right where he belongs—even if Lyle needed kicking. But . . ."

Gloria's heart was carried away and back in his long pause as he waited, thinking it over. ". . . I will do this: I asked Warden Haddock to give him twenty lashes. May be too late now, but I'll call over and tell him never mind."

Gloria smothered a sob in her throat. Twenty lashes! Papa mostly only threatened with his belt, so Robbie had barely had a whipping in his life except a paddling or two at school. She shivered with grief and outrage. Even after boxing Robbie's ear and having him sent to the Reformatory, Mister Red hadn't been satisfied?

"Thank you, sir," Gloria choked out. "Yes—please do that."

"And that's the end of this matter. Don't you come by here again." He gestured toward Lyle with his cigar. "Lyle, you step outside. Close the door."

Gloria looked at Lyle, startled, and he was as confused as she. But his eyes dropped from hers and he quickly did as his father asked. The door dragged against the soil as it closed.

"Come here," Mister Red said, gesturing Gloria closer. Ash dropped from his cigar. Gloria fought every better instinct when she took three steps toward Mister Red, expecting him to hit her too. She didn't like his eyes on her—assessing her up and down like she was in the display case in the window at Lily's Dress Shop on Main Street. Or the butcher shop. He looked at her the way Lyle did.

"You knocked up?" he said.

It was the most shocking question anyone had ever asked Gloria Stephens—so shocking that, although she heard him clearly and knew his meaning, her mind wouldn't accept the words.

"*Speak up*, girl. If you're knocked up, I'll send Doc over to take care of it."

All Gloria could do was shake her head no. Mister Red scowled, not quite believing her. "Brown sugar's one thing, but Lyle's not claiming no babies. So if you get knocked up, I'll send Doc—but that's all you'll get. You won't see a penny otherwise. You hear? And don't wait 'til your belly shows."

Gloria's face flared hot. Her own mother had never discussed such things with her: Gloria was a virgin, and this kind of talk came before marriage from a parent, not a stranger.

"We're not . . . doing nothing." That was all Gloria could manage.

Mister Red shrugged, not hiding his skepticism. He walked back around the table to his monstrous saw. "Remember what I said. Otherwise, just keep clear of here. *Lyyyle!*"

His raised voice made Gloria jump. The door opened again, and Lyle stuck his head in. "See to it she gets back to the road. And latch the gate."

"Yessir," Lyle said.

Sparks flew again as the saw roared.

Gloria and Lyle scurried in the dark across the field back toward the road, Lyle's flashlight beam leading the way. Neither of them spoke, and Gloria noticed every detail about Lyle: his shallow breaths, a half whistle that sounded too merry, his five inches of height above her, a football player's build. Gloria walked faster, and he matched her pace. She would take Mister Red's advice and never set foot on his land again.

At the gate, Lyle moved in front of her, blocking her path. "He slapped me pretty good," Lyle said.

"I heard." If Gloria weren't so angry about Mister Red's outrageous statements, she might have told him how she'd felt sorry for him.

"I knew he would, or worse. But I did what you asked, Glo. And if he says he'll call the warden, he will. So it's good Robbie won't get those lashes, right?"

Gloria blinked away tears. "If it's not too late."

He touched her shoulder. "Come on, now—you stop that crying."

The tenderness in Lyle's voice made her queasy. "Okay," she said. "Good night, Lyle."

But he did not let her pass, and his hand rose from her shoulder to the back of her neck. His palm was callused and rough. "Well, before you rush off . . . don't you think I deserve a kiss? And I'll make sure he don't forget to call the warden."

Gloria wanted to slap Lyle McCormack more than she wanted to kiss him. He'd made a threat sound like an invitation. But she'd kissed a boy once before: Henry Dooley behind the schoolhouse when she was fifteen. That had been all right.

"Then you'll leave me be?" Gloria said.

"Quit stalling," he said, and moved his face close to hers.

Gloria tried to keep her lips tight, but Lyle's kiss was wet and eager and he kept angling to pry her lips open. His tongue was a limp, warm worm. Gloria felt herself gagging.

Lyle pushed her back against the gate. His full body pressed to hers, both hands holding her shoulders still. He rubbed his belly against her, then she was shocked to feel him press his groin to her. She shifted away. His hand traveled from her neck to her shoulder, then dropped to her breast. He squeezed childishly. No one had touched her chest that way before.

Gloria stomped on Lyle's foot, and he cried out, surprised. "*Stop it*," Gloria said.

"You promised me a kiss."

Gloria wriggled free, scraping her back so hard against the wooden gate that she rubbed her skin raw beneath her dress. "I never said you could put your hands all over me!"

"I just thought—"

"There's nothing between us, Lyle. Leave me alone!" Gloria said.

"Why are you so sore about it? You're real pretty, Glo. Don't you like me saying that?"

Gloria was careful to keep a two-foot distance between her and Lyle so she could dash from his reach. She would climb that gate if she had to. She was more certain than ever that Papa had never behaved this way. If Lyle got hold of her again, she might not be able to get free. If she screamed, only his father might hear. And what would her scream be to Mister Red?

"Open the gate," Gloria said. "Let me go."

Gloria's future sat waiting in the long seconds she waited for Lyle to respond. She worried that if Lyle touched her again, she would find her way back to that waiting shotgun like Isaiah Timmons over his missing boys. She imagined the gun now, still leaning against Red McCormack's work shed.

With a sigh, Lyle flipped the latch and opened the gate at arm's length. Gloria hesitated; she still would have to pass too close to him to get by.

"Daddy's sure right about you," Lyle said. "You Stephens niggers are so uppity. Even a white man's not good enough for you."

"I'm engaged," Gloria lied.

Lyle didn't answer. Lyle sighed again and stepped away from the gate. In his icy silence, Gloria wondered if he meant to tell his father not to call Warden Haddock. She wondered if a kiss was Robbie's only chance. But she could not kiss Lyle again.

"Thank you, Lyle, for doing right," Gloria said. And she ran past him through the open gate. One of the dogs barked at her, matching her pace inside the fence.

Lyle slammed the gate behind her. "Don't come back! Just like he said!"

Gloria barely heard him. Her hearing was swallowed by the barking, the pounding of her feet on the road, and her frantic heartbeat as she escaped McCormack Farm.

She could almost—almost—hear the footsteps of others who had run before her.

III

THE FUNHOUSE

11

Crabgrass whipped against Robert's shins as he ran, sharp through his pants. On the Negro side of the campus, the grass grew taller and thicker between the stands of swamp pines. The walk to the Negro dorms on the west side of the campus had taken longer than he expected, or he'd have panicked at leaving the kitchen with only five minutes to spare. He, Blue, and Redbone had started running when the two-story brick building came into sight fifty yards ahead. This close to curfew, no one lingered outside of the dormitory door.

Robert had only seen the fuller grounds in frantic glimpses: a baseball field with bleachers, a church. And fences, fences, all around, a maze of them—the outer ones topped with barbed wire. Even in his hurry, Robert mapped the campus in his head: the main gate, the long driveway, the warden's office, the ghost fire, the schoolhouse, the kitchen. The rest of the Negro side of the campus grew in the weeds, still a mystery in the shadows of waning daylight.

A far-off clock chimed, and they cussed and ran with all their might until they reached the brick path to the rectangular dormitory, which seemed as big as Gracetown Memorial Hospital. Robert flung himself up the stairs and past the columns to reach the double doors. The last toll of the bell sounded as their feet pattered the steps.

Boone waited at the top of the stairs, a clipboard in his hand. Behind him, the boys already inside hooted and laughed. Could laughter be waiting for him too, ten steps ahead?

"Somebody must want a whupping, huh?" Boone said.

"No, sir!" Robert, Blue, and Redbone said.

They all braced for what was next, until Boone said, "Ya'll locked up that pantry?" and they all insisted they had, and they knew they had escaped punishment because Boone's thoughts already had moved on past their tardiness.

"Sweeting, sir," Blue said from the head of their line. Redbone followed next—"Montgomery, sir"—and Boone checked off his name on his clipboard. Then it was Robert's turn, and he tried to imitate them: "Stephens, sir." A squeak in his voice.

Boone scowled. "We got more'n one Stephens. First initial?"

"R.," Robert said.

"That's what you say every night: Stephens—R.—sir. And you raise your voice so I can hear over these fools."

"Yessir."

"Go stand over there."

Two teenagers waited at the end of the foyer, also holding their ties. They did not meet Robert's eyes, and he kept his eyes away from them. He might have been scared of them if they hadn't looked so scared themselves, shifting their weight from foot to foot.

Redbone and Blue gave him small, secret waves as they vanished into the line of boys of all ages crowding the dormitory hallway. Robert felt sad and alone now; the dormitory might be the biggest building he'd ever set foot in, aside from the courthouse. Again the laughter of boys floated from the hall; easy, relaxed, even happy. Maybe it wouldn't be so bad, then. Maybe the worst of the day was done.

"Y'all follow me," Boone said. He sounded weary, no thunder left in his voice. He yawned behind his clipboard and led them behind the crowd of boys. "We got Lincoln wing and Washington wing. Lincoln this end, ages six to thirteen, Washington the other side, fourteen to twenty-one. Bunks, rec rooms, lockers, showers, all either Lincoln or Washington. Stick to yo' own sides. Hear?"

"Yessir," they all said.

The windows in the dormitory lobby had no bars. Mr. Loehmann had told him the Reformatory was a prison, but the windows were no different than the tall, sturdy windows he cranked open at Miz Lottie's house. These windows had screens, but screens were easy to cut or take out. He'd climbed out of Miz Lottie's window almost every night to play bid whist and sometimes craps in a shed with his cousins Walter and Priscilla. They had often played long past midnight, and neither Miz Lottie nor Gloria had heard him climb in or out.

"*Stephens,*" Boone said, his voice a bullet. "Which wing you in?"

Robert couldn't keep his shoulders from jumping, and one of the teenagers snickered and mimicked Robert's nervousness. Robert wanted to shove the stranger against the wall hard enough to rattle his teeth. For a moment, he was afraid he might.

"Lincoln," Robert answered Boone.

"That's the only thing you need in yo' head," Boone said.

Could Boone *know* he'd been thinking about climbing out of a window? Robert made sure not to look at another window as long as Boone was with him. Instead, he gazed at the polished floors and emptying halls.

Boone pointed out the locker room, rows of metal doors closed tight, wooden benches askew in the narrow walkway. "Pick an empty one, write yo' name in chalk—and that's yo' locker. You hang up yo' school clothes and tie at night, fold up yo' pajamas in the mornin'. But they don't got locks, so yo' stuff's gonna get stole. You don't want your stuff stole, don't put nothin' in there worth stealin'. You want peace, then don't have nothin' ev'rybody else ain't got. You get caught stealing, you go to the Funhouse. I find anything in yo' locker ain't supposed to be there—cigarettes, gum, anything even *looks* like a weapon—you go to the Funhouse. Don't tell me somebody else put it there, neither. If it's got yo' name on it, it's yo' whupping."

The rules were so unfair! Maybe no one could avoid the Funhouse, Robert thought.

Maybe that was why the whole table had gone quiet at dinner.

Boone took them to the bathroom doorway next, and Robert felt weary at the sight of rows of open shower stalls that surely meant he must wash naked in front of other boys. It was bad enough he'd stripped in front of the warden. He hadn't even liked Mama seeing him naked!

"You will shower *ev'ry* night—but grow eyes in the back of yo' head. You go in, wait your turn, wash, come out. If I hear a ruckus in my showers, it don't matter who started it. All o' y'all gettin' whipped. Trust in that. That's straight from the warden. Y'all will learn. Any dumb animal can learn from pain, so you will too."

"Yessir," Robert whispered. And he would have to shower tonight! Robert's stomach dragged against his ribs like a sack of stones.

Next, separated by a wall from the bathroom, the large sleeping quarters: rows of dozens of iron-frame beds made up with white sheets and thin folded blankets pushed too close together. Each bed had a tiny Bible on top of the blankets. The beds were so close, it would be easier to jump from one to the next than find a path between them. Miz Lottie used to let him sleep with his bedroom door closed because her snoring across the hall kept him awake. Quickly, he counted the rows and calculated: twelve beds times four rows. Forty-eight boys in one room! He would hear boys breathing and snoring on all sides. Would this dormitory also be crowded with ghosts like the kitchen and the field? Robert hadn't spied any yet or smelled any smoke, but his stomach pinched with dread at the sight of so many empty beds.

"This is the bunk room. Lights out means lights out—no talking, laughing, playing, fighting. You mess up in the bunk room, you'll see Warden Haddock. He likes to work late, and he walks these halls. You'll be dealing cards one minute, staring him in the face the next. And then you'll *wish* he took you to the Funhouse. The Funhouse ain't the worst we got."

Boone's low, tired voice was worse than his shouting, which had seemed for show. Now he sounded like he'd just set him and the other boys off on an island with no food or water, and monsters were hiding in the thickets.

I can't do this, Robert thought. He squeezed back tears just as laughter exploded from somewhere nearby. Dozens of boys seemed to be mocking him.

Boone tapped Robert's shoulder. "I'll leave you in the rec room 'til eight. Lights out eight thirty. That means you're in and out of the shower and in the bed. Hear?"

"Yessir."

The source of the laughter was the Lincoln wing's rec room next to the bunk room. Now Robert knew where all the others had vanished: they were crammed in the rec room, the boys his age in folding chairs, the younger boys sitting on the floor with their knees pulled to their chests, squeezed tightly against the others. Their attention was turned to the radio cabinet at the far end of the room, and no one was squirming or talking. The radio volume was up high enough to hear from the doorway. Heads turned when he first stood in the doorway, but nobody watched him long. Robert was so careful not to look anyone in the eye that he didn't see Blue or Redbone, his gaze skating away from any faces. Instead, he looked at the painted Indian shields on the wall.

One red, one blue. He studied the lines of paint to avoid anyone's eyes.

"Tell him she's the Jack the Ripper of canasta," the radio actor said, and the boys laughed with the radio audience. Robert knew the show right away: *Amos 'n' Andy*. He used to listen to the show until Papa snapped it off and told him those were white men playing Negroes, making Negroes look lazy and silly so white folks could laugh at them. In truth, Robert had always liked the show; he just couldn't tell Papa.

"I ain't never seen him befo' in my life, is I, Andy?" Kingfish said. Lying, no doubt. There: with a quick glance, Robert finally saw Blue on the floor by the far window, and Redbone near him. Neither of them smiled, but Redbone raised his chin slightly. Robert's stomach relaxed. Robert turned to glance at the hallway behind him: Boone and the other boys were gone, making their way to the other end of the long building. Boone had left him alone in the doorway. No eyes on him. Robert wanted to run outside into the overgrown grass so badly that his legs twitched. Not running made his eyes sting.

But he squeezed himself inside the doorway, careful not to jostle or touch anyone. He had just enough room to cross his legs, his back pressed to the wall. The floor was hard and cold through his thin dungarees. The boys who had worked in the sun hadn't showered yet, and a musk floated through the hot, crowded room. Robert could smell his own armpits too after sweating in the kitchen. They all breathed air hot from one another's sweat and lungs.

On the radio, Kingfish and Andy were pretending to be doctors, examining the mouth of Kingfish's aunt after Andy accidentally dropped his flashlight down her throat. Robert remembered why he'd liked the show so much: he could *see* them bumbling.

"I've got to put some antiseptic on my arm before I go in there," Kingfish said. "Ain't no use for her to catch what *we* got mixed up with what *she* got."

Robert's chest jumped with a chuckle. He didn't want to—didn't know how he could—but he laughed. His laugh brought tears to his eyes. Andy's voice was like a friend's, and he made Robert laugh again from old jokes, even when he remembered Mama saying, *We told you not to listen to that nonsense,* and it hurt like fire to remember her scolding. But he looked over at Blue and Redbone, and they were laughing too, and so was nearly every boy in the room.

Robert couldn't tell if his belly was cramping from laughter or sorrow.

The locker room bustled as boys rushed to undress and shower. Luckily, most of them paid Robert no mind, but several stared as they passed him, especially the bigger ones, probably trying to decide if they could whup him or if Robert could whup them. Robert could imagine how a careless gaze in the locker room could turn into a beating in the shower, so he looked at no one except Blue and Redbone, listening as they pointed out an empty locker across from theirs, probably still unclaimed because the wooden door swung unevenly on its hinge. The door closed, but barely. It was just enough for Robert to finally feel at ease about where to lay his tie to rest on the waiting hook. He found a nub of chalk on the floor and scribbled his name on the panel, over the names that had been rubbed away: *Stephens, R.*

"I leave all my clothes in here?" Robert asked.

"No, you flush them down the toilet," Blue said, sneering. "You ask dumb shit."

Robert cut a look at him; at his school, a boy who spoke to him that way would have to answer for it. But Blue was obviously trying to sound funny, so Robert let it go. Robert was just glad he wasn't as tiny as Blue, who barely reached his shoulder, like he was seven or eight instead of twelve. He seemed younger to Robert all the time.

Redbone pointed to a folded stack of towels rapidly dwindling by the door as boys took them. "Grab a towel, take it to the shower, come back with the towel, put on your white pajamas. That's what you sleep in. Drop your towel in the bin—*not* on the floor. Get in bed. And do it 'fore eight thirty. Watch the clock."

"How will I know which bed?"

"He don't know *nothing*," Blue complained.

"I'll point at an empty one," Redbone said. "Don't take nobody's bed."

"Anybody knows that," Blue said. Then Blue's eyelid slid down in a lazy wink to Robert, his signal that he was playing a part. Nothing personal. The wink made Robert's stomach burn less, but he was still mad. His face was tight. He remembered Blue locking them in the freezer and wished he'd smacked him at least once.

"Don't let nobody see they makin' you mad—even Blue," Redbone whispered.

That was all anyone said: Don't let anyone know or see anything about you. Don't be.

Redbone grabbed a towel, so Robert took one too. When they stood in front of their lockers and began undressing, Robert did too. He imagined everyone's eyes on his "chicken legs," as Gloria called them, so his hands were unsteady as he undressed. He wrapped himself with the towel before he took off his jeans. Then he slid his feet out of his boots.

The boots were slightly muddied from the field, but they obviously were brand-new.

Even the laces were bright in the dim colors of the locker room. Why hadn't he appreciated such fine boots when he first opened the box from Papa? He shoved the boots into the locker as fast as he could, but this time he was *sure* other boys were watching. Papa's new boots would get stolen and there was nothing he could do.

A white slip of paper was stuck to the sole of his foot, damp from sweat. He peeled it off and saw that it was the business card from David R. Loehmann, State of Florida Children's Services.

Like he could pick up a phone anytime he wanted. Like Loehmann would take his call.

Loehmann had pretended to be nice by giving him a sandwich and advice, but if Loehmann gave a damn, he never would have brought him. Robert pursed his lips so tightly that his teeth hurt. He ripped the card in half, and again, and again, until the pieces floated to his feet.

"Better not leave no trash," Blue whispered, a peace offering. "I was just playing."

Robert collected the torn card and threw it into the dented gray metal trash can on his way out of the door. He didn't hang close enough to Redbone and Blue for anyone to notice, but he never strayed far in the stream of boys he did not know. Robert had fallen into a dark tunnel, and his new friends were the only light.

‖‖‖‖‖‖‖‖

The line for the shower room barely allowed Robert inside the doorway. A husky boy's jostling sent Blue and Redbone four or five places ahead, so Robert tried to vanish into the line, staring at the mildew-veined walls, his fingers pinching his towel around his waist so tightly that his fingers cramped.

The cloak of steam wasn't thick enough to fog the chipped mirrors, so his own wide eyes stared back at him from the mirror above the sink. The sight of his own face startled Robert, his eyes so big, his shoulders so small. He forced himself to straighten up, to stop standing like a turtle in a shell, to narrow his eyes into a glare. No, too much: someone would take offense. He softened his glare into a thoughtful scowl, alert but unafraid, practicing which face to wear.

The shower room had ten showerheads on each side divided into five stalls, all of them crowded. Everyone shared a stall with at least one other boy, sometimes two. And he was trapped. Robert wanted to turn around and take his chances in the bunk room, but Boone had said everyone had to shower, and he was already afraid he smelled bad from peeing himself in the warden's office. He had learned from Mama's bedsheets that urine smelled worse over time.

Pumpkin, you've got no reason to be so shy, Mama used to say.

Or had she just said it again now? Robert had heard her voice in his ear, somewhere buried in the hissing water and low, quiet taunts and the memory of her soiled bedsheets. Her voice came to him again, somehow *inside* his ears: *Don't be scared, Robert. This is only a season, and it will pass. No matter what happens—it will pass.*

Her voice was as plain as the smell of the smoke, real enough to touch. Mama was here!

Miz Lottie and Papa's kin talked about haints and spirits, but for the first time Robert understood: *Death was not the end,* just like Reverend Jenkins said when he quoted from the book of John. Mama was stronger here than she'd been at home, somehow. Closer, somehow. Maybe because he needed her more.

"Ma—" he started to call for her, but buried his blurting as a phony cough. The boy behind him sniggered. Robert coughed again to be more convincing, but Mama's voice had set his heart racing. *What* will pass? Her voice had seemed urgent, a warning.

"Mama?" he whispered.

And a pipe above him made a small ringing sound. *Ping.*

It was soft, but Robert's ear caught it. He stared behind him and found a whitewashed water pipe nestled in the wall, traveling the length of the room. *Ping.* The tiny notes raced faster, nearly identical in pitch, but not quite—enough to sound like movement and life. For him alone.

Pingpingpingping.

"Mama?"

Ping. Clear and strong, the loveliest note yet. It sounded so much like a yes that tears came to Robert's eyes. His heart raced him dizzy.

"Forget you, then," the boy behind Robert said, and shoved past him in line. A second boy followed. A third might have too, except that he was smallish, so Robert stood fixed and dared the boy to try to butt ahead of him. If he let himself get pushed out of the line, it would happen again the next night. And the next. He didn't need Blue and Redbone to tell him that.

"You cryin'?" the boy behind him said. "Crybaby."

"No."

The boy tried to pass again, but Robert blocked him with his hip, more forcefully this time. "What you gonna do?" the boy said, biting his lower lip to try to look meaner, or taller.

"Guess you'll find out," Robert said.

But the boy never did find out. He fell back to his own place to wait. Robert listened for another ping from Mama, but none came.

Instead, a smell answered him. The odor floated from the steam itself; something wet and rotting, as if dozens of rats had died in the pipes and the water was washing away bits of stewed flesh and fur. From the smell, the shower water should have been brown or gray, but instead it sprayed clear like any other. Robert gagged.

No, not rats. Worse than rats. Robert couldn't name the foul smell. For a moment, the smell made him forget who and where he was, a blanket smothering him.

"You goin' or what?" a voice said behind him. Someone gave him a small push, and he stumbled forward to a shower stall where only one other boy was bathing, his back bare except for streams of soapy water. Robert thought about how he had undressed in the warden's office, the uncomfortable memory holding him still so long that the lukewarm water pelted his towel. He finally took off his towel and flung it over the stall wall like the others. He hoped no one could see him trembling. He lifted up his chin and closed his eyes beneath the showerhead's stream so no one would see his tears. The water was lukewarm, almost cool.

And sour.

He spit out the taste as the stench in the water spilled across his skin. Robert kept from throwing up only because of his fear of ridicule and his worry that Boone might take him to the Funhouse for making a mess. None of the other punishments were fair, so why would it be different for getting sick? He glanced quickly at the boy beside him, who was slapping his soapy hands under his arms without a care.

Maybe no one else could smell it. Maybe it was a ghost smell, like the fire.

I hate this place, Robert thought. *I just want to go home, Mama.*

PING.

The sound came so loudly that Robert jumped. Even the boy beside him turned his head to look at the pipe that ran across the length of their stall. But the boy looked away, not interested. Robert laid his hand on the pipe, as warm as human flesh, coursing with water like blood. Mama was here, somehow! Whatever gave the water its terrible smell, it wasn't from Mama. She was fighting *through* the smell to get to him. Robert didn't know how he knew, but he knew that plainly. Robert leaned against the slimy shower wall nestling the pipe. He wished he could climb into the wall, through the concrete. He wanted to feel his mother's hug again. He wished she would appear like the stabbed boy in the kitchen, solid enough to lay eyes on. A sob—part joy, part sorrow—clawed from his throat.

"Hey," the boy beside him said. "You can't act like a sissy in here, dummy."

"My mama's ghost is here," Robert whispered. "Right now."

"So?" the boy said. "Be glad it's only your mama, stupid."

Robert swallowed back his sob and stood up straight. He grabbed a chalky bar of soap from the dish and tried to make enough lather to wash. No one had given him a washrag like Gloria always insisted he use at home, so he did his best with his hands on his face, under his arms, between his legs, though he barely brushed his privates because he didn't want anyone to see him washing there. Robert was shivering as he grabbed his damp towel and tried to rub himself dry.

The bunk room was hotter than the shower room even without steam.

Redbone led Robert down the length of the beds pushed so closely together that he could barely avoid bumping them. Robert took small steps, hips to the side. Many of the boys were already on their beds, either sitting or lying down. Talking was more fevered, everyone squeezing in their last bit of living while the lights were on, some playing cards or dominos, some sharing jokes. He heard a crack of marbles. A few were so tired they were already curled under their blankets, trying to sleep in the din. A handful were thumbing through their New Testaments, reading with their lips moving, as if memorizing the words could set them free.

Redbone pointed out a bed in the middle section, almost dead center, far from doors or windows. His neighbors were so close, they might as well be sharing one bed. One boy had glasses that made his eyes look like an owl's, listening to their every word with his chin propped on his elbows like they were a shiny new television screen in a store window. The other was sketching on a pad with black chalk, seeing and hearing nothing. Neither one looked like trouble.

"If a bed opens up by a window, grab it," Redbone said. "But you'll have to fight somebody for it. Ev'rybody likes windows for the breeze. Hot as hell in the middle."

Redbone glanced back at Robert and must have felt sorry for the look on his face. "You git used to it, though. We all start in the middle."

Robert stared at the windows lining the room, amazed again to see no bars. And most of the windows were cracked open. Did they sleep beneath open windows every night? The panes were too narrow to climb through, but with a screwdriver and time to work on the frame, maybe over days, he could get out. The windows were high, but he could stand on his bed. He almost said it aloud: *Why don't more of y'all run away?*

Redbone saw the unspoken question in his eyes.

"Oh, you might hear barkin' from the dogs," Redbone said casually. "The dog boys march up an' down outside with those hounds all night long, an' sometimes a squirrel or a possum riles 'em. But you'll git used to the barkin' too." Robert nodded that he understood: more boys didn't flee through the dorm's open windows because they were afraid of the dogs.

Redbone left him to go to his own bed in a far corner, beneath a window. Blue's bed was beside Redbone's, so close they could be sharing one, and Robert envied how they must whisper jokes in each other's ears. Blue gave him a nod. Robert almost smiled.

He was relieved Cleo and his friends weren't hidden anywhere in the room of nearly fifty boys. Cleo's gang was older, so they must be in the Washington wing. The first good news: he wouldn't have to be afraid Cleo might attack him in the night. He couldn't forget Cleo's terrible stare in the cafeteria. Some people never forgot a slight, no matter how small or unintended.

Robert noticed Owl still staring, wondering what to expect from him. "You don't bother me, I won't bother you," Robert said.

Owl shrugged.

"*Shhhhh,*" said the boy who was drawing. He was sketching a cypress tree standing alone in the swamp, and it was good enough to be a photograph: fat trunk squatting in the water, tendrils hanging like string, the water shining the tree's reflection back at it. Robert wished he could draw himself away somewhere else too. He sat on his bed and watched the boy's sure strokes as he drew shadows like a magician. A wiry boy in the bed in front of the artist's was leaning back to watch too.

"When you gonna draw me?" the other boy said.

"When you gonna cough up that dollar?"

Owl snickered. "Nobody's payin' you a dollar for that. A nickel, maybe."

A voice roared from the doorway: "*Prayer!*"

Everything shuffled around him. The artist shoved his pad under his bed, playing card decks fanned closed, marbles rolled stray on the floor. Everyone kneeled on the right side of their beds, folding their hands in a prayer position. For a moment, Robert only watched before he remembered to kneel and pray too. The cool floor was his only relief from the heat.

"The Lord is my shepherd . . . ," a boy began, and then the room was one voice, matching the tempo and monotone: "I shall not want. He maketh me to lie down in green pastures . . ."

Robert heard officious footsteps and peeked through a half-open eyelid: Boone and Crutcher were pacing the rows of beds. Boone was carrying a long wooden ruler. A thwack sounded as Boone smacked a boy across his back. Robert squeezed his eyes closed and recited in rhythm with the others, afraid to scratch his itching ear: "Yea, though I walk through the valley of the shadow of death, I will fear no evil: for thou art with me; thy rod and thy staff they comfort me. . . ."

Thwack. A brief, startled cry of pain somewhere behind him. That boy sounded very young. Robert was so nervous, he nearly forgot the words to the prayer he had recited in front of his entire congregation when he was only six while Mama, Papa, and Pastor Jenkins stared on with pride. He'd imagined that God was staring down at him with pride too—but he could barely think about God with a prayer interrupted by ruler strokes. The words seemed a boldfaced lie. ". . . Surely goodness and mercy shall follow me all the days of my life: and I will dwell in the house of the Lord for ever."

What goodness and mercy? But Robert said "Amen" with everyone else. He was grateful not to feel the ruler across his back for wrongdoing he didn't know was wrong. What had those boys done? Squirmed? Not prayed fast enough?

"Lights out!" Boone shouted, and the overhead lights switched off. Robert hadn't realized how bright the lights had been until they were gone. The only light left in the room streamed in from the hall. Around him, everyone hurried back into bed.

"Try me tonight," Boone warned from the doorway. "Somebody try me *just once*. I can't wait to take some of y'all out to the Funhouse with Warden Haddock. Who's it gon' be?"

The room was a tomb, no one breathing. Robert's folded blanket had fallen to the floor beside his bed, but he was afraid to pick it up. Would Boone take him to the Funhouse for dropping it? For reaching for it? The footsteps snapped down the hall, and they all sighed and breathed together. A couple of boys snickered, trying to be tough, but hardly loud enough for anyone to hear but themselves. Robert waited to hear if the footsteps would return, but in time even the echo was gone.

In the dark, Robert couldn't ignore the heat. His thin sheet clung to his sweaty skin so tightly that he felt like a bug trapped in a giant spider's web. He flung the sheet away. His house let in breezes in the summer, but this heavy heat was like someone lying on top of him. Was it truly this hot, or was this heat a memory from the fire? The heat sat so hard that Robert was sure his lungs were filling with hot water instead of air.

A mosquito landed on his shoulder, invisible in the dark. He ignored it and glanced right and left at the other boys, who still seemed afraid to move although Boone and Crutcher were gone. When the mosquito bit him, Robert slapped lightly at his slick skin. Every movement made the heat worse, a rippling current. No wonder everyone lay so still.

But despite the heat—or maybe because of it—Robert's sore, weary bones sank into the thin mattress and made him so drowsy that he didn't notice the return of the terrible smell for a long time. And when he did notice, he thought he was only remembering the shower room. But then the sharpness seared his nostrils—burned, rancid flesh—and Robert jolted awake.

The banks of windows and beds were not familiar when he first woke, and when he remembered—*The judge sent me to the Reformatory, and I'll be here six months*—his heart thudded and then sank with such misery that only the threat hidden in the awful smell kept him from whimpering. He heard someone crying softly in the vast room, smothered against a pillow. An angry "*Shhhhhh*" and "Damn baby gon' get us all whipped" silenced the crying.

Robert hoped the smell would fade, but instead it grew stronger. A slow, rough scraping across the floor was much louder than the buzzing flies or soft snoring around him: moving and halting, moving and halting, coming closer to him from the center row where his head lay. The object dragging sounded like . . . a bum leg, his foot dragging slowly? The smell and the scraping sound were tied together; when one came closer, so did the other.

It definitely wasn't Mama.

Robert warred with himself: Should he turn his head to look or not? Would it go away if he waited long enough, like the stabbed boy in the kitchen? What had Redbone's advice been about ghosts? His head swam as he tried to remember.

"Go away," Robert whispered, staring up at the ceiling's dark, sleeping light bulbs. "You're dead. So just stay dead."

The dragging came closer, the smell so powerful that it brought tears to Robert's eyes. He locked his throat to keep from vomiting. It was the worst smell he had ever known—worse than the deer carcass bloating in the creek bed he and Papa had found when they were hunting, its body a gross whitish pink from swelling. Papa had pulled him away, tried to cover his eyes. Just like then, everything inside Robert told him to keep his eyes away, but he had to see it. He had to *know*. (*Had* it really been a deer? Or had it been a child wrapped in wet clothing?)

Robert's neck gave a tiny crack as he turned his head toward the insistent scraping. The shadow was the size of a boy not much bigger than he was, the shape so black that it was darker than night, leaching colors from everything it passed. Too-white eyes stared at him from the blackness. The figure moved slowly, so slowly, with the scraping sound: the boy, or whatever the shadow thing was, dragged a lame leg behind.

Robert's heart tried to fight free of his ribs. He thought he would faint, but he couldn't stop staring even as the shadowed boy came closer. When the figure was close enough to touch—and when the smell was choking him—Robert saw glimmering on the figure's face and skin and realized he was burned all over, charred like meat on a grill. The alien eyes stared.

Robert's teeth chattered. It must be one of the boys who had died in the fire. Maybe he had followed him all the way from the field.

"I'm sorry . . . ," Robert whispered. "But you're dead. I can't help you. Go away."

For good measure, he closed his eyes tight and counted to ten. *One . . . two . . . three . . .*

He took his time counting, because counting was his last plan to keep from screaming. His heartbeat rocked him as he counted, as if a part of him knew the shadow would be staring him face-to-face when he opened his eyes. . . . *Eight . . . nine . . . TEN.*

He held his breath. And peeked.

Nothing but a bare floor and the empty row between the cots. Even the smell was gone. Robert's relief was so great that he gulped at the air and shuddered when he exhaled. He might not have breathed for two minutes. A mad giggle tickled the back of his throat and almost escaped. He was giddy with the thought of it: ghosts came to him, yes, *but he could make them leave*. Maybe no ghost could hurt him.

Robert was still smiling when the lights glared on, waking everyone, and Boone yanked him from his bed.

12

"Y'all must be the dumbest bastards ever born," Boone said.

Robert would have been sure he was having a nightmare, except for the way his shoulder smarted from Boone's rough handling. He'd been shoved out in the hallway, blinking in the bright lights. He, Redbone, and Blue stood lined up with Boone and Crutcher tall over them. At first he thought he'd been roused for Warden Haddock's twenty lashes, but why all three of them? Was it for swiping the apple tarts in the kitchen? Playing in the freezer? Arriving a few seconds late for curfew? With each thrum of his heart, Robert thought of a new reason he, Blue, and Redbone might be in trouble.

He dared a quick glance at Redbone and saw how afraid he was too: the hard set of his jaw, and a nervous swaying, like a scarecrow in a storm. Blue was already crying, his silent jaw quivering. Why couldn't this night, this whole day, this year, just be a dream? Robert felt himself pushing himself back against the wall as if he were a ghost who could vanish through it.

"Mister Boone, we didn't think we was late, sir," Redbone said, voice hardly above a whisper. "We ran here fast as we could."

Redbone braced for the crack across his shoulder from Boone's ruler. He flinched, but barely. Robert didn't see even a blink.

"You so dumb," Boone said, "you don't even know."

None of them could say they did. None of them dared to ask.

Crutcher leaned close enough for Robert to smell smoke on his breath. "What were you talking about at dinner, gentlemen?" he said. "Maybe that would ring a bell."

Dinner! Robert realized he was panting only when he opened

his mouth to speak. "I w-was j-just asking questions 'bout this place."

"That's not what we heard," Boone said. "Boy over in Washington says he heard you talking 'bout running away."

All three of them let out wails: realization, horror, shock. Boone's charge sounded so much worse than anything they had imagined. Tears streamed freely down Blue's face, and he shook his head as if it might fall loose. The memory crashed back over Robert: how Redbone said not to talk about how boys ran away, but how Blue had pressed on. The way the other boys at the table had jumped up and walked away, too wise to stay close to them.

"We wasn't plannin' nothin'. It was just stories. I just got here, Mister Boone—" Boone's blow with the ruler landed on Robert's crown and grazed his ear—not the one Red McCormack hurt, but the thin wood smarted enough that he dodged away and won a second blow across his hip, which made his teeth hiss. The second blow was harder, like a snakebite through his thin pants, stinging long after the ruler was gone.

"You don't even say the word *runnin'*," Boone said. "You don't *think* about runnin'. Some things is common sense, or ought to be if you ain't dumb as hell."

"It was me," Redbone said. "Robert didn't ask nothin' 'bout where to run. I was just talkin' 'bout those stupid boys at Boot Hill. Why I wanna run now? Wouldn't make no sense. You know me, Mister Boone, sir. I ain't like these simple boys out here missin' their mamas, cryin' 'cuz they never held a plow or rode a thresher. You know how I tell stories, Mister Boone."

Redbone's voice was a low, quiet begging, but he was so persuasive that Robert doubted his own memory. Hadn't it been Blue who told the stories about running away? Hadn't Redbone been the one who'd tried to shush him? Redbone had seen this horror coming.

"You talk too damn much," Boone said. "I told you, ain't I? Talkin' all the damn time."

"*All* the time," Crutcher said. He mimicked talking with his hand. "Yak yak yak."

"Yessir. I'm sorry, sir," Redbone said. "I didn't mean to get nobody in trouble."

Blue's head wobbled up and down as he tried to nod despite his shaking. "I didn't do *nothin'*, Mister Boone. I can go back to bed, sir?" Robert heard Blue's homeland thick in his accent, parts of him already fleeing far from Gracetown. When Boone didn't say anything or give him a glance, Blue ventured a step toward the door and scurried away. And he'd talked more than anyone at dinner!

Robert's heart ran with Blue, but he didn't dare move. Robert hoped he would be next, that Boone would say *That true?* and he'd say *Yessir,* he hadn't known what he was asking, and Redbone had told him about a stupid boy who ran and ended up getting buried—because that's what happened when you ran.

"Can we go back to bed?" Redbone said. "We'll work extra hours. We wouldn't try nothin' like what you said, Mister Boone. You know I ain't that way."

The long night and a day and another night seemed to pass while Boone studied them, making up his mind. A clock ticked on the wall behind them, the seconds impossibly slow.

"Naw," Boone said to Redbone. "You know better. You goin' to the Funhouse." A thunderclap shook Robert's head. For a flash, his vision went white.

Boone's eyes came to Robert next. Robert was praying so loudly to himself, he wondered how everyone couldn't hear him begging God to let him go back to bed.

"You too," Boone said. "Best learn early so you'll never wanna go back."

Robert looked to Redbone: *What now?* But Redbone's face was empty as he sagged against the wall, all swaying gone. Boone grabbed Redbone's arm with a meaty fist and pulled him to his feet. Crutcher took Robert's arm and shook him into motion.

"Go back to sleep or you'll be next!" Boone shouted as they passed the bunk room's open doorway. A dozen faces stared from the nearest beds. His comrades had pity in their eyes.

Somewhere in the dark, Blue was crying.

Boone ordered them to climb into the bed of the dusty white truck with a State of Florida seal parked outside of the dorm's rear door. Redbone climbed in right away, but Robert paused so long that Boone hit him with the stick, a flame across his buttocks. Robert whimpered and climbed into the truck, tumbling beside Redbone when his foot slipped. The truck's grooved metal was warm from the day's sun beneath a thin layer of dirt and straw. Crutcher stood watch over them from the doorway ten feet away while Boone went back inside the dorm.

"Where he goin'?" Robert whispered.

Redbone didn't answer, staring away.

"Why we gotta get in a truck?" Robert said. "Where they gonna take us?" His imagination flooded with his parents' stories of the woods and trucks and the night.

"Shut up," Redbone said.

"How come you covered for Blue?" Robert said.

"You started it, not Blue." Redbone's voice hitched, and Robert's guilt made the air wet in his lungs. If Redbone cried now, he would scream.

"Why wouldn't Blue shut up, then?" Robert said.

"Blue's Blue, that's why." Redbone glanced toward Crutcher, who was still waiting by the door, wrapped in a halo of smoke from his long cigarette. "Blue can't go to the Funhouse. You and me can."

"I can't neither." Mama's hand had stayed Papa's strap many times. Papa had said it would make him weak, and maybe Papa had been right.

"Yeah. You can," Redbone said, looking him in the eye for the first time since they'd been in the truck. "But Blue, he *can't* go. This ain't nothin' to me, long as they don't add to my time. And you'll get some marks, but you'll heal up fine—just like I did when I went one time. Blue's not like us."

Redbone turned away, his eyes distant again. Blue was everything to him. Blue liked to play pranks and tell jokes, so maybe Blue was everything to all of Lincoln. And *he* was nothing to any of them. No one here cared about him the way Redbone cared about Blue.

"But I can't neither," Robert whispered. He'd been tender-headed even when Mama pulled a comb through his hair.

Redbone leaned back against the truck's panel. "You better figure out how. You and me both." His sad eyes were raised to the moon.

The truck rumbled to a stop at the far end of the campus, on the white side, within sight of the cornfields behind the fences, gray in the night. Chains clattered as the teenage boy beside them kicked his feet in rage. The older boy was the only one of the three of them whose legs and wrists were bound. Boone had carried him out of the dorm over his shoulder like he was a side of beef and dropped him into the truck while the boy screamed his ribs hurt. The boy hadn't stopped cussing the whole time the truck sped them away from the dorm, bumping over rocks and knots of grass, every building ahead a fright in the headlight beams. The older boy's lower lip was bleeding, or maybe his gum, the blood trickling down the right side of his chin. Neither he nor Redbone asked him what he'd done, although Boone and Crutcher would not have heard them over the engine's rumble. The boy was scary, even in chains. Robert thought he might be one of Cleo's friends who'd jumped him after class, but he wasn't sure. That memory was a blur of shoes and fists.

"Don't look at me, sissy," the teenager said, so Robert kept his eyes away.

The truck passed the kennels, a strip of fence where at least half a dozen dogs the size of Old Man McCormack's barked from behind the wires. The dogs ran to keep pace as the truck drove past, eager for a chase. The dogs sounded angry, not playful. Robert wondered what the dogs did when they caught you.

When the truck lurched to a stop, his heart bloated to his throat. The engine clicked after it was turned off. The small wooden structure glowing in the bright headlights looked hardly bigger than Miz Lottie's backyard gardening shed, painted bright white.

Two white boys sat on a bench just outside the closed door. Not far off, a white man in a billed cap kept watch over them. Robert thought maybe the Funhouse couldn't be so bad, with white boys here too—until he saw their eyes. They looked terrorized. From inside the shed came a crack of leather striking flesh, and a child's scream after. Robert had never heard anyone scream that way except Mama, when she'd been dying. Or the voices from the fire.

"Get 'im out," Boone said. "Haddock wants him next."

Robert's body shook in his corner where he sat. He scooted closer to Redbone as Boone pulled down the truck's door with a sharp, rusty whine. Their hearts galloped with relief when Boone and Crutcher pulled the teenage boy out first and set him on his feet.

"I'm not goin' in there, you sick sons of bitches!" the boy yelled, lunging away. Boone hit him with a knee in the stomach so fast that Robert barely saw Boone move. The teenager doubled over while Boone and Crutcher pulled him to the Funhouse door.

"You've all got the devil in you!" the boy screamed.

"Git on in here, doggie doggie," the warden's voice charged through the closed door.

"Fuck you—" the teenager started to shout, but Boone smacked his mouth. The pain turned the teenager's rage to deep sobs instead. "Please. *Please—*"

"Shut the hell up," Crutcher said. "These babies are more a man than you."

Robert and Redbone looked at the white boys then, who in turn looked at them, mirroring them. Robert could swear he knew them although they had never met. The taller of the white boys, sandy-haired like the ghost in the kitchen, was turning a marble over in his palm. Robert wondered if he meant to use it as a weapon, but it was too small to be anything except a charm. Would he carry it through his whipping? Robert wished he had a marble—any toy—to hold.

The Funhouse door opened just as Crutcher signaled Robert and Redbone out of the truck. Robert saw only glimpses of a bare light bulb inside, the warden's silhouette, another man behind him. The wailing Negro teenager was dragged in. A crying young white boy was led out to the white man in the billed cap, who pulled him by the arm. The boy was having trouble walking, stumbling over his feet. In the shaft of light from the doorway, Robert thought he saw streaks of blood on his back. Robert's veins flushed with ice as if he were still in the freezer.

"Negroes wait on the other side," Crutcher said, gesturing. He said *Nee-GROES* with emphasis, and Robert realized he had never heard Crutcher say the word *nigger*. He might hate that word as much as Papa.

Robert walked where Redbone led him, but he turned his head to lock eyes with the white boys as long as he could, as if they could stare a plan into each other's minds. But soon he and Redbone were on the dark side of the shed, where six empty metal chairs waited, askew. Boone did not come with them. He'd gone inside the Funhouse too.

Crutcher straightened the chairs to a line and gestured for them to sit. Then he went off to pace by the fence, lighting another cigarette in the moonlight. Behind him, corn stalks shook in the breeze.

Robert's knees still trembled after he sat. Warden Haddock was lecturing inside the shed, but his voice was too low to make out. Robert heard only the sobbing.

"Maybe they'll get tired," Redbone said.

They? Robert's body tensed so much that his chair's legs rattled.

"Two or three hold you, one beats you. They lay you on a table and take turns."

"*No talking*. Talking's what got you here," Crutcher said, hushed. "If you can't learn here, where will you learn?"

"I've learned, sir," Robert said.

"Me too, sir."

"Shush—you haven't. There's worse than this waiting for you in the world. It's a shame for the new one, but I hope you see now to stay far away from the Funhouse."

"Yes, sir, I see," Robert said. His throat was crammed with tears. He wanted to say he was sorry for what he'd done, but he couldn't remember: Was it for asking a question about running away or because he'd eaten the apple tart from Blue? Was it because he'd been late to the bunk room or because he'd kicked Lyle McCormack on Tobacco Road? He couldn't count everything he was sorry for.

"Don't go in there arguin'. Learn the lesson, say you're sorry," Crutcher said. "Put it behind you. Have a chance to grow up." His voice seemed to crack, or had Robert imagined it? "Can't be like your daddy, fighting battles you can't win. His way don't work here."

Robert looked at Crutcher, startled. He couldn't make out his face, so far off at the fence. "You know my daddy?" Robert said. "Sir?" Crutcher didn't answer, so Robert asked again. "Mr. Crutcher, you know my—"

"Course I do—from the mill," Crutcher said. "Nobody in three counties don't know the name Robert Stephens." Robert heard admiration in his voice. Crutcher's orange cigarette ash flared to the ground. "You two choose which one goes first."

Perspiration sprang out on Robert, everywhere at once. "I'll go first," Redbone said. "Waiting's harder."

Inside the shed, the floor creaked. A sharp whistle, then a lash. The teenager yelped, crying. His whipping had begun. Two lashes. Three. Four. Five. The higher the number, each as hard as, or worse than, the previous one, the more Robert's own shoulders and knees whined with each one. The sound rocked through him. Would it never stop? He thought the twentieth lash would end it, but it didn't. Or the thirtieth. But after thirty-five lashes, when tears dripped from Robert's face, the whipping stopped. The sobbing was gone too, and the silence was worse. Robert was dizzy from not breathing. He sucked at the air. The chair's seat beneath him was so damp, he couldn't tell if he'd wet himself again.

Crutcher went to help bring the older boy out. Robert stared at the cornfield, wondering if there was a place to scale the fence or a hole someone might have left unrepaired in overgrown brush. He would have cut off his arm to know. He would have tried to outrun dogs.

"They give you a wood chip to bite on," Redbone said. "Don't spit it out. Better use it."

Crutcher signaled from around the corner, and Redbone rose to go to him. Robert burned to say something to him, but he couldn't make his mouth move. Redbone didn't look toward him anyway. Robert couldn't see the door from where he sat, or the waiting white boys, but he saw Boone and a white man drag the older boy out of the Funhouse by the shoulders.

Was he moving? Was he dead?

Robert's chair rattled when he craned to see the two men lift the teenager back into the truck. He was relieved when the teenager bucked and cried out again. His legs and wrists were still chained. Boone clapped the truck's panel shut and patted the door, and the white man drove the teenager away, toward a part of the campus Robert did not know. Maybe they were taking him to the infirmary.

Then Boone pulled Redbone's arm, and Redbone vanished behind the clapboard wall.

The door slammed closed. Crutcher strolled back toward Robert, but this time he posted himself so he could see the white boys on one side and Robert on the other, a good fifteen yards away.

Robert knew he could easily outrun Crutcher at this distance, if only he knew where to go.

Inside the shed, the warden's voice sounded jovial, as if he were meeting an old friend. No delays. No scuffles. Redbone's lashes began right away.

Liquid fire. That was the feeling of the strap. Robert felt it in Redbone's scream, loud and anguished and somehow surprised. By the second lash, the surprise in his scream was gone. For his third lash, Redbone must have gritted down hard on his wood chip, so his scream sounded more muffled. But whether they were loud or soft, Redbone's screams chafed Robert's ears raw and wrung out tears that drowned his face. His chair legs clattered when he sobbed.

I can't do this, he thought. He remembered the shower room and the pinging he'd heard from the wall, when he'd been so sure Mama was there. Was she still watching him? His fright in the shower room was long ago and silly now.

"Mama?" he whispered to the shadowed corn. "I need you. I can't do this. I can't."

The breeze picked up and dry corn stalks whispered, and Robert remembered when such things used to feel like a sign from Mama. If he saw a red bird (Mama's favorite). If he found the tiny silver cross Mama had given him on his floor in the exact same spot three days in a row. If he heard a creak on the floorboards when his eyes were closed. Even the shadow across his window. But whispering corn wasn't enough to comfort him now.

"Please, Mama. I know maybe it's hard to come, but I need you."

The ping sounded just below his pinkie where he was resting his weight on his chair. He heard it both from the metal and between his ears, amplified, and this time he *felt* it too, a pulse.

"Why I gotta be here, Mama? I can't do this. It ain't fair."

Another ping, and this time he cupped his hand over the vibration so it tickled his palm. In that touch, Robert felt how sorry

Mama was to see him like this, how she wanted to help, but couldn't. *Ping*. This time, he felt her arms wrap around him and sway with him.

This isn't everything, he heard Mama's voice say inside his ear. *Mama's here. There's more ahead for you than this. This is only a moment.*

LASH! Redbone must have dropped his wood chip. He howled.

"This isn't everything. There's more than this," Robert said.

The ping tickled Robert's palm, and his ears fogged, the howling far away.

13

True to its carnival name, the Funhouse looked twice as big on the inside, an endlessly long shed with the table at its center lighted from an overhead bulb as if it were a main stage. A transistor radio on the shelf by the door played a cheerful song like a county fair: a fiddle and a guitar and a singer who sounded like a cowboy. Laughter snapped Robert's head around; two shirtless, sweating white men were dealing cards over wooden crates in the corner, their bare bellies jiggling when they laughed. Everyone else was busy: Crutcher was wiping down the table beneath the lights, Boone was locking the door behind him, and Warden Haddock was rinsing his leather strap in a small sink. Robert tried not to notice how the water washed down pink.

Methodically, Warden Haddock wiped the thick strap with a towel.

This isn't everything. There is more than this.

"Didn't 'spect I'd be seeing you tonight," Warden Haddock said. His low voice rumbled the pit of Robert's stomach.

"S-sir?"

"After I got that call from Red McCormack saying hold off, I didn't 'spect to see you."

"No, sir." Robert tried to hold his tears at bay, but why couldn't he escape bad luck?

McCormack had changed his mind—Gloria had a hand in it; he was sure of it—but he might be worse off despite whatever miracle she had performed for him.

"Not getting off to a good start, are you?" Warden Haddock said.

"No, sir." Robert could barely speak through the coat of phlegm in his throat.

Warden Haddock slowly wiped his strap. "You know what you did wrong?"

Robert longed to argue, but he remembered Crutcher's warning. "Asking stupid questions, sir. I'm sorry, sir."

Warden Haddock laid his strap down on the table and picked up a lighted cigarette from a clay ashtray. Robert held a wild hope he might say, *Well, never mind all this, then. Go'n back to bed.* Instead, Warden Haddock studied Robert with his eyebrows raised, as if he might have heard wrong.

"'Stupid questions'?" Warden Haddock said. Exaggerated, the phrase seemed monstrous. "That what you call it?"

Boone made a chuffing sound, glaring at him. Robert didn't know what to say, so he dared not speak until he learned his mistake.

"A 'stupid' question would be 'Does the sun rise in the west?'" Warden Haddock said. "'Do pigs like slop?' Those are stupid questions. Way I hear it, 'less you're fixin' to call Boone a liar, you were asking how to run away."

In the corner of his eye, Robert noticed the men at the card table flexing their arms, exercising their fingers like Mama had before she taught him scales on the piano at Miss Anne's house. They had put their cards down. They were preparing to hurt him.

"Not for *me* to run, sir," Robert said. "I was just asking if anybody ever did . . ." Robert's voice dropped away. Crutcher had told him not to argue. Keep his mouth shut.

"Why would you want to know if a thing was possible, Robert, 'less you thought you might want to try it? Explain that to me."

Everyone's eyes came to Robert. Under the room's gaze, his mind spilled empty. "I dunno, sir," Robert said.

"Since you're the one who brought it up, you'd better explain it." Warden Haddock picked up the leather strap again, wrapping it from elbow to palm.

"Like . . ." Robert imagined the ping from Mama beneath his hand and said the first thing that came to him, as if she were whispering in his ear: ". . . like how, in picture shows, people fly to outer space and can look down on the whole Earth. Or how Joe Friday chases down crooks on *Dragnet*. I ain't never gonna be on no rocket ship, no police detective, but I still want to hear it like a story."

The room was still while the men waited to hear what Warden Haddock would say. The white men waited too. One of them was chuckling, sure it was a lie.

After a time, Warden Haddock nodded. "'Like a story.' A kind of fairy tale."

"Yessir," Robert said.

"You believe that, Boone?"

Please please please please please. Robert's heart thundered with hope again. Boone shrugged. "Dunno, boss. That's what they both said. Like it was just a story."

"Bullshit," one of the white men said under his breath.

"Stories are dangerous, Stephens," Warden Haddock said. "They can get you hurt bad. Get you killed. Your friend the storyteller just got thirty lashes. It's not his first time here, and he should know better. I have to teach you too, and I'm not sure yet how many licks that'll take. But however the Lord leads me, from now on, if you're smart—and I think maybe you are—you're not gonna want to hear no more stories."

"No, sir." Robert's words were only air whistling between his chattering teeth. Crutcher gently cupped his elbow like an usher leading him to the front of the church, and Robert's body seized up but he walked with Crutcher anyway—one step, two steps, three—closer to the table where he would be whipped. Blood rushed in Robert's ears from the tremor of his heartbeat, and his knee joints fought against his weight. Boone was almost gentle enough to fool him into wondering if he might still be spared. Hadn't Mama's messages to him already been a miracle? And another: Red McCormack already called the warden once—so why shouldn't Mr. Loehmann come bursting through the door to tell him Judge Morris said it was all a mistake and to let him go? Robert had learned at his mother's bedside that God tested you.

"Gimme your shirt," Crutcher said. Robert hesitated just long enough for him to add, "You don't want to wear it. Fabric gets in the skin." For the first time, Robert thought of his skin breaking; not bruises, not welts, but slashed-open flesh. As if he were no different than the dead side of beef hanging in the freezer.

Robert looked at Crutcher with pleading eyes: *You know my daddy and you know this is ain't right,* and Crutcher's eyes blinked away.

Boone tugged at Robert's shirt, impatient, so Robert quickly pulled on the button beneath his chin, trying to tame his fingers' strange dancing. Robert heard shuffling, all of the men moving to their places, penning him in. Ready to catch him if he ran. Warden Haddock's boots snapped closer against the floorboards, loud in Robert's ears.

"He always so polite and quiet?" Warden Haddock said.

"Seems like he was raised nice enough." Was Crutcher arguing for him?

"I don't think you wanna bring up his rearing," Warden Haddock said, and Crutcher's face puckered as he tried to hold his expression blank. Crutcher wasn't the only one in Gracetown who knew Papa's name. "But I'll say this: he's lucky I'm the superintendent and not some of those county boys, or he'd be out in a swamp with the Klan. My boys are already grumbling. Don't try to say I don't play fair."

Boone and Crutcher agreed they had never met any man fairer, white or colored.

"I'll take it one more step . . . ," Warden Haddock said, and spat to build up anticipation like Reverend Jenkins encouraged excitement from his flock. Robert stood in amazement while a conversation bloomed like when men had come to Papa's back porch, or when his grown cousins gathered under Miz Lottie's oak tree, playing with her old truck's engine to try to make it run. Like an ordinary day in an ordinary place. "I'd bet five dollars that gal was never raped by anybody, white or Negro."

Thunder might have shaken the walls. The two white men groaned with disapproval, and Boone and Crutcher shifted uncomfortably. Their amen corner was silent now. The room felt weighted down.

"Know what? Make that *ten* dollars," Warden Haddock said. "What you think . . . Robert Stephens? Did your daddy rape that white lady?"

Robert's mouth was so dry that his tongue and cheeks felt glued to his lips. He could not open his mouth. To speak, he thought, might mean dying. White men talking about rape always led to a rope. That's what Papa had said right before he left.

"Sir, the boy don't know nothin' 'bout that," Crutcher said, quiet as an undertaker.

"He's not shy," Warden Haddock said. He nudged Robert with the tip of his boot, heavy pressure on his bare toes. Robert felt one of his toe joints crack. "Go on and say. Did your daddy rape that white lady?"

The word *rape* was profane. He and Gloria had overheard Mama telling Miz Lottie she'd been raped by her employer when she was seventeen—the reason she'd decided she'd never work for anyone but herself again—and Gloria had run off with horror in her eyes, but she'd never told him what it meant. The first time he'd learned had been last year, when the sheriff came looking for Papa. He'd asked the older boys at school what *rape* was even though Gloria wouldn't tell him. *It's when a girl doesn't want to, but you force her anyway,* the sage eighth grader, Pastor Jenkins's son, had said. *Sinners and cowards and drunks do that.*

"No, sir," Robert whispered. "My daddy wouldn't hurt nobody. He'd never do that. He ain't a sinner or coward or drunk."

By the way the warden's head canted to one side as if to see him in better lighting, Robert realized he should have thought before he spoke. Only fright had made his words tumble out.

Neither Crutcher nor Boone would look at him. Crutcher took one step away, pretending to search his vest pocket, as if hearing talk of the white lady would conjure her.

"So . . . you think she lied?"

Robert knew better than to say *lie*. "I think like you think, sir."

Warden Haddock slapped Robert on the back hard enough to sting and then rubbed the spot to soothe it. "There ya go," he said. "Everybody knows it. Just a bunch of vile talk the growers put Lorraine up to. Pete McClain's been blacking her eye for a year, and everyone knows 'cept that dim wife of his. Pete prob'ly paid her and her loudmouth daddy and mama a pretty penny to make up a story. All of y'all know it and won't say. And leastways, I won't visit the sins of the father on the son. The son pays for his own. Ain't that right, Robert Stephens?" Warden Haddock continued to rub at the spot on his shoulder until a new alarm grew in Robert he could not put a name to. Slowly, Warden Haddock slid his hand away.

"Your daddy has a big damn mouth and thinks he's good as a white man," Warden Haddock said, "and that's crime enough in Jackson County."

"I don't know for sho' what happened with my daddy, sir," Robert said, and his heart died a thousand deaths, and he wondered if somewhere in Chicago, Papa might have heard him.

"Hush. Yes you do," Warden Haddock said. "A young man stands by his convictions. The good Lord has seen fit to give me this opportunity to steer you to the right path. Hop up on the table." He said it so kindly that Robert almost missed the words.

A white man yanked Robert so hard that the tabletop dug into his stomach and made him lose his breath. The man's red caterpillar eyebrows frowned. Robert smelled sour beer on the man's breath, in his sweat; he worked drunk most nights—

—like the men on the night of the fire in 1920. Knowing what he shouldn't made Robert dizzy.

There is more than this. Mama's voice in his memory gave Robert the strength to pull his leg high enough to try to hoist himself onto the wooden platform. It was truly as if he'd never worked his body before, every part difficult to manage, like his newborn cousin, Jackie, who had been named for Jackie Robinson. He thought of Jackie's wobbly arms and legs as he nearly slipped from the plank, which was slick with sweat.

No, not sweat. The sharp, prickly scent was blood.

He looked behind him to the mud-splattered wall and realized the tiny dark dots in random patterns were *not* mud. Blood patterns were sprayed like paint droplets against the dull planks. He would bleed here. His blood might fly.

"Take this," Crutcher said, and shoved a thick, uneven wood chip into Robert's hand. The chip was dry, fresh from a storage bin. Robert's fingers shook around it. Crutcher leaned closer and whispered in smoky breath, "Bite down. Lie still as you can. It'll be over quicker."

Robert didn't know when he had started crying. Warden Haddock made a *tsk tsk tsk* sound and Robert bit back a sob and wrestled with it. The room seemed as cold as the freezer now that his shirt was off. But not his pants, thank goodness—not his pants.

"What you waitin' for, Robert Stephens?" Warden Haddock said. "Lay down."

Robert tried to lower himself, and his limbs disobeyed, his elbows locked as if he were holding the tabletop against gale winds from below.

"Do what he say, boy," Boone said.

When Robert felt Boone grab his left arm, he hurriedly shoved his wood chip into his mouth. The wood almost jostled loose as three men grabbed and arranged his body with rough hands, but Robert flung his head high so the chip would fall against his molars. He imagined ants or wood mites crawling in his mouth, but his teeth sank into the soft wood, fused. Robert's hot breath hissed in and out against the wood, faster and faster, but his jaw held on so hard it ached. His whole body heaved with his breathing.

The edge of the table cut into Robert's collarbone—his neck muscles had to support his head to keep it from dangling forward—and Robert suddenly knew that boys had died on this table during their beatings, their voice boxes crushed and necks snapped during careless handling. No, he would not move. He would do as Crutcher had said and lie still. He would do as Redbone had said and bite on the wood chip.

"There is more than this," Robert whispered against the wood in his mouth.

The floor creaked under the warden's boot. A low whistle and snap sounded above Robert, and then pain tore across his back as surely as if it had claws. *Fire,* Robert thought. Most of his scream stayed bottled in his throat. His jaw clamped down so hard on the wood chip he thought he loosened a tooth. Just as Robert began to think the pain wasn't so bad, the numbness wore off his back in a wave and he felt surely his skin must have peeled in two.

Robert writhed and screamed. Then came the next, laid across the first. He would have spat out the wood if he could, if it weren't so fixed to his teeth, because pain was choking him. Wild in him.

"Stop—" Robert tried to say, muffled, but the whistle and snap sounded, and his body went rigid, and when the lash came, it seemed to snap his spine apart. Robert's head flung right and left as he screamed, and if not for the wood chip he might have bitten his tongue off when his chin hit the edge of the table so hard, he saw sparks before his eyes.

By the fourth lash, or the fifth—he lost count, one fire burning into the next—his throat was raw and his jaw pulsed and he was sure his back must be a solid pool of blood streaming to the floor. Pastor Jenkins's threats of hellfire could be no worse than this! Boys got beat like this for being late to curfew or fighting or talking too much at night? Boys got beat like this for everyday things his teacher might rap his wrist with a ruler for? The wrongness rang in his head.

"This ain't right," Robert tried to say, a mush against the saliva-drenched chip in his mouth, which still would not budge no matter how much he tried to scream. "This ain't right!"

His outburst met another lash—a harder one. His skin melted open beneath the cutting leather, and he knew it was far worse than the rest as he flopped on the table. To hold him in place, a man clamped each arm harder on either side of him, another held both of his legs. The edge of the table dug into his throat, and for the first time Robert stopped screaming. His nose was clogged. The new panic from not breathing was worse than the pain, so he remembered to slow his hitching breaths: *Don't move. Don't move. Don't move.* And soon the men loosened their grip a bit, and he could shift his neck enough to keep the table from crushing his throat.

For the next five lashes, maybe six, he whimpered but could not scream. He was melting from the table, beneath Boone's muddy work boots and Warden Haddock's pointed shiny snakeskin ones, beneath the floor, into the red-brown soil, past the long-forgotten ashes from the fire in 1920, all the way to the bones buried at Boot Hill. Vibrating pain coiled across his back, but no pain could touch him where he was buried in the soil. His body was far above him, the world black. He hoped he had willed himself to die.

Kindred spirits awaited him here: boys who had been afraid of beatings and dogs, whose skin had been torn or charred, whose bones had snapped, spirits circling the site of their shared tragedy. They rose from the stink of the wrong done to them, and he could almost see them in the dark: blinking eyes around, straining to have their faces remembered.

I see you, he told them, and it almost wasn't a lie because sometimes he *did* see shadows of noses and chins in rows around him. *I see you.* And when he did not see their faces, he saw their stories: Jim, who had run away one too many times and his family never saw him again after they found a note from the sheriff tacked to their front door. Jesse, whose family had sold him to the Reformatory for fifty dollars because they thought it would teach him not to sass back. Russell, who went truant each fall to help his uncle paint houses. And Reynaldo and Justin and Emory and John, who had done nothing beyond being left alone by their parents, torn away by drinking or sickness or death, just like him. The dead boys were called every name except *Murdered*: accident or oversight or cautionary tale.

"He fainted dead away," said a voice he remembered was Crutcher's.

Robert heard, but did not feel, the final lash do its unholy work across his tattered skin. "Guess fifteen's enough, then," the warden said. "I've got a headache anyways."

It was Mama, Robert knew. Mama was giving the warden headaches when he wanted to hurt him, just as she had in his office. A fiddle's whine from the radio niggled at Robert's ear, bringing light through his closed eyelids. Even half senseless and full of rage and pain, he knew better than to open his eyes, or the warden might change his mind and keep whipping him. And if the warden spoke a single word to him, Robert worried he would spit in his face. Oh yes, he would. Robert never had wanted to kill anyone—before now. He wished he could summon a grenade to burn through the shed's roof and split Haddock in two. If Robert were a conjurer, Haddock would be dead already. The entire shed would be burning, even if he were still inside to burn with it.

There is more than this. In the grainy light of his returning, Robert Stephens heard his heartbeat, and the frantic pumping helped him remember: no, he wasn't like the sullen ghosts who roamed this place. The warden hadn't killed him—not yet—and Robert vowed he never would, just like Papa had escaped the lynch mob.

He was alive.

There is more than this.

He would learn.

There is more than this.

Like Papa, he would find a way to be free.

14

". . . That's why Fatima has more than doubled its smokers coast to coast."

A familiar voice; a message he knew from home. After the commercial, the brassy theme to *Dragnet* played from a radio past the open infirmary doorway. *Dragnet* told Robert he was still alive. He woke to the rocky seas of pain across his back, cinching his shoulders, throbbing in his hurt ear. He lay shirtless on his stomach, his back swathed and bandaged, but the pain had not washed away. The bandages across his back were strips of burning sand, and breathing or moving raked Robert's skin. The strap's *SNAP* still rang where Mister Red had hit his ear too hard on McCormack Road. The warden had whipped him too hard.

Rage made the pain flare worse.

Morning. New pink-gray daylight brightened the drawn blinds over the windows. He probably couldn't stand yet, much less walk, but even so, he noticed that the windows had no bars. This room was less than half the size of his dormitory, with twenty beds instead of forty-eight, all of them hospital white. No, not white. Nothing in the room was quite white: the sheets were gray in the daylight, the dingy walls closer to a sad, pale yellow and veined with dark cracks. Robert's eyes tracked a row of tiny red ants marching in formation from a crack in the wall nearest him to the floor beneath his bed. The ants swarmed something sticky on the floor, battling the flies.

Redbone was far across the room, also on his stomach, snoring loudly. Somehow, Redbone had slept most of the night. Robert had barely slept at all, waking again and again to the drumbeat of his agony, hearing whimpers of three younger boys in the infirmary and the sound of the restless radio just out of sight.

Dragnet might get him through the next thirty minutes, at least. His thoughts buried themselves in the story on the radio: Detective Joe Friday and his partner, Ben Romero, are called to the city hall. (That's not how it usually goes!) A man says he's holding a bomb in a box on his lap, and he'll blow up City Hall if police don't release his brother from prison.. (Holy cow!) Taking his bomb away will be a tough job, but Friday and Romero volunteer to go in to try to talk the bomber into giving up. The bomber gives them twenty-four minutes to set his brother free. (No way Friday will agree to that!) Friday and Romero tell the bomber they will never free his brother. They're not even sure the bomb is real. (Could be a fake all along!) "You'll let me blow up ten million dollars of taxpayers' money?" the bomber says. Romero secretly tells Friday and the captain that he can go in and clip the bomber with his gun—or just shoot him dead.

Robert started to feel bad for the bomber. He was only doing anything he could to try to get his brother out of jail. Robert's heart pounded at the idea of Gloria—or Papa!—trying to free him. Did Papa even know he was locked up yet? Would Papa try something as wild as this? Mama always said Papa would do anything to right a wrong.

The voices on the radio rose in a rare argument between Friday and Romero. Friday: "You can't just walk in there and shoot him down. You have to warn him." Captain: "No, a gun's not the answer. We can't shoot him until we're positive."

The captain was nothing like Sheriff Posey. The sheriff and his deputies wouldn't think twice, or even once, before shooting Negroes—like they had shot Mr. Clement's son in the apple orchard when all he'd stolen was a sack full of apples. They would shoot even if their mama was watching. Even if their children were watching. Even if they had no weapon like a box that might or might not be a bomb. In the radio world, everything worked like it should, a pretty lie. Robert's eyes already ached, too puffy from his crying, but more tears leaked out. Now that he'd been arrested and seen the lie up close, he could never like *Dragnet* again.

Joe Friday wasn't real. The Funhouse was real.

A shadow from the corner of his eye made Robert look up to the ceiling above his bed, where he saw a blurry dark mass. He blinked the tears away and saw that the mass was not on the ceiling; it was hovering a few feet above his bed, weightless, and it was a young boy, maybe six years old, limbs splayed as if he were swimming. Studying him. He was real enough to touch, down to the snot crusted on his nostrils and the knotty, uncombed curls on his head. The boy looked like he would drop on top of him.

Until the Reformatory, Robert had never known that ghosts could look so much like regular people—well, except they could walk through walls or float in the air. He wished Mama would appear to him in a flesh state instead of strangers. But maybe she couldn't: maybe Robert could only see the boys who had died here. At least this one wasn't ruined like the one who had found his bed in the dorm and made him want to scream. Now that he knew what real screaming was for, he was only bothered by the ghost, not scared. Mostly, he was mad it wasn't Mama.

Robert started to say, *Go away, you're not real,* but those two eager, real-boy eyes stopped him. For a haint, maybe spying on the living was entertainment like listening to the radio. At least he didn't smell bad like the burned-up boy. Robert had to strain his neck to see the boy so high, so instead he relaxed to his flat pillow and closed his eyes.

"You can stay," Robert whispered. "But don't touch me. And don't say nothin'."

Robert felt the boy bobbing above him; he didn't have to open his eyes to know he was still there. He could have learned more about the dead boy if he concentrated: the facts of the boy's life bubbled just beneath the surface of Robert's knowing. The dead boy was trying to tell him, a chorus of I was, I was, I was. *Pneu-*

monia. One word screamed through before Robert made himself listen to the radio again. He had enough pain by himself.

"Hush," Robert said.

On *Dragnet*, the bomber is excited and angry. He might set off the bomb at any time.

When the captain asks Friday if he's scared, Friday says, "Yeah," and the captain says that makes them even. After a wrestling match with the bomber—no one gets shot—Friday grabs the bomb and drops it in a bucket. He rushes it outside, but he trips, and the bucket hits the ground at the same time he lands. But no explosion. The bomb never goes off! Friday is lucky; it was wired wrong. Has Joe Friday ever come so close to dying?

Robert felt like Joe Friday at the end, waiting for the explosion. He was still waiting when the theme music came on and the episode was over.

Robert whispered to the ghost, "I'm sorry you got pneumonia." Wasn't that all haints wanted? For someone to be sorry?

When Robert craned to look back up, the floating boy was gone.

A blink later, Redbone was standing over Robert's bed with a clean, unbloodied shirt buttoned over his bandages. The daylight was brighter, so Robert must have slept for an hour, maybe two. Someone had turned off the radio. The three other living boys had stopped crying and were eating breakfast from trays in their laps. Robert noticed a tray at the foot of his bed: applesauce and runny eggs that looked gray. He checked the ceiling: no one floating.

How could Redbone be on his feet?

"See?" Redbone said. "Told you."

His voice was strained, his only sign of suffering.

"Told me what?"

"You could take it. How many stripes you get?"

"I dunno." Robert remembered Warden Haddock saying fifteen lashes, but he didn't want to sound proud of it. Redbone had him twice beat, anyway. "Don't you hurt none?"

Redbone sucked his teeth. "I don't give nobody the satisfaction of seein' me hurt, son."

But he lost his big talk at the sound of footsteps approaching from the doorway. Redbone hobbled back to his bed, and Robert heard his *Sssssss* hiss of pain as he lay on his stomach.

Then Redbone began moaning in a way he never moaned when they were alone.

The Negro nurse who pushed a cart into the room was old, maybe nearly as old as Miz Lottie. The wobbly, squeaky wheels on her metal cart made Robert's bad ear scream, igniting every piece of him that had bled. He moaned too, following Redbone's lead. He was always moaning in his head anyway. His bed was closest to the doorway, so she stopped beside him.

"Hope we won't see you back here, huh?" the nurse said matter-of-factly. Moaning and whippings were a regular part of her job, nothing to change the look on her face over.

"No, ma'am," Robert said. He hoped he wouldn't have to talk more.

"You're hurtin'?"

"Yes'm."

She picked up a tin of Bayer aspirin and shook two pills into her hand. "You're big enough for the adult dose. Swallow those down."

Robert hated taking pills of any size, but he would do anything to keep from hurting so much. The old Robbie was dead, he reminded himself. Dead and gone on McCormack Road.

"Aspirin won't seem to do much good," she said. "But better'n nothing."

The aspirin was chalky, and the tepid water the nurse gave him in a plastic cup didn't help much when he tried to swallow. Fear sealed his throat when he felt the pressure from the pill, but to his relief the water washed down. He discovered a trick of moving the second bitter pill toward his gum, and he swallowed it easier from there. Still, he gasped when he was done. He'd been holding his breath.

Redbone let out a cry as if he'd just felt Warden Haddock's lash, trying for sympathy. "How many this time?" the nurse asked Redbone.

"Thirty, ma'am."

"Well, gracious. I expect you'll behave now, won't you?"

"Yes'm," Redbone said.

"Both of you boys from Lincoln," she said, glancing back at Robert, "you'll stay here today and then back to your dorm tonight. Then it's out to the fields in the morning."

"Ma'am?" Robert said, startled. "We work in the kitchen."

"Not anymore," the nurse said. "Not for at least a month after the Funhouse."

Robert glanced at Redbone's face for a sign she was lying, but Redbone looked glum, so they would go to the fields after all. Papa had told him he should never spend even a minute picking for white men. And how could he work at all with his back hurting so much? He could say none of this to the nurse, who didn't much feel sorry for him, so he began to eat to smother the lump in his throat as she rattled away with her cart.

His eggs were cold and bland and didn't taste much like eggs. The applesauce seemed more sour than sweet. Maybe nothing could have flavor today. He might not *really* taste anything again until he left this place, was back at home with Gloria or at Miz Lottie's kitchen table. Thinking of home brought tears to his eyes, but he didn't want Redbone to see him crying.

The kitchen had been his one good thing, and now that was gone.

Redbone was back at Robert's bedside as soon as the nurse left. "The lucky thing is, we don't got to go to school today if we're in the infirmary," Redbone said slyly. "Work neither." Redbone had already found something to be happy about.

Not Robert. "Why we got to work the fields for a whole month?"

Redbone's lips tightened and a shadow overtook his brow. Instead of answering, he slapped down a deck of playing cards on Robert's mattress. "Spades or bid whist?"

In his misery, Robert didn't want to play cards with Redbone or anyone else. At least the ghost floating above him had been quiet.

"I wanna play!" one of the young boys called out. He wheezed when he talked. Did he have pneumonia too?

"Shut up," Redbone said. "You're too little. And hush 'fore you bring the nurse."

"She can't hear nothin'," another boy said. And he laughed far too loudly, testing.

The other two joined the laughing.

"All of y'all hush or I'll whup your hides," said Redbone, and the boys fell silent. Redbone's eyes came back to Robert. He patted the deck of cards, impatient.

"You my friend now?" Robert said. "Like . . . if I needed you to, you'd cover for me like you did for Blue? I'd cover for you."

Redbone considered it, staring at the marching ants on the wall. Then he nodded. "We been to the Funhouse together now. So . . . hell yeah."

Robert had never needed to have someone declare his friendship so badly. Redbone's *Hell yeah* made the dingy room's walls seem brighter. Dulled the sharp edges of his pain. He felt his mouth twitching to smile. Almost.

"Bid whist," Robert said, deciding.

Redbone grinned. "You *really* 'bout to get yo' ass beat now," he said.

"We'll see who gets beat." Robert's smile snuck out.

Redbone dealt out cards, his hands as fast as a hummingbird's wings.

The infirmary, despite its griminess and chemical smells, was a sanctuary for a day. Robert and Redbone snuck in card games between the nurse's halfhearted rounds when they both put on a pathetic display for her eyes, which wasn't really only for show. "If you don't act sick enough, they send you to school at twelve thirty," Redbone advised him.

Whenever the nurse was gone, Redbone told stories: more adventures from his joy ride, his rabbit-hunting skills, his baseball card collection, and how his daddy sold liquor and paper sacks stuffed with fried catfish from his pickup truck. Robert couldn't bring up anything Redbone didn't already have a story about. Redbone was only a few months older, but his life was so much fuller than school and church and Papa's meetings. Redbone's back porch had been a place for play, not for work. And since Gloria had warned him never to talk about Papa, Robert didn't tell Redbone about Papa's back-porch meetings, everyone stiff and silent when they thought they heard a car. Or if a hunter's rifle sounded too close. He didn't talk about Mama dying either. Those weren't stories to make you feel better like Redbone's.

Robert checked the ceiling for the floating boy. Still gone. "You see the haints?" Robert said finally.

The question caught Redbone so off guard that his lips dropped apart. He didn't speak at first. "They don't mess with me too much," he said finally.

"I already seen three," Robert said. Four if he counted the fire. Five if he counted Mama. And then the ones in the Funhouse, too many to count. He settled on the three who'd looked real.

"In one day? That's a lot," Redbone said. He wanted to say more about the haints, but he wouldn't. As if it might be bad luck. "So, you scared?" Redbone said after a long wait.

"Of haints?" Robert said. "No." It wasn't even a lie. Not anymore. He was only scared he'd be like them, trapped.

"Good thing, 'cuz they may not let you alone."

"Why?"

Redbone shrugged. "Some people draw 'em like magnets. That's what Blue says."

Maybe Blue could teach him everything he'd learned about haints. Robert might have to forgive Blue for talking so freely about runaways hiding and ducking his whipping.

"Two of them . . . at *least* two," Robert went on softly, "they were killed. Murdered." Redbone raised his eyes and gave a small shake of his head that meant *Shhhhh*.

"I guess they want someone to know," Robert said quietly. "That's all."

"Better worry about your own self," Redbone said. " 'Fore you're a haint too."

That sounded like something sensible Gloria might have said, and Robert missed his sister, his life, so fiercely that he could hardly catch his breath. Haints must miss their lives too.

A new Negro woman appeared in the doorway, and his heart jumped. She was Mama's height but a bit thinner, her skin darker. Mama had worn her hair pressed and long down her shoulders, but this woman's hair was pinned in a high, tight side bun. Robert stared, wondering if her features would change and she would become Mama. But, no, her cheekbones were smoother. Her forehead was higher. She was a bit younger than Mama, dressed in a gray skirt and prim white blouse Mama never would have worn because it looked too much like a uniform she had vowed never to wear even if she *was* doing wash. Was she a haint too?

"You see her?" Robert whispered to Redbone, to be sure.

Redbone turned and quickly hid the playing cards under Robert's sheet; he saw her.

The woman was wearing heels instead of soft soles like the nurse, and her feet made polite clicks on the floor as she walked closer. She seemed as surprised to see them as they were to see her.

"Oh," she said. "This is the infirmary? I was looking for the school."

"School's down the path a ways, closer to the cornfield," Redbone said.

"I'm all turned around, then," she said. "No matter. You boys all right?"

She asked the question with care. Robert wanted to blurt out an inventory of his pain and troubles, but instead he only nodded while the others mumbled, "Yes'm."

She smiled at them. And what a smile! Mother, aunt, sister. But then she took her smile back just as quickly, turning to walk back out the way she'd come.

"Who's that?" Robert said.

"I ain't never seen her," Redbone said. "Maybe they got a new nurse."

Rattling came from the hall, and the woman returned with a large cart packed with musical instruments, still shiny through their dents. A large round drum was alone on the bottom shelf, painted GRACETOWN BOYS' SCHOOL in faded red. On the top shelf, Robert recognized a trumpet, a saxophone, a tambourine, a flute, and a sticklike black instrument he couldn't name. The three younger boys flocked to her cart.

"No touching," the woman said firmly. "They're not toys. Who's twelve or older here?"

Robert and Redbone looked at each other, not sure they should volunteer. But Robert wanted to touch the trumpet, so he raised his hand. Redbone followed his lead.

While the younger boys complained, the woman wheeled her cart to the foot of Robert's bed. For the first time, Robert learned that instruments had a *smell*: brass and oil and maybe spit.

"All right," the woman said, and took a breath. "My name is Mrs. Marian Crutcher Hamilton, and I'm the new band director for the Gracetown Reformatory Negro Boys' Marching Band. Did you know the Reformatory has an award-winning band? For the past five years, it has marched in the Gracetown Christmas Parade."

Robert shook his head. Every word out of her mouth was more amazing than the last. A Negro woman was leading a band at the Reformatory? Negro boys marched in a town parade? Negro families were not welcome to attend the Christmas parade, shooed away by deputies.

Negro children who were willing to wait could gather by the trees at the end of the street, where everyone in the parade was tired of putting on a show. But you could see the pretty costumes.

"You kin to Mr. Crutcher, ma'am?" Redbone said.

Her face brightened. "Yes! Mr. Crutcher is my brother. Do you know him?"

Redbone's shoulders sagged with bad memories. "Yes'm."

"Well, what's your name?"

"August Montgomery." Redbone's given name sounded like a storybook character.

She turned to Robert. "And you?"

"Robert Stephens." He figured if Mr. Crutcher knew and respected his papa's name, his sister might too. And she did: something stirred behind her eyes.

"From the mill?"

"Yes'm." He wanted to add, *He didn't do what people say,* but a woman might take another woman's side anyway. Even a white woman's side.

"I see," she said, lowering her chin to study him. "Do you boys play an instrument?"

"I can play that drum," Redbone said, which Robert was almost sure was a lie.

"Yes, everyone loves the drums," Mrs. Hamilton said. "And you, Robert?"

"Mama taught me the scales on Miss Anne's piano. I know most of 'em."

Now her eyes were afire. "Oh! Can you read music, then?"

Her excitement made Robert afraid to say the wrong thing. Was knowing the notes on the lines on sheet music were E-G-B-D-F and the spaces were F-A-C-E the same as reading? Knowing where the letters told his fingers to go? Mama had taught him that much.

"I can read it some," Robert said.

"Well, unfortunately, there's no piano in marching band . . ." When she spoke the word *un-for-tu-nate-ly,* it sounded so pleasant that it didn't seem disappointing. ". . . but if you have a musical foundation, maybe I can help fill in the rest. Do any of these instruments on the cart look interesting to you?"

For the first time in hours, Robert sat up. His back screamed at him. If the aspirin he'd taken had helped at all, it wasn't helping now. But the *trumpet* helped: it was tarnished and the wide bell had dents, but it called out to him from pictures he'd seen in Papa's *DownBeat* jazz magazines. He'd always wanted to play one. Shyly, he pointed.

"You can't play without a mouth," she said. "Use it, please."

"The . . . trumpet. Please."

Mrs. Hamilton picked up the trumpet and gave it to him, keeping both hands on it firmly until Robert had taken it into his own, like passing a baby. Most of its weight was in the center, where the three columns were lined up for the keys. It was somehow both lighter and heavier than he expected. Robert felt perspiration dampen his fingertips. The three younger boys had gathered as his audience, envious and mesmerized.

Mrs. Hamilton pointed out the rounded narrow end. "This is the mouthpiece. Raise it up."

While Robert raised the mouthpiece to his lips, Mrs. Hamilton gently arranged his right thumb and fingers; his thumb beneath the thin bar, three middle fingers resting lightly on the keys, pinkie hooked around the ring. With his left hand, he grasped the columns to support its weight. The trumpet seemed to fit in his hands just right.

"Now give it a try," Mrs. Hamilton said.

Robert puffed his cheeks out like he'd seen in pictures of Dizzy Gillespie and blew. Silent air traveled through to the other end. No sound at all. The boys laughed. Even Redbone hid a smile behind his hand. Robert's neck flared with embarrassment.

Mrs. Hamilton snapped her fingers for quiet, the loudest finger snap Robert had ever heard, a crack. The laughter stopped.

"Your lips go like this," Mrs. Hamilton said, and pursed her lips to demonstrate. "But don't press too tightly against the mouthpiece. And you don't blow air from your cheeks; it's from your belly. What's called your diaphragm. Try again, please."

Robert almost said he didn't want to try again; she was sure to lose interest in him once he failed. But he pursed his lips the way she'd shown him, pressed the mouthpiece to his mouth, but not too hard, and took a breath from his belly. Then Robert blew. He was already pushing out as much air as he could from his stomach before he realized he'd forgotten to press down any of the keys. Yet . . .

The pure, high-pitched note was so loud that Robert almost dropped the trumpet. The note rang against the windows and ceiling and circled the room, unbroken and steady. It sounded to Robert like both a peal of laughter and the world's saddest cry. Redbone grinned and slapped Robert's knee. The three other boys cheered. Mrs. Hamilton's eyes grew wide, and she was smiling too.

"Well, listen to that," Mrs. Hamilton said. "That was a high C."

Robert's face was hot. "Yeah?"

"It can take students weeks or months to hit that note. You're a natural, Robert. In fact, there's a young man like you from New Orleans who was sent to a boys' home. And he picked up a trumpet, just like you, and could play it right away—a cornet, actually, but they're much the same. You know who it is?"

Robert shook his head. He didn't know.

Mrs. Hamilton leaned closer. "It's my friend Louis Armstrong. He may just be the greatest trumpet player in the world. Do you think you'd like to be like him?"

Robert was almost too frozen in place to nod his head. He knew that name, of course.

Mrs. Hamilton was *friends* with Louis Armstrong? She didn't fit the picture he'd had in his head of jazz people: women in sparkly evening gowns, smoking cigarettes in nightclubs.

"Good. Then I'd like to see you at band practice tomorrow." She glanced at Redbone. "You too. So I can hear you play that drum. Maybe you play like Art Blakey."

"But . . . ," Redbone began, and Robert looked at him wildly, hoping he wouldn't ruin it. "We got to work the fields tomorrow, ma'am."

Robert's spirit quaked. He'd been so hypnotized by talk of music that he'd forgotten.

"I'll take care of that. You'll work in the morning and go to school. Band practice is at oh sixteen hundred—that's two hours before dinner. Every day. The colored music hall is directly behind the bleachers. Don't miss practice or you're out of the band. Understood?"

"Were you in the Army?" Robert said. Mrs. Hamilton wasn't a ghost, but she wasn't ordinary. Only soldiers in war pictures told time in such high numbers.

"As a matter of fact, I was—the 404th ASF Women's Army Corps. Good guess."

"The Army!" Redbone said, as if she'd said *the sun*. "How come you're here now?"

"This is home," she said. "I grew up on Lower Spruce before the war. I'll be teaching at the high school in the fall, but I'll come here after school to teach music. And this summer you can get a head start for the parade. Feeling proud of yourselves will make your time here easier. Once you leave, you can take music wherever you go. And learning something will help you realize you can learn anything—anything else you put your mind to."

Her words were so soothing that Robert's bloody welts stung a little less and he almost forgot the pain that still lingered in his ear from when Mister Red had hit him.

The nurse peeked in from the doorway. Mrs. Hamilton noticed her and reached for the trumpet to return it to the cart. Robert hated to let it go. The younger boys' laughing stopped when the nurse stuck her head in.

"Sorry for the noise, Nurse," Mrs. Hamilton said. "I just found a trumpet player for my band. This young man has a very promising embouchure."

"Those boys are violators," the nurse said.

Mrs. Hamilton glanced at Robert and Redbone, especially the bandages on Robert's back. Her jaw flexed hard before it relaxed again.

"I can see they're being punished. But I'll clear it with Superintendent Haddock. He wants to show off this Christmas."

Robert noticed Mrs. Hamilton had brought up Warden Haddock's name to overrule her.

And the nurse, like him, had no idea what that word *embouchure* meant, and maybe Mrs. Hamilton had used the fancy word on purpose. Robert tried to keep his smile from showing.

"This is an infirmary," the nurse said, "not a juke joint. They're here to rest."

Mrs. Hamilton gave Robert and Redbone a warm look, as if their faces gave her strength. "You're absolutely right." She turned, precise on her heels. "If you could direct me to the schoolhouse . . . ?"

They watched Mrs. Hamilton and her cart of instruments until she pushed it out of sight. The younger boys stayed in the doorway to see her as long as they could. Once she was gone, it was harder for Robert to imagine Mrs. Hamilton than the ghost floating above his bed.

Redbone pulled the sheet back to gather up the playing cards.

"Won't band be fun?" Robert said.

Redbone shrugged. "Band might be all right."

"You really play drums?"

"Can't be hard to learn to bang sticks."

"She's nice, huh?"

Redbone scowled, cut the deck, and fanned the cards facedown on the mattress before he shuffled them. He never cut and dealt directly; he always put on a show. "Don't be fooled."

"What you mean?"

As Redbone scooped up the cards and began dealing, his look reminded Robert of the story he and Blue had told in the kitchen—a year ago in a day—about how Crutcher had held his head under the hot sink water. And the band lady was Crutcher's sister.

"No one stays nice," Redbone said. "Best remember it."

A shadow moved up high, from the corner of Robert's eye. The boy who had died of pneumonia floated above him again, staring down while he waved his arms beside him, like swimming. Robert jumped, but not even enough for Redbone to notice. The gently bobbing haint made him imagine himself at the bottom of the deep Atlantic, looking up at an ocean of the dead.

They were not allowed to stay in the infirmary for a second night.

The nurse brought Robert and Redbone a bland dinner of peanut butter sandwiches and canned peaches; then at seven she told them to go back to their dorm to sleep. Redbone had warned Robert to expect it, but after six thirty, with the skies getting dark, he'd gotten his hopes up for the peace and safety in the infirmary, especially after the younger boys were gone.

The nurse came in after dinner and told them to walk back to their dorm. They were both barefoot because they'd been in bed when Boone took them to the Funhouse, wearing nothing but pajamas, but they walked in a hurry so they wouldn't be late. The walk back to Lincoln was long, across at least twenty acres of the field from the school side to the dorm side, and then over to the Negro area of the campus. Robert was glad his soles were tough. Redbone kept hissing at pebbles and pine cones. *City boy,* Robert thought.

Since his feet weren't tender and hurting, Robert noticed the world of free space around him. They were by themselves! At this late hour, so close to curfew, no one else dared to be outside. He scouted the vast tracts of grass and ragged, bark-shedding pines between the buildings. Tall fences stood at the outer edges of everything he could see. To the west, the painted steeple of a church glowed white in the dark. A Reformatory *church*! Robert hoped he would never have to sit in any church where Warden Haddock prayed, or else the devil might glimpse him too.

Every touch, every lash, became real again. Robert had to curl his lips to keep his anger from flooding into tears. As Robert thought of Haddock, he recognized the warden's brick office building in the distance, a dim light inside a far window still on, and the open space beyond it in the field where the ghost fire burned.

He couldn't see as far as the front gate, but he knew the road was that way too, open and waiting. Every muscle in his body knew he was walking in the wrong direction, *away* from where he needed to be, and he felt an ache worse than the welts and cuts from his beating. His stomach growled too. He wished he could have eaten his real dinner in the cafeteria. He envied Blue, who probably was still working happily at his job in the kitchen, stealing sweets instead of washing dishes, getting away with everything because he was quick and small.

Long rows of fenced kennels ran between the white and Negro dormitories, and barking dogs mocked their approach. Robert had always known he would run from dogs. He'd been dreading it since Mama first told him how white men sent dogs chasing after runaways in the swamps, and how sometimes the water could fool a dog's nose. Even when he'd been much younger, he'd felt like it was worth knowing how to escape dogs. The McCormacks' dog Duke, as a puppy, had snapped and snarled when Robert tried to take back his own bread he'd dropped. Duke had gone from wagging his tail to chomping his sharp teeth with a growl in his throat. That had taught Robert everything he wanted to know about dogs. He wasn't fooled by wagging tails or Rin Tin Tin.

Robert had assumed the McCormacks' dogs would be the ones to chase him—he had nightmares about running from those dogs sometimes. But, no—*these* were the dogs who would chase him. His body wanted to take a wide arc away from the kennels as they walked, but he wouldn't let himself be scared. Even Redbone hesitated to walk so close to the runs, where dogs stood on their hind legs against the gates with mean barks saying what they would do to them if they could. Robert felt adrenaline prick him every time a dog's paws clanked the fence links.

Hard, like the shake of a grown man. The kennel smelled like dog shit.

Most of the dogs were two-toned German shepherds like Duke, but one was a bloodhound with drooping skin. Spittle sprayed from the nearest dog's teeth as he barked. Robert counted six in all.

"Don't stare 'em in the eye," Redbone said. "We're too close."

Robert followed Redbone a few paces away from the dog runs, but only after he'd proven he wouldn't panic at a dog's bark. He had never let himself jump.

"Is this all the dogs?" Robert said.

"Shut up," Redbone said, in a hushed voice.

Just past the kennel's far corner, a white teenager was filling up water dishes. Redbone shot Robert a look: *See?* And gave Robert a small shove that hurt more than it should have as they hurried past him, silent. Robert had been careless. *Sorry,* he mouthed.

When they were long out of earshot, Redbone said, "If you get me sent to the Funhouse again, I'm gonna whip you myself." He didn't sound like the same Redbone who'd played cards with him. "Blue talks too much, but you were stupid to ask him. Everybody thinks they'll run, but nobody gets out. And if they get out, they don't stay out. Six months is the end of my time. It's all you got, but it's the end for me. If Haddock gives me more time 'cause you mess up again, you and me ain't friends. And I'll knock out your teeth—just watch."

"I'm sorry—"

"Sorry don't heal my back up. Sorry won't get me home. Just don't be dumb no more."

"Okay." Robert had never been sorrier. What if he'd said something even worse the white boy might have heard? Papa said people got paid for snitching on their own, so of course a white boy would snitch. He'd been talking like only the dogs could hear him.

"And I better not never hear you say Blue's name to Boone—not about *nothin',*" Redbone said. "No matter if it's his fault or not." Again, Robert envied Blue for Redbone's fierce friendship.

"I didn't say nothin'," Robert said. "I could have, but you know

I didn't. Did I? Did Blue go to the Funhouse? I only counted me and you laying on those hospital beds."

Redbone walked ahead of Robert, deliberately outpacing him. Redbone had been in a better mood in the infirmary, Robert realized, but now his good mood was gone as they got closer to his everyday world. The food was terrible, but the infirmary hadn't been as hot as the dorm room, and no ruler swats or late-night intrusions. It didn't feel so much like jail.

"We already had a bath," Redbone said. "That's what we'll say."

"Okay," Robert said, although he felt a ball of dread in his stomach. He didn't want trouble, and now Redbone wanted him to lie right off. As much as he had hated the shower room and being naked, Mama had found him through the shower pipe. Robert hoped to hear Mama again. And even if Mama had been able to visit only once or twice, he'd rather go to the shower room than the Funhouse. But he owed Redbone; he was his only friend.

"Don't mess it up," Redbone said. "A shower'd hurt like hell. Boone don't care."

Robert was too scared to speak again as they quickened their pace toward the looming dorm ahead. Vines clung across the bricks like they were trying to strangle the building. Boone was waiting with his clipboard at the top of the stairs. Boone had helped hold them down while Haddock beat them worse than horses, and Boone didn't ask how they were feeling. The waiting lie sped Robert's heart.

"Montgomery—A.," Redbone said.

Robert remembered how he should say his name: "Stephens—R."

As Boone checked off their names, Redbone said casually, "We had a bath already."

"All right." Boone didn't blink or give them a second look, already checking in the older boys who'd run from around the corner and smelled like cigarettes. Robert felt sure Boone would notice, but if he did, he didn't say anything. Robert couldn't help smiling a bit. The radio show was already playing, so laughter filled the hallway: Bob Hope, who was so funny he'd even made Mama and Papa laugh.

Redbone slipped into the rec room doorway. "You comin'?" he said. He didn't seem at all like he'd just threatened to knock out his teeth.

Robert shook his head. "I gotta check on my boots."

"They prolly gone," Redbone said with a sad look.

Robert nodded, but he had to know. He'd thought about Papa's boots a lot while he was in the infirmary: how ungrateful he'd been when they arrived in the box; how he'd been so mad at the boots that he forgot himself and kicked Lyle McCormack. He'd felt powerful in those boots, teaching Lyle never to touch his sister. The boots were Papa's last gift to him, the last part of him from home.

The locker room was empty. His locker door was the only one standing wide-open. He could see his name he'd written in chalk on the rusted door.

Tears came fast. Tears always came fast when no one was watching. Robert ran to his locker, afraid his tie would be gone too.

But his boots were still there, untouched. No—not untouched. He'd thrown them in as far back as he could, hoping no one would notice them. Now the boots were upright, side by side, their toes at the closest edge of the locker. His tie and clothes hung on hooks.

"Mama?" he whispered.

Inside his boot, he saw a thin napkin wrapped around something warm to his touch. He peeked around the locker door to make sure no one would see, then he opened the napkin: it was corn bread. And sweet like cake, the way Miz Lottie made it. He shoved it in his mouth whole.

"I'm sorry."

The voice scared Robert so much that he nearly choked. The room *wasn't* empty; Blue had been waiting at the end of the lockers, out of sight. Blue's sad-eyed look reminded Robert of the boy floating above his bed, full of sorrows he didn't have words for. Robert's anger tried to swell, but Blue's eyes melted it down.

"You didn't mean it," Robert said, mouth full. "Thanks for the corn bread."

"Does it hurt real bad?"

"What you think? You don't know nothin' about it." Robert felt bad as soon as he said it: Blue was an orphan. That was worse than the Funhouse.

"That's what you think," Blue challenged. "*You* don't know nothing about it."

They sounded like they might be teasing each other, except they weren't. Blue's stare felt chilling now. Blue's eyes spoke of something so final and awful that the corn bread lost its taste. Robert turned away to gather his new pajamas from the hook, purposely hiding from Blue's eyes on the other side of his open locker door. Why was his heart pounding?

"Go on," Blue said, voice husky. "Ask me what I know about this place. Ask me."

No way. The last time Blue had told him a story, Robert had gone to the Funhouse. Either Blue hadn't learned anything or he was playing a dirty game of chicken. Robert had been glad to eat the corn bread, but he rubbed his lips clean and scoured the floor by his locker for crumbs. A bright yellow crumb stood out, so he bent over and he popped it into his mouth, ignoring the faint bitterness of the floor's dust.

"Let's go find Redbone, huh?" Robert said. "Radio's on." He spoke loudly in case anyone was searching for wrong to tell Boone about.

But by the time Robert closed his locker door, Blue was already gone.

IV

THE COURTHOUSE

15

"Did you talk to her? The law student?" Gloria asked as soon as she was inside the house, but Miss Anne hushed her and gestured *hold your horses*. Gloria noticed that Fred and Nell were within earshot, and although they all lived in the same house, Miss Anne did not like to share a bit of her life with them if she could help it.

"Soon," Miss Anne said, and that was all.

Every time the phone rang, Gloria hoped it was Loehmann calling with the news that he'd spoken sense to the judge. Miz Lottie always said to make her prayers specific, and that was what she wanted most: a chance to start the week again. A chance to keep Robbie out of trouble. She wanted Miz Lottie to drive her out to the Reformatory so they could take Robbie home. They'd already driven there once, so the journey there from Route 319 to Marianna Road was so clear in Gloria's mind that it felt certain as she mapped the route. But although the telephone rang three times that day—much more than usual—Miss Anne never called for her, and she spoke sharply when Gloria reached to pick up the hall phone ahead of her.

"Go make yourself useful and trim the chicken," Miss Anne said, taking the receiver.

The phrase tumbled in Gloria's head—*Trim the chicken*—and she got madder with each repetition. In the kitchen, she thought the three words every time she chopped through the gristle. Her baby brother, Mama and Papa's youngest child, was locked up and hurt, and Miss Anne's answer was to trim—*CHOP*—the—*CHOP*—chicken? Only anger kept Gloria from crying, but her anger felt like a mountain too big to fit inside her. If Miss Anne knew how mad she was, she'd never have sent her to the kitchen to pick up a knife.

Miz Lottie had warned her. Mama had warned her. Miss Anne might be related to them from slavery days, but the Powells should never be mistaken for family. Gloria remembered every story she'd heard of salaries shorted, holiday requests denied, and unreasonable demands imposed when they were fresh from a sickbed or the undertaker's. The Powells would promise the moon to help ease a bad time, but their promises fell short, especially since Councilman Powell had passed. Miz Lottie said he was the only one who never failed to keep his word, or who *almost* didn't see them as Negroes first. He had been voted off his seat when he signed a petition against lynching that got printed in the *Gracetown Herald*. Miss Anne had once told Gloria he probably died distracted on the road because he worried too much about what people said about him, but Papa had said the Klan probably got to him.

Of course Miss Anne would not want any extra risks or responsibilities, and she would take her sweet time when she did. Gloria felt foolish for expecting anything from her. But what could she do next? Leave another message for Loehmann to ignore? In her overtired state, she couldn't think of a single idea, and as the hours passed, her anger simplified to grief again. Her skin was hot to the touch; she'd worked herself into a fever.

Gloria was about to fix a supper plate for Ma Ma when Miss Anne came to her, pocketbook in hand, wearing dungarees and a sleeveless blouse instead of her usual home sundress. Fred and Nell were eating boisterously in the dining room, and Gloria could tell from Miss Anne's rushed walk that she had come down the back stairs to avoid being seen.

"Come on," Miss Anne said. "Nell said she'll feed Ma Ma. I'll drive you home." A day's waiting for an offer to drive her home?

"No, thank you," Gloria said. "I'm going to Miz Lottie's." She couldn't spend another night worried and alone in her bed a stone's throw from McCormack Road. Miz Lottie would have ideas for what to do next.

"Fine," Miss Anne said, cheeks red. "I haven't seen Auntie Lottie since Easter." And she breezed out of the door toward the carport as if she had an invitation.

Gloria decided she would quit. No amount of money was worth the aggravation, even if no one else would hire her. She would move back in with Miz Lottie and start going back to school like Miz Lottie said she should. What good was saving a few extra dollars when she didn't even have Robbie to care for?

Miss Anne was already in the driver's side of her blue Buick Coupe when Gloria walked to her window. Boss lady or not, she was about to hear the truth. "Miss Anne—"

"Channing's ready to see you," Miss Anne said, whispering although no one was nearby to hear them except the mockingbirds on the telephone pole. "She's already talked to Mr. Loehmann. She's out waiting for us at the fishing hole at Misery Swamp."

Until the days right before Papa left, when he considered Gracetown's roads too dangerous for Gloria even in daylight, Papa used to say, "Come ride with me, jelly bean." Negroes they passed all through Lower Spruce waved at his old black Plymouth, and so did the Negro pickers up and down McCormack Road, on the farm-to-market roads between Gracetown and Marianna, through the peanut farms near the county line and the Reformatory and mill, and all the way down to the fisher folk in Misery Swamp, if the road wasn't too muddy for driving. Even on paved roads, Papa drove at a parade pace, never speeding. Except for his last night in Gracetown, he had rarely seemed in a hurry, bringing smiles with a wave of his hand.

Instead of talking about whatever business he was driving to—

and Papa's drives always led to a quiet huddle or loud meeting—he pointed out things he wanted her to notice. *See this tree? When I was a boy, this was a hanging tree. We had to walk past it to go to school even if a man was still swinging. See this street? Used to be a cow pasture. These houses were all built by Elmore Bryant one at a time so folks could move out of the McCormacks' shacks like that Jimmy Stewart picture* It's a Wonderful Life. *See this bench? This is where your mama was sitting eating ice cream the day I realized I'd better marry her 'fore someone else did. It's whites only, and she was sitting there in broad daylight like she didn't know no better. A hardheaded woman was just the woman for me!*

Every tree, thicket, and alleyway had meaning to Papa, and Gloria had tried to remember it all, a secret language of history between them. Gloria now understood that Papa hadn't just been trying to teach her; he'd been giving her stories to remember him by. Papa's leaving had only been shocking because Mama had gotten sick and died first. But they had known he would have to leave or be killed. One day.

So Papa's voice filled Gloria's head as Miss Anne navigated the road to Misery Swamp, which became less a road every eighth of a mile as it wound between the pines and crabgrass, more swamp than solid ground. The car drew closer to a makeshift dock and inlet ringed by mangroves. Two Negro men sat at the dock with rods and reels. One of them was Mister Paul, who was selling bait from rusty cans because he couldn't work after he hurt his arm at the mill.

Farther out, standing in knee-deep water in fishing boots up to his thighs, a white man in a plaid shirt and pale fishing hat cast out a cane pole. He did not turn at the sound of the engine. Why was a white man here fishing with Negroes?

The car jolted as mud from the rutted road sloshed beneath the undercarriage. "You driving us in the water?" Gloria said, sounding sharper than she'd meant to.

Miss Anne didn't answer, flustered and embarrassed.

"See if it'll reverse," Gloria said. "Papa always parked by that dead oak."

The oak was ten yards behind them, its rotted trunk reaching high like gnarled gray fingers. Miss Anne surveyed the distance in her mirror. Mud tried to pull at the tires when she reversed, but she revved the gas until the car lurched. Mister Paul and his friend stared as she parked. Gloria peeked to see; the white man had turned and was watching them too. Dammit.

"Chan says I'll get my car stuck out here one day."

The only other car was an empty red Ford pickup nestled between the trees, probably the white man's truck. No women in sight. "Did she leave?" Gloria asked.

"No, she's right there."

Miss Anne pointed toward the white man. He took off his hat to wave with it, and yellow hair tumbled out. A woman, then. Gloria had been fooled by her dungarees and man's shirt. She was also tall for a woman, nearly six feet. Gloria hadn't realized how much she'd tensed her body at the sight of the white man so close until her back relaxed against the car seat.

Gloria took off her loafers and bobby socks before she got out of the car, since she didn't want to lose them. Every pebble and twig was a bother as she followed Miss Anne toward the dock. Mama had scolded her against walking barefoot, and Gloria had sworn by the lesson.

Twilight made the leaves and the water's ripple golden orange.

"'Bout time y'all got here!" the woman called across the water. "Annie, have her bring me some worms. These bream out here are laughin' at me."

The nickname "Annie" sounded childish in a way she'd expect Miss Anne to hate. But Miss Anne was unbothered, already slipping Mister Paul fifty cents for a can. Mister Paul's easy smile with Miss Anne through his salt-and-pepper beard made Gloria realize she had been fishing here before, although Gloria hadn't known Miss Anne liked fishing. And whites in Gracetown fished the town harbor or the roadside canals, not the swamp, which had too many mosquitoes and gators. Miss Anne gave Gloria the can of wriggling, mud-slimed worms.

Mister Paul nodded to Gloria; an entire conversation unfolded in his unblinking eyes. Then he said, "How you doin', Gloria Stephens," in a way that was not a question but a comfort, an encouragement. Papa had huddled many times with Mister Paul on the dock at Misery Swamp to talk about his hurt arm and his "recourse," Papa's favorite word. Mister Paul's granddaughter, Priscilla, was in Gloria's class, probably learning geometry by now.

"All right, Mister Paul, thank you," Gloria said, the worst lie she had ever told. Mister Paul's eyes said he'd already heard about Robbie, but there was nothing he could say or do.

"What's that she's wearing?" the woman in the water called. "She can't fish in that."

The woman had not yet spoken to Gloria directly, that peculiar habit white people had of treating Negroes like store mannequins even if they were talking about you. Gloria looked down at her plain gingham dress, one of her only three good dresses, and the other two were back at her house so near the McCormacks'. She didn't want to go wading in that muddy water, but Robbie was more important.

"I brought her straight from work," Miss Anne said. "I forgot to have her change."

"Have her grab Daddy's boots and pole. We'll make do."

It took Gloria much longer than she wanted to arrange her bare feet and legs into the stiff, scratchy boots, which felt hot on her thighs and of course were too big for her. Her dress hem hung lower than the boots, so she gathered it and tied off the fabric as high as she could over the boots without showing her thighs. The knot was loose and sure to drop her dress dragging into the water eventually, but Gloria did her best to protect her precious clothing.

The honey-colored cane pole was new but similar to Papa's

older faded one, strung with a red-and-white lure. Gloria checked the hook, which was shiny and bare.

"You know how to bait a hook?" the woman called out, finally directing a question to Gloria, although she did not look back.

"Yes, ma'am."

"Then do me a favor and teach Annie? And call me Channing. Or Chan."

"All right," Gloria said, thinking she would call her no such thing, even if they weren't in Misery Swamp with hardly anyone to overhear. She never addressed adults by their bare Christian names without a "Miz," "Miss," or "Missus," much less a white woman she'd just met. She couldn't help glancing at Mister Paul, who gently shrugged and shook his head.

"Pay that no mind at all," Miss Anne whispered behind her, knowing Gloria's thoughts. With the bait in one hand and her pole in the other, Gloria waded slowly into the sun-warmed marsh to get closer to the fisherwoman. She nearly stumbled in the grown man's boots, but at least her feet weren't bare. Miss Channing hadn't seemed so far out from the sound of her voice, but it took more than ten strides to reach her. With each step into the soft swamp bed, the water climbed higher, to Gloria's knees. Gloria swayed, holding out her arms for balance. It would be easier to swim. By the time she reached the woman, Gloria's face was dripping with sweat and maybe tears.

"You made it," Channing said with a grin. The day's sun had burned a red stripe across her forehead and matching crescents beneath her eyes. She was a young woman, no older than Miss Anne. She took the can of worms and nestled it in her large front pocket. Then she took Gloria's hand and gave it a long, firm shake. "Good to meet you. Annie's told me a lot about you, even before this latest horseshit from that jackass Judge Morris."

The profanity and Judge Morris's name nearly made Gloria drop her pole. She'd thought worse by herself, but it startled her to hear her thoughts fly from someone else's mouth.

"What about Robbie?" Gloria said.

"Bait your hook, and then I'll tell you what I know. I wish I could say I had good news . . ." Gloria's insides withered. If it wasn't good news, it was bad news—and Gloria didn't have room for more bad news about Robbie. The imaginary drive to the Reformatory to claim Robbie had felt so real that a sob burned in her throat.

Channing sighed. "I know. None of this will be easy for me to say, or easy for you to hear. Get a good cry out if you want, but I personally feel like there's too much crying. If it was me, I'd want to hear everything I could and maybe get that kid out of that hellhole. Even if it won't be today. Or tomorrow. So—here."

Channing dropped a fat, squirmy worm into Gloria's trembling palm. The worm was flipping back and forth and might have slipped away if she hadn't tightened her fist. Gloria caught her hook with her right hand and pincered the worm with her index finger and thumb. She hadn't been fishing since Mama had taken her out on a rowboat at the church's Founders' Day picnic the year before she died, when her pain was only a twinge in her back from time to time and no one yet knew it was cancer. Somehow, Gloria had only let herself think about Papa today, when Mama was the one who liked fishing and had taught her how to hook a worm. Gloria picked her spot and slipped in the hook, curving the worm across the way Mama had coached her. Gloria's bait never fell off. Mama had always been more squeamish with worms.

"Shoot, you need to do mine too," Channing said, so Gloria repeated her technique and they both cast their lines. The water bobbed with ripples from hungry fish. One leaped out high five yards from them, its silver scales glittering in the golden twilight before it dove back down.

"See that? Told you," Channing said. "They're laughin' at us."

Gloria's line tugged gently, but she knew the difference between a passerby's nibble and a hooked fish. Fishing was all about waiting, Mama had said.

"Miss Anne said you talked to the social worker?"

"Sure did," Channing said. "He's a waste of time, but I suppose he means well enough. Jews are more reasonable on race most times, so we'd best not give up on him entirely. But he spent most of the time on the phone telling me what he *can't* do."

"What'd he say, then?"

Two lifetimes seemed to pass before she answered. Channing glanced over her shoulder, looking for listeners. "Said the sentence seemed too harsh. And he thinks Judge Morris and Sheriff Posey are too harsh on coloreds overall, like that's a news bulletin."

"My father's not a rapist," Gloria said.

"Oh, I know."

Gloria's heart thumped her chest. "How do you know? Who said so?"

Miss Channing glanced back at her, deciding what to reveal. "I'll just say I know. For a fact. Nobody raped Lorraine. It's a damn shame for the girls who *do* get raped when someone lies. But she had her reasons—felt like she had no choice but to lie. Quickest way to cut off a snake by its head, at least in their way of thinking. A whole lot of folks wanted your daddy strung up in a tree or at least run out of town. It won't matter much to you, but she feels awful about it. She only knew him in passing, but she knew him enough to feel sorry."

Sorry! Gloria's body went so stiff that she shook. "Then she should take it back."

Channing yanked her line out of the water to check her bait: her worm was still there. She sank her line again and went on: "She hopes he'll stay gone, and then she can let the whole thing rest and not have to swear on a Bible. But if they catch your daddy, I'd bet Sheriff Posey'd be willing to look the other way when it comes to justice by rope. And hell, I guess a jury in Gracetown would convict a Negro if a hog snorted his way. Your daddy in particular."

What had sounded at first like shocking honesty was only icy cruelty now. How could this woman know these things and say nothing? Why protect a liar?

"You know her," Gloria said as she realized it. "Don't you?"

"She's my cousin. More like a sister." Miss Channing's voice was low.

"Is that why you're here?" Gloria said. "You feel bad about it?"

Miss Channing did not answer her. "She'll stand by that story 'til her dying breath because she's so scared of the one who really beat her up, so I can't help you with that. But I want to help you, if you'll accept my advice. Maybe we can keep this from getting worse."

"Does Miss Anne know she's your cousin?" The idea of it rocked Gloria. She could imagine the three women sipping Coca-Cola in a booth at Meg's Diner on Main Street.

Channing turned to give Gloria a look like surrendering. Like a secret. Of course Miss Anne knew. "I were you, I'd be mad as a hornet too," Channing said. "But from what I understand, your daddy's safe in a big city now. Isn't he?"

Gloria didn't answer. She didn't trust this woman with Papa's secrets. How he moved from job to job, couch to couch. Always afraid.

"They're too lazy to chase him," Miss Channing said. "They don't want federal scrutiny anyhow. But they're not too low to try to lure him back with Robbie. I'm not sayin' they were smart enough to plan it that way; that's just how it's worked out."

"Who's 'they'?"

"The sheriff. The judge. The growers. The town council. The White Citizens' Council. Chamber of commerce. The Klan, of course. Hard to think of anyone with sway in Gracetown or Marianna who isn't gunning for Robert Stephens. He scared them, that's why. He walked tall, didn't stoop his shoulders." It was odd to hear Papa addressed in the past tense, as if he were already in a grave beside Mama at Christ the Redeemer Baptist Church. Miss Channing's voice grew gentle. "First thing'll happen is your brother's six-month sentence will turn to a year. Or two years. However long they want to keep him, that superintendent will make up a reason. By law, that bastard can keep him until he's twenty-one. And that's only if—"

"If he lives that long." The blood in Gloria's veins grew hot with sorrow.

"Yes," Miss Channing said soberly. "If the SOBs don't kill him first. I guess you've heard some children don't come out. White or Negro."

Gloria wanted to ask about the haints Miz Lottie had mentioned, but her instinct told her Channing knew the world of men better than the world of spirits. She swallowed her anger about Papa, and her fishing rod stopped shaking. Papa was safe, for now. Robbie wasn't. And this woman was offering to help, no matter how much her daily silence hurt Papa.

"Maybe Miss Anne can pay for a lawyer," Gloria said. It was the least Miss Anne could do for letting the lies against Papa stand for so long.

"She would—to a point," Miss Channing said. "She's told me as much. But the problem is finding a lawyer willing to come speak up for Robert Stephens Junior. I've talked to one or two, and I'll tell you for a fact there aren't any willing within fifty miles in any direction. The boy's growin' up to be trouble like his daddy, they say. And Miami lawyers aren't too keen on stirring the Klan up here."

"What about you?" Gloria said. "You're a law student."

"Oh, I'd love to see the look on Judge Morris's face," she said, "but until I pass the bar, there's a world of difference between me and a lawyer. Not for another two years."

"Then I'll find one," Gloria said. "A Negro lawyer."

"In Florida," she said, "there's no such thing."

"There are Negro lawyers in New York," Gloria said. "There's got to be one in Florida somewhere. More than one."

Channing's face didn't fully agree or disagree, but she didn't say anything right away, so Gloria figured she didn't have much faith in finding a Negro lawyer. Maybe she had never seen or heard of one. She wasn't as smart about the world as she thought she was.

Channing's line went taut, and her lure raced away as a caught fish tried to flee. Deftly, she pulled out the line, and a good-sized bream veered toward her. Miss Channing caught it and hissed when the stiff dorsal fin poked her, then she slipped the fish into the sack slung across her shoulder. She sucked her finger and swung her empty hook back to Gloria for more bait.

"You mind, Gloria?" she said. "You're good luck."

Good luck! Gloria wanted to tell her to go to hell. Miss Channing was going about her fishing while Robbie's life was in danger. But when Miss Channing handed her another worm, she took it in silence. This one was barely moving, or maybe it was already dead.

"My mentor told me," Miss Channing began, "that if the dean of my law school caught word I was talking to you, I might find myself expelled as a communist. And I could be blackballed out of any law school in the state if he wanted it that way. The whole South, in fact."

Gloria jabbed the hook into the worm so hard that she almost pricked her fingertip when the hook poked through the worm's flesh.

"I don't expect you'll feel sorry for me," Miss Channing said. "I just want you to realize how serious this all is. If you can find a lawyer—or even if you can't—it's not safe for you in Gracetown." She said it like a secret.

"It's never been safe."

"But now I'm hearing bar talk about Robert Stephens Junior kicking Lyle McCormack. How they should have burned down *both* of your houses, not just the new one out by the lake. Should have burned down Lower Spruce. No good talk starts in a bar."

Gloria had known such talk happened, but this was a report from an eyewitness. Her heart and stomach curdled.

"Annie and I have a commercial property; it'll be a winter resort with a few cabins for folks on a budget, very discreet. We haven't opened yet because we're still fixing it up. The way we've been delayed, you could stay there two or three months with no one to bother you. Give this time to blow over."

"Where are the cabins?"

"Near Orlando. Not too far outside Eatonville. That's about—"

Gloria knew about Eatonville because Zora Neale Hurston grew up there. She'd always hoped to visit one day, but not now. "That's way downstate," Gloria said. "Hours and hours."

"Five hours. I drive it in four and a half, but I drive fast."

"You think I'm gonna run off and leave Robbie here? Just run and give up?"

"It's not giving up. You can still pursue legal channels from a distance."

"Is that what you would do?" Gloria said. "If it was your kin? Or 'Annie'?"

Miss Channing gave her a startled, sad-eyed look. Her face would make a *yes* a lie. Gloria went on: "Then you know I won't either. So, thanks all the same for the very kind offer, but no. I won't leave Gracetown. And I'm already planning on moving out of my house."

Miss Channing looked back at her line, relieved. "I'm very glad to hear that."

Gloria stared hard at Miss Channing's profile tall beside her, so serene as she fished.

Mama used to say that unaired feelings ate you up inside.

"A word," Gloria said. "One word from you is all it would take to help my papa. One word from you saying what happened."

"That's not true, Gloria," Miss Channing said. "I know you think it is, but me telling isn't what counts. There's a legal term for it: hearsay. It's *her* word that counts. And I can't sway her. I offered to send her to stay at the cabins too if she'd recant and wanted to be away from that man. I promise I'll never stop trying."

Gloria didn't understand how Miss Channing couldn't see: it didn't matter if a judge accepted her word—she could still talk to a reporter at the *Gracetown Herald*. She could mention it every time she ran into other white ladies in town, at the market, at the diner, at church, at the picture show. She could write it on a sign and carry it from one end of Main Street to the other. Someone would listen to a white woman, surely. Wouldn't that stop some of the bar talk if white men's wives took Papa's side?

But Channing kept secrets, like Miss Anne—who had a friend and business associate even Miz Lottie knew nothing about. Gloria was almost sure Fred knew nothing about Channing Holt either. Did he know about the cabins near Eatonville? Did he know a woman called his sister "Annie" with softness in her voice and face? Robbie and Papa were lost inside these women's other secrets from Gracetown.

"One day," Channing said, "things will be different for everyone. You'll see."

"I don't think so," Gloria said. "Papa said we'd be farther along now if people weren't so scared to tell the truth. Is that gonna change too?"

Miss Channing didn't answer. Gloria hadn't caught any fish, and the oversized boots were itching her sweaty thighs. She tried to think of anything else she could say to convince her to clear Papa's name, which might help get Robbie free. She closed her eyes and listened to the herons fussing and the chorus of night frogs, waiting for the words, but none came. Her only thought was: Miss Channing's scared. Maybe *she* should be more scared too.

When she opened her eyes, she realized how much darker it was now. A splash made her turn her head in time to see a leaping fish fall back into the water behind her, the sparkle gone from its gray scales. It was too dark for her to stay in the water. Gloria turned to trudge back toward the swampy shore. "Watch for gators," Gloria said. "G'night . . . Chan."

She said it because other white folks would gasp if they heard. "Good night to you, Gloria. I really am sorry about this mess."

"Thanks for troubling yourself about Robbie," Gloria said, an afterthought. She'd meant it sincerely, but Mama had been able to cuss people out using the politest words possible clenched between her teeth, and in that moment Gloria had sounded just like her.

"Did Channing tell you what you needed to know?" Miss Anne said once they left the dirt road from the swamp and returned to smooth blacktop.

"She said what she wanted to."

"And you still want to go to Miz Lottie's? You think that's enough?"

Gloria nodded, and Miss Anne looked relieved. The grand escape to the secret cabins probably had been Channing's idea, since it was hard to imagine Miss Anne as that daring. But she might be more daring than Gloria knew. Gloria had questions about Channing and the cabins they owned together, but she wasn't curious enough to ask. It wasn't her business.

"Do you . . . want me to drive by your house with you first? Pick out some things?"

The offer was tempting; it wouldn't take Gloria much time to pack her clothes and toothbrush and sanitary napkins, and a few of her favorite books she'd brought back after she left Miz Lottie's, carrying them between the two houses like memories. No McCormack, or probably anyone else, would bother her with Anne Powell standing watch—would they? But any offer from Miss Anne was sullied by her silence about Papa. And Gloria felt sullied too, because she needed Miss Anne. And Channing too. And Loehmann. No matter how little they had brought her, she couldn't turn away anyone's help. But she didn't want to spend another moment with her while her mind was screaming about Miss Anne's silence.

"Not tonight," Gloria said. "Not while it's dark." Again Miss Anne seemed relieved.

"You'll pay for a lawyer?" Gloria said. "If I find one for Robbie?"

"As much as I can. To a budgeted amount. But, yes."

"What's the budget?" Gloria said. Miss Anne snapped to look at her, startled. Gloria was too tired to use her daytime voice where Miss Anne was her boss. "I'll need to tell the lawyer, won't I, Miss Anne? If he's deciding if he can take the case?"

"Two hundred fifty dollars," Miss Anne said. "That's all I can afford."

Two hundred and fifty dollars! If Gloria had had that much money, she would not have quit school to take care of Robbie. Yet, as grand a figure as it was, Gloria doubted it would be enough to entice a lawyer, or to keep him interested. Papa had said court cases could cost thousands of dollars, which was one reason so many Negroes went to jail. No one in the courtroom was truly speaking up for them.

"Thank you," Gloria said. "When can I get it?"

"As it's needed. If you find a lawyer, just tell them to—"

Tears pricked Gloria's eyes, and even the car's crisp air-conditioned air felt hard to breathe. "I can't do it like that," she said. "I can't wait on you to do things for me. Like today, at your house—I can't stand by and wait."

"I'm sorry, Gloria, but you know how my brother runs his mouth," Miss Anne said. "I couldn't call Chan and make all the arrangements and keep you apprised at the same time." She sounded more hurt than annoyed. "It's all very sensitive. If Fred said the wrong thing in the wrong place—"

"I understand you feel like that. And what if something happens that makes you think, 'Maybe I'd better not hire that lawyer'?"

"I would never do that. You have my word."

"Miss Anne, I know what I'm asking doesn't sound right to you. But I need to make the decisions about Robbie's money. *Me.*

I need to have it—and it's best in cash. I can't work for you now, while Robbie's in that place. I can't spend my whole days not working for him. I need to have the money for Robbie to spend as I see fit. Please."

Miss Anne's blinker flickered golden light across the weeds growing at the railroad crossing, where the town landscaping crew stopped trimming on Lower Spruce. The brush grew so wild that whites and Negroes alike called the crossing "the Jungle."

"Am I hearing you right? You're asking me to give you more than two hundred dollars—in cash—and you don't want me to consult with you?"

"Yes. That's the best way. If you hear of a lawyer or have an idea, I'll be grateful to hear it. But I don't want to have to come begging you."

"Does that sound like me?" Miss Anne said. "Really, Gloria, you make me sound like Ma Ma. Like I would lord the money over you. Your parents knew me better than that. They knew my father better than that. Name one time I haven't done right by you."

She was the one who said it: *Name one time.*

"Do you think my papa's a good man?" Gloria said.

Miss Anne didn't answer for a moment, driving at a crawl on the dimly lighted road. She veered to avoid the gaping pothole the town had never bothered to fix. "I've told you many times: Robert Stephens is a good, honorable man."

"Yes, you've told *me* many times," Gloria said. "But I never hear you say it in front of Fred. Or at your bridge game on Wednesdays, when Miss Nell brings her brother to try to woo you. I've never heard you say it to anyone but me."

"Gloria—"

"I understand plenty from Miss Channing. *Plenty.*"

Gloria saw Miss Anne's cheeks flame red. "I don't know what you mean," Miss Anne said. Her hands were tight on the steering wheel. She was worried Gloria was about to ask questions about

Channing. That was the first time she *knew*: Miss Anne and Channing were sweet on each other, not just friends.

"About Papa," Gloria clarified. "And how sorry you feel for him. But not saying it where other white folks can hear—keeping those thoughts secret—doesn't help him. It would take somebody brave to help Papa. And it'll take somebody brave to help Robbie. You're not brave, Miss Anne. That's why I have to be the one, not you. I may not be brave most times, but I can be brave for Robbie."

Miss Anne drew in a ragged breath. "I am brave, Gloria. You don't know how brave." She sounded ready to tell how much courage it took to love Channing instead of a man.

"That's enough for you, but it's not brave like I need it," Gloria said. "Not enough for this. She's not brave enough either."

For the first time, Gloria realized exactly why she'd asked for the money: her plans for Robbie might involve a courtroom, or they might not. Miss Anne's money might go to a lawyer, or it might pay bribes to Reformatory guards. Or buy train tickets to Chicago. Miss Anne wouldn't agree with all of Gloria's ideas.

"It's dangerous to carry cash," Miss Anne said. "If you lost a check, I could write you another one. When cash is gone, it's gone. That's the last of Daddy's insurance money. Nearly the last of my cash savings. I put all my money in the cabins."

"A check doesn't do me a bit of good," Gloria said. "I need it in cash, Miss Anne. And it can't be in big bills people will look at funny. Make it fives, please. I'd be grateful if you'd pick it up from the bank tomorrow."

Miss Anne half laughed, although she wasn't smiling. "They'll look at *me* funny," Miss Anne said. "I'd sound like a bank robber. I haven't taken out that much cash at once since Daddy died. For his funeral." But she nodded.

Everyone on the street noticed their approach, wondering what had brought a white Powell to the colored side of town. Miss Annie's father had been considering a run for the Florida

Senate, and his car had appeared on Lower Spruce so Negroes would know they had a friend. Gloria wondered if Miss Anne had ever heard the rumor that William Powell had been run off the road by the Klan the night he died or if she should be the one to tell her.

Gloria noticed the watchers who seemed most interested: mean-tempered Mr. Grady, who was on a ladder clipping his magnolia tree by porchlight. And holier-than-thou Miz Etta Mae, who was staring at the car's slow progress through her window while she dried dishes at her sink. Not all skin folk were kin folk, as the saying went. Gloria had seen it a hundred times. The growers wouldn't have known about Papa's meetings if someone hadn't told. And probably someone couldn't wait to go run and tell how they'd seen Gloria in the car with Miss Anne, never mind that Gloria worked for her.

"If you have to quit, promise me you'll go to school," Miss Anne said. "You should train to be a teacher, Gloria. That's the best chance you have for yourself. I know that's what your mama wanted for you. She couldn't stop talking about how smart you are."

Gloria's eyes clouded. "I will," she said. "But not 'til Robbie's free."

"If you ever change your mind about the cabins, let me know. And I'll withdraw the money tomorrow, first thing. Daddy would have been proud to help."

The car was at a stop sign, and the world felt frozen too. Having money meant she had a chance. Robbie would have a chance. She wanted to hug Miss Anne, but she was still too angry. A tear ran down her cheek, squeezed from the space between gratitude and rage.

"All right, now," Miss Anne said quietly, her eyes darting up and down the street, noticing how so many people were watching. "Everything will be all right, hear?"

Gloria nodded, wanting to believe it. Even pretending to believe made her feel better.

But when Miss Anne turned the corner to Miz Lottie's street, something already felt wrong. Miz Lottie's front door at the end was wide-open, her clutter and stacks of newspapers and magazines visible to the street in the light from inside. Miz Lottie was too proud to leave her door open for strangers' eyes. And Uncle June and Waymon were leaning against Miz Lottie's truck as if they were waiting for her. They both straightened as the car approached, wary of the slow-moving headlights.

"Let me out here," Gloria said a hundred feet shy of Miz Lottie's.

"Is something wrong?"

"I don't know," Gloria said. "I'll see you tomorrow. Lunchtime. For the money."

She climbed out of the car and looked back once at Miss Anne's sad-eyed face through the windshield, wishing she could trade places and be the one driving away. *Please let Miz Lottie be all right. Please don't let there be any bad news about Robbie.* The what-ifs were a ball in Gloria's stomach as she ran on the uneven, grass-choked sidewalk toward Miz Lottie's yard.

Uncle June and Waymon jogged to meet her.

"Where you been? Mama's worried," Uncle June scolded.

"I'm sorry. I was with Miss Anne."

"You wasn't there," Waymon said. "That mouthy cracker there said you left ages ago."

Gloria had never known Waymon to go to Miss Anne's house. The Powells lived on Juniper Street, where the mayor, the sheriff, and old-money families lived in the town's Victorian Row. Negroes avoided Juniper and Main Street near dark or else be locked up for vagrancy, or a worse fate. It was best not to cross the railroad tracks at all after suppertime, much less to Juniper, where any Negro men were treated like robbers and rapists, even on the Powells' more modest end. But Waymon had come back from the war without a scratch and stripped of his fear of white people. She imagined Waymon knocking on the Powells' front door.

Gloria's alarm returned. "We went for a drive. What's wrong?"

June pressed his hand to Gloria's shoulder and spoke directly into her ear. "Maybe he's still on the phone. Your pops called from Chi—"

Gloria didn't hear the rest. She was already flying up Miz Lottie's front porch.

16

"I don't have time to go into it," Papa kept saying. "This call costs too much. But you never should've left and taken Robbie away from Lottie's. Don't you know that? I set you up that way for a reason. I don't know what you were thinking, I just really don't. What did you think would happen, up under the McCormacks' thumb? And Lottie says you went back out to our house last night too? Girl, you've gone out your head. Never again, you hear? But I don't have time for your foolishness. I don't have time."

Each word of Papa's was a slashing blow, but *I don't have time* cut the worst. He had not spoken to her in at least two weeks. He'd missed two Sunday calls to Miz Lottie, when she and Robbie had lingered late in case he might call. Chicago was two hours behind Florida, so Papa was always coming off work while Mister Randolph—the only one on Miz Lottie's party line they did not trust because he cared too much what white folks thought of him—was leaving for his late-night shift at nine thirty.

Papa sighed hard into the phone receiver, a gale in her ear. "All righty now," he said, calming himself. "All righty. Lottie says you aren't hurt, are you?"

"No, sir."

"And you're not setting foot near our place again unless June's with you?"

"No, sir."

His anger poked out again. "I just expected more from you, Gloria. Now look where we are! But I don't have time." Hot tears rolled from Gloria's eyes. She could be six years old again. "Anyway, pumpkin, I'm glad to hear your voice. We'll get this thing fixed." Tenderness only made Gloria's tears flow harder. Papa was fighting for his life in Chicago and she'd brought this new grief for him to carry. "You hear me?"

"Yes, sir."

"Say it like you mean it, gal."

"Yes, sir."

"Like I told Lottie, I think I found a lawyer. There's another colored fella I know in Jacksonville, but he won't do pro bono. I want you to try this one first."

Gloria's despair vanished, and she remembered she was talking to Robert Stephens, the leader people trusted to address the wrongs done to them as far as three counties. She was surprised he'd heard about Robbie's arrest so soon, and he'd already found a lawyer too? And knew of another?

Miz Lottie thrust a notepad and a pen to her, so Gloria rested the phone's heavy receiver on her shoulder. She used the pen to trace the squiggles of ink at the top of the page where Miz Lottie had tested it. Miz Lottie had taken notes, but her handwriting was a mystery.

"Bob, tell her what you told me," Miz Lottie called to the phone. "She'll take it down."

"His name is John Dorsey," Papa said. "D-O-R-S-E-Y. He's in Live Oak on another case, but if you can find him, he'll listen. He's with the NAACP in New York."

"Where's he staying?"

"Nowhere for Negroes to stay 'cept the Kinsey boardinghouse," Miz Lottie said, at the same time Papa was saying it. "And only other place he'd eat is at Belle's."

"I can't hear him, Miz Lottie," Gloria said, shushing her. She was magically in the bosom of family again, with Papa and Miz Lottie talking over each other like they always did at the table. She'd felt horribly alone last night in her empty house, but no more.

"Does he know Robbie's case?" Gloria said.

"Not 'til you tell him," Papa said. "I've never talked to him.

But when I called the New York office, one of the boys let it slip this Dorsey fella's nearby. Maybe it's a lucky break. He'll give you the same rigamarole they give me about how they're looking for capital cases, but I bet he'll listen. He'll know more'n we do about our recourse."

"Papa, Miss Anne's giving me money for a lawyer. All cash."

The phone line crackled in Papa's stony silence. He did not want to take money from the Powells. She waited for him to ask how much, but he didn't.

"You damn well earned it," Papa said. "Keep that money. But those NAACP lawyers don't charge like other lawyers. And this won't be the end of the line for us, but I'm hoping it's a start. It's a plan. Save that money for later."

When Mama took sick, at first she'd thought her backache was from bending over with the washing, but after a year it drove her to bed and they learned it was cancer all along—and the whole while Papa had rallied the family with his plans: *Give her a few days off her feet and she'll be all right* and then finally *I just read about a new treatment called chemotherapy* and each time they said, *Yes, Papa*, and hoped for the best, but the best never came. The days grew grimmer, the sunshine less bright, and Daddy's plans that helped so many others in Lower Spruce and Marianna and Quincy did nothing to help Mama, the one he loved most.

"I'm sorry, Gloria," Papa said, because he seemed to know her thoughts even now. "It wasn't your burden. I've got no right to blame you."

Gloria had never agreed with anything more, but she said, "It's all right, Papa," because his voice had knotted in a way that alarmed her. She didn't know what she would do if Papa started crying.

"We'll set it right," Papa said, forcing new oxygen to his words.

"I know we will."

"Lottie said Robbie looked good?"

"He looked fine," Gloria said. But all that meant was he'd avoided a beating from the sheriff's deputy and she'd seen him so long ago. She could have told Papa about her strong feeling last night that Robbie was taking a terrible whipping, a bloody one, but all day she'd tried to tell herself she'd imagined it. It wouldn't do any good to worry him, or herself.

Then Papa said what she feared most: "I should catch a train—"

"No," Gloria said.

"What he say?" Miz Lottie asked.

"Just to Live Oak," Papa said. "Not to Gracetown."

"*No,*" Gloria said, as angrily as she'd ever spoken to him, or as frightened, or both.

"He better not be talking no foolishness 'bout coming down here," Miz Lottie said. "On my damn line, for half the street to hear." Papa had heard her. He went quiet.

"We'll go early in the morning," Gloria said, speaking tersely for any listeners. "We'll find him."

"How's Miz Lottie holding up? Don't let on I'm asking."

"What's he sayin' now?" Miz Lottie said, aiming her ear toward the receiver, but Gloria gently pulled it away while she answered Papa: "You hear her for yourself. Like always."

"Don't let her drive. Have her tell Waymon—"

"Is he talkin' 'bout my driving?" Miz Lottie said loudly toward the phone. "Bob, hush. I told you to let off with that. Waymon can't miss work; neither can Junior. It ain't safe for them nohow, 'specially not Waymon. I'll take her. I can drive to Live Oak with my eyes closed." Her voice tremored with irritation.

"Remember what I said," Papa whispered to Gloria, a hiss across the phone line from Chicago. "She's more than eighty years old."

"We'll get there the best we can," Gloria said. She agreed with Miz Lottie: they would attract less attention than a big Negro man like Junior or wild-mouthed Waymon.

"Tell him to quit wasting his money goin' all the way 'round Adam's barn like we're a couple of fools who can't do nothin'. We *been* doin'." Miz Lottie smarted from Papa's every other word. She loved him as if she were Papa's mother, no doubt, but half her love was fussing.

A knock sounded on the front door, and they both whirled to look as the door flew open.

It wasn't Junior or Waymon; the door opened clumsily, pushed too far. On the umbrella rack behind the door, a bright red hat in the tangle of clothing tumbled down. Miz Lottie's neighbor Earl Hatchett, Gracetown County's NAACP vice president, stuck his gray head in. His moustache grew up his cheeks. He lived two houses down and shared Miz Lottie's party line.

"Tell Bob he better not come to Live Oak," he said, "or they'll catch him on the county road. They already out lookin'."

"See?" Miz Lottie said toward the receiver, loudly enough for Papa to hear. "Don't tell your business on my phone. And don't you dare come to Florida. Hatchett said they're looking for you to come."

It dawned on Gloria that Papa had not spoken in a long while. Had the phone cut off? Had he already left for the train station? "Papa?" When she heard an empty line and its clicks and buzzes, Gloria's chest tried to wring out her breath. She'd just gotten used to his voice again.

"All right," Papa said, as if remembering her. He'd still been thinking about it until Mr. Hatchett spoke up. His thoughts often took him away when other people were talking, which had annoyed Mama to no end, one of their last arguments until Mama stopped speaking and her own thoughts took her away. "I won't come." His voice was soaked in grief. He did not sob, but Gloria could hear the tears on his cheeks.

"I'll go, Papa," Gloria said. "I'll make sure Robbie gets out."

And she prayed she was not the liar tomorrow might prove her to be.

The bedroom was pure dark when Gloria felt tight fingers shaking her shoulder, and when she gasped to wakefulness she saw Lyle McCormack standing over her. When she blinked, it was Lyle's father and his bright red hair. Then Miz Lottie flicked on the bedside lamp, and she saw only the room stashed with Miz Lottie's fabrics and antiques. "Wake up, sugar," Miz Lottie said. "We leave early, we'll just be two headlights on the road. Get your clothes on. You should have slept ready-roll. Let's go."

The glowing hands on the bedside clock said it was not quite four thirty in the morning, so early that the cranky rooster next door was still sleeping. But Miz Lottie was already dressed, her pocketbook on her arm and white pillbox hat on her head like they were going to church. Miz Lottie wore this hat on special occasions or trips to the bank, when she would be on display. The only fresh clothes within Gloria's easy reach were an old pair of overalls she used in the garden, so she would look plenty common and didn't care. Miz Lottie frowned at Gloria's clothing, but she was more interested in leaving in a hurry. Anyway, Gloria had muddied her dress at the swamp.

Miz Lottie waved to her from the truck's driver's-side window. The engine was already running. "Grab the gas can case we need more to get back. Come on."

It was so early that the world felt blurry on the sleeping street. She and Miz Lottie could be the only two creatures on earth except the mosquitoes and crickets. Gloria hauled the half-empty gas can and set it in the bed of the truck alongside the gardening equipment Junior stored there. She wondered where Robbie was at that moment. Was he asleep too? Was he at peace or in pain? Gloria tried to imagine her brother, but she couldn't fix on him. Maybe she never had. Maybe he'd never been whipped.

"Girl, git your head out of the clouds," Miz Lottie said. "Come on!"

Gloria was so tired, she'd nearly fallen asleep on her feet. She hardly had room to squeeze beside Miz Lottie in the cab of the truck because two large laundry baskets were in her way: one on the floor and one beside her on the seat.

"Whose clothes are all these?" Gloria mumbled, trying to close her door without pinning her leg. The baskets smelled like mothballs. She glanced at the one beside her and found bedsheets that smelled like Miz Lottie's bedroom. "No more room in your closet?"

Miz Lottie slapped her hand away from the linens. "Hush." In her irritation, Miz Lottie backed out of her dirt driveway too quickly, bouncing over the exposed tree root at the curb. "Anyone asks us, we're delivering laundry like your mama used to. You hungry?"

Gloria *was* hungry. She'd barely eaten any dinner, so her mouth watered when she found a biscuit wrapped in a napkin on the dashboard. It wasn't warm, but the butter inside had melted. "Did you sleep last night, Miz Lottie?" she asked, mouth full.

"Enough," she said. "I'll sleep after Robbie's home."

"Who are we delivering laundry to?" Gloria said, testing the cover story.

"An NAACP lawyer named John Dorsey who fights these crackers in court." Gloria gaped, and Miz Lottie looked at her sidelong with a smile. "We'll just say it's for Ruby and Sam McCollum. Sam's a big man, and Ruby'll vouch for me if I ask. She's colored to boot. We pretendin' to do laundry, we might as well wash for our own."

Gloria's laugh startled her so much that she nearly choked.

Their laughing and talking stopped after they passed the railroad trestle, leaving Lower Spruce. Even the truck's engine seemed to quiet. A sheriff's car was parked in the shadow of the cypress tree twenty yards beyond the trestle, which was dangling its curtain of aerial roots. If not for the white coloring of the hood, Gloria would not have noticed the car. The dead headlights gleamed dully like a jungle cat's watching eyes.

"Miz Lottie—"

"I see him. Don't turn your head."

Gloria forgot her half-eaten biscuit. Her hand tightened on her leather seat, fingers curling. She studied her side mirror as they passed the sheriff's car. Leaving before dawn had seemed like a good idea until now. People disappeared in the dark.

Miz Lottie did not slow her driving or speed up. Gloria glanced at the speedometer, and she was driving at precisely twenty-five miles per hour, which Papa had called the Negro speed limit even though the sign on the road proclaimed it was thirty-five.

The clay road separated the deputy's car from them by ten yards, fifteen yards, and the car still did not move. But when they reached the paved road that became Main Street, the car crawled from the bushes, bright headlights flicking on, lighting up the truck's cab like morning.

Gloria jumped. *But it's not the red lights,* she reminded herself between throbs from her heart. They only had to stop for the flashing red light.

"He stops us, you leave the talking to me, hear? Don't you say a word."

Gloria only nodded. She'd already forgotten the proper names to cite. "He doesn't have the right to stop us. We haven't done anything."

"Hush that damn foolishness."

Only their two vehicles rolled past the darkened storefronts on Main Street, where even the neon Coca-Cola sign at Meg's Diner wasn't yet lighted red. Mannequins were ghosts in the windows. The parking spaces were empty. Miz Lottie tested her speed, creeping higher to thirty miles per hour.

"Don't speed up," Gloria said.

"They stop you if they think you actin' scared too. Just sit tight."

Miz Lottie had borrowed all of Gloria's courage. Papa had been pulled over time after time with Gloria under one pretense or another, and she could not remember being more afraid. She did not feel like the same person who had marched to Red McCormack's yard. *Trespassing,* he'd called her visit. What if the sheriff was looking for her? Her head swiveled to peek back.

"What I just tell you?" Miz Lottie said, so Gloria stared ahead as their truck crawled past the darkened courthouse and the hanging tree.

At the end of Main Street, Miz Lottie drove to the empty farm road toward State Route 90. Still the deputy's red lights did not come on. And the tailing headlights drew farther and farther behind until Gloria's mirror showed the sheriff's car turning around and heading back toward the sleeping town. Gloria stared a long time to make sure she wasn't only wishing him away.

Gloria's stomach seized, nudging her throat. "Pull over," she said. "Quick."

"Don't you be sick in my truck."

Miz Lottie lurched to a stop just in time for Gloria to retch into the crabgrass below.

When her tears from the strain of vomiting cleared, she saw how close they were to a deep ditch that might have tumbled them both to their deaths, hidden behind the thick grasses.

"You almost ran us in a ditch, Miz Lottie."

"Good thing I'm driving, or you'd run us in for sure. Close that door. Let's go."

An eerie feeling of being alone in the world smothered Gloria again on the open road as the wind fanned her face, still hot although it was dark. Even the logging trucks and tractors were gone, and it made her feel small. And hopeless. What could the two of them do in Live Oak?

What if they never found John Dorsey? Or he couldn't be bothered with a case that seemed so small? They might be heading toward another disappointment as big as Miss Channing or the social worker. Sometimes the worst thing happened—usually, in fact. Gloria couldn't remember a single time the best outcome had won out.

Miz Lottie began singing loudly, probably to stay awake, Mahalia Jackson's "Walk with Me," which was always playing on the record player Uncle June had bought her for Christmas. She sang at a faster tempo than the recording, tapping out a rhythm on the steering wheel, her voice throaty and mostly on key: "I need you, Jeeee-sus . . . walk with me . . ."

Gloria joined in, tentatively. Her voice was not as good as Miz Lottie's—she'd inherited Mama's singing voice, not Papa's—but she raised her voice to sing loudly to try to banish the gloom in her thoughts, trying to believe that the same Jesus who had forsaken Mama might help them get Robbie back. She felt trapped into singing, almost, like begging instead of worship, but she sang until her throat hurt. Until daylight was glowing pink and yellow at the horizon. Gloria thought she recognized God in the birth of new light and longed to pray, but her relationship with prayer had not been steady. Maybe she could pray through her eyes, with the pink golden light of dawn waking the colors all around her.

"How do you still believe in God, Miz Lottie?" she said. "With all the bad things."

"Don't you?"

She tried to, she'd tried hard for Mama, but she also knew it was possible that the sun was just a burning rock and had nothing to do with God. "Sometimes I do," she said. "But since Mama . . . sometimes I don't. Seems like the McCormacks in this world get all of God's love."

"You think no McCormack ever got sick and died?" Miz Lottie didn't wait for an answer. "*Seems* like, that's what you said. Nothin' ain't never what it seems. This whole world is a lie—the bad things, the good things. Only God's kingdom is the truth. And when I meet Jesus face-to-face, you can bet I'll have some questions. But 'til then, I *don't* know why some got so much and we got so little. Could be a test. But I feel God blessing me, Gloria."

"But how do you *know*?"

"It ain't my head that knows," Miz Lottie said. "But my heart do."

Gloria wished she could catch hold of Miz Lottie's unbroken faith and wrap it around herself like Joseph's blanket. Sleepiness stole over her, although she jolted awake to bumps and turns.

The tires vibrated with ruts as they crossed the bridge over the Suwannee River. Each time Gloria woke, Miz Lottie was still singing under her breath, a personal song to her Lord.

Gloria woke to the sound of women's sad, sour laughter.

Her vision rocked as she straightened. The world was dust and too-bright light. The dust was smeared across the windshield of Miz Lottie's truck, she remembered. Miz Lottie's seat on the other side of the laundry basket was empty, the door open. Gloria rubbed away the tension from her neck, which was sore from deep sleep against her door. She stared through her window.

The yellow two-story house where the truck was parked was a style unlike any in Gracetown, walls ribbed with markings that made it look like it belonged in a faraway place, like a Spanish mission in St. Augustine. The house was halfway hidden behind thick palms planted at the curb. Even Miss Anne's house wasn't as big and didn't have the exotic half-moon carving atop her chimney or the attic window's flourish. The house was dressed like a mansion. Most of the houses on the street were no better than Miz Lottie's, and some reminded Gloria of her cabin with strips of rusting tin. And Miz Lottie was talking to a woman in the doorway. The *front* door. Was this a Negro woman's house?

"Oh, she's sixteen now. Actually, turned seventeen in May. Out there 'sleep. Worn-out, po' thing," Miz Lottie was saying. And as much as Gloria liked knowing what other people were saying about her, she nearly dozed off again. She'd had little sleep three nights solid now. She was so tired that her limbs and eyes ached. She dozed again. When she woke up, the laughter was gone and the door to the house was closed. Miz Lottie had gone into the house. *I should get up and help Miz Lottie,* she thought, but sleep took her again.

The next time Gloria woke up, a stout woman was standing directly at her window, round face peering inside as she studied Gloria, scowling in the sun. Gloria gasped. Miz Lottie chuckled, hoisting herself back into her seat by tugging on the steering wheel.

"Well, she's awake now. Jumpin' at shadows. Gloria, this here's Ruby McCollum."

The woman at the window smiled wanly at her. Gloria recognized the woman's name from the cover story she and Miz Lottie had devised—but couldn't smile right away because she was swallowed by *knowing* Ruby McCollum, although she'd never met her before now. Mama had called it déjà vu: you think you've done something before. Except, for Gloria, it was always more like seeing the future. Like the time she'd seen Mama standing at the sink and thought, out of thin air, *Mama's sick.* Or when she and Robbie had run into Lyle McCormack on the road, a sad inevitability from the second she'd seen his stupidly grinning face. Ruby McCollum's eyes twinkled, fresh from laughter, but Gloria tried to hide her sudden tears.

"Don't worry none, you'll get your brother back," Ruby McCollum said, and Gloria couldn't explain she wasn't crying for Robbie: she'd seen something in this woman's eyes like a long ribbon into her life, and the feelings as deep as feelings went: grief and rage and a long, slow dying. Gloria knew this woman told lies, and was lied to. She was boastful, but only as a mask over feeling like nothing her whole life. And she could hold her temper longer than some, but if she was pushed too hard, if she hurt too much, she might shoot a white man down—a white doctor, even—and not care who saw her do it. Gloria tasted the stranger's future rage and thought about Lyle McCormack putting his hand on her, and she almost said, *I know what you did and what he did to you.* Ruby McCollum would kill a white man who touched her. She was living her last good year in her pretty house and didn't know it. Soon, every Negro in Florida and Zora Neale Hurston herself would know Ruby McCollum's name.

Gloria's hands trembled in her lap.

"Miz Lottie, I'll slap you if you're drivin' up and down Suwannee County without protection," Ruby McCollum said.

Miz Lottie patted the laundry basket. "Shoot, I got my protection."

"Just making sure. I hope Bob don't have you tangled up with communists."

"Ruby, now you sound just like *them*. Don't forget: I know where you started, chile. I got stories all the way back to grade school."

"Works both ways," Ruby McCollum said. "We both got stories, then."

"We sho' do," Miz Lottie said, and they both laughed again.

Ruby McCollum slapped Gloria's door as if to share her cheer. "Yeah, go talk to 'im. Like I said, he seems all right to me. Seditty like all northern folks who come down here like it's a safari in Africa; thinks he's a big man. I don't think he wants nobody to know he's here, but Belle says every other word out of his mouth is 'N-double A-C-P.' "

The lawyer was real, not a myth or a hope! And he *was* in Live Oak. Gloria squirmed, flushed with blood from her celebrating heart.

"Good thing you always in e'rybody's business," Miz Lottie said. "And e'rybody's always up in mine and Sam's."

"Don't give 'em so much to talk about, then."

Miz Lottie turned the key and the engine choked and died. As usual, it didn't catch until her second try. Gloria's legs bounced anxiously against the laundry basket and the glove box. If she had known where to run, she'd have jumped out of the truck. She couldn't help what she knew, or thought she knew, about Ruby McCollum's future, but she could help change Robbie's. Gloria kept her eyes cast down from the woman's face, avoiding the mask of coming grief that hovered over the woman like a cloud of fruit flies. The truck pitched backward as Miz Lottie reversed. She made a perfect half-U shape to the roadway, barely missing Ruby McCollum's elegant brick columns and her bright, well-tended grass. Gloria's neck snapped back as the old truck's brakes whimpered and moaned.

"Learn who you can trust," Miz Lottie told her. "You wouldn't know it, but Ruby and Sam is the richest Negroes you likely to meet. They pay off the sheriff, ev'rybody, with that bolita money. She couldn't do none of that if she didn't know how to keep secrets."

Ruby McCollum waved as the truck drove off, and Gloria almost saw the secrets spilling at her feet: the secrets of others, and her own.

17

Gloria spotted him right away. As soon as she and Miz Lottie walked into the roomy, steam-filled kitchen of Belle's wood-frame boardinghouse, she knew the young man sitting at a corner table in a dapper gray suit, a cigarette balanced on careless fingers, had to be John Dorsey. She had expected him to be fair-skinned like Thurgood Marshall, the way she imagined all NAACP lawyers must be, but he was as brown-skinned as she was, his curly hair conked. He was well shy of thirty, no more than twenty-six or twenty-seven. And he was holding court with two men standing over him at his table, one in overalls and a thinner man closer to Papa's age in a black suit and tie. Neither man moved to sit in the table's two empty seats.

John Dorsey spooned teaspoon after teaspoon of sugar into his coffee, punctuating each sentence. On the table before him lay a long yellow pad crammed with writing.

Yes, he was the one.

All colors, smells, and noises orbited him: the frying bacon that rumbled her empty stomach, the phonograph near the open window playing "Am I Asking Too Much" by Dinah Washington like Mama used to, and the din of a dozen other people, mostly men. Aside from the small corner tables, customers were shoulder to shoulder at the counter or eating at two long tables as they passed biscuits and gripes. Many of the men wore mill shirts. Two or three, like John Dorsey, were dressed like travelers who had found Belle's in the *Green Book*. A Coca-Cola sign glowed in the window like Belle's was a five-and-dime.

Gloria took two steps toward the lawyer's table before she felt a sharp tug on her arm. "I see 'im too," Miz Lottie said, keeping a firm grip at Gloria's elbow. "Be still. You don't jus' run up on a meeting, chile."

A middle-aged mill worker tipped his hat as he rose from his seat at the corner of a nearby table, making room for Miz Lottie. The boy her age who was with him reluctantly rose too as he glanced over Gloria's overalls, doubting she was worth the inconvenience. Gloria's cheeks flared. She hated to be on display to boys, but she patted down her hair. She'd had thick French braids from Miz Lottie for more than a week, and they were loosening at her scalp and forehead.

"Why, thank you very much," Miz Lottie called after the father and son as they carried their plates away. The boy gave Gloria one more glance, half grinning when he caught her fussing with her hair. Gloria looked quickly away. Her friends at school, Doris and Rose and Pat, were forever discussing such clues from boys: what they meant, how to behave if a boy smiled, if a boy *didn't* smile. Her bigger worries liberated her from that care.

Belle, a sharp-boned woman in a long apron, was already wiping the table with a damp, brown-stained cloth. "Just coffee? Breakfast?" she said, impatient. Gloria stared at the lawyer while Miz Lottie rattled a long food order.

Another spoonful of sugar. Then another. The two other men were speaking over each other, voices rising. Were they arguing?

"I'm not hungry," Gloria said, but her stomach roared.

"Might as well eat," Miz Lottie told her. "You see he's a talker. He ain't goin' nowhere. That's the state NAACP president with him, Harry Moore—another one I been tryin' to reach about Robbie. But the lawyer's from the New York office, which has more clout. So we'll kill two birds with one stone." Excitement wavered Miz Lottie's voice.

Gloria's stomach loosened with relief, and she was suddenly hungry again. "Sausage and biscuit, please," Gloria said, trying to guess how much that might cost, if Miz Lottie could afford it. She'd left Gracetown too early to get her money from Miss Anne.

Gloria slipped her eyes to the lawyer again. While the man in the overalls spoke close to his ear, the lawyer was nodding, head bowed low, almost as if in prayer. "I know it," the lawyer said. "I know." Like a pastor would.

"So what about it, then?" the man in the tie said. "Been near *six* years—"

The lawyer looked sorry to his core. "Harry, the national office put everything down in Lake County and those Groveland boys—"

"What's that gonna do for Willie?" the man in the overalls said, more loudly. The entire room rocked still, or seemed to. Bacon grease popped from the skillets, impossibly loud. Gloria wasn't the only one eavesdropping on the lawyer; most of the men in the room, especially the ones from the mill, already had their heads turned his way, nursing coffee cups as they seemed to stare at the window just right of his head. Yes, they *were* watching his window as much as they were noticing the lawyer, tracking each passerby. How hadn't she recognized it? Belle's was a meeting place. Sometimes Mama had fried up chicken wings and made biscuits and stayed out with Papa and his meetings on the porch long into the night. The awful things they spoke of had been banished from the house.

The man in overalls wiped his brow with a napkin from the table. Or maybe he'd wiped the corner of his eye. "They been *bragging*," he choked out. "Bragging how they did it."

"I heard it with my own ears." A testimony floated from the table behind Gloria, a man across the room. The silence grew heavy with unspoken stories.

"And he's still the postmaster," the man said. "Like it ain't nothing. Not an ounce of shame. Not a goddamn ounce of shame between none of them."

Belle made a shushing sound. "Don't blaspheme in my house,"

she said. "And we got company, gentlemen. I don't know them like I know y'all."

She nodded across the room, and Gloria noticed the only jovial faces: the two suit-wearing strangers and their lady companions in private conversations at smaller corner tables. Disconnected, without a care. A few curious eyes studied Gloria and Miz Lottie but quickly moved on, as if they already knew Robbie's story as well as they knew the story of the unlucky boy named Willie.

Willie was dead. Gloria could have squeezed more knowing out of the room because it hung over her like rain clouds bloated purple and ugly, but she did not want their sorrows to drown her. They shouted their sadness to her anyway. Willie had been fifteen, only three years older than Robbie. Fifteen and dead.

The lawyer stood up—he was taller than Papa—and put his hand gently on the angry man's shoulder to will his grief away with his touch.

"Thurgood is hurt over Willie," the lawyer said, aware of his audience too. "Real hurt. All of us are. Up to the governor. But you know as well as I do . . . *they* won't." He motioned out the window, past the Coca-Cola sign, toward the street. "Those 'decent' friends and neighbors of the postmaster out there, they won't do it. No indictment, no trial. We already tried. They saw Willie's father's statement saying they made him watch at gunpoint while they forced a child with hands and feet bound to jump from the bridge, and we still couldn't get an indictment. There's nowhere left to go. Not on this case. Our hands and feet are bound . . . same as Willie's." The silence in the room became terrible.

"What y'all gonna do in Lake County, then?" The man snatched his shoulder away from the lawyer's touch.

"Maybe nothing," the lawyer said. "But those boys still have a chance. The way this happened with Willie . . . we couldn't help him. I wish we could. But if we can do something in Lake County, maybe it'll make even a lowdown murdering coward like Phil Goff and his cracker thugs think twice. When word gets around that

Negroes can get justice in Florida, maybe we can spare another family from what you've been through. Spare another town."

His pretty words were plausible, stirring Gloria's heart to pounding. A gray-haired man at the end of Gloria's table clapped his hands slowly, both admiration and a call for quiet. "Y'all just picking at it," he said. "Makin' it bleed. You don't watch out, it'll bleed you to the grave."

"He was my baby cousin!" the man in overalls said.

"Lemme ask you this," the older man went on, speaking slowly, "and you know I don't mean your family no disrespect . . ." Gloria expected him to say something especially disrespectful, of course. "What if the girl had made up a story, said Willie'd touched her or some such instead of just writing a li'l note? We lucky they didn't burn down 'Nigger Hill'—*all* of us. I'll say what y'all won't: the child had no business sending a love note to a white girl. Some of y'all ain't raising these children to know these crackers like they need to." He settled behind his newspaper pages, ignoring the groans around him.

"You wrong for that, Clement," the man in overalls said. But eyes in the room looked away and voices fell to private grumbling.

The man in the black suit, Mr. Moore, sighed. "The national office got me out here trying to sell memberships at double the price—and folks say, 'For what? Register to vote for what?' "

John Dorsey winced. "I know," he said. "I hate the politics. But the Legal Defense Fund isn't the problem. Thurgood is the first one to tell those fools at national that Harry T. Moore is the Negro's hardest-working friend in Florida."

"Don't forget Harriette." When Miz Lottie broke in, the man in the suit took off his hat.

For the first time, their talking stopped. Gloria felt sorry for the boy who'd died, but she was glad Miz Lottie had wrested away their attention.

John Dorsey turned and saw Gloria and Miz Lottie for the first time. "No, ma'am," he said. "I could never forget Mrs. Moore and her cobbler."

"The school system didn't fire her for her cooking," Miz Lottie said. When Harry Moore leaned over to greet Miz Lottie with a kiss to her cheek, Gloria thought she smelled soot in his hair. "You and Harriette still givin' 'em hell?"

"You mean they're giving *us* hell, Miz Lottie."

"This is my goddaughter, Gloria Stephens. Bob's oldest. Gloria, this is Harry T. Moore."

Harry Moore's face clouded a bit at the mention of Papa, but he smiled for Gloria and shook her hand. Gloria drew her hand away as fast as she could. His palm had seemed to rub hers with ashes; she tried to wipe it on her overalls. As she stared at his weary face, sparks danced at the edges of his hair. She expected the dishes to rattle from a sudden shaking of the floor, as if from a bomb.

But no one else had felt the shaking, and Gloria couldn't see ashes on her fingertips. The future was shouting again, and this time Gloria felt sick to her stomach. She had seen a ribbon of sorrow into Ruby McCollum's life, but Harry T. Moore's was already close to gone.

"Be . . . careful," Gloria blurted out. "They'll try to bomb you. You and your wife both." She spoke so quickly, she startled herself. Mama had said to consider anything she told. But it was like he was standing on train tracks and she could see the engine bearing down.

"Oh, you damn right they will," Harry Moore said, hardly bothered. And he winked.

"You sound like Bob all right. Same thing he always said, almost word for word." His mouth worked itself as if to go on, but he glanced between Miz Lottie and Gloria and thought better of it, sad-eyed. Even in a room with an NAACP lawyer and so many others carrying their grievances, he did not want to say more about Papa.

"Harriette told me you called," Mr. Moore said to Miz Lottie. He sounded sheepish. "I didn't mean for you to drive all this way—"

"I'd 'preciate an introduction to Mr. Dorsey," Miz Lottie said. "He's the one we came to see. When y'all finish up."

"Oh, we finished, ma'am," Willie Howard's cousin said, flipping his cap back on his head. "I don't think Mr. Dorsey's got nothin' else to say to me."

Harry and the lawyer exchanged a look. "I'm sure sorry, Mr. Howard," the lawyer said. Mr. Moore patted the dead boy's cousin on the back as he walked away. Other men patted him all the way to the door.

The lawyer sighed and scooped his spoon in the sugar dish again.

"You keep putting in all that sugar," Gloria said, "and you'll have to eat that coffee." John Dorsey lowered his spoon, found Gloria's eyes. Smiled. She rose from her seat. "Too much sugar will rot out your teeth."

"You sound like my wife," the lawyer said.

"I'm Gloria Stephens," Gloria said. Her stride to him did not betray the way her pounding heart made her knees watery. She outstretched an unsteady hand. "I'm from Gracetown and my brother needs your help."

John Dorsey shook her hand with a cool palm, only glancing over her face. "Pleasure, miss," he said. "I'm sorry for your circumstances." He glanced to Mr. Moore for guidance.

"Juvenile matter," Mr. Moore muttered. He gave the lawyer a private shake of his head she almost couldn't see. The lawyer nodded in a way that seemed to sweep Gloria from his sight. His eyes pulled more deeply behind their lashes. He was looking at her and *past* her.

"Mr. Dorsey's got a full plate today," Mr. Moore said to Miz Lottie, as if it were she, not Gloria, who had spoken. "I'll make some calls for the boy, see what we can do."

The lawyer rested a light palm across Gloria's and said, "With a sister like you working for him, I don't have a worry, Miss Stephens." Then he squeezed her hand and let her go.

Suddenly his pretty talking offended Gloria the way it surely had offended the dead boy's cousin. Dismissal lay at the core, just like with Loehmann outside of the Reformatory. They wanted to seem nice, as if niceness could bring Robbie home.

"Robbie needs a lawyer," Gloria said.

Miz Lottie stood up while Gloria held her steady. "We got up 'fore dawn and drove a long ways, Mr. Dorsey," Miz Lottie said. "And don't you worry, Harry—I'm not gonna ask you nothin' about Bob's case. Though I'd be lyin' if I said I don't have questions 'bout what the hell the NAACP is doing for *him*."

Mr. Moore pursed his lips. "Not much we can do . . . yet, Miz Lottie." He meant Papa would have to give himself up and stand trial first, or at least get arrested and put in jail.

"Robert Stephens?" the lawyer said to Gloria. "You're his daughter? Robbie is his son?"

Gloria did not like how many eyes were on them; even the travelers in far corners were watching. Papa had warned her not to claim him in public, even to denounce him when she needed to, though she never had, or would.

"There's too many people here," she said quietly.

The lawyer nudged his sugar-choked coffee aside and stood. "Let's go somewhere we can talk."

Belle's had a screened-in porch just beyond the kitchen's back door instead of a yard, crammed with wicker tables and chairs smudged gray by time. Thickets of bougainvillea bushes in bright blooms of dark pink and purple hid the porch from the road, which was busier with passing cars than Main Street in Gracetown. The lawyer settled into the cushion of a throne-like chair next to a table with an ashtray, where he set down his half-burned cigarette. He seemed to be mulling Robbie's case over. Miz Lottie sat near the lawyer while Mr. Moore paced, checking his watch. A rust-colored, overfed cat took to Gloria and twined between her legs, mewing.

"He got six months," Gloria said. "Six months for a kick that wasn't anything."

"A kick to Red McCormack's son," Mr. Moore said, correcting.

"I don't care if he kicked the Virgin Mary," Miz Lottie said. "It don't make sense."

"Oh, it makes sense to them," the lawyer said. "To sentence a child to six months over a schoolyard kick is to willfully ignore that child's humanity. To rebuke it."

Gloria was tired of sad, angry words. "How do we get him out?"

"Where is Gracetown?" the lawyer said.

Only now, starting to hope, did Gloria feel afraid of what he might say next. "Outside Marianna," Gloria said, while Miz Lottie said, "Couple hours' drive."

"Northwest," Mr. Moore said, to make it clear. "Not south. *Two* hours northwest."

John Dorsey pointed his cigarette at Mr. Moore. "But setting distance aside . . . let's look at all the angles of this thing, Miss Stephens, Miz Lottie." He leaned closer to them, using a secret-keeping voice. "We can't expect justice in a racist court," he said. "It happens from time to time, but most times it won't. White juries are afraid of Negroes, so even our children seem dangerous on sight. That was the trap laid for Robbie before he ever kicked anyone."

"Lyle pushed Robbie first," Gloria said.

"A push is also an assault," the lawyer said, nodding. "By law. But I'm gonna take a wild guess that the son of a wealthy white planter and business owner didn't pay a price for assaulting your brother?" He didn't wait for her answer, which was bubbling as a sob in Gloria's throat as she remembered that awful morning on McCormack Road. "Of course he didn't. The law, by design, is to protect the McCormacks. Not us. Not Robbie. That's the reason no grand jury will indict the postmaster who murdered a child here in town." His voice cracked and he sat back in his seat. He seemed to have a sob buried in his throat too.

"Welcome to Florida. That sick feeling's gonna stick with you all the way down to Lake County and probably get worse after you get there," Mr. Moore said. "But sometimes folks just need to tell their sorrows and all you can do is hear them." Gloria felt Mr. Moore was talking about her and Miz Lottie, eager to steer the lawyer back to their day's plans far away.

John Dorsey shook his head to say, *It's okay,* and brought his eyes back to Gloria's, fully focused. "How old is Robbie?"

She had him. Mr. Moore knew it too. He hung his head. "Twelve," Gloria and Miz Lottie said together.

The lawyer winced. "Twelve-year-olds in prison . . ."

"They beat Robbie with a whip," Gloria blurted before she remembered she had only sensed it; she couldn't prove it. Miz Lottie gave her a surprised look.

The lawyer's eyebrows jumped. "Flogging's not legal in Florida prisons, is it?"

Mr. Moore was nodding. "It is at Gracetown Boys' School. They've got a whipping shed. I've heard about it. Half my calls from parents are about the Reformatory."

"They got a damn *cemetery* out there," Miz Lottie said. "They're buryin' them boys. And doing who knows what all else. Workin' 'em like grown men besides. Like slaves. Last I heard, Lincoln set us free."

Every word Miz Lottie spoke made the lawyer's jaw tighten. Gloria suddenly knew the exact words to steer him: "You couldn't help Willie," she said, "but you can help my brother, Mr. Dorsey."

Mr. Dorsey and Mr. Moore shared a long conversation with their eyes. "Gracetown's a lot like Lake County," Mr. Moore said to the lawyer. "They need to know the whole size of it, Johnny."

Mr. Dorsey nodded and looked back at Gloria. "Say we threw around the NAACP's name in Gracetown; that'll get their attention, all right. But will it be the attention you want?"

"We just want Robbie free," Gloria said. "I don't care if people are talking about us."

"This isn't about talk," Mr. Dorsey said. "In a case like your father's—when a white girl is telling the sheriff she was raped by a Negro—it's never just about talk."

Gloria's face felt hot to hear Papa's story from his mouth. "This isn't about my father." She hated the whine in her voice, just when she'd convinced them not to treat her like a child.

"What he's saying, we've got two strikes against us," Mr. Moore said. "One, he's Robert Stephens's son. That hurts us with the judge." Miz Lottie started to argue but he cut her off. "It's just facts, Lottie. On top of that, there's Superintendent Haddock: he's a special case. Spoils for a fight. He'll keep a boy for ten years out of spite—until the very last minute of the very last day he can keep a boy by law, and sometimes when he can't. Sometimes the children are only seven or eight. He'll keep them ten, twelve years. I've seen it. And the governor has the same answer: 'discretion of the superintendent.' There's always a witness willing to say they saw the boy do wrong just before it was time to get out: those boys say what they're told to say. That gives Haddock a whole lot of sway, always an excuse."

"Who does Haddock answer to, then?" Gloria said. "He answers to somebody."

The lawyer patted his suit pocket for a cigarette although the one in his ashtray was only half burned. "The judge," he said.

Mr. Moore let out a sigh. "NAACP showing up at the courthouse?" He leaned over to clasp Miz Lottie's hands, voice gentle. "For Robbie's sake, I think it's better to let him quietly do his time. You don't know what could get stirred up. Lake County's ugly, Lottie." He lowered his voice. "You don't want to see it in Gracetown. Send the girl somewhere for a while. It'll keep her from harm's way . . . and may help Robbie get out quicker."

"*If* he gets out," Miz Lottie said.

"How many folks got a child buried at Boot Hill?" Gloria spoke to the lawyer. "What would the judge have to do?"

"Easiest thing, I guess, would be to say he's reconsidered his sentence, wants to commute to time served. Or he has the power to rescind his sentence entirely."

"I know this judge," Mr. Moore said, again directly to Miz Lottie. "Bob knows this judge, and *well*. It's a miracle he only gave Robbie six months." Gloria remembered the judge's smile when he sentenced Robbie: he'd been so pleased with himself, thinking how he'd been so fair to a Negro, especially a Negro who was Robert Stephens's son.

"But here's the thing about these racist cracker judges," the lawyer said. "They don't *know* they're racist cracker judges."

"And don't give a damn," Moore said.

"Some do give a damn how they look anyway, Harry," John Dorsey argued. "They want to be the good guy. I've sat in their chambers and told a few jokes and they told a few right back. That's a tactic Thurgood taught me. Once you're man-to-man, sometimes you can get through."

"These Florida sheriffs laugh with you on Friday morning and set the Klan on you Friday night," Mr. Moore said. "You're not from here, Johnny."

"I'm from Indiana. We've got crackers too."

"So you'll do it?" Gloria said to the lawyer. "You'll speak up for Robbie with the judge?"

"Now you're getting their hopes up," Mr. Moore chided him.

"If that's what you want me to do," the lawyer said to Gloria, then he repeated it for Miz Lottie: "If you want me to, I'll go to Gracetown. But I can only do it today. This morning."

Mr. Moore gestured *Come here* to the lawyer, flapping at the air. "A word?"

The lawyer shook his head. "Tell him we're rescheduling. Make it dinner instead."

"I don't like that drive into Lake County at night, Johnny."

"We'll drive fast," the lawyer said, and smiled. "We'll get there."

Mr. Moore hurried toward the sliding glass door to the house.

"Lemme at least call and see if Judge Morris is at the courthouse today."

John Dorsey dragged on his cigarette and petted the cat, who was now rubbing against his shiny shoes. "Let's bring him a hot plate for lunch, ladies," he said. "Everybody likes to eat."

He winked at Gloria, and she laughed in a childish way that startled her. "There's fried chicken in Gracetown that's good as hoodoo," Miz Lottie said.

"Good, I'll try a piece myself," John Dorsey said.

Gloria almost giggled again but caught herself as she noticed the way the lawyer's eyes shifted away, mired in his thoughts, and how his mirth was only on the surface. For the first time, she realized he was afraid. Doubts assailed her: as much as she wanted to free Robbie, maybe Mr. Moore was right. Maybe it was better not to rile them and bring up Papa's name. If the warden was as evil as Mr. Moore said, Robbie might not get out until he was a grown man.

"Thank you," Gloria said, but she really wanted to ask if he thought they were foolish. Or how someone who had so little faith in the law could feel any hope for Robbie. Maybe it was like Miz Lottie's faith in Jesus. And Mama's.

John Dorsey stubbed out the cigarette and rose to his feet. "We'll see, Miss Stephens. I'll do my best, but I can't promise how it'll fly. Might fly wrong." He glanced at Miz Lottie. "Harry's right about that. These crackers are gonna try to kill him one day."

A sharp knock from the glass door made them all jump like a gunshot. They turned and saw Mr. Moore giving the thumbs-up sign, cradling the phone on his shoulder. In her excited imagination, Gloria thought he had somehow arranged to get Robbie free. Then she realized his true meaning: the judge who had sentenced her brother was at the courthouse in Gracetown.

She and Miz Lottie had found Robbie a lawyer, like she'd promised Papa she would.

18

For the next twenty minutes, nearly thirty, Gloria felt proud of herself—excited, even. The lawyer said his goodbyes at Belle's, hearing two last requests for legal advice. He handed one young man a folded five-dollar bill, slipping it so deftly that Gloria might have been the only one to see.

While the lawyer gathered his bags, Mr. Moore filled Miz Lottie's tank from the gas can and explained they would drive separately to the Gracetown courthouse so neither car would draw attention to the other. They were all likely being watched, he explained, and he didn't want anyone to guess their plan before they reached the judge. Miz Lottie and Gloria would set out first, and then Mr. Moore would follow with the lawyer in his car ten minutes later. They agreed to meet up in front of the courthouse by noon.

Under the hanging tree, Gloria remembered.

The plan gave her oxygen. For the first time since Robbie's arrest, Gloria felt like she knew anything at all again. She could imagine Robbie at Miz Lottie's house, and maybe all three of them could go away to Miss Anne's secret cottages. Or maybe to Chicago. Yes, to Chicago—to join Papa. She should have insisted on it long ago. They would have traveling money now.

On the road, Miz Lottie's hand felt uneven on the steering wheel, the truck veering too far into the center. She had lost her songs and energy from the morning drive. She looked small and frail beneath her glamorous hat. Worry over Robbie was stealing days, maybe weeks or years, from the end of Miz Lottie's life.

"You want me to drive?" Gloria said.

Miz Lottie's head snapped up. "Hush. You don't know nothin' 'bout drivin'."

"Papa taught me enough to go up and down an empty road."

"Not Ole Suzy," she said. "Drivin' Ole Suzy ain't like drivin' nothin' else."

"Well, you look like you're about to fall asleep."

"Nobody could sleep with all yo' fussing. If I nod off, gimme a nudge."

Gloria hardly noticed the billboard advertising Minute Maid orange juice until she saw the sheriff's car parked behind it, a sight so sudden that they both sucked in breath. Gloria leaned over to check the speedometer: thirty miles per hour, slowing slightly. And Miz Lottie was in the proper lane again. Maybe it would be all right—

"Dammit, dammit, dammit," Miz Lottie said, and Gloria saw the flashing red light as the sheriff's car raced to the road behind them, kicking up dust behind it.

Gloria had an impulse to outrace the sheriff's car, to yank the steering wheel from Miz Lottie's hands toward the thicket of pines west of them to take their chances. But Miz Lottie slowed down while the sheriff's car barreled in on them and flashed its headlights.

"Don't look so scared," Miz Lottie said, calm. "We was just pickin' up laundry from Ruby. They prob'ly gonna let us alone if we say that. Most o' these boys is on Sam's payroll."

Gloria only nodded. She didn't want Miz Lottie to know how scared she was.

"Don't say nothin' 'less they ask you," Miz Lottie said. "Don't give 'em no lip either 'bout what right they got to do this or that. Hear me?"

Gloria nodded again. She craved an hour's more advice from Miz Lottie, but there was no time before the deputies' doors flew open. The truck barely had rolled to a stop before the driver was lumbering toward Miz Lottie's window. He was as bad as Gloria had feared: fireplug stocky with a barrel chest, big jowls, and unkind creases across his brow. He stomped rather than walked. He carried a stink of violence sharp to her nose.

When the deputy reached her window, Miz Lottie summoned a grin so wide that the gaps from her missing back teeth showed. "I sho' hope I wasn't speeding, suh," she said. "We can go up to thirty up where I lives at." Miz Lottie exaggerated her lack of schooling, dipping into a lulling, obedient singsong.

Gloria tried on a smile, but her lips were too tight and trembly, so she gave up. A second deputy approached her. This deputy was younger and softer faced, peering at her through her window. His hair was cut short to blond fuzz. He loosened his shoulders when he saw she was a girl, not a boy, despite her overalls. He glanced at her feet, at the basket. Looking for something.

"Where y'all from, Auntie?" the deputy at Miz Lottie's window said. He gestured to his partner toward the back of the truck, so the deputy left Gloria's window.

"Gracetown, up a ways," Miz Lottie said, still grinning.

"Suwannee County's a long way from home, ain't it?"

The second deputy climbed into the bed of the truck, and Gloria bristled. He needed a search warrant to look at anything in Miz Lottie's truck—she'd learned this from plenty of radio programs and picture shows, from Papa, even from school—but she remembered not to say so. Metal clanged as he searched. Miz Lottie was particular about anyone handling June's gardening equipment, since that was his weekend living, but she didn't say that either.

"We take laundry from Sam and Ruby McCollum," Miz Lottie said. The frowning deputy glanced at the basket that sat between her and Gloria. The linens were neatly folded, fresh from Miz Lottie's closet. Under scrutiny, the story felt flimsy.

"That laundry don't look dirty," the deputy said. He noticed alarmingly fast. He was not an unseasoned deputy like the one who'd arrested Robbie. He talked like the poor whites who lived in Misery Swamp in houses built barely above the water, but he was not stupid.

Gloria leaned forward with the effort of trying to think of an answer about the laundry, but Miz Lottie answered first, tapping Gloria's knee to remind her to be silent. "I didn't think so either, suh, but she's awful particular. Wants it washed again."

"You drive a long ways to make a few dollars."

"She pays real good, suh. Makes it worth my while."

Gloria expected him to say Miz Lottie was too old to be driving—that almost would have been a relief—or to ask to see her license, but instead he said, "Funny you mention Gracetown," and Gloria's heart fell to her stomach.

"You got folks there?" Miz Lottie said, still grinning. Oh, she was an actress!

"Naw." He spat over his shoulder. "But you do. Nigger name of Robert Stephens?"

Miz Lottie gave up her grin. The skin on her face sagged, old and tired again. "I ain't got nothin' to do with that man, suh," Miz Lottie said. "Kin or no. He ain't in Gracetown no mo'. He been long gone."

The deputy's eyes came to Gloria: pale irises that felt like blades, alien and dangerous. "So y'all got no idea where Robert Stephens is? He ain't in Live Oak? You ain't plannin' on hidin' him in your truck? Sneak him back home, maybe?"

Gloria shook her head. She thought she should answer, but her tongue was limp.

This deputy had created a fantasy about her and Miz Lottie that was absurd and yet seemed so real that she wanted to look back at the truck's bed herself to see if Papa was hiding beneath Waymon's weather tarp. Who had told the sheriff they were in Live Oak? Was it someone who'd overheard Miz Lottie's party line? Someone at Belle's? The deputy who had tailed them out of Gracetown? Gloria wished she could know to slap them blind.

"No one's back here!" the younger deputy called. "Maybe some stolen tools, though."

"Those are my grand-nephew's tools," Miz Lottie said. "I got bills of sale in the glove box." Her voice's pitch had climbed; she couldn't hide her nervousness.

"You got an answer for everything, don't you, Auntie?" the deputy at the window said, and Miz Lottie had no answer for that.

Gloria wanted so much to relieve Miz Lottie with clever remarks, to shame this man into letting them go, but she kept her lips pinned. Her heart banged against her breastbone.

The truck shuddered as the second deputy jumped down. The first strolled around the front of the truck as if inspecting it for sale while the other watched and waited, clearly a subordinate. The deputy in front of the truck stared at Gloria through the windshield, his eyes heavy above stern jowls. Gloria wished she could duck from him. She hated her body in his eyes: breasts loose beneath her undershirt and thick denim because Mama had not been there to remind her to put on a bra before going to town. He stared as if her clothing could not hide her. She would have made herself invisible so he could not see the dark skin across every inch of her.

The deputy looked over his shoulder toward the woods where Gloria had imagined she might outrun them. Gloria didn't like him studying the woods, which grew thicker thirty yards from the road. A path was rutted through the mud and high grass toward the trees, plunging into shadows. This deputy hurt Negroes in the woods. He had done it many times.

How? How had the day gone so wrong? She had plunged into the worst trouble of her life, just like Papa had worried, and no one was with her but Miz Lottie, who was too frail to raise a hand to defend her. And Gloria could not run and leave Miz Lottie, even if running would not get her shot from behind.

Gloria's eyes fluttered, blinking, as she fought to think of what to do. "Shhh," Miz Lottie whispered between her teeth. "Sit real still."

While Gloria forced her frantic blinking to stop, her back straight, she noticed Miz Lottie's hand creeping to the laundry basket, hugging it to her. Miz Lottie burrowed her hand into the pile of linens, an inch at a time, her eyes fixed on the back of the deputy's head as he gazed at the tree line.

When he looked back toward Gloria, his thoughts were plain on his face. The deputy began his slow walk to Gloria's window, feasting on her fear, bent down so he never lost sight of her. Miz Lottie kept her hand in the laundry basket as his ruddy face appeared in Gloria's open window. A twig beneath his boot sounded like a breaking bone. He came so close that Gloria could see the too-big pores on his shiny nose, the sweat on his brow. She smelled chewing tobacco on his breath.

"You're his daughter, ain't you?"

Gloria moved her mouth to answer, and at first it made no sound. "Yessir." A whisper.

The deputy tugged on her car door, but it did not yield. Gloria had never been more grateful for a lock to hold. The obstacle was temporary—he only had to reach through the open window to pull up the lock himself—but it held him at bay for precious seconds, long enough for him to think it over. Gloria's pounding heart wanted to leap outside of her body.

"How you feelin' today, Jimmy?" the deputy said, calling to his partner while his eyes stayed on Gloria. Jimmy didn't answer. "You feel like a ride real quick?"

In her peripheral vision, Gloria saw Jimmy take off his hat, smooth his hair back, put it back on. "Not too much." She could barely hear him over the rush of blood fogging her ears.

The deputy's glare smothered Gloria, but she was afraid to look away. Her eyes itched from wanting to blink, from tears frozen just out of sight. She knew what a ride meant to him; she could hear the woods' whimpers, women and men helpless beneath white skin and badges.

"How come you dress like a damn bull dyke?"

"I . . . don't know," Gloria said, the only words she could think of.

"Is the Nigger Stephens's daughter a bull dyke? You sure look like one. Don't she, Jimmy?" Again Jimmy was silent. Gloria wished Jimmy would say, *Come on, leave her be.* But Jimmy was not going to help her and Miz Lottie. Whatever this deputy did or said, Jimmy always went along, or at least covered for him. Always.

"No," Gloria said. "I'm not. Sir."

Gloria couldn't help pausing before she said *Sir* to make it an afterthought, to strip its weight and even mock it. The deputy's eyes flared. He heard it too. He tugged at the door handle again, like rattling a cage. Gloria refused to jump. Her body was calcifying in her seat. If he touched her, she swore, her body would be a stone and not her body at all.

"You don't wanna mess with that girl, Mister Deputy, suh," Miz Lottie said.

Her words and voice were quiet, beyond calm. Gloria noticed Miz Lottie's hand buried inside the laundry basket again, and the deputy did too. *Shoot, I got my protection,* Miz Lottie had told Ruby McCollum, and Gloria remembered what Miz Lottie called her "pea shooter," a little .22 she kept under her bed for squirrels that ravaged her garden or stole her birdseed. Miz Lottie had her gun! Her hand was already on the trigger. Gloria knew it as plainly as if she could see through the basket's braided brown wicker. Miz Lottie's face was all pleasantness, but her eyes told the deputy a story of sudden death.

"What's that, Auntie?" The deputy sounded as confused as if a hound had spoken words.

"You want to leave that young gal alone, suh," Miz Lottie said. "You surely do."

The deputy glanced at Miz Lottie's hidden hand, and knowledge burned between them as they stared at each other over Gloria and the neatly folded linens. So much anger churned inside the deputy that his jowls shook. His hands were on the door, not at his holster, and Gloria was amazed to realize he was too scared to move. Scared of Miz Lottie!

Time slowed to molasses. Miz Lottie's engine coughed, weary

from idling. Nearby, loud birds quarreled. A car was approaching from town, close enough to hear its tires humming on the road. The deputy spat on the floor of the truck, the brown glob falling into the laundry basket at her feet—and backed away from Gloria's window. He kept his hands away from his gun. He circled widely around the back, toward Jimmy.

"Stay the hell out of Suwannee County!" the deputy called out to them, out of easy range. "You hear me? I better not see no kin of Robert Stephens here again!" Gloria heard the petulant child hidden inside his anger.

"Yes, suh," Miz Lottie said. "We won't come back, suh."

Gloria braced for the deputies to try to shoot them from the rear, but they didn't. Maybe pride had saved them: the deputy who'd menaced her couldn't confess to Jimmy that he was scared of an old Negro woman, or why. Or maybe Miz Lottie had shamed him. Was it over?

The approaching car finally reached them—a timeworn black Model T—and didn't slow before passing. But Gloria glimpsed John Dorsey watching with grave interest from the passenger window before Mr. Moore drove on. Neither deputy looked the passing car's way. At least the NAACP knew where they were. That was something.

Gloria and Miz Lottie waited in tense silence while the deputies returned to their car, doors slamming. Miz Lottie moved her hand out of the laundry basket and brought out her gun, a wink in the sunlight, and nestled it between her legs before she cranked the truck into gear.

"Thought I was gonna have to kill both of them crackers today," Miz Lottie muttered. She said it like she had avoided a sudden rainstorm or a nail in the road. She glanced sidelong at Gloria. "It's all right now, pumpkin."

Gloria nodded, but her heart hadn't slowed. Her imagination was lost in the woods; her hair caught in brambles, bare skin chafing against pebbles and soil. So real. So close. Gloria shivered in the heat like Mama in her sickbed.

"Least I'm awake now," Miz Lottie said, giving Gloria a laugh for show.

Miz Lottie coaxed Ole Suzy back to the road to follow the lawyer to Gracetown.

Since they got back to Gracetown at eleven twenty and they weren't due at the courthouse to meet the lawyer until noon, Miz Lottie stopped by her house so Gloria could change. Her good dress was muddy, so Gloria went through the tight stacks of hangers packed in Miz Lottie's closet, one fabric nearly glued to the next, until she found a black dress that seemed better suited for a funeral. The dress was nearly too long for her and far from fashionable, but it might make the judge feel sorry for her. She couldn't come in wearing too nice a dress anyway or the judge or anyone who saw her would say she was putting on airs. Lyle's words in his yard, in the dark, lanced at her: *You Stephens niggers are so uppity. Even a white man's not good enough for you.* How many others, white and Negro, felt that way about her family? How would they feel when they saw her in the courthouse with an NAACP lawyer in a New York City double-breasted suit?

Gloria stared in the mirror while she patted down her hair with the unmarked jar of pomade Miz Lottie kept on her kitchen sink. She looked tired-eyed and sullen, so she tried on a smile for the judge. Each smile looked more forced than the last. *Imagine Robbie coming home,* she told herself, and her face filled with a grin. Then tears stabbed her eyes because it wasn't real. Not yet. Her shivering had not stopped since the deputies. She didn't want anyone's eyes on her. She wanted to be invisible in an old woman's funeral dress.

By eleven thirty-five, Gloria and Miz Lottie were parked in front of the courthouse while they waited. The truck smelled like cold fried chicken from Miz Rita's refrigerator, the best Miz Lottie had been able to gather on short notice. It would be better hot, but Miz Rita's lunch window wasn't open yet—it was supposed to open at eleven thirty but she often didn't have food ready until noon—so they'd taken yesterday's leftovers: a large breast and a couple of wings. From time to time, Miz Lottie patted Gloria on the knee, as if to apologize she couldn't have made a better world for her.

She and Miz Lottie did not speak in the parked truck. The time for talking had passed.

A familiar car inched by, and Gloria recognized Miss Anne on Main Street, heading back toward Juniper. Maybe she had been to the bank!

"Be right back," Gloria told Miz Lottie, and she jumped out of the truck to catch Miss Anne at the stop sign at the intersection.

There, Miss Anne seemed startled and eager to drive on until she recognized Gloria in the dress so long that Gloria nearly tripped on the folds.

"Gloria? What in the world—"

Gloria leaned into Miss Anne's window, excited. "We found a Negro lawyer. He's coming to talk to the judge right now."

"That's wonderful news," Miss Anne said, looking left and right, with no celebration in her voice. Now every parking space was filled on the street in front of Meg's Diner, the Main Street Pharmacy, and the *Gracetown Herald* office while whites strolled the sidewalks. "But don't make it a spectacle."

Gloria spotted the light green envelope marked FIRST BANK OF GRACETOWN on Miss Anne's passenger seat. "Is that for me? The two-fifty?"

"Yes—here." The envelope was fat and heavy. Gloria had felt none like it. "You asked for it in fives, but I got a hundred in tens. Just imagine the queer looks I got. Don't walk with it out in the open. Slide it under your arm. Hurry." Miss Anne's hand trembled as she helped Gloria adjust the envelope beneath her arm, tucked out of sight. Miss Anne looked from corner to corner to make sure they weren't being watched. The sidewalk and center courtyard with the Confederate statue of Captain Powell were empty. Gloria wondered what the long-dead captain would think of his great-granddaughter giving money to Negroes. "Get out of the street, Gloria. Go on, now."

Miss Anne drove off before Gloria could thank her. Without wishing her good luck, even.

She was scared out of her head—a white woman! Councilman Powell's daughter. Miss Anne must truly believe the Klan had run her father off the road. Or that the statue was watching her.

Standing at the intersection, Gloria realized she was ignoring every warning, just like Papa had. She was a *Stephens*. The town had expected to chase her and Robbie away, to force them to hide like mice, and she was in the middle of the street in the noontime sun. She was like Mama eating ice cream in broad daylight on the Whites Only bench.

Mr. Moore's black Model T drove up. As Mr. Moore inched past her, John Dorsey's window was closest, so he called out, "Where's the marching band?"

"Girl, get out of the road," Harry T. Moore said. "What's wrong with you?"

Nothing was wrong, not at that moment. Gloria's trembling from Suwannee County had stopped. She gazed past the hanging tree to the courthouse's regal clock face—noon, the Roman numbers said—and her face was washed in the dizzying rush of sunlight.

The bell tolled through Gracetown as if she had willed its song, a reckoning come at last.

19

Miles away, back toward town, the courthouse bell was ringing so faintly that Robert's ear missed every other toll. But the thin breeze carried the bell like a memory of long ago. Was Mama ringing to him? Was music her way of watching him? He strained to hear the bell's song, not wanting to miss a note—and the music carried an image of Main Street's colorful awnings and Miz Lottie's house on Lower Spruce. With every toll, he forgot about the sun burning through his thin work shirt to his scarred and bloodied back. He floated away free in the chimes.

Then the bell stopped, and the day's heat smothered the endless cornfield. The corn stalks were already tall in late June, up just past Robert's eyeline, shiny green tips as far as he could see, except where two muddy trucks were parked near the fence on the farm road back toward the gate. The corn wouldn't be ready for harvest until fall, so none of the corncobs had grown in. The field looked like rows of giant weeds.

Tall enough to walk through. Tall enough to disappear in, especially if he stayed low.

Imagining himself sneaking off unseen in the stalks helped Robert keep up his pace although his hands were still raw from his previous day's work tugging bare-handed at the spiky, spindly ragweed nearly as tall as the corn. Yesterday, his first day in the field, his back had felt like it was ripping apart when he bent over. The ragweed was taller than the water hemp for grabbing, but weeds needed to come up by the root. Boone had promised a smack with his strap for every half-pulled weed he found anywhere. Some of the older, trusted boys had tools, but Robert only had his sore hands. No amount of scrubbing would clean the mud from his fingernails. Mama would have a fit if she could see. Papa too. Robert had wondered what it would feel like to be a sharecropper like his grandfather, or a slave in a history story, and now he knew. His skin knew. His back knew. His hands knew.

And no one he could whisper to or call a friend. Another dozen boys were to the left of Robert, heads bobbing through stalks in the field as they worked, but Robert did not know them. None had been as friendly as Blue and Redbone in the kitchen his first day. The field was not a place for talking. Redbone was three rows to the right, no more than fifteen steps away, but his back was always turned away from Robert. Redbone had not come near him yesterday either.

"Hey, Bone," Robert whispered.

Redbone shifted to another row, another direction, and glared at him over his shoulder, reminding him it was his fault they were pulling weeds in the sun. Each time Redbone glared, Robert wanted to cry.

But he couldn't cry. The night before, Boone had sent a boy to the Funhouse for no reason other than crying at bedtime, and promised he'd do the same to any sissy he saw crying all day long. At least Robert's back wasn't hurting as much as the first day. At least he had to work only four hours in the sun and not all day like grown men did, and in chains. At least he wasn't *really* a slave, with no end to the work for his whole life, or his children's. Robert tried to think of every reason to feel glad so he would not cry. He would never go to the Funhouse again.

Boone was watching. Boone had a crew of three men with him—one on horseback, two with hound dogs—but Boone was the only one whose eyes always seemed to be following Robert. It was as if Boone could see every thought in his head, like how Robert wanted to run away every time he bent down. Hell, he might have tried if not for the dogs.

"Fill up those sacks!" Boone called. "You don't fill your sacks, you stay 'til suppertime!"

Unless he was punished for working too slowly, Robert could have his lunch break soon and then go to school and then to band practice. And the day would be over, like yesterday, ready to start again. He hadn't gone to the Funhouse yesterday, and he wouldn't go today.

He and the other boys he'd ridden the truck with were working a small swath of the field, headed toward the fence, but older boys had clustered farther ahead. Most of them had taken off their shirts to wrap them around their heads to block out the sun. Their muscles were hard like grown men's.

Robert was wondering when his own muscles would grow so strong when he saw Cleo. A pale reed hung from the corner of Cleo's mouth like a cigarette, and he seemed twice as tall as Robert, who was close enough to see the dark, splotchy mole on the side of Cleo's nose. He'd seen a glimpse of Cleo at dinner last night, but he'd managed to keep out of his sight. Now one of Cleo's friends tapped Cleo and pointed at him, and Robert nearly gasped. Robert bent down right away and hoped Cleo would forget about him, but Cleo was still staring when Robert straightened up with a fistful of weeds in his clenched palm.

Robert saw the tool in Cleo's hand—a curved hand fork that looked like claws. The boys huddled near Cleo were faces he knew from the schoolhouse, the ones who had jumped him on his first day. Dammit. Dammit, dammit. What had he ever done to them? He didn't want another beating, especially if those tools could be weapons. Just as bad, if Cleo started something, he might go to the Funhouse again. Walking slowly, Robert changed direction slightly, away from the fence where he'd been heading. Toward the open corn.

"Was you makin' up stories on me the other night?" he heard Redbone call out to Cleo.

Redbone's voice surprised Robert so much that he froze. He

wondered if Redbone was snatching Cleo's attention away on purpose. "He gave you a pat on the head like a good doggie, huh?"

Cleo let out a hooting, angry laugh. "Did you and that sissy hold hands in the Funhouse?" Redbone didn't answer Cleo's taunt, but he glared daggers at him.

"You ain't gonna do nothin'," Cleo said. He slashed his claw-like tool at a corn stalk, shredding leaves. "Come on, then, boy."

Again Redbone said nothing, and Robert was glad. If he had to go help defend Redbone, they'd both go to the Funhouse for sure. After giving Cleo a long stare, Redbone veered away from Cleo, closer to the comparative safety of the gray-bearded white man riding his horse up and down the path between the stalks.

"Yeah, just like I thought!" Cleo called. Robert wished he and Redbone both could sock Cleo in the nose, but not if it meant more time for Redbone. Or another night under a leather strap. Robert bent just long enough to try to fool Cleo's eye. He counted to ten before he raised himself. Sure enough, when Robert took another peek, Cleo had turned his back to him. Robert crossed rows to keep out of his sight.

But the corn to the left of him swished as if a pack of dogs were moving toward him, or a horse at a full gallop, the tips dancing wildly. The swaying stalks rustled as if to swallow him—

A hand curled around Robert's ankle, and his throat caught his scream. Had Cleo come after him so fast? Robert was so startled that he lost his balance and fell.

But the laughter was a smaller child's—Blue's! Blue was rolling on the ground beside him, gleeful, holding tight to Robert's ankle when Robert shook his boot to try to free it. Blue had crawled through the stalks to surprise him, and somehow he'd made the corn shiver and quake. Maybe he'd used a hoe to make the corn sway. Blue was supposed to be in the kitchen!

"I scared you, huh?" Blue said.

"What—what—" Robert couldn't speak right away, imagining the quavering corn stalks. He stood up on his tiptoes and saw Boone calling out instructions to the boys working closer to the fence with Cleo. "How'd you get out here? You're supposed to be—"

Blue finally released him. His grip had been tight; Robert's ankle vibrated, raw from Blue's cool grasp. "I go where I wanna go."

"You tryin' to go to the Funhouse? And get me sent too?"

Blue laughed, standing up. Blue seemed no taller than a seven- or eight-year-old, not quite reaching Robert's shoulder, but Robert pushed down on Blue's knobby shoulders to make him hunch lower.

"You better not let nobody see you," Robert said, hushed. "Not even Redbone. Go back where you s'posed to be."

"Kitchen's not the same without you and Bone," Blue said, pouting.

Had Blue hidden in one of the trucks? Crawled through the fence because he was so small, maybe a hole hidden in weeds? Robert wanted to ask him to draw him a map of how he'd done it, but he knew better. Soon, but not now—not with Cleo and Boone and the dogs so close.

Robert couldn't decide if Blue was the most daring kid he'd ever met or the stupidest. Stealing dessert and locking him in the freezer were bad enough, but sneaking out to the cornfield could get him hurt bad. Or killed.

Tears stung Robert's eyes. Blue's risks were a bad omen. "Just go, Blue—please. Go back the way you came. Quick."

"What you cryin' for?"

"What you think?" Robert said. "Blue, you don't know what the Funhouse is like. Redbone jumps in and takes your licks for you. It's bad your parents are dead, but you don't wanna be in a shed gettin' whipped. And me neither."

"Don't talk about my parents," Blue said. His voice was a knife. He'd become the Blue from the locker room, all hard edges. "Don't talk like you know anything about me."

He and Blue would have to fight, that was all. A certain kind of boy didn't learn until his nose was bleeding. Robert had been in only one fight: Papa had said if he bloodied Randall Lawrence's nose, Randall would stop tripping and punching him every chance he got. Randall had still been laughing before Robert stood back up and hit his nose with the side of his fist as hard as he could. Randall didn't laugh after that. Papa said you fought if there was no other way. Robert wanted to hit Blue so badly that his lips shook.

"Don't you *never* come back out here like this," Robert warned him.

"I came for you, stupid," Blue said. "You think I'd come if it wasn't life-or-death?"

Life-or-death. Robert glanced in every direction: Boone was still fussing near the fence, and the graybeard on horseback wasn't close enough to hear. Redbone had outpaced him by a long way by now.

Robert's mouth and throat dried out as he held his breath. "What?"

"Never, *ever* be alone with Haddock," Blue said.

Robert's heart shook him. He thought about the old photo of the dead baby in Haddock's lap when he was a child. He hadn't liked how proud Haddock had been, bragging how he was the only one with guts enough to hold the dead sister he never wanted.

"That strap?" Robert said.

"Forget the strap," Blue said. "The whippings ain't the worst. You don't even got the brains to think it up yet. You've never thought of nothin' as low as Haddock. You wouldn't even know how."

"*What*, then?"

"He does his worst things at night—after the teachers and workers go home. When it's only the dorm masters—who do anything he says. *Anything.* The Funhouse ain't the worst. You don't go to Boot Hill from the Funhouse. The Funhouse don't make you *want* to curl up and die."

"Stop trying to scare me," Robert said, although he knew Blue wasn't lying. He'd known when he stood naked while Haddock studied him head to foot. The memory shivered his skin.

"He treats the band special," Blue said. "Likes to win the Christmas parade. So that's good for you, but there's bad mixed in. He'll be watching you. Don't forget."

"Did he ever bother you, Blue?" Robert whispered. He remembered Haddock rubbing his shoulder in the Funhouse. Too hard. Too long.

"The worst of the worst of the worst," Blue said. "That's what he is. What he'll do."

"Stephens—who you talking to?" Boone's voice boomed.

The sky seemed to veer from daylight to night. Robert turned around fast, trying not to look as surprised and scared as he felt, but his mouth was hanging wide. Boone thrashed past the corn stalks to face him, and Robert blinked, hoping Boone was only in his imagination. But he smelled the stink of Boone's sweat and the cigar pinned between tight, angry lips.

When Boone reached for his belt as if to grab his strap, Robert said, "What?" Any empty word to try to slow time or turn it back outright.

"You deaf?" Boone said.

Robert glanced back to look toward Blue—but Blue was gone. None of the corn swished or swayed to betray his path. Blue had run off, as quick and quiet as a snake. That meant Boone hadn't seen him! Robert's heart hammered with relief. He looked back at Boone, who was still threatening, his hand on his belt. A crow cawed overhead, sounding as angry as Boone.

"I was only singing, Mister Boone. Trying to sing real quiet."

"Singing?" Boone said, frowning. His hand fell slowly away from his belt buckle.

"Yessir," Robert said. "My mama used to wash clothes and she would sing to pass the time. I think I musta got it from her, sir. I sing when I work. And I've been workin'—see?" He opened his bulging sack to show him.

Boone leaned over to examine his weeds, noting the soil-tangled roots. He nodded, satisfied. Robert knew he'd pulled more weeds than most of the other boys, that he'd been more careful. He had to: the marks on his back were still fresh.

"But I sing it real quiet, so no one can hear," Robert went on. "So it sounds like talking, I reckon, sir. I'm sorry if I was singing too loud." He measured his voice: not too easy, not too soft. Then he waited. He'd said enough—maybe too much. Papa said sometimes you had to be quiet to let a man think over what you said.

Boone's eyes went to the place where Blue had been standing, as if he could still see his shadow. He stared at the place a long time. Robert's heart quailed again.

"You ever see anybody who don't belong?" Boone asked him.

"Sir?"

"Ones you ain't seen before," Boone said. "Faces you don't know."

Robert shook his head. "No, sir." He didn't feel like he was lying—until he remembered the boy who'd floated above his bed at the infirmary.

Boone leaned close to him with the fierce look he'd had in his eye when he drove Robert through the smoky ghost fire. "You ever do see somebody like that—somebody who ain't s'posed to be here, who makes your skin crawl—you be sure to let me know. Ev'rybody won't see 'em . . . but you might. Hear? I know how to get rid of 'em."

He reached into his shirt pocket and pulled out a small leather pouch. He laid it in his palm and displayed it to Robert as if it were jewelry, or a gun. The brown leather was frayed, the residue of gray powder at the pouch's mouth.

"This sends 'em gone for sure—the way they was s'posed to be gone already," Boone said. "You can help me find 'em. Finding 'em is part of my job, and I like to do my job well. You do right by me, you won't have no worries in here."

"Find . . . who?"

"Haints," Boone said. "Don't act like you ain't seen none. You from Gracetown, ain't you? I know who you is. I know yo' people."

Robert didn't answer. He only nodded, hoping Boone wouldn't bring up Papa. Or what the white woman had said about him.

Boone put his pouch away, buttoning up the pocket. "They all around here," Boone said. "Like rats. They come mean and jealous 'cuz you still got life and they don't. They lie. They whisper 'run' in yo' ear just to see if they can fool you into dying. Then you stuck like *them*."

That didn't describe any of the haints Robert had seen at the Reformatory, but Boone wasn't just trying to threaten him: he *believed* it. And Boone wanted to make a deal with him! Did that mean Boone would never send him to the Funhouse again? He wouldn't tell Boone about Mama, of course. Or the floating boy in the infirmary. Or the ones in the Funhouse. But . . .

Robert pulled his parched lips apart. "I saw a . . . white boy . . . in the kitchen."

Boone grinned. He patted Robert's shoulder, excited. "When? Where?"

Robert told Boone about his first day in the kitchen and how he'd seen a white boy stirring a giant pot. He kept Blue and Redbone out of his story in case they might get in trouble, telling as little as he could. As Boone listened, he rubbed his pouch through the pocket's thin fabric as if touching the place where it rested gave him pleasure.

"Hot damn," Boone said. "Hot *damn*. I'll get 'im today!"

"How?" Robert said.

"Long as it ain't been more'n three days, you can draw a haint to a spot where he's been. If I sprinkle my powder back where he was, he'll come. And 'cuz of my blessing over the powder, he'll be trapped. And he'll shrink down to a pile of ash. A tiny li'l anthill."

Boone was talking nonsense, except it wasn't nonsense to Boone. He spoke as if he were telling stories he'd always known. Robert had heard about people who used powders and potions, even if Miz Lottie said it was foolishness. Boone grinned more widely than any man he'd ever seen, stretching his teeth from one side of his face to the other: Boone loved hunting haints the way Robert's grandfather had loved hunting wild hogs, almost child-like. Robert was sorry he'd told on the white boy in the kitchen; it wasn't his fault he'd had a knife in his back.

What if Boone's powder touched Mama and her spirit got turned to ash? What would happen to her soul? Robert felt sick to his stomach, beyond tears.

"Maybe . . . I got the place wrong," Robert said.

"Naw, boy, them big pots is up against the back wall just like you said. Only one place he could've been. You done good! Keep doing good like that and Boone will make life here easy. I get what I want, you can go back to the kitchen early." Boone winked. "You can go back tomorrow. You and Redbone too. The warden's real good to me when I bring him ash for his jar. I'm his Collector."

Blue had been right: Robert never could have guessed how low a man Haddock could be. He wasn't satisfied with beating and hurting boys who were alive: he hunted dead ones too.

20

The clock on Judge Morris's desk was a shiny copper oddity that seemed to come to life in the bright light through the tall corner window. The face was embedded in the image of an old-fashioned carriage pulled by a horse beneath a driver holding a whip coiled in mid-lash. The clock's muted ticking was the only sound as they waited. Everything in the office, it seemed, was made of wood and smelled like long ago.

The chamber was cramped. Only two wooden chairs sat before the regal desk, so Miz Lottie and Gloria were sitting while the men stood behind them, no one moving or fidgeting. Miz Lottie now wore gloves that matched her pillbox hat.

Silence was a clamp in the room. The judge's secretary outside had said Judge Morris told them to go right in, but she had left the door wide-open, and the office felt fraught with waiting accusations of snooping and stealing. Gloria glanced at the headlines in the *Gracetown Herald* folded on the judge's desk—"Cape Canaveral Preps for Launch" in one column and "Tensions Rise in Korea" on the other. Gloria had always found it silly that so much effort went into trying to send humans to space instead of learning how to get along on Earth. Rows of law books stuffed his shelves, brown with regimented black and red stripes across the spine, gilded with gold accents. The books' order held a kind of beauty. These were the books of spells and incantations from John Dorsey's mysterious world. The lawyer was so close behind Gloria that for the first time she noticed his pleasant cologne, an exotic scent she had never encountered in Gracetown. She was surprised, and a bit annoyed, at how much the scent pleased her.

When John Dorsey's stomach rumbled, Gloria smiled at their shared secret.

"Thought some of that chicken was for me," John Dorsey muttered. He reached over Miz Lottie's shoulder toward the chicken in foil she was holding in her lap.

Miz Lottie snatched the food out of his reach. "Shoulda had more'n sugar for breakfast."

A voice broke into the room from the doorway. "Well—we've got a convention in here."

Judge Morris had slipped in so quietly behind them that his tobacco-roughened voice startled Gloria. Chairs scraped the floor as Gloria stood up and helped Miz Lottie rise quickly to her feet. Mr. Moore and John Dorsey took off their hats.

Judge Morris turned his back to them as he hung his black robe on the wooden coatrack behind his office door. Underneath, he was wearing a wrinkled white shirt and black tie. His armpits were ringed with sweat.

"Tell you one thing," Judge Morris said, as if continuing an earlier conversation, "whoever designed these dang robes wasn't from Florida."

John Dorsey laughed like Judge Morris was Bob Hope on a USO tour. Judge Morris was the shortest of the men in the room, and John Dorsey stood tall over him as he extended his hand. "John Dorsey, Your Honor," he said. "From the New York office. It's a pleasure, sir."

Gloria would never have thought to say, *It's a pleasure.* None of this was a pleasure.

"Your Honor, I'm Harry T. Moore."

"Must be in trouble now," Judge Morris said, although he was smiling—almost too much. Up close, his teeth looked like rows of new corn kernels, more yellow than white.

"Oh no, sir, no one's in trouble," Mr. Moore said. "We're grateful for the time."

Judge Morris closed his door, where his secretary was peeking inside. His smile had wavered, but it brightened as he faced them to go to his desk. "Y'all promised me some of Rita Mae's fried chicken?" the judge said, his eyes on the foil in Miz Lottie's lap.

Miz Lottie extended her foil package to him. Gloria saw her hands tremor slightly. "Last night's batch, but every bit as good."

"Now who would *you* be?" Judge Morris asked Miz Lottie as he took the foil. He sounded like Santa Claus talking to a child on his lap at the Gracetown Christmas Fair.

"Lottie Powell, Your Honor. I'm a deaconess at Christ the Redeemer Baptist Church." Miz Lottie was taking pains with her enunciation. "I'm the legal guardian of Robbie Stephens."

The judge's smile wavered again, a tic in the corner of his mouth. But he peeked inside the foil and nodded. "I'll eat this with my bare hands, if y'all promise not to tell my wife. I'm still a country boy fresh from Misery Swamp." And he was: Gloria noticed a tobacco stain on his shirt. Mama never would have let Papa leave the house with a stain like that.

John Dorsey chuckled. "Tell the truth, Your Honor, I don't trust a man who eats fried chicken with a knife and fork."

Judge Morris pointed at John Dorsey soberly. "Amen."

"And if there's a piece left," John Dorsey went on, "I can take it off your hands."

"Not much chance of that, Attorney Dorsey," the judge said, and laughed.

Gloria tried to keep her astonishment from her face. John Dorsey sounded like he had been meeting with the judge for years. Had she ever heard a white man—never mind a judge—call a Negro man anything except his first name, or just *boy*? She searched her memory, from Papa to her teachers to the reverend, and she could not remember a single time. And John Dorsey was so much younger than the judge, who might be at least fifty. Was it because Dorsey was from the North? Or because he represented the national NAACP? Most whites in Gracetown hated the

NAACP—or were they afraid? Was that possible? Gloria thought so as she watched Judge Morris wipe his sweaty brow with a handkerchief also stained with spots of tobacco spittle.

"Y'all have a seat," Judge Morris said. He noticed Gloria, an afterthought. "I do b'lieve I remember you from my courtroom."

"Yes, sir," Gloria said. "Gloria Stephens. I was there to speak for my brother." John Dorsey squeezed Gloria's shoulder slightly and Gloria remembered the judge had told them to sit down.

Judge Morris was already taking his first bite of the fat chicken breast, with a coat so crispy that it crumbled to his touch. "Y'all tell Rita Mae she should have a chicken stand on every corner. I've been sayin' it for years." His mouth was half-full.

"Yessir, she ain't humble," Miz Lottie said, and the judge laughed.

Gloria knew chatting was a part of the lawyer's strategy, but their lighthearted voices were insufferable, no one saying why they all knew they were there. Who knew where Robbie was, or what was happening to him, and the judge and John Dorsey were talking about the humidity in New York and then rumors that Joe Louis was coming out of retirement because of tax troubles. Gloria tried to read impressions from the judge the way she had from Ruby McCollum and Mr. Moore and that terrible deputy on the road, but she'd never been able to command her knowing like a radio dial. The more she tried to read, the less she could see—just the judge's smile.

When Gloria exaggerated a sneeze from the room's dust, all eyes came to her.

"God bless you, young lady," Judge Morris said—and no one else, because they all knew she was faking. Miz Lottie scowled at her.

"I'm hoping for sure He will bless me, Your Honor," Gloria said. "That's why I'm here."

Harry T. Moore moved from behind Miz Lottie's chair to stand beside it, a step forward. "We want to discuss the case of Robbie Stephens, Judge Morris."

The smile stayed frozen, but the judge was already shaking his head. He gestured toward Gloria. "Well, this young lady was in my courtroom when I sentenced him to six months. Most boys get at least a year. It's half the time." Every time he said *young lady*, it sounded to Gloria like a curse. Was he trying to impress the NAACP lawyer with his politeness to Negroes? He was already saying *no* and they had barely started talking. The judge found a legal pad on his desk and flipped a couple of pages, ready to argue facts.

"I didn't get the chance to tell everything that happened, Your Honor," Gloria said. She ignored John Dorsey's hand squeezing her shoulder more urgently.

"Nobody's saying he should have kicked the young man—" John Dorsey said quickly.

"That boy's in the trouble of his life," Miz Lottie said. "I'll see to that."

"—but he's twelve years old," John Dorsey said. "No trouble with the law before. So now he's spent a couple of nights away from home, maybe got a few licks. Your Honor, we were hoping you might reconsider the sentence. I understand even the young man involved didn't want Robbie charged."

"A juvenile's parents make that decision," the judge said. "You ought to know that, you call yourself a lawyer." The judge's smile made his words sharper.

"I don't think there's a name I haven't called myself," John Dorsey said, matching the judge's smile. "But, yessir, 'lawyer' is one. And I also understand the sheriff's office never formally pressed charges. I'm just pointing out maybe it seemed like everyone knew this boy couldn't do real harm to a strong football player like Lyle McCormack. And Robbie Stephens, wrong as he was, knew that too. In fact, I'm thinking if word had gotten around too much about it, Lyle might get cracks at school. I wouldn't have wanted that going around about me in the schoolyard—or the locker room—when I was sixteen, seventeen. I expect you wouldn't either."

Judge Morris chuckled. "Heavens no."

Lawyers were wizards. The judge was listening to him. *Agreeing* with him.

"Now, I know Robbie surely won't be talking about it if he comes home, but I can only imagine what kind of talk goes on at the Reformatory. And what talk comes *out*," the lawyer said.

Judge Morris shrugged. "Bird told Red to leave it be." Gloria held her breath.

"Bird?" John Dorsey said.

"County sheriff," Harry T. Moore told him quietly.

"Red boxed the boy's ear," the judge said. "The whole thing with Lyle happened in the quiet: nobody there to see. Bird said if he picked Robbie up like Red wanted him to, word might get out. You're right, Mr. Dorsey, that's why there weren't formal charges. But I still have discretion to impose that sentence." Despite his smile, his eyes were flinty with challenge.

"I had no doubt of that, Your Honor," John Dorsey said. "I'm only asking whether you can see fit to let this child go home to the discipline of his family so he's not locked up so long with boys who might influence him wrong. And who most likely talk too much."

Miz Lottie spoke up. "My grand-nephew, June, lives with me—he's working today—but he's like a father to the boy. June will see to it his lesson stays learned. And I'll keep him close to the Lord. I'll have him in church twice a week."

The judge stared at his notes. "I don't like to reverse a sentence. No judge does."

"*Commute*, Your Honor," John Dorsey said. "Not a mistake—a mercy. A lesson."

How did his pretty words come to him so fast? John Dorsey lobbed gentle words like grenades, so hard to argue against.

"Nothing breaks my heart more," the judge said, "than when I don't believe a defendant should be locked up, especially a child. Sometimes I sentence people I've known my whole life. But I'm bound by the law. I gave him half the time."

Gloria was dizzy before she realized how long she had not drawn a breath.

"Lyle pushed Robbie first," Gloria said, more like gasping. "Lyle was . . . making advances at me." Gloria had never known that words could fill her throat and choke her, but she could barely go on when she saw the judge's eyebrows knit close, incredulous. "Robbie thought he was protecting me. He was . . . confused. Just ask Lyle and he'll say so. Even Mister Red knows it. Lyle admitted it to Mister Red. I was there. I heard him. He slapped Lyle's face over what he did." Her last words were almost a whisper.

Judge Morris was no longer smiling. Telling the truth always broke the peace.

Miz Lottie wrapped her arm around Gloria's shoulders, vise-like. "She's plenty upset about her brother, Your Honor. She's almost like a mama to him too. She's a trusted house girl for Miss Anne Powell. She left school to work after their mama died of cancer."

But Miz Lottie's bids for sympathy did not soften the judge's face as he stared at Gloria. "Young lady," he said, "you are sitting in my chambers, telling McCormack family business."

Was that all he'd heard? "Yes, sir, I'm sorry," Gloria said. "It's only for Robbie's sake."

"You of all people," the judge said, not satisfied, "should understand why people don't want their family business told."

Too late, Gloria realized the lawyer was frantically tapping her shoulder to quiet her.

The judge looked back at the lawyer. He slipped on reading glasses that transformed his face, making it hard to remember his smile. "What's the NAACP's interest in this case?"

"Just to bring a young child home, Your Honor," John Dorsey said.

"You came all the way from New York for that?" The judge's sarcasm called him a liar.

"These two ladies caught up with me while I was here in Florida, and most lawyers won't work pro bono." He hesitated just enough for Gloria to notice; he didn't want to say the next part. "I'm in Florida on my way to Lake County with Mister Moore."

A bigger picture snapped to focus in the judge's eyes. Gloria remembered Papa's stories from Lake County—about Negro homes and businesses shot up and burned as mobs of whites rampaged after four black men, the Groveland Boys, were accused of raping a white woman. At the time, it had seemed like other people's problems, long before she'd imagined someone would accuse Papa too. Now Gloria remembered that mobs had swarmed in Gracetown in the past. Mama had told her. Miz Lottie had told her. Mobs came when Negroes stood up for themselves, a bonfire of pent-up hate and envy sparked by the lie *rape*.

"Y'all got a mess down there," the judge said.

"Sure do," said Mr. Moore.

"And I do *not*," the judge said, raising his voice, suddenly red-faced, "want that kind of mess up here."

Gloria jumped at his outburst. Miz Lottie grabbed her hand, squeezing tight. Her bones were knotty and felt nearly bare of flesh. Miz Lottie was halfway to a skeleton already.

"We are all agreed on that, Your Honor," John Dorsey said.

"Funny how it don't look that way." Judge Morris gestured toward Gloria. "She's here telling me—what? Lyle grabbed you and kissed you? Well, good for you: you're the envy of every white girl at Gracetown High, my daughter included." Gloria winced at his mocking distortion, unable to answer. Her face burned.

"It wasn't that," she whispered, but trying to explain felt dangerous.

"She has the nerve to be sitting here with her lip quivering when her daddy's a fugitive for forcible rape of a white woman? And y'all must know where he is—probably each and every one of you in here. Bird would love a meeting with y'all too." His threat to call the sheriff sucked oxygen from the room. Would he send an old woman to jail to try to get her to talk about Papa's telephone calls? Try to learn the address of the friend who took in Papa's mail? Gloria wondered if she would say the address if someone beat her hard enough and she were out of her mind with pain.

John Dorsey was the first to gather words. "Your Honor, we're not harboring Robert Stephens Senior. We're only here on behalf of the son." Quiet wariness steadied his voice.

Judge Morris studied them one by one. He scolded Gloria with his eyes before looking away. "I'll spend my lunch hour with anyone who's interested in peace, whites and nigras alike—but y'all do not want to go to war. Not with me. Y'all hear me?"

They all nodded and assured him they had heard.

"All right, then." Judge Morris took off his glasses. "You ask me, Sheriff McCall is a showboat who likes the sound of his name. But he called Bird asking why Robert Stephens hasn't been brought to justice when he had to catch *four*. And seems like the NAACP would rather set every rapist loose."

"No, Your Honor," John Dorsey said. "We choose which cases to back very carefully. Only cases where we strongly believe the defendant is innocent."

"Like men who had confessions beat out of 'em in Sheriff McCall's jail," Mr. Moore said. "Or got hunted down and shot like a wild dog in the woods—" He stopped in mid-thought. Maybe John Dorsey had stomped on his foot.

Judge Morris's face tightened. The unspoken words scalded Gloria's mouth: *Just ask and you'll find out Papa didn't do what that girl told the sheriff. Just ask Miss Anne. Just ask Channing. Go ask the girl herself when no one's there to scare her.*

But she had seen how angry he got the last time she spoke the truth, so the unspoken words scarred her tongue and filled her eyes with tears. If she called that white woman a liar now, Robbie might never go free.

"*Boy,*" Judge Morris said to Mr. Moore, "don't mistake my remark about Sheriff McCall as an invitation to slander. That jury spoke. Don't try to re-litigate that case in my chambers."

A pause came before Mr. Moore said, "I'm sorry, Your Honor."

Mr. Moore had unsettled the judge, who flipped through his pad, not pausing for reading. "So now I suppose y'all will come back to try to speak up for Robert Stephens Senior. Or send Thurgood Marshall. Get us in all the papers too." Gloria's heart leaped. Thurgood Marshall himself defending Papa?

"Thurgood hasn't been briefed on the particulars of Robert Stephens Senior's case just yet," John Dorsey said as soon as her hope rose. "But, Your Honor, since you brought it up . . ." Judge Morris waited for him to go on. "One of our concerns is that with feelings running so hot about Robert Stephens Senior, it'll affect the boy's stay at the Reformatory. I'm sure the superintendent does everything he can, but—"

"Might be safer in there," Judge Morris said. "You think of that?"

Mr. Moore cleared his throat, a reflex. His tongue must be hurting his mouth too.

"I've thought of it," John Dorsey said placidly, "but we believe he's much better off with loved ones. It feels like this thing is a spat between neighbors—kids, really. It's not the boy's fault it's tied to so much else."

Judge Morris sighed, rubbing his forehead. For the first time, he checked his oddly shaped clock, its whip threatening to strike. It was already twelve forty-five, almost the end of his lunch hour. He folded up his foil over his stripped chicken bones and tossed it into his wastebasket. Then he swiveled his chair to gaze out of his tall window at Main Street below, past the ancient, gnarled branches of the hanging tree.

"I was born and reared in Gracetown," Judge Morris said. "My father opened the five-and-dime when this town was hardly more than a dirt road on the way to Tallahassee. These are good people who've worked hard to make Gracetown worth something. We're not Lake County. Bird isn't Sheriff McCall." He seemed to need to hear them say how much Gracetown was different.

"I was born and reared in Gracetown too," Miz Lottie said. "I was kin to Claude Neal just over the way in Marianna." The judge's chair squeaked as he turned to glance at her over his shoulder. His lips were pinned tight, nearly gray. Harry T. Moore's breath fluttered with a quiet sigh. In the 1930s, Claude Neal had been lynched after he was accused of raping and murdering a white woman. Miz Lottie had told Gloria about it after Papa left.

"One thing I've learned," Miz Lottie went on. "Everything seems fine until it ain't. And then we come to see it wasn't never 'fine.'"

"No good citizen of Jackson County is proud of that past," he said. "But it's the *past*. It's done with. No one strung Robert Stephens by a tree, did they? Everyone forgets how Flake tried to keep Claude from harm, even got him out of town—" He stopped, voice hitching. He searched their faces and gave up on helping them understand. White and colored in Gracetown had never been easy since Claude Neal. In Marianna, anyone bearing his name had fled.

She should have fled too, Gloria thought. Papa should have taken them with him. No one had accused him of murder, but he should have known his family wouldn't be safe.

The judge stood up. As if they were in a courtroom, Gloria and Miz Lottie rose to their feet with him. Gloria watched the judge's face, looking for signs of mercy or anger. His smile returned, but it wasn't a smile meant for promises.

"This has been quite a visit," he said, as if they had only come for a casual lunch. "Mighty nice talking to all of you folks. I don't want my town in the headlines, but if Thurgood Marshall's ever passing this way, Attorney Dorsey, I'd like to know what's he like in person." He was asking about Thurgood Marshall as if he were Joe Louis.

For the first time, John Dorsey seemed surprised. "Depends on whether you see him in the courtroom or at the bar after."

Judge Morris laughed, his eyes sparking. "You know, I'd heard that," he said. "I heard he's a man you'd want to have a drink with. Too bad Gracetown is dry." And even if it weren't, Gloria thought, where could a white judge and Negro lawyer drink together?

"About Robbie Stephens . . . ," John Dorsey pressed.

While Gloria waited for his answer, so much time passed that her heartbeat made her light-headed. Judge Morris made his way past their huddle to open his door. Footsteps scurried away from the other side, so Gloria wasn't surprised to find the secretary and a young man in round eyeglasses who might be a clerk standing just beyond the doorway, eavesdropping. The clerk stared, moon-eyed, through his lenses.

"I'll take everything you fine folks said into consideration," Judge Morris said, loudly enough for his audience. "Y'all have a nice day."

As they all walked past the watchers, Gloria saw grimness on the faces of Harry T. Moore and John Dorsey: they knew. She wanted to believe the judge had said *maybe*, but as she took one last glance at Judge Morris's smile, she realized it was a weapon, not a mask. Judge Morris would not set Robbie free. He and the sheriff would not risk making Red McCormack angry. How many times had Mama and Papa told her that Red McCormack owned so much of Gracetown that no one wanted to cross him? And anyway, everyone was so mad at Papa.

It had been foolish to come, just like Mr. Moore said.

Tears were stinging Gloria's eyes as they emerged from the colored stairway downstairs even before she noticed how many whites had gathered in the hall to observe them, lined up on either side of the shiny marble floor, a Red Sea parting. Their eyes were sharp with scorn as they assessed the four Negroes: John Dorsey in his smart suit, Harry T. Moore with his unbowed head, Miz Lottie in her pillbox hat, and Gloria Stephens—*that* Gloria Stephens. Their angry thoughts hissed in the courthouse's stale, ancient heat.

"Know what N-A-A-C-P stands for?" a woman's voice called from a window booth. "National Association of Communists and Pickaninnies." Several people laughed. *Most* people. John Dorsey paused as if to answer, but he could not return the joke. His good humor was gone.

"That's right—git on back to New York!" a man said.

"Where's your rapist daddy at?" another called. A rock bloated in Gloria's belly.

"Walk faster," Miz Lottie muttered as she leaned on Gloria for support.

Mr. Moore touched Gloria's elbow to urge her to hurry, and Gloria pulled Miz Lottie beside her. The rear door by the COLORED sign seemed miles away, but finally they were outside in the rear parking lot where Mr. Moore's Ford Model T waited, Miz Lottie's truck just beyond it at the curb. Gloria turned to make sure no one from inside was following them. No. She'd almost been certain they were.

"Damn it to hell," Harry T. Moore said.

"Had to try." Miz Lottie's voice was small.

"We don't talk here," Mr. Moore said. "Get to your truck and get home. Quick. I'll call you later tonight." Gloria followed his glance to the rear courtroom door, which was now propped open with two men staring out, watching.

John Dorsey rushed into the old Model T, door slamming. Mr. Moore went to the driver's side and opened his door, keys jingling and ready. Gloria and Miz Lottie had gone to Live Oak and found the lawyer like Papa said, and it wasn't enough. The money from Miss Anne, now hidden in Miz Lottie's pocketbook, would not be enough. Nothing might be enough. It was worse than before.

Mr. Moore hushed his voice. "Gloria's not still sleeping out in those woods by the McCormacks', is she?"

"She's with me," Miz Lottie said. "Nobody's comin' past Way-mon and June."

"Keep clear of Main Street," Mr. Moore said. "Tell your other kin too. Let it settle." He looked at Miz Lottie like he wanted to say he'd warned her, but he only sighed. "We've gotta move on down the road to beat the dark. I'll tell Harriette I saw you. Come here, sweetheart."

When Harry T. Moore kissed Gloria's cheek, the phantom smell of his skin's charred ash plugged her nose. The certainty of his death was a breathing thing. But not today. He and John Dorsey would be all right today. But would she and Miz Lottie be?

"All right, now," John Dorsey said, seeing Gloria's face. He reached to her through the passenger's-side window and she took his smooth, dry hand, the one with his golden wedding band. His palm was soft from paper and pen and book pages. Mama's hands. Papa's hands had never been so soft. "It'll be all right, Glow Bug. They'll simmer down."

Mama had never allowed her nicknames, but Gloria liked "Glow Bug" because John Dorsey had given it to her. And now John Dorsey was leaving like a ghost she had conjured, and she was afraid to forget a single detail: his handsome face she might try to sketch for herself, the Pall Malls he smoked, his slicked-down, curly jet hair, the shiny buttons on his suit coat.

And his scent, a smell like freedom.

V

HAINT CATCHER

21

Mrs. Hamilton raised her thin baton, and Robert lifted his trumpet to his mouth the way she'd instructed. Twenty-five boys with their horns and clarinets and saxophones in a half circle around him did the same. But not fast enough. She tapped her baton on her desk, and they all lowered their instruments, with only a stray rattle from Redbone's snare drum in the back.

"Remember what I told you: your instruments should *snap* to attention. Again."

They repeated the exercise once, twice, three times more. The third time, Robert jerked his trumpet so fast that he bumped his lips, knocking against his teeth. But he didn't move to betray the sting, as frozen as the rest. Mrs. Hamilton smiled.

"Yes, that's it," she said. "All right, on the count of three, we'll play the scale."

As she counted, Robert never took his eyes off of her bouncing baton. When the time came to play the first note, most of them started at the same time, with a couple of stragglers. The first note in the scale was Robert's favorite because he didn't have to remember to press a key. The last note, high C, was still his strongest, strung in the air as if it could hang Christmas lights.

Mama. Yes, it *had* to be Mama, hidden inside the trumpet's peal.

Mrs. Hamilton smiled at him as she had in the infirmary. The music lifted her lips. "Robert Stephens, you've never played before?"

Robert didn't know what he should say: the last time he'd answered a teacher in front of other boys, he'd gotten jumped after class.

"Young man, I asked you a question." Her smile faded quick.

"Yes, ma'am—I mean no, ma'am, I never played before."

"Speak *after* you've chosen the words," Mrs. Hamilton said. She'd been in the Army all right. "Don't let your words spill out willy-nilly. Express yourself clearly." From the back, someone sniggered. Maybe Redbone was laughing at *willy-nilly*, not at him.

"Ma'am, I don't want to sound like I'm boasting, that's all."

"You're a talented beginner, Robert," Mrs. Hamilton said. "There's nothing to boast yet. You won't be here by the time you'd be ready to play first chair, God willing. But, yes, you have a talent and I'd like to see you nurture it once you're back at home."

"Yes, ma'am." His face burned, then cooled, from the pleasure of her compliment, yes, but more from hearing her say he would go home. After the Funhouse, he had begun to doubt it.

Robert glanced farther down the row to Darren, the husky teenager who played first trumpet, and Darren nodded at him, raising his trumpet's bell in salute. Robert smiled. He wished he'd been in band his first day, or that band time didn't speed by so fast.

Robert was still smiling when he saw a shadow from the open doorway—tall and lean, with a wide Stetson stretching clear across the floor—and then Warden Haddock was standing at the band room entrance as if an instant's joy had summoned him. Robert's shoulders drew close to his neck so he could disappear.

Mrs. Hamilton saw their eyes on the doorway, so she turned to see who was there. Robert thought she stiffened when she saw Warden Haddock, but only a little. Like Mama, she did not seem afraid of white people, even one who was her boss. Or at least she didn't want *them* to see if she was. Her smile in her profile was polite but tight, as if her jaw might clench at any time.

"Supervisor," she greeted him from behind her smile.

Warden Haddock took off his hat and cradled it to his chest in a way that made Robert think of Haddock's dead sister. "Heard the boys, thought I'd pop in."

"Nearly half are brand-new, some only yesterday," Mrs. Hamilton said. An apology.

"Nonetheless," Warden Haddock said, and only then, for just a flicker, did his eyes skate to Robert's, finding him right away, just long enough to thrash Robert's heart. "I thought I'd take a looksee. Whole town will be watching on parade day. You'll march past the mayor's booth."

"I certainly aim to make the Gracetown School for Boys proud." She had never said *sir* to him, even though in every war picture Robert had seen it was always *yes, sir, no, sir*.

"I wager you'll do just that, Marian."

Mrs. Hamilton's smile sharpened from the extra force behind it. She did not like to be called by her first name. She was itching to say it, but she didn't. Mama had been the same way.

Warden Haddock stood in a silence so long they all heard a hog's dying squeal from a faraway chopping block. Some boys worked with the butcher, leaving the aluminum sink in the dormitory pink with blood when they washed their hands at night. The cry was horrible and so human that Robert wondered if it was only a hog dying. He was glad when the squeals went quiet. "Help you with something else, Supervisor Haddock?" Mrs. Hamilton said, and Robert felt the other boys let out gentle breaths with him. None of them had breathed while he stood so close.

"Any of these boys giving you trouble?"

"No, the boys in band are very well-behaved."

He leaned over and said something into her ear as quickly as he'd glanced Robert's way. While Mrs. Hamilton listened, only the smallest piece of her smile remained. When she nodded, he grinned and put his hat back on.

"I'll be waiting," he said for the class to hear.

"I'll see to it," she said, and an unspoken *sir* softened her voice. She didn't like what he'd said, but she would do it anyway. And knowing that made the warden grin. He spun away to leave the room, playful in a way Robert had never seen. The light through the doorway was brighter without his shadow.

For the rest of band practice, Robert wondered what the warden had said in Mrs. Hamilton's ear. Blue had said things in the cornfield that made Robert wonder if Warden Haddock did whatever he wanted with women who worked for him. The Reformatory had polluted Robert with ugly thoughts.

Mrs. Hamilton seemed to know he was thinking about her because from time to time her eyes came to his and then quickly away as if they had a secret. He got a funny feeling when she looked at him; like he wanted to be with her all the time and see her the entire day, and like he would kick anyone who tried to bother her, even if it was Warden Haddock. She made him feel like he mattered the way Mama and Gloria and Miz Lottie did. Robert's distracted thoughts made him fumble through the exercises in the music primer, and he thought she would chide him when band class was over.

As he walked close to her to leave—by himself, since Redbone was still ignoring him—Robert tried to think of something more interesting to say than *Bye, Missus Hamilton* and wondered what she would think if he said something like *Your hair looks very nice*. His face flashed hot again as he imagined saying it.

"Missus Hamilton," he said, lingering near her as the last to leave the practice room, "I'll practice my scale in my head before I got to sleep. Like I did last night."

She smiled, but her smile was flimsy and sad. "Robert, stay behind, please. Supervisor Haddock wants to see you."

Robert's ears rang from his heartbeat. Redbone, who was already halfway down the steps outside, turned his head to look back at them.

"What for?" Robert said.

"He didn't say," she said. "Can you think of why he might be calling after you?"

Robert glanced at Redbone, who looked away, his face stormy.

Maybe Redbone thought Robert would snitch on him because he covered for Blue the night of the Funhouse. If Redbone thought he was so low, he was no kind of friend. Maybe nobody made any friends here. And Robert had been so careful not to get in trouble! He didn't talk to anyone or play around, so he hadn't been late to the farm truck, the band room, the classroom, or the dorm. Not once. He'd been first in line. He'd picked more weeds than the other boys; he'd seen it with his own eyes.

"I don't know, ma'am." It took all of Robert's resolve to hold back his tears.

But Mrs. Hamilton saw his tears. She put her hand on his shoulder, and the sob fighting from his throat died, although his throat still burned. "There's no reason to assume the worst. I just thought you might know about something. If so, please tell me."

Then, suddenly, Robert knew: someone must have seen Blue talking to him in the cornfield! Blue was the worst of the worst of bad luck. Mrs. Hamilton saw Blue in his face too.

"There's something and you just don't want to say," she said. "Is that right?" Robert couldn't shake his head to deny it.

She went on. "And it involves another person you don't want to get in trouble."

Without wanting to, Robert glanced toward Redbone, who loved Blue so much that he'd taken his licks for him. But Redbone darted away and was out of sight.

"Now, you listen carefully to me, young man," Mrs. Hamilton said, and her voice was so commanding that he couldn't have stopped listening if he tried. "I don't have to tell you how badly boys get punished in this place. I don't like it, but those are the rules. And since you just got out of the infirmary, I hope you'll remember how you ended up there. If Warden Haddock ever asks you a question direct, you tell him the truth—every time. He won't ask you a question unless he already knows the answer. Do you understand?"

Robert shook himself from paralysis and nodded his head.

"I can't hear you," Mrs. Hamilton said, just like a drill sergeant in *Sands of Iwo Jima*.

"Yes, ma'am. I'll tell him the truth."

And why shouldn't he? What had Blue done for him except get him in trouble? No one had told Blue to come out in the cornfield when he wasn't supposed to. Blue said he had come to warn him about the warden, but Robert wouldn't need warnings if Blue would leave him alone. Warden Haddock might give him double the lashes this time! Or worse: drag him away like the teenager he'd seen in chains. Robert had watched every older boy's face in the cafeteria to try to see that kid again, but he hadn't found him yet. *Ev'rybody don't go home,* Boone had said.

"Stand up straight, Robert," Mrs. Hamilton said, "and wipe away those tears. I'll walk over to his office with you. And I'm going to wait until he's done and walk you to the schoolhouse." Then, quietly, she said, "Be strong like your father. Can you try to do that?"

Robert nodded again, almost smiling. Crutcher had spoken kindly of Papa too.

"Come on, then," she said, and she held out her hand to him. Robert was startled: Miz Lottie still held his hand when she crossed Main Street with him, but he had already forgotten how adults treated children, or at least how they were supposed to. He hesitated so long that he was afraid she would pull her hand away, so he curled his fingers around hers harder than he meant to.

"It'll be all right," she soothed him. "As long as you tell the truth."

And he would, Robert vowed. He would tell everything. As Robert walked hand in hand with Mrs. Hamilton down the steps, he couldn't stomach Redbone's burning, wondering eyes as he passed. Redbone brushed close, pretending to trip on the stair, and he brought his lips to Robert's ear for a whisper as faint as a breath.

"Better not say nothin' 'bout Blue."

22

"You like Coca-Cola?" Warden Haddock said. "I don't mind mine warm, but I picked you up a cold one from the machine." He offered the green-tinted bottle across his desk of files and neatly stacked photographs, past his candy jar. Sunlight from the window behind Haddock made the bottle glow.

"Thank you, sir," Robert said, although he didn't like Coca-Cola since Mama died. Mama had kept a bottle or two in their icebox, stashed in the back. If you drank Mama's Coke, there'd be hell to pay. The taste of it made him miss her.

Haddock's teeth were frozen. "If you like a thing, you smile, don't you? When the superintendent gives you a cold Coke?"

Robert tried a smile and failed. Then he imagined Mrs. Hamilton sitting close to the door, watching the time passing on the clock, waiting and listening in case anything went bad. She had said to tell the truth, so Robert said, "I'm too scared, Mr. Haddock. I feel like you think I did something wrong."

He smiled. "Relax and drink your Coke, Robert. You're not in trouble." Warden Haddock said it like the idea was ridiculous, as if he hadn't just beaten his back bloody while two men held him down. As if the boy bound like a hog hadn't called Warden Haddock the devil himself.

Robert didn't believe Haddock, but he sipped at the frigid bottle anyway, and the sugary syrup stung his mouth while he imagined Mama pouring Coke over ice in one of her good glasses at dinner, her treat at the end of the day. He would have preferred tap water to the fizzy Coke, but he swallowed half the bottle before he knew it because Warden Haddock was watching. His throat was grateful for the cold, at least.

"Boone tells me you have a gift, son." The word *son* made Robert nearly cough. Warden Haddock's eyes melted with what seemed like affection. "You're a spotter."

Now it was coming. Now Haddock would ask him to betray Mama. "Sir?"

"A spotter. You ever seen war pictures? When snipers up on a hill or in the window want to kill an enemy, they need a spotter to make calculations so they can do it right." Warden Haddock crossed his elbows across the desk, leaning closer to Robert, ready to tell secrets he didn't want his secretary to hear. Or Mrs. Hamilton, even if she was listening as hard as she could. "This school is stinking with haints, Robert. All of Gracetown stinks with 'em, but here most of all. Anyone who grew up here knows that. Don't pretend you don't."

Robert tried not to think of Mama to keep the tears from his eyes, but Mama was all he could think about, as if she were hiding behind Warden Haddock's door. And wasn't she? Would she give the warden a headache now to save him from having to lie?

"Yessir," Robert whispered.

"I need someone who sees 'em regular, not just once in a while. Someone who can track 'em and show me where they've been. I haven't had a good spotter in a long while. Boone says you're the best he's ever seen, and he's been here since '45. Going on five years."

Robert's hearing phased in and out as his heart pounded, and he fought against tears and held his face steady as the awfulness twisted his stomach. The social worker had told him to be invisible to the warden, and somehow he'd become an outright marvel. Bad to worse in a heartbeat. He would never get out in six months now!

Robert tested a lie. "I've only seen the one in the kitchen, Warden Haddock."

"That's not true, son," Warden Haddock said, and Robert

swooned in his seat at being caught. His mouth lost all moisture. He shook his head to try to explain.

"The fire," Warden Haddock said. "You *felt* the fire. Not all haints are human, Robert. A big enough corruption can be a haint too. Boone said you flinched in those flames like the fire was still burning. Like you could see every face. He knew what you could see as soon as he met you."

"I didn't see faces in the fire," Robert said after the warden waited for him to say more. He had seen faces in the Funhouse, but he didn't want to tell on those. "It just felt . . . hot. Smoky."

"But chances are, you will—you will. I want you to visit the spot each day. Just like one of our tracking dogs, I want you to get familiar with the scent. Learn the stink of the dead. I used to see 'em as a boy—a lot of us Gracetown boys do, don't we, Robert?—and if the moon's right some nights, I still see a shadow in front of my window just the size of my baby sister. My wife can't see her—only me. You don't know angry 'til you've met an angry baby, Robert Stephens. *There's* something they don't teach you in church." Warden Haddock winked, a flutter of his right eye. "Now, I know what you're thinking . . . she's got the right to haunt me *of all people*. I'll give her that one."

Robert froze his face so his eyes wouldn't widen to show his shock. He'd thought maybe, just *maybe*, the warden had done something bad to his sister when he had seen the old photo proudly on his bookshelf—but was Warden Haddock admitting it to his face? And who would believe his word against the warden's if he tried to tell? Robert's heart sped as he feared the warden might spell out exactly how he had done it and force him to hear about whatever dark room he had killed his baby sister in. Robert didn't want to hear another word. Would the warden beat him if he asked to leave the room? Send him to Boot Hill after he knew?

"I think it's only right," Warden Haddock went on, "for me to leave my sister's spirit alone. In my mama's memory. A young'un like I was can't see all the bigger pieces of a thing. She's still blood kin, temper or no. No real man is afraid of a few broken windows or a missed night's sleep."

He waited to see if Robert would speak, but Robert could only stare at him, forgetting he should never look a white man in the eye. Even when he remembered to look away, he couldn't. Warden Haddock said he wasn't afraid of his sister's ghost, but another story was buried in the creases of his quivering crow's-feet.

Warden Haddock looked away first, tapping a pencil on his stack of photos. "It's the other haints, on *this* land—those are the ones I won't tolerate. They're tryin' to give my school a bad name. All a man has in the world is his name. Your name outlives you. You might as well know, Robert . . . boys died here. Quite a few have, in fact."

When Robert's throat closed, he remembered his Coke and tried to force down another sip.

The cold glass made his hand shake.

Warden Haddock picked up a file folder in front of him and fanned through the pages, a breath of hot dust. "By my research . . . I'd say there's about sixty in the official records since the school opened at the turn of the century. Another, I don't know, thirty or so may not be so official." He said it in a singsong, a math problem that puzzled him. He studied the page his finger had stopped on. "Give or take, let's call it a hundred haints on this land. I'm sure I'm still missing a few. The truth is, no one knows for sure." He threw the file down, sending more dust into Robert's nose.

Robert finished the rest of the math in his head: that meant two boys died a year. At least. "Now, before you get the wrong idea," Warden Haddock said, stern again, "those numbers got jiggered way up by the fire. One fire in 1920 killed twenty-five boys. It's the biggest tragedy in the history of this county. Maybe worst in the state. I don't know of any tragedy worse, do you?"

Rosewood was worse, according to Miz Lottie's stories. But he hadn't *felt* the killing fires in Rosewood the way he had here. Besides, Rosewood's screaming Negro men, women, and children wouldn't count as a tragedy to Warden Haddock.

"No, sir," Robert said.

"You're damn right. It's a hell of a thing for an institution to bounce back from. Tongues are still wagging thirty years later. The mayor, the town council, the governor's office—they all wanted to shut down Gracetown School for Boys. It was my first job—I was a bricklayer—and good-paying jobs weren't easy to come by. Still aren't, Robert—not for swamp boys like me. I put down the foundation for your dormitory with these two hands. Then, just like that, they wanted us gone. We're too big to shut down now, but the wrong kind of stories make it hard to keep order, Robert. It's all meetings, meetings, meetings, instead of seeing to my boys."

Warden Haddock wanted Robert to feel sorry for him, so Robert nodded. "And about your daddy . . . ," the warden went on.

Robert couldn't keep from squirming.

"You know this about me by now: I'm a man of God and duty," Warden Haddock said, an outrageous lie. Warden Haddock was a master of lies. And maybe a baby killer too! Still, Haddock gazed at Robert with soft, wet eyes. "The Funhouse, what happened between you and me, was duty. I didn't lay down that strap as hard as I could have. Every lash gave me a goddamn headache, Robert. And I respected the way you defended your father, when you spoke your mind. You knew good and damn well you could say the wrong thing and swing from a rope, but you said, 'Yessir, that white bitch is lying.' "

The room spun until the warden winked again.

"I've even told the story a time or two, how you spoke your mind. Half the town, including the sheriff, knows she only made it up to cover bruises from her drunken boyfriend, and the other half are swamp trash who couldn't spell 'investigation' with a dictionary. Now, there's plenty I don't like about your daddy, who is a communist—make no mistake. But the Constitution says 'free speech,' and I'd be a hypocrite to lay a finger on you over a lie. I'm saying all this, Robert, because you need to understand I'm not a monster. Like all God's creatures, I've made mistakes; I made my worst one when I was younger than you." Robert thought of Warden Haddock as the boy in knee pants holding the baby he'd killed on his lap . . . with a smile. "I'm only saying this because . . . if you can get your heart around this endeavor, being my spotter, we can be a great help to each other, Robert. You can help me clear the stink out of the Gracetown School for Boys, and I will ask the judge to let you out early."

He pushed a form toward Robert and turned it right side up so Robert could read it: PETITION FOR EARLY RELEASE. Followed by, on the next line: STEPHENS, ROBERT E. JR. It was the first time Robert had ever seen his name from a typewriter, so official and important. Only the blank signature line waited. The white paper shimmered like gold.

"Spotting is an honor system, Robert. Boone says spotters sometimes don't tell all they could. See it as bein' 'tattletales.' Start to feel like they're hunting down innocent boys." He searched Robert's face, nodding when he found the floating boy from the infirmary in Robert's eyes. Or, God help him, maybe Warden Haddock saw Mama too.

"So you'd better know this: there's nothing innocent about haints. They say one thing to your face and whisper how to die in your ears when you're sleeping. They want you to keep 'em company. What's six months or a year or ten years to a haint? The worst haints are children: always bored and wanting to play. Haints only want what *they* want, not a damn thing *you* want. They can't be bargained with. Can't be trusted. Haints will sure enough get you killed."

Robert's memories of the pathetic haints he'd seen must have been plain on his face. "Ah, I see," the warden said. "They're already getting to you. Trying to make you feel sorry."

"He didn't want to get stabbed in the back," Robert said, thinking of the white boy in the kitchen. He tried to make himself believe the boy was a bully like Lyle McCormack or the ones who yelled *Nigger!* as their shiny yellow school bus rolled past him and Gloria on the road. But more likely that white boy in the kitchen had been just like him, another boy who had waited to get whipped at the Funhouse and wanted to go home so bad that his stomach burned. Tears came to Robert's eyes before he could stop them.

Robert flinched when Warden Haddock reached toward him. A fresh white handkerchief lay in his hand, embroidered like a doily Mama had put under drinking glasses for company.

"Wipe those tears, son," Warden Haddock said. "Those are the last tears I want to see. Don't worry: I'm not sore at you for crying. Least now you see how haints'll trick you, fool you with their form. I've been working here long enough to tell you no boy has been stabbed to death in that kitchen. I bet it was a big knife he made you see, huh? He's just tellin' you spook stories." Yes, it *had* been a big knife, like a butcher used to chop through bone. But the boy had died somehow, hadn't he? He wouldn't be a haint otherwise. And Robert had felt the past flashes of pain as soon as he'd walked into the kitchen. More than one boy had been stabbed there. He had to keep reminding himself that Warden Haddock's lies sounded so sweet and true.

"You know how he probably died?" the warden said, again as if he could hear Robert's thoughts. "I'd wager a hundred dollars he died running away. Now, this is where my hands are tied: the state says we can't tolerate running. How would that look? The state can't leave boys in our care and then we let them run loose. And sometimes boys who run die; it's a nasty fact. They have poor judgment, cross the street wrong, get hit or dragged trying to jump the train, fall in a ditch. There's hypothermia in the cold, heatstroke in the summer, and sometimes a dog will catch 'em before the dog boys can pull 'em back. That's an ugly business. But even with all that, they still try to run. It's the scourge of my work here, Robert. My duty in the Funhouse was to try to save your life. And now we'll start again on a different foot, you and me."

Warden Haddock reached down and raised another Coke bottle from his lower desk drawer. He extended his half-empty bottle across the desk, waiting for Robert to clink it.

"Let's collect those haints," Warden Haddock said. "Once and for all."

Robert hesitated, knowing with every part of him that he should not toast with Warden Haddock. He finally did because the warden's eyes narrowed, his anger ready to return, and his leather strap was in plain view on the wall. The *ting* of their glass bottles as they touched was off-key in Robert's ear, making his stomach roll. It felt like the worst thing Robert had ever done. He imagined Mama screaming out in pain. Music was *her* place with Robert, not the warden's.

Was there a way to take it back?

"But . . . what if I only see one, sir? That one in the kitchen?"

"Oh, you'll see more than one," Warden Haddock said. "If you're half the spotter Boone says you are, I guarantee it. Especially if you want that early release."

Robert glanced down at the form again, typed up with his name. He thought of his soft bed and Gloria's rabbit stew served in his favorite bowl. No more Funhouse—ever.

"And," the warden went on, hesitating as if he hated to put the next part in words, "that's the only way to be extra sure that nothing happens to your friends. The warden's spotter gets extra protections, Robert. You'll see that right away." Robert heard the threat in the words the warden had disguised as a favor.

Warden Haddock lifted up a large mason jar from somewhere under his desk and displayed it on the desktop. It was empty except for about two inches of red-gray ash at the bottom so fine it could be dust. The jar was maybe eight inches high, with a sealed top and a raised image of a king's crown on the glass. The word *Crown* stabbed through the glass below the picture. Haddock kept his hand across the top of the jar like he thought it might fly away.

"This was a jar for a pint of liquor," Warden Haddock said. "But now it's my collection jar, Robert. Take a good look at it. Believe it or not, that's about ten years' work. We haven't got far, as you can see. We've only collected a handful. But once you set Boone loose with his traps, we'll have more. They leave evidence behind once they're gone. That's how I'll know you're doing your job right. Each one you help Boone catch, that's a day you go home early. But don't you worry: like I said, this place is stinking with haints. You can help Boone catch twenty, thirty, without half an effort. Once you've caught ten, I'll take off a full month's time."

The ash sat dead in the sunlight burning through Warden Haddock's window. Robert peered more closely to see if even a fleck would stir, but none did. The ash was truly dead.

"What . . . happens to them?" Robert said.

"Nothing happens; they're just the way they were supposed to be. Gone. Like it says in the Bible, Robert. Does the Bible talk about haints roaming free? Does Jesus say 'Bless these haints and let them prosper'?"

Robert wasn't sure, so he shook his head. He didn't think so.

"You're damn right it don't. Haints are unholy, Robert. A good church boy like you can see that. You can't capture a person's soul in a jar. The soul belongs to God. This is just what's left: the parts that should have been gone already. A shadow of the flesh."

Robert felt himself nodding his head. He had heard Pastor Jenkins say *Ashes to ashes, dust to dust* at Mama's burial as they lowered her wooden casket into the ground. Maybe Warden Haddock didn't lie about everything. He had told the truth about killing his baby sister, after all.

But ten! Could he betray the haints he'd seen in the Funhouse? The boy who'd died of pneumonia floating in the infirmary? The charred boy who'd walked near his bed? Could he betray all of them so he could get out? Robert started counting the haints he'd seen in his head, adding up the cost of his freedom.

"I'll even help you, since sometimes it's hard to tell haints and the living apart," Warden Haddock said. "I'd like you to start with this one—he's awful dangerous. He died in the 1920 fire."

Warden Haddock picked up a photograph from the pile on his desk. This time he stood up and walked behind Robert's chair, leaning over him to place the photo practically under his nose. All of Robert's skin prickled with the warden so close, like a bear was standing behind him. When Warden Haddock rubbed Robert's shoulder, Robert's eyes stared at his long, pale, pink fingers instead of the image on the photograph. The warden wore a gold wedding band. Robert wondered if the warden's wife knew him even a little bit.

"Go on," Warden Haddock said. "Take a look."

The photograph was charred blackness, a burned shell of a wall and a circular heap of bones tangled together. The charred bones reminded Robert of a football game when both teams piled on a ball that had gotten loose, except they were in a perfect O shape, in swirls like the pattern on a peppermint lollipop. Because Boone had driven Robert through the ghost fire, he knew things the photo didn't say: they had all hugged each other when the fire surrounded them. They had died together, not apart.

But he couldn't see faces. The faces had been burned away.

"I don't—" Robert started to say, and then Warden Haddock let go of Robert's shoulder and pointed to the center of the pile with his index finger.

"Middle of the pack—that's the one. Name's Kendall Sweeting. Must've died from suffocation, from the smoke. Hardly had a burn on him. Maybe the rest were trying to protect him. He was the youngest in the shed. God as my witness, Robert, I want this one most of all."

Robert followed Warden Haddock's finger to a clear portion at the center of the circle, where a child was curled on his side as if he were in a womb, his face upturned, perhaps posed that way. He might have only been sleeping. Robert's throat drew shut as if he too were gagging on thick smoke. He could not breathe—could not remember ever breathing.

The boy in the photograph was Blue.

23

Robert could barely catch his thoughts after he left the warden's office and told Mrs. Hamilton everything was fine and saw relief soften her kind face. His shock at seeing Blue in the photo made him doubt the sight of the twilight sky above him and every blade of grass beneath his feet. Warden Haddock wasn't lying this time: Robert had seen with his own eyes! If Blue wasn't alive, if Blue wasn't *real*, could he trust in anything he thought he saw? He had *touched* Blue. *Talked* to Blue. Robert's skin rang with the memory of Blue's fingers around his ankle in the cornfield. And the way he'd laughed and laughed.

Who was real and who wasn't, then? What about Redbone? Did Redbone know Blue was long dead? Of course he did! So many things made better sense: how Redbone had lied to Boone the first night and said *he'd* been the one telling stories about boys running away, not Blue. How Boone had ignored Blue when he took him and Redbone out to the Funhouse. How Blue had slipped out to the cornfield. And Redbone's last words to him had been *Don't say anything about Blue.* Robert wondered if Redbone might be a ghost too.

And who else? Was he a ghost himself?

Robert didn't want to be near the other boys until he saw Redbone, so he stood waiting for him beside twin pines outside of the cafeteria near the supper line. He stood near the garbage Dumpster that was so close to the cafeteria door that it was hard to separate the smell of their dinner and rotting food, both clogging his nose. He'd been hungry most of the day, but now his appetite was gone.

As they passed him, two boys he'd warned in the cornfield

when Boone and the watchers were near nodded and said, "Hey, Robert," but Robert barely noticed them. He also barely noticed when Cleo brushed past him with a rough bump of his shoulder and a sneer. He'd been afraid of Cleo in the cornfield, but not anymore. Robert didn't glance Cleo's way, staring straight ahead, and he barely heard Cleo say, "Yeah, you better not do nothin'," before he moved on. Robert stood statue still while all around him boys jostled and joked in line for supper. Robert kept looking for Redbone, afraid he'd see him, afraid he wouldn't.

But he was more afraid he might see Blue.

As soon as Robert thought Blue's name, Blue appeared like the ghost he was in a row of boys walking toward him, grinning from ear to ear. But when Robert gasped aloud, choking on his own tongue, he realized the boy was much younger than Blue, and he and his friends had nearly identical plaid shirts he had never seen Blue wear. No, it wasn't Blue, Robert reassured himself three or four times to try to calm his heart.

Robert had considered Blue *almost* a friend, at least on the way to being one, but now every moment he'd spent with Blue felt like a violation. Blue had locked them in the freezer, slamming the door behind them, and . . . then what? Floated in the air? Marched back and forth through the wall until he was bored? And in the locker room, he'd appeared like a phantom from behind Robert's locker door. And then there was the cornfield. Robert had known something wasn't right about Blue being in the cornfield the moment he'd felt his touch.

"Stephens!" Boone called.

Robert spun, afraid everyone within earshot knew. He might have jumped ten feet high if his muscles didn't feel like rocks. No, no, no—this was all wrong. He was supposed to see Redbone first, not Boone. He wanted to undo and unsay everything that had happened in the warden's office.

Boone wore a leather pouch around his neck. He gestured. "Come on," he said, and pushed through the line toward the cafeteria's double doors. He stopped walking and turned, frowning when he saw Robert hadn't moved. "Show me where it was at. It ain't gonna hurt you none."

All eyes were on him now. Robert had imagined a meeting in secret at the rear kitchen door, not a proclamation in front of every boy in line. Robert darted toward Boone to keep him from saying the awful thing out loud, that he was a haint tracker. He helped the warden hunt down boys who had already died—boys the warden himself might have helped kill like he'd killed his sister. Some of them *did* seem to know, the way they cleared a path for Robert and stared questions at him. Even the boy who reminded him of Blue was staring.

"Let's go," Robert whispered, mostly to be away from their eyes.

Inside the doors, heat and the smell of over-steamed vegetables swamped Robert as he followed Boone to the building's left side, away from the cafeteria and toward the kitchen in back. Redbone was in his white cap, pushing a mop; Warden Haddock had already put him back in the kitchen. Redbone stopped mopping when he saw Robert. Boone was so intent on walking to the big metal vat against the rear wall that he didn't tell Redbone to get back to work. Boone surely hadn't seen the loathing in Redbone's face.

Robert gave Redbone a shrug he hoped would look like an apology, but Redbone's dark eyes sharpened on him as if he knew his every secret thought.

"Where was it again?" Boone said. "Show me where you saw that haint."

Why had he said it aloud? Redbone's face changed to a pale shade, melting away into an expression that reminded Robert of Papa's when he had sat at Mama's sickbed.

"That floor's wet!" Redbone called out. "I just mopped it."

"Don't seem wet to me," Boone said, and kept walking, and Robert had to follow. He couldn't make himself look at Redbone.

The floor wasn't a bit wet, or even clean—it had tracks through spilled flour in places—but Boone didn't catch Redbone in the lie because Boone was only interested in the vat where Robert told him a haint had stood. Why had that white boy shown himself? Why hadn't he been more careful? White boys didn't belong in the kitchen—not even as haints. Robert tried to convince himself this was all the haint's fault. He even tried believing Warden Haddock's claim that the haint hadn't been stabbed in the back; he only showed himself that way to make people feel sorry for the victim of such a low-down, cowardly act. Or to try to scare him. All the storybooks and picture shows were about haints scaring people. Hurting people, even.

"Tell me where he was at and I'll sprinkle all around. If I had enough powder, I could do the whole kitchen." Boone surveyed the floor and finally frowned. "He said he mopped this damn floor." But instead of yelling or threatening to send Redbone to the Funhouse, Boone reached into his pouch, the floor forgotten, and pulled out a saltshaker full of red-brown powder.

"What's that?" Robert said, although he knew everything except its name.

"Goofer dust," Boone said. "Fresh batch I just scooped from my grandmama's grave. That's what draws 'em. Sprinkle goofer dust where you saw 'em last and they'll come right back. Must smell like frying bacon to a starving man. Long as the trail's fresh, they'll come back an' get caught. And they sure 'nough turn to dust like a li'l anthill."

Robert felt sick to his stomach as he remembered the warden's proud jar of dust. *If you're dead, stay dead,* Blue had said. With his own mouth.

"Right there," Robert said, all the while praying that Mama had never come near this spot, that she had stayed far away from the kitchen.

"Speak up, boy. I can't hardly hear you."

Robert didn't move his arm from his side as he stuck out his index finger ever so slightly to point to the corner beside the vat. Robert could still remember the boy's freckles as clearly as the knife. "That's where he was standing, and then . . . he walked through the wall."

"That right?" Boone caressed the wall nearest the corner as if he might find a soft spot and walk through the wall his own self. "This spot here?"

"Yessir." Robert wasn't sure. He hoped not, but it might be.

Boone rubbed his palms and paced like he was about to feast on the beef stew simmering in the large pots on the oversized stove. The carrots had been overcooked to a dull, sickly shade nothing like orange, and the meat alongside them had turned gray. The smell made Robert feel sick. This day, this week, this year, made Robert feel sick.

Boone was squatting in the corner, and ordinarily Robert might have laughed because his pants were tugging down low past his butt crack. He looked back at Redbone to see if he might be smiling, but the crushed look on Redbone's face lashed Robert, so he turned away as fast as he could. Redbone would never be his friend now. Tears nearly snuck from Robert's eyes, but he wiped them away while Boone wasn't looking.

Boone was shaking powder from the saltshaker, oh, so carefully. He could have been drawing a picture with the grave dust, the way he took his time. "This here's my trap," Boone said, and backed up a step, still shaking dust out in a careful way so he wouldn't spill a fleck, "and I'll lay out a trail from where he was standing. Right here?"

Robert nodded. "Right next to the big pot, like he was stirring it."

Robert had to admit he felt a twinge of excitement now, the way he'd gotten past feeling bad for the rabbits Papa had hunted with him and concentrated instead on the thrill of finding their hiding places and timing the buckshot just right. Once he'd shot a rabbit's head clean off, leaving the rest perfect for stewing, and Papa had put his hand on top of his head and said, "*Great* shot, Robert"—not Robbie, not Junior, which he hated (and reminded him too much of Uncle June), but his full name spoken aloud as if to remind him they were both the same.

Boone surveyed his work when he was done: a thin, barely visible line of dust about twelve inches long led from the spot in front of the vat to the corner of the wall, where, indeed, Boone had drawn what looked like a loose circle. The trap was obvious if you knew what you were looking for. The haint might catch the scent and follow it to the circle like a lit match.

"What happens now—" Robert started to ask, but his words were snatched away by a keening scream between his ears like nothing he had ever heard before. *Heard* wasn't the right word, because it wasn't his ears; it was in the place where he'd heard Mama's voice in the Funhouse, a secret place beyond hearing. But it wasn't Mama, not this time. The sound was barely human, but Robert knew in his bones that it was the boy with the knife in his back.

"Well, I'll be . . . god . . . damned . . . ," Boone was saying. Robert thought he was hearing the sound too, but instead Boone was pointing at the wall. "Look! Look here!" Boone raised such a fuss that other boys gathered behind them, curious.

At first, Robert didn't see anything except the circle in the floor, but then Boone raised Robert's chin to look *up*, and he saw what looked like pale dust motes gathered in the air above the circle with lazy swaying as they floated toward the floor, the way Papa had described snowfall. These fell with a loose order *inside* the circle, never outside, clinging more tightly as they fell, until they grew to a small pile: an inch-high gathering of gray, dead dust. With a peak at the top like a mountain. And small as it was, it *seemed* like a mountain because the air had conjured it.

"He was right here!" Boone said, slapping Robert's back so hard that it hurt. But Boone hadn't meant any harm, because his face was full of that too-big grin. "Musta been standing close by the whole time! I ain't never seen one caught so fast! Ain't never *seen* one, not like that."

Boone looked at Robert with wide-eyed wonder the way a small child might. "I knew it," Boone said, nearly whispering. "Soon as I drove you through the flames. Most boys, they don't feel a thing, maybe just get an itch. But you? You felt it all right. You felt every lick."

Boone watched and waited to see if more dust would come or the pile would grow, but it had all happened within a few breaths. If either of them had turned their heads, they would have missed the falling dust and only seen the pile left behind.

Boone's hands were shaking as he reached into his back pocket and pulled out a laboratory tube and a brush like the one Mama used to paint her cheeks and a miniature dustpan. Working carefully again like an artist, he swept up the dust and shook it into the jar, hissing behind his teeth if he dropped a single speck. The dust wasn't as impressive in the jar, a thin layer across the bottom, but it was perfectly visible. Boone admired the jar in the light, and all of the boys behind them tried to see it too. At the bottom of the tube, the prick of a miniature firefly's flare came and went so quickly that Robert was sure he was the only one who'd seen it. He couldn't have named the color: not golden, not bronze. Something in between.

Robert turned to look for Redbone among the watching boys, but Redbone was gone. "Lookit, he's a haint catcher!" Boone said. "All of y'all hearin' bumps and jumpin' at shadows can rest easy now. We won't have no more haints in the flour bags and under your beds." The boys—now ten or twelve of them at least—let out a cheer. The sound of their celebration helped unlock Robert's stomach and make it seem less like he might throw up. Instead of thinking about the white boy with the knife in his back, who had *actually* died long ago, Robert took in the happy eyes and smiles all around him. Would it matter if Redbone wasn't his friend? He would have many friends now.

When Boone looked down at him, Robert wondered if it was sweat or happy tears falling from the big man's eyes. "Warden Haddock's gonna be so pleased," Boone said. "When the warden's happy, we all git a piece. You go an' eat—have all the sweets you want. No more cornfield. No more kitchen. The only job you got now is catching haints." His face glowed.

Before Robert could finish fixing his plate of stew and runny mashed potatoes, the younger boy who'd fooled him because his height was so close to Blue's was tugging on Robert's shirt to ask if he could sit at his table. "Haints keep me up all night," the boy said. Up close, he was gap-toothed, nothing like Blue.

"Me too," said another. "Bad enough we stuck in here, but we got haints too?"

Robert had filled a table before he took his seat. A crowd of boys raced for the seats nearest to him, then at the edges, until all eight seats were taken and a few boys were left standing with their trays, jostling for space behind him.

"You got some nice boots," a cross-eyed boy told Robert. "Where'd you get 'em?"

"From my papa," Robert said. He was glad to speak of Papa with pride instead of shame. Every boy agreed they were the finest boots they had ever seen.

"You gotta have good boots to be a haint catcher, you know," one said wisely.

Robert told the boys how he'd caught the kitchen haint, although it was a flimsy story because he'd only pointed the way. He remembered how Redbone exaggerated his stories and added, "I could smell where he was. Like a coal burning in the stove."

Two or three boys gasped like it was the most amazing thing they had ever heard. In return, the boys told Robert how the captured haint had surprised them around corners and hidden in the cabinets and whispered curses in their ears. How once it had spilled a whole bag of rice on the floor and gotten three boys sent to the Funhouse. How it had left a burner lit and caused a grease fire. Every wrong they could imagine, it seemed, was laid at the feet of the haint Robert had caught.

Robert almost believed every word.

Sleep was impossible. Robert didn't feel natural sleeping on his stomach, but his back was still sore. And the awful heat in the dormitory still hung everywhere, made worse because every breath he took felt used up by someone else. And Robert's mind was racing in circles. All he saw when he closed his eyes were those odd flecks of dust falling from the air into a pile. And he heard the awful scream. He remembered the freckled face of the boy with the knife in his back. A stranger had stabbed that boy to kill him, but Robert might have stolen his soul. Thinking of it, Robert trembled despite the heat. "I'm sorry," he whispered through tears.

Redbone had not looked Robert's way once before bed, avoiding him in the shower room, the radio room, and the dorm before the lights went out. Robert had hoped to explain himself to Redbone, but what could he say? He was a haint catcher. Everyone knew it now. And what if Mama was drawn to that spot like the stabbed boy? Would he return to the kitchen tomorrow and find another small pile of dust? Robert was so anxious to know that he wanted to fling off his thin blanket and sneak out to the kitchen to see. Only his memory of the Funhouse kept him in bed, his mind wide-awake and worried.

Although Robert was on his stomach, his scarred back sweating in the dark, he *felt* someone above him, just out of his sight. The tiny hairs across the back of his neck quivered, and the sweat on his back changed to ice water. He hoped it was Redbone ready to talk to him at last—a daring move after lights-out—but even before he turned his neck slightly to try to see, straining his muscles, he knew it wasn't Redbone visiting his bed. Robert's eyes looked up, only his eyes moved, and he was relieved no haints were floating above him in retaliation.

But then he saw a kneecap. Someone was sitting cross-legged

on his headboard, someone small with impossible balance, and he didn't have to look further to know it was Blue. Blue still smelled like the cornfield. Now that Robert noticed it, he smelled faintly of soot.

"Don't you touch me," Robert whispered, "or I'll call for Boone." He sounded braver than he felt; his heartbeat was banging hard against the mattress.

"That was wrong," Blue said, not a whisper but not loud. "What you did to Clint."

Well, if that didn't beat all. A haint telling *him* he was in the wrong when a haint had no business trying to talk to living folk! Robert was ready to tell Blue to go back where he'd come from, but hot shame clamped his mouth. Another tear came to the corner of his eye.

"I tried to tell you, didn't I?" Blue said. "Haddock's the worst of the worst. And now you doin' just like he said, so that makes you the worst of the worst too."

"Leave me alone," Robert whispered.

"That was real dumb, making it look so easy," Blue said. "All you had to say was 'Oh, the ghost was *here*, not there.' Played him along. But I guess you wanted to look good, huh? Lick Boone's shoes. Now it's gonna look way worse when you can't find no more. He's prolly gonna send you to the Funhouse pretty quick."

"I know where there's plenty more," Robert said. He didn't want to say it—he knew Blue was right—but he didn't want any haint to have power over him.

Blue leaned over then, his neck impossibly long as he forced himself into Robert's view.

Blue's face waved in front of him like a snake's head at an impossible angle, and Robert squeezed his eyes shut to try to keep from fainting.

"Go away."

Hadn't Blue told him he only had to tell a haint to leave him be? Had that been a lie? "You scared?" Blue was closer than ever. If Robert had opened his eyes, he might see Blue's eyes staring right back at him. The sooty smell was stronger now.

"Shut up 'fore I call Boone on you too." Robert could only manage a whisper.

Robert heard a *CLANG* so loud that he almost fell out of his bed. Two boys near him stirred in their sleep but they didn't wake. He wondered why everyone didn't sit up, but then he realized no one else had heard it. Just him. Blue had made the noise somehow, tweaking Robert's nerve endings just enough to make his eardrums vibrate inside. What else could he do?

"Okay, stop," Robert said, his eyes still squeezed shut. "Sorry, sorry. I won't tell Boone."

"You sure are dumb," Blue said, as if Robert's dumbness were as big and vast as the night sky. Admiring it, almost. "Not the dumbest I've ever seen, but pretty damn dumb. And I've been here thirty years. Thirty-one, really. You know what we call y'all? 'Thumpers.' 'Cause we hear those heartbeats goin' *boom boom, boom boom*. Like yours right now." He laughed.

Robert opened one eye just a little, and he saw Blue's teeth in the moonlight hardly an inch from his face as he laughed. Those teeth looked too white, and *sharp* like a wolf's fangs, but maybe he imagined the pointy tips. Haints weren't like Count Dracula, were they? He squeezed his eyes shut again. When he opened his eyes, Blue's teeth didn't look like fangs anymore. They were only baby teeth. He looked younger all the time.

"You got a problem now, all right," Blue said. "You gave 'em a taste, but they can't have no more. Clint's the only taste they get. You could live the whole rest of your life and never make up for what you did to Clint. Not in a hundred years. You might go to hell already."

Robert smothered a sob into his pillow. Part of his anguish was feeling sorry about Clint, especially now that the haint had a name, but mostly he was scared of the Funhouse. And, more distantly, he was afraid of the hell he'd heard Pastor Jenkins talk about from the pulpit.

"Have you seen hell?" Robert heard himself ask.

The *CLANG* assaulted the inside of Robert's ear again, burning where he couldn't touch it. "What you think? Dang, you're dumb. Did he show you his photos of the fire? I bet he did. He's so proud of it. You think that wasn't hell? Burning alive?"

"Was Clint . . . in the fire?"

"*Shut up,*" Blue said, hissing soot into his face. "You don't get to ask about Clint. We ain't none of your business. Don't you say his name again. Do it. I dare you."

Tiny drops of pee escaped between Robert's thighs, but he clamped his bladder tight before he could wet his bed. He held his breath, but he couldn't quiet the *thump-thump* in his chest he was sure Blue could hear. Each heartbeat seemed to shake the world.

"Since you're so dumb, I'll put it like you can understand," Blue said. "If you tell Boone where to put down any more of his poison dust—you so much as point in my direction or anyone else—I'll make sure your mama gets trapped too. I'll call her right to the spot."

"*No—*" Robert said, too loudly, sitting up in bed.

A boy across the room shushed him with an angry *Shhhhhhhh,* but Robert was the only one in the dorm sitting up in the rows of beds. Blue wasn't sitting on his bed's thin brass headboard—of course not; he was floating above it, legs still crossed like he was at a campfire.

"You heard me," Blue said, bobbing as he floated, "and there ain't nothing you can do about it. She follows you around—but you know that, don't you? You can feel her, can't you?"

Robert felt himself nodding his head.

"She don't belong here," Blue said. "She ain't like us: she didn't die here. That's why you can't see her like you see me. She's just fighting to be here, trying to look after *your* dumb ass instead of moving on like she should. She smells sweet as cream—nothing evil 'bout how she went. Bet she went with all of y'all around her saying 'Oh, Mama, how we love you so much,' didn't she? Holding hands and singing songs. It would be a mighty shame, wouldn't it, if she got caught in a trap that wasn't meant for her? If your mama was in Haddock's jar too?"

Robert nodded again. Tears flooded his face. Blue's mockery of Mama's dying was unbearable. "Please don't," he whispered. "Please."

Blue grinned, still nothing but baby teeth. How had he ever thought Blue was the same age as Redbone? Blue had been only seven or eight when he died, nowhere near twelve like him.

"*'Please, please,'*" Blue said, mimicking him behind his smile. "You're no haint catcher now, are you? Now the haint's caught *you*."

Robert breathed faster, trying not to sob too loudly, his throat afire with grief and dread.

Blue stared at him awhile and finally seemed to feel sorry for him. "Do what I say," Blue said, "and I'll leave your mama be."

Robert nodded so hard and fast that he dizzied himself. "What can I do? I never wanted it. He made me—"

"Shut up," Blue said with that hiss in his voice again, the grin gone. "I'll help you stay out of trouble with Haddock. You messed up bad already, but I'm gonna fix it so Clint ain't in that jar for nothing. I'm gonna get him out—and every other boy he's caught so far."

"They're not . . . gone?"

"No thanks to you," Blue said. "But they gotta be buried and prayed over, or set free in the creek." The words *set free* electrified Robert. Of course! "But none of them will want to go while Haddock's still here. Before he's paid for what he's done."

This time, the pounding of Robert's heart had nothing to do with fear of punishment. The idea dawning on him was so awful that his heart sped just to imagine it. "The . . . fire?"

"That's right, Albert Einstein. Course he set that fire."

"But why?"

Blue scowled at him. "There you go being dumb again. 'Cause he's a killer, fool. He's a raper and a killer. He's been a killer his whole life. He poisoned his daddy's favorite hunting hound. He smothered his baby sister with her blanket. You haven't figured that out yet? Why you think he stays on here where nobody troubles him? Where he has say over everything? He took it too far killing us all at once like that—people noticed—so now he does it a little at a time. And he's scared to death of the haints coming back, in case we might tell. In case we *prove* it."

"Can you?" Robert whispered. "Can you prove it?"

"No, I can't—but you can."

"Prove it how?" Robert said.

"He showed you pictures, didn't he?"

"Just one. The one . . . with you. The circle all around you. Everybody burned up." Blue didn't say anything for a few seconds, and Robert expected to hear the terrible *CLANG* again from the way his face turned so hard.

"That ain't the only one. There's more: the ones he looks at in private. The ones he doesn't want *anyone* to see. He's got his own darkroom in his shed 'cuz he can't take that film to a five-and-dime. Him with naked boys. And other ones from the fire. Posing and grinning. He can't help it, see? He needs to look at all his pictures every day. He's too scared to keep them at home 'cuz he thinks his wife might find them. So he locks them in a drawer in his desk. Nobody has the nerve to go near his drawer, not even his secretary. Not even me: he's got a haint trap under his desk. Everyone's scared of Haddock."

Robert was scared of Haddock too, and more scared now that it was dawning on him that Blue expected him to somehow steal the warden's most precious hidden possessions.

"So, for now, you keep playin' along," Blue said. "Act like you're out hunting haints. I'll try to find you at least one more—one of the SOBs who used to work here died in the fire too, but by accident. He didn't know if he chopped open that door the flames would come flying out. He's not so bad now, I guess—keeps clear of us—but he did plenty of bad while he was living. I'll let you know where to tell Boone to put the dust down so it won't catch nobody but him."

"When?"

"You just gotta wait. You'll see me when it's time. Then Boone will keep on hooting and hollering, and Haddock will feel like he's on top of the world. Then you gotta get those photos and his jar of dust. You'll climb out his window when he's not looking."

Blue made it sound like he only had to snap his fingers. Blue might as well have said he would need to storm Omaha Beach without an army.

"Then what?" Robert said.

"What you think, dummy?" Blue said. "Then I'll help you run away."

VI

LOWER SPRUCE

24

Gloria was shaking again by the time she got back to her cramped room at Miz Lottie's and burrowed beneath the quilt to cry, a slow unraveling. This guilt was a new feeling, enflaming her grief about her family's dead and missing—a hot spear stabbing every pain she'd tried to bury. She saw Mama's slack-jawed face on her deathbed pillow, where Gloria had sat and stared too long, wanting to look away and yet not able to, chronicling each missing movement and breath while Robbie wailed and kicked the wall and Papa paced the garden outside Mama's window, saying, "Oh dear God. Oh dear God," in a stranger's helpless voice. Until Mama died, he had never stopped believing she would get better.

Papa had been good at everything outside of the house but almost nothing inside except to threaten a whipping. He could not make himself wash Mama when she was too weak to use the outhouse or the corner tub, so Gloria had wiped away Mama's watery stool and seen to the folds between her legs. When Gloria had needed the back-porch Robert Stephens to help her, instead he had leaned on *her*—he had come home less than before, working longer hours ("We'll need the extra money," he always said), and moved his meetings farther away. A sob tore at Gloria's throat as she remembered how she'd been robbed of school, which Mama had said was her only chance every day for the last three months of her life, her last words to her before her mind was gone: *Don't quit school. Go to college.* When Mama was senseless with pain and medication, Gloria had begun lying to her, promising her she wasn't missing class. Every lie to Mama haunted her now that Mama was gone. Gloria had been so good a liar that Mama had believed her. It was a new, loathsome idea: she could lie to her own dying mother.

Gloria wailed, her face hot in the pillow to stifle the sound.

Because that wasn't even the worst. The worst—the *worst*—was how instead of freeing Robbie like she'd promised Papa, she'd ignored the advice from Mr. Moore and even John Dorsey, who had known better too but hoped to make up for a boy in Live Oak he couldn't save. She had stirred up the courthouse, which meant she might have stirred up the town.

This day felt worse than Mama's dying. She hadn't *caused* Mama to die. If she and Robbie had stayed on Lower Spruce in Miz Lottie's house, they never would have met a McCormack on the road. Thinking of Lyle touching her while Robbie watched with shock, then the way Lyle had pushed her up against his gate at night and rubbed his body against hers, made her remember the deputy on the road and the plans in his mind. She smothered herself in the pillow to try to contain her scream. Gloria only quieted when she was afraid Miz Lottie might come to check on her. She couldn't stand the thought of adding a single ounce of burden to Miz Lottie.

"Hurry—check the back." A man's voice.

When she opened her eyes, the sky had dimmed through the sheer curtains and she heard a burr of voices from the living room—June and Miz Lottie, but also others witnessing trouble. Gloria sprang up and tottered to the doorway.

The living room was crowded. Except for June and Miz Lottie, all of them were peeking through the front window facing the road: Mr. and Mrs. Hatchett and Leroy Jenkins, the pastor's brother. June took off running—full-out running—toward the kitchen the other way. Mr. Jenkins was heaving up and down with a wheeze at the window. He'd been running too.

"All of y'all get away from that window," June barked, angry. "Get down low."

"What's going on?" Gloria said.

No one answered, which made the scene more troubling. Mrs.

Hatchett took Miz Lottie by the arm to lead her to her couch. Miz Lottie looked tired, as if she'd been asleep too. "Gloria, go fetch Miz Lottie a glass of water. Go on."

Gloria worried for Miz Lottie and wanted to demand to know what the fuss was, but the fear in the room was thick and urgent, so she turned to follow June to the kitchen.

"Truck down at the corner," she heard Mr. Hatchett report. "Big red one."

"Told you," Mr. Jenkins said, still breathing hard. "There's five, six riding in back."

A strange truck in Lower Spruce might mean the Klan! In the kitchen, June was pulling down the blinds to block the jalousie windows in Miz Lottie's rear kitchen door. He'd grabbed his shotgun from its hiding place behind the fridge, had it propped on his shoulder, finger on the trigger. Gloria's heart clamored.

"They said there's a truck," Gloria told him, though he looked like he already knew.

"That light," he said, pointing, and she flipped the kitchen switch off. The kitchen went dark, and the crickets chirped more loudly through the open windows, but there were no other sounds. The curtains glowed faintly with gray light. Gloria hazarded a peek from the window's opposite corner: nothing was moving between Miz Lottie's clothesline and the mango trees where her truck was parked. Even June's work shirts hanging from the clothespins were petrified and still.

"What you doin', Glo?" June said.

Gloria let the curtains fall shut. She'd forgotten about Miz Lottie's water. "Sorry, I'm—" She reached into the fridge for Miz Lottie's cold mason jar. Her fingers *were* shaking again.

"What I mean is, what you *doin'*?" Uncle June said. "You better decide. You gonna curl up an' cry? You gonna go hide under the bed?"

"Is it the Klan?" she said, speaking her worst fear. "What will they do, Uncle June?"

"You done cryin'? Tell me yes or no."

From the living room Miz Lottie's phone jangled. Mrs. Hatchett answered, and she sucked in her breath from whatever she heard. Then she slammed down the phone. No doubt someone had called with a threat, or bad news. Miz Lottie asked who had called and Mrs. Hatchett said no one.

"I'm done crying," Gloria said, although her eyes wanted to flood.

"All right, then, you carry Miz Lottie her water," June said. "Real calm like. Don't get her excited, hear?"

"Yessir."

June spoke so quickly, she had to strain to hear him over her heart's pounding. "Then you take her to her room. Make sure she's clear of that window. Keep the lights off, or they'll see you better'n you'll see them. That old oak blocks her window pretty good, so you peek out from time to time. See what you see."

Gloria nodded.

"Look for fires," June said. "If you hear gunfire, try to see the muzzle flash." Uncle June was telling her the things he would tell a soldier, she realized. "You know where Mama's peashooter is?"

The laundry basket was in Miz Lottie's room, on her bed. She'd carried it in herself when they returned from the courthouse. "Yessir." Gloria's slamming heart made the room seem dimmer. Papa had taught her how to shoot squirrels and rabbits with buckshot, but she wouldn't trust her aim with a pistol. Shooting into the dark.

"Don't even think about firing that gun at a white man unless you're about to die first—not 'cuz you got scared an' jumped."

"Yessir."

"But if you got to shoot, don't shoot blind. Eyes open. And *keep* shooting. And all of us, we'll get to the truck. I parked it out back. Tank's full and I've got the key in my pocket. I been stayin' ready for these SOBs. If you see me run for that truck, follow behind. No matter what, you get Miz Lottie to the truck. That's your only job, even if you got to carry her."

"Why don't we just go now?"

"Too late now," Uncle June said.

Outside, a vehicle's tires growled across the road. A man yelled something Gloria couldn't understand, but she knew the angry sound. The strange truck might be right in front of the house. "Remember what I said," Uncle June said, hushed. "You squeeze that trigger by accident, they'll burn down Lower Spruce. But they might anyway. So don't fire it until we're all done for. All you can do then is take a few of them too. God sorts out the rest."

"Yes," Gloria said, fully agreed. She wished the deputy from the road in Live Oak would come, a wish so fierce it sped her heart. But then she saw ashes—a heralding, not a memory—and her heart iced. *There would be burning tonight.* What would Papa do if he were here? Gloria knew the answer: he would run. Papa had run already. Running had been the answer for Robbie all along, and she'd been foolish enough to go to the courthouse.

"Go on," Uncle June said. "Get Mama out of the front room."

"Where's Waymon?" Gloria asked. June and Waymon were not Miz Lottie's biological children, but she had raised them both since the time they were Robbie's age. While they were gone for the war, at times Gloria had wondered if Miz Lottie would worry herself to death. June was kin, and Waymon had found his way to her somehow. They both talked about how she cut switches from her yard to keep them in line as if she'd done them a great service, just like Miz Lottie said her mother, in her slave cabin, had cut switches to beat her children because she said it was better if it came from her instead of Massa.

"Waymon can take care of himself," June said. "*Go*, Gloria. Hurry."

Miz Lottie walked slowly, so Gloria tried to take her time walking with her despite her anxiousness. Gloria flicked off the bare bulb in the hallway, and the house beyond the kitchen went dark except a faint glow from the windowless bathroom. Gloria held Miz Lottie's slightly trembling hand as she led her through the dark. She knew the house from memory enough to reach Miz Lottie's open doorway. Her room was an inky cavern.

Miz Lottie had so many clothes that two racks of dresses lined her bedroom doorway to make a path to her pink canopy bed, a long-ago retirement gift from Councilman Powell, so high she needed steps to climb to it. The bed was more regal than the bed where Ma Ma said Miz Lottie had kept Ma'am's feet warm. Gloria led Miz Lottie through her collection of memories to her bed. "Where's my water?" Miz Lottie had sworn she didn't need more after two sips, but now she sounded panicked. Gloria had kept the mason jar, knowing better. "I've got it."

Miz Lottie drank in thirsty gulps, her hands struggling with the jar's weight, so Gloria helped her steady it.

"Do you need your heart pills?" Gloria said. "They in the bathroom?"

Miz Lottie shook her head. "Stay here," she said. "With me."

Outside, a white man was shouting. He was too far to make out his words, except *niggers*. "Is Waymon in the kitchen with June?" Miz Lottie said. "Did he come back yet?"

"Yes," Gloria lied, the easiest thing to say. Uncle June had said to keep Miz Lottie calm.

Headlights swept across Gloria's face through the open blinds, as if God wanted to shine a light on her lies. And Miz Lottie knew: Gloria saw it in the flash of her wide, probing eyes. Gloria rushed to the window to close the blinds like Uncle June had told her to. The headlights were coming from the back, not the road. Who was driving in Miz Lottie's yard?

Once the blinds were closed, Gloria rushed back to the bed to find the laundry basket, feeling for the ribbed wicker. She banged her ankle on Miz Lottie's steps to the bed, but she barely felt the pain while she looked for the gun.

"Gloria—" Miz Lottie said sternly. "Is Waymon here or not?" More angry shouts outside.

"No, ma'am." Gloria did not want her dying words to be a lie.

"What?" Miz Lottie's voice rose in alarm.

"Waymon's not here. Not yet."

"Then why'd you say . . ." But Miz Lottie did not finish, anguished. Worse than a rebuke. Gloria wished she could take back the truth when she heard Miz Lottie's whimpering sob.

She had seen Miz Lottie weep only once, at Mama's funeral. Miz Lottie's crying twisted her insides with shame and dread.

Gloria wrapped her fingers around the butt of the .22. She didn't have the time or light to check the chamber, so she went to the window, led by the moon.

"This loaded?" Gloria said, hoping Miz Lottie could hear her over her crying.

"Five shots. Bullets in my closet, top shelf, in my hatbox." Miz Lottie held back her sob. "You see anybody?"

Gloria looked for movement in the shadows. "No."

The silent hulk of Miz Lottie's truck waited in the moonlight, ready. *We should have run.* Gloria *saw* herself in the truck in another time, racing the truck along the railroad tracks past rows of slash pines, Miz Lottie beside her. Racing toward—

—the woods. Someone waiting in the shadows.

"Where's Robert Stephens?" In the backyard, a stranger let out a yell.

Gloria almost dropped her gun when her knees buckled in fright. The voice sounded not farther than ten yards away, maybe fifteen. Instinct made her pull back from the window, but she remembered Uncle June saying to watch for fire. She peeked out again, trying to see past the tree. Glass broke from the other side of the house, probably the living room window. Out front, Mrs. Hatchett screamed and her husband told her to stay down. Someone was out back; someone else was at the front. Maybe the house was surrounded. Cold facts came to Gloria, lining up.

"Gloria?" Miz Lottie said, still a whimper. "You smell kerosene?"

"No, ma'am." But the entire room might smell like kerosene. Gloria's nose was plugged with her own hot breath as she panted by the window.

"You tell me the truth," Miz Lottie said. "I can't smell anything. I was in my bed, an' I thought to myself, 'Who's that fussin' outside? Who's out there yellin' to raise the dead?' "

"You mean now?"

"My mama say, 'Lottie, you smell that kerosene? They pour it to make the fire burn quicker.' They'll pour it on your skin, you give them a chance. Then you'll be blacker'n black."

Miz Lottie was talking out of her head and white men were circling the house. The world folded in on itself, and Gloria held her breath until her dizzy feeling passed. She'd almost forgotten the lesson she'd learned from Mama's illness: people seemed fine until they weren't fine at all. Just like towns. Like Gracetown.

Gloria watched the truck, waiting to see if Uncle June would start shooting or give her a signal. To keep from being afraid, she felt herself *wanting* it to happen. The nozzle of her gun tapped lightly against the edge of Miz Lottie's closed window.

"You're not in old times with your mama anymore, Miz Lottie."

For a moment, Miz Lottie was silent, mulling that over. "Don't die in no fire," she said. "Any way but that."

"Yes, ma'am," Gloria whispered, not sure what she was promising. She was just glad Miz Lottie sounded in her right mind again. Maybe the broken window had taken her mind back to the old days, like Waymon sometimes jumped when he heard loud noises since the war.

"They don't care who it is—man, woman, or child," Miz Lottie said. "Once it starts—they don't care. They'll treat you like you ain't from the same God as them. Like they the devil."

Gloria thought of the hard-eyed deputy on the road who wanted to drag her to the woods. "I know, Miz Lottie."

"If you gotta run, go on and run," Miz Lottie said.

"Uncle June said—"

"And *I'm* telling you: Don't wait on me. Please, Gloria—please, child." She was begging. "It's bad enough Waymon's out there. They burned it all—my grandpa's house. His barn. I was a child—I was fast, and so was Mama—so we lived. We ran to the woods and hid. That's what you'd better do. You only live through it if you're quick."

"They're not going to burn us," Gloria said.

"How do you know that?" Miz Lottie hissed, both a whisper and a shout.

Gloria didn't know how she knew, but she did. She saw fire—plumes of black and gray smoke and excited golden flames—but the fire was not destined for Miz Lottie's. A fire was burning somewhere else. Was Robbie on fire somewhere? The Reformatory?

But no. That didn't seem right either. *That* fire had been in 1920. This one was new.

"I just know it," Gloria said. "Same way I always know. Mama used to ask me things."

That satisfied Miz Lottie. She went back to her quiet whimpering over Waymon. She'd told Gloria that whites had remarked to her that Waymon had "changed" since the war, how he unnerved people as he paraded to church in his Army uniform every Sunday. Waymon said he liked to remind people he had shed blood, and he might shed blood again.

"Is Waymon all right?" This was the first time Miz Lottie had ever tugged on Gloria's knowing like Mama used to.

Gloria tried to know about Waymon, but part of her didn't know *how* to try. Her flashes came on their own. The harder she tried, the less she knew. "I can't see that now. I can't see everything."

Another window broke. It might have been the window in Gloria's room—right beside them, where she had been sleeping until only minutes ago. Gloria peeked through the blinds again, toward the truck. Still no Uncle June, no headlights, no engine. But the light-colored shirt at the end of the clothesline was flapping unnaturally, coming to life.

Gloria peered more closely, trying to see. Was her eye fooling her?

A shadow bobbed in front of the shirt, closer and closer. Rapid footsteps crushed twigs and leaves as someone, a man, was running toward her—right *at* her, as if he could see in the dark.

What was the point of yelling a warning? Gloria raised her pistol and backed up two steps, waiting for the window to break. She kept her hand steady on the trigger by remembering Uncle June's advice: she couldn't shoot just because she was scared. If he just threw a rock, she would not shoot. If he just yelled out epithets, she would not shoot. But if he had a gun, or tried to climb into the room, or if she saw fire—

"Let me in!" the man said at the window. He tapped hard, but not enough to break it. Gloria's plans left her—trigger finger tightening—

"It's Waymon!" Miz Lottie said.

Before Gloria could move, Waymon already had coaxed the window halfway up. When Gloria added her strength, the window squealed in its frame, raised high enough to let wiry Waymon through. Then they both slammed the window behind them. Waymon locked it.

"Goddamn crackers—one of 'em tried to come right out back," Waymon said. He saw the gun in Gloria's hand and snatched it from her. "Girl, gimme that 'fore you hurt somebody."

Then he stumbled out of the bedroom, crashing through Miz Lottie's clothes racks. Miz Lottie called after him, but his footsteps were racing to the front of the house.

Waymon smelled like smoke.

The Klan had burned down her cabin.

Gloria guessed before she saw the thin gray smoke rising out from the McCormacks' way: her knowing sharpened and she fixed on a sadness that told her everything she owned was gone. But she had to wait through the night to hear the story because the cars and trucks never stopped their ruckus up and down the street. Gloria thought Sheriff Posey might come, but Miz Lottie told her he wouldn't unless someone got killed—and maybe he wouldn't come even then. They all agreed his deputies probably were the ones making the most noise. Gloria wondered if the deputy who had taken Robbie to the courthouse was outside with the rest of the angry white men.

When no fire came at Miz Lottie's, Gloria slept beside her in her bed fit for a queen. At first daylight, Gloria woke beside Miz Lottie and walked past Mrs. Hatchett sleeping open-mouthed on the couch and went outside to join June and Waymon on the front porch. It was strange to see so many people milling early in the morning up and down the street in the sad sunlight, no one going anywhere, men in sleeping clothes in their yards or on their front porches at every house. Waymon had put on his Army private's uniform, his Sunday clothes, and sat on Miz Lottie's porch rails with his legs swinging, a sentry daring someone to trespass. Uncle June stood beside him with his shotgun in plain view. Across the street, Clyde Frazier, the barber, had his hunting rifle, and Mr. Hatchett paced his porch with a baseball bat over his shoulder.

Lower Spruce wasn't ducking and hiding anymore. Let the Klan come, then.

The last of the whites were congregated near a truck at the far end of the street, about ten or twelve who looked like teenagers. A few of them had shotguns or hunting rifles. It felt like a standoff in a western picture, except everyone had been up all night and was too tired for shouting. Still no sign of the sheriff. But she saw the smoke's haze to the east. She turned away, trying to ignore the acid twisting her belly. "What are they doing?" Gloria asked.

Waymon spat. "Wishing they had more nerve. Look at 'em. What we been so scared of?"

"We'll see," Uncle June said, watching.

Then Uncle June and Waymon shared a look, and Gloria figured what was coming. "Just say it," Gloria said. "You think I don't see the smoke?"

Waymon looked surprised, mopping his face with a handkerchief, and soot came off. In the daylight, she could see his hair was flecked with white ash. He nodded, glad she had guessed so he would not have to tell her.

"What happened?" she said.

"I was cutting grass over on Grove Street when this guy, Jake, grabs my arm and about pulls me off my feet. Looks scared like Mantan Moreland in *King of the Zombies*."

"Just get to it," June said.

"Jake says, 'Klan's headed down to your little cousin's house.' And I say, 'Come on with me to see after her, then,' and he just looks at me like I'm crazy. These scared country Negroes, I swear. I didn't know if you was in that cabin or not, so I went as fast as I could."

He told her how he'd borrowed a friend's car and driven out in time to see two or three trucks turn off McCormack Road to the rutted dirt path that led to her cabin. He'd parked behind a fallen tree and gone the rest of the way on foot. The trucks had parked at the front of the cabin, so he'd gone around back and whispered her name, tapping on the windows. Trying to rouse her.

"I saw this on the wall and snatched it through the window," he said. He picked up a small gold-tinted picture frame he'd been keeping beside him on the railing. Mama and Papa's wedding photo had been on the nail next to the stove. The frame's glass was cracked, but the photo was untouched. Mama had a laurel wound into her hair and Papa's hair and moustache were styled like Nat King Cole's. Waymon must have carried it with him through the woods and through Miz Lottie's window and had kept it with him to give to her when she woke. Waymon had never done such a kind thing for her.

Gloria hugged him. When soot rubbed off on her, she wondered which room the ashes had come from. Which memory was touching her lips?

"That's all I got, sorry, cuz," Waymon said.

Gloria nodded, trying not to think of her bedroom, or Mama's clothes, or Robbie's toys. And the other photos, lost. Thinking would make it real. She'd promised Robbie she would bring him home, and now she had no home to bring him to. She pulled clear of Waymon's smoky scent. "Then I got the hell out of there. I stayed hid while it burned in case they'd leave—thought I could go in and save some things—but they stayed to watch. All of 'em took bets on if you were hiding and you'd come running out on fire. 'She'll come through that window.' 'No, it'll be the door.' I tell you, if I'd had June's gun—"

"We'd *all* be burned up," Uncle June said. "Or swinging from a tree."

"Red McCormack finally drove out, told 'em to go home 'fore they burned down his turpentine farm. He was madder'n a hornet. He had a truck, made 'em douse it with water."

"Dumb as hell, setting a fire so close to McCormack land," June said, shaking his head.

"Did he ask after me?" Gloria said.

"Nah—they just said, 'Nobody's home.' But I didn't know my own self 'til I saw you."

They fell into a hard silence, all of them realizing how close she'd come to dying. What would the men have done to her if she'd tried to escape? Or if they'd seen Waymon? Gloria let herself remember Mama's bookshelf behind the dinner table—her Zora Neale Hurston, W. E. B. Du Bois, Langston Hughes, Lewis Carroll, and Anna Julia Cooper books, some of the pages marked with old receipts, grocery lists, mementos. Gone. Gloria would remember one shelf, one cabinet, at a time. That was as much as she could let herself think of it. Already, her stomach was withered.

Uncle June reached over and tousled Gloria's hair like a boy's and Gloria ducked her head away. "We can't take none of it with us," he said. "That's what I'm always tryin' to tell Mama."

"Shoot—one match and Mama's house would go up like the

Fourth of July," Waymon said, peeking over his shoulder at the window, not wanting Miz Lottie to hear.

"Mama all right?" Uncle June asked Gloria, already moving on from the fire.

Gloria nodded. "Sleeping."

"Then we blessed it wasn't worse."

"Aw, shoot," Waymon said, peering down the street. He jumped down from the porch.

At the intersection down the street, Sheriff Posey's car was pulling up beside the pickup truck. His sheriff's car had a gold stripe across the side that made it noticeable from a distance, shiny in the sun. His lights and siren weren't on.

"Took his damn time," Uncle June said.

"He's prolly the one sent these crackers out here," Waymon said. He whistled to the neighbor and pointed toward the sheriff. Up and down the street, the men lowered or hid their weapons. Grudgingly, June set down his shotgun across Miz Lottie's empty porch rocker, out of sight from the road.

Sheriff Posey wanted to run for governor one day, or so Miss Anne said, and he comported himself as if he already had the position. He wore a dark suit and tie, with only his gray Stetson as his police uniform. He walked down the street instead of riding in his car, touching the brim of his hat as he passed one house and then the next on the way to Miz Lottie's. The Hatchetts' big-bellied yellow hound followed him, sniffing after his two-toned boots.

"Shouldn't y'all be gettin' ready for work?" Sheriff Posey called out as he walked. "Kinda late in the day to be out on the front porch, ain't it?"

No one answered him.

The air was already hot before 7:00 a.m., so Sheriff Posey was sweating by the time he reached the end of the street at the edge of Miz Lottie's grass. He folded his suit coat over his arm.

His face looked as if he were smiling even when he wasn't. A face where you couldn't guess his age. The broken living room window was staring right at him, but he ignored it.

"They'll be looking for you at the mill any minute, J.W.," Sheriff Posey said to Uncle June.

He did not greet Waymon or speak to him, and Gloria was glad. Waymon had bowed his head to hide his glare, but he might say anything. Gloria kept quiet too.

"Can't leave my godmama's house with hooligans breaking windows up and down the street," Uncle June said. "We've got property damage all up and down. They were shoutin' and raising a ruckus all night."

Sheriff Posey glanced back at the pickup truck and the gathered white men and boys as if he had just noticed them. "Don't you worry none about those fellas back there," he said. "I'm sending them back on home."

"You send 'em home, Sheriff, an' we'll go to work all right," Uncle June said. Gloria wondered when the sheriff would say something about the fire.

Sheriff Posey sighed. He took off his hat and rearranged it on his head. Gloria understood why he was nicknamed "Bird"; he was fidgety, his eyes skirting here and there. "From what I can gather . . . lots of folks are wondering why Robert Stephens hasn't been brought to justice. That was a nasty business, what happened at Pixie's. But here we are, a year later—and no trial. If you could help us find him, I'm sure they'd settle down."

Now he was looking straight at Gloria.

"He didn't do what they say—everybody knows it." Gloria had been afraid to say it to the judge, but Gloria was too weary to be afraid. She had lost Papa, Robbie, and her home. What else could they take?

"That's what the trial's for," Sheriff Posey said. "She'll say her side, he'll say his."

Waymon chuckled beside Gloria, almost out of her hearing. No jury in Gracetown would side with Papa's word over a white woman, even if half the town knew she was lying.

"We ain't seen Robert Stephens since he left," Uncle June said. "Might be in New York."

"I hear Chicago," the sheriff said.

"Then you know better'n I do, suh," June said.

"He might be out in California," Waymon said. "Lotsa folks go out there too."

Sheriff Posey gave Waymon a sour look. "War's been over for five years, boy." Miz Lottie was right: few things riled white men more than a black man in an Army uniform. Maybe it was knowing they might have killed white men overseas, even if they were Nazis. Or the white girlfriends in France so many Negro soldiers had stories about.

"Yessir," Waymon said. "But looks like a new war's comin'."

Sheriff Posey's lips formed a tight line and his face got redder. Before he could say anything, Uncle June said, "Papers say Korea's heating up."

"Then both of you go on and re-enlist," Sheriff Posey said. "Anyway, you should all think real hard on getting out of Gracetown 'til this business with Robert Stephens is settled. Take this gal and the old woman too. Nights will get a whole lot quieter for everyone in Lower Spruce."

None of them answered. Mild voice or not, they knew the sound of a threat. Gloria was so angry that her teeth clamped tight. Sheriff Posey backed up a step, as if he could see Uncle June's shotgun waiting on the rocker. Or the little peashooter in Waymon's pocket.

"By the way," Sheriff Posey said to Gloria, "I'm sorry to report there was a fire last night. Looks like your daddy's house got burned to the ground. Nothing but ashes left. Thank goodness you were here—safe and sound. I'm guessing maybe you left something cooking on the stove? Those grease fires get out of hand fast."

"Wasn't no grease fire," Waymon said. "Ask Red McCormack. Might be he saw Mister Earl and some swamp boys out there last night." He didn't say Klan, but he didn't have to.

Sheriff Posey froze, surprised. He wasn't used to answers to his lies. He turned to scan the street, where everyone was posted on their porches or by their windows. Miz Lottie and Mrs. Hatchett were awake now, listening by the living room's broken windowpane. Sheriff Posey suddenly busied himself with wiping his shoe in the grass. Gloria hoped he'd stepped in dog shit.

"Y'all heard me, now," Sheriff Posey called out. "It's time to get dressed and out to work."

No one moved or answered him. He hadn't come to hear their complaints about broken windows or threats keeping them up all night. He hadn't come to promise justice for the fire.

Sheriff Posey went on, his voice angrier. "If I come back and see y'all here in an hour, I'll have my deputies run you in for vagrancy. See how you like it when you get locked up like her brother. And locked up is where he's gonna stay—until someone helps us find his daddy." He spoke more loudly so the crowd of whites could hear at the end of the street.

Gloria was so angry, the world went red. Then Sheriff Posey turned to look at her—and winked. A true politician, he was performing for his audience.

"Be smart," Sheriff Posey said, gentler. "I'll see he makes it to trial and the trial's fair."

Sheriff Posey took his time during his long walk back to the intersection, careful not to show fear. As he walked, he signaled to the waiting white men and boys at the end of the street. Most of them climbed into the truck, and a few walked to their cars. A chorus of car doors slammed just out of sight.

"Fool," Miz Lottie muttered from the window. "Ain't fit for a badge."

"You shouldn't have named Mister Earl," Uncle June chided Waymon. Mister Earl, who ran the tack and feed, was Klan to his bones. Negro farmers drove to Marianna or Quincy when they needed feed, fearful Mister Earl might poison their stock.

"But I did it, huh?" Waymon shrugged. "He's the sheriff, ain't he? Fighting crime?"

"Now *you* sound like a damn fool."

Slowly, as the whites left, neighbors waved at June and went inside.

Gloria had not moved since Sheriff Posey's wink, rigid with anger. But she realized she was grateful to him for confirming everything she had learned yesterday: Gracetown would not free Robbie. She could stop wasting her time with lawyers and judges.

Gloria waited until she saw the sheriff climb into his car, and then she said, "Uncle June, you worked at the Reformatory. Didn't you?"

Uncle June's jaw tightened. He wasn't proud of his time at the Reformatory. He'd never told her what he'd done, but she felt something near his mind almost as bad as his war memories. Worse, maybe. "Few months," June said, voice low.

"So you know how boys would run sometimes."

Uncle June looked at her. "If they wanted to get whipped, shot, or ripped up by dogs." Knowledge of things he'd done flared quietly, but she didn't want to know. Not yet.

"But those boys . . . they didn't have help, did they? They didn't have someone who worked inside once who could tell them how to go. Or someone to drive them away once they were out."

Waymon let out a joyful hoot, patting Gloria's back too hard. "You sho' is kin to Robert Stephens. I'll say that much."

June glanced back at Miz Lottie. If he was looking for an objection in her face, he didn't find one in Miz Lottie's steely eyes. "Told you," Miz Lottie said to June. "She's just like Bob and her mama."

June turned back to Gloria. "Naw, I guess they didn't have nobody helping them like that."

Gloria gazed at the smoke rising where her home and family had once lived. For the first time, she understood the liberation of having nothing left to lose.

"We're gonna help Robbie run," Gloria said.

"'Bout time," Waymon said. Maybe he and Uncle June had argued about it already.

Uncle June glared at the morning, making sure the last trucks at the end of the street had driven away. "It won't be pretty. We can't count on no one else. We sure we're ready for that?"

"Damn right," Miz Lottie said.

Deciding was that easy. But the rest, Gloria knew, would be, oh, so hard.

25

Miss Anne showed no surprise, only relief, when she opened her kitchen door and saw Gloria waiting on the rear stoop. Without a word, she stepped aside to let Gloria in, lingering to scan her backyard for spies watching beyond her prize rosebushes that ringed the house. The kitchen smelled like brewing coffee, but no one else was up. Only Fred's wife, Nell, had a job, but Miss Anne always got up early and dressed as if she expected visitors. Gloria could tell by the stricken look on Miss Anne's face that she knew about the trouble on Lower Spruce, and she might even know about the cabin. But Miss Anne didn't say anything, gently closing and locking her door with a sad sigh Gloria barely heard.

"Can I use your phone?" Gloria said, keeping her voice low. "I want to call that place. The social worker said I have to get on a list to see Robbie on visiting day."

Miss Anne didn't ask why she couldn't use the phone at Miz Lottie's house. Instead, she led Gloria to the wooden telephone chair just beyond the kitchen entryway. She gestured for Gloria to sit down. She didn't want to be too loud either.

Miss Anne picked up the handset on the small tabletop and dialed the operator. "Hi, Maddie," she said, and Gloria thought about how all the Gracetown ladies knew each other and Miss Anne was friendly with the woman who had lied about Papa too. "Good to hear your voice, too. Gracetown School for Boys, please." After the operator's answer, Miss Anne handed the receiver to Gloria.

The ring was loud and grating, as ugly as the place itself.

When the phone stopped ringing, Gloria noticed tears in Miss Anne's eyes. But no time to worry about it; the woman who'd answered was already in a bad mood, and she was repeating herself because Gloria missed what she'd said after the distraction of Miss Anne's tears.

"I'd . . ." Gloria straightened her shoulders to sound more confident. "I need to make an appointment on visiting day, please."

"Your name?"

Gloria's confidence melted. Not for the first time, she wanted to lie. "Gloria Stephens," she said. "I'd like an appointment to see Robbie Stephens, please." *Robbie*, not Robert. Not Papa.

In the long silence, Gloria noticed Miss Anne flick a tear away while she pretended to straighten an old framed map of Florida hanging on the wall.

"Too late to book an appointment for tomorrow," the woman said. "Tomorrow's full."

"But . . . the social worker, Mr. Loehmann . . . he said I could see him." Loehmann had also said something about how she would need to rush to make an appointment, but she'd been so busy with Live Oak and John Dorsey and the courthouse and worrying about Lower Spruce and her cabin burning down that she'd forgotten to plan for visiting day.

"Not tomorrow you can't," the woman said. "I don't care if the man on the moon says it. You'll have to wait a week." She was so snappish that Gloria thought she might hang up on her.

"Can I get my name on the list for next week?" Gloria said, biting back tears. This was wrong in every way: she wanted to see Robbie *tomorrow* to tell him he would be all right because they were going to figure out how to break him free. She had hoped she might even be able to share seeds of the getaway plan Uncle June was mulling over based on what he remembered about the grounds. Uncle June had promised to help her draw a map.

The woman's voice became muffled, and Gloria realized she was talking to someone else, muting the phone. Then she was back. "Oh no—we don't take new appointments until Monday. And you have to come in person to put your name on the list."

Drive to that awful place just to put her name on a list? The Gracetown Reformatory was a *state* school, not just for the county. Parents who lived hours away couldn't be expected to come in person just to make an appointment for a visit. This woman didn't *want* her to make an appointment. The woman probably expected Gloria to be too scared to come in person—and maybe she *should* be scared.

"I can't make an appointment to see my twelve-year-old brother until Monday—for *next* week. And I can only make an appointment in person," Gloria recited, to make sure Miss Anne heard. Miss Anne's mouth dropped open, indignant.

Not liking the sound of her own words, the woman hung up.

Gloria wanted to scream or cry, but somehow she only slipped the phone back to the cradle, her hand trembling with rage and disappointment and too many other emotions to name. She thought of Mama's photo albums and Sunday dishes and carefully folded hand towels embroidered with strawberries she'd kept in the drawers by the sink burning in the fire and could barely catch her breath.

"You lure a fly with honey, Gloria," Miss Anne said, her voice sounding far away inside Gloria's boiling thoughts. Siding with a stranger. Of course. "I only mean, you know how—"

"Yes," Gloria said, "I know what you mean. I'm supposed to pretend like it's fine."

"I know it's not fine," Miss Anne blurted. "Fred came home drunk as a skunk a couple hours ago. He was out all night in Lower Spruce. He told me he went to see it didn't go too far, but I don't believe it and I'm so ashamed. Daddy would . . ." She didn't finish, wiping away another tear.

Fred had always been trash. Mr. Powell had known it better than anyone. Gloria was not surprised and had nothing to say, so she stood up to leave.

"Wait," Miss Anne said, grabbing her arm, and Gloria's flesh turned taut as she waited for Miss Anne to go on. Miss Anne braved the anger in her eyes. "What will you do now?"

"Miz Lottie can drive me," Gloria said. "I have to see Robbie. I have to get on the list. I won't wait until Monday."

"I don't think you should go there, Gloria," Miss Anne said. "I think you should keep out of sight altogether for a few days." She hushed her voice. "Is it true you hired a communist lawyer with the money I gave you? And went to the courthouse?"

"The NAACP isn't communist," Gloria said, yanking her arm away. "You sound just like all the rest, Miss Anne. And that lawyer didn't charge me a cent."

Miss Anne's eyes fluttered with embarrassment. "My phone was ringing off the hook last night from people asking me about you and a lawyer at the courthouse," Miss Anne said. "Gloria, who was that you mentioned on the phone? Mr. Loehmann?"

"He's the social worker who drove Robbie to the Reformatory. He's from New York."

"*Yes*. I know that name. Chan and I went to a meeting of Christians and Jews in Tallahassee, and I think he was there. His wife's name is Rachel, if they're the same ones. They must be. She was telling me how her kids get teased. Let me call her. Or, better yet, I'll try calling him. Please let me do something to help."

Gloria didn't remember Loehmann's number or have his card, but she remembered the agency he worked for, so Miss Anne took Gloria's place in the telephone chair to try to get through to him. Gloria knew she could make the tedious call herself, but she was tired. *They wear you down one wrong at a time,* Mama used to say.

"Yes! Mr. Loehmann," Miss Anne said, so giddy that she nearly giggled. She clutched the bulky phone receiver close to her ear. As soon as she introduced herself, Gloria heard Mr. Loehmann's faint voice say, "Why yes, Miss Powell, it's indeed a pleasure," like he was Cary Grant at a cocktail party. He went on some about his wife, but Miss Anne cut short their small talk. "Mr. Loehmann, I have a frustrating dilemma . . . It's about Robert Stephens Junior, the boy at the Reformatory. I have his sister, Gloria, here with me . . ."

The line went silent as he listened.

IIIIIIIIIII

David Loehmann's fingers tightened across his coffee mug when Anne Powell mentioned Robert Stephens's name.

The son's name carried his father's every bit as much as Anne Powell's name carried her late father's in the circles he was navigating in Jackson, Gadsden, and Leon Counties. Rachel couldn't stop talking about how kind Anne Powell had been to her, that they might actually have *lunch* at the Silver Slipper, like it was an invitation to the White House. Driving home from that meeting, they both had confessed they finally felt a slim claim to their community, a promise to the end of their sons' misery at school, at least one day. Bit by bit, they might fit in.

His heart had soared at the sound of Anne Powell's voice ("Wait until I tell Rachel!")—until she said why she was calling and he realized her call might be related to the gossip about Klan activity and a fire in Gracetown last night. As he listened, Loehmann massaged his temples with his thumb and index finger. His heart quickened in his veins beneath his skin.

"Is that right?" he said, his mouth dry. "No, that's not the procedure. She should have been able to get on the books by phone." He hated his perfunctory words, as if the issue were banal bureaucracy and not the lingering stranglehold of the Confederacy.

"We're hoping you can help us," Anne Powell said. "This is a terrible ordeal for them."

"Of course!" he said brightly. "Anything I can do." *Shit.* He had made a promise now.

She went on: "Mind you, nothing has been proven about the accusations against his father." Loehmann was shocked to hear his doubts about the case against Robert Stephens echoed by a woman, especially a white society woman. "Many of us here . . . believe he's innocent. But that's not even the point. This is a child, and he needs to see his family."

"Understood."

"Can you get her on the list for tomorrow?"

"Miss Powell, I certainly will try."

"I've known him his whole life. He's a good boy, Mr. Loehmann."

"He seemed like a fine boy to me too." *Ask her. Ask her about it.* His tongue felt bloated and dry. "I heard . . ." How could he put it? Were there polite words for *siege* and *terrorism*? ". . . there was some excitement last night?"

I heard there was a rainstorm. I heard the new DeSoto is out. I heard the Dodgers lost in extra innings. I heard the Ku Klux Klan nearly burned down the colored neighborhood in Gracetown and I'm afraid they'll come for my family next.

"Yes," she said, clipped, but did not elaborate. "That's all the more reason we need your help. I'm worried about his sister's safety. She looks like she hasn't slept in a month. She only wants to see her brother and make sure he's all right. I can go with her—"

"No," Loehmann reminded her. "The visiting areas are segregated by race."

For the first time, she went quiet. "Even if I want to see him too?" She'd grown up in the Jim Crow South her whole life, and she sounded like segregation was just dawning on her.

"Yes, Miss Powell," he said. "You too. *Colored* means colored unless you want to apply for an exception from the warden, and I don't recommend we involve him. Let's try hard not to." Too late, he thought to jump up and close his door, the receiver's wire tugging across his neck.

His colleagues were fielding calls about other families' miseries, but you couldn't be too careful.

She sighed. "I can only imagine what you think of us down here."

"Segregation isn't unique to the South," Loehmann said, thinking of how often he'd seen colored children chased from his Lower East Side library. "Just . . . more flamboyant."

She gave a thin, sad laugh. "That's a way of putting it, all right. I'll tell you honestly, Mr. Loehmann . . . this doesn't feel to me like the country we say we are."

"No," he said. His head slumped at the memory of the WHITE ONLY signs he'd had to explain to his boys, and they'd said, *But isn't that like the Nazis?* And how could it be so? And why didn't they just take the signs down? Loehmann would have said so much more to Anne Powell if he hadn't been worried J. Edgar Hoover might be listening. Rachel thought it was a silly worry, but it wasn't silly to him. His cousin Josh, a screenwriter in Los Angeles, had just been thrown in jail for refusing to testify for McCarthy's witch hunt for radicals and communists. You're a radical if you sneeze, Josh had complained at his father's funeral.

"Anyhow, he doesn't belong in that place," Anne Powell said. "Maybe no children do. Locking up children is barbaric."

"I agree." He had so much more he could say! According to the files he'd studied after he was hired, the Gracetown Reformatory had been riddled with complaints since the day it opened. Loehmann realized he had lied to that child while he'd driven him to that place. He'd lied to himself. The Reformatory was still flogging children when the state had outlawed flogging adult prisoners years ago. Warden Haddock often lashed those boys personally—and he did far worse, if the whispers were true.

"I'll call the warden's secretary right now," he said.

By the time Loehmann hung up, his nervousness had transformed to resolve. Smart people of good conscience lived everywhere, if only you looked for them. No wonder Rachel had been so excited when she showed him the bulletin about the meeting. He'd spent his childhood on picket lines with his father, but instead of feeling inspired like his brother, he'd noticed the toll at home. At his father's funeral, trying to collect his favorite memories, he always came back to that Dodgers game because there had been *only* the Dodgers game, unless he counted the silent dinners with his father's thoughts miles away. How could Loehmann have married Rachel if he thought he could do that to her? Or to their boys? If he were labeled a radical, God only knew what could happen to his family. The deputy in Gracetown practically had called him a commie on sight.

But doing nothing wasn't a choice anymore. After a year of keeping most of his thoughts to himself, he had an ally. So he dialed the number for the Reformatory.

Doris, Haddock's secretary, could be standoffish, but sometimes she cracked a smile when she saw him. Without any fuss, he would ask Doris to add Gloria Stephens's name to the next day's visitors' log—and the old woman too. The log was on Doris's desk, so all it would take was a flick of her pen. She might grouse about the short notice, and he would smooth it over with a joke. Like always.

The phone stopped ringing, but no greeting came.

"Hi, Doris, this is David over in Children's Services," he said.

The line was still silent, although the silence was alive. Someone breathing?

"Hello? Doris? This is David Loehmann. I'd like to get Gloria Stephens on the visitors' log tomorrow." He sounded less casual the second time, more like reading lines from a script.

"You don't say." The voice was a deep-voiced man, not Doris. Not close to Doris.

Breath rose so quickly in Loehmann's throat that he almost gasped. Haddock! Until that moment, Loehmann hadn't realized that Fenton Haddock honest-to-God frightened him, but his fingertips tingled across the phone's receiver. He'd only dealt with the man twice: once to introduce himself, and once to bring a mother's complaint that her son's back was scarred from a beating. Both times, Haddock had listened intently and smiled wide, but his pale blue eyes had twinkled with an unsettling blend of bemusement in one blink and barely muted rage in the next. A likely anti-Semite, yes, but Haddock's eyes brought to mind a word he'd learned in Intro to Psychology at NYU: psychopath.

"Good morning, Supervisor Haddock," Loehmann said, trying to recover. "I thought Doris must have a frog in her throat." He had learned in elementary school that even bullies liked jokes. But not this bully. Not that joke. The silence was heavy with irritation. "We're calling to get Gloria Stephens on tomorrow's visitors' log. She wants to see her little brother."

He added *we* for extra weight although he knew his boss, Martinson, would string him up for making this call. Everyone had been talking about Gracetown over coffee that morning. The Gracetown NAACP had called to complain about the danger to children at nine o'clock sharp.

Haddock cleared his throat loudly, taking his time—mocking him, Loehmann realized.

Bastard. Haddock's reformatory was too big, had too much local influence. Made too much money. Even Governor Warren needed a drink when Haddock was on the line, his boss had said.

"Deadline's passed, I'm afraid," Haddock said with a smile in his voice.

"I know that, Supervisor," Loehmann said, although the Reformatory made so many exceptions that it was a deadline in name only. "He's a good boy, no other trouble, and it feels like Judge Morris overstepped a little here. So we're asking as a favor to the state of Florida."

His voice sharpened a bit at the end, when he invoked the state. Martinson would be livid if he had to hop on the phone with Haddock to clean up an unauthorized request. Martinson liked to save his favors.

"Well," Haddock said, and Loehmann imagined his eyes laughing at him, then glaring, "you know I'm always happy to accommodate the state, Mr. Loehmann. Two o'clock. After church. Tell her don't be late."

Loehmann exhaled with a silent prayer. "Thank you, Supervisor. She might bring an old woman with her too. We appreciate—"

The Reformatory superintendent hung up before Loehmann

could finish. Loehmann pushed his chair away from his desk to give himself a foot's distance from the telephone.

Despite the growing heat in his office from the morning sunlight filling his east-facing windows, he felt chilled to his toes.

Gloria had no time to celebrate the news of her two o'clock visiting time before a knock came at Miss Anne's front door. When the knock sounded, Gloria had barely finished the toast and orange juice Miss Anne had fixed for her at the kitchen table. Disdained, Miss Anne looked at the clock on the stove: nine thirty. Too early for salesmen and too late for the milkman.

"Someone gonna get that?" Ma Ma yelled from upstairs, excited and confused by the knocking. "Daisy's come home! Someone let Daisy in the house!"

Gloria wondered if one day she would be like Ma Ma, an old woman always missing Robert long after he was gone. "I'll go shush her," Gloria said from habit, standing up.

Miss Anne turned back to her from the doorway. "No," she said firmly. "Stay here."

Gloria sat again. Her chair gave her a clear view down the empty hallway to the living room, but the front door was out of sight to the right. Miss Anne scurried back into her view from the hidden foyer and raised her finger to her lip for Gloria to see: *Shhhhh.* Then she ducked back to open the door.

"How are you, Bird?" Miss Anne said loudly.

The sheriff! Gloria jumped to her feet and scurried farther out of sight, her back to the refrigerator door. She jumped when the teakettle on the stove whistled behind her. She reached over to shut off the burner so quickly that she nearly seared her arm on the hot kettle.

"Been better, tell you the truth," the sheriff said. Was he in the house? Would Miss Anne be clueless enough to offer him coffee or tea?

"I'm sorry, Sheriff," Miss Anne said. "Fred told me what he was up to last night, and we'll pay for any property damage. He's upstairs sleeping off whatever he was drinking. It sounds like a whole bunch of them were up to no good."

"Actually, Anne . . . I'm not here about Fred. I'm looking for Gloria Stephens. They say she works here as your house girl."

Gloria felt rocked. Wasn't it enough he'd just seen her on her front porch at dawn? Or had he been afraid to make her go with him then? Maybe he'd waited until she left. Maybe a deputy had followed her when Uncle June dropped her off at Miss Anne's in the truck.

"Is she in some kind of trouble?" Miss Anne said.

"No, but other lawmen are burnin' up my line after last night, and they say I'd better ask her where her daddy's at. Right now, this whole thing's a lost ball in the high weeds. If folks in town feel like I can't bring them justice, they try to get it their own way."

The cold seeping through the refrigerator door froze Gloria in place. She wanted to run, but she expected a deputy's knock at the kitchen door behind her.

"He rode off and left them in the night," Miss Anne said. "I'm sure she has no idea."

"If it's all the same, I'd like to bring her to my office."

He would hurt her, or another sheriff would. What if he called in the sheriff from Lake County, whose deputies had beaten confessions from three men and shot one dead in the woods? *That* got her moving. Gloria made it halfway to the back door.

"Gloria quit working for us after her brother got locked up," Miss Anne said. "I haven't seen her today."

Miss Anne was lying to the sheriff for her! And she'd said it just as smoothly as if she lied every day. Gloria decided not to try to flee outside, where another deputy might see her. Instead, she moved to the pantry, careful to pull the frayed rope handle slowly, slowly, so the door would not click too loudly into place. In the dark, tight space, her breathing grew faster. A broom handle was jammed between her shoulder blades, but she did not dare move or she would knock over the pantry's tightly packed tin cans and jars of preserves. She tried to hold her breath so she could hear their conversation through the thin wooden door.

"Any idea where she might be?" the sheriff was saying.

"I don't have the faintest, Bird. I just know she's very upset, with her brother locked up. Taking a child away from his family is excessive for a schoolyard kick, isn't it? And Lyle McCormack three times that boy's size?"

"That may be, but I don't make the law—I only enforce what they tell me to."

"Seems to me this whole fuss has more to do with Red McCormack's money and Robert Stephens Senior than it does with his children." Miss Anne's voice turned fiery in the way she usually reserved for Fred. "I'm going to write a letter to the newspaper."

"Anne, I wish you wouldn't do that," the sheriff said. "I'd hate to see you get mixed up in the hurt feelings around this whole mess. That's just pouring gas on the flames."

"I know the Stephens family," Miss Anne said. "I'm already mixed up in it. Their mother, God rest her soul, gave them both piano lessons in this room. They're like family."

"She knows more than she's saying, Anne. I'm supposed to let a fugitive run loose?"

"You don't have a case, Bird. You know you don't. Show me a deputy or councilman who thinks Robert Stephens gave her that black eye. Tad's been beating her bloody for years."

To Gloria, the floor seemed to shake. Yesterday, Miss Anne had sounded as meek as a mouse, and now she was testifying to the sheriff's face. The sheriff said something in a whisper Gloria couldn't hear no matter how she held her breath silent. Then the sheriff said, "Sorry again to bother you, Anne," and Miss Anne closed the door and locked both locks. The sound of Miss Anne's quick, rapid breathing filled the house. She sounded scared, or angry. Probably both.

Gloria didn't peek her head out of the pantry until Miss Anne came and called for her. Gloria didn't come out until she saw with her own eyes that the sheriff hadn't followed her.

"Sonofabitch," Miss Anne said, the first time Gloria had heard her cuss. Miss Anne paced the kitchen, grasping her flaring dress with her palms so hard that she might rip it. "The *nerve*. That goddamned sonofabitch. That sorry excuse for the law—"

"What did he say?"

At first Miss Anne shook her head as if she didn't want to repeat it. Gloria thought it might be something about Miss Channing. But she was wrong.

"He said, 'Remember what happened to your father.'"

William Powell had driven his car into a ditch on a rainy night, and Papa had said it was the Klan as soon as he heard the news. Councilman Powell had signed a petition against lynching and his name had been in the *Tallahassee Democrat*, not just the *Gracetown Herald*. He'd met with the governor and called the Klan an embarrassment to business owners in the New South.

"Was it . . . a warning?" Gloria said. "To help you keep safe?"

"I don't know," she whispered. "The way he said it, the way his voice changed . . . Gloria, it sounded like an actual threat. Against *me*. I'm shaking."

The sheriff was always on the side of white people, Papa had said, until white people tried to help Negroes. Miss Anne clasped Gloria's elbows, and Gloria clasped hers back. They stared at each other wide-eyed with growing understanding of how deep their troubles went.

Heavy footsteps on the rear staircase made them jump and look up. Fred was leaning on the railing halfway down the stairs, unshaven and bleary-eyed, still wearing last night's rumpled clothes as he watched them. He lit a cigarette.

"Turns out, you're not the smart one," he said. "Matter of fact, I see you're dumb as shit."

He could be talking to either of them, or both. Miss Anne moved in front of Gloria, an impulse to protect her, and for a terrible moment Gloria expected Fred to go running outside to tell the sheriff she was hiding there. But Fred only gave her a dead-eyed look, not blinking, before he turned around to go back upstairs.

26

The Reformatory

All morning, boys came to Robert to tell him their haint troubles, even the teenagers who looked like men. Even two *white* boys stole away from their side of the campus to meet him after breakfast to tell him which lockers were haunted, where they heard whispers in the cornfield, which mules could talk like humans, and which tractor powered itself when no one was driving. Robert couldn't keep track of all the promises he made to check out this place or that.

It was a fine morning until Robert saw Boone waiting by the cafeteria door with his leather haint satchel. Robert's stomach bloated into his throat when Boone gave him that too-wide grin.

"Warden Haddock's tickled to death," Boone said. "Let's head on over to that old fire spot and see what you see."

"I can't," Robert said before he'd thought up a good reason. Boone's grin vanished, replaced by glowering eyes. "I . . . need time. It's too quick. Like . . . when a car is out of gas."

Boone scowled, only halfway believing him. "How much time you need?"

Robert remembered Blue hovering over his bed like a vulture. Blue had said he would find him another haint to track, but when? "Maybe . . . only a day? A day in between. I think."

Boone leaned over so his eyes were only an inch from Robert's, as if he could see his lies. "You get *one* day," he said. "Go wash dishes in the kitchen, then. But don't you let down the warden after you got him all excited. He'll skin you alive out in the Funhouse."

Robert promised he wouldn't, but he could barely look Boone in the eye or hide the way his stomach clamped at the idea of making Warden Haddock mad.

During band practice, Mrs. Hamilton announced that they would spend twenty minutes polishing and repairing instruments, so Robert volunteered to polish the brass instruments on the rack on the rear wall while Mrs. Hamilton tinkered with the piano strings to coax them back in tune. Mrs. Hamilton was strict during practice, but she allowed them to talk during chores, so the hum of conversation started right away. When someone sidled up to Robert, he said without looking up, "No more haint stuff today. Tell me tomorrow."

"Missus H. said to put a few drops of oil on your trumpet keys so they'll stop sticking." To Robert's surprise, Redbone was beside him offering him a small plastic bottle.

Robert hesitated before he took the bottle. "You still mad?"

Redbone shrugged. "Blue said you're too dumb to know any better. So I guess not." He said it quietly, just below the other boys' playful chatter.

The mention of Blue's name both electrified and angered Robert. Blue's neck had stretched abnormally long, like an ostrich's, and his teeth had seemed sharp at first glance. Maybe Blue had been playing tricks on him, changing how he looked.

"You shoulda told me," Robert said. "I had to hear it from Haddock."

Sickly alarm rose in Redbone's face. "What you mean?"

"He showed me a picture of him from the fire. You shoulda told me he's . . . like that." He didn't want to say *dead*.

"Did you tell on him?"

Robert shook his head no, and Redbone's shoulders fell with relief.

Redbone glanced around, but the room was too noisy for eavesdropping. "You would've believed me?"

Robert couldn't lie and say he would have, but he felt betrayed. He rubbed the tarnished bell of the old bugle he was polishing almost hard enough to dent it. The bugle was just like a trumpet but without any keys. Robert could play it as easily as a trumpet, his lips tripping across the notes, but Mrs. Hamilton said it was only good for playing reveille and at funerals. She said she didn't like the sound of a bugle anymore.

"Blue said not to tell nobody," Redbone said. "He's the only one I see, mostly. He says he has to try real hard with me. And sometimes . . . I can't see his face. It's all blurry, a shadow. But with you, he said he doesn't have to try at all." Redbone ran his cloth listlessly across a trombone, and Robert wondered if he was envious over Blue.

"I wish I *couldn't* see him," Robert said. Should he say it? He felt he shouldn't, but he couldn't help himself. "You know what he wants me to do?"

Redbone nodded. "Shoot—I wouldn't."

Robert wondered if they were both thinking about the same thing, if Redbone knew about the photos Blue said the warden had hidden in his desk. "He asked you too?"

Redbone spoke from behind his teeth, nearly impossible to hear. "Oh, sure, he tried to make it sound so easy. But no way I could get close enough to get inside that desk. I told him only a fool would try it, and he said he found his fool. You let him put *you* in a trap."

An explosive clattering on the floor made them both jump. Boys laughed as a cymbal rocked from side to side with a racket before it stilled. Mrs. Hamilton called out a reminder to be careful, but she didn't sound angry. Band time was the only time they weren't scared. Mrs. Hamilton would never send one of them to see Warden Haddock. She hadn't said it, but they knew.

"You should've told me," Robert said again, bitterly.

"How'd I know you was gonna start huntin' haints?"

"*HE* made me," Robert said, not speaking the warden's name.

"Why would I want to? Boone said I had a nose for it and told him and then *HE* said I had to." Robert didn't care that he was whining. He didn't mention the warden's early-release form, but what difference did it make? He'd never had a choice with a strap on the wall.

"You got all of 'em singing your name now—the Great Haint Catcher."

"Shut up," Robert said, ashamed, then softened his voice. "They just blame haints for every li'l thing." Robert wanted to tell Redbone he'd missed him, but instead he said, "Why'd you get so sore at me?"

Redbone shoved one hand in his pocket and rocked back on his heels. "I thought . . . you would tell on Blue."

"You already told me not to talk about him. Before."

Redbone shrugged. "Sorry, but I don't know you that good yet. Well, I *didn't*."

"I *ought* to tell on him," Robert said. "After what he said about my mama."

Redbone couldn't deny it. Blue must have told him everything. "He says an eye for an eye is even in Scripture. He's mad as a hornet you put his friend in the jar. But I think if you try to do what he says . . . you could end up at Boot Hill, Robert. Buried under the ground."

So they both knew Warden Haddock was a killer. "I know," Robert whispered.

"But Blue says he'll make you pay if you *don't*."

Schoolyard taunts from a haint. If Robert hadn't been so miserable, he might have laughed.

Redbone shook his head the way an old man might. "He's helped me out of jams lots of times, but I guess a haint can't be a real friend. He don't care a lick what I say now, won't listen to nothin'. I don't know him neither, not really." Redbone's grief wavered his voice.

"I thought he was nice at first," Robert said. "Even after the freezer, I wasn't too mad."

"No one stays nice," Redbone reminded him in a faraway voice, speaking to himself just as much. "Anyhow, I'm sorry I played along when Blue wanted to trick you like he was just another kid. Nobody else could see him, and . . . I don't know, when he talked to me, I felt like more'n just another sorry nobody counting off time in here. He's been the best thing about being here. And when he tells how he dies, it's the most awful story you ever heard. I never want to see Blue go in that jar, but it's his fault we got sent to the Funhouse—not yours."

Robert nodded and savored two good breaths before his ribs started cramping again. "What am I gonna do?" Robert whispered. He didn't care that he sounded like he was crying. Redbone had heard him do worse than crying.

All around them, instruments peeped and squealed while boys enjoyed their moment without troubles. Many boys were practicing their scales like their lives depended on it.

"I dunno," Redbone said. Now his voice was an old man's too. "But we'll figure it out."

We was a mighty and beautiful word.

All around him—among the oak, pecan, mulberry, and cedar trees on the hill that overlooked his campus—Fenton James Haddock heard the complaints of the dead. The grave sites were pits in the soil imperceptible unless you knew where to look. But every insect at Boot Hill hissed in a frenzy, as if to try to drown him with their rage. A slight burning sensation on the soles of his feet made him shuffle from side to side. Oh, those bones under the soil were mad.

Lucy deviled him at home too, but his baby sister's dissatisfaction was more inchoate, veering between anger and playfulness as she'd been in life, giggling one moment and then screaming when he tugged on her thin strands of hair or slapped her cheek to make a perfect outline of his fingers in bright red. Watching her skin return to milky porcelain had been his favorite magic trick. "Fenton, why's the baby screaming?" his mother had called out to him, pretending she didn't know, unwilling or unable to rise from her whiskey nap.

In some ways, Boot Hill was the place that knew him best and honored him most. The soil recognized his footsteps and warblers in the treetops sang his name. A cloud of mosquitoes and gnats followed him, so Haddock opened his bottle of 6-12 insect repellent and lathered his bare arms where he'd rolled up his white shirtsleeves. Mosquito bumps were already rising. No matter. If angry spirits couldn't do more than rile up a few mosquitoes, let them have their taste of his blood. Fair was fair.

The slight elevation at Boot Hill gave Haddock his best view of his campus, which was why he took a long uphill walk from his office with his thermos of coffee in the mornings. He surveyed the Negro dormitories he had helped lay bricks for, the infirmary he offered patients to, the kennels (*God bless those dogs*), the kitchen (*he found one there*), the Funhouse. He could just make out the white steeple of the white boys' church past the baseball field on the far end of the campus, closer to his administration building, which he could not see from this distance at all.

Years ago, the Reformatory grounds had been half this size, and now they stretched a thousand acres between the campus and the fields. What other state-run school could boast its own printing press? The bushels of corn his boys harvested? Their famed Christmas display? How many other schools taught their boys to be bricklayers, butchers, and farmers in addition to his harsher lessons on becoming men?

And a haint was trying to wrest it all away. The mealy-mouthed governor, who grasped at his skirt after every complaint from a parent or an investigator, would try to take the school from him at the first whiff of an opportunity. Gossipers and reporters from the *Gracetown Herald* had written the governor letters with sob stories and accusations, hinting not only that Haddock should be removed but that the entire Reformatory ought to be shut down. The fire had been thirty years ago, with a second world war and the atomic bomb behind it, but the memory rang fresh at the town council and governor's office. That damned fire.

Haddock spit bitter coffee into the soil. "What'd you go and do that for?" he said.

He'd been drunk on cheap corn liquor when he lit that match. No question about it. He'd blamed intoxication, so he'd given up corn liquor and whiskey, or even wine with his dinner or a Falstaff at a ball game, suffering every missed sip. But he couldn't blame drink for how he'd balled Lucy's blanket between his hands and shut up her crying for good when he was a boy.

Even sober—and he was *never* drunk at work—he'd been furious at those boys goading and defying him when he was a dorm master with peach fuzz. He'd whipped some of them in the Funhouse two or three times over and they still kept trying to run. Since those white boys wanted to act like coloreds so bad, let them be locked up in the shed with the coloreds. Let them piss on the floor, sleep on the cold ground, and feel their stomachs howl with hunger. Let them pound on the wood until their hands bled. Let them choke on black smoke and scream until their throats burned to ash.

No, he couldn't blame the drink. Even now, knowing the consequences, he could feel the young man he'd been arguing how he was *right* to do it. For a long time after, no boy had tried to run. With all the grumblers and agitators gone, hadn't the rest fallen in line? With less energy spent on chasing runaways and more on building the school, look how far they'd come. The state football championships. The Christmas parades. God help him, if Haddock could go back in time and counsel his younger self, he might light that match stone sober.

The real truth: This Place had told him to burn the shed. From the moment he'd set foot on the Reformatory's grounds, fresh from the turpentine camp he'd hated after high school, This Place had found his dreams and shown him how he didn't need to tolerate shit from anyone ever again. This Place had shown him images of how these boys must be molded and corrected, and sometimes correction wasn't pretty.

If he could change only *one* thing, he would have kept Robicheaux from breaking that door down so the flames wouldn't have eaten his friend's face and sent him screaming in circles, clutching at his burning ears. But other than Robicheaux, God rest his soul, the memory of the fire helped Haddock sleep at night. He'd been 4-F on account of his bad knee after Grandpa thrashed him when he was ten—which pained him even now, standing so long on the hill—but he envied the men who'd traveled overseas where killing was just another day's work. Where you got a *medal* for it, if you did it in high enough numbers or with a brave enough story. He could have had a Silver Star pinned to his lapel. Instead, he was worrying about what would happen if anyone found out how he'd soaked the wall with kerosene before he lit the match.

"What you got to say now, you little bastards?" he'd called inside to them, and their pounding fists against the planks with the first wisps of smoke had rolled like glorious thunder.

No surprise that one of the haints was after him now. Kendall Sweeting, that was the one. Haddock remembered him well, with his odd, careful speech from the islands, like he thought he was King George of England. He'd seemed like a little black gnome at first, a man dressed as a boy. That fussy little imperious boy hadn't learned yet how to talk to white men and had petitioned for a meeting with him. By right, Sweeting used to say. He should meet with the superintendent *by right*. He shouldn't be at the Reformatory *by right*.

Of course Sweeting was the one. If Robicheaux hadn't held his strap hand back, Haddock might have beat Sweeting to death on the Funhouse table instead of locking him in the shed. All week long he'd surveyed those boys' faces, white and colored, and collected each one who'd cut their eyes at him, or laughed at the wrong time, or was uppity like Sweeting. Twenty-five of them all locked up in a hot house with no windows, built of aged but sturdy

Florida pine. When Robicheaux and the others wanted to tip over to Leon County to get beer, like they always did during the Friday night shift, Haddock had stayed behind with his private corn liquor jug.

That was his favorite time, when almost everyone was gone. The time he came alive.

After the fire, when the burned shell of the shed still smelled like frying ham, he'd photographed Sweeting at the center of the circle with other boys fanned all around him, and no hint of a burn on his skin. No blisters or boils or pooling, charred blood. Haddock had expected Sweeting to sit up from where he lay and say *by right* Haddock should get the electric chair.

And Sweeting knew his weakness: the photographs. Haddock could have buried them in the woods, or put them in a safe-deposit box in the bank, or even under the loose floorboard in his bedroom closet he used when he brought them home over a long weekend. But he liked to see at least one photo *every day*, or all of them if he could, and that meant keeping them at arm's reach—at his desk. Sometimes he only unlocked the drawer to see the envelope and feel the rush of electric joy, but it was so much sweeter to peek in for a glimpse in the light. He often woke from nightmares about his photo collection blown up as banners, swinging from the telephone poles at the Christmas parade, the whole town gasping and pointing, but he could not let go of the fire. The dead boys. The boys without clothes.

The first time Haddock had found his desk drawer not only unlocked but *open*, he'd thought he'd only been careless and cursed himself the whole day. The next time, he found his packet of photographs sitting on top of his desk in plain sight—and he'd known it was the work of a haint. But the third time, the boldest time, Sweeting had shown himself by leaving *his own photo* in the ring of charred bodies on top of Doris's desk. She would have been sure to see it if she hadn't arrived late that morning on account of her son's visit from the doctor for flu.

Haddock had never come closer to a heart attack, pain cramping his chest. Sweeting's photo had been on top, but even worse ones were tucked underneath. Haddock had barely had time to sweep the photos under his arm before the dorm masters came in for their staff meeting and Doris arrived red-cheeked and full of apologies. He'd asked Boone to lay fresh haint traps under his desk without telling him why, and since then his photos had been untouched.

But Sweeting, a ghost, had almost ruined him.

Three times this year alone, Haddock had taken his packet of photographs to the clearing in his yard where he burned leaves each fall, ready to drown them in gasoline. But he'd only made himself burn *one*: the boy he'd thought was only unconscious before he pulled off the boy's pants and grabbed a broom handle to teach him a lesson. That was the only memory that made Haddock feel sick; he should have checked for a pulse first. He was not a desecrator of corpses. *He* had been the one to dress Lucy with such precision and detail for their immortalized photo with her on his knee, her dress sleeves puffed just so, her wispy hair brushed and neat.

Could Mother? His father? Certainly not. They couldn't even watch him dress her, just as they'd never noticed her enough in life. *He* had more respect for the dead.

Rustling fluttered above him. Squirrels? Haddock's ear caught any sounds of scurrying or motion. Sometimes boys hid in the trees to elude the dogs, or while they waited for the nerve to run. And sometimes—

A muffled *CRACK* sounded high above Haddock, left of him, and he raised his eyes just in time to see a sharp branch from a nearby pine come flying toward him from above like a spear, heavy with green needles. It stabbed the soil at least six inches deep barely a foot from him, standing as upright as the broom handle until it fell over from the needles' weight. It was a long branch—four feet tall. It would have hurt him, maybe killed him, if he hadn't dodged it.

Although his heart was wound up, his breastbone constricting enough to notice, Haddock laughed. He backed away from the canopy of treetops overhead until he found clear sky, slightly unsteady on his feet.

"You there, Sweeting?" he whispered. "That was you, wasn't it?" Another hearty laugh swelled from his chest. He ignored the barely hidden hysteria in his own voice. "I'm not gonna let you do that, son. You're not gonna kill me or drive me crazy. If Lucy couldn't do it after all these years, you don't stand a chance in hell." But his voice quavered.

He might be surrounded by them. How many *were* buried out here in the woods? Haddock was glad to see the white truck pulling past the colored boys' dorm below, headed toward the rutted path to climb up to Boot Hill. The truck rounded the red-clay walking path flanking the Negro schoolhouse toward the mudhole, gaining speed as it got closer. Good ole Boone was on his way.

Boone had called him at home at dinnertime last night with the news: Robert Stephens caught a haint. On the first try! Boone had helped Haddock set traps over the years, and occasionally they'd seen tiny dust piles waiting the next morning that might be a haint, or might just be plain dirt. But Boone had said, *Boss, it was the damn'dest thing I've ever seen.* And the grandson of a bona fide Gracetown-roots woman had seen a lot.

"We've got a haint catcher now," Haddock whispered to the woods on Boot Hill, his nervous smile splitting into a grin. "Drop those branches while you can—maybe break a window in that truck when it gets here. Hell, have a damn ball. But you're gonna be in my jar soon, along with all the rest of you. Then what will you little bastards have to say? Huh?"

He raised his voice at the end, more anger than mirth, and a flock of pine warblers flapped away from the treetops, thrashing the branches.

Haddock's boots were still clean because he'd walked on stones and grass patches alongside the mud, but mud splashed the truck's undercarriage as Boone drove toward him on the uneven road. Haddock made his way down the deer trail to meet the truck, balancing himself on pine trunks as his knee tried to give under him. He wasn't long past fifty, but he could already imagine a time ahead when his bad knee would force him to walk with a cane. And Robert Stephens Jr. had the gall to kick Lyle McCormack—the town's leading rusher who'd already signed with Florida State—*in the knee* right before his senior year of high school. What were the odds of it, the boy appearing just when Haddock needed him most? Maybe Boone had summoned Robert Stephens somehow. Maybe they both summoned the boy together.

Boone swung his girth out of the truck by the handrail. His leather pouch was cupped in his hand instead of where he usually wore it around his neck.

"Boss," Boone greeted him, already grinning. After a haint left Haddock's photos out in plain sight, Haddock had punched the burly Negro across the jaw and reminded him of his promise to cleanse the grounds, the reason he'd hired him. Boone had averted his eyes like a whipped dog whenever Haddock came near, but now Boone's eyes were fixed with glee. If he'd had one, Boone's tail would be wagging.

"Whatcha got for me?" Haddock said.

Only a few steps uphill winded Boone. He was more muscle than fat, but he had never learned to carry his own weight. "See for yo'self, suh," Boone said. He reached into his pouch and pulled out a small tube from the high school chemistry lab. "It ain't much . . . but you'll see. Look there at the bottom."

In the past, Boone had brought him dust piles half an inch thick, but barely a quarter inch of film lay across the tube's flat bottom. Maybe not even that. But Haddock's disappointment vanished when he held it closer to his face. This *was* different, pure golden-brown dust that turned darker or lighter depending on how he angled it in the light. He had dust like this in his main collection jar, but not all of it—too much of that dust was red, like the soil on the grounds. But now he knew the difference between debris and haint dust. He wondered if Boone had tried to fool him with fake dust a time or two, but he decided to let that suspicion rest. Boone had found him Robert Stephens, and that made up for a multitude of sins.

"Told you, boss," Boone said. "In all my years, I swear, I'll never forgit that swirling from thin air. Even Nana couldn't do nothin' like it." His panting was from excitement now.

"Where's Stephens hunting today? Back in the kitchen?"

Boone frowned, his grin forgotten. His stare fell to his feet. "He said . . . he needs a day after to rest. Just one day, he said. So he'll see more." He spoke low to the ground.

"Repeat that, please." Haddock tried to keep anger from his voice, sweet as candy. Boone didn't repeat it, not daring to.

"And you said all right," Haddock said. "Like . . . a vacation."

Boone winced at the word *vacation* as what he'd done dawned on him. Haddock had told him he was in a hurry to clean out the haints. His *number one priority*, he'd said.

"I'm sorry, boss, but, yes, I did. Let me explain: he did so good at it, no trouble at all, I thought it couldn't hurt to rest him up. Sometimes Nana didn't get up for days at a time after she read cards, 'specially when folks' fortunes was hard to see. Hard on the spirit, I mean. If . . . their futures wasn't clean. So one day off, well . . . I hoped that would be all right with you. A reward."

Boone had reasons for everything he did, as diligent with a carrot as a stick. Haddock nearly had come to blows arguing with his swamp redneck cousins over the intelligence of Negroes, since white trash forever liked to say, *They're so dumb.* They'd said as much about Robert Stephens Senior when Haddock had pointed out the holes in the rape story—primary being that not a soul worth trusting had seen him with Lorraine at Pixie's that night and that Negroes were not served there. He was supposed to believe Stephens had been passing by in his car everyone knew on sight and offered a drunk white woman a ride? What Negro man in his right mind would offer a ride to any white woman, much less a councilman's girl, even if she was only Tad Hurley's mistress?

Whites thought Negroes were dumb because they didn't let them say their piece—or didn't listen when they did—but Haddock had been working alongside Negroes his whole life, and any white man who underestimated one might end up with a bullet in his back. Negroes were talented pretenders. Robert Stephens Sr. wasn't dumb and neither was his son. Maybe the boy really thought he needed a day to rest, or maybe he wanted to quit catching haints.

"Next time," Haddock said, "get my permission."

"Yessuh, boss."

Haddock tilted the test tube and the dust seemed to spark in the sun. The hairs on Haddock's neck stood tall. Overhead, pine needles hissed and swayed as if an army of squirrels were marching across the treetops. Boone looked up at the racket too. Haddock nearly warned him to watch for flying branches but thought better of spooking him. Still, Boone wrapped his arms around himself as if he were cold. He could feel those angry spirits too.

"Stephens seemed at peace with it?" Haddock said. "What he's done?"

"Seemed real proud of himself," Boone said. "He was tellin' all about it at dinner. Boys was sayin' where to find haints under their beds and whatnot. He was laughin' and grinnin'."

Haddock nodded, more at ease. That was typical of the boys: Give them special privileges and attention and they would betray anyone, much less the dead. Stephens hadn't seemed at peace in his office, but maybe he'd told Boone the truth about needing to rest. Or . . .

"You don't think one of 'em got to him, do you?" Haddock asked Boone. "A haint?" Lucy's spirit was just a baby, but she knocked picture frames off his dresser and made his bed's headboard shake. A haint or two might have given Stephens a sleepless night.

From Boone's blank face, he hadn't considered it.

"Every action, Boone, has an equal and opposite reaction," Haddock said. "That's science. And that's haints too. They ain't gonna just sit still for it. They won't be idle. If I was a haint, I wouldn't let the new haint catcher sleep another wink."

Worry crept across Boone's face. "You right. Nana used to say spirits she crossed bedeviled her sometimes."

"He might not tell you, so watch him real close. Pay attention to everything."

"You know I already do that, boss."

Out of the blue, Haddock thought of Kendall Sweeting. Almost as if the young man he'd been—the one who'd set the fire—had whispered in his ear. If any haint was troubling Stephens, it was Kendall Sweeting.

"Does Stephens have friends yet?" Haddock said.

"He stays close to Redbone—I mean August Montgomery. That's about the only one." Of course. Stephens and the bright-skinned one they called Redbone had gone to the Funhouse together on Stephens's first night. They were blood brothers now.

"That's the one we'll use, then," Haddock said. "They'll do things for friends they won't do for themselves. As long as Stephens chases haints like he's supposed to, hands off Redbone. Otherwise, Redbone pays. And if Stephens tries to cross you or con you . . . Redbone *really* pays."

Haddock could devise a number of punishments for Redbone beyond the Funhouse or more time on his sentence, especially if he used a broomstick. Or he could give Redbone to Cleo, who was happy to do anything to avoid another night with Haddock in the shed. And Cleo was good with a knife. He could rip a hog's belly from end to end without blinking.

"Only if it comes to that," Haddock said for clarity. "Don't jump ahead of me, Boone."

"Gotcha, boss," Boone said. He scratched the bridge of his nose, glancing toward the pitted soil without headstones. That was another thing about Boone: nothing that should remain unspoken needed to be said. If Haddock were still a drinking man, he'd rather share a beer with Boone over at Pixie's than the swamp scum he'd hired as dorm masters for the white campus, Negro or not. Any damn day.

"You've done real good with this one, Boone."

"Yessuh, I pegged him," Boone bragged. "He's part bloodhound. Saw that right off."

Just when you thought you understood Negroes and their place in the world, a special one came along and made you rethink everything you knew. Haddock had seen how scared McCormack and those Juniper Street blowhards looked when they heard reports of Robert Stephens and his union meetings right under their noses. *That* was power. As Gramps used to say, once you saw a talking dog, you never looked at a dog the same way again.

Robert Junior had a different kind of power. Haddock had felt an odd pull to him right away. He *wanted* to tell him things. He'd wanted to open his heart to this boy who stood one step closer to God's mysteries the way Catholics confessed sins to their parish priests. Haddock was mostly Baptist, and Baptists only liked telling other people's secrets, but Haddock had felt unburdened when he showed the Stephens boy the photo of Kendall Sweeting and the fire. He wanted to show him more—so much more. Because what could Stephens say or do? Even if he had the foolish courage to try to tell, who would believe him?

But someone *might*. And even if they didn't, any wild claims from Robert Stephens Jr. might give fuel to those who wanted to shut down his school or run Haddock away from his duty to his boys. Telling Stephens about Lucy had been an indulgence, a moral and rational weakness, like keeping the photos close in his drawer. Grief and shame stirred and tightened beneath Haddock's breastbone, the way he'd felt when he stared at the photograph of the broomstick his conscience had compelled him to burn.

Boone had his own ugly secrets from the hunts after boys ran, but Haddock didn't want to air out his new plans at this restless graveyard. He didn't want to hear his plans with his own ears. He'd told Stephens he could get an early release, and Stephens had sat there with wide, believing eyes despite Haddock spelling out to him how he'd killed Lucy—not all of the words, but enough. Stephens had seemed to know as soon as he'd seen Haddock's photo with his dead baby sister on the wall, his confession in plain sight.

Haddock had come close to confessing the first time Stephens had set foot in his office with those scrawny arms and knobby knees, pissing in his pants. On Stephens's next visit, after he *did* confess, Haddock's hand had itched with the desire to spread his entire photo collection across the desk and show each one to this boy who saw haints. If Stephens had the wisdom of a grown man, he would have blubbered, *Don't tell me no more. Please don't tell me.* A grown man would have expected to be shot on sight.

How many ghosts would Robert Stephens catch before he would have to die?

27

Robert waited all night for Blue to appear and tell him which haint he could point out for Boone, but Blue never came—unless he was the tree branch scraping against the dormitory window in the wind or the shadow that flew across the ceiling once, but it was probably an owl hunting in the moonlight. When the sky grew lighter and Redbone finally stirred and sat up in his bed, Robert gestured a shrug: Did he come? Redbone shook his head. Blue was right: he'd come up with his first haint too fast, and Boone would expect him to catch one right away. He might go to the Funhouse again if he didn't catch another one today.

It was Sunday, church day. Could he ask God to help him find a haint who deserved to go in the jar? Was it a sin to ask? The church bell tolled as if to answer him, and Robert could have sworn he felt Mama say, *It'll be all right, Robbie,* or his ears only wanted to hear her. Robert looked out for Boone, nervous, but only Crutcher came to snap his ruler against the wall to get them out of bed. After he and the other boys were in button shirts and ties—which hardly dressed up stained pants and scuffed shoes—Crutcher lined them up for the walk to the church.

"Superintendent Haddock believes the house of God belongs to everyone," Crutcher said, overhearing them as they marched two by two. "Today he'll preach the Word to you boys himself. That's the kind of man he is."

Robert knew what kind of man Haddock was. He was itching to share a look with Redbone, and knew Redbone felt the same, but they both stared straight ahead across the field that looked like a grassy version of the Red Sea between their campus and the white side.

Robert had been afraid he might go to hell for setting foot on any church on these grounds, but he would go for sure if Haddock was preaching.

"Silent reflections on God's blessings as we walk to church," Crutcher said. "No talking."

Their walk in the hot morning began, everyone fidgeting and no one speaking. Robert tried, but he couldn't think of a single blessing to be thankful for—not even Papa and Gloria, who seemed too far away to be real. Thunder rumbled above, a low growl. The sky was graying as dark, bloated clouds floated past the sun, trapping soupy heat below. Robert's armpits were drenched with sweat after only a few yards.

A colored boy stood alone in the high, empty grasses thirty yards ahead, arms outstretched like a scarecrow. He was dressed like a deacon in a dark suit, white shirt, and tie. His shirt ruffled in the warm breeze but the boy didn't move, arms frozen akimbo. Robert knew it must be Blue before he was close enough to see his face. Still, the sweat under his shirt turned cold as he and Redbone walked past Blue without stopping or turning their heads. The bell kept ringing, past counting.

"You see him?" Robert whispered. Redbone nodded.

Blue matched their pace, walking beside them—or floating, anyway. Robert looked away from Blue's bare feet skating across the grass—*flying!*—because it made him feel like he was Alice falling down an impossible rabbit hole like in Mama's book.

"Did I look like Jesus?" Blue said. "I bet I did, didn't I?"

The belly of a gray cloud sparked white. Lightning would strike them all before they made it to the church; Robert was sure of it.

"Don't be sore," Blue said. "We can still be friends. You just have to do what I say now."

Redbone made a snorting sound, and Blue looked hurt. The only sound other than Blue was the tolling bell, which finally came to a rest. It must have rung twenty times.

"Don't you want Haddock to pay for whupping you?" Blue said. "Get what's coming?"

"I need another one, like you promised," Robert mumbled, staring at the ground.

"Oh, you'll see him," Blue said. "At the church. He kneels at the altar every Sunday like he can make up for all he's done. Name's Robicheaux. He's more decent now than he was, but better to be sacrificed in a church than in the kitchen. Tell Boone where you see him—but *only* him. You put anybody else in that jar and I'll make you sorry, all right."

"What does he look like?" Robert said, impatient with Blue trying to make him feel bad.

"No talking," Crutcher called from behind them. The boy behind Robert kicked the back of his heel to shush him.

"You'll know him," Blue said while Robert limped through the pain in his foot. "Haddock's gonna be so happy, he'll think nothing can touch him. And that's when you're gonna use his spare key to find his snapshots in his drawer. And you're gonna take them. Every single one."

Robert shook his head. Hell, no. The plan sounded more dangerous all the time.

"Yes you are," Blue said in a singsong, and when Robert looked up to challenge Blue, Blue was gone. Robert couldn't guess how long Blue had been nothing except a voice in his ear.

Robert had never visited a finer church, identical to the church on the white side of the campus. The white paint looked fresh from the top of the steeple to the wide double doors. The shiny golden cross above the doors was as tall as a tree. Miz Lottie's church was filled with memories and people who loved him, but those pews were shabbier; it had only a handful of worn Bibles and hymnal books, and no stained glass rinsed color into the gray morning light.

This sanctuary had carpeting and these pews had thin cushions instead of bare wood. The church's prettiness was startling.

Inside the church, the organ set high beside the pulpit was fitted with large pipes to make it louder as Mrs. Hamilton, dressed all in white, played "Amazing Grace," Mama's favorite hymn. Robert hoped the haint Blue wanted him to catch wouldn't go near the massive pipes because he doubted Mama could resist them. Mama was probably wrapped inside the brass, making the powerful music swell. Mama had said most people didn't know "Amazing Grace" had been written by a slave ship captain who saw the error of his ways. Anyone can change with help from God, she'd said.

The first rows of pews were filled with a dozen colored employees in their Sunday best with their families, including babies. *That* was a surprise. After Crutcher led the boys to their rows, he joined a round-faced woman holding a young girl's hand and kissed her on the cheek.

Even Boone was dressed for church in a tight-fitting suit with straining buttons, although he had no family with him. Robert was sitting at the edge of his pew across the aisle, so Boone tipped an imaginary hat to let Robert know he was watching. And tapped the leather pouch hidden just under his suit coat.

Robert only mouthed the words to the hymn while the others sang. He looked up and down for the haint Blue had promised him, but the only people kneeling at the altar were two colored boys in tatters giggling while they took turns blowing on the nearest candle to make the flame dance. Even Redbone didn't see the boys—only Robert. Was he supposed to point out one of these boys to Boone? If so, which one? Maybe even Blue didn't know they were there.

"Please remain standing," an officious colored woman said at the shiny wooden pulpit, "as we prepare for a special address from Superintendent Fenton J. Haddock."

Warden Haddock appeared from where he had been sitting just out of sight, wearing a preacher's crimson robe embroidered with a yellow cross. His robe was far too short for his long legs, barely reaching his knees. Robert noticed rumbling thunder above again, closer than it had been. Warden Haddock's boots boomed across the wooden planks, then he clasped the woman's hand with a smile and took his place at the pulpit. Mrs. Hamilton's organ went silent.

"Good morning, Gracetown School for Boys family," Warden Haddock said.

"Good morning, Superintendent," the church said in unison, although Robert called him *Warden* instead of by his proper title like the rest. That was what he was, wasn't it?

"Today we greet the promise of not only a new week, but a new era," Warden Haddock said. "An era of trust and growth. An era when we can truly leave the darkness of the past in the grave where it belongs and walk together to a better future." His eyes came to Robert's and stared, and Robert's fingers tightened on the smooth wood of the pew in front of him. His knees trembled with relief when Warden Haddock looked away from him. "No more whispers. No more questions from Tallahassee. Only all of us, hand in hand, making the Gracetown School for Boys the marvel it deserves to be in this great state and nation."

Thunder outside mingled with the happy amens and applause inside the church, most loudly from the employees' pews. The grown-ups stared at Warden Haddock as if he were Jesus in the painting hanging above him—except Mrs. Hamilton, who could barely keep the scowl from her face on her organ bench. Maybe she had expected him to talk about God. Maybe she didn't know yet that Warden Haddock wasn't fit to speak God's name.

"So on this Sunday, during this moment of reflection and prayer . . ."

Warden Haddock's voice retreated into a tunnel, muffled noise, when Robert smelled smoke so strong that it stung the lining of his nose. His eyes followed thin wisps of smoke twirling beneath the pulpit and then to the left end of the altar. There, on his knees, sat a grimy white man with smoke rising from the back of his faded blue groundskeeper's uniform. His hands were clasped in prayer as he stared up toward the ceiling as if he could see the sky.

Robert couldn't help gasping loudly enough for Redbone to hear and stare at him with confusion. Robert gestured toward the praying man: *Don't you see?* Redbone leaned over slightly to look, but he only shrugged and frowned: *What?*

Robert checked again to make sure the man in smoking clothes was still there. The back of his head was peeling and burned in patches as smoke rose from his scalp. His ear was burned away. Robert squeezed his eyes shut to see if the white man's image would fade away, but the smoky smell was only stronger. A cough forced itself from Robert's throat. Then Robert whispered his name: "Robicheaux."

The man snapped his head around so fast that Robert jumped and coughed again. The man's face was shadowed beneath his forehead, so Robert couldn't see his eyes or tell if he had eyes at all. Still facing Robert, the kneeling white haint rose to his feet, more than six feet tall and growing as he straightened his spine one bone at a time. Was he *seven* feet? He looked like he could fill the church! The man's mouth dropped open in an accusing *O* that could be rage or anguish, or both. Robert tried to back up so fast that his legs caught on his pew's seat, and Redbone had to hold him steady so he wouldn't fall.

"Cut it out," Redbone hissed. "Boone's lookin'."

Robert glanced toward Boone, who was studying him with eagerness, then Robert looked back at the altar: the white man was gone, only his smoky odor left behind. Robert glanced around the rest of the church to be sure the giant white man wasn't hiding behind him.

"*What?*" Boone mouthed when Robert looked his way again.

"*Haint,*" Robert mouthed back.

"*Where?*" Boone mouthed, massaging his leather pouch.

Thunder boomed above. A window in the rear rattled. A young boy whimpered, and Robert heard the thwack of a ruler as a watcher corrected him.

". . . our shared mission to carry out God's duty to right the paths of troubled boys . . ." Warden Haddock's voice floated at the edge of Robert's awareness.

Robert raised his finger and pointed to the farthest left corner of the altar, near the gold-colored vase holding artificial flowers faded gray from time. Robert could still see the haint when he closed his eyes and remembered. Yes, he'd been standing next to the flowers.

"*Altar?*" Boone mouthed.

Mrs. Hamilton followed Boone's gaze and realized he was talking to Robert. A frown soured her face. Robert nodded to Boone, ignoring the questions in Mrs. Hamilton's eyes.

Boone jumped to his feet, making his way through his row to get to the left side of the altar. Robert hadn't expected him to move so fast or to try to catch a haint in the middle of the Sunday service. Mrs. Hamilton watched Boone with interest, trying to guess what communication was flurrying between them. From the pulpit, Warden Haddock noticed Boone's sudden motion too, but he never missed a word of his talk.

". . . through discipline and that God-given feeling of self-worth from a job well done . . ." Boone posted himself at the end of the altar as if he were only listening to Warden Haddock's talk with enthusiasm, but Robert noticed him pull out his leather pouch. Gently, like salting his food, he shook powder to the floor, checking with Robert again. Robert pointed to the space directly in front of the potted plant, and Boone sprinkled dust there too, inches to the left.

Too late, Robert remembered the boys he'd seen playing with the candle at the altar's opposite end. They were gone now, but had they been close enough to be caught in the haint trap too?

He barely had time to wonder before a horrible *SCREECH* circled the room. Robert stared with amazement while the giant haint appeared in the rear of the church on the carpeted center row, pulled backward toward the altar as if a truck were dragging him, arms flailing. His charred fingernails caught the rounded edge of Robert's pew, clasping hard, and for a horrible moment Robert thought he might climb up to sit beside him. His face was charred to the bone.

Robert pushed himself against Redbone, away from the long, scrabbling fingers. Could no one else see? Not even Boone? The warden? Robert checked the faces around him, and no one else seemed to see the terrible spectacle of the man being pulled toward Boone and his trap.

With another terrible *SCREECH*, the man's fingers wrenched loose and he tumbled to the front of the church with a *THUNK, THUNK, THUNK* on the floor as he turned end over end before he vanished to nothing. The row of candles at the altar whiffed out at once. Warden Haddock stopped in mid-sentence, and people *did* look at the aisle after they heard the thumping that might have been running footsteps, but now nothing was left to see. Except . . .

Boone was grinning. Robert followed Boone's gaze to the altar cushion, where sunlight streaming through the stained glass showed a small cloud of ash, as if someone had beaten a rug, but it swirled a spiral pattern like the one in the kitchen, all of the ash clinging and settling.

Warden Haddock was looking too from the pulpit. His face turned chalky white. "*Hallelujah!*" Warden Haddock said, fevered, raising his arms. His voice was so loud that some of the employees in the front row jumped. "A new day is arriving before our very eyes!"

"Hallelujah!" Boone echoed.

Robert was afraid Warden Haddock would ask him to stand up and point him out to the entire congregation as the new haint catcher, and then how would he meet Mrs. Hamilton's eyes ever again? But Warden Haddock just stared at the little sparkling ash cloud most of the people in the church could not see. Warden Haddock's face wrenched as if he might cry.

"Children, say 'I believe!' " Warden Haddock said.

Everyone repeated the warden's words except Robert, who could not make his lips move. "Say 'The past belongs in the past. I rebuke evil spirits who dwell in history!' "

Robert felt unsteady and had to sit down although everyone else was still standing. He was trembling like he had when Blue locked him in the freezer.

Warden Haddock whipped the congregation into a frenzy of amens and *"Yes, Jesus."* But Mrs. Hamilton stared at Robert, still trying to guess what was troubling him. She didn't play the organ again. The rest of the service passed in a blur until the congregation showered Warden Haddock with applause. The colored woman got up to make announcements.

"The following students should report to the recreation hall at two for Visiting Day . . ." Robert was so eager to leave the church that he almost didn't hear her say his name.

28

A crooked Sunday tie. A wide grin. An unbruised face. When Gloria first saw Robbie, she only let herself notice everything right with him, the things she'd prayed for since his confinement. He *was* alive. He was healthy. He wasn't babbling with fright. He was sweaty but he was clean. His cheeks *might* be fatter than the last time she'd seen him. She pinched his cheek and rubbed his knotted hair and laughed as she hugged him and swung him from side to side.

But when Robbie winced while Miz Lottie circled her palm across his back, Gloria noticed Robbie's sleep-starved eyes, his stiff shoulders, and . . . something else. He avoided her eyes.

"What happened to your back?" Gloria said. She wanted to scream and throw chairs. Had the Negro guard reading a magazine with his chair tilted halfway over in the doorway been the one who hurt Robbie? If so, she wished she could knock his chair over with her mind.

"Nothing." Robbie pulled away from Miz Lottie and sat on a wobbly chair at the wooden table meant for small children.

The visiting area was a playroom with cartoon murals on the wall and board games with torn covers stacked on the back shelf. Another colored woman was visiting her weeping son on the opposite side, and he had climbed into her lap despite the petite chair. So far, his mother just kept saying, "It's all right. God will get us through." The boy looked only nine or ten.

Robbie wasn't weeping on the outside, but he was just as miserable.

"Brought you some of your favorite food," Miz Lottie said

cheerfully, and he watched while she unwrapped her foil, which was leaking on the tabletop. "A turkey wing, greens, macaroni and cheese, corn bread. And that hunk of sweet potato pie like I promised! Didn't have to make most of it myself, the way folks brought food plates yesterday." Gloria gave her a worried glance, but Miz Lottie didn't say why people were bringing plates—because of the cabin burning down. Because of the Klan. Most of them didn't have money to give, so they brought food instead. Like a repast.

"It's Thanksgiving?" Without a smile, Robert sounded mocking.

"It sho' is for us, Robbie. We're so glad to see you."

Miz Lottie had to be instructed to leave the fork and butter knife she'd brought at the desk, so Robbie clawed into the food with his fingers. For a long time, he concentrated on eating. Gloria itched to correct him about crumbs and juice he should wipe away with the crumpled napkin Miz Lottie offered him, but the intensity of his hunger kept her quiet. She and Miz Lottie looked at each other with the same mind: *Let him eat in peace. Let him enjoy something.*

Already, Robbie was a different boy. The deputy and the judge and the warden had stolen away the brother she knew. Even if he'd been the same boy, the life he'd known was burned to the ground. What would she give to curl in Mama's lap? But she would not cry, although her insides were rending and the sobbing boy across the room captured the exact sound of her pain. She *would not* cry. Robbie was the prisoner, not her. She would walk free after their visit even if a part of her would still be locked inside with him.

"They feed you in here?" Miz Lottie said.

Robbie nodded, still filling his mouth by the handful. "Not good food. Not like this."

Gloria and Miz Lottie laughed too brightly to create a sound other than crying and the sad pattering of rain against the window.

"At least he's got his appetite," Miz Lottie said.

"They let me work in the kitchen. Well . . ." Then he stopped, not wanting to tell.

"What, Robbie?" Gloria said, leaning closer.

"I had to pull weeds in the cornfield two days. But then I got back in the kitchen."

Gloria felt rage again, remembering the boys she'd seen loaded on trucks as labor, but she made herself smile. He knew where the cornfield was. Good. That would make it easier to help him understand the plan Uncle June had worked out with her.

"What do you know about a kitchen?" Gloria said, making small talk. "You're not back there cooking, are you? No wonder you're so hungry." Robbie had sometimes helped Mama stir flapjack batter so he could lick the bowl, but he was a stranger in the kitchen.

There! A small smile peeked from the corner of Robbie's mouth. "Nah. Just dishes."

But it wasn't just dishes. Every word Robbie spoke rang with deliberate silences. Gloria couldn't contain her question anymore: "They beat you, Robbie?"

He looked up, startled. She saw him want to lie, but that was the thing about her and Robbie: he could lie to Mama and Papa to keep out of trouble, but not to her. Maybe it was because she so often knew things without being told, so why lie?

Robbie nodded. Under the table, Miz Lottie squeezed Gloria's hand so tightly that it hurt. "Bad?" Gloria said.

Robbie shrugged. He didn't want to say how bad with Miz Lottie there. "Where? Your back?"

Robbie nodded again. "It's not just me," he said. "Lots of boys get beat."

Gloria stood up so quickly that her knees banged against the tiny table. After a glance at the doorway where the guard still sat tilting back on a chair, she went to Robbie and lifted up the back of his shirt. At first she didn't see any evidence of a beating, so she lifted higher—revealing crisscrossing patterns of at least a dozen lash marks. The blood had dried, but thin scars remained. The grooves seemed shallow, so maybe they would heal. Maybe he would not carry the marks the rest of his life. If not for last night's meeting with June and the Bible in Miz Lottie's lap, Gloria might have stormed to the husky Negro man guarding the door and said things she would regret. Instead, she took a breath to make her hand stop trembling as she touched her brother's skin.

Miz Lottie looked to Gloria's face for her reaction, but she would not lean over to look at Robbie's back. She didn't want to see. Gloria lowered Robbie's shirt with care.

"Why'd they beat you?" Gloria said.

Robbie shrugged, a kind of lie. He knew full well and didn't want to say. Gloria tried to make herself know everything, but Robbie felt like a wall. She only knew he was surrounded by danger, with no room for mistakes.

"Be sure you don't act up or sass back," Gloria said.

"I didn't do *nothing* wrong," Robbie said, his voice rising with anger. The watcher in the doorway glanced up from his reading.

"Course not, pumpkin," Miz Lottie said.

"I know," Gloria said. "I'm sorry. None of this is your fault, Robbie. Okay?"

"Two minutes!" the guard called out. Gloria panicked until she realized he was talking to the mother in the other corner, and her son wailed more loudly. Gloria hated to feel glad for someone else's sorrow, but the clock said she still had ten more minutes with Robbie and she would wade through a river of tears for every second of her time with him.

Gloria glanced back at the distracted guard again and whispered, "I talked to Papa."

Robbie's eyes grew wide. His smile beamed. "He knows?"

"Yes. And I got money to find a lawyer. So don't you worry. This will be over soon."

No need to smother his smile by telling him about John Dorsey and the courthouse and Miz Lottie's broken window, or that his baseball mitt had burned up. No need to tell him that she was on the run from the sheriff herself and was sleeping on a cot in Miss Anne's basement, where even her brother didn't know she was there.

But she had to tell him the rest. And they didn't have much time.

Gloria looked at Miz Lottie and nodded, their signal. Miz Lottie moved her Bible from her lap to the tabletop, one hand planted firmly on top. With her other hand, she pulled out the small jar of petroleum jelly Uncle June had told them to give Robbie.

"So your legs don't get ashy in here," Gloria explained, sliding the jar next to him. "And Miz Lottie wants to sing you some church songs and pray."

"I just came from church," Robbie said. "They got one here . . . kind of." He wanted to speak of it so badly that Gloria could almost see a man kneeling at an altar, a shadow. Almost see . . . something that seemed nothing like church.

Gloria stared at Miz Lottie to make sure they were ready. Miz Lottie's eyes glittered with encouragement, eyes young and defiant inside her folds of wrinkled skin. Gloria glanced back at the guard, who was staring at his watch, counting down the seconds before he would separate the weeping boy from his mother.

Gloria slid the Bible from beneath Miz Lottie's hand and slowly fanned open the pages. Miz Lottie brought this black leather-bound Bible with her to church every Sunday, although she could barely read it. Gloria saw the small crease she had made in the pages, but it wasn't time for that yet. She jumped instead to the book of John, to the passage she had underlined.

"That's time!" The guard stood up to come inside the visiting room. Gloria's heart whaled in her breastbone. She wanted to fling the Bible closed, feeling exposed, but what was wrong with reading a Bible?

The boy did not take the news well. His sobbing turned to shrieking. His mother told him he would be all right, but the guard was annoyed and pulled on him sharply.

"Lord have mercy . . . ," Miz Lottie muttered, appalled at the boy's treatment.

Gloria wanted to jump up and help his cowed mother defend

him and tell the guard to take his hands off that child, but she could only think about the Bible in her hands and the things she needed to say.

"Can you listen to me, Robbie? Every word?"

Robbie nodded. Like her, he ignored the sobbing beside them.

Gloria leaned close to him and read the passage she had chosen for their mission. " 'The Father hath not left me alone,' " she read, and Robbie blinked, both of them already fighting tears, " 'for I do always those things that please him. As he spake these words, many believed on him . . .' " She skipped a sentence and took a breath to speak the important passage as fiercely as she dared. " '. . . And ye shall know the truth, and the truth shall make you free.' "

Free. The word was breath and light. Together, they drank the word. Basked in it.

Robert understood. Robbie looked ready to tell her everything he had withheld, his wall tumbled down. Near them, the child was shrieking in terror and his mother was begging for mercy on him, but the world felt emptied except for her brother.

"Free," Robert murmured, tasting the word.

Hand still shaking, Gloria flipped ahead a few pages until she found the crease—and the onionskin-thin paper she and Miz Lottie had hidden there. She moved the Bible to show Robbie the hidden paper and its pencil markings: a series of drawings a young child might have made. A house. A tree. An ear of corn. A river. A train car.

Robbie knew then: a map! He was so startled that he jumped. On cue, Miz Lottie began to sing, her voice uneven but sure. *"Waaaaade in the water . . . Wade in the water, children . . . Waaaaade in the water . . . God's gonna trouble the waaaater . . ."*

Mama and Papa had taught them how slaves who planned to escape hid their plans in their songs. Did Robbie remember that "Wade in the Water" was a spiritual about running away? They had sung the song together in the children's sketch at their church on Founders' Day, pretending to cross the river with knapsacks across their shoulders when Mama still conducted the children's choir. Oh, she hoped Robbie remembered.

He did. He smiled only a little, but his face glowed. He bounced in his seat. Gloria shook her head, and his bouncing turned to gentle rocking.

"That's the Bad Place," Gloria whispered in code, pointing carefully at the map. "But they named it for a good place. You know what I mean? A place that's supposed to be fun, but it's not? I think you've seen it, Robbie." What kind of monstrous place would call a whipping shed the Funhouse? But that was what June had told her.

Miz Lottie sang louder. The guard was in the doorway with the departing mother, but Gloria and Miz Lottie might both go to jail if he heard a word of what she said. And who knew what might happen to Robbie?

Robbie nodded. "I been there."

"Uncle June said to tell you hi," Gloria said casually. "He said he knows the grass grows high against that fence. That fence by the bad place. Real high."

"Yeah," Robert said. He looked so excited that Gloria was afraid the guard would notice.

"Sometimes it gets broken," Gloria said. "Over by the chairs on the colored side." He nodded. He *knew* the chairs!

Robert's eyes tracked her finger as she moved it to the corncob. "There's a big corn patch out there, huh?"

"Yeah," Robert said. "I been there too."

This was the hard part. She had to be specific without getting caught, and she could not leave him with paper that anyone might see. Uncle June had said that boys sometimes tried to escape through holes in the fence, but when they got to the cornfield, they made the mistake of heading toward the road and the farms scattered at the edge of Gracetown, trying to reach the famed peanut mill to hide. Too many neighboring motorists and eager farmers were ready to collect the fifty-dollar reward if they caught a runaway, and sometimes drivers patrolled the road. Uncle June said Robert should go the *opposite* way, toward the woods. Toward the creek, which he could follow to Miz Lottie's waiting truck.

"You think you might have to pull some more weeds?" Gloria asked, tapping the corn.

"Yeah," Robbie said, but she could tell he was only playing along.

"You could get lost out there," she said. "If you go the wrong way." She dragged her fingertip from the cob of corn to a tree at the top of her map.

Robbie's brow knit with confusion. She'd been afraid to draw a forest, which would look more obviously like a map, but the tree wasn't a good enough symbol. She would just have to say it. One last glance for the guard, who wasn't visible in the doorway, and she whispered it all to Robbie in a single breath while she hugged him close: "Uncle June's gonna cut the fence by the Funhouse. Follow the cornfield fence. But out of sight. Don't follow the fence to the road: Go the other way, toward the woods. The water's only waist-high in that part of the creek. Walk up the creek. Upriver, not downriver. To the railroad trestle. The creek passes under it."

"*Waaaaade in the waaaater . . . ,*" Miz Lottie sang.

Oh! Gloria had almost forgotten. She leaned close again. "Rub that Vaseline over yourself before you go. *All over,* even your hair. Don't forget." Uncle June said it was a myth that dogs couldn't track through water, but Vaseline might help, especially if he got a head start.

"But . . . when?" Robbie whispered.

"Next Sunday. Instead of going to supper. While it's still daylight, but almost dark." Uncle June said most of the boys were so hungry that no one ran at suppertime. If he timed it right, Robbie might have an hour or ninety-minute head start, long enough to get to the truck before anyone realized he was late for dorm check-in. Before Haddock would go for the dogs.

Robbie's heartbeat was shaking his tiny body. Or was it hers?

Gloria quickly pulled away, breathless, expecting Sheriff Posey and his deputies to storm into the room.

Robert's face, so excited before, looked crestfallen.

"You can do it," Gloria said, meaning the long wait, not the escape itself. "It sounds hard but just look at the Bible." She tapped the drawing with her fingernail—from the Funhouse to the cornfield to the woods to the creek to the train car. "Just walk two miles . . . in Jesus's shoes."

"Why so long?" Robert whined.

Gloria had expected arguments, but the new Robbie had outgrown fear. Or his only fear now was the Reformatory, making an uncertain escape through the cornfield and a creek a happier thought. "We need time." She coughed the words and turned her head away from the doorway, mouthing their destination: *CHI-CA-GO*. Robert's eyes widened. "We all need to be ready, Robbie, for the day you can come home."

"*Tomorrow*," Robbie whispered.

"Too soon." Waymon and June were waiting for their wages, and Miz Lottie needed to settle her house to leave without arousing attention. They knew Gloria's two hundred and fifty dollars from Miss Anne wouldn't get them far, but it would buy them all train tickets to Chicago and lodging for at least a couple of nights. It would buy food. Then they could find Papa.

"Wednesday," Robbie bargained.

"Five minutes!" the guard called, back in place in his chair in the doorway. He was no longer reading. His arms were folded across his chest as he stared at them. Had half of her time vanished so soon, or was the guard suspicious? Dammit. The guard had given them his full attention just when Gloria wanted to warn Robbie about the danger of the dogs. Uncle June had said to be *sure* he understood he had to stay in the creek or else he would be caught. Even with the Vaseline, the dogs were likely to catch his scent as soon as he set foot back on land. He said he'd learned in the war that dogs could track *better* with a water trail.

"I know it's hard, Robbie," Gloria said. "But you'll be home soon. Be patient."

"There's haints here," Robbie whispered.

Miz Lottie stopped singing but caught herself and hummed while she tried to listen. "Ghosts aren't real," Gloria said, repeating the tired story adults told children in Gracetown to help them sleep at night. But why were adults so eager to make children forget the lessons they themselves had learned when they were young?

"That's not true," Robbie said. "You know it's not." His belief vibrated from him. "Mama's here sometimes."

Gloria had envied Robbie's stories about Mama's gentle ghost coming to visit him while he slept, since Gloria had never once sensed her. Was she too old to see haints? At least she didn't have to worry that somehow Mama's spirit was tangled in their cabin's ashes. Gloria grinned, trying to cheer Robbie, squeezing his hand. "Well, see? She's guarding over you."

"I'm not scared of Mama," he said. "It's the other ones."

"But haints can't hurt us, Robbie."

"They can too," Robbie said, certain. "They can lock you in the freezer. They can get you whipped. They can make you do things you don't want to do."

"Like . . . what?" Flashes of Robbie's terror undulated between them in mute waves.

Robbie shook his head, unwilling to go on. Back to the silence where he had started.

She would get him out *today* if she could! "Okay, Robbie . . . ," she sighed in his ear. "Friday." At least Waymon and Uncle June would have their pay by then. Waymon wanted to wait until Saturday to cut the fence, when there would be less traffic on the road, but he would have to take a chance and cut it sooner.

Robbie still looked disappointed. When they were silent for a long time, Miz Lottie stopped singing and took Robbie's hand and held it to her cheek, and Gloria held his other one. They sat in stoniness like Gloria had sat at Mama's bedside during the wake, her mind tossed, wrestling to remember who she was in this vengeful new world.

She'd expected to feel good after this visit with Robbie, or at least better. Instead, Robbie's scarred back and unspoken horrors were proof that the baby brother she had come to visit was gone. At any instant, the guard would bellow that their time was finished, and Robbie might say a stoic goodbye or he might wail and scream, or she might, or they both might. And Miz Lottie's tired heart might falter from the strain of being chased since the time she could walk. And Papa might hang from the courthouse tree.

Each one of Gloria's terrors felt as real as the ticking of the clock on the wall.

29

After Gloria's visit, Robert was so excited, he could hardly get to sleep Sunday night.

When the heat finally drove him to doze off, he had nightmares, dreaming he was running alongside the tall grass of the fence by the Funhouse, tugging the wires and searching for the hole, but he never found it—not even when his hands bled. In his dream, he was trying to catch a train on the other side of the fence, as if there were no woods or creek to cross. He woke with a gasp. Being awake in the dark was worse, searching for signs of Blue, expecting to see sharp teeth or too-big glowing eyes.

Then daylight came. A few boys in the row closest to the church altar had seen the swirling dust just like Warden Haddock had, so Robert caused a commotion wherever he went on Monday, his best day at the Reformatory so far: everyone smiling and patting him on the shoulder, more dessert than he could eat at supper (since five boys offered him their butterscotch pudding in exchange for a story), and, best of all, permission to roam the campus with Redbone in search of haints as their *only* job. Once they were free to talk, Robert and Redbone mostly made up *Flash Gordon* adventures so they didn't have to think about the dead boys.

Robert didn't mind that he had to ignore every haint who surprised him around a corner, or in a reflection shimmering in murky sink water, or barely visible in the dark spaces in room corners and cubbyholes where haints apparently liked to hide. Never mind that the scars on his back still ached when he bent down or flexed his muscles. Never mind that Boone and Warden Haddock would expect another offering soon.

Monday, nothing bothered Robert—not the cold water in the shower, or the rain-slick grass and cloudy skies, or the horrible taste of the morning oatmeal. Everything was different. Because, for the first time, *Robert knew he would not have to stay at the Reformatory for six months.* Even better, he would *not* have to sneak into Warden Haddock's drawer like Blue wanted him to; he only had to put off Blue for a few days and then he would run away.

He was going home. Better than home: he was going somewhere *new*. Chicago!

Robert had never heard of a haint being able to follow anyone out of the state. No matter what frightful images Blue tried to make him see in the cornfield or the woods, he would not turn back. He would run every step until he saw Miz Lottie's waiting truck by the railroad trestle. When Robert closed his eyes, he could see Gloria's drawings on the map.

Robert dreamed about his escape most of the day Monday while he and Redbone played hooky from the world. Being paired with Redbone to walk the campus with no one else within earshot seemed almost like being free.

But Tuesday was different.

Tuesday arrived with sad, gray light and thunder rumbling the sky, and Robert felt certain that Blue had been staring at him all night from the shadows. He couldn't *see* Blue, but he felt his stare. He called for Blue, a whisper, just in case he might offer him another haint to catch.

Robert's stomach locked up as he realized how far off Friday was, somehow farther than yesterday, more dream than real. If Blue didn't sacrifice another haint, Warden Haddock might take him to the Funhouse again. And Blue could appear at any moment making demands and threats against Mama without another offering. Anything could happen in the next three days.

And Robert felt like a kind of liar, or at least a bad friend, because he hadn't told Redbone he would be running away—or offered him a chance to come. Robert's stomach twisted when Redbone cheerfully joined him after breakfast with the pen and notepad he'd begun carrying so he would look busy while he roamed the campus with him. Robert wanted to pretend to look for haints near the Funhouse so he could check the fence to see if a hole was there. If he dared.

But Boone met them outside of the cafeteria with an assignment: he said some white boys had complained about haints on the other side of the campus, so he and Redbone should go check out the baseball bleachers. He handed Robert a written pass. "Be back by lunch," he said. "Nobody better catch y'all goofing off."

And so they were off, just like that, wandering at their own pace toward the church and the dormitories beyond it on the white side of the campus. The other boys were headed to the cornfield or the kitchen, or to the butcher's block or the henhouse, or to lay bricks, or tend mules, or one of the other endless chores they were assigned that gave them blisters, calluses, and sore muscles. But he and Redbone were lucky for another day.

And no sign of Blue yet: still more luck.

Robert almost held his breath until they were past the church and the sharp memory of the giant tumbling haint. Miniature train tracks ran between the pines, too compact for a real train. Nearby, linked mini train cars were large enough for little kids to ride in, tied to an engine car painted bright red. If the cars had been running, bells ringing, this would look like it belonged in the Main Street Christmas parade. And here it was, sitting quiet in the warm drizzle while the tracks wound in a large circle among the pine trees.

On the white side, the Reformatory felt more like a place for play than for work. The grass beyond the train tracks was clipped short just like in downtown Gracetown. Above the ridge, a fenced enclosure looked like a large dog kennel, but it was actually penning in a swimming pool larger than Robert had ever seen, equipped with a diving board. The water rippled in a kind of blue that belonged in a painting, a color of water he had never seen.

"Look at this!" Redbone said. "They're livin' like kings over here. A damn pool like they're training for the Olympics."

"They go to the Funhouse same as us," Robert said. "Die like us too, sometimes." Most of the haints Robert saw were Negro, but not all of them. White boys died here as well, even if they were allowed to go swimming or ride the miniature train first.

"So? It still ain't fair."

True, Robert didn't see as many haints on the white side. None on the train, anyway. None at the pool enclosure, with its ring of empty chairs for observers. He walked to the pool fence and peeked down as far as he could into the unnatural blue, looking for shapes that didn't belong. He even stared at the waving ripples of water from the rain droplets. The haint at the church had taught him that a haint could take many forms. Nothing unusual was in the pool . . .

But *there*—

At the baseball diamond fifty yards farther down the slope, he saw a vague image of a solitary person sitting at the top of the stands. He'd have to get closer to see if he was a haint. Probably. No one would be sitting up there in the middle of work time, even a white boy.

"You see anybody sittin' over there?" Robert said, pointing.

Redbone gave half a glance and shook his head. Robert had asked him a dozen times yesterday and Robert could tell he was already irritated by the question, even if answering it was his only real job. "You do?"

Robert shrugged, but the figure was clearer as they walked closer. A teenage boy. Robert didn't want to betray him by pointing him out if Redbone couldn't see him.

"I gotta tell you something," Robert said. The words popped out without planning.

"Tell me, then."

Robert glanced all around to make sure no one was listening. He and Redbone seemed so alone on the vast, well-tended campus that he might have tried to run right then if Gloria hadn't already told him the plan. And he couldn't trust that the haint in the bleachers wasn't a regular boy who would tell the warden. Hell, a haint might whisper his secret to the warden to get even.

"A secret," Robert said. "But if you tell anyone, we could die. Both of us."

Redbone's eyes mooned. "Worse than Blue?"

"Not worse—better," Robert said. "But you can't tell. You have to swear to God."

"Oh, okay, swear to God," Redbone said carelessly.

Robert held Redbone's arm to keep him from walking ahead of him past the pool toward the baseball field. "I mean it, Bone. Swear it on your life. Your mama's life. It's the biggest secret you ever heard."

Redbone nodded, sober. "Swear on my life," he said. "I won't tell."

Robert told him in pieces while they walked, from time to time falling silent to make sure no one was coming near. While Redbone listened, not asking questions, taking it all in, Robert told him every step of his plan for Friday, even if a hurricane came: instead of the supper line, he would go to the kitchen as if he were looking for a haint. He would go to the very back, near the freezer. And the rear door. With the supper lines in front, no one would see him leave by the rear. And even if they did, so what? He could say he was haint tracking and tell anyone to leave him be. Then he would walk toward the Funhouse like he was tracking—no big deal. Why else would anyone *want* to go to the Funhouse? Once he got there, he would hide behind the narrow building, which no one used in the daytime. And peek right and left to make sure no one was watching. Then go to the high grass by the fence and look for the promised hole.

"I wanted to try to find the hole today," Robert said, "but Boone sent us here."

"Maybe it's better to keep clear 'til it's time to go," Redbone said, voice smooth and untroubled. “Don’t draw nobody’s eye. I’ve never seen no hole. Maybe they’re gonna cut one from the other side.”

Robert had worried that Redbone would be too excited, or might get angry or scared, but he was only talking it through the way they had talked about *Flash Gordon* stories they would write. Redbone was used to laying plans. He had been laying plans for years. He thought more like Robert did than any other friend he’d had, and Redbone was smarter than any of his school friends too. It was almost—*almost*—worth coming to the Reformatory to have met him.

“I had a bad dream I couldn’t find it,” Robert confided. He’d tried to forget Sunday night’s dream about shaking the fence until his palms bled, with no way out. He tried not to believe the dream was a message from the future, like Gloria said her dreams were sometimes.

“It’ll be there,” Redbone said then, quietly. “Probably. But maybe not yet.” They walked in silence for a while, the bigness of the plan rattling their heads.

“We should use a code to talk about it,” Redbone said, “like Joe Friday. Starting now.”

“Good idea.”

The silence became solemn while they thought about it. Operation Freedom and Project Escape wouldn’t work, but those were Robert’s only ideas. He was too excited to think of others.

“Christmas,” Redbone said. “That’s what we’ll say.”

“I sure can’t wait ’til it’s Christmas!” Robert said, raising his voice so that it skated across the water of the empty pool behind them. They both laughed, although Redbone smothered his laughter behind his arm to leave no witnesses.

Robert suddenly missed Blue—the old Blue. If the old Blue were here, he would push the joke further and further, and laughing from his tummy would feel good. But they stopped laughing at the same time. The living weren’t allowed to play the same games as the dead.

"He's not gonna let you," Redbone said quietly.

"Who?" Robert said, although he knew.

"He's not gonna let you run off 'til you do what he says first."

Robert glanced around again, and no one else was in sight except the haint sitting in the bleachers. He had changed position, from center left to dead center, sitting at the top. He wasn't a regular boy for sure, since he moved too fast, but could he be Blue in disguise?

"Who says he even knows?" Robert said.

Redbone gave him a look: biting, almost angry. Then he sighed. "Come on."

"Did he say something to you?"

"He knows everything here," Redbone said. "*Everything.*"

"Are you gonna tell him?"

"Hell no, but I don't have to. He probably knew before you did, soon as they drove up. He's a *haint*. You thought you could keep a secret from him?"

Embarrassment flashed hot on Robert's cheeks. He'd misjudged how much he could evade Blue then. What else had he misjudged? Even a small thing would get him caught.

"You better be sure Haddock don't know too," Redbone said, lowering his voice when he said the warden's name.

"No chance," Robert said, his fervent hope. But what if the guards had searched Miz Lottie's Bible? What if they had found the drawing and realized it was a map?

"Better hope not," Redbone said. "I'd rather meet Blue in a bad mood than those dogs."

Friday seemed like an even more impossible time away. Robert felt dizzy.

They stood at the red clay entrance to the baseball park, facing home base with bleachers on each side of them. The haint was still there—Robert didn't look closely at his face—but he pretended to scan the places where he saw nothing but empty rows.

"How many haints we got now?" Robert asked Redbone. Anytime they logged an imaginary haint, Robert was hoping to throw Boone off the trail of real haints he'd seen. Blue had warned him not to capture anyone else, and Robert never wanted to see anyone else turned to ash before his eyes.

Redbone flipped through his notebook. "We said three yesterday."

"I could say I saw one at the pool."

"So Boone has to crawl out on that diving board to put down his dust," Redbone said, and they laughed. Laughing felt reckless, so they both stopped right away, looking over their shoulders. Again Redbone's eyes looked straight past the haint in the bleachers.

"He's gonna know," Robert said, realizing he had misjudged Warden Haddock as much as he had Blue. "When there's no ash pile, he's gonna know. We can't do it three or four times: he'll know after *one* time. He'll look me in my face and see with those . . . those . . ."

"Those devilish eyes," Redbone said, and nodded, although they didn't tell each other their stories about being with Haddock. Neither of them wanted to.

He had to get past Warden Haddock too, not just Blue. His escape was a fairy tale! "You gotta come up with a story and stick with it," Redbone said. "Say you're messed up since church. 'Cuz a spirit can't dwell in God's house. But you're praying you'll feel better." Ooh, that sounded good! Clever words flew out of Redbone's mouth like rainwater.

Robert tried the words on, remembering the frightening sight of the haint tumbling end over end down the aisle, shaking the church floor. He could sound convincing to Warden Haddock. He *could*, if it meant he could run away on Friday. He could even endure the Funhouse again if it meant he could run away on Friday.

"Do you think . . . I can do it?" Robert said. "Christmas?"

Redbone knocked his head back as if giving it thought for the first time. His pause made Robert's heart pound. "You damn well better do it," Redbone said. " 'Cause now I gotta go too."

He sounded like he had no choice, almost sad. Annoyed, even.

"Not if you don't want to," Robert said. He'd hoped that Redbone would want to come because he was a quick thinker; maybe that was why he'd burned to tell him all along. But the plan might not work for two. Gloria hadn't said he *couldn't* bring someone with him when he ran, but she hadn't said he could. She'd trusted he would have the good sense not to tell, and Robert felt he'd let her down. But he could have convinced her if he'd had time. He *could* have.

"You don't know how it goes here," Redbone said, his voice still sad. "They'd put me out in the Box. They'd whip me and starve me to try to make me tell where you went. They do it all the time when somebody runs."

"You could say I didn't tell you."

"Wouldn't matter if you did or didn't: punishment's the same. They make you an example. 'If you run away, this is what happens to your friends.' "

The worst of the worst of the worst, Blue had said. Blue had been right: Robert couldn't think like them enough to imagine how low their wrongdoing could go.

Redbone slapped his forehead with his palm. "Oh, damn. I get it now."

"Get what?"

"Boone's been grinning at me, telling me, 'Have fun!' I thought he'd been switched with a robot or something, he's been so nice—" He stopped himself short, his eyes filled with new, scary realizations. "Haddock *wants* us to be friends."

"Why?"

"So you'll think twice about messing up," Redbone said. "Or running. Trust me, if you get in trouble, I'll be the one who pays first. You sure you don't see another haint here? 'Cuz Haddock's gonna want his ashes, Robert. Remember, they're already dead."

The boy in the bleachers was wearing a gray baseball jersey with the number 13 in white.

Robert tried not to look at his face, but he couldn't help seeing his hair matted to his forehead, his missing jaw glistening red in the sun. Dogs had gotten to him. He was half-*eaten*. Robert looked away, feeling his throat fighting vomit.

"Blue said I can't," Robert said. "He'll hurt my mama, Bone."

"Tell your mama to go away," Redbone said. "She'll go if you say so."

"How do you know?"

"Blue told me she has to fight to be here," Redbone said. "Most times haints can't go to places they've never been—unless there's an object, like something they owned. That's you, I guess. But if you tell her to go away, I bet Blue can't hurt her."

"Won't matter. Boone's haint dust is good for *three days*. That's what he said."

"Boone can't hardly count to three."

"Well, he got it from his grandmama, and I bet she can count to a million."

Redbone stared around him, trying to spot a haint on his own. "Then you better cry your eyes out when you tell Warden Haddock you're trying your best," Redbone said.

"Would you tell on me?" Robert almost wanted to say it would be okay to tell if Haddock was hurting him enough, but he was afraid to. He was afraid to ask what the Box was. Or what Boone and Blue had meant when they said the Funhouse wasn't the worst.

Redbone shrugged. "You never told about Blue, so I'm not gonna tell anything about you, then," Redbone said. "But if I see any haints, I'm telling where they are—except Blue. And if they punish me *too* bad . . ." He didn't finish. Maybe they were both realizing at the same time that he would tell on Blue if he had no choice. "I'll do what I have to do. Then maybe I'll be the new haint catcher. Since maybe your luck ran out."

Even standing side by side with Redbone, Robert felt miles away from him. He had never felt that way about a friend. And wasn't Redbone Blue's friend too? This new, harder kind of friendship cut through his skin like Haddock's whip.

"What if Blue hurts my mama's spirit 'cuz of you?" Robert said. "What if he lets Haddock trap her? You should've heard the things he said, Bone."

"I'm not trying to hurt nobody," Redbone said. "I won't tell on you—not *ever*—but I wanna remember who I am when I leave this place. Some boys, they get this look in their eyes and you know they'll be old men still in this place 'til the day they die. I might go to the Funhouse or stay in the Box a night or two, but I won't go to the shed, so that's that. You should be ready to give Blue up too if you have to. Your mama would want you to do it no matter what. She wouldn't want Haddock to touch you. No mama would want that. We just gotta get by day-to-day."

Robert knew he could ask about the most terrible places and punishments, but he didn't want to know. He had vague shapes and outlines in his mind, but he didn't want to see the pictures hidden in Haddock's desk even in his head.

"Until Christmas," Robert said.

"Yeah," Redbone said, cheerless. " 'Til Christmas."

Was Blue's spirit hovering somewhere near them, invisible? Was that what Redbone had meant when he said Blue knew everything? The next time Robert checked the bleacher, the haint and his mangled face were gone. He had only wanted Robert to see his injury. To be a witness.

"You need to call out for Blue," Redbone said. "Call him by his real name: Kendall. That's how you know he'll come for sure. He told me they love having their names called. He said for them it's a feeling like we don't even know about. Like a new life, almost. It's like hearing it from outer space if someone calls them."

"Why should I?" Was Redbone already laying a trap for Blue?

"Tell him you're ready to hear his plan for getting in Haddock's drawer—a *good* plan. You have to do what he says, Robert. It's the only way he'll let us go."

Tuesday night, Redbone and Robert were still wrapped in their bath towels, straight from the shower, when they found Boone waiting in the hall, beckoning for them. They looked at each other—Redbone was as clueless and wary as Robert—and then followed him, dripping down the hall toward the lobby. Robert's bare foot slipped slightly on the floor as he tried to catch up to him. Boone hadn't hollered at them with threats about the Funhouse, so maybe it wasn't that, but Robert thought about how the whip would hurt against wet skin.

In the hall, three boys from the teenage wing stared from a distance in a huddle.

Boone hesitated by the front door as if he were about to walk outside. "Y'all didn't see no other haints?"

His voice suggested a last chance, but Robert and Redbone both shook their heads. One of the watching teenagers sucked his lip, angry. Robert had never met those older boys, so why did they care? After dinner, Boone had made a ceremony out of sprinkling his haint dust near a brick pile not far from the cafeteria after Robert lied and said he'd seen a haint there. A crowd of boys had waited around him, holding their breath, but Robert had ducked away even though Redbone had whispered that it would be better for him to watch too.

"Did the ash come?" Robert said, trying not to sound like he already knew the answer.

Boone gave Robert such an ugly look that he wanted to give up Blue right then.

"Come on, then," Boone said, and he opened the door to the twilight.

Robert's feet were more tender because they were damp, so the sharper stones and twigs poked like straight pins as he kept up a fast pace to follow Boone across the field. All around them, boys with late passes were streaming back to the dormitories. Only Robert and Redbone were walking away from the laughing, away from the rest. The air was soupy and warm, but Robert felt cold in his wet towel, as if everyone were seeing him naked as they stared.

But they were walking *away* from the Funhouse; that was what mattered. Instead of veering right, Boone veered left and led them through an open gate toward the horse stables Robert had not visited yet. Here, the air smelled like hay and manure. None of the horses were in sight, which at least might have been an unexpected treat, but Robert heard them snuffling and pawing at the ground behind the barn walls. He thought it was his imagination at first, but the horses stirred as they passed, a chorus of worry. Robert had ignored his fear as much as he could—*At least we're not going toward the Funhouse,* he told himself again—but the horses' nervous whinnies felt like the worst kind of luck. His damp back shivered with the breeze upsetting the leaves, hissing at him from above.

Were Redbone's eyes glistening in the dimming daylight?

Grass gave way to rocky soil and then soft dirt and then concrete warm from the sun.

Robert thought about everything his feet touched to try to keep from being afraid.

"Tell him, Robert," Redbone said. "Tell him what you were telling me, about how it was so unsanctified at the church. You said you saw the devil's shadow, remember?"

"Yes!" Robert said, admiring Redbone's quick thinking. Robert wished he had added more details in his earlier report to Boone. "I left that part out by accident, sir." He tried to imagine a *Flash Gordon* story of a great battle between good and evil, except it would be a story about him. "The devil got the upper hand at the church, Mister Boone. While you and Superintendent Haddock were looking at the dust, I saw something out of the corner of my eye on the wall: the devil's shadow. It was gone quick as lightning, but I knew right then he'd come to try to stop me from finding haints. And I'm praying him away and praying him away, and I just *know* I'll find another haint tomorrow. But I'm not strong enough to fight off the devil himself in one or two days, Mister Boone. Maybe I could lick him in three or four."

"Maybe you know a potion, sir?" Redbone said. "A potion that could help him beat the devil down? I'm praying too, but some hoodoo would sure help."

"Yessir, sure would," Robert said. "That would speed it up."

In the past two days, talk of hoodoo had created a kind of secret club between them, with Boone telling stories of learning to mix teas and salves at his grandmother's knee, boasting of his skills as a haint catcher in his own right. But Boone didn't look back at them as he led them across the concrete. Boone's walking slowed as his breathing got louder. Nothing they said would turn him around, so they fell silent. Robert hoped they hadn't made him madder with what might have seemed like obvious lies.

Finally, Boone stopped walking beneath a stand of pines. Robert looked at Redbone, confused, until he saw where Redbone's eyes were staring: two wooden doors like cellar doors were lined up side by side in the midst of the pine needles, propped up by about six inches to show the darkness below. Two eyes stared out at them from the closer propped door, but Robert couldn't make out the face in the dark. His chest began heaving as he understood: the Box!

"Guess you're feeling good and sorry you ain't found no more haints, huh?" Boone said.

Robert and Redbone both swore how sorry they were, how they would do better, how the devil had bested them in their hunt. Robert's bare knees trembled beneath his towel. The underground space looked so tiny! Would they be forced to spend the night there? Or longer?

"*Shut up*," Boone said, and no living thing within earshot made a sound, not even the unlucky boy who was locked in the Box. The crickets and nearby horses were silent too.

"Don't make no promises to *me*: Talk to *him*," he said, pointing toward the Box and the staring eyes. "'Cuz until you find me another haint for Warden Haddock, that's where he's gonna stay."

Robert couldn't grasp Boone's words at first. Someone else was in the Box because he hadn't shown Boone how to find the haints? *The worst of the worst of the worst,* Blue had said. Again he tried to look at Redbone, but Redbone's eyes were locked with the boy in the Box.

"We're sorry," Redbone said to the boy. "We didn't know he was lockin' somebody up."

"We'll . . . try harder," Robert said, his throat lined with sand as he spoke the lie.

"You'd better!" the boy's rough voice came, vicious. Robert knew his voice! It was Cleo.

That was why the teenagers had been staring at them back at the dorm: they already knew. "What you look so sad for?" Boone said. "Didn't you tell me how he was botherin' you out in the cornfield the other day? Ain't that so, Redbone?"

Redbone's mouth fell open, shocked. "*No*, sir," he said. "I never said . . ." But he looked mortified that he had contradicted Boone, so his words fell away.

Cleo had threatened them in the cornfield, true, but Robert had never told anyone, and he doubted Redbone had either. Why would Redbone be a fink and tell on Cleo when everyone knew that was the worst thing to do? If you finked on a bully, a bully would hurt you.

"Tonight he's the only one out here," Boone said. "There's nothin' in the Box 'cept a bucket to piss and shit in, and he's gonna be mighty hot when the sun comes back out. And ev'ry minute he sweats in there and his stomach rumbles 'cuz he ain't got no food and his throat burns 'cuz he ain't got no water, he's gonna be madder 'n' madder. And he ain't never gonna forget why he got put in there—'cuz y'all are playin' around. Keep it up, and tomorrow night I'll throw Redbone down in there with him." He said this directly to Robert as if Redbone weren't standing beside him.

Blue's name stirred in Robert's throat, and Redbone seemed to see it; he bumped hard against Robert as if to knock Blue's name away.

"Just give us a chance, Mister Boone," Redbone said. "Don't put him down there. Cleo didn't do nothing to be down there like that. I never said to put nobody in the Box."

"You worry about your own self," Boone said, grinning sideways at Redbone in the meanest way Robert had ever seen. "That's what I'd do if I was you."

Boone nodded toward a steel water pail not far from Cleo's coffin-like cage, this time looking back at Robert. His mean grin softened to a smile that didn't look real, not with the way his eyes gleamed in the lamplight. Robert realized he didn't know Boone at all, that Boone could do much worse things than laying stripes in the Funhouse. "Go on. Give him a scoop of water if you feel so bad. But remember he's down there. You better show me a haint tomorrow. Hear?"

"Yessir," Robert whispered, and he rushed to the pail as if giving Cleo the water quickly would somehow make him forget his anger. Make it better to be in the Hole, alone in the dark.

One lamp on a post cast enough light for Robert to see that the water in the bucket wasn't clear like he'd expected. Pine needles floated on top, and a big black drowned beetle on its back. When was the last time this water had been changed? But Robert pulled out the scoop and tried to fill it with only clean water, without bugs.

"Hurry up," Boone said. "I ain't gonna stand here all night."

Robert spilled half the water in his scoop in his rush to pull it out, but he kneeled beside the raised opening of the Box and saw Cleo's angry jawline, not much more, in the dim light. He could smell Cleo's sweating skin, gleaming with the heat still trapped in the Box from the long day. Robert offered the scoop to him. "I'm real sorry, Cleo," he whispered. "I didn't mean to—"

Cleo knocked the scoop away, and it landed with a *clink* on the concrete ground. Then Cleo spat at him. Most of the warm spit missed, but some of it hit Robert's ear. The bad ear.

"You're dead," Cleo hissed at him. "I'm gonna kill you both."

"We'll get you out of here, I promise," Robert said, finding words somehow, voice gentle like a parent's, hoping there was something he could say or do to quiet Cleo's rage. Gloria could look in anyone's eyes and know almost anything about them, and maybe this was how she felt every day. He stared straight to the heart of Cleo's life story, all of it bad and sad and wrong.

And now all of the blame was on *Robert*, somehow.

Cleo's going to kill us, he thought, trying on the words, his head almost quiet. He could see his future plainly in Cleo's eyes.

30

Tuesday night

Because their feet were caked with mud and pine needles, Boone said they could shower again after the visit to the Box. Redbone decided he'd rather join the laughter with the boys listening to the last few minutes of Jack Benny and Rochester's raucous, throaty voice. "I never give up a chance to laugh," Redbone told Robert after he changed into his pajamas.

But Robert couldn't imagine laughing at anything, so he went back to the bathroom since all the boys were gone and he wouldn't have to be naked in front of anyone. Maybe Mama would come to him. Maybe she would look more like Mama this time, not just a tapping sound on the pipes. She always came when he needed her most. His throat ached from the effort of keeping his sobs stifled. His heart still hammered from the idea of Cleo locked in that dark hole like an animal. No, worse than an animal: no one would even keep a dog somewhere so terrible. The horses in the stable would have a more comfortable night.

The bathroom was a sad collection of corroded sinks and leaking showerheads, with too few toilets lined against the tall, narrow rear windows—hardly any privacy for boys who needed to sit and take their time. Robert took advantage of the empty bathroom to visit the toilet first, and not a soul disturbed him. He pressed his feet against the slick tile and curled his toes, ignoring the smell of pee and a stain that looked, to him, like blood. By the time Robert flushed the toilet, he didn't feel like crying as much. His senses were also coming back to him. He couldn't visit with Mama: Redbone had said that it was hard for her to come to a place so far from anywhere she'd ever been, and he should send her away if she did. He might have to give up another haint to Warden Haddock, and Mama shouldn't come anywhere near him in case Boone tried to lay down his dust in places of his own choosing. He was beyond Mama's help.

"Don't come to me anymore, Mama," he whispered. "Wait 'til I'm gone from here." The pipes were silent. Maybe she had heard him. Maybe that one thing was all right.

The water from the showerhead only dribbled and wasn't warm, but at least he didn't have to share. The cool water felt good on such a hot night, so he let the fat droplets douse his hair and face before he picked up the shriveled soap bar to wash. Only then did Robert understand why he was *really* in the shower room. Who he *really* wanted to talk to.

"Kendall," Robert whispered in the empty shower stall. "Kendall Sweeting." He shivered a bit when he called Blue by the name Warden Haddock had used; he thought of the dead boy in the photograph's charred fire circle, curled up like he was in his mother's womb.

He called Blue's name five times, six times, and heard nothing in response except the laughter from the radio room echoing against the bathroom's cement wall.

"Come on, Blue—*Kendall*," he said. "You gotta talk to me."

Again Blue did not come. The faucet complained in a howl when Robert turned off the water. He kept from crying by telling himself that he could call for Blue all night, now that he knew which name to use. But he would have preferred to see him in the light instead of the room's darkness, where Blue looked more like a ghost.

All of the towels were already damp, so Robert felt dissatisfied and only halfway dry as he rubbed a thin towel across his skin. He was drying his legs when he saw steam rising from the neighboring shower stall and the hazy figure of someone standing beside him.

Had someone come in to shower while he wasn't looking?

No. The water wasn't on, and even if it had been, it wasn't hot enough for natural steam.

And the cloudy shape was too small to be Mama. Finally—Blue had come. Robert thought he should peek around the stall's wall to see more clearly into the phantom steam, but he couldn't make himself go any closer to Blue. He liked the short wall between them. In fact, although he'd called for Blue, Robert's damp legs felt weak and trembly. As the steam grew thicker, impossible to see through, Robert was sure he would pee down his leg and need to rinse himself off again.

"Blue?" he whispered.

"I was a long way from here," Blue said. His voice was coming from the shower stall, but it also seemed to be nestled inside Robert's head. Robert tensed as Blue snapped, "You can't have more of us, if that's what you're asking. No one else deserves to be in that jar. Even Robicheaux didn't deserve it. Any one of us is better than ten of you."

Tears came after all as Robert poured out the story of how Boone had marched them out to see Cleo in the Box and how Redbone would be next if they didn't find more haints.

"Cleo looked mad enough to kill us, Blue," Robert said.

"Being dead isn't so bad," Blue said blandly, and Robert cried harder. Redbone was supposed to be his friend! "Just come up with a story to stall. Redbone's a whiz at talking stories. I'm working on getting you the key to Haddock's drawer—by tomorrow if I'm careful. The dust isn't as strong anymore, and I'll bet Boone will forget to refresh it. Finding you is the smartest thing Boone has ever done. Did you know that?"

"Are you even listening? I *can't* stall anymore," Robert said. "They know I'm lying."

But Blue went on as if Robert hadn't spoken. "So if I get you the key by tomorrow, Thursday at the latest, you'll have plenty of time to swipe the package of photos and that jar of ash so you can meet your sister. Isn't that what you want? To meet your sister by the railroad tracks Friday night?"

His voice seemed a shout to Robert.

"You thought I didn't know?" Robert heard the smile in Blue's voice. Blue's laugh spilled from the ceiling.

"*Shhhhhh,*" Robert said.

He rushed to the next stall to try to shush Blue, maybe even try to shake him, but the steam broke apart like parting curtains and Blue wasn't there.

"I'll do what you say," Robert said to the empty stall. "But you have to help us too. If you don't . . ." He *almost* told how Redbone might give Blue up. Hell, how hard would it be to tell Boone to come sprinkle his dust in this shower stall? *The first stall he'd used when he arrived,* he reminded himself. *The one where Mama had found him in the pipe.*

"If I don't *what*?" Blue's voice said in his ear.

Robert whirled around, terrified at the idea of Blue standing behind him. But when he whipped around, Blue wasn't there—just the empty bathroom and the row of sinks. Except . . . in the reflection in the cracked mirror above the sink, Blue was standing beside him. He was dressed in a blue work shirt so big on him that his head barely poked out, like a turtle's.

Gasping, Robert took a step back, looking right and left for Blue. But the only Blue was in the mirror, staring intently at Robert with glowering eyes. "You'll tell Boone about me?" he said, the voice still close to his ear. "You'll bring him in here to trap me?"

"No," Robert said, swatting Blue's voice away from his ear. "You know I can't." Only because of Mama, although he didn't say it. "But I called you," Robert said, fumbling for any words that might sway Blue. "I called your name."

Now Blue looked intrigued. "So?"

"If something happens to me or Redbone, who's gonna call your name then? Does anyone remember you except me and Redbone . . . and Haddock?"

Blue's head lolled to one side, his ear resting on his shoulder. He stared at Robert from that odd pose in the reflection for a long time, no longer sneering. His head had fallen too far, with no bones to hold it. Was he trying to scare him again? Or just thinking it over?

"You need me just like I need you," Robert said, lowering his voice so no one in the hall would hear him and so Boone wouldn't come running with his leather pouch. "I'm the only one you can talk to whenever you want. Redbone can't even hardly see you sometimes." Blue pursed his lips. He didn't like hearing *that*. Or maybe he didn't like that Redbone had told him so much. "So you need to be nice to me, Blue," Robert said firmly.

Blue's reflection disappeared, an empty space. A corner of the mirror cracked away, shattering a triangle of glass tinkling into the sink.

"Stop it," Robert hissed, rushing to retrieve the broken pieces. He wrapped them inside a crumpled paper towel he found in the trash can and buried it at the bottom. Would someone notice the new damage to the mirror? He hoped he wouldn't get blamed for it. He turned on the faucet to wash any other slivers down the sink. "You want Boone to come in here? I know you don't, so stop doing . . . haint stuff."

"That's an ugly word," Blue said. This time he was sitting on the floor of the shower stall behind Robert in solid form, like any other boy, watching him work to clean up his mess.

"*Haint*. Evil-sounding word. Like I'm a jumbee trying to walk in your skin the way talkers say in the old stories. I'm not the one who set the fire, am I? Am I the one dragging boys out to the shed?" The island lilt in Blue's accent was clearer now. Blue was revealing more of his true self.

"What should I call you, then?"

"Trapped," Blue said. "Dirtied. We died dirty—until *you* fix it."

Robert wrapped his towel around his waist and sat beside Blue, careful not to touch him so he wouldn't feel that too-cool skin that wasn't living flesh. Even the space beside Blue felt colder than the rest of the shower stall.

"I can't do anything until Friday," Robert said. "Until it's time. You said you'd help me."

"Sure I will. Any small thing'll get Haddock to go running out of his office. I can set the dogs off barking and yelping, I'll scare 'em so bad. Dogs lose their mind around haints. I know he'll come look after his dogs. He'll think someone gave them rat poison. Then you can get in through his window."

"But I need a hai— . . . I need someone else," Robert said. "For the jar." Blue shook his head, firm.

"Blue, listen: Redbone's going with me," Robert said. "I told him all about it. He's so smart, we're sure to get away. You said I just have to set the ashes loose in the creek, right? And then they'll be set free?"

"That's right."

"And you'll be set free too?"

"I'm already free," Blue said. "I'm more free than you! We have a pact: we all stay until Haddock's gone. We stay until everyone knows how dirty we died."

"Then it doesn't matter who goes in the jar, right? They'll come right back out."

"Only if you get away," Blue said, shrugging.

"We will. You said you'd help."

"I'll try, but the running and hiding, that's up to you. Two's not easier than one. You think you're the first two who ever tried it? One wants to go this way, the other wants to go that way? The dogs barking and snarling behind you all the while?"

The cold floating from Blue seemed to gather in Robert's chest. He remembered Haddock telling him how boys got killed trying to run.

"Can you keep the dogs off?" Robert whispered.

"Not if they're on your scent in the woods. Especially Haddock's."

"Can you slow 'em down at least?"

"I can fool them from time to time, but those are tracking dogs. Haddock trained most of 'em so they *want* to hurt you. That's all they want in the wide world. And the dog boys, the dorm masters, the farmers, everyone—they love the hunts. Fifty dollars per boy, dead or alive. It's like they're on holiday, all the whooping and hollering."

Robert's bare back trembled against the damp shower wall. Did Gloria and Uncle June know how hard it would be? Had they planned it out as well as they should? What if there was no hole in the fence? What if the dogs started chasing them as soon as they were in the cornfield?

Robert's plan to run terrified him anew.

But that was Friday's terror. First, he had to get past Wednesday's.

"Someone has to go in the jar tomorrow, Blue," Robert said. "Just *one* more. Maybe that will get me all the way to Friday. Somebody brave has to go in just for a couple of days."

Blue chuckled, his voice turning sour again. "A couple of days. You say that like you know anything. You don't know. You think any of us want to be locked up again? Like *that*?"

"You said they're trapped already. Isn't a pact a trap too?"

"That's different than the jar. In the dark. Shrunken to ash and screaming." He sounded angry now. Robert had heard the boy in the kitchen scream, and the giant haint at church. He couldn't say Blue was lying, or that what he was asking was fair.

"But I'll let them out," Robert said anyway. "You said I can. Who's the bravest? See if they'll do it. Otherwise, Boone might make me go to the fire spot—"

"So?" Blue laughed. "Memories, that's all you saw there. You'll never find us at the fire spot or the Funhouse. They're profane to us. You got lucky in the kitchen, that's all."

"The infirmary," Robert said. "I saw one there. And at the ball-field. Number thirteen."

Blue was silent at that, his eyes narrowing like he might break the mirror again. Or worse. "I don't wanna hurt nobody else," Robert whimpered. "But if I can't get somebody for the jar . . . Haddock's gonna kill me. Or Redbone. Or both of us. I *know* it. You think I wanna end up in one of those photos in his drawer too?"

For a long time, the bathroom was silent except for dripping from the showerhead in the stall where Robert had washed himself. Finally, Blue said, "You know where the old well is?"

Robert shook his head. He'd never seen a well on the campus.

"By the butcher's," Blue said. "Out in the back, by the cedars. You'll see it."

"Okay," Robert said, sure he could find it. He had heard enough horrible squealing of pigs to know where the butcher's block was.

"He won't like it . . . but there is one, maybe," Blue said. "He was almost twenty-one when Haddock shot him dead running. He doesn't scare easy, always bragging he was a grown man. Maybe he'll go to the well if I ask him. Maybe he won't be afraid of the jar."

"What's his name?" Robert said, remembering Redbone's advice about calling haints.

Again Blue was silent. He didn't want to give out the name. "Henry Jackson," he said. "He went by Hank, but call for Henry Jackson. No one's called his name in years, probably."

"It has to be tomorrow," Robert said. "By dinner. Please. Boone's gonna want to set his trap, and he has to see the ashes come. Tell Hank I'll let him out Friday—I promise."

"Maybe he will, maybe he won't," Blue said, shrugging. "I'll try to dare him into it."

"He *has* to do it or I can't help any of you," Robert said. "Boone never waits any later than six to put down that dust. I'll push him off as long as I can, but he has to come by six." This time Blue didn't answer.

"What's in that goofer dust?" Robert whispered. "Why does it make y'all come back?"

"Grave dust," Blue said. "You can't understand. It's just dirt to you."

"I could try."

Blue sighed. "It smells like . . . rest. But it's a false rest, a fishing lure, and it's a hex instead. Most people hex the living—but Boone and Haddock hex the dirtied and the dead."

Robert heard footsteps approaching quickly outside of the doorway. As soon as Robert rushed to his feet, he saw Redbone facing him. Robert's own reflection was clear in the mirror behind Redbone, but Blue was no longer visible beside him.

"He here?" Redbone said. He looked older since he'd visited the Box. Tired.

Robert couldn't help looking over his own shoulder to see if Blue was still there behind him despite his missing reflection, but Blue wasn't in sight. Blue had been Redbone's friend first, but now Blue was shunning him. If Redbone knew Blue had just been with him, he might yell for Boone as loud as he could to avoid going to the Box.

"Who?" Robert said, his voice thinned by his pretending.

"Who you think?"

Robert shook his head, hoping he didn't look like the liar he was. "It's just Mama," he said. "Like you told me . . . I was asking her to stay away."

Redbone's face softened a bit. He would never betray his best friend's mama, at least not yet. Would he? For a moment, Robert's heart caught when Redbone didn't say anything. Then Redbone took a step back to give Robert privacy. "Oh . . . okay. Be sure to call for Blue and tell him we need a haint. Call him all night if you have to. You heard what Boone said."

Robert nodded and promised he wouldn't stop calling for Blue until he came. He wished he could calm Redbone's anxiousness and tell him he and Blue already had a plan to collect another haint. But not here. Not in the shower stall where Mama had come to comfort him in the pipe. Not where Blue's presence was still so fresh that the tiles beneath Robert's soles were as cold as the water at the bottom of the well.

31

No one was bringing food plates or even calling Miz Lottie's house to check on Gloria since the deputies had begun patrolling Lower Spruce. Neighbors stayed in their houses, peeking out of their windows at every strange car that rolled down the street at random hours of the day and night—some with police stripes, some without. Miz Lottie had predicted that the patrols would let up after the memory of the courthouse visit died down, but Gloria was still living like a fugitive. And wasn't she one, with the sheriff looking for her?

Gloria had spent two uneasy nights in Miss Anne's basement, but she hadn't felt safe there. She hated being on alert for creaking stairs signaling that Fred might be coming downstairs to cuss her, threaten her, or worse. She'd spent last night with the Hatchetts, who lived two houses down from Miz Lottie, but deputies had knocked that morning asking about her while Gloria slipped out of the back door, careful not to rile the laying hens in their coop. Mrs. Hatchett was afraid to let her spend the night again because she didn't like lying to the police, so Gloria was back at Miz Lottie's, the one place deputies might not think to look for her because it was too obvious. While Miz Lottie prayed, Waymon and Uncle June kept their guns close.

Someone had thrown rotten eggs against Miz Lottie's door before screeching away at dinnertime, so the sour smell had sunk into the porch's floorboards and seeped through the door into the house despite Uncle June's scrubbing. Rotten eggs smelled like death. The smell made Gloria angry, mounted upon her anger over Robbie's imprisonment and her father's banishment. Papa used to say he was so mad that he sometimes got headaches, and now Gloria felt an ever-present tightness at her temples that made it easy to snap at Uncle June or Miz Lottie or throw dishes in the sink too hard, chipping them. It was all so unfair!

Only three more nights, Gloria promised herself. Three more nights and they would pack up Miz Lottie's truck and drive out to meet Robbie at the railroad tracks in the moonlight. Three more nights and she would leave Gracetown behind forever.

"What about this one?" Miz Lottie said, holding up another dress for Gloria to examine. This had been their ritual for the past hour as they tried to forget about the patrols and the sour smell invading every corner of the house despite the rosewater perfume Miz Lottie had sprayed. Gloria's decisions about what to preserve from her old life had been wrested away from her by the men who had burned down her cabin, but Gloria caught Miz Lottie's eyes chronicling everything in her room she would lose. After the sheriff learned they had helped Robbie escape, a mob might come burn down Miz Lottie's house too.

This dress was faded pink, a bit more fashionable than the others Gloria had seen, but it still looked like it belonged to a flapper during Prohibition, with puffed sleeves and a large collar, and it was much longer than a modern dress. Mostly to humor her, Gloria held the dress up to her chest and examined herself in Miz Lottie's bureau mirror, another once-ornate gift from the Powells. Where would she wear this? Gloria realized that many of Miz Lottie's dresses must have belonged to the Powells too. How else would Miz Lottie have afforded the clothes?

"I think . . . I like this one," Gloria said, barely avoiding a lie.

"Put it on your pile, then. You can make your final choices 'fore we go."

"Don't you want to keep your favorite dresses for yourself?" Gloria had never been interested in looking at clothes, no matter how often Mama had asked her to go window-shopping with her on Main Street to stare at dresses they could neither try on nor afford. Gloria had always felt foolish standing on the sidewalk staring at the clothes on white dress dummies while she saw the frowning reflections of white people passing behind them. If Mama had seen the frowns, she'd never let it bother her, taking her time to stare as long as she wanted.

"Can't take it with you, child," Miz Lottie said quietly. "If I make it to Chicago, I won't need much." Gloria tried to unhear the word *if*. She wanted to say *You'll make it, Miz Lottie,* but she couldn't be sure. In her only vision about their escape, Miz Lottie had not been driving the truck. Neither had Uncle June nor Waymon. *She* had been driving the truck. And she had learned from Mama that she should listen when someone talked about dying because death was as real as breathing. Death might be more real than living, since life was over so soon.

"And a coat!" Uncle June called from the hallway. "That's *all* we need in Chicago, come winter. They say it's cold enough to freeze a—"

Keys jingled from the kitchen and the back door hinge creaked. Gloria clutched at the dress's fabric until she heard Waymon call, "Just me!" Relief fluttered from Miz Lottie's lungs.

Waymon had been out to the cornfield. He'd said he wouldn't cut the hole in the fence yet, but he'd borrowed a car to drive back and forth past the cornfield to do what he'd called "recon," short for *reconnaissance*, another word from the war. Waymon was excited as he filled a water glass from Miz Lottie's chilled mason jar and gulped it down before refilling it. Miz Lottie and Gloria sat at the kitchen table to listen while June stayed by the rear window, watching.

"Anybody see you?" June said.

Waymon shook his head. "Nah. It was real quiet. Hardly nobody else on the road. Maybe we oughta just have him meet us at—"

"No," June said. "Just 'cuz you don't see nobody don't mean they ain't watching."

"And we can't change the plan," Gloria said. "We already told Robbie to go to the creek."

Waymon nodded toward June. "So Thursday before dark, you and me'll go out there just the same as I did today. We'll take Clive's car again—"

June looked angry suddenly. "You didn't say nothin' to that drunk fool, did you?"

"No, I didn't say nothin'! How come you always askin' did I say something?" They stared each other down for a moment, their eyes boiling with old memories. Waymon looked away first. "It ain't like that time at the base. You gonna hold that over my head forever? I didn't say nothin'. I just pay him for gas. He don't ask where I'm goin'. Can I finish?"

"*Stop it,*" Miz Lottie said. She rested her head in her hand as if to block out the light. "I swear and be damned, if you two jackasses don't stop all that fussing!"

"I'll drive us out in Clive's car," Waymon went on, "and you'll hop out into the cornfield. It ain't gonna be nothin' for you to crawl under that barbed wire out front. But the fence on the Reformatory side, that one's tougher. Wire cutters gonna work?"

"Should," June said, thoughtful. "I'll just need time to cut a hole big enough."

"But not big enough for nobody to see it before it's time," Waymon said.

"Robbie's small," Gloria said.

"I'll let you out, drive off," Waymon said. "I'll go a ways down the road, then I'll turn and drive back. If you ain't back yet when I whistle for you, I'll drive off and come back again."

"You can't park," June said. "No matter what. Those farmers will call the warden before you can count to three."

"What did I just say?" Waymon asked. "I'll drive off."

With a silent sigh, Gloria surveyed Robbie's escape team: an old woman who looked ready to faint and two grown men who argued like schoolboys. *God help us,* she thought. In the kitchen light, the plan seemed foolish in every way. If not for the hope she'd seen in Robbie's eyes, she would have called it off. Instead, she said, "We have to make sure Ole Suzy is ready by Friday. That engine keeps clicking and goes off on a dime. We can't be stranded out there."

"I'll fix it," Uncle June said. "I just got the parts from—"

A knock on the door interrupted him. The *front* door. Then the doorbell rang. It wasn't the proper code: Uncle June had told the Hatchetts to knock twice, pause, and then knock twice again so they would know who was there. Gloria leaped to her feet, and June's shotgun had appeared from nowhere in his hands. He beat Waymon to the kitchen doorway and gestured for him to stay back. "I'll get it," he said.

Waymon nodded, reaching for his waistband. "I got the window."

Gloria grabbed Miz Lottie's hand and squeezed. Miz Lottie did not squeeze back. All at once, Gloria's mouth and throat felt sucked dry. No wonder Waymon had been so thirsty: constant worry stole everything from you, even the spit in your mouth.

"Can I help you?" Uncle June said, slightly gruff but polite. No hint of danger.

The stranger at the door spoke with clear confidence, her voice raised loudly enough for all of them to hear: "Why, yes, I'm so sorry to disturb you after dinnertime," a woman said. "Is this the family of Robert Stephens Junior?"

Robbie! The stranger's voice sounded like a War Department notification. Gloria tripped on the hall rug in her hurry to get to the living room. The woman's voice went on: "My name is Marian Hamilton, and I'm the director of the Negro band at the Reformatory. Robert is one of my star students." *Is* one of her students, the woman had said. Not *was*. He couldn't be dead, could he? Surely she wouldn't have chosen that word if Robbie was dead.

The woman standing silhouetted in the porch light could have been Mama, from her hair to her shoulders to her posture. If she hadn't spoken and said otherwise, Gloria would have believed she was seeing Mama's ghost. Gloria could only stare.

"Somethin' bad happen to him?" Uncle June's voice came out small, from a cavern of waiting grief. He sounded helpless despite the shotgun just beyond the door.

"Oh no—I'm sorry—nothing like that," the woman said.

The living room's foul stink, which seemed to have wrapped Gloria in a cobra's grip, let her go. She could breathe again. And move. And *think*.

"Sorry for the smell," Gloria said. "People came and threw spoiled eggs and drove off." She felt a sting of self-consciousness, eager to let the stranger know that this was not how Robbie lived, in stink and clutter. Gloria's cheeks went hot when she realized the woman could see inside the living room at the stacks of newspapers and magazines climbing the wall.

Now that the woman was no longer in mystery and shadow, Gloria noticed the crispness ringing from every part of her: the gleaming part in her well-oiled hair, the tightly wound French braids, her blouse and collar starched and free of wrinkles. She spoke like she'd been to college, or somewhere even more exotic than college, carrying music in her words, like a march that must be followed. Gloria felt only twelve inches high in front of her. Was this woman writing some kind of report on Robbie? Had their family just failed a crucial test?

"Some of you came to visit on Sunday, but I see him every day, so I thought you might like to know he's all right," the woman said. She cast a quick glance over her shoulder, toward the road. For the first time, she seemed uneasy. "May I please come in?"

"No—" Gloria started to say, but June was already stepping aside to give her room.

"Yes, ma'am," June said. "Watch your step."

Miz Lottie did not like strangers in her house, especially "seditty" strangers, as she called the Negroes who lived in the new houses on the hill built from VA loans. But although she was watching from the hall, Miz Lottie did not complain as the woman came inside, where the sprawl of clutter was in plain view.

"Marian Hamilton?" Miz Lottie said. "You one of Bo Crutcher's grandbabies?"

Mrs. Hamilton smiled. "I am indeed, ma'am," she said. "I'm the eldest."

"You the lady who went to war?" Miz Lottie said. June looked surprised by the question.

"Me again. My late husband and I enlisted together. We hoped it would make a difference at home."

Waymon poked his head out from the hall. "But it didn't work out that way, huh?"

No one answered that. Mrs. Hamilton pursed her lips. Her face seemed to lose color. "Sorry for your loss," Uncle June said. He cleared away a folded pile of blankets from Miz Lottie's couch to make room for her to sit. The couch, like every other surface, was mostly for storing things. If Mrs. Hamilton was shocked by the condition of the living room and its collections of Coca-Cola bottles and piles of mail, she kept it from her face. The room looked like a long life turned inside out.

"You say Robert's doing fine?" Gloria probed.

Mrs. Hamilton smiled. "He's a natural on the trumpet. I hope he'll keep up his music study once he's out."

So many surprises at once: learning that Robert played the trumpet, which he had never mentioned, and hearing a stranger talk about him getting *out*. Gloria couldn't help exchanging glances with Uncle June and Waymon. Did she know about the escape plan?

"Why're you callin' on us?" Waymon said pointedly. "What do you want?"

"Did Haddock send you?" Uncle June said, and noted her surprise that he knew the name of her boss. "I used to work out there. Groundskeeping crew."

"No one sent me," Mrs. Hamilton said. "I'm here on my own accord. I just . . ." She paused, choosing which words to share. "I'm a longtime admirer of the work of his father to try to make Negro lives better in northern Florida. He once helped my father get a job. So . . . since I have an inside view, I thought you'd appreciate hearing that someone is looking out for him."

"Looking out from what?" Gloria said.

"The Reformatory can be a dangerous place, especially for colored boys," she said.

"He told us he got beat," Gloria said.

Mrs. Hamilton gazed down at her folded hands as if she had held the strap herself. "Yes . . . I know," she said, raising her eyes to Gloria's. "He spent a night in the infirmary. That's where I met him to recruit him for the band. I'll do my best to see it doesn't happen again. The last time Superintendent Haddock called for him, I accompanied him to his office. I'll advocate for Robert at every opportunity."

Uncle June was agitated, shifting from side to side. "What'd Haddock want him for?"

"I'm not quite sure," she said, and hesitated. "I thought I might ask you. The superintendent has taken a special interest in him. I admit I tried to listen through the door, but I couldn't quite make out what it was."

Uncle June took a step toward her, so sudden that she jumped. "What did that SOB—"

"He didn't hurt him," Mrs. Hamilton said. "But the superintendent has excused Robert from regular work detail. The rumor is"—strangely, she almost smiled—"Robert's helping the superintendent find ghosts. That's what all the boys are saying."

"The *hell* you talkin' 'bout?" Waymon said. "What're you really doin' here, lady? Did the sheriff send you? That boy don't play no trumpet. You need a better story than *that*. Ghosts? You must think we're some real dumb country folks, huh?"

Gloria's ears were buzzing with a rush of blood as her heart sped. She gazed back at Miz Lottie, who was still standing in the hall entrance. Miz Lottie took a step closer to her.

"He said he was seeing haints," Miz Lottie said. "He looked scared out his mind."

"Mama, don't listen to this bull—" Waymon started, but Gloria cut him off.

"If he says he's seeing haints, he is. You don't know, Waymon."

"I don't know what? Crazy talk?"

"You ain't from here," Miz Lottie told him. "You was too old when you moved in with me. So you don't know 'bout Gracetown. Young people here, they can be touched by spirits."

"Y'all are 'touched' by something all right," Waymon muttered.

"Robbie could feel Mama's ghost," Gloria said. "He said it all the time."

"If any place ever should be haunted," Uncle June said quietly, "it's that one."

Waymon looked at all of them, lips curled with scorn. "I'm not listening to this . . . ," he said, and retreated to the back of the house, walking with exaggerated heavy footsteps toward the kitchen and complaining all the while about backward country folk.

"How long did you work there?" Mrs. Hamilton asked Uncle June.

Uncle June flinched at the question. "Five months. Three weeks. Six days."

"And then you left?"

"Yes, ma'am, I was sorry I ever set foot there. My advice is, once Robbie's out, you should get out too. That place . . ." He shook his head, not finishing.

"My brother is Robert's dorm master," Mrs. Hamilton said. "And I understand. I feel like Percy's been working there too long too. He told me after a time you start to have—"

"Dreams," Uncle June finished. "You wake up mad. Pictures in your head. You . . . do things and later it seems like it was somebody else. Not at first. But by and by."

All at once, Gloria *knew* that Mrs. Hamilton was who she seemed to be. The woman's presence radiated courage and honesty—and raw strength she had not known since Mama. Maybe Uncle June knew too, because she had never heard him talk about his time at the Reformatory beyond a clipped word or two. He had never told her anything about dreams.

"Thank you," Gloria said, near tears. "Thank you for coming to tell us about Robbie."

"He calls himself Robert now," Mrs. Hamilton said. "Like his father."

"And that's all?" Uncle June said. "You just came to give us a report? You sure Haddock ain't done nothin' else to him except set him off after haints?"

"As sure as I can be," Mrs. Hamilton said. "But . . . I heard your family tried to use an NAACP lawyer to get him released. And I've heard about the backlash: how the Klan burned down his house. It's a disgrace through and through. As an admirer of your family, I just wanted to offer my services in case there's anything I can do to help."

Help us get him free, Gloria thought so fervently that it felt like a shout.

Instead, Miz Lottie said, "The sheriff won't let Robbie's sister, Gloria, alone since we went to the courthouse. They tryin' to use these children against their daddy. I can barely sleep at night 'cuz I'm 'fraid she'll be locked up too."

Mrs. Hamilton brought her eyes to Gloria's, shining with kindness. "You need a place to stay," she said, as if she had torn the thought from Gloria's mind. "And I have a spare room. I would be honored, young lady, if you would stay with me."

SUNNY HILL, a sign promised in the headlights as Mrs. Hamilton drove Gloria to the new Negro housing development near the county line, far from downtown Gracetown. Lights glowed in evenly spaced squares and rectangles from windows in two blocks of houses that looked identical, painted the same variations of lighter and darker brown. As Mrs. Hamilton squeezed her DeSoto into the narrow carport of a house on the corner, Gloria saw a splash of a lighter color bordering her bright-shingled rooftop. Mrs. Hamilton's yard had no grass or any growth except weeds and saplings planted in rows, half-starved and browning in the summer sun. Like Lower Spruce, the road was packed dirt, but the newer cars in the driveways, fresh paint, and patterned curtains in the windows—like in a Sears catalog!—felt as far away from Miz Lottie's street as Chicago.

As soon as Mrs. Hamilton's car rocked to a stop and Benny Goodman's orchestra on the radio went silent in mid-flurry, Gloria heard someone playing a piano a few houses down, tapping out the notes in a scale slowly, uncertain. Gloria was carried away by the music, imagining herself squeezing her narrow hips beside Mama's thicker ones on the piano bench at Miss Anne's house, Mama's hand over hers, guiding her fingers along the grooves of the keys. Gloria felt a grief so sharp that her breath hitched.

"You all right?" Mrs. Hamilton said.

Gloria nodded. She didn't trust herself to speak without tears.

"Well, I doubt that's so, but sometimes we say a thing to try to believe it," Mrs. Hamilton said. "How many times a day do people ask me how I'm doing and I say, 'Just fine, and you?' as if that wasn't the biggest lie ever told." She gave a sour laugh, shaking her head. "Come on inside. I won't ask you any more foolishness like that."

Despite her sad heart, Gloria smiled a little.

A small dog was barking from across the street, from *inside* the house, paws scrabbling on the window. Gloria had never known anyone who pampered a dog inside. Even during winter, Papa's dog, Freedom, had slept under the cabin with a blanket. This dog was trussed up with ribbons like a doll! She couldn't wait to tell Miz Lottie that now she'd seen a seditty dog too.

"You like dogs?" Mrs. Hamilton said.

"No, ma'am. Especially big ones."

"Me neither," she said. "Not one bit."

When Mrs. Hamilton opened her front door, Gloria smelled paint and promise, the way the new house Papa had been building by the lake had smelled. But she stopped shy of the doorway. Gloria felt like a hex on everyone she touched, anywhere her feet walked.

"You're not scared of the sheriff?" Gloria said.

"Did you break the law trying to get an attorney?" Mrs. Hamilton asked. "Did you set fire to your own house?"

"No, ma'am."

"Then why should I be afraid of the sheriff?"

"And you're not scared of losing your job?"

"I don't work for them," Mrs. Hamilton said. "I'm a volunteer. If the wrong person caught wind, could they get mad and tell me to stop coming? I suppose so. But, no, I'm not afraid."

No, that *wasn't* the worst that could happen, not to Robbie. But maybe it would be all right, since Robbie was running away Friday night. The thought was so big that Gloria ached to say it aloud. Miz Lottie had whispered in Gloria's ear while she was packing her suitcase: *She seems all right, but don't fool yourself into thinking you can tell her. You better not, no matter what. Hear?* Uncle June's cheerless stare had echoed Miz Lottie's feelings as he helped Gloria hide in Mrs. Hamilton's back seat, where she had lain flat so no passing deputy or neighbor would see her through the window: *Don't tell about our plan,* his eyes had said. And she had nodded.

But as soon as Gloria's foot touched Mrs. Hamilton's polished wooden floor, she wanted to tell this woman everything. Gloria scanned the living room's perfect order—not a flower petal or sofa cushion out of place—and ached to share the plan to see if Mrs. Hamilton would spot any imperfections that might hurt Robbie. She saw a framed photograph on the fireplace mantel—just like the mantel at Miss Anne's house except smaller—of a uniformed Negro man with an American flag behind him, and another of *both* of them in uniform smiling at a table in a music club, and thought,

She was in the Army too and we could use another helper on the inside and almost had to clamp her hand over her mouth to keep quiet. Mrs. Hamilton seemed so much like a younger version of Mama that Gloria wanted her to know.

Maybe—*maybe*—she could tell her about the escape plan, but not today. She would obey Uncle June and Miz Lottie tonight, but it might be safe to tell by tomorrow, she told herself—the only way she could push the ready confession out of her throat. Out of her head.

A piano was nestled in the corner beyond a small dining table that looked well-kept but older, perhaps a family heirloom. The piano had a candelabra. On a glossy wooden shelf in the living room was a record player combined with a radio dial, and the biggest speakers Gloria had ever seen, almost a foot high. A bookshelf was crammed with record albums. But what was . . . ?

"You have a television set," Gloria said, surprised. She had seen one only in a shop window. Even Miss Anne didn't have a television yet. The picture tube and wooden box stood on four legs across from the living room's sofa, not much bigger than the radio. Gloria stared at her dim reflection on the darkened screen.

"That was a gift from a friend in California," Mrs. Hamilton said, chuckling. "Nearest station's Jacksonville—too far for a signal. So I guess I'm waiting to see what the fuss is about."

Gloria couldn't stop staring at her face, elongated and aged.

"Go on," Mrs. Hamilton said. "You won't get a station, but you can turn it on." She pointed to a silver-colored dial. "Turn it to the right."

Gloria turned the dial, felt it click beneath her hand. The screen flared bright white so suddenly that she took a step back. Then the image settled to wavy gray lines, with a hissing sound from the speaker. She watched the chaotic screen, hoping to see a glimpse of a face. The screen reminded her of how her head felt when she tried to see the future and couldn't. But wait . . . Hidden in the waving lines, a solid dark form seemed to be taking shape.

Gloria was almost sure she saw a railroad trestle! Blinking turned it to wavy lines again.

"Guess we've got to wait for the times to catch up," Mrs. Hamilton said, and turned the television off. The image vanished to a star burning in the center of the screen before it went dark again. Had Gloria's vision been a sign? Should she—

"I want . . . to tell you . . ." Gloria began, but headlights lit up the front window. Gloria glanced around the sparsely furnished living room for places to hide and saw none, unless she crouched on the other side of the piano.

Mrs. Hamilton leaned over her couch to look outside her window. "That's just Percy, my brother," she said. "I'll put you in your room until I see what he wants."

Her room. No one had ever called an entire room hers. They hurried to the narrow hall while Gloria clung tightly to her suitcase stuffed with Miz Lottie's old clothes and the photo of Mama and Papa on their wedding day. Mrs. Hamilton closed the door of the room, which was the same size as Miz Lottie's sewing room but empty except for a four-poster bed and a new chest of drawers. Mrs. Hamilton's tiny house was full of empty spaces, with so much room to grow, looking ahead instead of behind.

While Mrs. Hamilton greeted her brother, Gloria glanced through her window and saw the house next door, built close, separated by a picket fence. Her window was locked, but she could climb through if she needed to, even if she left her suitcase behind. But nothing she heard set her on edge. The brother sounded so jovial, laughing over a plate of food she'd saved for him, that Gloria expected Mrs. Hamilton to call her out to introduce her. But she never did.

So Gloria sat on the made-up bed and its taut floral bedspread to wait. Before she knew it, she was lying down fully clothed, her eyes heavy from lost rest. She might have dozed off, but their conversation woke her.

". . . all this foolishness with ghosts?" she heard Mrs. Hamilton say. "Why can't he let the boy serve his time without all those hoops to jump through? Then I suppose he'll blame the boys if . . . what? They don't find ghosts?"

"Boone's all wrapped up in it too with his hoodoo talk," the man said, his mouth full. "It's none of our business. Don't bring none of it home with you, Marian. Told you that. Might as well quit right now."

"Was that why you took him to the whipping house? This ghost business?" Gloria smothered a gasp. This was one of the men who had whipped Robbie?

"Had nothing to do with it," the man said. "He was talking about running. Asking about it, anyway. So that's that. Never hurts for them to learn early. Good dose of medicine, that's all."

"Haddock whipping him until he needs *actual* medical treatment? That's medicine?"

"Better than dying! Haddock's right: a Negro boy without better sense won't live long. That's his daddy's bad influence, not knowing when to keep his mouth shut. If it wasn't for me speaking up for him, Haddock might have beat him twice as long."

Mrs. Hamilton was silent for a moment. Maybe she'd been thinking about telling him about Gloria and changed her mind. "Well, one thing you're right about," Mrs. Hamilton said. "I *will* have to leave before long if it means I'll start sounding like you."

"Don't forget, those boys are locked up for a reason," he said. "Every single one."

Gloria sat upright again, too angry in her bones to keep lying down. If not for worries that he might turn her in, she would have rushed out to tell him Robbie hadn't done anything to be locked up, and if he had, then Lyle McCormack should have been locked up too.

Mrs. Hamilton's voice softened. "Deep inside, you still know better."

The man exhaled a laugh, dismissing her. "Tell Mabel this potato salad is dry."

"Tell her yourself," Mrs. Hamilton said, and their voices grew muffled as they moved closer to the front door and then out of the house. Gloria paced the room, agitated. Imagine a Negro man whose family owed them a debt talking about Robbie and Papa that way! Gloria felt such loathing for the man that she tried to see a glimpse of him through the window, but she couldn't see anything except a sliver of the empty road and the house next door.

But at least Mrs. Hamilton wasn't like him, she told herself to slow her breathing.

Robbie had someone at the Reformatory on his side.

A polite knock at her door, and Mrs. Hamilton poked her head in before Gloria could answer. "I thought I might find you at that window," she said. "Don't worry, he's gone. I'm sorry you had to hear all of that. I keep to myself when I'm out there. They all sound the same, like they're talking about movie gangsters instead of children."

Gloria tested telling the secret. "Robbie should run away."

Mrs. Hamilton's face cracked to alarm. She rushed to Gloria and grabbed her shoulders. "*No,*" she said firmly, as if Gloria had told her the entire plan. "Never say that to him. He can't talk about running—can't even *think* about running. They hunt down runaways, Gloria—do you hear me? *Kill* them, sometimes. Just because the lawyer didn't work out at first, don't lose hope. Trust in the system to find a way to get him out."

Gloria's knees tremored from a combination of disappointment and renewed terror at their plan to free Robbie. "Yes, ma'am," she whispered. Mrs. Hamilton searched her eyes like she was looking for the truth before she let Gloria go.

Mrs. Hamilton offered her food, but Gloria wasn't hungry. Then Mrs. Hamilton gave Gloria a folded washrag and towel and told her to knock on her door if she needed anything. She said she would be listening to music in her room and that Gloria should let her know if the sound was disturbing her. Gloria lay in the strange new bed with a mattress harder than she was used to, maybe because it was so new. A brass band played a march through the wall on Mrs. Hamilton's record player like it was the Fourth of July.

The system, Mrs. Hamilton had said. *TRUST in the system.* The words lanced her. How could she trust in a system that would lock up her brother over nothing? A system that would leave arsonists unpunished after they burned down her house? And chase Papa out of town?

Gloria felt safer than she had in nearly a week, but she had never felt more alone.

VII

BOOT HILL

32

Wednesday

The stone block well, about three feet high, was set back from the butcher shop in a clearing near a stand of cedars, ringed by dead leaves and pine needles. Robert took a step closer to the well to try to peer down beneath the faded wooden hutch, but the opening was covered with a tarp like a lizard's skin, cracked from the sun. Would the haint try to come from *inside* the well? Should he move the cover? Robert tried to remember every word Blue had spoken, but he wasn't sure, so he backed away a step. The well gave off a feeling he didn't like, in a way that reminded him of the knife pricks he'd felt when he first walked into the kitchen. Maybe some boys had thrown themselves into the water down there—or been thrown. The skin-like tarp wasn't moving, but the well felt restless enough to shake the ground. The uneven ring of stones looked like a hoodoo circle from Boone's conjure stories.

"What time did Blue say it would come?" Redbone asked.

"*It* is a person," Robert corrected.

"A haint, you mean."

"Blue said they don't like being called haints," Robert said.

Redbone spat. "I don't like being called 'nigger,' but that's life. And death too, I guess."

"*Cut it out,*" Robert whispered. "With you running your mouth, I wouldn't come either."

Redbone tipped an imaginary hat toward the well. "What time is this poor, sad soul coming to meet us, Robert? We supposed to stand here and wait?"

"Blue didn't say when exactly. I just told him Boone checks by suppertime."

"*Suppertime?*" Redbone groaned, leaning back as if to curse the sky. He ran his fingers through his short-cropped hair. "I gotta wait the whole day to find out if I'm goin' in the Box?"

"We don't want to bring Boone 'til we're sure. I don't even know where to put the dust."

"If it was you was the one goin' in, I bet you'd know."

Robert's jaw tightened with irritation, but he knew Redbone was only scared of how pathetic Cleo had looked down in the Box without food, water, or a bed. And Redbone didn't even know the worst of it: Robert hated every moment he stood in this place. The slaughterhouse fifteen yards behind them reeked of shit and rotting meat and blood, and a hog was snuffling against the wooden planks, trying to get free. Robert didn't want to imagine himself as that hog in a pen, but he felt the same desperation to be free . . . and a dread hanging over him as grim as the butcher's knife. Why did the well have to be so close to the slaughterhouse? The hog would scream. The haint would scream. He would scream when the dogs caught him after he ran. Death was everywhere, a taste like poison in his mouth.

He didn't want to be here. Blue had said the haints had cursed the fire spot and the Funhouse, but this spot felt cursed too. A lone green clover was pushing through the decay circling the well near Robert's feet, so he squatted to pick it up, hoping it was a lucky one with four leaves. But it was a regular one, of course. He and Redbone had spent an hour near the well that morning trying to call for the ghost, and nothing about this place felt lucky. Robert tossed the clover away.

He had to try again. He had to try to convince this stranger to sacrifice himself so he and Redbone could sleep safely in their beds another night. It wasn't fair, but it was a fact. Robert blinked to keep from crying. He couldn't stop his nose from running, the snot thin and warm.

"Henry Jackson!" Robert said, calling for the dead man again. "Please come out. Please come to this well, Henry Jackson."

Redbone shuffled beside him, unsure what to say. "Yeah, man, if you could please—"

"You have to call his whole name," Robert reminded him.

Redbone gave him an annoyed slap against his shoulder and sighed. "Henry Jackson!" He called so loudly that Robert jumped. Redbone cupped his mouth with both hands, shouting toward the well, "Come on back, Henry Jackson! *Henreeeeeeeee!*"

"Sounds like you're slopping a hog."

Redbone's voice lingered in the treetops, and Robert was sure no haint could have missed it. His sore eardrum popped, and a strange silence wrapped around them, filling both of Robert's ears with deep and steady nothingness. No birds singing. No leaves whispering. No whir of insects. Something—*something*—seemed to be holding its breath.

"Please come, Henry Jackson," Robert whispered, coaxing.

A large twig snapped from the tree line in front of them. Redbone heard it too; he looked at Robert, then shielded his eyes from the sun to stare toward the cedar trees. A twig spiraled from a higher branch and fell to the ground. Was it a coincidence, or . . . ? *There.* A man stood back beyond the trees, half hidden behind two trunks on either side of him. He was a young Negro man with a billed cap, tall, but too far to see his face. Was he real?

"Hello . . . ?" Robert called out.

A shriek as loud as an air raid siren made Robert cover his ears. Redbone grabbed his arm hard, startled. But the shriek was *behind* them, not in front. The hog pounded itself against the wood slats, shaking the whole shed as boys inside yelled to hold it still. The hog's next shriek, full of terror and agony, sounded like a child begging for its life while one of the boys laughed.

Then the hog was quiet, silenced by a blade.

When Robert looked between the trees again, the man he

thought he'd seen was gone. Now he couldn't remember *which* trees he'd been standing between, they all looked so alike.

"Did you see him?" Robert whispered to Redbone, hoping.

"Where?" Redbone said, anxious. "At the well?"

Robert pointed toward the cedars. "He was . . . far back. I couldn't really tell . . ."

Redbone sighed and shook his head. "Dammit. Do you know where to put the dust?"

"He was gone so fast," Robert said, although the whole truth was that he had turned his head because of the dying hog. As Redbone's eyes got teary, Robert's heart raced. "Maybe it wasn't him. He's supposed to come to the well. It's still a long way 'til supper, Bone."

"Hey!" A boy of about fourteen leaned out of the slaughterhouse through a window without glass. His shirt was covered in blood. Robert wondered if he was a friend of Cleo's, since Cleo worked there too. "What y'all doin'?" the boy called out. "Y'all catchin' haints?"

"You seen one?" Redbone said.

"Sure I did. A haint turned over the slop bucket last month and I got beat for it!" Robert and Redbone had heard dozens of stories like it, most of them doubtful, but Robert would have been desperate enough to ask for the exact place if the story weren't a month old. Boone's haint dust wouldn't work that far back. When they didn't answer him, the boy ducked back inside the slaughterhouse to return to his bloody task.

"Henry Jackson!" Redbone called out again, his voice hoarse.

Another man appeared, rounding the corner of the slaughterhouse at a fast pace, and Robert held his breath until he realized it was only Crutcher in his suit coat and vest. Crutcher dressed like he was invited to a fancy dinner party every day, no matter how hot it was. He looked angry, so they both took a step back at his fast approach. Robert couldn't forget how Redbone had said Crutcher had dunked his head under hot water in the sink.

"You boys—what are you doing here?" Crutcher said.

"We got a pass to—" Robert began.

"I know about that bogus pass, but what are you doing *here*?" Crutcher cut him off. "You've got Boone fooled, but I won't have you here with your theatrics distracting these other boys who have real jobs to do. Move your hoodoo coon show somewhere else." He checked his pocket watch, which swung from his vest. "In fact, you should be in the schoolhouse, getting your lessons. This is shameful. I'm telling Boone no more of this during school hours. You need to put some learning in your empty heads so you can be something in this life."

Robert and Redbone stood frozen, trying to think of what to say to his stormy face. He clearly did not believe in haints, but what other excuse would he listen to?

"Sir . . . ," Redbone began, and fumbled for words. "We just . . . need to . . ."

"Move along," Crutcher said, "or I'll take you to the Funhouse myself."

The sun felt hotter, burning Robert's arm as he and Redbone mumbled "Yessir" and backed away. Robert took a last look at the well in case Henry Jackson was floating beside it or standing tall beyond it with the trees. It would be such a simple thing if Henry Jackson would come like he was supposed to—so, so simple. *Please come, Henry Jackson,* he thought.

Crutcher was watching them, so they walked away so fast, they were nearly running. Robert felt like he was racing toward a burning field, away from air and breathing. For the first time, Robert heard Redbone stifle a sob.

"If that was him behind the trees, I'll show Boone where he was," Robert said. "Okay?" Redbone didn't answer, pulling far ahead. Walking alone.

Dinner was runny stew and corn bread missing its flavor. The silence between him and Redbone made Robert's stomach tight, so he only ate a bite or two before he pushed his tray away. He didn't touch his chocolate cookie, so Redbone took it and Robert didn't mind. A few boys had asked if they could sit at the table with them, but they had said no. No one else could hear what they had to say.

"You know what I gotta ask you," Redbone said. "In case it's not there."

Robert knew but he didn't want to. He tried to pretend Redbone wasn't thinking about turning on Blue or that he wasn't thinking about it himself. He would hate to betray Blue, who had already been wronged by Haddock and the guards like the other haints. But on the good side . . . *with Blue gone, he wouldn't have to sneak into Haddock's office*. He could offer Haddock the ash from Blue and that might make Haddock happy until Friday. It wasn't his fault all of those haints had been caught in the jar. He wasn't the one who'd killed them. If only he hadn't seen Blue in the bathroom so close to where Mama had been! More than three days might have passed since she'd been there, but how could he take the risk of trapping her by mistake?

Robert stared at the table. Letting Redbone down felt worse than the Funhouse. "I can't."

"Who says you can't?" Redbone said.

"You said the Box wouldn't be so bad."

Redbone's eyebrows knit in anger. "You shut up! You ain't even been here a week, talkin' 'bout how the Box ain't so bad. You felt all sad for Cleo, but it's worse to be in there than it is to be looking down. When they close it and there isn't but a little air coming through that hole, it's like you're buried in your grave. You've gotta give me the choice, Robert. Let *me* decide what happens to me if the ash doesn't come—not Haddock. Maybe I won't tell, but I need a choice if it gets too bad. I'd do it for you."

That hurt. Blue had come between them for a time, but Redbone had been a good friend when he needed a friend more than any other time. He felt like he had known Redbone for years.

"We saw him on the way to church . . . ," Robert offered.

"Come on! Like you're gonna trap him out in the grass? And that was *Sunday*. It's three days already. You told me you talked to Blue after that. Last night. You talked to him fresh."

Robert tried to raise his eyes to look at Redbone, but his skin felt heavy on his bones. "The baseball field," he whispered. "We can take Boone to the bleachers. I saw one there."

Robert felt Redbone staring. Redbone didn't believe him. "I *did*, Bone," Robert said. "I was afraid to tell you."

"Which seat?" Redbone said. "Where was it at?"

In his memory, the haint had been sitting in a center bleacher. And then he had moved to one side. Midway up? Or up on top? Every time Robert tried to remember the boy with the mangled face, he was sitting in a different place. And Robert had been too far away to count the rows, to know which seat.

"*Look at me,*" Redbone said, and Robert raised his head again at last. Redbone's red-rimmed eyes bored into him. "I know where you saw him." He said it with such certainty that Robert blinked, startled. "I heard you talking to him in the bathroom, Robert. You lied and said it was your mama—maybe she was there too—but that's the reason you won't tell. Ain't it? He was right where you were standing in the shower. If it's a lie, call me a liar."

Robert didn't answer, but his unsteady chin told Redbone everything he needed to know. In the dining room doorway, Boone stood waiting.

The hog was strung up on a pole beside the slaughterhouse, a long, bloody slit carved across the length of the carcass. A cloud of flies circled the head and snout as two sightless eyes stared toward the sticky ground. Robert had seen Papa hunt and skin deer, but the dead hog hanging like a bad omen made him think he might never eat ham, bacon, or pork chops again.

Talk had spread about a haint at the well, so a crowd of about thirty boys had followed Robert and Redbone while they led Boone back there. A few of the boys were blood spattered from the slaughterhouse and Robert recognized a few from his dorm, and some from the cafeteria, and some from classroom and band. He did not know their names, but he knew them. Crutcher was there too; he stood, arms folded and face pinched, on the side of the slaughterhouse, away from the bloody hog.

"You saw a haint here?" Boone said, patting the rusted bucket hanging over the well on a frayed rope. The bucket swung slowly back and forth, twirling.

"No, sir," Robert said, and rushed on when Boone frowned, "but I . . . *feel* one. I think so."

"You *think* or you *know*?" Boone said.

Robert tried to feel confidence that Henry Jackson couldn't resist the sound of his name.

Blue had said he would tell him to come to the well. "I . . . feel like a haint was here. Maybe he came before I got here, or after I left."

Boone studied Robert a long time. His eyes seemed gentle, almost pleading. "You've been wastin' up my dust day after day. I better see something tonight—you hear? I better see a li'l anthill of ash like at the church and in the kitchen. Or you're gonna be sorry to your soul." The threat frightened Robert more because of its sadness.

"He maybe was by those trees," Redbone said, pointing. "We might need to try twice."

All gentleness leaked from Boone's eyes when they snapped toward Redbone. "No-bo-dy," he said, drawing out each syllable like a blow, "was talking to *you*."

A hush fell over the observers. At first Robert thought the sudden venom in Boone's voice made their hearts skip too, and no one wanted to make him mad. But when he glanced over his shoulder at the crowd, he saw that Warden Haddock was walking up behind them, and boys were alerting each other with anxious taps to be quiet and still. In the setting sun, Haddock's long shadow stretched far ahead of him in the grass as he walked in his snakeskin boots. His shadow made him bigger. Crutcher stood up straighter when he saw him, no longer leaning against the wall.

"Children . . . ," Crutcher prompted loudly, and most of the boys knew to join him when he said, "Good evening, Superintendent Haddock!"

A few, caught off guard, didn't say anything, only mouthing at the end. Redbone greeted Haddock loudly with the rest, his voice clear and steady, but Robert couldn't make his mouth move. Warden Haddock was looking at Robert, and his eyes seemed to know everything in Robert's mind: about the photographs, the key, his desk, the false reports. Then Haddock shifted down the slant of his cowboy hat, and a shadow fell over his eyes. Robert's bladder had bothered him a little during the walk to the well, but now it bloated. Haddock was carrying his haint jar under his arm.

"Good evening, boys," Haddock said, still staring straight at Robert. "I understand our new haint catcher wants to put on a show for us. To help you boys sleep a bit better at night. Is that so, Robert Stephens?"

Haints might enjoy hearing their names, but Haddock calling Robert's name soiled him and Papa with the sound of his voice. The closer Haddock walked, the more Robert wanted to take a shower and wash him away. Somehow, Robert nodded his head. When Redbone nudged him, he remembered to say, "Yessir, Superintendent Haddock."

"That's what he says, suh," Boone joined in. "Says there was one at the well."

"Or by the trees . . . sir," Redbone said, and speaking up might have been the bravest thing Robert had seen him do, the way Boone's eyes burned into him after.

Haddock made a fluttering gesture with his hand "'By the trees'?" he said. "That sounds mighty vague. There's two dozen trees out here. I surely hope it's not as vague as all that."

Boone's jowls shook, he was so mad, and Robert knew Redbone

had accidentally made a fool of Boone somehow, that Warden Haddock had come because it was *solid*, not vague.

"Henry Jackson," Robert blurted. Haddock knocked his hat back on his head, unable to hide his surprise at hearing the name: Haddock knew him, of course! He likely had killed him.

"Go on."

"His name's Henry Jackson," Robert said. "I feel him at the well, but . . . I might have seen him by the trees. He's a grown man. He's tall. About six foot."

Haddock's eyes shifted to Boone, whose face had gone slack, shocked instead of angry.

The buzzing of the flies from the dead hog rose nearly as loud as its dying shriek.

Robert glanced around to make sure Henry Jackson had not turned up in the watching crowd, that he wasn't hidden behind the hay bales or a corner of the slaughterhouse shade.

Haddock looked around too, raising his hands slightly in readiness. Haddock didn't want to show it, but he was scared. Soon the crowd was glancing around with murmurs, more afraid of Henry Jackson than they were of Haddock.

"You all *hush*," Crutcher said, and everyone was stone silent again.

Two crows landed on the fence post nearest the hog. One made a caw that seemed like a warning. Could that be Henry Jackson too? Could he have come in the form of a crow? Why didn't he fly to the well, then? Or had he already been?

"It may be," Warden Haddock began, "that I remember a young man by that name. Do you remember that name, Boone?"

Boone nodded. "Yessir," he said. "Went by Hank. Could sing pretty good."

Warden Haddock nodded, snapping his fingers. "That's right—Hank Jackson. He could sing sweet as Nat King Cole. Then that big dumb fool tried to run. Now, that was a sad day."

Again he was staring straight at Robert. Redbone, beside him, went rigid. Robert was sure one of them was about to confess their plan to run away as Haddock's pale eyes studied them. Not only did Haddock already seem to know the plan, he seemed to be trying to drive Henry Jackson's spirit away. What haint would stay to hear his name mocked by his killers?

"Yessir," Robert said. "He's the one."

Haddock nodded toward the well. "All right, then. I would love to help put him to rest."

Boone pulled his leather pouch from his pocket. "Come on, then, boy. Tell me where to put it down just like before."

Robert turned to Redbone, maybe for a sign that he should go to the cedar trees first and take a wild guess about the exact spot where he might have seen the haint. But Blue had said *the well*. Redbone gave him a small nod. Robert glanced around for Blue to see if he might show himself to give him a hint, but Blue only wanted to help himself, never anyone else.

"I might not get him on the first try," Robert said. "But . . . maybe toss the dust inside?"

"You saw him way down there?" Boone snapped.

"No, but—"

"Then why you wanna drop my dust thirty feet down?"

Robert felt like he was swimming in the ocean, every limb weary and no land in sight. This was all just a wild guess, and Boone knew it.

"Put it on the cover," Robert said, trying to sound firm. "Right in the middle."

After giving him a glare, Boone followed Robert's instructions, sprinkling the powder from his sack in a loose circle on the canvas covering the well. He looked back to Robert, and Robert nodded. Then they stepped back as if he had just planted dynamite. The crowd stepped back too, all of them craning their necks to see.

Nothing happened until a breeze blew some of the dust outside of the circle on the canvas and Robert's heart raced with exhilaration until the dust settled again. The silence was eerie except the flies' buzzing. The silence told Robert that Blue *hadn't* convinced Henry Jackson to come to the well—might not even have tried to. But he'd come anyway, when Robert had called his name and stood out in the cedars—

"Maybe it's been too long since he was at the well," Robert said when he saw Boone's angry lips start to move. "But I saw him by the trees *today*. One second and he was gone."

Boone grabbed Robert by his collar roughly, yanking him close to his dark shaving bumps and whiskey breath. "Lemme tell you somethin' . . . ," Boone said. "I gotta drive all the way out to Jacksonville to get dirt from my grandmama's grave. If you make me waste any mo' dust, you're gonna wish *you* was dead."

After he let Robert go and pushed him away, Robert's skin still felt knotted in Boone's phantom grip. Boone was strong enough to snap his neck without a thought.

"He was there. I saw him. That's how I know what he looked like."

"Let the boy work," Haddock said. His voice was quiet as the hot breeze.

Robert pointed straight down the center of the cedar grove, or he tried to—but was he standing in the exact same spot where he'd been when he thought he saw a man? And had the man been standing just beyond the other side of the grove, or closer to the center, in the shade?

With the sunlight waning, the cedars' trunks looked different now, the colors wrong. Too many shadows tricked his memory. Each new spot Robert studied looked like where the man had stood, the trunks separated just enough to hide half of his face.

"Don't just point," Boone said. "Show me."

Robert walked toward the trees and Redbone started to follow, but Haddock said, "Not you. Stay where you are." Robert looked back at Redbone, half expecting to see tears again, but Redbone was staring toward the sunset. Redbone probably didn't think he would find the haint and was thinking over what to do next. Redbone always had a plan.

Robert's stomach twisted. He should have marked the spot by the trees somehow! Why had he put all of his faith in *Blue*? If only Crutcher hadn't made them leave, he would have remembered to mark the spot. Robert blinked away tears because he couldn't turn back time and fix something so simple, just like he couldn't go back to the road and not kick Lyle McCormack and sleep in his own bed tonight. Would he sleep in the Box with Redbone?

Dry leaves splintered beneath Robert's boots as he walked in what he hoped was a straight line to where Henry Jackson had stood. This felt as hopeless as looking for blades of grass Blue had floated above on the way to church, every inch as vast as a mile. Was it here? No, wait—he didn't remember seeing a rotted tree stump so close. Robert adjusted his position three or four feet to the right. The two trunks in front of him now seemed to be the correct distance apart, not too close and not too far, like the ones that had framed the haint. Robert tried not to notice how many other trunks also might be the right ones. He felt nauseous as Boone's heavy footsteps followed him. And Haddock's, moving more slowly.

"You sure?" Boone said. "You better be sure."

"It just has to be close, right?"

"Better be within five, six feet," Boone said. "That's why they don't trap easy."

And Robert knew Boone was right because in the church Robicheaux had been caught at one end of the altar and the laughing boys at the other end hadn't been touched at all, or at least he hadn't heard them screaming. Robert surveyed the trunks and closed his eyes to try to remember where the man had been standing, and thought just *maybe* . . .

Robert pointed just beyond the twin trunks in front of him. "There. Right between."

The spot was grass and twigs and dead leaves. Haddock leaned close, inspecting it. The soil was marshier here. "Hold on," Haddock said, and reached into his shirt pocket for a small notebook. He ripped out a sheet of paper and gave it to Boone. "Set the dust on this."

Robert braved another glance back at Redbone, and this time Redbone was watching too. Waiting. Neither of them smiled, but something in Redbone's eyes, beyond words, was the only language that could make Robert feel less afraid, as if he were floating above it all like a haint.

A small brown beetle crawled across the paper Boone had laid on the ground. Robert watched its tiny legs scurry from one end to the other before forever passed and Boone finally said, "Here we go."

Robert's stomach cramped so tightly that he suppressed a cry and couldn't keep from hunching his body like an old man. But Boone and Haddock didn't notice, they were so busy over the spot beyond the cedar trunks where Boone was shaking out some of his dust. Robert heard every grain patter across the paper. The crow behind them seemed to laugh.

Then the awful, complete silence came again. No terrible screeching Robert would have welcomed with all of his heart. And no dancing ashes emerged anywhere near the paper where the haint dust lay still.

"Maybe this isn't the exact right place," Robert said. "But I *know* I saw him."

Haddock's eyes narrowed at him. "I'm very disappointed in you, Robert," he said, gravel replacing the earlier kindness in his voice. "These other boys are too. But I'm quite sure you'll do better tomorrow."

Haddock turned to walk back toward the slaughterhouse. Toward Redbone, waiting on the other side of the cedars. Redbone backed away a step from Haddock before he remembered himself and stood still, his arms rods at his sides. Redbone was breathing fast. Haddock slowed, studied Redbone, and then walked past him. The other boys cleared a path for Haddock, avoiding his eyes.

Redbone hung his head and sighed, relieved to be out of Haddock's sight.

Boone spent some time arranging the haint dust on the paper, salvaging it by making a funnel to tap the dust back into his pouch. Robert watched him work, hoping his mood would improve. At least nothing had been lost! Boone groaned slightly when he leaned on the trunk to bring himself back to his feet. His brow and nose were sweaty.

"Go on back to the dorm," Boone said. "Get washed up."

"I tried my hardest, Mister Boone," Robert whispered. "I swear I did."

Boone wiped his brow with his shirtsleeve, still strangely calm. "Do what I said." Boone sounded like Papa when he was too tired to lecture. Robert followed Boone back toward the clearing, where the crowd was still gathered. "All of y'all—show's over! Go back for check-in."

The boys scattered quickly to obey, some of them running, all of them veering far away from Haddock's solitary path as he walked across the campus ahead of them. Redbone waited for Robert, shifting his weight nervously. They had taken only a step together when—

"Not you, Redbone," Boone said. The quiet in his voice was awful now. Robert remembered Boone's promise that Redbone would pay if anything went wrong.

"Mister Boone . . . ," Robert said, pleading. "It's not his fault. We could try another tree. I did my best, I swear on my—"

Boone's lip curled like he wanted to hit Robert, but instead he snatched Redbone's arm so roughly that a joint cracked and Redbone hissed in pain. Crutcher was still watching from the shade of the slaughterhouse's tilted rooftop. Robert hoped he would step in and say something like Mrs. Hamilton would, but Crutcher only watched. If only she were here! If only someone could see—

"Shut up and go do like I said, or I'll break his arm," Boone told Robert.

"Okay," Robert said. "Yessir."

He pressed his forehead to Redbone's. Redbone's skin was so hot, it felt feverish like Mama's. He was so much more scared than he looked.

"But Mister Boone," Robert said, unable to stop his streaming tears, "I saw another one last night, in the dorm, the one—"

Boone wrenched Redbone's arm, pulling him backward, and Redbone cried out, but he never looked away from Robert. "Shhhh," Redbone said. "*Shut up*, Robert. I'm not scared." It was a lie and it was not a lie, because although fear had pounded a fever into Redbone's skin, his eyes were not afraid. He even smiled a little. "It's okay. You'll get one tomorrow. I know it." Redbone knew Boone was taking him to the Funhouse, the Box, or maybe somewhere worse, but his eyes were unblinking on Robert's telling *him* not to be afraid, that he shouldn't tell on Blue or say anything that could mean his mama might get caught in Haddock's jar. Robert kept staring to be sure, and Redbone nodded his head. "It's okay," Redbone said again.

"Oh, no it ain't," Boone said, pulling on him to get him walking, and Redbone stumbled with him in the direction of the horse stables. Toward the Box.

Crutcher sighed. "I don't know what game you boys are playing with Superintendent Haddock," he said, "but it's a dangerous one. You'll see that now. He's not the sort to play games with, Robert."

"It's not a game." Robert forgot to say *sir* and didn't care. "We weren't playing."

Robert watched Redbone being led away by Boone until they were around the corner and out of sight. When Crutcher turned to leave too, Robert was left alone with the hanging hog carcass and the flapping crows landing beside it. Loneliness was so thick in the air that Robert's lungs rattled with sand. He tried to draw in deep breaths but could not. When he sobbed so deeply that his stomach clenched, his mouth made no sound. It was the purest grief he'd felt since Mama had died—or maybe worse, since he had let down his only friend.

The crows flapped away in a sudden flurry while Robert waited in the growing shadows. At first he barely noticed Henry Jackson standing at the left corner of the cedar grove, still in his cap, as if he'd always been there. He wasn't floating like Blue or the boy in the infirmary or a giant like the man in the church; he just looked horribly ordinary. Robert heard a low-pitched voice singing words he could not hear, a song of the dead. Even after the man was gone two seconds later, his voice carried in the breeze until it died away. Still sobbing—for Redbone, for Henry Jackson, for himself—Robert ran to the spot where the dead man had stood. He ripped a grimy shoelace from his boot and wrapped it around the trunk, wishing again he had done it sooner. *Tonight* had mattered.

He called for Blue all night in bed, whispering in the dark, but Blue did not come to him.

Robert never saw Redbone again.

33

Thursday

At breakfast time, Cleo was sitting in the cafeteria, eating lumpy grits at a table by himself. It was the same table where Redbone and Robert had last sat together, so at first Robert thought he was imagining Cleo—or maybe he was a haint already! Cleo raised his eyes to watch Robert approaching but didn't acknowledge him otherwise, eating hungrily. His face was gaunt and pocked with mosquito bites. He sat in a cloud of stink. After a time, Robert decided he was real. Cleo's fingernails were black and stained with what looked like blood, but he only seemed dirty and starving, not the way a haint might try to look to scare him.

"I'm glad they let you out," Robert said. "We never told nobody nothin' about you. Boone was lying to set you against us."

"I'm eatin'," Cleo said, irritated, his mouth half full. He picked up his fork and turned it over in his hand like a weapon, but Robert wasn't afraid of Cleo when he saw how his hand was shaking. Cleo's eyes were so red that he might not have slept in a week.

"They let Redbone out too?"

Cleo's eyes turned away, glaring at the wall.

"They took him to the Box last night? You see him?"

Cleo's cheekbones turned sharp as knives. His jaw was clenched so tightly that it looked like his teeth could break.

Robert whispered so Cleo wouldn't get madder. "We were at the well and then—"

"Shut up," Cleo said. He rattled his tray, so Robert became quiet. "Ask *them*, not me."

The worst feeling didn't come until Robert realized Cleo's eyes were red from crying, his eyelids puffy with tears. All this time, Cleo had been sad, not angry. Worse than sad.

"Did something happen?" Robert heard himself speak before he felt his mouth move. Cleo's nostrils flared slightly. His damp lashes were matted with mud. His teeth were yellowed, one of his front teeth turning brown. Details about him flooded Robert's panicked mind while he waited for one breath, two, to hear what Cleo knew and what he did not yet know. Cleo only stared down at some ketchup hugging the corner of his plate.

"Robert! Come here!" Crutcher's anxious voice called sharply from across the cafeteria, hushing the room. He was standing in the cafeteria doorway, waving his hand to Robert in urgency. "Don't go near that boy."

Mrs. Hamilton stood close behind Crutcher in the doorway. Her face, afire with alarm and grief, filled Robert's mouth with a sourness he had never tasted. He looked back at Cleo, trying to understand before Mrs. Hamilton could tell him what she knew and he did not yet know. The story was in Cleo's eyes, if only he knew how to read them.

"What did you do?" Robert whispered.

Cleo pinned his lips together to keep his story from spilling out. He rocked slightly back and forth. Even now, Robert wanted to feel sorry for Cleo. He didn't want to feel the pressure rising in his chest that must be a scream.

He felt himself lifted up by his shirt collar, his feet not touching the floor. "Didn't you hear me?" Crutcher said, pulling on Robert the way Boone had pulled on Redbone, half dragging him. His chair rocked back and forth. "Leave it alone."

"What'd he do?" Robert said.

"I'll tell you outside." Crutcher looked to see if any other adults were witnesses and saw none. "Lower your voice."

Outside, Mrs. Hamilton waved them farther away from the door. Her eyes told the same story as Cleo's, only different details.

Robert nearly gagged on the smell of rotten meat from the garbage bin. He remembered the dead hog and its ring of flies.

"I'll take him to the band room," Mrs. Hamilton said.

"Sticking your head in only makes it worse."

"Percy, *hush*," she said. "I'm taking him. I'll tell him."

Mrs. Hamilton clung to his hand and urged him to walk faster as they crossed the field toward the band building. The cornfield fence was in sight and Robert wondered if the hole was cut in the fence. He wanted to pull free from Mrs. Hamilton and run so he would never learn the sad story in her eyes.

"I have awful news, Robert," Mrs. Hamilton said as they ducked into the band building, where the empty chairs and music stands stood in neat rows. "I've had to give this news many times, but you're so young to hear it and I'm truly sorry to tell you."

New horror gripped Robert: maybe it was something he'd never considered! "Gloria?" he said in a mouse's voice.

"She's fine. I know this personally." Mrs. Hamilton steadied herself. "But your friend has died. August was killed last night. He got into a fight in the Box and he was hurt and bleeding, and he died."

Robert did not know anyone named August. His chest swelled with relief. Even when he remembered that Redbone's real name was August Montgomery, he could not be sad because he could still feel Redbone's warm forehead and see his smile, so he could not be dead.

"Did you hear me? Redbone—isn't that his nickname? He's gone." The name lashed Robert with grief.

"Is he at the hospital?" The nearest hospital for Negroes was in Tallahassee, and Papa and Mama had forever complained about how people in accidents died on the way. No white hospital would let you set foot inside, even if you begged and screamed and bled all over the floor. But maybe Redbone was only hurt, and an ambulance racing with a siren had saved him.

"No, sweetie. They found him this morning. It was already too late for a doctor."

The scream he'd swallowed when he was sitting with Cleo tried to erupt from him as he imagined Redbone bleeding on the dirt floor in the dark. His throat cinched with a sob.

"Where is he?" Robert said when he could speak again.

"He's still here. They're burying him today."

"Who . . . did it?"

"It doesn't matter who," Mrs. Hamilton said. "It's another boy. He said it was self-defense. It was a fight. A piece of scrap metal they got in somehow. Boys fight here, Robert. They're scared, and they fight."

"It was Cleo, wasn't it?"

Instead of using words, Mrs. Hamilton answered with a sigh. "You see how upset he was. He was sobbing all morning. He said it was self-defense."

The earth and sky pulled away. Redbone *could not* be dead, and yet he *was* dead. And he had died in a cloud of outrageous lies. Redbone never would have attacked Cleo first! Cleo had promised to kill both of them, and Boone had put Redbone in the Box with him to die. Then Boone and Haddock had set Cleo free to eat breakfast like it was an ordinary day. Instead of punishing Cleo for killing Redbone, they *stopped* punishing him. And Mrs. Hamilton, with her soft eyes and voice, was telling their lies. Cleo had said, *Ask them, not me.*

"They killed him," Robert said. Once he started talking, he said the rest in a hurried breath. "Boone and Haddock. They made Cleo do it. They tricked him by telling him lies to make him mad at us. They did it on purpose. They kill people here. There's haints all over this place—did you know that?"

Mrs. Hamilton gave him a pitying look. She didn't believe it any more than her brother did. "We've all heard the stories."

"Well, they died here, or died running from here. Who do you think does the killing? It's *them*. They come to work every day like killing people is nothing. How can they do that? How can they kill kids and nobody does anything?"

Mrs. Hamilton strained to think of a good answer, or maybe another lie, but she couldn't reply to him for a time. "It's wrong," she said. "As wrong as anything I've ever seen."

Hearing the truth made Robert's bones heavy. He sobbed into Mrs. Hamilton's arms. If she'd been Mama, she would have hugged him for a long while, patting the back of his neck, saying, *All right, try to be brave like your papa,* and then let him lie down and miss his chores. But she wasn't Mama, so when the hug was cut short, he could barely stand.

"Listen to me," Mrs. Hamilton said, her words steadying him. "I *know*."

She'd spoken as if she'd seen it all: the dead boys in the photographs, Gloria's map, the haint at the church. Every secret thing that only Redbone knew—*had* known. Robert felt dizzy when he remembered Redbone was dead.

"I know what it is to have someone killed by violence—the injustice of it. It's the worst feeling there is. My late husband, he didn't die in the war: he got pulled off a train and beaten to death after he got back home. He never made it back to me. I carry that, Robert." Her eyes were bright with tears. "This is yours to carry. There's lots of people working to get you out of here, but you won't find justice in here. If there's any kind of justice, and I do mean *if*, it's waiting outside. After you're out, you can tell everyone about Redbone—how you played in band together and he helped you cope with being here. I saw you two laughing together in the infirmary. That was a special friend who could make you laugh in here, especially when you were new."

"He was covering for me!" Robert confessed, each word fire. "I didn't tell everything—"

"That's behind you now," Mrs. Hamilton said. "Friends protect each other. That's the only meaning of friendship in a place like this. And he knew that, Robert. Only he didn't know it would turn out so bad—"

Robert sobbed, imagining Redbone bleeding and wide-eyed as he realized he was dying, maybe calling for his mama. Had Cleo taunted him and called him names while he died?

"—but if he made that sacrifice, you need to keep your head so you won't get hurt too. Friends die for each other, Robert. The secret to war is the sacrifices friends make for each other, and this is your war. Don't let your friend's sacrifice be for nothing. Don't vex Haddock or make accusations. Promise me that, son. It's the most important promise you might ever make."

"He should go to jail!"

"You've told me, and I heard it. I promise you—*I heard it*." She held his face then, grasping his cheeks tightly, and his neck gave itself over until the weight of his head rested in her hands. "They're going to bury Redbone today," Mrs. Hamilton said. "At Boot Hill. They tidy these things up fast. His family's not coming; I don't even know if they've been told. That's the first thing I'll see about: making sure they're told. But you need to be there to say goodbye, Robert. And I can help you."

"How?"

"You'll play four notes on that trumpet you play so beautifully. It's taps, holding that lovely high C the way I know you can. It's a sound only God could have created. I do believe Redbone will hear that horn all the way in heaven."

"He will?" Robert whispered. He hadn't been sure that a boy who stole a car and got sent to the Reformatory could go to heaven. He was glad Mrs. Hamilton thought so.

"I played it for my husband," she said. "And I do believe he heard."

Robert remembered that Redbone might be a haint now! He might find Redbone leaning against a tree. Or at the well. Redbone might come to his own funeral to watch himself be buried, legs swinging from a fence railing, making funny faces. He almost smiled.

"Teach me how," Robert said.

Something rattled when Robert lifted the trumpet from the shelf. A small key fell to the floor. Mrs. Hamilton's back was turned, so Robert kicked the key away and watched it spin across the room until it slid under the bass drum. He was so angry, he was panting. Was it the key to Warden Haddock's desk drawer? Only a haint would choose such a silly place to hide it. How dare Blue try to give him the key *now*, of all times! Robert was far angrier with Blue than he was with Cleo, because Blue should have been able to stop it. And if Blue had delivered Henry Jackson like he'd said, Redbone never would have been sent to the Box.

"I don't want your stupid key," Robert whispered under his breath. "Leave me alone. I'm *never* talking to you again. *I hate you.*"

Instead of thinking about Blue and the rage he could hardly keep bottled inside, Robert spent his day learning how to play taps. He remembered the fingering easily enough with Mrs. Hamilton's patient instruction, but he struggled with fixing his mouth properly up and down the octave. His high C squealed and stuttered, and his lowest note rumbled. For hour after hour, as Redbone's memory charged him from every direction—even from the tiny bottle of oil he'd given Robert, which was still standing on the chalkboard rack—Robert drove away his thoughts with his trumpet. When he imagined Redbone dying alone, or Redbone's reflection in the mirror on the wall, he couldn't breathe except through the trumpet. He played to forget. He played to remember. His lips grew puffed and sore, but he never stopped practicing: middle C, middle C, F—pause—repeating middle C, F, A—slightly longer pause—F, A, high C—the longest note, his high C, which he often could hit just right before his descent down the scale—A, F, middle C—and then repeating middle C, middle C, F, allowing the final note to float to silence. The music felt like a kind of prayer. Mrs. Hamilton had said he was in a war, and Redbone was a fallen soldier as surely as if Haddock had shot him down instead of walking past him near the well.

Had Haddock known even then? Had he walked past Redbone thinking to himself how Cleo would take care of him because he could do anything he wanted to Cleo too? When the scream tried to rise in Robert's throat again, he blew his hot sobs into the trumpet.

"Again, please," Mrs. Hamilton said. Her voice always came just when he was about to forget he wasn't alone.

Two firm knocks sounded on the door, impatient. Robert looked around to try to see who it was, but only a shadow moved beneath the closed door.

"Keep playing," Mrs. Hamilton said.

Crutcher and Boone stood at the door. Robert's heart raced, but he started taps again, keeping the notes smooth, an accusation in the sad beauty. He kept his eyes on the wall and Mrs. Hamilton's charts of music scales. If Boone tried to touch him, Robert thought he would hit him as hard as he could with his trumpet and didn't care what happened to him afterward.

Crutcher spoke first, gentle and familiar. "Marian . . . the boy needs to stop playing that. He's played it a dozen times. More."

"He's practicing for his friend's burial."

"He sounds good enough. The other boys can hear . . . and it's upsetting."

"They can dig a grave and bury a child, but they can't hear music?"

Robert had played taps an entire time again before Boone took over, less gentle and familiar. "He's got chores. He needs to come on with me."

"Chores?" Mrs. Hamilton said. "That what you call telling this boy when he's chasing ghosts?" Robert kept playing but glanced back at Boone's angry jowls. Crutcher took a step away from Boone, closer to his sister, as if to protect her. The middle C that

Robert played was gravelly and flat as his attention fluttered. But he played on.

"You may not be aware of what emotional stress does to young people," Mrs. Hamilton said. "August and Robert were in band together, so I've seen their bond up close. I'm not sure what all this ghost business is or how you're caught up in it, Mister Boone, but I will tell you that this boy needs time to grieve in a safe environment. And I am providing him with that."

"But, Mr. Haddock—"

"And if that's a problem for the superintendent, you tell him he is free to come here and tell me so personally."

"Marian . . . ," Crutcher said, whining.

"But while he is here, I assure you I will have some questions about why August Montgomery's family has not been notified of his passing. And how a weapon ended up in those boys' hands. Or the fitness of that punishment—the Box—on a boy hardly thirteen years old."

Robert had to stop playing then. His hands were trembling too much.

"He won't like that kind of talk," Boone said with the same weary sadness he'd had in his voice when he knew he was leading Redbone to his death.

"I'll just bet he won't. But if anything happens to Robert Stephens, that's exactly the kind of talk he's going to be hearing—and not just in here."

"*Marian,*" Crutcher hissed, tugging at his own vest so hard he might have torn it.

Boone was faking a smile suddenly. "Naw . . . ," he said, his eyes heavy on Mrs. Hamilton. "She's right, she's right. Terrible thing, what happened. It's a damn shame."

"And Henry Jackson too!" Robert called out. The words that had been bottled up in him flew free. "And the boys from the fire! A lot of terrible things happened! That's why they're *everywhere*. That's why he wants them in his jar! *Isn't it?* Does he think I'm gonna put Redbone in his jar now? Well, I'm not!" Blue too, he remembered. Blue had suffered a terrible death. It wasn't Blue's fault he was a haint. Robert's face itched from his tears.

Speaking the truth had loosened Robert's lungs. Boone was staring at Robert as if he were a haint floating ten feet high, his lips parted and slack. Even Mrs. Hamilton and Crutcher were wide-eyed.

Boone was the first to recover from his outburst. He took off his hat as he ducked inside the band room, taking a step closer to Robert, who remembered how much it had hurt when Boone grabbed him and twisted his shirt. "Yeah, I see now he's talkin' foolishness," Boone said. "He needs time to get his head back on straight. So he don't say nothin' to get in trouble." His eyes dared Robert to say another word, and Robert raised his trumpet to his lips to play taps again, staring back. Robert blew.

"We goin' to Boot Hill at five o'clock, you and them other boys he knew," Boone said, raising his voice over Robert's trumpet. "Here, you bury your friends. And you try to learn so you don't end up in the ground right next to 'em."

If Robert could have killed a man by squeezing his eyes closed, Boone would have dropped dead where he stood. And Haddock. And Crutcher too, although he wasn't the worst. If he could, he would set the entire Reformatory on fire and let all of the boys run with him.

"He'll be there," Mrs. Hamilton said.

When it was time for the band to meet, Robert sat with the sad-faced band students and then helped straighten up the band room. No one mentioned Redbone's name. Robert nudged the big bass drum marked GRACETOWN SCHOOL FOR BOYS to the side and found the tiny glistening metal key he had kicked beneath it, just the size for the lock on a desk drawer. Robert slipped the key into his sock and enjoyed the solid feeling of his secret. He didn't feel fear. Even the grief that had sliced his belly all day was squashed to a low pulse of pain when he remembered his plan.

Friday—*tomorrow!*—he would find a way to sneak into Haddock's office and open his drawer. He would steal his photographs and his haint jar, even if it meant he needed help from Blue like he'd promised. He wouldn't do it for Blue—he would do it for Redbone, so his true killers wouldn't try to trap his spirit in this awful place.

And then he would run. With the jar. With the photographs. With his stories. Even if he died trying.

34

Fourteen boys came to bury Redbone, most of them from their dorm, where his bed sat empty, but also a couple of older boys who had just met him in band. They took turns with four shovels they shared between them to scoop into the ground, clearing room for the pale plywood casket in the back of the white truck. None of them looked toward the truck. Once, Robert saw the simple casket in the corner of his eye, the darker wood whorls like eyes staring back, and he remembered riding with Redbone in that same truck and how Redbone had given him advice about the Funhouse, and he couldn't understand how Redbone was lying dead when he could still hear Redbone's voice in his ear. That was the only time he almost cried again, so he made sure he didn't look at the truck anymore. As they worked, the thin grass on the surface gave way to red-brown soil that grew redder and more like blood the deeper they dug. Like Mama had said.

When it was Robert's turn to take the shovel, he pitched it hard into the packed soil, and his elbows and palms rattled. Maybe he'd hit a rock. Digging was hard work, but Robert welcomed the effort because it gave his anger a place to go as he grunted with each strike. The boys working beside him created a *chop-chop-chop* chorus as they worked, and an older boy from the band started singing a work song none of the rest of them knew, but they caught on and sang the words: "*I said I need more power—power, Lord—I need an everlasting power—power, Lord . . .*" And before they knew it, Crutcher said quietly, "That's deep enough, fellas."

And the hole for Redbone was dug, a lonely pit in the soil that looked impossibly small beneath the cedars and pines on Boot

Hill. Robert noticed that this graveyard had no crosses or headstones like the cemetery behind his church. No flowers or wreaths or favorite items marked where a person was buried or honored their living. They were about to lay Redbone in the ground like he was a dog. He felt so angry again, the sky above him flared bright pink.

"Come on, Tex, you're big and strong," Crutcher said to the boy who had led the singing. "You too, Calvin. Let's go carry him."

Robert felt like he should have said he would carry Redbone's casket too—he remembered Papa's tight face when he'd been a pallbearer at Mama's funeral—but he couldn't make himself speak up. He didn't want to touch Redbone's casket or think about what he looked like inside. Instead, while Crutcher and the two other boys lifted the box out of the truck to move it to the freshly dug hole, Robert looked around desperately to see if Redbone's ghost was watching from somewhere in the trees. But no other haints or people were in sight. Boone wasn't there either, of course. Or Warden Haddock. They were cowards.

Crutcher cursed when they dropped the casket too hard into the hole, and it wasn't even properly nailed shut, because the top flew open a few inches and there was a *thunk* sound as Redbone's body jumped, and in the shadows inside, Robert saw a glimpse of Redbone's thin arm, almost like he was trying to wave to him, and then the casket fell closed again. Robert almost threw up, but he swallowed the sour taste back down into his throat.

"Lord," Crutcher said as they all stood in a circle around the casket in the hole, "we are gathered to lay August Montgomery to rest. Please bless this soul and forgive him his trespasses, for he was young and had lost his way." Robert expected a better prayer or a passage from Scripture, but none came. "Do any of you boys have any remembrances of August?"

Stone silence except for quiet sniffling. Robert tried to open his mouth but couldn't.

Even now he was letting Redbone down.

"He made me laugh," said the boy with round glasses Robert had nicknamed Owl.

The other boys nodded and agreed with murmurs.

"He never wanted to see nobody get in trouble," another boy said.

More agreement. Each one who spoke gave strength to the rest. Another boy remembered Redbone dressing his wound when he cut himself on a saw on lumber duty. A boy from band said Redbone kept good time and would have loved marching with the bass drum on Main Street, struggling to say something although he had not known Redbone hardly at all.

"He was a child of God," Tex said, which was better than Crutcher had done. "He shoulda had a chance to live his life."

All of the boys agreed.

"He . . ." Robert fought to force language from his burning throat. He wanted to say *He died because of me*, but he couldn't confess in front of so many mourners. "He was my best friend." Five small words cost so much effort that Robert wanted to curl on the ground.

"It's time to play now, Robert," Crutcher said. He handed him his trumpet, which had been resting against the trunk of a tree.

Robert hesitated. He could barely feel the breath in his lungs. How could he play?

"You want me to?" Tex said. He was first trumpet, after all. He would play it better.

Robert shook his head, taking the trumpet from Crutcher. Blinking acid tears from his eyes, he tried to blow. No sound came at all through the instrument except ragged breath.

"Take your time, son," Crutcher said.

Tex put his hand on Robert's shoulder, and Robert imagined Tex was Redbone standing tall and alive beside him, and his lungs opened up. Despite all of his practicing, the notes were unsteady and wavered in and out of key, but no one seemed to mind. Robert remembered what Mrs. Hamilton had said about how Redbone might hear him all the way in heaven, so he took a deep breath from his belly before he played his high C, the saddest sound of all, and even Crutcher looked at him with startlement because the note was so sure and strong. Birds flapped out of the trees, shamed by its perfection. Robert held the high C for an impossibly long time, until Tex was nodding and smiling at him. The last six notes were easy, his lungs emptying out. The memory of his music floated over them long after he had laid his trumpet down.

Mrs. Hamilton had said Redbone died like a soldier in a war, so Robert saluted him the way he'd seen in picture shows, and the other boys all saluted Redbone's casket too. Then Crutcher said, "All right, let's cover him up now," and their shovels flurried to return the soil they had taken and slowly hide the pale wood of the casket. Although tossing loose soil was less work than digging, Robert's shovel felt heavier in his hands as he watched the last traces of Redbone buried under the dirt. The triumph of his high C note was too small a solace, especially when he realized that no one from Redbone's family was with them. Would his mama just get a letter in the mail saying *Oh, well, he's dead, sorry you missed the funeral*? If he died here too, would that same letter go to Gloria and Miz Lottie? Would his family come to Boot Hill one day without knowing where to find him because his grave wasn't marked?

None of the boys were crying. Since crying on an ordinary day could get them sent to the Funhouse, they had trained themselves to hide their crying. All of Robert's crying was hidden in the plan in his head, which was the only thing that got him through burying Redbone. Once the crater dipped only a little less level with the rest of the ground, they patted the soil with their shovels. And then it was done.

"Anyone who wants to ride in the truck, climb in back," Crutcher said. "If you walk, no one's holding supper for you. So walk fast. And don't miss dorm check-in."

Most of the boys raced after Crutcher to ride in the truck, but Tex and the two other band kids decided to walk together. They waited to see if Robert wanted to walk with them. Robert only shook his head. If not for his plan, he might have tried to run right then, headed blindly into the woods far from the spot Gloria had shown him on her map. To stop thinking about running, he remembered laughing with Redbone by the swimming pool at the idea of Boone crawling on the diving board after haints that weren't there.

"I'm sorry, Redbone," Robert whispered. "I didn't know what they would do."

A twig snapped from behind him, and Robert whirled around with a gasp. He was so eager to see Redbone's ghost that his knees went weak.

But it was only Blue, shoulders hunched inside too-big mourning clothes. "I'm your best friend now," Blue said.

Blue hadn't come when Robert called him to try to help with Hank Jackson, but now Blue wouldn't leave Robert alone, walking ahead of him as they headed back to the cafeteria. When Robert tried to veer right or left, Blue instinctively knew which way to veer to mimic his path, like a shadow in front of him. Robert tried kicking the back of Blue's leg as hard as he could, but although Blue appeared as solid as any other boy, Robert's boot passed straight through him. Robert almost lost his balance from kicking so hard at thin air.

Blue looked back over his shoulder. "You think you can lick a haint? You think this is *me* walking here and not . . . me just wishing I was here? Making you see me?"

"Where's Redbone?" Robert said.

"Where you just put him."

"Shut up!" Robert said. "You know what I mean! Don't you care about him?"

Blue was silent so long that Robert thought maybe he *didn't* care, but Blue finally said, "I didn't know Redbone would get cut like that. By the time I knew, it was done. And I told Henry Jackson to go to the well just like I said. Haints don't always know how to find one place, especially if they're not visiting somebody they know. It takes practice to get it right. You saw him, didn't you? He came like he was supposed to. You messed it up, not him."

Robert could hardly see for his tears, since Blue was saying exactly what he'd been saying to himself: it was his fault. The hog's cry had distracted him, and he'd missed his chance to catch Henry Jackson just because he hadn't come exactly to the well. Why hadn't he ever thought the haint might just come *close* to the well because it was all the same to him? For the first time, with no one but a haint to hear, Robert's sob rose to a wail.

"Crying won't get you free," Blue said, and the promise of freedom was enough to stop Robert from wailing. "And I miss him too, you know."

"He's a haint now, ain't he? He's not with you?"

"We don't all sit around in a clubhouse. Is that what you think? Everyone who dies doesn't come back; most just move to what's next. They die cleaner, or don't feel like there's anybody left here to look after, so they don't get stuck. Sure, Redbone might come around to see after you, but he won't look like me—not at first. He might come to you in a dream, though. Dreams are the easiest way. But I don't dream like you, so I can't talk to him yet until he learns how. He knows you're gonna make things right here, so he might be long gone without a care. We don't get vexed about everyday things."

"If he's gone . . . is he in heaven?"

"After I'm not here anymore, maybe I'll know. But after I know, I bet I won't be able to tell you. You'll see what heaven is about for yourself, just like me, I guess."

Robert wrestled in silence with the idea that Redbone might be happily away from the Reformatory, which felt good, but his grief deepened knowing that he might never be able to see him like he saw Blue. He'd been *counting* on seeing him, he realized now. How could he see haints he'd never met and not Redbone? No part of life felt fair since the day Lyle McCormack pushed him.

Robert had a hard time remembering why he'd expected fairness at any turn. Mama used to say *Life isn't fair* when he cried over not getting his way, but he hadn't known then that unfairness was so big, covering the world.

The steeple of the Negro church appeared to signal how close they were to the campus. With a downward slope, his pace quickened. He was still mad at Blue, but he didn't have time to waste. He had one chance to get his escape right.

"Do you have a plan?" Robert said.

"Sure I do. First thing is to put Haddock in a good mood."

"How?"

"You know how," Blue said. "You already tied a shoelace around the tree. Call Boone out and put Henry Jackson in the haint jar like we planned. He'll let you keep looking for more."

The unfairness of giving Boone and Haddock what they wanted after they had arranged for Redbone to get killed roiled inside of Robert. Could he trust himself not to cuss them out? Or grab a knife from the butcher shop to see how *they* liked getting stabbed?

"Do it tomorrow. Early. They'll leave you alone tonight."

"Then what?" Robert said.

"Did you get the key?"

"Just lucky I saw it," Robert said. "That trumpet was a dumb place to put it."

"You found it, didn't you?"

Arguing was giving Robert a headache. The sunset's red fireball glared through his skull. "Yes, I have the key. Now what?"

"We'll do it like we said," Blue said. "I'll draw him away so you can get in through his office window. He likes fresh air, and that screen on his window is loose enough to break. I rattle it sometimes, right behind his head. So I can cause a fire in the kitchen at suppertime—that's what I'll do. It's so easy, with all the flames. I can tip over some grease and do that real quick. I know he'll go running if it's big enough. He'll be scared the governor might hear."

"Don't hurt anybody!" Robert said. "You're just as bad as them."

"I won't burn up any thumpers," Blue said. "Not on purpose. Not if they're quick."

"I won't do it if you hurt anyone," Robert said. "Quick or not. You sure don't sound like somebody who died in a fire."

Blue sighed as if Robert were being unreasonable. "I guess all your talk about sacrifice is just for your own kind, but fine. I'll set the fire when no one's nearby."

"Redbone's not enough of a sacrifice?"

"You're right," Blue said more softly. Maybe Blue loved Redbone after all; Robert would be less mad at him if he thought Blue had feelings. At least he could trust him a little more.

The cafeteria was in sight ahead, with the line out the door of boys who had made it late or who were on punishment so they had to stand at the end, where Robert saw Tex and the band students who had returned from the burial. They were still at least fifty yards away, but Robert reminded himself not to be obvious about talking to Blue, in case Boone saw him.

"Grab a satchel from somebody's locker," Blue said. "You'll need it to carry the haint jar and the photos so you won't drop them. But don't carry *anything* else: it'll just slow you down." For an instant, Blue *did* seem like Redbone, who was always so quick with plans. But Blue knew about things and places that Redbone hadn't known about. Blue looked and acted like a boy, but he had been learning and watching for thirty years.

"Okay," Robert said. "Then, when I grab it, I'll just climb back out of the window and run for the hole in the fence?"

"Do everything else just like your sister said."

"How do I know the hole is there?"

"It's there," Blue said, certain. "Right behind those weeds near the chairs behind the Funhouse."

"How do you know?"

"I saw your uncle June, that's how," Blue said. "He cut that hole today."

That night, when the dormitory was quiet and dark except for moonlight through the windows, Robert opened his eyes when he heard pages flapping.

Redbone was sitting at the foot of his bed reading a *Flash Gordon* comic book. The moonlight was bright enough to see the red of Flash's costume as he battled a green-clad figure from another planet. Robert was so intrigued by the comic—he hadn't seen one the whole time he'd been at the Reformatory!—that for three whole seconds he forgot Redbone was dead. Then he sat up, clutching his sheet to his chin.

"Bone?" he whispered.

Redbone flipped the page before he looked at Robert and smiled. "Damn right."

No sign of blood or cuts on him. Redbone was wearing his normal pajamas. Robert checked to make sure no one else was stirring and that Boone wasn't spying in the doorway to try to catch Redbone.

"You're a haint now?"

"Guess so," Redbone said. He didn't seem interested.

"Did it . . . hurt?"

Redbone looked away, flipping another page. "Hey, you know who Ming the Merciless reminds me of? Haddock. Right?"

Robert nodded. "Yeah. They're the same." He was going to say more, but he remembered Redbone was a haint and he felt unsure of what he should say. Had Redbone heard all of the nice things everyone said at his burial? But Robert didn't think Redbone wanted to talk about that.

Redbone suddenly closed the comic and put it down on the mattress. He looked at Robert again, his expression serious. "It's a big deal, what you're gonna do," Redbone said. "You're gonna tell the whole world about this place. You're gonna get it shut down."

Robert nodded. "Yeah."

"You scared?"

Robert started to shake his head, but that wasn't the truth. "Kind of."

Redbone grinned. "Well, that's why I'm here: to tell you not to be scared. And one other thing . . . You're not gonna like it, though."

"What?"

Redbone sighed, ruffling the comic pages. He was suddenly wearing his work clothes, not his pajamas, but haints could change the way they looked easily. "It's about Blue."

"That little rat—" Robert started, but Redbone raised his hand to make him quiet.

"He's not a rat," Redbone said. "He's like . . . Jack Johnson. He's a fighter." Robert studied Redbone closely, trying to see if he was really Blue in disguise, since that sounded more like something Blue would say, not Redbone. He went on: "You know how he said he's your best friend now? It's really true, Robert. He is. You need him to get into that office and you'll need him after the dogs start chasing you. He'll help you get away."

"I'll be gone before the dogs even know it," Robert said.

Redbone sighed sadly. "No. You won't. You better trust him. That's what I came to say. Even if deep down you don't want to, you *have* to trust Blue. What happened to me, that's not Blue's fault. Trust him like he's your brother. Don't fuss with him, Robert."

"But I don't need him," Robert said. "You can help me now."

Redbone shook his head. "Nah . . . I can't."

"Why not?"

Redbone pointed toward the window. "Just look. You'll see."

Robert followed Redbone's pointing finger and looked toward the windows, where the light was starting to glow like morning. The brightness turned to a flare and—

Robert sat up in his bed with a gasp in the near-dark dormitory. Everything suddenly felt more solid, from his mattress to the sweaty clothes matted to his back. He knew before he even looked back at the foot of his bed that Redbone would be gone. The comic book was gone too. He patted the mattress and looked over the side of the bed to be sure.

Redbone had just been a dream. Robert's chest heaved a few times as his body decided if he would cry again, but he didn't. Redbone had come to visit his dream just like Blue had said!

"Okay," Robert whispered just in case Redbone could hear him. "I promise."

The daylight was so new that Robert calculated he still had at least half an hour before he had to get up. He needed his rest for the day ahead. Robert was even smiling a little as he turned on his side, away from the window, to try to go back to sleep.

Tomorrow night, he would not be in this bed. Tomorrow night, with Blue's help, he would be gone.

35

Friday, 8:05 a.m.

Gloria recognized the sound of Ole Suzy's chugging motor outside the house before she jumped out of bed. Mrs. Hamilton was always gone before eight in the morning, so Gloria knew she was the only one in the house. She'd been dying to call Miz Lottie because she hadn't spoken to her yesterday, but she had heeded warnings not to use the phone and give away her location. She had barely slept because of her anxieties that Robbie's escape might go wrong.

Miz Lottie stood on the front porch, ready to ring the doorbell, when Gloria flung the door open, making Mrs. Hamilton's chimes sing frantically. Miz Lottie was dressed up in her pillbox hat again, no doubt to look nice for Mrs. Hamilton's monied neighbors.

"Come in," Gloria said before she could ask about the harried look in Miz Lottie's eyes.

Miz Lottie only stepped in far enough to allow Gloria to close the door behind her. "Get packed up. Then lie down flat. Time to come back with me."

"Did Uncle June cut the hole?" Gloria said.

"Yes. Now get your suitcase," Miz Lottie said. "I'll tell you the rest in the truck."

"Maybe we should both stay here, Miz Lottie," Gloria said. "She's gone all day."

Miz Lottie seemed to consider it, peering around the room but stepping no farther than the entryway as if she didn't want to be tempted by its comforts. "No," she said. "She might come home early. Leave her a nice note, but it's time for you to go. Hurry so we can get back."

Gloria finally saw the worry in Miz Lottie's brow that she had been trying to hide—something more than her arthritis and sore joints—so she rushed to her room to dress from the suitcase she had not yet unpacked. When she peeked into Mrs. Hamilton's empty room, she found a pad on her desk, so she slipped in to hurriedly write a note.

Thank you so much for all of your help during our family's hard time. I will never forget you.

Gloria Stephens (sister of Robert Stephens, daughter of Robert Stephens Sr.)

She felt unexpectedly sad writing the goodbye note to a woman she'd just met. In Chicago, few people would know the name Robert Stephens or how Papa had tried to help families in years past. For the first time, Gloria let herself feel how hard it would be to leave a place she knew and that knew *her*: her family, her history. She thought about Miss Anne and how she'd never written her a note of thanks for the cash still hidden in Miz Lottie's house, which they would use to buy the five train tickets to Chicago from the station.

"Don't look so sad," Miz Lottie said when Gloria emerged ready to go. But Miz Lottie looked sad and small herself.

The truck's engine struggled less than usual as Miz Lottie turned the key, but Gloria still wondered how such a rickety, complaining truck would make it to the railroad trestle beyond the Reformatory and then all the way to the Tallahassee train station.

"June said he was gonna fix it," Gloria said.

"June did the best he could with it," Miz Lottie said. But her voice was thin.

"What's wrong?" Gloria said. "There's something you're not saying."

Miz Lottie didn't answer at first as she peered out of her window to back out of the driveway. Luckily there weren't any other cars on the street, since her swings in reverse were always wide. Once the truck was driving forward and had passed the neighborhood's cheerful sign, Gloria said again, "What's wrong, Miz Lottie?"

"Tonight at the railroad trestle, it's just gonna be you and me looking for Robbie."

"What do you mean?"

"June and Waymon can't come with us."

Stoically, Miz Lottie told Gloria that a deputy had seen Waymon pick up Uncle June on the road by the Reformatory and pulled them over. When he didn't like their answers about what they were doing out there, he locked them up for vagrancy. Miz Lottie said she'd gotten a call from Waymon at the jail and had gone to try to get them out, but Sheriff Posey had threatened to lock her up too and sent her away.

Such terrible news! "But Uncle June really cut the hole?"

"Yes," Miz Lottie said. "Waymon was at the cell door and nodded his head at me like everything was all right. Course, I couldn't ask him on the phone. They hung up that phone on me 'fore I barely heard his voice."

"You know for *sure*?" Gloria said. "If there's no hole, we can't send Robbie there."

"Waymon wouldn't have nodded like that if it wasn't done. I know him, pumpkin. He even smiled at me. The sheriff beat him up a little, but he had a look in his eyes like he'd won."

Waymon rarely smiled, so a smile was signal enough. Still, tears warmed Gloria's cheeks. He always said he would end up in jail because it was the white man's trap for him: he just didn't know when.

She had counted on having Uncle June and Waymon with them. She hardly knew how to imagine the escape without them. And what would happen to them after the escape? Even helping

Miz Lottie manage the steps from the platform to the train would be a challenge.

"Guess the Lord only wanted three of us in this truck tonight," Miz Lottie said.

"Why would the Lord want that?" Gloria snapped, and Miz Lottie stayed silent. Gloria thought about taking it back, but she was too mad. Or scared. Or both.

"No sense turnin' on the Lord now," Miz Lottie said, although to Gloria it felt more like the Lord—or some other powerful force—had turned on *them*.

Unthinkable words came to Gloria's throat. She could probably find a way to get a message to Mrs. Hamilton, who could get a message to Robbie. "Should we . . . call it off for a couple days? See if the sheriff lets them loose after the weekend?"

"*No,*" Miz Lottie said firmly. "Spiteful-ass crackers might kill that boy in there. Now, lie down out of sight. We're on the main road."

Gloria obeyed, curling her body down low so that her eyes were level with the glove box. "I'm scared with just the two of us, Miz Lottie."

"No sense in bein' scared. Ev'rything else is the same as before. You can get Robbie to Chicago fine. Don't you worry. Without payin' for those extra tickets, you'll have money for clothes and a boardinghouse, at least 'til you find your papa."

"What do you mean 'you'? *We* can get Robbie to Chicago." Miz Lottie clicked on her turn signal, with its regimented rhythm matching Gloria's heartbeat. Miz Lottie didn't answer, so Gloria said, "You're still coming to Chicago too, aren't you?"

Miz Lottie sighed. "Pumpkin . . ."

Gloria felt as if she were melting through the truck's warm floor to the road below. "You *have* to come! We're all supposed to go together."

"Gloria, you know how much I love Robbie, but he's your responsibility now," Miz Lottie said. "That's what you told me that day you packed him up and moved back out to your cabin, ain't it?"

"I didn't mean that! I was just—"

"No, pumpkin, you was right," Miz Lottie said. "Robbie is yours. And June and Waymon are grown, but they're mine. I can't jump on a train with no one left behind to see after them, make sure they get out in one piece. Besides . . . child . . . I don't got but a few years left. No sense in me going up in all that cold when my life is here in Gracetown. That's not so for you and Robbie. Your life is as far from this place as you can get, with your papa."

Gloria knew better than to argue; if anything, Miz Lottie had never planned to take that train and leave behind the house she had stuffed with memories. And Gloria *had* worried that Miz Lottie might not be strong enough for the challenges of the trip—that moving away might cut her life short. But she might never see Miz Lottie again, an idea that hurt so much that she sobbed until she gasped for air.

"Let it out," Miz Lottie finally said. "I already cried enough for the both of us. But when you're through crying, we gotta go over the plan. We'll get it just right for your brother."

Gloria's breath hitched as she wiped her face against her dress sleeve. "Do we have enough gas?" Gloria whispered. She couldn't make out the gas gauge from her angle on the floor, but Miz Lottie's truck usually hovered right near empty.

"That's my girl," Miz Lottie said, smiling down at her. She lurched to a stop at a traffic sign, flinging Gloria back against her door. "Filled up Ole Suzy last night."

The Hatchetts sent a traveling suit for Robbie that looked fresh-bought, just his size.

Since all of his other clothes had burned with the cabin, Gloria just packed his new suit, an old pair of Waymon's dungarees that might fit him if he rolled up the cuffs, and a faded mill shirt Miz Lottie thought might have belonged to Papa. It wasn't much to begin a new life.

Once the suitcase with their meager belongings was safely stored under the tarp in the bed of the truck, Gloria set her attention on ways she could be helpful to Miz Lottie: washing and drying her dishes, cleaning old food out of her icebox, pinning her laundry on the clothesline . . .

When she'd lived at Miz Lottie's house while she was working for Miss Anne, her days had felt like one long set of chores. Miz Lottie rarely asked for help, but Gloria had never been able to stand spending so much effort making Miss Anne's life easier while Miz Lottie had no one to help her. Waymon and Uncle June were good about fixing whatever was broken, but Miz Lottie did her own cooking and washing, although it took her more time and forced her to spend long parts of her day dozing. If Uncle June and Waymon got sent to Raiford for a long prison sentence, Miz Lottie's life would be twice as hard.

But the plan was set, so there was nothing left to talk about. Miz Lottie's kitchen radio played *Fibber McGee and Molly* while Miz Lottie shook chicken pieces in flour and seasoning in a paper bag before putting them in a skillet to fry. Gloria watched her at every stage, memorizing the amount of flour, how much salt and pepper, the dusting of paprika. Miz Lottie had never written a recipe down for her, but Gloria wanted to remember them all. Gloria savored the scent of the grease as it heated. Only then did it dawn on her that Miz Lottie's kitchen was her favorite place left standing in the world.

They would not head out to the railroad trestle so early that they would be more likely to be spotted before Robbie made it to them, but they could not arrive too late, when he might have dogs and guards at his heels. Five o'clock, they had decided. They would make sure the burners were off and the curtains were drawn and they would drive out to the old railroad trestle that stood over the creek near the county line to wait. The time was six hours away when they set it, but the day whittled away an hour at a time until it was only four hours, and then three.

For now, grease from the skillet was popping halfway to the ceiling and Miz Lottie was laughing at Fibber McGee and Molly fussing on the radio and Gloria was torn between her eagerness to rescue Robbie and her wish that she could root time still, each drive equal and ferocious inside of her, slowly sawing her to the bone.

36

4:30 p.m.

Henry Jackson came moaning back to the spot where Boone put his powder down like it was nothing, a further insult after Thursday's failure in front of Warden Haddock. After Boone had carefully swept up his ashes, he looked back at Robert as if to say, *Too bad you couldn't do that yesterday,* and Robert wanted to kick him. No one else witnessed the appearance of the ash hill, not even the boys at the butcher's. Robert missed Redbone so much that his insides ached. He hid tears while he replaced the lace of his boot, yanking it tight.

His boots would need to be tight for running. The boots from Papa.

Boone didn't ask about putting down dust where Redbone had died, although maybe he had already tried on his own. Redbone hadn't been a haint yet when he was in the Box, so it probably wouldn't have worked anyway, and at least Redbone was safe from Boone's traps in Robert's dreams. But Boone said Robert could spend the rest of the day hunting for haints if he wanted to, so Robert walked back and forth across the campus making sure everyone saw him in case Haddock asked about him later. He passed the schoolhouse where Owl and other boys from the dorm were copying from the chalkboard, and Owl smiled at him through the window. He passed the doorway of the band room, where he saw Mrs. Hamilton writing music on the chalkboard, and he only said "Fine!" when she asked how he was doing before he hurried away because he didn't want her to see his escape plan in his mind. He was proud of himself for never telling her, although he had wanted to—but Gloria would have been so disappointed. Besides, he'd told Redbone and then Redbone had died, so telling was bad luck.

He was too close now for mistakes.

The dormitory was mostly empty and unlocked during the day, except for a couple of boys who had earned privileges in the rec room, so Robert snuck into the locker room to organize his supplies. He found a small satchel in a locker piled with junk at the far end, which seemed fine except for a small tear in the corner. Blue must have known it was there.

When Robert opened his own locker to stash the satchel until later, he found a drawing on a sheet of paper: Redbone! The likeness was so good that Robert recognized him from the part in his hair and the tip of his nose. The goofy grin on his face captured him too. At first he thought Blue might have drawn it, but it must have been the artist from their dormitory. A cloud sketched behind Redbone's head implied that he was in heaven—but the artist didn't know about haints. Robert slipped the drawing into his satchel and hoped it wouldn't wrinkle too much. Now he could show Gloria a picture of his friend. The artist rarely spoke, but that boy could draw! Maybe if the Reformatory shut down, he might get out and be a famous artist one day before somebody beat him too bad and broke his drawing hand, or just broke the part of him that liked drawing.

He checked for the jar of Vaseline he'd hidden at the rear of his locker, under his tie, and found it untouched. The jar might fall through the hole in the satchel, so he would stuff that in his pocket instead. He would need it when he got out of Haddock's office, crouching in the bushes. *All over, even your hair,* Gloria had said. Redbone had said the dogs would chase him, but that didn't mean they would find him. His uncle June had been a soldier for real. He had help from the living, not just the dead.

When Robert heard footsteps in the hallway, he slammed his locker shut—too loudly.

Since it didn't have a lock, the door flew back and almost hit him. He was pushing it closed tight again when he heard boys' voices passing in the hall. No one stopped. No one noticed him.

No one knew.

"Blue?" he whispered. "What time you gonna set the kitchen fire?"

But Blue did not answer, of course, so Robert could only wait. Robert stood at the dormitory window beyond the rows of empty beds, staring across the overgrown field toward the cafeteria. Did haints even follow time? Did Blue understand how important it was that Robert must start running before check-in? Before dark?

Redbone had said to trust Blue, so Robert tried to trust the haint with all his heart.

He didn't know how much time passed before he saw handwriting emerge from the dust on the windowpane near his nose, one letter at a time like a crawling snail: *B-U-R-N-I-N-G*. No one was writing the letters—they appeared from thin air—so Blue's signal had come in his own way.

Robert stared until the slow writing stopped and the word stared back. He'd expected to bolt out of the dorm as soon as it was time, but even with so clear a message, he stood staring longer than he meant to. Being this close to his bed reminded him that he could just curl under his sheet and go to sleep tonight instead of risking his life in the woods—if he even got as far as the woods. He had to go to Warden Haddock's office first or Blue would trip him up for sure. He'd been whipped bloody just for *asking* how anyone ran away. How many hidden graves of boys who had tried to run had he walked over already?

He didn't see any smoke from the cafeteria yet, but he thought he saw a small crowd. He had to hurry! Why wasn't he moving?

Finally, thinking of Gloria helped. She would be so worried if he didn't come! He slipped to the empty hall to go to his locker. He shoved the petroleum jelly in his pocket and slung the satchel with Redbone's portrait over his shoulder. He untied and retied his laces, making sure to yank them tight. The warm key to the warden's desk still lay safe inside his sock, the only place he dared to keep it.

Why hadn't he eaten more of his cheese sandwich at lunch? He was already hungry. He hadn't slept well, so he was tired too. Robert's stomach was a ball of knots. Maybe this was how Papa had felt when he climbed into the trunk of the reverend's car to leave them, forehead creased as he thought about the danger and how it might be a mistake to go.

Right before he was free.

Robert's nostrils tingled from a smoky smell. But he was walking *away* from the cafeteria, so this smoke was from the ghost fire, the cursed spot where a shed once had stood, the place where Blue had died. The field seemed to shimmer, so Robert stayed at the spot's outer edges, but sometimes his foot landed so close that his toes felt singed, making him hop away. Would the fire keep burning after he set the haints free? After he showed everyone the photographs of what Haddock had done? Maybe he could finally put the fire out.

Distantly, a bell began an excited, tinny clanging: a fire alarm at the cafeteria! He couldn't see the cafeteria from this side of the campus, but he was sure that must be it. Ten minutes at least had passed since Blue's writing on the dirty window, and maybe the fire was good and big now. If Blue had started the fire in the back, where he'd seen the haint who'd been stabbed, maybe no one had been close to the burners when Blue set them on fire. And since it wasn't dinnertime yet, the cafeteria would have been mostly empty. Robert wished he could see the fire to be sure—both how big it was and to be certain no one was hurt. "Trust Blue," he whispered, a reminder. If no one would be hurt, he hoped the fire was *big*. He hoped they'd have to shut the kitchen down and the judge would send everyone home.

The brick administration building stood ahead as pretty as a church, but the white truck parked outside that had carried Redbone's body reminded Robert that it was a deadly place. He slowed his pace when he saw a white woman step out of her parked car to go inside, but she never noticed him. Robert ran toward the rear of the building, looking for refuge in the neatly clipped hedges that hugged the length of the wall, so thick that he was hidden from anyone who might pass except for his boots, and maybe even they were not visible.

A line of six unevenly spaced windows loomed above, vines crawling up the walls between them, and he realized with horror that, with all of his planning, he had never figured out which window was Haddock's. Breathing fast, he crawled to the first window and peeked inside: the lobby. The woman who had left the car was sitting directly in front of him, her back turned.

Robert ducked down fast. If she saw him, his escape would be over already. His heart was pounding so hard that he was sure it must be shaking the windowpane. Robert took a breath and tried to remember the layout of the lobby. If the first window was for the room where people sat down and waited, the next window might be behind the secretary's desk.

As if to confirm his memory, the secretary's phone jangled from the next window, which was cracked open to let in a breeze. She picked it up on the first ring. "Superintendent Haddock's off—" But the person on the line cut her off. "Wait a minute—just slow down . . . ," the woman said. Robert inched slowly down the side of the building behind the hedges, the jutting bricks scraping his skin white with scratches like claw marks as he moved. "Oh my! Oh my, yes."

And she hung up the phone with a clatter. "Mr. Haddock, there's a fire in the kitchen!"

The third window was dark, but it was halfway open, and Robert was wondering if that third window was Haddock's when he saw movement and the curtains were flung open. *He was there.* Robert couldn't see Haddock's face from his angle below the window, and he prayed Haddock couldn't see him, but a palm was pressed to the upper window as Haddock stared outside, looking toward the kitchen. Robert wondered if he could see some of the smoke . . . and if he *liked* seeing smoke that reminded him of the fire he'd set.

"Just go," Robert whispered, hardly louder than a thought.

As if Robert had willed it, Haddock's palm disappeared and his footsteps landed hard across the floor, mingled with someone else's. Haddock was speaking rapidly, a few words flying out of each window as he passed from his office out to the lobby. "Don't call . . . until I say so . . . I'll . . . you round up Blake . . . call you back . . . a report." Haddock slammed his office door closed. Keys jingled as he locked it. "You hear me, Doris? Don't call anyone 'til I take a look." His voice was in Robert's ear as he passed the lobby window.

Haddock sounded scared. For the first time, Robert understood the power of enjoying someone else's fear. Haddock had told him the town hadn't forgotten the 1920 fire, so maybe he was afraid a new fire would shut him down. Robert's own fear was gone—he was smiling as he savored Haddock's fear, feeding on it.

Robert waited until he heard the white truck's engine start up and Haddock raced off.

Even then, Robert counted to ten to make sure Haddock wouldn't come back.

"Bit of excitement?" the visitor inside said through the window, sounding chipper.

"Always something on Friday," the secretary said, pretending to match her cheer. But this woman who had called him a "scrawny little nigger" the first day he came was probably scared because her boss was scared. Robert hoped her heart was racing so hard that she might faint, the same way he'd felt at the Funhouse.

Once he was sure Haddock wasn't nearby, Robert inched past the secretary's window to the third, where the curtains were parted like an open mouth. After checking to make sure no one was watching him, Robert stood on his toes to peer inside. The back of Haddock's desk and leather chair were nearly close enough to touch. He could see far across the empty office to the photo of Haddock with his dead baby sister on the wall. The window was open enough for him to squeeze through without touching it or making a racket, but when he jiggled the loose screen, it held instead of falling. Dammit. He pushed inward harder and it gave an inch more, but he realized he should have brought something sharp to cut the screen. How had he forgotten?

One more glance around, and Robert reached inside the screen to try to feel for a pin that might be holding it in place. Nothing at first, and then—there! With his fingertips, he tried to jiggle the pin left and right. He raised himself higher on his tiptoes for more reach and it finally gave . . . and the screen widened maybe six inches more into the room. He knew he should try to be patient and feel for another pin, since the screen was still dangling, but Robert suddenly felt desperate to be inside the office and out of sight from outside. Unevenly jutting bricks gave him the footing to lift himself a bit higher, and he began a headfirst slide. Gloria used to call him "li'l skinny bean," and now he was glad to be so small. He felt himself catch below the waist and wished he had hoisted his leg in first: at this angle, he would tumble to the floor! But the leather chair's back was close enough to help him gain balance, even as it twirled slightly and rolled forward on the wood floor and hit the side of the desk with a *THUNK*. Robert held his breath until his vision dimmed, but no one came to Haddock's door.

He was still only halfway through the window, so he arched his back against the wobbly rim of the screen, which scratched him as he raised his leg to climb inside. The scratch felt deep enough to bleed, but Robert moved more quickly, hanging on to the thin shelf above the curtain rod to keep his balance until his feet landed on the floor. The screen finally came loose on his back, but Robert caught it before it fell to the floor. Perspiration ran into his eyes, stinging him as he panted and waited once again to see if anyone would come.

No one. And he was inside! This was the hardest thing he had ever tried, an act so bold that Haddock would never imagine it, and he was actually *doing* it. Rushing now, Robert sat on the bare wooden floor behind the desk to fling off his boot, which he'd tied so tightly that he spent nearly a minute fumbling with the knotted lace with sweaty fingers. He heard the clock on Haddock's wall tick as the minute hand moved up, so he noticed the time: 4:55 p.m. It was almost dinnertime, so more boys would be flocking to the cafeteria soon, fire or no fire. He might go unnoticed on an ordinary day, but maybe not today. If he didn't make it to the hole in the fence before someone noticed he was gone, he would have no chance to get away. While he worked to untie his lace, Robert glanced at the space under the desk and saw traces of a circle of powder on the floor he recognized from Boone's leather pouch: a trap was laid to keep Blue away just like Blue had said. If he could just get his boot off—

The knot answered his prayer and came loose, and Robert pulled off his boot and sock to find the key buried in the meat of his foot's sole, where his calluses were thickest.

The center desk drawer and its keyhole stared Robert in the face.

With a trembling hand, Robert slid the key into the lock, but he knew even before he tried to turn it: the key was too small to catch. For a few seconds, Robert refused to believe his bad luck, trying again and again. The keyhole was so oversized that he almost pushed the key inside, but he yanked hard to retrieve it.

As if it were playing a game, the drawer began rolling open. It wasn't even locked! Robert raised himself to his knees as he rifled through the drawer's neat rows of pencils, blue ink pens, red ink pens, staples, and paper clips, everything eerily neat. The only papers were two certificates from the state of Florida with blue designs in the margins. He reached as far back as he could . . . Nothing except a ragged old cigarette.

"It's not the right drawer," he whispered to himself, imagining what Blue or Redbone would say if they were with him. And why *wasn't* Blue with him? This was all Blue's idea!

Cursing Blue under his breath, Robert finally noticed the sets of drawers on both sides of the desk, but none of the drawers seemed to have a lock. Leaning down, he saw that the largest drawer on the desk's left side had a keyhole hidden close to where Haddock's knee would be, on the *side*, not in front. The keyhole was much smaller than the one for the center drawer.

"Please, please, please . . . ," Robert whispered. The longer he sat in this office, the more he was daring Haddock to catch him.

The key clicked and turned easily. Leaving the key in the lock, Robert pulled on the drawer. It was too heavy to give at first, so he pulled harder . . . and it rolled toward him. A wooden case of Coca-Cola bottles came into view, the bottles full except for two empty ones. The case was so large that it filled the entire drawer . . . except in the very rear, where Robert saw a large envelope as golden yellow as firelight, sealed with a string wound at the top. Robert was so excited to see the envelope that he almost forgot about the haint jar, and he worried about where the jar was hidden as he pulled out the tightly packed envelope. He smiled. The haint jar was hidden behind it.

This time, his good luck froze him still. It was here! It was all just like Blue had said.

". . . the Fourth of July . . . ," said Haddock's secretary, passing close to his door. "My family's in Clearwater, so I'm thinking we'll . . ." The rest was muffled.

Robert held the envelope but did not open it. The horrible images inside pulsed against his fingertips like a writhing snake. He was sure that if he glimpsed one more photo, he might see Haddock's profane work every time he closed his eyes. Instead, he crammed the envelope into his satchel, barely leaving room to squeeze the haint jar in beside it. Robert turned the jar's lid to make sure it was closed tight, so none of the ashes would fall out.

"I've got you," Robert said to the haints inside, not sure if they could hear. "I'm gonna take you to the creek to let you loose."

With the window screen set aside, it was much easier to climb back out of the window than it had been to climb in. The bulky satchel caught in the corner of the window as he jumped down, but it came loose with a tug. He hid behind the bushes, heaving and light-headed as if he'd just run a mile, dizzy with the size of what he'd just done. Robert patted his pocket and found it empty: Where was the Vaseline? He panicked until he realized the jar had fallen out of his pocket, landing a foot from his boot in the dirt.

Robert took his time, careful. By the time he'd slathered his hair and face with the warm goop, except for his eyes, he wished Gloria had given him two or three jars. He slickened each of his arms and legs with it beneath his shorts, then reached under his shirt to try to smear it across his chest. He thought of several spots he'd missed even as he scraped out the last of it with his index finger. Damn! But it would have to do. Through the window, Robert heard the woman visitor say maybe she'd better come back on Monday if it was a bad time, but the secretary said she was sure Haddock would be back soon, her voice still pretending everything was fine.

Robert had to leave, and *fast*. He didn't want to bring the empty jar, but he also didn't want to leave it behind, so he scooped up some loose soil under the warden's window and buried it, a sour memory of burying Redbone. That done, he peeked from behind the bushes to see if anyone was in sight. From there, he had a clear view all the way to the Funhouse about sixty yards away, which was always empty and locked until after dinner. Beyond it stood the cornfield fence where he prayed the hole was waiting.

Robert wanted to take off running, but he couldn't draw attention to himself, so he emerged from the hedges as casually as he could, scanning the rear of the building as if he were searching for haints. As much as he wanted to go directly to the Funhouse, he decided to walk in the direction of the Negro side of the campus, which wouldn't look strange to anyone—and then he would veer toward the Funhouse in a wide loop. His heart slowed with each step he took, the plan seeming less dangerous and easier with every stride.

Since he wanted to avoid the fire spot this time, his walk took him past a small supply shed that looked locked. But it wasn't locked. The shed door opened and Crutcher emerged holding a large custodian's broom. Robert was so close to the door that they stood face-to-face.

"Robert Stephens!" Crutcher said. "What in the world are you doing?"

"Catching haints," Robert heard himself say before his brain caught up, when he was still hoping Crutcher wasn't really there. "Mister Boone said I could." He prayed Crutcher wouldn't demand to see inside his satchel, which hung heavy behind his back. But what if he did? What would he do if he saw the shocking photographs inside?

Crutcher frowned, dabbing at Robert's shiny forehead. "What in the world . . . ?"

Sand seemed to clog Robert's mouth. Why hadn't he waited until he was at the Funhouse to cover himself in petroleum jelly? All he could think about was Gloria waiting for him and how he couldn't go to her if Crutcher caught him so soon. Even if Crutcher reported the photographs to the sheriff, which he might be too afraid to do anyway, that didn't mean Robert would be free. And he wouldn't be able to free the haints trapped in the jar.

"I asked you a question," Crutcher snapped.

"Haint . . . grease," Robert said. "It pulls them to you. That's what his grandmama said."

Robert couldn't see Crutcher's face clearly as he stared up because the sun was shining behind him, so he shifted slightly and saw grim disapproval glimmering in Crutcher's staring eyes.

"Be careful," Crutcher said, and he paused so long that Robert was *sure* he knew Robert was running, until he added, "Don't go to work at the kitchen today. There's a fire."

Robert let his eyes go wide with the surprise he'd been trying to hide. "Yessir. I won't. I'll go wash up at the dorm." The dormitory was the farthest place from where Robert was going and might delay anyone looking for him. He was proud of himself for the lie.

Robert expected him to say more, but Crutcher jogged off toward the kitchen, holding his broom with two hands in front of him like a weapon. Robert watched him go, breathing fast, and leaned against the shed to regain his balance after his scare. The shed's ragged wooden door was still partially open to reveal a dark space inside that smelled humid and sour, but—just like with the envelope—Robert knew better than to look too closely. Hadn't Redbone or Blue warned him about the shed? He crossed to the opposite side, where he would be out of Crutcher's view, and changed his path to walk directly to the Funhouse. He'd already explained himself once. He could do it again.

Full of confidence from his successful evasion, Robert walked steadily, even quickly, in direct strides. The Funhouse's long white building had seemed so large that first night, but in daylight it was puny and sad. The truck had made ruts in the grass from driving back and forth so often, so Robert followed the ruts until he noticed that his boots were leaving a pattern behind him in the packed soil. *That* wouldn't do! He went back and kicked at the soil to cover his tracks, reminding himself that he had to be careful about leaving tracks out in the woods too. He would have to pretend he was a Seminole Indian warrior evading cowboys, or a slave running for the North on the Underground Railroad. Robert walked carefully in the thickest grass beside the ruts, leaving no visible signs of his path. With each step, the Funhouse drew closer, until he could see the chipped paint on the walls.

Two chairs were arranged for the white boys in front, and six for Negro boys in the rear.

Instinct took Robert to the chairs where he and Redbone had sat, just in case Redbone came. But the chairs were empty in two neat rows, waiting for that night's unlucky boys. The luckiest of them would go only to the Funhouse, not to the Box. Or the shed. Since Redbone wasn't waiting for him, Robert concealed himself behind the far side corner of the Funhouse, near an old tire and broken beer bottles hidden in the shadows near the cornfield. The cornfield fence was barely ten yards from the Funhouse walls, stretching in both directions as far as Robert could see. In his imagination, he'd thought only one clump of weeds might be growing wild against the fence, but weeds seemed to be everywhere along the fence line except for patches where boys had pulled them. There was no marker to help him find the hole!

He tried to remember everything Gloria had said; he'd recited her words from visiting day over and over in his head: *By the chairs on the colored side.* He stayed hidden in the corner of the wall closest to the six empty chairs, scanning the fence again. Would they have cut a hole by a fence post? Where the weeds were thickest? The minute he left the shelter of the Funhouse, anyone might see him squatting by the fence, so he didn't want to root around for the hole in plain sight. But of course he couldn't see it from a distance; Uncle June was too smart for that.

A voice clawed through Robert's calm: *Maybe there isn't really a hole—Blue just* said *there's one to get you to steal the haint jar,* and Robert's heart thudded with dread, then sped with rage. Redbone had said to trust Blue, but maybe that had just been a dream, or Blue playing a trick on him. Blue's treachery felt so obvious that tears came to Robert's eyes.

"You said you were gonna help me!" he shouted as loudly as he dared. "I don't see it!" Only the wind answered, rustling the corn plants growing beyond the high fence.

Robert wiped runny snot from his nose on the back of his hand, and some of the petroleum jelly smeared on his lips with the taste of medicine. Would it sting if it got in his eyes? Or blind him? What if he got as far as the woods and couldn't see? The escape plan felt hopeless in a hundred ways. Robert's stomach cinched tight. If Warden Haddock found him with his photographs and haint jar, he would kill him. It seemed obvious now, but Robert wondered how he had forgotten that part while he was sliding back out of Haddock's window, almost grinning. Even if he didn't run away, what would he do if he went back? Could he hide the jar and photos somewhere? Robert wondered if it would be worse to run and be chased by dogs or to stay and be afraid he'd be discovered. Could he put the stolen items back in the drawer? Was there still time?

A crow cawed near him. When Robert looked up, the crow was only Blue, leaning on a wobbly fence post. Blue was wearing a cap and striped tie that looked out of date, maybe the way he had dressed in life. The fence post he was leaning against was the only one that wasn't standing completely upright, like a loose tooth. Robert should have known to look there first; the weeds were thick around Blue's feet, to his knees.

He meant to say thank you but instead he said, "I would've found it. I just didn't want anybody to see me." He was so relieved that his heart was racing.

Blue shrugged.

"Did anybody get hurt in the fire?" Robert said.

"Hurry up and get through the hole or you're wasting the whole point of the fire."

But Robert had to know. "Tell me."

"Not because of *me*," Blue said. "Someone got stupid and ran at it with a towel and he ran too close. He's all right, though. His hand's sore, but it'll heal. He jumped back fast."

Robert imagined a boy engulfed in flames, screaming like the boys who had died with Blue. He would hate himself if he made someone hurt like that or if someone died for him. "You swear on your mother?" Robert said.

Blue frowned but he nodded. "Yes. On my mother. You have the jar?"

Robert tapped the satchel he was carrying.

Blue grinned. "Told you it would work. And you were so scared."

"I'm still scared," Robert confessed.

He expected an insult, but Blue's face softened. "We'll make it—promise. Like I said, you're my best friend now. I wouldn't let my best friend get caught."

"But"—Robert hated to say it—"you couldn't help Redbone. He was your best friend before me."

Robert waited, hoping Blue would point out a dozen ways he was a different case, but Blue never answered. So Blue couldn't promise safety, only his help. Maybe that was enough.

"Will I still be able to see you in the cornfield?" Robert said.

"It's hard to show all the time, but I'll come when I can."

"And in the woods after that? At the creek?"

"Yes," Blue said. "All the way to the railroad trestle. I'll be watching even if you don't see me. And when I want to call you . . ." He croaked like a crow again, his eyes turning black like a bird's before he blinked and they looked like normal eyes again.

"How will I tell you from the real crows?"

Blue laughed. "Real crows get scared! Crows love pecking at dead things, but they sure don't love spirits. If you hear a crow near you, you'll know it's me."

Uncle June had cut the cornfield fence links in a neat, regimented line, the loose flap hanging by a nail on the fence post so no one could see it sagging. When Robert unhooked it and pushed the broken fencing down flat in the weeds, he had more space to crawl through than Warden Haddock's window, although his face itched from the ground. Once he had gotten through to the other side, he propped the fencing up, trying to make it look as natural as Uncle June had. He could tell it was sagging, but it wasn't obvious. If no one knew which way he'd run, they were most likely to think he had headed toward the farm road beyond the Negro side of the campus. Maybe they would send the dogs the wrong way.

Just like that, Robert was in the cornfield. He would have loved the cover from fuller fall corn, but even the summer corn rows were tall enough for him to crouch down unseen as he walked parallel to the fence's straight path toward the woods, which still weren't in sight in the massive field. He occasionally found broken or abandoned farming tools in his path, but none of the work crews or supervisors were in the cornfield so late in the day, so close to supper. Robert tried to stay clear of the fence in case any groundskeepers were working on the other side, but as he ran he saw glimpses of the Reformatory campus through the fence: an old water pump, a storage lot full of large crates, a parking lot with two more old white trucks.

But he was alone in the cornfield—*truly* alone. No sign of Blue now, but he trusted Blue's promise that he was with him even when Robert couldn't see him. He didn't run fast enough to wear himself out or to trip over his feet in the boots from Papa, but he ran at a steady pace between the cleared rows of corn stalks, weeds, and leaves lashing at his arms. The satchel on his back was uncomfortable as it bumped harder and harder against him the faster he went, but Robert Stephens breathed through his tightly gritted teeth and ran for his life.

37

5:10 p.m.

Thick black smoke billowed from the kitchen's side door like a rearing dragon's head. A scream from inside was a thirty-year-old echo in Fenton Haddock's ears. He was no stranger to screams, to be sure, but a scream from burning sounded like no other. Haddock had not stood this close to any burning except a bonfire since That Night thirty years earlier, when he had sworn off both liquor and flames, and time both peeled away and slowed, making each footstep interminable as he walked through the wall of smoke to behold the fire's work.

Smoke battered his eyes, but he blinked to see tendrils of flames scrabbling like fingers to reach toward the outer kitchen from the fire's nest on the stovetops that were now hidden behind mist. Instead of the pounding fists from behind the burning shed door (*Let us ouuut!*), footfalls surrounded him as kitchen workers and boys scattered and groundskeepers ran inside to help douse the flames. Crutcher led a screaming boy through the doorway. A towel the boy had been clutching was left smoking on the floor. The boy's face was bright with terror and agony.

Haddock wished he had brought his camera. The fire was glorious. And terrible. But glorious. Haddock's mind felt cleaved in half: one part excited, the other mortified. The hungry flames were a delight, but, dear Lord, if the fire spread and burned down the whole kitchen, or the cafeteria—

"Grab those extinguishers!" Haddock shouted even as the gleeful part of him whispered: *Let them all burn.*

Luckily, or unluckily, his men were well trained, and fire extinguishers hissed foam in the burning room as groundskeepers beat back the flames. Boone was a quick thinker, using the garden hose to fill a large tub because the hose wasn't long enough to reach the fire. Boone gestured for a burly teenager to help him lift the sloshing tub closer to the smoky doorway.

"One . . . two . . . three . . . ," Boone and boy counted in unison, and they groaned with their exertion as they swung the tub of water with all of their strength, drenching the smoking stovetops. The wall within hissed and crackled under the gallons of water, sending more steam and smoke into the adjoining rooms, but Haddock felt the fire die. A groundskeeper stepped in with an extinguisher to spray foam anywhere left smoking. He coughed as he worked.

Time was, Haddock would have grabbed a fire extinguisher or the other end of that tub, but he stood watching his men work as if the scene were a picture show high up on a screen. He felt grief that he had arrived so late. Despite what a beautiful monster the fire had been, Haddock could not have invited it to dwell with him today. New stoves and remodeled walls would be covered by insurance, but if the fire had grown any bigger, Tallahassee might close him down. As of now, the entire kitchen *hadn't* burned down—just one of the back rooms. The fire hadn't even reached the shelves of food sacks in the storeroom beside it. And it hadn't reached the new, costly freezer, thank God.

"Anyone else hurt?" Haddock called out. The boy who'd tried to swat the flames was sitting just outside of the doorway, still sobbing as Crutcher wrapped his burned hand with that oh-so-fancy white handkerchief always stuffed in his front coat pocket.

"Naw, suh, we got ev'rybody else away," Boone said, huffing from his efforts.

In his half-fugue state, Haddock observed his men at work opening windows, sweeping smoking debris—*Wasn't that his favorite broom from the shed?*—foaming down every inch of the now-ruined back room with his best cookstoves. Fire lived in raging beauty and died in silent ash, painting everything it touched black. For a time, Haddock regretted only that it had died so soon. After the sadness came anger.

"What the hell happened?" he shouted, and the flurrying motion around him stopped.

"I don't know, suh, but we 'bout to find out," Boone said, his face no less angry. "I was hangin' meat in the freezer and next thing I knew, the room was on fire. I told all them boys in here to line up outside. The Funhouse is gonna be busy tonight. The Box too."

When Haddock ducked through the doorway to go back outside, twelve shivering, sniveling boys were lined against the wall, in rough order of height. One stoic teenager stood at the far end, staring straight ahead with tear-pooled eyes—Kendrick, who was due for release at the end of the month and had avoided a day of trouble until now—and then a pathetic collection of wiry younger boys shaking like pine needles in the wind. Kendrick was sixteen or seventeen now, and from his size he was long overdue for a trip to the shed. The smaller boy with the burned hand was still crying, lined up with the rest, holding his bandaged hand over his heart.

The injured boy looked weakest, so Haddock started with him. "What's your name?"

"Tuh . . . Tuh . . . Tuh . . . ," the boy said, struggling to speak. "Turner."

"Let me see that hand." The boy stuck his wrapped hand out, and it wavered, trembling.

"Hold still," Boone warned him, and the boy tried.

Gently, Haddock rested the boy's hand on his left palm and unwrapped the loose handkerchief with his right, until the blistered black and red peeked through. The burn was a doozy, maybe second-degree, or closer to third. The burned flesh smell teased Haddock's nose.

"How'd this happen, son?" he said in his Pastor Haddock voice.

"When I . . . suh-suh-saw the fire, I ran in with a tuh-tuh—"

"The towel," Haddock finished for him. "You ran in with a towel to try to beat the fire out."

The boy nodded, relieved to be understood. "Yessuh."

"Then what happened?" The boy hesitated, lip trembling. Haddock moved his face closer to loosen the boy's tongue. "I said *what happened*?"

"It jumped up at me!" the boy said. "It was . . . luh-luh-little . . . on the stove . . . and when I hit it, it jumped up tuh-tuh-twice as big and cuh-cuh-climbed up the wall to the ceiling! Like it was . . . alive!"

"Mr. Haddock, that's just what happened, sir," Kendrick said at the far end. His voice rumbled like a man's now, not a boy's.

"That right?" Haddock said to Turner. "All right, son, you told it well. Go on and run to the infirmary. Tell the nurse to look after you."

"Should I take him, Mr. Haddock?" Crutcher said.

"I expect he knows the way," Haddock said.

Crutcher watched the boy as he scampered off, nearly tripping on the cement steps because he was half-blinded by tears. Crutcher, that impertinent SOB, wanted to challenge him like his bitch sister did at every turn. Crutcher hadn't worked at the Reformatory a full year yet, and Boone said he coddled the boys too much. A black eye or loosened tooth might fix that—later.

Haddock strolled the length of the line of boys until he reached Kendrick at the end. "Did you see the fire start?"

"No, sir," Kendrick said. He looked over Haddock's shoulders, avoiding his eyes. "I only saw Stutterin' John run in. Then he got burned."

"Who's responsible for the cookstoves?" Haddock said.

"You talkin' to him right now," Boone said with venom in his voice.

"Me, sir," Kendrick said. "I'm over the cookstoves."

"And you didn't see the fire start?"

"No, sir. I was helping the boys chop carrots on the counter."

Haddock stepped closer to Kendrick until he could smell the fear baking from the sweat on his brow. "You're in charge of the cookstoves. But you didn't see it start."

"Wasn't none of us in there, Mr. Haddock," Kendrick said.

"You left my goddamn stoves burning unattended?"

"No, sir. I swear it on all my people. On my grandmama. None of them burners was on, Mr. Haddock. We was still choppin' carrots. They . . . was running late. We hadn't started boiling yet. Wasn't nobody in there."

Haddock pressed his palms in a prayer position, his fingertips to his lips. He leaned closer to Kendrick, reminding himself that he could be gentle now because he would teach Kendrick's lying ass a lesson to remember him by in the shed later. "So . . . you're trying to have me believe . . . that fire started all by itself? Is that what you're telling me?"

Kendrick didn't have the nerve to repeat the words out loud. He only nodded, his stoicism giving way to a tiny tremor of his jaw.

"Explain to me," Haddock said, "how a fire starts by itself."

Kendrick wanted to answer but didn't. Haddock surveyed the boys' faces and saw their absolute agreement, not only that the room had been empty but that they *knew* the fire had started itself. Awareness brushed the back of Haddock's mind. He stepped away from Kendrick as if to escape his own fledging thoughts.

"The first one of you who can explain to me in plain English how that fire started by itself won't go to the Funhouse," Haddock said. "The rest get fifty lashes."

A small, gap-toothed boy raised his hand. Haddock blinked to make sure he wasn't hallucinating: except for his gapped teeth, the boy was a ringer for Kendall Sweeting, who had died in the fire in 1920. Again Haddock felt himself slipping through time. One by one, all of the other hands went up. They all knew. Haddock realized he knew too.

Haddock pointed toward the boy who looked like Sweeting. "You," he said.

"A haint," he whispered.

Haddock shot a look at Boone. The anger in Boone's brow had caved to nervousness.

"It's true," Kendrick said. "I never seen one, but . . . the younger boys . . ."

"That room's haunted," another boy said. "Always cold, even with all the burners on."

"We used to see him sometimes, that white boy with the knife in his back," said the boy who looked like Kendall Sweeting. "We thought it was done with, ever since . . ."

The ground rocked beneath Haddock's feet. Haddock turned to Boone. "Was that where you found the haint in the kitchen?"

Boone nodded. "Yessuh. That very room. Like I told you, I never saw nothin' like it." Clint Newsome, that had been his name. Just like Cleo, Boone had promised a slow-witted boy he would never go to the shed again if he buried a butcher knife in that swamp-trash troublemaker's back when no one was looking. Clint Newsome had died on that kitchen floor in a mess of his own blood at least four years ago. And Boone had *just* captured him for his jar.

Haddock knew haints could touch objects in the physical world—hell, Lucy had taught him that. Broken windows and rattling lampshades and slamming doors had followed him all his life. But he had never heard of a haint starting a fire . . . until now. Could it have been Clint? Had he escaped the jar? Or was another haint taking up his cause?

Haddock realized his heartbeat had sped up while the boys were watching, so he took a deep breath until he felt his heartbeat slow. If a new haint had set the fire, he'd put that haint in his jar too. That was what his haint catcher was for.

"Where's Robert Stephens?" Haddock said.

"He didn't come to the kitchen today," Kendrick said.

"I saw him by the schoolhouse before," one boy said. "But he didn't come to class."

"I saw him by the band room," said another. "Outside the window."

"So he's everywhere and nowhere, is that it?" Haddock said, raising his voice.

Finally, Boone explained: "I said he could go hunt haints today."

"But where is he *now*?" Haddock said. The pinched look on Crutcher's face made Haddock's eyes land on him. Crutcher fussed with his pocket, looking for his missing handkerchief. Instead, he used his sleeve to wipe sweat from his brow.

"I saw him not twenty minutes ago," Crutcher said. "Out by the . . . shed." In that instant's pause, Haddock could have sworn the man's skin was turning gray. "I grabbed the broom after I heard the fire alarm, and that's when I saw Stephens. I told him to stay away from the kitchen and he said he'd go to the dormitory to wash off the grease."

"What grease?" Boone said.

Crutcher hesitated. "On his face. Maybe it was dirt. He was filthy from looking for haints. I was rushing to the fire, so I didn't get a good look."

Crutcher was lying: Haddock could practically smell his lie, but it was apparent in his uncomfortable fidgeting. "What the hell was Stephens doing in my shed?" Haddock said. The shed would no doubt be a good place to hunt for ghosts, but Crutcher had no business nosing around. Crutcher, unlike Boone, had never been invited with him into the shed. He brought only men he trusted most, as a treat. Could Crutcher had taken Stephens back there for a quick ride himself? *That* would be impressive. Maybe he'd misjudged Percy Crutcher.

"No, sir," Crutcher said. "He was just outside. Twenty or so minutes ago, as I said."

"Find him," Haddock said. "Bring Robert Stephens to me right now."

Marian Hamilton was having a crisis of faith.

Not faith in God: if the war and Walter's murder couldn't shake that, nothing could. But her own judgment was suddenly suspect, making her rethink every decision she had made in the past six months, starting with coming back to Gracetown instead of moving to Los Angeles to play in a studio band, an offer straight from Louis Armstrong. And buying a house in a community where so few people could afford to buy it from her, or even rent it, if she wanted to leave. And taking in a fugitive girl.

No, *that* was no mistake. She was proud to shelter Gloria Stephens.

Her biggest mistake—perhaps her *only* mistake—had been to start volunteering at the Gracetown School for Boys. She and Percy had heard stories of the horrors at the Reformatory since they were children, and after she'd seen the troops' powerful reaction to music during the war, she'd thought music might help heal these boys too. But their horrors were smothering her now as well, interrupting her sleep, making her wonder if she recognized her own face in her mirror.

She was changing—she was sure of it. If she were the same person she'd been when she first came to work at the Reformatory, she would have quit on the spot and gone to the sheriff or, even better, to the FBI. Haddock was covering up a murder—probably more than one. August Montgomery's death was the first she'd experienced in her short tenure, and she'd *known* him, even if it was only a few days. And no punishment for the boy who'd killed him? No visit from the sheriff to file a report? A rushed, unmarked burial in the woods with children digging his grave while his family still did not know he was dead? When she'd asked Haddock's secretary the day before, she'd brusquely pointed out the typed envelope sitting in the outgoing mail bin, too late for the afternoon pickup. The boy would be buried for days before his family knew he was dead. Marian had tried to read the name and address, but that spiteful heifer had covered the envelope from her view and told her to stop sticking her nose in the superintendent's mail.

Despite all of this, she'd gotten up and dressed for work and driven to the campus like it was an ordinary job on an ordinary day. If she tried to air Reformatory business with Haddock's friends in the Gracetown establishment, she might end up behind bars herself on goodness knew what ridiculous charge, or have her house burned down. She knew better than to waste her time talking to that redneck sheriff, but why was she still here? Who was she becoming?

"For the boys," she whispered to herself in the empty band room, among the rows of trombones, trumpets, and drums she had hoped would deliver joy. "I'm here to help these boys."

But was she? *Could* she?

Marian didn't usually leave the campus before six in case boys wanted to practice late, but she pulled open her desk drawer and began cramming the contents into her handbag: a hairbrush, a pack of Wrigley's gum, her palm-sized photo of Walter. She had come to work as usual today, but no more. She had to tell Percy—

Marian sensed someone in her doorway and almost gasped at the shadow, convinced it was Warden Haddock ready to confront her and make good on the malicious promises in his eyes. But it was Percy, his hat in his hand across his chest. His face was wretched.

"I saw it," Percy said softly. "The door was open, so I walked right in. I saw, Marian."

Marian didn't want to guess what horror her brother might have seen, so she waited for him to explain. "That shed. The one behind the administration building? I went inside."

He looked pale enough to faint, so Marian pushed a wooden chair to him and he sank down. She closed the door behind him and pulled down her blinds so no one would spy on them.

"What did you see?" Marian said.

Percy's glassy eyes stared ahead, miles beyond her. "I've driven boys there bound up like hogs," he said, his voice cracking. "I did it just the other day. I thought it was just another punishment like the Box."

"What's worse than the Box?" Marian said. "We couldn't have put prisoners of war down there without violating the third Geneva Convention. I've been telling you, Percy!"

"After what happened to August Montgomery, I had to go try to see about the stories. A boy told me Haddock rapes them in that shed." He'd lowered his voice at the end, but not enough to blunt the shock to Marian's ears. She'd heard of beatings and disappearances . . . but rape too?

Percy nodded to confirm the ugly truth. "Boy called Haddock the devil like he meant it. And I saw it, Marian. Not where the brooms and tools are up front—but in the back. Past a bedsheet hanging like a curtain. There's a filthy, bloody mattress on the floor. And chains. Just like the boy said. He was telling the truth all along. Haddock's barely trying to hide it. The door wasn't even locked! I think Boone knows. Maybe they all know. *And I drove that boy there.*"

"Oh Lord," Marian whispered, the silent prayer slipping from her lips. "Lord have mercy. We have to be away from this place, Percy. We have to tell."

"I don't have proof," Percy said. "But after what I saw . . . I just know in my bones."

"What about August Montgomery? Maybe we can call the NAACP . . ."

"The NAACP almost got Lower Spruce burnt down the other night!" Percy stood up, his strength returned. He rubbed his face as if his veil of conscience weighed too heavily upon him. "You're talking foolishness."

"Then we have to leave," Marian said. "We have to leave and never come back. We can't be a part of it, Percy! Every day we come here, we make what they do here seem all right. We're no better than them!"

To her great relief, Percy was nodding. He had made up his mind before he came to her. "Yes," he said. "But we can't leave right now. There was a fire in the kitchen . . ." At her start, he held up his hand. "No one hurt too bad. Haddock is blaming a ghost."

"That explains it all, doesn't it?" Marian said. "With all the filthy, immoral things he's done, no wonder he's half-crazy with ghost stories."

"He told me to find Robert Stephens. That's his 'haint catcher,' or whatever nonsense."

"Where is Robert? Is he all right?"

"I don't know, Marian, but I saw him covered in Vaseline, carrying a bag on his back. I was so busy worrying about what I'd seen in the shed, I didn't think twice. But now that I look back on it . . . he might be running away."

THE HUNT

38

5:25 p.m.

The whole world was summer corn plants. When Robert strayed away from the fence to try to avoid being spotted as he ran, he lost his bearings and thrashed through the stalks in a panic, like the time he almost drowned after jumping from the Misery Swamp dock and Gloria reached down to save him. He wasted valuable time trying to veer back toward the fence rather than running straight ahead in what he guessed was the direction of the promised woods, but even tracking the position of the low-hanging sun couldn't keep him from getting lost and tangled in the endless green field. He wished he had a compass to guide him north. When he found the fence again, he was *too* close. A loud argument between two white boys on the other side reminded him to duck low. He hoped they wouldn't hear his ragged breathing.

And he was sure he heard dogs. Every few steps he stopped running to listen past his heart's roar to be sure the hounds weren't chasing him. Usually the barking was only in his imagination; once, the yapping dog he heard from the road behind him sounded far too small to be a tracker, but he started running faster to be sure. But the quicker he ran, the more he lost track of the columns of corn, panic coursing through his body like lashes from Haddock's whip. How could he make it through the woods if he couldn't even find his way in the cornfield?

Haddock was probably chasing him by now, releasing the dogs from their kennel. Soon Robert was crying from the horror of what he'd done and the hopelessness of trying to run. His legs buckled and he tumbled down, skinning both of his knees white in the fall. The haint jar landed so hard that he was afraid he'd broken it, so he rifled quickly through the satchel to be sure it was intact. It was all there: the slightly wrinkled drawing of Redbone, the tied pack of photos, the jar of ash. Nothing was broken or lost, except maybe him.

"Blue!" he called out to the sky. "You here? Which way do I go?"

A crow cawed from above. Robert looked up: a single crow he hadn't noticed before circled him like a buzzard waiting on him to die. If not for what Blue had told him, Robert would have thought it was bad luck and shooed the big crow away. He couldn't stop imagining the crows gathered near the slaughtered hog the last time he'd been with Redbone.

"Is that you?" Robert called. He expected the crow to land near him and take a human form, but instead it flew ahead . . . and then circled back, a shadow passing over him. Almost like an ordinary crow, but not quite. The crow was trying to lead him. It was Blue! Or seemed to be. Crows had always looked ugly and fearful to Robert, but this one had jet-black feathers that shined in the sun, and it struck him that crows had always been lovely. This one was, anyway.

That was enough to get Robert back on his feet and dry his eyes. Robert followed the soaring crow toward the woods.

The longer Fenton Haddock waited for someone to find Robert Stephens to take care of his newest haint problem, the more he was convinced something was badly, badly wrong. The certainty was an itch in his brain, the voice of his younger self—his less disciplined self—that whispered his worst thoughts to him. *You let them get the best of you,* the voice said. *They're all making a fool of you. You should've let these burn too.*

His staff had blocked off the cafeteria door because it was so smoky inside, so dozens of waiting boys were sitting in the grass, organized by dormitory, waiting for sandwiches the kitchen crew was working on from folding tables hastily set up against the wall. Boone said no one else had been hurt in the fire, but Boone was calling off names from his ledger just the same, getting a head count. No boy ever missed dinner unless he was up to no good.

And Robert Stephens was still nowhere in sight. Haddock watched for Stephens as every new boy streamed toward the cafeteria, but he did not come.

Crutcher had gone looking for Stephens at the dormitory, but Haddock didn't trust Crutcher to the task alone, so he'd sent a couple of other dorm masters out to drive around the campus and look for Stephens too. Boone said he hadn't given him a pass to the white side of the campus, so he shouldn't have been so hard to find—unless he didn't *want* to be found. Had Stephens taken advantage of the excitement to try to disappear? The voice inside him posed an even more alarming question: *Did Stephens set the fire somehow so he could run?* What if a haint hadn't set it at all? The plan seemed cunning and far-fetched for a boy of twelve, but Haddock couldn't let go of it easily. The thought made him so nervous that he patted his back pocket for his billfold to find the spare cigarette and matchbook he kept hidden in the folds.

The cigarette was crumpled and stale, but he never kept fresh ones because he didn't like the way cigarettes made him cough at night, no matter what the doctors in the radio ads promised about the new filters. His parents had smoked and then coughed themselves to death by the time they were sixty, so doctors be damned. But a jolt of nicotine cleared his mind, so from time to time Haddock allowed himself one spare so he could get enough of what he needed but not enough to like it. The cigarette was so deformed that he could barely light it, but it finally took.

Haddock had almost slid his billfold back in his pocket when he remembered his ritual of checking the zippered change compartment where he kept his spare desk key. His main key was snug on the ring strung to his belt, where he touched it at least a dozen times a day, but he checked on his spare only when he used his billfold.

The compartment was empty. His spare desk key was gone.

Haddock's lips pulled apart so fast that the cigarette fell to the grass. Haddock tried to slow his quickening heart by quizzing himself calmly on when he might have last used the key; no more than a couple of days could have passed since he'd seen it. Had he left it on his dresser at home? Spilled it out with the change he'd put in the change jar on his kitchen counter? Had his wife been rifling through his wallet and pulled it aside without knowing what it was? He'd slapped her more than once for touching his things, so he doubted she would have the nerve. But it was possible—wasn't it? Because where else—

The smoky smell that clung to his clothes and hair answered his question. If a haint had started the fire, couldn't a haint also have stolen his key? Kendall Sweeting had already pulled his photos out of his drawer more than once, before Boone laid his trap. What if . . . ?

"Shit," Haddock said, all calm stripped from his mind. The day's events felt inextricably linked in such an obvious way that Haddock didn't need to hear the voice in his head say, *He's made a damn fool of you. And you better do something about it.*

Haddock ran for his truck, which was still parked near the kitchen door. He gestured for Boone, who put down his clipboard and stopped his roll call. Haddock was in a hurry, so Boone hurried too. Haddock wished he had ten men like him.

"I don't think any of this is an accident," Haddock said as he drove across the grass to the field that led to the administration building, the truck going so fast that even Boone looked uneasy. "I need to check something in my office . . . then we're gonna find Robert Stephens ourselves."

"I would've seen Stephens by the kitchen," Boone said, not yet understanding, but Haddock didn't have time to broaden his thinking. No, Stephens probably had not set the fire; in fact, he'd been smart enough to steer clear of the kitchen altogether. But that didn't mean he hadn't had anything to do with it—that he hadn't helped coordinate it in some fashion. Haddock had ordered Cleo to kill Redbone to break Stephens and motivate him to trap haints without lies or disobedience—but what if Stephens really was like his daddy at his core? What if he made plans instead of getting scared? Stephens was only twelve, but Haddock had learned not to underestimate children the same way he knew never to underestimate Negroes.

He hoped he hadn't underestimated this one.

Doris stood up behind her desk, startled, when Haddock and Boone came bursting in from outside. The woman he'd been scheduled to interview as a schoolteacher was also in the lobby, her mouth in a surprised *O* at the sight of them. Business as usual in Haddock's office.

No accusations or repulsion in their eyes. No sign of the sheriff. No photographs in view. "Is everything all right?" Doris finally said.

Haddock slowed his pace, holding his arm out to bar Boone from moving so quickly. In the small room, Haddock realized how they both reeked from the fire. He could only hope he had no ash on his face as he forced a grin. "Someone left a burner on and we got some smoke," he said. "Everything's fine now. The boys are eating dinner as usual."

Doris's shoulders sagged with relief. She relied on this job to put food on her family's table, like all of the Reformatory's employees. That was the thing none of the Tallahassee blowhards wanted to consider: Without the Reformatory, where would the town get its corn? Who would run the printing press? He wasn't just trying to protect himself: the Reformatory was like a town unto itself, and his town could perish. It could perish *today*.

He shook the woman's hand and apologized for being tardy, asking if she wouldn't mind coming back on Monday. He even assured her the job was probably hers, and the way her face lit up put his mind even more at ease. As he reached for his main key ring to unlock his office door, Haddock heard Doris offering appointment times, so he gave Doris a warm smile over his shoulder and she smiled back at him, her ears turning pink at his rare affection.

But his smile died as soon as he opened the door. "Come in," he whispered to Boone, and he quickly closed the door behind him. Something *was* wrong, but at first glance Haddock couldn't have said what, even at gunpoint. He scanned every corner, trying to spot it.

"Stay here," Haddock said to Boone, leaving him standing close to his photo with Lucy.

When Haddock walked closer to his desk, he saw that his screen had been removed from his window and propped against the back wall. The curtains swayed enough to remind him that he'd left his window wide-open. He usually closed his window when he left his office for long periods, but not always. And not if he didn't expect to be gone long.

Haddock ran behind his desk and saw the specter that had dogged his nightmares for thirty years: his bottom drawer yawned and the space behind his bottle crate was a dark, empty maw. He leaned over and felt inside to make sure it was empty. Quickly, he tugged on the other drawers to check them. Had a haint only moved his things around to scare him?

No. Nothing. The haint jar was gone. Even worse: *his photographs were gone.*

"Boss?" Boone finally said, worried.

"Someone broke into my office," Haddock said. "Stole the haint jar."

"Jesus, help," Boone said, more frightened than outraged. Ordinarily, he'd come up with a plan to flush out the thief and how to punish him—but, like Haddock, Boone wasn't assuming the burglar was living. What did you do if the burglar was a haint?

"Jesus ain't got nothin' to do with this, Boone," Haddock said. He went to his window and looked outside at his limited view: he could see only the cornfield fence and a small swath of the campus that included the shed, about thirty yards down.

The shed! Crutcher said he had seen Robert Stephens near there.

Boone had walked closer behind him. "Came in through the window!" Boone sounded relieved when he saw the discarded screen. A window screen probably wouldn't matter to a haint. "Let's go see what's outside."

Boone's mind was working more quickly than Haddock's, and why not? He didn't know the whole of it, the terror in the missing photographs. Haddock trusted Boone with many of his secrets, but not the worst of them. Nervous perspiration stung Haddock's eyes, so he mopped his brow with his shirtsleeve and followed his most trusted man outside.

The thief had obviously hidden in the hedges, with fresh footprints—*They look like a grown man's!*—between the first three rear windows, leading to Haddock's. A few leaves had fallen from the shrubs, and scuff marks on the bricks showed how he'd climbed inside.

"I'm gonna call and get you bars for that window, boss," Boone said, still not understanding that there would be no need for bars across the windows if those photos were made public. If a child had stolen the photos, he had a better chance of finding them, but a grown man might be long gone. Boone was crawling under the hedges like a detective, but Haddock's rib cage constricted so hard around his lungs that he had to think to breathe.

"These look to me like boot prints, boss, and I bet I know who's wearing these boots," Boone said, like a miracle. "Robert Stephens. Just like you were saying before."

"This big? He's only twelve—"

"Naw, suh, he had brand-new boots when he came in, so we didn't have to give him no shoes. They looked big, just like these. Nobody can't find him, right?"

"Right," Haddock said, and his lungs opened for a flood of oxygen. "And Crutcher said he was out by the shed! So he can't be far."

With his panic receding, Haddock leaned over to examine the soil beneath his window in the patch of sunlight evading the hedges. A scoop of soil was missing near his window, with a lumpy pile of dirt beside it that didn't look natural. It might be nothing, but—

"Boone," he said. "Back up. Let me see if something's buried."

"Good eye, boss," Boone said, noticing the apple-sized lump. He gave Haddock room to kneel beside him. Haddock knew better than to pray to God for his photographs, but he prayed just the same to whatever spirit ruled over the Reformatory and fueled the voice that had told him to set the fire: *Please let it all be buried here*. But whomever he was praying to spat his prayer back at him, because he unearthed only an empty jar of Vaseline with a blue label.

"Stephens!" Boone said. "Crutcher said he was covered in this. What'd he do, grease himself up to slide through your window like a pig at a county fair?"

Slowly, Haddock shook his head. Quick as he was, Boone still didn't see. It *couldn't* be a coincidence that Stephens had broken in at the same time he'd run off to see about the fire.

Haddock's earlier panic was replaced with rage: this little son of a bitch had somehow staged a distraction while he invaded his private chamber and stole from him. *You better make him pay*, the voice that had told him to set the 1920 fire rumbled, a voice very much like his own. *Make him watch while you spill out his guts. Don't leave it to somebody else: you better kill this one yourself.*

"Ring the big bell and rouse the dog boys," Haddock said. "Time to hunt."

5:45 p.m.

"Ladies and gentlemen, this program is for you, not your children," Jack Webb's voice said gravely on the radio between the crackles on Miz Lottie's old receiver in the truck. "The subject is of vital importance to you as parents. This is the story of a vicious man . . ." The familiar dramatic horn music came on, and then an announcer's voice: "Fatima cigarettes, best of all cigarettes, brings you . . . *Dragnet*."

Gloria switched the radio off. The music program playing while Miz Lottie had been driving on the main road had soothed her, but she couldn't abide the tension of a police show while they were idling near the railroad trestle, just off of the deserted gravel road that had jounced them for the last ten minutes of their drive. If Joe Friday were real, he'd be chasing after Robbie right now because the judge said Robbie deserved to be locked up. Even Joe Friday, who never made a mistake, would be on the wrong side of justice in Gracetown.

The creek that ran under the rusting old railroad trestle was so dry that it was mostly a mud puddle with reeds growing high. Gloria hoped the water flowed more like a proper creek closer to the Reformatory to help cover Robert's scent as he ran. The water near them was so shallow that he would barely splash, and he would leave footprints. And while Robert would be able to climb up the bank to the truck, it was steep for a hurried climb. She wished she had scouted ahead instead of relying on Uncle June's memory of how it had looked before. With Uncle June and Waymon in jail and the creek so pathetic, Gloria felt certain that the day would end in sorrow. If it all went wrong, she would tell the judge that she had led Robbie and Miz Lottie astray and he should punish her instead. Maybe there was no way for a Negro with fixed ideas to avoid being sent to jail.

"That water sho' ain't much," Miz Lottie said, sharing her thought.

"He'll get away before anyone even notices." Gloria kept her fears to herself, since Miz Lottie was sweating too much, her forehead dripping even though all of the windows were down. Worry made the air hotter and thicker. Gloria felt her own cheeks, sure she had a fever.

The truck sputtered and coughed before the engine ticked off. Dammit!

"Don't worry," Miz Lottie said, pulling out the key. "Prob'ly the heat. We'll let her rest."

"We have to keep it running so we'll be ready when he comes."

"Give Ole Suzy a minute or two," Miz Lottie said. "She's earned it."

A mosquito landed on Gloria's nose and she swatted it away. "I can't sit here anymore," she said. The drive hadn't taken as long as they expected, so they had been waiting for twenty minutes, watching the creek for signs of Robbie through the archway of leaning cypress trees over the creek bed that might have looked majestic on another day. Gloria opened her door and climbed out of the truck and onto the rocky soil on the side of the road. Miz Lottie whistled to her, reaching over the seat to hand her the pearl-handled .22.

"Take it," Miz Lottie said. "Just in case. But don't . . . shoot Robbie." Even if Gloria hadn't heard her odd halting speech, she noticed the tremor in Miz Lottie's hand as the gun passed between them, warm from Miz Lottie's clasp.

Gloria didn't ask Miz Lottie what was wrong. *Everything* was wrong. Before Mama died and she'd seen how brutal life could turn, she would have fretted more over Miz Lottie, but she discovered a frozen piece of her mind reminding her that she couldn't leave Robbie even if Miz Lottie got dizzy or sick, or even worse. It was too late to change the plan now. Like Miz Lottie had said, Robbie was her sole responsibility now.

"Can you . . . reach in the back and . . . hand me June's canteen?" Miz Lottie said.

Gloria didn't answer, her face too stony for words. She felt around under the tarp in the far corner, beyond her suitcase, where June kept his Army canteen with the green fabric cover he'd brought back from the war. Gloria took a swallow herself first to moisten her mouth and throat. The water tasted slightly metallic, but it was still cool from Miz Lottie's kitchen faucet.

"Thank you," Miz Lottie said primly, her lips pinned, when Gloria handed her the canteen. Gloria knew Miz Lottie could have made a dozen complaints, but instead she only swallowed from the canteen and laid her head back against her seat, her eyes closed. Gloria did not ask Miz Lottie if she was all right because she already knew she wasn't. But she had to watch the creek.

Gloria walked a few steps down the embankment, trying to find the most obvious path for Robbie that he could climb quickly if dogs were at his heels. She spotted what looked like a deer path winding past jutting roots and weeds not far from the truck. Was it too steep for him?

Gloria remembered the rope coiled in the back of the truck she'd seen near the canteen.

"Miz Lottie, I'm gonna tie a rope here to help him climb up," she said. Miz Lottie said "All right" so faintly that Gloria almost didn't hear her.

Gloria shoved the gun snugly into her deep front pocket, half afraid it would explode in her dungarees. Then she tied the rope securely around a sturdy tree trunk at the edge of the road and tossed the rest of it down to watch it uncoil. The rope got caught in branches halfway down, so Gloria tugged on it to test her knot and then began climbing down herself, holding the rope taut with her right hand while she unraveled the rest on the sharp descent and shook it loose with her left. While her loafers were solidly supported on a jutting boulder about fifteen yards above the creek, she shook the rope to unfurl it as far as it would go. The tip didn't quite reach all the way down, but it would be easy enough to see from below. Gloria looked up, imagining it from Robert's viewpoint, and saw the rear of the truck where Miz Lottie had parked it just before the trestle, half hidden in wild weeds. The truck was obvious if you were looking, but it wasn't directly over the creek where anyone might see it from a distance. Robert would see the trestle before he saw the truck, but he *would* see it. That was what she told her pounding heart, anyway.

Gloria slipped on her climb back up with the rope, and she was glad she was wearing too-big Levi's jeans she'd borrowed from Waymon's drawer instead of a dress, since she was already muddy at the knees. She was eager to check the clock in Miz Lottie's truck, to see if two hours had passed instead of two minutes, the way it seemed in her imagination.

When she climbed back up to the truck, Miz Lottie had moved to the passenger side, hunched over as she went through the glove box. The part of Gloria that secretly had expected to find Miz Lottie dead over the steering wheel rejoiced. She loved Miz Lottie, but that also would have meant pushing Miz Lottie's body aside to be ready to drive off with Robbie no matter what.

"You see him?" Miz Lottie said, eyes hopeful and childlike.

"Not yet. What are you looking for?" Now that Gloria had mapped out a safer passage for Robbie, she felt guilty that she hadn't doted on Miz Lottie more.

"I got it," Miz Lottie said, weakly holding up her black pillbox with a rose image Mama had bought her. Miz Lottie's doctor had prescribed her pills for her chest pain from angina. Miz Lottie raised the canteen to her lips to swallow the pill, and Gloria helped her hold it steady despite Miz Lottie's irritated glance because she hated to be treated like she was helpless.

"You okay?" Gloria said, the question she had avoided.

"Dizzy spell. You'd better drive, pumpkin. Don't want Robbie to get this far for me to drive us off the road."

Her voice was casual, but Miz Lottie had never confessed that she was not fit to drive, not once, although Papa and Uncle June had been telling her for years. Whatever was troubling Miz Lottie was worse than dizziness. Gloria was partially relieved but also terrified to see new pieces of the plan crumbling away. She'd laid the road map to the train station on the dashboard, but she didn't trust that she could steer the old truck well enough to make the sharp turn back to the main road with such steep ditches on either side. But she said, "All right," the simplest thing to say even if it wasn't close to true.

Gloria took a step away from the passenger's-side window to peer toward the creek again. Not even rabbits or raccoons stirred in the stillness of the woods. Robbie wasn't going to come: the feeling was so certain that she was sure it was the future whispering in her ear.

Then a bell began to ring. The bell from the courthouse had a stately and reverent sound that probably would not reach this far, certainly not as crisply. This bell was a sharp, frantic rally with a higher pitch, probably rung by hand, so loud that it had to be much closer than Main Street. The bell sounded like they had been caught already.

Lottie straightened up in her seat. "The runaway alarm," she said. "He's out! And they know he's gone. All these cracker farmers out here will be looking for him. Hope he's quick."

Robbie *was* quick, but the bell's sound was quicker. Another flaw in their plan: Robbie might not make it alone if he'd already been missed. She checked her pocket for the assuring mass of her hidden .22 and stared at the quiet creek bed where Robbie had not yet appeared no matter how much she tried to summon him.

"Oh no," Miz Lottie said miserably, and before Gloria could ask what was wrong, she heard the barking. Dogs! The barks were faint, but there was more than one. They might just be excited by the bell, but one bayed so loudly that it could only be a bloodhound.

"Miz Lottie, stay here," Gloria said. "I'll drive, but get the truck running."

"Where . . . are you going?" Miz Lottie said, barely a whisper. She was in pain, but she would not say so and Gloria did not ask because they only had room for Robbie.

"Down to the creek," Gloria said. "I have to find him."

39

5:50 p.m.

Colonel was Haddock's favorite tracking dog, a bloodhound personally trained since he was a rambunctious pup. Colonel didn't like to use his teeth the way the German shepherds did—he found runners with his tail wagging like the hunt was a game of hide-and-seek—but it was a forgivable flaw, because Colonel was never wrong. He never gave up. Colonel was the best tracker in the kennel. He knew the bell meant it was time to work, and he'd track all night and through the next day if it meant he'd get his favorite hamburger steak when his job was done.

Colonel came tumbling out of the bed of the dog boys' truck, loose brown jowls flapping, along with the three German shepherds Haddock had ordered special and two Lab mixes who had better noses than they should. They barked and ran in circles, glad to be free of the kennel.

Jasper, the willowy, ginger-haired dog master who had started as one of the prisoners and graduated to staff, spoke sharply to keep the dogs focused as they barked, eager to run and chase. The three other dog boys who lived in the cottage at the edge of the campus with Jasper were strapping on their overalls and buttoning their shirts like firemen as they jumped from the truck. Jasper clipped Colonel's leash to his harness and handed it over to Haddock.

"Where was he at, sir?" Jasper said.

Haddock pointed to his window. As embarrassing as it was to admit he'd been careless enough to leave his window unlocked,

Haddock had called the dog boys to the hedges where Robert Stephens had hidden while the kitchen burned.

At Haddock's prompting, Colonel sniffed studiously under the window. Haddock put the empty jar of Vaseline under Colonel's nose and watched his dog's nostrils quiver as he caught the scent of the last person who had touched it who wasn't Haddock himself.

"You got him, boy?" Haddock coaxed. "That's it. That's the one."

Colonel strained on his leash, nose on the ground. If Haddock let him loose, he'd have to search for both Stephens and his dog, since Colonel wouldn't pay attention to a hurricane, much less Haddock calling after him, once his nose had a scent. Even Haddock's training couldn't trump this stubborn dog's instincts to follow a trail.

Holding tight to Colonel, Haddock gave the closed, empty jar of Vaseline to Jasper for the other dogs. "This is all he left behind," he said. "No time to go run and fetch his clothes. But this should do. Let 'em smell the window too."

"What the hell'd he use *this* for?" Jasper said, wrinkling his freckled nose at the jar.

"Maybe somebody told him dogs couldn't smell him with that," Haddock said. "It's not completely a fool notion, but he didn't have near enough to cover him." He pointed to a footprint in the mud beneath the window. "I'll bet fifty bucks he didn't put none on his boots."

Jasper looked bewildered that a Negro boy would have thought so far ahead, but he didn't know Robert Stephens Jr. Hell, a haint might have taught Stephens the trick. But with any luck, Stephens hadn't found his way off of the campus yet. He might be hiding in a tree until after dark, when he might believe he could make it out to the road undetected. Haddock hoped this whole ugly event could be put to bed fast. If Jasper or another dog boy found Stephens first, they might see the photos. He might be damned either way.

Right on time, Boone drove back up in his white pickup after his trip to the gun cabinet.

"Colonel's already on him!" Haddock called to Boone, and Boone grinned before he went to pull out the rifles. The younger dog boys got .22 rifles, but Jasper always hunted with a shotgun. Haddock decided to forgo a shotgun and use the Colt .45 instead: less weight to carry to vex his knee. And he was a good enough shot that he wouldn't miss the extra accuracy he would get with a rifle. Colonel would get him close enough to Stephens to shoot him in the face.

Haddock noticed that Crutcher was finally returning from his search for Stephens at the dormitory, his sister hurrying beside him. They were both breathless and sweating from rushing. He'd hoped that Crutcher might have thought to bring some of Stephens's clothing with him from the dorm, but Crutcher was empty-handed. Useless! Crutcher was already shaking his head that he hadn't seen any sign of Stephens. In the distance, the boys from the cafeteria had followed the commotion to gather and watch the start of the hunt.

"What's going on?" Crutcher's sister asked.

"Hunt," Haddock told her. "We got a runaway." He only answered to see that uppity bitch squirm. He made a show of checking the rounds in his chamber as loudly as he could before he secured the gun in the back of his pants. Haddock handed Crutcher a leftover .22 rifle while she watched, and Crutcher held it as if he'd never seen a gun despite the requirement that all dorm masters knew how to shoot. The shock on his sister's face nearly made Haddock smile despite everything. She was hanging a few yards back, far away from the dogs.

"Anything moves, you shoot it," Haddock said to the dog boys, but he kept his eyes particularly on Crutcher. "If Robert Stephens gets loose, there will be hell to pay. And if anybody shoots one of my dogs, I'll beat you senseless myself."

Crutcher's eyes were wide with horror he could not conceal. He had never been on a hunt, but everyone had a first time. Haddock winked at him. "Don't worry," he said. "That rifle's for hunting rabbits. You probably won't blow his head off."

Haddock noticed how Crutcher glanced back at his sister and she was shaking her head at him, mouthing *No.* Boone patted Crutcher on the back with encouragement and pulled him away from his sister's eyes, since the man looked so sick. Crutcher held tight to his rifle, not refusing his orders. Haddock didn't quite trust Crutcher on the hunt, but he needed every hand. A posse of seven with almost as many dogs should be able to collect Stephens just fine.

"All right, let's move out!" Haddock said. He unwrapped the leash he'd wound around his hand, giving Colonel more room to move, and the dog took off so fast toward the shed that Haddock's shoulder joint snapped and his feet nearly tangled. When Haddock's knee flared, he yanked back on the leash to try to slow Colonel down: sometimes it worked, sometimes it didn't. But Haddock was so eager to find Stephens and his photographs that he didn't care how sore his knee would be. "Good boy, Colonel. Git him!"

The dog boys whooped behind Haddock, adrenaline sizzling between them. Boone drove behind them slowly in the truck in case they needed more speed. The trail took them close to where the burned outbuilding had been thirty years earlier; all traces of it were gone, but Haddock would always know that spot in his sleep. Colonel seemed to know too, avoiding that place. At first, Colonel steered as if to go to the Negro side of the campus, like Crutcher had claimed.

But then Colonel headed straight to the shed. The dogs were barking in a chorus by the time they reached the closed shed door. Colonel's nose was still pointed down into the grass, but the other dogs were sniffing the air. Haddock pulled the shed door open—*Could it be this simple?*—but Colonel backed away from the shadowed space, keeping his nose down near the wooden wall planks. He yanked his leash toward a corner of the shed's exterior, sniffing furiously. The other dogs ran eagerly inside, though, pulling their handlers behind them. Haddock hoped those dogs weren't just excited for the exercise.

"I don't think he went in," Crutcher said as he caught up, out of breath. If not for Colonel's lack of interest inside the shed, Crutcher's uneasiness might have made Haddock suspect he was covering for the boy. But Colonel would never lead him astray.

"Come on back out of there!" he called to the dog boys, banging on the shed wall. He didn't need a crowd trampling on his business if Stephens hadn't been inside. He'd barely gotten his order out before Colonel tugged on him again, taking him to the grass beyond the shed, following the trail. The watching crowd of boys in the distance had grown, on both the Negro and the white sides of the campus, separated by the large field between them. *Let them watch and see what'll happen to them,* Boone thought. *I oughta bring Stephens's head back on a stick.*

Colonel picked up speed as he reached the rutted path in the grass from the truck's tires. His heart celebrated. "Look!" Haddock said, pointing. He yanked on Colonel's leash with two hands and had to dig in to prevent the dog from charging ahead.

Before him lay a perfect front half of a boot print; the other half was lost in the grass. The size of the large boot matched the print beneath his window. His progress delayed, Colonel sniffed at the boot print and wagged his tail.

Haddock scanned the ruts to see if any other footprints had been captured, but all that remained was a disturbance in the soil that looked like Stephens might have tried to cover his tracks. Smart goddamned boy, but not smart enough. Colonel still had him.

"Make sure the rest of 'em get that scent," Haddock said to Jasper. "All they're smelling is each other's assholes."

"Yessir," Jasper said, red-faced. He had pride in his dogs. Tracking was harder in the warm months, especially if it was dry, but that was no excuse. Only Colonel was on the trail. The other handlers crowded around the footprint with their dogs, giving irritated commands.

"All right, Robert Stephens," Haddock said, half to himself. "Where you headed now?"

Colonel knew. As soon as the pressure on his leash eased, Colonel's nose led him to the grass parallel to the rutted soil, as if Stephens had stepped aside a few feet to hide his tracks.

Colonel quickened his pace until Haddock had to jog to keep up with him, but he was glad they were running when he saw the Funhouse in their direct path. Another clever place to hide!

Behind him, the dog boys echoed Haddock's excitement with whoops and hollering. "He's in the right place all right!" Boone called from his truck, keeping pace beside them.

"Here, doggie doggie doggie!" Haddock cupped his mouth. "We got you, Stephens!"

Taunting the boys in their hiding places was half the fun of the hunt, pricking their terror to flush them out. He hoped Stephens would get scared and bolt from the Funhouse so the dog boys and their trackers could get the chase they wanted. Colonel didn't have a taste for blood, but those German shepherds would eat that little bastard for dinner when they caught him, especially Scout. Stephens couldn't tell anyone about the photographs with his face eaten off.

And if half the boys at the Reformatory saw it happen, all the better. No one else would run in a long while, would they?

The growing grin on Haddock's face faded when Colonel avoided the Funhouse entrance and followed the scent toward the rear. He nosed around the chairs assembled for the Negro boys, knocking one aside in his fervor, but then Colonel paced the rear wall, back and forth.

Haddock glanced nervously at the adjoining hundred-acre cornfield, glad a tall fence topped with barbed wire separated the field from the campus. He'd had to fight to pay for that fencing a few years back, but the peace of mind was worth every penny. He scanned the barbed wire for signs of torn clothing just the same, but no child in his right mind would try to climb that fence. Again Jasper and the other dog boys were clambering inside the Funhouse in search of Stephens even though Colonel had already told Haddock they would not find him there. But *where*, then . . . ?

Haddock wished he had a cigarette or even a swig of water. The panic that had smothered him when he first discovered his photographs were missing was cooling from his cheeks and fingertips. He prayed Colonel was about to round the Funhouse and go to the front entrance after all, but instead the dog's nose sniffed at the grass on the way to the cornfield fence.

"No way!" Boone called out from the truck, idling just off to the side. "Maybe he lost it."

"Colonel doesn't lose a trail," Haddock muttered, but he hoped Boone was right as the dog sped up again, pulling Haddock toward an iron fence post. Colonel plunged his head into the weeds around the fence post, snuffling like a hog. As Colonel burrowed, a large panel of the fence hooked to the post shivered more than it should.

"No," Haddock whispered.

"Damn, boss—lookit!" Boone said.

Colonel was pushing himself *through* the fencing as the panel trembled until a flap fell away from the post, flattened. Colonel's front paws were already on the other side, his thick haunches sliding across the grass as he slipped through what had become a gaping hole more than large enough for a bloodhound—and a twelve-year-old child.

"He got through the fence!" Boone called to Jasper and the dog boys. "Git out here!" The cacophony of barking sent Haddock's head spinning, his thoughts hard to catch. If Stephens had crawled under this fence close to twenty minutes before, or longer, he might have made it to the road already. How had this happened? How had he been bested by a child?

Colonel was already on the other side of the fence, pacing as far as his leash would allow through the hole. He looked back at Haddock as if to say, *I thought you wanted to catch him.*

"I'm going under with Colonel!" Haddock said. "Boone, load

up the dog boys on the truck and drive around the fence. I want the dogs covering the field and the truck covering the road. Let's make up for lost time and catch him before dark."

"Boss, you want me to call on the Hewitts and—"

"No," Haddock cut him off. The last thing he needed was for those photographs to land in the hands of Lance Hewitt, who was with the state highway patrol and beyond Bird's jurisdiction. Some of the Reformatory's neighbors might already be patrolling because of the bell and the standing fifty-dollar reward, but he wouldn't tempt fate. "We'll get him ourselves."

"You sure, Boss?" Boone said. He didn't question instructions often, but of course he was worried that Stephens was already to the road and beyond, if he'd been running fast.

"Yes. I'm counting on you, Boone." Ideally, Colonel could lead Haddock straight to Stephens without a pack on his heels to see the photos. But if Stephens had too much of a head start, Boone would see him on the road or another dog would catch him hiding in the corn. "He has my private belongings. No one sees my private things except you, hear? Not the dog boys, not Hewitt. *Nobody.*"

"Yessir." Boone honked his horn in a long, persistent note that sent Jasper and the dog boys scrambling to climb back into the bed of the truck with their dogs.

Crutcher stood watching. He wasn't Boone by a long shot, but Haddock wanted to keep an eye on him during his initiation. "You come on under the fence with me," Haddock said. "Take off that coat so you don't dirty up that pretty suit."

"Yessir," Crutcher said in a defeated mumble, taking off his coat and draping it over a branch. Crutcher might not survive this hunt if he couldn't get his heart behind it, or if he saw too much. Haddock had warned Crutcher the day he interviewed for the job that he could not be soft on the boys or they would be ruined as men. Today was Crutcher's first real test.

Haddock lowered himself to his knees, pushing the loosened

fence panel down as far as it would go, while Colonel tugged on his leash, barking impatiently for him to hurry up. Colonel pulled so hard that a sharp edge of the severed metal gashed Haddock's upper right arm as he crawled through, leaving a red stripe of blood through his torn shirt. The cut wasn't too deep, but it hurt more than any injury in years and would likely leave a scar. When Haddock roared a curse, Colonel whimpered and looked back at him with hangdog eyes, snapped from his scent euphoria. Colonel lost all his passion for hunting if Haddock yelled at him. And of course Haddock had never hit Colonel. Haddock couldn't train his bloodhound the way he trained the boys.

"It's all right, boy," Haddock hissed between his teeth, patting Colonel's head and running his hand down his flapping ears. "I'm not mad. I promise." Then his command: "*Git him.*"

Colonel's tail wagged. He pressed his nose back to the soil.

Once again, Haddock's celebration was cut short as he followed Colonel's lead. He'd expected Stephens's trail to turn south toward the road, but the dog was tracking north through the crops and more or less parallel to the fence. Haddock thought Stephens might have run the wrong way at first and would correct his path, but Colonel's pace north only quickened.

"What's back this way?" Crutcher said.

Haddock mapped it in his memory, since he had considered purchasing that land for the Reformatory: the cornfield ended on the unincorporated property beyond the county line that was still mostly untouched woods. Nothing was out there except a creek, once a river, that ran out just beyond the abandoned railroad track and was long overgrown with weeds. This route held none of the promise of the peanut mill or the main road leading back to Lower Spruce. But if Stephens thought the Vaseline would keep the dogs off of him, maybe he thought the water would too.

"The creek," Haddock said as it dawned on him. "That little sonofabitch."

Crutcher quickened his pace to try to catch up with Haddock. "Should I tell the others?"

"They'll figure it out if those dogs are worth a damn. If not, I don't need 'em." Haddock reached back to pull out his Colt so it would be ready in his hand.

"Superintendent . . . ," Crutcher began gently. "Why the guns? Surely he doesn't have one." No, Crutcher would not pass this test.

"I'd 'surely' love to know who cut my fence," Haddock said, mimicking him. "Stephens didn't do that by himself. You got any idea?"

"No, sir, not at all."

Haddock waited a moment to decide if he believed Crutcher while Colonel sniffed at another boot print beside a browning plant. By God, Colonel *was* on Stephens's trail!

"How'd you like what you found, Crutcher?"

"Sir?"

"Out in my shed. You said you were messing around in there. How'd you like it?"

In the long silence, the other dogs barked a racket, still heading the wrong way. He and Crutcher would be alone, at least for a while.

"I found a . . . broom," Crutcher said. "That's all."

"That's the trouble when you go through another man's things," Haddock said. "Did it dawn on you to wonder what I use it for besides sweeping?"

"Maybe I'm just . . . dumb," Crutcher said, an almost laughable claim from a man as haughty as he was, "but I don't understand your meaning, Superintendent Haddock."

Haddock hated being lied to. He considered turning on his heel, raising his Colt, and seeing what kind of mess he could make of Crutcher at close range. He'd tell Bird he was so surprised by the footfall behind him that he'd shot Crutcher by accident. Not that Bird needed more than half a reason. But he didn't want to slow down Colonel's momentum; a gunshot would upset his dog.

"Only two things you need to know on a hunt," Haddock said instead. "Number one, you make an example of the runner or others will try it. Number two, you keep your mouth shut and don't ask questions. Don't make me tell you twice. Some mistakes you don't come back from."

Crutcher did not answer, even to say *Yessir*. Haddock heard his silent loathing and judgment behind him, but if Crutcher wanted to shoot him in the back, so what? Crutcher would have a hell of a tough road explaining the shooting to Bird, even if he tried to claim it was an accident. Negro men didn't shoot down white men if they wanted to live another day.

Haddock ventured a glance over his shoulder so he could see Crutcher's tight, angry lips and let him know he didn't give a damn. Haddock smiled. "Watch and learn," he said.

The leash snapped as Colonel ran faster, leading them toward Robert Stephens.

40

On the unfenced end of the cornfield, Robert ran into a wall of trees. With dogs barking behind him—*real* dogs, not the noises that had fooled his ears as soon as he was under the fence—Robert had hoped that liberation from the corn plants meant he could wade straight into the creek. Instead, he was wading into a tightly packed thicket of thin tree trunks and nests of brush beneath them, barely passable and harder to see past than the ordered rows of corn. If not for the dogs, and Gloria waiting for him, he would have turned back.

These weren't the tamed woods where he lived, thinned by traffic paths to the turpentine camps, with easy gaps between the trees for games of tag. He never would have played with Gloria in these woods, where any toy would instantly be lost and every step was met by twigs poking and scraping his chest, arms, and shins. If not for the dogs and maybe snakes, the thick woods would be the perfect place to hide. But they were not good for running or for finding his way. For the first time since the crow had appeared in the cornfield, Robert was forced to slow down until he wasn't running, and then he was hardly walking, fighting against the underbrush, his arm raised to protect his face.

But it was impossible not to get scratched, and Robert pressed one hand over his right eye after a twig smacked his face so hard that he thought he'd poked his eyeball out. The sting almost made him cry out, but the barking behind him reminded him not to make a sound. Was the barking farther away? Robert was afraid to trust his ears because he wished it so much and wishes weren't real, but at least the dogs didn't sound closer. Not yet.

He didn't see the crow anymore either. The crow had come in and out of sight in the cornfield, but Robert hadn't seen it in the web of trees. Now Robert wondered if the crow had been Blue or if he'd only hoped it was, and despair licked at his stomach again. He felt let down both by Blue and by Gloria, although it pained him to admit that he was frustrated with his sister. She hadn't described the woods this way at all! She'd promised a creek, and instead thick woods were a trap slowly catching him like a spider's web to hold him for the dogs.

And holding him for Haddock. Robert knew he must be coming too.

No wonder most runaways ran toward the road instead! Why hadn't Blue told him what to expect? Or did Blue know these woods himself, after being trapped at the Reformatory? Blue might not have ever set foot in the land behind the cornfield, or even known how to get there. Robert's doubts and worries cramped his lungs as he gasped harder for air, although his pace had slowed to a crawl. The more slowly he moved past the thickets and fallen timber crisscrossing his path as if to block him, the harder he breathed, as the air was hotter and thicker.

But his fear of Haddock and the dogs kept his feet moving despite his aching muscles and overworked lungs. He squeezed himself past the pine trunks and tried to duck as many branches as he could, ignoring the scratches. As he was finding his rhythm, he was yanked backward so hard that he almost fell from his feet. He turned around in terror, afraid Haddock had somehow snuck up behind him, but his satchel had only caught on a broken limb. When he pulled to try to free himself, he realized the limb had caught in the satchel's hole, not the strap, and had ripped the hole so big that the haint jar fell to the ground, with the envelope beside it.

"No . . . no . . . no . . . ," Robert whispered.

He didn't know if he was more afraid of breaking the haint jar or seeing Haddock's photos, but he rushed to collect everything that had fallen out. The jar had a chip in the glass now, but it had not broken enough to release the ashes inside. The envelope was still tied tightly, but Robert tightened the string a little more just to be sure. He would have to carry the torn satchel in his arms like an infant.

A dog bayed behind him, shockingly close. He heard Haddock's voice calling in the wind, saying, "Here, doggie doggie!" Haddock was going to catch him!

Despair froze Robert where he crouched. He was afraid to move or lift his head too high.

When he was still, his breathing and heartbeat were so loud that he was sure Haddock would hear him a mile away. He started to crawl forward in the prickly brush, but he noticed that the drawing of Redbone had flown free from the bag, lying ten feet to his right. The drawing was more wrinkled than it had been and seemed to have a tear, but Robert would not leave Redbone's drawing behind. Leaving it behind would not only be a sign for Haddock on the trail; it would feel like leaving Redbone's spirit behind too.

Still breathing fast, perspiration falling into his eyes, Robert crawled toward the drawing, which had landed on a flat stone beyond another fallen tree trunk. He strained to reach through a gap beneath the fallen tree to try to grab it, but as soon as his fingers got close, the paper shivered . . . and flew out of his reach, hopping five more feet away in a light breeze.

Cursing, Robert climbed over the tree trunk to try to reach it again. This time the paper whirled up higher and away from him like it had been snatched and was dancing eight feet in the air above him, rocking gently back and forth before it got stuck in a tree branch and flapped there.

"No . . . ," Robert whispered again, near tears. He didn't have time to climb up and—

The paper freed itself, hovering above Robert so that Redbone's face showed. Then it floated farther ahead, rocking lazily on breezes that Robert could not feel.

"Redbone?" Robert whispered, hardly daring to hope. "Or . . . Blue? Is that you?"

An invisible crow cawed.

Robert was so excited that he nearly shouted for joy. "Will you show me?" he whispered. "Can you show me where to go?" The floating paper whirled in a circle and then charged forward, nearly out of sight past the treetops. "Wait—not so fast!"

But he followed. If Blue or Redbone or both of them were driving the paper's path as he hoped they were, they had saved him a harder time, because his direction had shifted slightly. He fought past untamed brush until the floating and dipping paper revealed a deer trail he had not seen from his previous position. He might *never* have found the thin trail of orange soil, where it was so much easier to run and seemed more likely to lead to a creek. He noticed that his boots were leaving prints on the path, but the loud baying behind him told him he didn't have time to cover his tracks. The dog knew where he was. He only hoped he had enough of a head start to outrun the dog and locate Gloria and the truck.

But did he?

Clasping the broken satchel and its contents to his chest, Robert begged his aching, pulsing legs to keep running just a bit farther and faster. He was quick in short races, but he wasn't used to long distances, and his entire body was complaining. His feet were sore, chafing against the insides of his too-big boots, and his lungs were howling for rest. When his stomach lurched, he braced himself against a tree trunk with one arm while he bent over and threw up the food he'd eaten that day, splattering the mess against the soil. He kicked at pine needles to cover it. He didn't want to give Haddock the satisfaction of knowing how tired and scared he was.

"Heeeeere, doggie doggie doggie!" Haddock's voice called.

Haddock sounded close enough to tap him on the shoulder, so Robert stumbled into a run again. And the dog! The howling sound wasn't like the choppy barks from Red McCormack's dog

Duke when he chased you down the fence; the low, wounded baying sounded like Henry Jackson's song by the old well, as if the dog were telling stories about Robert's short, sad life.

Where was the paper? He had lost sight of it when he threw up, but he noticed it caught in some branches overhead, more torn than before. For an instant he was sure it was just an ordinary piece of paper that had been blown by the wind—and maybe he was completely off track by now. Why had he ever believed he could steal from Haddock and get away? Why had he believed that Gloria could rescue him when she'd barely been able to feed him? Or that haints could lead him to freedom when Blue was trapped himself?

But as Robert ran on the faint trail, the paper yanked itself free from above and sailed a few yards ahead of him, twirling. The paper's frolicking reminded Robert of newsreels he'd seen of Air Force jets doing tricks in the air. Robert laughed with a hysteria he could not control as he gasped for air. The paper *was* a haint somehow, and the haint was leading him just as Blue had promised, and every time he thought of it, he laughed harder, because no haint he had ever seen in a scary movie looked like a plain old piece of paper.

The treetops whispered as he ran, rustling so loudly that they obscured the sound of the barking. Gooseflesh sprang across Robert's arms as an energy like electricity jolted his skin, like being held and rocked and sung to. Like being *carried*. When the path cleared up and Robert saw an opening ahead he hoped led to the creek, his feet were moving with longer and longer strides before he touched the ground, and it dawned on him that he might be flying instead of running. Was he floating over the stones and dead leaves and pine cones, his legs freed from their burden as they churned above the ground? As soon as he looked down, Robert's feet landed on the path hard, but he didn't lose his balance, propped up by imaginary arms.

He leaped up again to see if he *could* fly just as his dreams had always promised, or some memory of long ago, and as his legs pumped, he felt himself rise until a tree branch above him thwacked the side of his head and a dead leaf went into his mouth, but that only made him laugh harder. His feet couldn't feel the chafing against his raw ankles anymore, gliding instead of running. Then he landed so hard that it hurt his soles and made him stumble, scraping his knees.

The path had led him to a clearing . . . and a Negro woman in a white dress like a church usher was standing twenty feet ahead. She was smiling at him, so familiar that he almost called Gloria's name—but the shape of her face and frame made him gasp as he realized—

"Mama?" Robert said.

Calling her broke the spell, or maybe it was the baying dog behind him, but the woman was gone when he blinked away droplets of sweat. The leaves' powerful rustling was gone too, along with the electric feeling Robert was now sure she had given him to help him move faster and find his way. She'd appeared in the middle of the creek ahead, wading in the water like the spiritual Miz Lottie had sung. A crow cawed, and this time Robert saw the bird perched on a branch above the water, close to where Mama had been.

Robert's knees gave way until he was kneeling at the edge of the path, panting, new tears mingling with the sweat stinging his eyes. His excitement at finding the creek couldn't overcome the pain of seeing Mama so briefly before she was gone. He had seen a dozen ghosts at the Reformatory, but only Mama's ghost truly mattered, and she'd been the hardest to find. Maybe it was because she had never visited the Reformatory in life, as Blue had said, and she had only appeared in a flash to let him know she was there, that he had reached the creek he was looking for. The unfairness opened new sorrow in Robert even as he whispered, "Thank you, Mama," because coming to him must have been so, so hard.

As if in comfort, the pencil drawing of Redbone floated back down in front of him and onto the ground. The journey had nearly torn the paper in half, but Redbone's grin still showed through the rips and creases. Sobbing now, Robert folded the paper as well as he could with shaking hands and shoved it into his back pocket, hoping it would be safe there.

The crow cawed again, sounding impatient, and Robert let go of any doubt it was Blue. "Okay—dang," Robert whispered. "I'm coming."

The creek stretched in two directions, lined by nearly identical trees and mud banks, but the crow was perched in a thin tree cracked in half like a matchstick above the water, so that was the way Robert went. *Upriver,* he remembered Gloria telling him, although, without the crow's help, how would he have known? The water was a still pool, not flowing in any direction, mostly clear but clouding from mud every time Robert took a step. Warm water seeped into his boots, soaking his socks and feet, making each stride heavier as the mud sucked at his soles.

Gloria had said the water would reach his waist, so he held the satchel high on his chest, but even after he'd waded several yards into the warm creek, the water barely reached his knees.

Was it enough to cover his scent the way Gloria had promised? Haddock would know he had come to the creek, but if he moved quickly, Haddock might not know which way he had turned. Robert tried to increase his pace, but he nearly tripped on something solid hidden under the placid green-brown water and he had to move more slowly so he wouldn't fall, trying not to disturb the water too much so the ripples would not betray him.

Untouched woods grew on either side of the creek, with debris clogging the center from fallen branches he had to walk around. The dog chasing him bayed mournfully again. A stitch in Robert's side stabbed him as he grew more anxious, straining to see the railroad trestle. He could smell every pore of his skin and drop of sweat on his body, but he hoped the dog would not. How far did he have to walk in the creek? Haddock would see him from a distance!

The crow's call sounded annoyed this time, although it was hard to tell with crows. The bird slowed ahead of him, circling, but Robert walked stubbornly on. If the crow was Blue, Robert knew what he wanted—but he didn't have time yet. The dog was too close.

"I'll set them free when I see the railroad trestle," Robert said, breathing hard. "I can't stop and let Haddock see me." But Blue wasn't satisfied. The crow made another annoyed sound and swooped close to Robert's head, making him duck by instinct. "Hey—*cut it out!*" Robert hissed. "You're gonna make me drop it."

It occurred to Robert that Blue *wanted* him to drop the jar in the creek so it might break and free the ashes. If Robert could be sure that would work, he would have tossed the haint jar away as soon as he got to the water. But if the glass didn't break, Haddock might find it floating. Redbone wasn't captured in the haint jar, but all of the spirits inside deserved to get away from Haddock.

But Blue had a different idea. The longer Robert hurried through the water, the closer the crow dove at his head. Hot air flapped from its wings and a talon scratched through Robert's hair to his scalp. He wasn't sure, but he might be bleeding. Robert was so startled by the pain that he tripped and splashed into the murky water, soaking his clothes. He held his satchel over his head, clutching the hole tightly closed so nothing would spill out. If the photographs in the envelope got wet, they would get stuck and the images might be ruined.

"You got my picture of Redbone wet!" Robert complained as he stood up as quickly as he could. He didn't have to look at his shorts to know how wet they were; his clothes clung to him like a second skin. He didn't try to pull the drawing out of his pocket because he was sure he would only tear it up worse now; he would have to wait for it to dry and hope he could still recognize Redbone's face so he would never forget him, even when he was an old man.

The crow landed atop a pile of branches collected in front of Robert in the creek, gazing in a way that dared him to keep moving. Robert never wanted to see another haint his whole life unless it was Mama. If he had time, he would have cussed Blue out good.

The barking behind him was still too close, but no closer than it had been before he reached the creek. Had Haddock seen the water yet? Was he trying to decide which way to go? The creek had turned with a slight bend, so Haddock might not see him when he emerged from the woods. Maybe Blue was right: maybe he did have time to set the ashes free first.

"If I get caught, it's *your* fault, Blue," Robert muttered, pulling the jar from the satchel.

The crow shook water from its shiny black wings, waiting. Robert was sure it was Blue because it had grown to be the biggest crow he had ever seen, the size of a young turkey.

Robert had to keep one hand on the satchel, so he pressed the jar against his belly as he tried to open it with his free hand. The lid was *tight*. Dammit again! Even when he maneuvered his left hand to hold the jar steady, he could not make the metallic lid budge. Petroleum jelly had greased up his fingertips, so he couldn't get a good grip.

Somewhere behind him, the dog bayed again.

Panic made Robert's mouth taste rotten. He plunged one hand into the water, feeling around. At first he only clutched pebbles, but finally his fingers landed around a fist-sized stone, slimy with algae. He cradled the haint jar against the crook of his arm and smashed at it with the stone as hard as he could, more afraid of Haddock and the dog than he was of cutting himself.

With the first try, the blow only vibrated across his arm with a dull ache, leaving the bottle intact. His second try, even harder, made a large crack across the word ROYAL in the glass. The third blow with the stone finally cracked open a hole the size of a silver dollar. Still breathing fast, Robert shook the bottle to fling the ashes out. A breeze flew some of the powdery ashes across the bridge of his nose, and Robert coughed, panicked, turning his face away. When he had shaken out as many of the ashes as he could, he submerged the bottle to let the water soak inside and poured out the gray mixture of creek water and ash until the bottle was cleared.

That done, Robert thought maybe he should say something like everyone had done at Redbone's burial. He had not known the boys, not even Henry Jackson, so he remembered what Tex had said, declaring, "They were children of God. They deserved to live their lives." Then he added something he had heard Pastor Jenkins say at Mama's funeral: "Please lead your children home."

"Amen," a voice said, and Robert jumped.

Blue was standing on the creek's bank in black mourning clothes, a crow no more.

Robert forgot his anger when he saw Blue. It was good to see him looking like a regular boy again. Emptying out the haint jar might have been the most important thing he had ever done: bigger than breaking into Haddock's office. Bigger than running away.

"Did it work right?" Robert said. "Are they free?"

"Yes," Blue said. "See?" Blue pointed to the water at Robert's feet, which bubbled as if dozens of tiny guppies were feeding, the circles of ripples colliding. The guilt Robert had felt for helping Haddock capture the haints melted as he watched the creek water dance.

"Are you free now too?"

"Yes," Blue said. "I won't have a reason to stay. Not after we're done."

"Done running?" Robert said. He tossed the empty, broken bottle into the creek, watching it sink so it would not betray his path. The glass didn't gleam beneath the water. Good.

Blue shook his head. "I'm sorry, no. I was afraid to tell you . . ."

Everything was a trick with Blue. Nothing was exactly what he promised. "Tell me what?" Robert said.

"About Haddock," Blue said.

Robert's bottom lip shook. "What about him?"

Blue stared at Robert with the same scrutiny as the crow, with eerily round black eyes. When Blue blinked, his eyes turned normal. "You're not the only one running," he said. "That kid Tex from band, when he saw the dogs after you, he led ten other boys with him to the woods on the other side of the dorm, headed in another direction. They're gonna try to make it to that side road while everybody's looking for you. And Haddock's got this kid from the kitchen, Kendrick, locked up in the Box so he can hurt him later. You're not the only one in trouble."

"When people see the photos—"

"They don't have time to wait for that," Blue said. "It's up to us."

"Up to us to do what?" Robert said, his heart racing with new dread. Whatever plan Blue had kept from him was bound to be terrible. Blue had never cared about him running away or whether he ever saw Gloria and Miz Lottie again.

"We've got to kill Haddock, Robert." Blue's garbled voice sounded half like a crow's, half like that of the young boy he'd been. "Before he hurts anybody else."

"Liar," Robert said. "You don't care about those other kids. You just want Haddock dead because of what he did to you."

"Don't you?" Blue said. "After what he did to Redbone?"

With all Robert's heart, he did. He'd wished Haddock dead since the night Haddock whipped him at the Funhouse, but especially since Haddock had sent Redbone to die. He'd always believed killing was wrong, but no jailhouse was good enough for Haddock. Not even the electric chair, although Papa said the worst punishments were mostly for Negroes. The photos he carried might not prove enough to put Haddock in jail; he might make up explanations other white people would believe. The sheriff wouldn't believe Robert's claims against Haddock, the same way he'd never believed Papa. Maybe no one would.

But Gloria was waiting for him. Boone was a liar, but had been right when he said haints whispered ways to die in your ear.

Robert knew he should still be running instead of wasting time talking to Blue in the middle of the creek. Haddock might see him at any time. He suddenly felt so tired that he wondered how he could take another step. Blue's demands were taking the wind out of him even while the dog's baying, so much closer now, made his skin itch to run.

"I don't want to kill anybody, Blue. Not even him. I just wanna go home."

"You don't have to kill him. I will," Blue said. "You only have to let him catch you."

41

The creek's bank was so choked with brush that Gloria stepped into the water close to the shallowest edge as she hurried toward the barking. Birdsong overhead and the gentle stirring of small creatures in the reeds concealed the true horror of the day. The bloodhound was closest, but at least two other dogs were audible now, although she didn't think they were in a pack. Not yet. Intuition flooded her as she ran, flowing freely with her breath: Haddock wanted to hide his secrets, but other dog handlers were catching up. And Haddock had a gun, his trigger finger untroubled by decency or conscience.

Haddock didn't only want to capture Robbie: Haddock planned to kill him.

Mama used to say Gloria rushed into plans without thinking, just like Papa, so she tried to think as she navigated the creek with all the speed she dared. As she ran, splashing her loafers and the cuffs of her denim dungarees, Gloria asked herself what she was willing to do to save Robbie. She could rescue him from one dog and one man, maybe, but she couldn't prevail against several. Could she die for her brother? The resolve pumping through Gloria's veins with her heartbeat was so fierce that she knew she could. She had not believed she might die today when she woke up in Mrs. Hamilton's comfortable guest bedroom on a quiet new street free from crowing roosters, but she might have reached the place where she would die. Not Miz Lottie, as she'd feared—*her*. She squeezed her eyes closed to try to see what was to come, but as always, she couldn't see when she tried. Gloria tested the idea of dying to see if it would paralyze her or make her want to turn back, but she only ran faster, her feet slipping slightly in unseen hollows. Until that moment, she had not known that she was not afraid to die.

But she *might* not have to. She could shoot a dog without thinking twice, and she was sure she could shoot a man too, even if it would mean going to jail. But could she shoot more than one man? She didn't know, but maybe she could. Newspaper reporters and the sheriff would claim she had lost her mind like they would say about Ruby McCollum in Live Oak one day soon, but her soul knew the truth: rescuing Robbie from a killing place would not be as immoral as leaving him there. The stench of pain and death from the Reformatory reached all the way out to this creek, dripping from aerial roots reaching toward the water. And if the law said she was wrong to shoot at the men chasing her brother, the law was wrong too. Uncle June had said he didn't think his killing in the war was a sin because those men were trying to kill him.

She would know the truth, at least. Miz Lottie, who had given her the gun, would certainly know. Papa would too. If she lived long enough, one day she would write a book about how she had helped set Robbie free. She'd tried the courthouse, hadn't she? She'd brought Harry T. Moore and the glorious John Dorsey to try that way, but justice in Gracetown didn't exist for Negroes. She'd told the judge about Lyle McCormack's true-life violations and all he'd cared about was Papa's imaginary one. No one was left to look out for Robbie except her.

Gloria heard a woman singing and realized the voice was hers. She didn't remember hearing it before, but the melody and lyrics popped into her head like a song she knew well and had sung with her arms clasped with others who were not afraid to die. She sang with a low, soft voice, keeping rhythm with her splashing feet: *"Ain't gonna let no-bo-dy . . . turn me 'round . . . turn me 'round . . . turn me 'round . . . Ain't gonna let no-bo-dy turn me 'round . . . I'm gonna keep on walking . . . keep on talking . . . Marching to Freeeeedom Land . . ."*

It was a freedom song! Gloria didn't know how she understood there was any such thing, but it was a song for church and also for street marches in a sea of determined Negro faces. No music had ever lifted her spirits like the song on her lips; she finally understood how Mahalia Jackson's praise music sounded to Miz Lottie. The melody was old-timey, but it was a song from the future. Maybe it was a song from *her* future. Or Robbie's. The song made her feel like she could remake the world. If she lived, saving Robbie might only be the beginning of what she could do.

The song led Gloria through twists and turns as the creek widened and deepened farther into the woods, away from the safety of the waiting truck, toward the chaos of the barking.

Nearly whispering, she sang her way past branches and stones, brushing off bugs and spiderwebs so thick and strong, they once would have made her scream when they touched her hair.

And then she saw him. Twenty yards in front of her, Robbie was standing dead center in the creek like a nature portrait on a museum wall. She grinned, but he was facing the bank instead of looking ahead at her. Whispers of his voice carried on the water's surface. Who was he talking to? Gloria crouched behind a shrub on the bank in case one of the trackers had found him. Gloria's heart stuffed her throat; shooting someone had been easier in her imagination.

What if it wasn't Haddock? What if it was some silly young boy hardly older than she was, like the deputy who had arrested Robbie, just doing what he'd been told?

But no one was in sight, although Robbie was so intent on his conversation that he hadn't noticed her approach. And Robbie's tone was measured, not scared, so soft she could not hear his words. The only other creature she saw on a branch above the bank was some kind of bird, maybe a raven or a crow. But even the crow was gone when Gloria blinked a gnat from her eye.

Why had Robbie stopped? Why wasn't he running? Was he praying?

After thirty long seconds of watching Robbie, Gloria decided it was safe to call for him.

She tried a whistle at first, but her lips were trembling and mostly blew out only breath.

Gloria opened her mouth. "Rob—"

The bloodhound was so loud that it could be in her ear, and brush rustled nearby. Gloria clamped her mouth shut with both hands to keep any sound from bleeding through. She ducked farther into a cluster of air plants growing against a mangrove trunk. Water sloshed a racket as her weight lurched, her knees suddenly unsteady and worthless as she clung to the tree. Her veins felt like they were filled with acid instead of blood.

But Robbie did not move or jump. As if he had been waiting.

"Here, doggie doggie doggie!" a deep, languid voice taunted—a voice she had never heard but knew as well as the song in her head. Then she saw Haddock, abnormally tall, wearing a western-style hat that made him look like every slave catcher from Mama's history lessons. She might have met him in her nightmares long before this terrible day.

Haddock was limping on the bank, pulled forward by a black-and-brown bloodhound that was squirming with excitement because it had tracked his target. Gloria dug into her pocket to pull out her gun. Haddock was too far to shoot with her little .22—and besides, with Robbie standing in the center of the creek, she might hit him by accident—but Gloria didn't see a weapon at first and hoped Haddock was not armed. Maybe she wouldn't have to shoot him. She could surprise Haddock from her hiding place and wrest control away from him.

"I got you now, boy!" Haddock called out. "Quit running before you get hurt!"

Something in Haddock's right hand gleamed in the golden sunlight. A gun! And much bigger than hers, from the shine. Haddock was hiding the gun from Robert's view, but Gloria saw it when he turned slightly to the side as he made a careful approach to the edge of the water.

Why didn't Robbie run? Why didn't he seem afraid? The water was shallow, but even if he dove down, Haddock would not have a good shot at him and Gloria might get lucky. The other barking dogs seemed much closer, picking up speed, but so far Haddock was alone—

Except he wasn't. A panting Negro man with a rifle caught up to Haddock and stood a few feet behind him when Haddock raised his gun hand to signal that he should stop. The Negro man eyed Haddock's gun warily, keeping his rifle pointed at the ground.

"I do believe," Haddock said to Robbie, his voice almost friendly, "that you broke into my office and took some things that don't belong to you, son." Robbie finally moved, turning away from the bank to face Haddock, his back to Gloria just when she'd been ready to try to signal to him that he wasn't alone. "I don't know who told you dogs can't track in water, but it isn't quite true."

"I broke your jar," Robbie said with a confidence that shocked her. "I set those haints free."

"Did you, now?" Haddock said, taking only one slow step forward despite the bloodhound's frantic pulling. "Then you must be real proud of yourself. Where's my envelope?"

"Does *he* know what's in it?" Robbie said, pointing to the Negro man.

"I don't share my private belongings with just anyone," Haddock said. One more step, until the water reached above both ankles. "I think you know that, Robert. Why would I tell everyone my business? I only told you because you're special. Boone was right about you."

"He's a killer!" Robert shouted to the Negro man behind Haddock. "He killed his baby sister! He takes photos of all the kids he's hurt. That's what he wants, so I won't show them!"

Haddock looked back at the Negro man as if they were sharing a joke. But even at a distance through the spindly plants, Gloria could see the sober concern in the Negro man's face.

"Quite an imagination you've got there," Haddock said, grinning back at Robbie.

"Robert," the Negro man said, pleading. "Don't talk back! Don't put up a fight. Just give the superintendent what he's looking for. Settle the rest later."

Gloria knew his voice: it was Mrs. Hamilton's brother, the one named Percy who had come to her house! Gloria longed to call out to him. He had a gun too, and if she could think of the right words, she could pull him to her side, the two of them against Haddock. Papa had helped their family! Gloria's lungs heaved as she tried to decide if it was smarter to act—or to wait for a more perfect moment. If Robbie had stolen something Haddock wanted badly enough, he might not kill Robbie until he had it back. Robbie must have hidden the envelope he'd taken; his hands were empty.

"You hear that, Robert? Mister Crutcher here is talking good sense." One more step, then two. Haddock was striding into the creek, less than twenty-five feet from Robbie. The dog was within fifteen feet of Robbie at the edge of his leash, trying to swim toward him since he could no longer run. The dog whined, frustrated, almost like he wanted to play. Robbie took a small step away from the dog, his first sign of fear. The water rippled gently around him, the wavy circles reaching the dog and then Haddock, enfolding them all.

"He set the fire in 1920!" Robert yelled to Crutcher. "He's got photos of all the—" Gloria's intuition showed her what would happen seconds before life imitated her vision, so she was suppressing a cry before Haddock turned to Crutcher with his gun raised and an explosion ripped through the woods. Crutcher grabbed at his chest with a muffled yell, more of surprise than pain, before he dropped his rifle and curled to the ground on the creek's bank. He didn't stir an inch. The distant barking grew frantic. Haddock's dog yelped, startled, wading in a confused circle back toward Haddock.

"Now you see what you've gone and made me do?" Haddock said, voice still languid as he turned back to Robbie.

Robbie was the only one who screamed.

The worst of the worst of the worst, Blue had said about Haddock, but that hadn't prepared Robert for the rose bloom of blood on Crutcher's white shirt after Haddock had shot him. Mrs. Hamilton had lost her husband and now her brother too, and it was Blue's fault. If he hadn't listened to Blue, he might be at the railroad trestle by now instead of only feet away from Haddock and his gun that stank of killing. Every path he took with Blue meant walking past someone else's dying.

Robert hated for Haddock to see tears in his eyes, but he couldn't hold them back. "You've got a big mouth, Robert. This is what happens when you say things you shouldn't," Haddock said. He almost sounded sad about it. "That's a good worker lying dead on the ground because you talk too much. That social worker from the state said you got done wrong by the judge, and I'll confess he had me wondering about it my own self. But it turns out you're a thief after all, like the rest of these dumb monkeys and swamp trash. And a liar. We had a deal, Robert. We *toasted* it, and anyone knows a toast is as good as a handshake. I'd say even better. Don't you remember our deal? You'd catch the haints; I'd let you go."

Robert sobbed. He still hated himself for toasting with Haddock and agreeing to be his haint catcher to help Haddock cover the wrong he had done.

Haddock went on: "But that isn't what you did, is it? You and your slick-mouthed friend Redbone made it into a game—"

"Shut up!"

"You had to know I wasn't going to let that pass," Haddock said. "You had to know you would pay the piper. So tell me where you put my photo collection and I'll let you die quick. If you don't tell me . . . when those dog boys find us—and you can hear 'em on their way—those leashes are gonna slip loose. Whoops! Have you ever seen somebody who got chewed up by a dog? Not a bite: I mean chewed down to the bone. I do believe Scout's palate has developed a taste for stupid boys. You're gonna taste real good to Scout, Robert. There's no good way to die except maybe in your sleep, but no one since the beginning of time wants to get eaten alive."

"I'm not scared of you," Robbie said. After the Reformatory, he doubted he could ever be scared of a new thing again.

"Really?" Haddock said, wading another foot closer. "I think you ought to be, and you know why? You're plenty smart, I'll give you that. But you're not as clever as you think you are. You made a mistake with that Vaseline: it didn't hold off Colonel here at all." At the sound of his name, the dog whined and wriggled against his leash, trying to reach Robert again. "You made a mistake with the creek—because here we are: you, me, and Colonel. And you got yourself good and wet, so I can see straight through your shirt It's all black skin except for one square spot right across your belly So I'm gonna guess that's where you hid my envelope. I'm fairl certain I can see the edges poking against that thin cotton. Ain' that right?"

Robert didn't answer, but Haddock had spotted the envelop he'd hidden: Blue had advised him to toss away the satchel an hide the envelope from sight to buy him time, since Haddock ha a sickness and would not be satisfied until his photographs wer in his hands again.

Be sure to get him in the water, Blue had said.

"You sure about that?" Robert said. "Then come and see. I dar you."

Haddock laughed. His smile faded with a moment's uneasines but then he smiled brighter than before. "You dare *me*?" he said. H pointed his gun at Robert so he could see the wide hole of the larg revolver's muzzle. Every part of Robert wanted to duck and ru but he held himself steady. Blue had told him to stay where he was no matter what.

"If you shoot me and you're wrong . . . you'll never see your stupid, nasty photos again," Robert said. "*Ever.*"

"But I'm not wrong," Haddock said. A gun sounded.

Robert thought he had died, until the water six feet beside Haddock sprayed and bubbled with a stray bullet and Haddock leaped away. Robert realized he had felt the bullet sail past him. He looked back at Crutcher, praying he was awake and alive—but Crutcher had not moved, his gun still abandoned. Of course not. The shot had come from *behind* him.

"Leave him alone!" Gloria's shaky voice said. "That was just a warning. Drop your gun, or I'll put the next one in your head!"

Robert whirled around, sure he had slipped into a dream. Gloria was standing near the bank, a small pistol raised like she meant it. Gloria barely seemed real, dressed in too-big men's pants, talking like a mobster with a gun in her hand. If he was dreaming his sister so vividly, maybe he'd dreamed these past days at the Reformatory too. If Blue hadn't told him to stay exactly where he was, Robert would have run to her.

The only person more shocked to see Gloria was Haddock, squinting his eyes in her direction, pointing his gun toward her instead. That was the only way Robert was sure she was real, and pain bloated his belly. He'd never thought Gloria would come to try to find him, although now it seemed he should have known he would lose everyone he loved. Mama first. Then Papa. And now Gloria was in a place she shouldn't be, face-to-face with a man who was the closest Robert had seen to the devil himself. Nothing had been right for him in the world for as long as he could remember, so of course Gloria was about to get killed while he watched.

"I'll be goddamned," Haddock said. "That explains this whole thing. You had help." He didn't sound the least bit concerned about the gun. He'd flinched at the gunshot, but now he was at his full height again. The bloodhound barked angrily at Gloria, tugging hard on his leash.

"Put the gun down!" Gloria said again, although her voice was less steady.

"Who is that, Robert?" Haddock said. "Is she kin to you?"

Robert didn't answer, as if telling would cause Gloria immediate harm. If he moved at all, Haddock might shoot her. Or he might shoot him to spite her. Gloria didn't have good pistol aim—she was just playing a part to try to seem scarier—but Robert was sure Haddock loved to practice.

"Ahhh . . . ," Haddock said, and a small smile returned to his face. "I bet that's the sister who came to visit on Sunday. Is that when y'all hatched this crazy idea? Is she the one who cut the fence?"

"*Drop your gun!*" Gloria said again, screaming with rage now, although clearly Haddock had no plans to obey her. Her gun seemed to mean nothing to him.

"With all due respect, miss," Haddock said, turning to Gloria, "I admire your gumption, but I will not. I'm betting that wasn't a warning shot; you just missed. Now, you can come closer and try to shoot me again with that little lady pistol, but I guarantee you Robert will be dead before you can get a bead on me. You're lucky you didn't clip your brother at that angle. I think we both know that, don't we?"

Robert heard Gloria breathing faster, frustrated and frightened. Blue landed on the tree branch, watching as a crow. He cawed so Robert would see him. Finally!

Robert's relief died when Haddock fired back at Gloria, and wood chipped from the tree trunk near her head. Gloria ducked away with a shriek, splashing in the water. Robert felt faint with worry that she'd been shot, but she was stirring behind the brush, climbing to the bank to hide. The dog barked and growled madly now, wading toward Haddock.

"Now, *that* was a warning shot," Haddock said. "See the difference? But I'm not gonna kill you yet, little miss. I want you to see this."

Robert covered his ears, which were ringing terribly from gunfire so close, especially the ear Red McCormack had hurt. "Gloria, get back!" Robert yelled to her. "I don't need your help!"

Again Haddock looked at Robert with nervous confusion. He was more worried about Robert than he was about Gloria. Maybe, deep down, he knew.

"What's got into you?" Haddock said.

"*Now*, Blue!" Robert shouted. "What are you waiting for?"

Haddock crouched slightly, looking over his shoulder to make sure no one else was coming. When nothing on the bank moved, Haddock canted his head as he glared at Robert. "You've wasted enough of my time. I'm getting that envelope back. Move an inch and I'll shoot you where it'll hurt most." Haddock waded toward Robert, so close that Robert could see his rage-reddened eyes. "First I'm gonna kill you . . . then I'll get your sister too."

The water around Robert's knees turned cold, as if he were standing in the freezer. He thought the cold might be from fear, his limbs losing sensation—until the fog began to rise.

In his last moments of life, Fenton J. Haddock thought about his baby sister.

It was a lie to say he'd never wanted a sister. The idea had seemed fine at first: someone to dress up, someone to tease who couldn't cuss him like his mother or beat him like his grandfather, who had once made a living whipping slaves he tied to an oak tree on the McCormack plantation. But he'd quickly learned that a baby drained away what little time and care his parents had for child-rearing, and it wasn't long before he'd hated how they only smiled at Lucy and never at him. They didn't notice whole days he missed school or the wild rabbits he caught to torture in cages in the barn. Lucy had been staring up at him with those giggles that turned so easily to tears, and one day he'd had enough of his parents' new favorite pet. He didn't plan it out or choose the day; he simply picked up her blanket and covered her face until her crying stopped. He wasn't sure she was dead at first, since he hadn't pressed the blanket especially hard. He was a little surprised at the new color of her face, how her breathing had stopped along with her wailing. But he made his peace with it.

He'd been more superstitious as a boy, thinking God would storm into his room and drag him straight to hell. But it never went that way. If anything, he gained more sweets and a later bedtime because his parents coddled him after Lucy died. Maybe he tried to make it up to Lucy by brushing her thin hair so pretty and heating up the iron all by himself so her dress wouldn't have a wrinkle on the photo-taking day. But while he posed with her on the sofa with her feeble weight on his lap, her skin cold, eyes closed, he felt certain that Lucy would exact her revenge one day. Sure enough, that very night, a drinking glass flung itself from his nightstand and broke to pieces on his bedroom floor. A piece of glass he missed when he tried to clean up the mess cut his foot so deeply that it had left a blood puddle that could never be washed away from the wood. That was the first of his long association with spiteful haints.

And this ordinary summer day in Gracetown might be his last. Haddock suspected it as soon as the creek turned to ice water, but he only *knew* when Kendall Sweeting appeared in front of him, blocking his view of Robert Stephens, solid as living flesh. Even Colonel saw Sweeting, the dog yanking so hard on the leash that he finally freed himself as Haddock's hand went slack.

"You," Haddock said, the last word he would ever speak.

Sweeting shook his head. "*Us*," he said.

The water, so still before, churned like rapids against Haddock's knees while the treetops swayed above, a sudden and impossible storm. Colonel growled and barked, confused and wild-eyed, but he was moving *toward* Sweeting as if for protection. Smiling at Haddock with perfect white teeth, Sweeting laid his hand across Colonel's head to scratch him behind his ears.

"Colonel knows me from the kennel," Sweeting said. "Colonel knows *us*."

The new cool fog hanging low over the creek should have been enough to warn Haddock to move out of the water, but it was too late now. He felt a small, short-lived victory when he put the rest together: Stephens had emptied out the haints' ashes in the creek, so he'd been standing in their midst the whole time. Who knew how many spirits were conspiring against him now?

Could Lucy be with them too? Haddock felt the greatest terror of his life as he thought he saw his baby sister's face framed beneath the bubbling water, laughing at him. Other faces shimmered beneath the pale creek water—some he remembered, some he didn't—but Lucy's was his greatest torment, a long-ago promise finally fulfilled.

Too late, Haddock turned to run toward the safety of the bank.

"Git him, boy," Sweeting said, his voice mimicking Haddock's, nearly buried by the water's roiling.

Colonel splashed after Haddock with savage growls, his sweet nature twisted by the haints, unrecognizable. Between awkward, stumbling steps in the water, Haddock reached over his shoulder to try to shoot the dog, which he now knew he should have done as soon as he'd seen Sweeting petting him. But Colonel sank his teeth into Haddock's wrist before he could squeeze the trigger. Haddock dropped his Colt in the dizzying blaze of pain as Colonel's teeth raked through his skin, snapping the bones of his fingers and wrist. Haddock roared with agony as he stumbled and fell into the hostile creek. One or two of his fingers might be gone, but he couldn't tell for sure in his hand's pulsing agony.

All he saw was fur and Colonel's bloody muzzle.

Haddock started to say, "*NO, boy—*" as he choked on the bitter water clogging his mouth, but Colonel's teeth clamped across his neck and stole his words, and his throat, clean away.

42

Gloria hadn't known dogs could feel shame until she saw Haddock's bloodhound, coat drenched soupy red, dragging itself out of the creek. The dog was shaking as much as she. Gloria raised a wobbly arm as she climbed over brush to get closer to the dog and Robbie, ready to shoot the animal if she had to, but the blood-spattered dog didn't look her way. It didn't sniff at Mrs. Hamilton's brother, who was now groaning and stirring on the bank as he raised himself to a sitting position. She knew the sheriff would put down any dog who killed a man, but she didn't have the heart to shoot the dog that had saved them. The dog trotted off to the woods, back the way he and his master had come, tail slung between its legs. Whatever strange fever had sparked the dog's attack against the Reformatory's warden had passed.

She'd felt the fever too. For a minute, maybe two, the world had slid off-kilter to a place where still waters churned white with foam and tree branches whipped without wind. Somehow, in the confusion, the dog had gone mad. Or come to its senses. Or . . . something.

But the other dogs were still coming, and she could not expect a miracle twice.

Gloria wanted to help Mrs. Hamilton's brother, but first she went to the edge of the creek to look after Robbie, who was staring at the mess left floating there. Gloria looked quickly away from the gore so it wouldn't sear her memory—although she would never forget the sight of a man's neck so thoroughly shredded. Robbie was standing only feet from the mess, still staring. He had not looked away once during the attack—had not seemed to hear her calling for him.

"Robbie!" she said. For the first time, his eyes snapped up—but only his eyes. He looked so much like he wasn't himself that Gloria tensed, afraid that whatever fever had gripped the dog might have infected her brother too. "Don't look!"

But his eyes went right back down to the mutilated corpse barely held together by clothing, half floating in the water.

"Hey!" Crutcher half called, half groaned. "I'm . . . I'm sorry I didn't shoot him when I had the chance." He let out a vigorous yell of pain as he used his rifle to try to prop himself up. His shirt was a bloody mess too, but not as bad as the one in the creek.

Gloria ran to him. "Are you all right?" she said, an empty question that ignored obvious answers. But she didn't know how to ask if he was dying.

He nodded, biting his lip. "Yeah," he said. "Mostly got my shoulder. I had to play dead. I'm sorry. I thought he might try it; I was waiting . . . and I turned just enough"—he heaved, peeking beneath his shirt at his wound—"just enough so he'd think he got me."

"Why'd his dog do that?" Gloria said, hoping he might know.

His eyes glimmered as if he might have the answer for the strange things she had seen, but he only said, "I don't know, but I praise God he did. You and Robert . . . you need to go. *Now.* They're close. They're at the creek by now, moving faster in the water. Stay in the water too. I'll point them the wrong way to give you time. Do you know where you're going?"

Gloria nodded. "My godmother's waiting."

He smiled a sickly, pained smile. "That's good. Get far away, as fast as you can. *Go.*"

"Thank you," Gloria said.

His face wrenched with pain. "Don't thank me. I didn't do nearly what I should have. Should've shot him first. I knew what he was deep down. Didn't want to believe the stories."

"Robert has proof, I think," Gloria said.

"Keep it," he said. "Take it with you. Don't give it to the sheriff. Take it to—"

"The NAACP," Gloria said, thinking of John Dorsey. She imagined what Thurgood Marshall would do with evidence that the Reformatory was hurting and killing children. Or Robert's testimony that Haddock had shot his own man and tried to kill him in the woods. Or an envelope filled with atrocities.

"I was gonna say the governor," Crutcher said with the same pained smile. "But that works. No doubt who your father is! *Go on*, now. They're almost here." He swatted her away with his good arm. He'd said Haddock only hit his shoulder, but he was sweating a river and looked ready to collapse. She tried to decide if he would be all right . . . and thought he would. The intuition didn't blaze as strongly as when she'd known that Haddock had murder in his heart, but it felt real enough. He would recover. He would survive. Maybe they all would.

Gloria could no longer ignore the urgency of the dogs drawing closer. Taunts and whistles skated across the creek water to accompany the barking. Half a dozen men might be on their way. Gloria gave Crutcher a last grateful look and ran back to Robbie.

Gloria tried to maneuver around the remnants of the man killed by the dog, but the water swirled bright pink in a ring around the body. Maybe that would keep the trackers busy, when they heard what the dog had done. They couldn't possibly blame such a gruesome killing on a man. She wondered what kind of tale Crutcher would tell to explain it.

Still, Robbie had not looked away from where he stood standing over the bobbing corpse. "Come on," she said, and tugged on his arm, trying to ease him from his thoughts as gently as she could, to wake him from this unspeakable dream. "Don't keep looking."

Robbie stared up at her with haunted eyes. "I just want to be sure he's dead," he said, his voice cracking—half man, half child. "If you're dead . . . *stay* dead." He whispered the last words to himself. Robbie was not the same. He would never again be the Robbie she had known. Gloria wanted to scream her rage and grief to the sky.

But he was alive, she reminded herself. She had found him. She would take him to Chicago, where they would find Papa. The future was waiting.

Robbie slipped his hand into hers, and she squeezed his. They ran in the shallows. A crow soared ahead of them, wings spread wide.

Blue was gone without a goodbye.

Robbie kept his eyes on the crow flying off as long as he could see it, but soon the black dot was out of sight, either too far or vanished into the air. Blue was headed somewhere Robert could not follow him—not yet, anyway. Robbie hoped wherever Blue was flying next would be a mystery for a long time. But he would write down the rules for haints so another kid who met another Blue would think twice before putting their life in a haint's hands: Haints can look different ways. Haints usually come if you call their full names. Haints don't like to be called haints. Haints can be fun as friends, but you have to look out for yourself or you might die like Redbone. Haints don't say goodbye, except when they visit your dreams.

And haints can kill you.

Robert's memory overflowed with red-foamed water and torn flesh. The entire creek seemed to fill with blood, splashing crimson against his calves and boots as he and Gloria ran. A nearly buried part of him almost screamed. But Gloria squeezed his hand when he tightened his grip, and the creek's water turned normal.

"Thanks for coming for me," Robert said.

Gloria rubbed his head. "You knew I wouldn't leave you here."

They had so much to say, but talking was hard while you tried to avoid tripping. The dogs were still coming, so they couldn't catch their breath. Robert guessed the trackers hadn't spent too much time with Crutcher, or maybe they hadn't believed him when he told them he and Gloria had gone another way. The barking was never far behind.

"There's only two trackers now," Gloria said. "Others did what Mister Crutcher said."

Robert glanced over his shoulder, scared the new trackers might be in sight already without Blue to help them, but the wild woods blocked his vision.

"How do you know?" Robert panted.

"Just do," Gloria said.

If anyone had a sister better than Gloria, Robert didn't know who it could be for all of time. She'd taken care of him after Papa left, she'd threatened to shoot Haddock down to save him, and she could see things other people couldn't, almost like a haint.

"I saw Mama," Robert told her. "When I first got to the creek. I think . . ." He almost—*almost*—told her he thought he'd been flying for a short time, but instead, he said, "I think she helped me get out of the woods."

Usually Gloria shrugged her shoulders when he talked about Mama's ghost, but this time she said, "I know she did."

"Did you see her?"

Gloria didn't answer for a moment, and Robert remembered how she'd pretended she didn't believe him when he first told her Mama was visiting his room when he slept, but he'd seen her jealous pout. "Nope," she said. "Just you."

"But you can feel her?"

"Every day."

"Me too."

More dead and broken limbs clogged the creek, so they concentrated on not falling. The water was so shallow that it barely reached the tops of Robert's boots. They would leave tracks. Robbie was about to ask Gloria if they should try to find places where the water was deeper when he saw a rusting metal column up high ahead, something unnatural in the woods. A bridge!

"There it is!" Gloria said.

"But where's the truck?"

"Maybe we can't see it yet. Come on!" Gloria tried not to sound as surprised as she looked that the truck wasn't there. He followed her out of the creek to the steep slope, which was just as thick as the woods toward the cornfield but much harder to move through because of the climb. His legs, only sore before, felt like jelly on the uphill hike.

"I tied a rope from the top—see?" Gloria said as she trudged closer to the trestle. He did not see the rope, but he trusted her in a way he had never trusted Blue, clinging to jutting roots and stones so he would not slip back down.

Splashing was coming from the creek behind them. So close now.

"Hey!" a reedy voice shouted from a distance, but not far enough. "Stop!"

They'd been spotted! The trackers' guns would start firing next. Robert imagined the bloody body in the creek again, but this time he saw himself. Gloria's gun fell out of her jeans in her hurry to climb; it tumbled down into the brush. Robert knew without Gloria saying so that neither of them could slow down to find it, just when they needed it most.

Gloria was scaling the hillside so fast above him that Robert worried he would not keep up. She could not hold his hand now like in the creek. The soles of his boots were slippery, sliding on the moss when he tried to get a good footing. He glanced up at the trestle again, the angle slightly different, and still saw no truck waiting.

"Is it Uncle June and Waymon?" Robert asked. "Maybe they drove off, Gloria."

"No," she said firmly. "They didn't." Robert wondered if she *knew* that or if she was just guessing, but he decided she knew the same way she knew Mama's ghost was watching.

Worrying would not help him climb faster or outrun the dogs.

Gloria grabbed the rope, which met them only halfway up. He

was relieved when he saw the ease with which she pulled herself up two-handedly like a mountain climber. After moving around a prickly dead tree, Robert finally reached the frayed end of the rope after her and held tight. His palms were no longer slippery, so his grip was strong. He held the rope with only his right hand so he would not drop the envelope he'd hidden down his shirt, pinned by the waistband.

Pebbles sprayed down from Gloria's shoes, but he didn't complain, trying to keep her in sight above him. Robert felt so much more scared now than he had facing Haddock in the creek, when having Blue on his side made him feel like he could do anything. The railroad trestle had felt like a fairy tale then, but now that it was real and solid, his desperation to reach it made it hard to catch his breath.

"Gloria . . . ," he said. "I can't breathe . . ."

"You're just scared," she said. "Me too. Keep climbing, Robbie!"

Red spots and shapes wiggled in front of Robbie's eyes as he felt dizzy, but he never let go of the rope, forcing his wobbly legs on. Gloria's silhouette blazed above him in the setting sunlight like an angel. He held on to the rope. He followed his sister. He tried not to think about breathing as his lungs and throat burned.

The rapid splashing in the water below did not sound like men. Robert risked one glance back down and saw two loose dogs running toward them, German shepherds like Mister Red's dog Duke, but bigger. And moving fast.

"The dogs!" Robert called to Gloria, and she did not look back before she somehow climbed even faster. She was already only three feet from the road.

"Come on, Robbie! The truck's here!" Gloria couldn't hide the relief in her voice.

When he looked up again, he saw the white paint on the back of Miz Lottie's truck. The brush below rustled with the dogs' approach. They ran as fast as demons.

Robert's foot slipped, and he swung wide on the rope, his feet wheeling as he tried to touch something solid. His weight pulled on Gloria as she grabbed the rope and cried out: for a long moment he was certain she would fall on him and they would both tumble into the jaws of the dogs. But his hands slid down only a few inches, scraping his palms raw, and he held on. Then he pressed one hand back against the envelope just as it was jarring loose.

"You okay?" Gloria called down to him. "Hurry up!"

Two more big steps, and Gloria was at the top. Robert thought she would wait and pull him up, but she vanished toward the road. He heard her say, "Miz Lottie! Dogs! Start it up!"

The truck wasn't even running? And Miz Lottie was driving?

"I got Ole Suzy turned around, but she needed another rest," Miz Lottie's voice said from where she sat just out of sight. "Where's Robbie?"

"He's coming! Start the truck! Hurry!"

One foot up, his other foot up, then the other again. While he climbed, Miz Lottie's truck choked as she tried to start it just out of sight. The second time Miz Lottie tried, the truck came to life, the engine as loud as an angry baby.

"Start driving slow. We'll catch you!" Gloria said.

"You sure, pumpkin?" Miz Lottie said. "Shouldn't I—"

"I'm sure!"

Gloria's face appeared from six feet above, open-mouthed and scared. She reached her hand down to him. "Robbie, look out!" Gloria said. Robert looked: pale brown fur moved past the brush with growls like death, close enough for Robbie to see gnashing yellow teeth. Robbie didn't have time to think before he kicked Papa's boot in the dog's face as hard as he could and the dog tumbled back down several feet with a yelp. The other dog tangled with him in the brush. His last piece of luck, he thought. Maybe his sure kick had been a gift from Blue. Or, more likely, Mama. Robbie could breathe again.

Carried by his memory of flying in the woods, Robert scrambled up the rest of the slope without the rope to support him. Gloria's hand was there to meet his, clamping tight. She pulled him with the strength of a grown man, and the ground was flat beneath his feet again. They emerged just below a railroad trestle that hadn't been used in years, wrapped in rust and weeds. The road under the trestle was just as old, more weeds than dirt. Miz Lottie's truck was chugging forward, already fifteen yards beyond them. She leaned out of her window to look back, waving with a grin only because she was happy to see them. She didn't know the rest. Her smile was so full of light that Robert vowed he would never tell her.

"We gotta go!" Gloria said, but Robert was already running behind her.

Gloria sprinted ahead of Robbie, grabbing the truck's rear panel while he trailed her by ten strides. Pressing his hand against the envelope so tightly was slowing him down. Gloria took a leap to hoist herself into the back of the truck.

"Robbie, come on!" Gloria yelled. "Don't look back!"

But Robert had to see for himself. One dog had made it to the road: the larger German shepherd, uninjured, at a full run while it barked ugly plans for him. Maybe this was the dog Haddock had said would eat him alive before he was eaten himself. A last burst of speed took Robbie within five strides of the truck, then four. Then three. Again his sister's outstretched hand waited. The truck's lurch made him miss Gloria's hand when he tried to grab it.

"Miz Lottie, drive straight!" Gloria said.

"Hit a hole!" Miz Lottie said. "Sorry!"

With the dog running behind him and gaining fast, Robert flung himself forward, and Gloria snatched his hand before he could fall, holding on even as his feet dragged on the road before he could climb up with help from Gloria's unbreakable grip. The dog panted and growled on his heels as if it might jump in the truck too.

"You got him?" Miz Lottie called back.

"Yes!" Gloria said. "Faster!"

The truck sped up so quickly that they were both knocked against the side, but Robert was too full of joy in his sister's arms to feel bumps or bruises. He watched the dog fall farther and farther behind until it slowed to a trot. Then the dog just sat still in the middle of the road, watching them go. Too late, the second dog and two handlers emerged, too far back to see well—and too far to get a good luck at the truck. The men yelled and shot their rifles in the air before the road curved and took them out of sight. Those men would hardly be able to tell the sheriff what color the truck was, much less who had been driving it. The sheriff would never expect the getaway driver to be an old woman.

"Praise the Lord!" Miz Lottie cried from the driver's seat. "Praise Jesus!"

"Miz Lottie, you're not sick?" Gloria called.

"Only with worry!" she said. "Better now! When we git to the state road, I'm gonna take the shortcut to Tallahassee. Those hillbillies don't know these roads like I do."

The truck swerved when Miz Lottie laughed like a young girl on a joyride like Redbone, and her laughter spread to Robert and Gloria as they hugged to keep from falling over. Robert laughed until Gloria rubbed his shoulder and said, "Don't cry, Robbie, we've got you back now," and he realized he was sobbing because Redbone was dead. Gloria's touch, so much like Mama's, made him vibrate with the horrors that had happened to him since the deputy picked him up and took him away from her.

The Reformatory was the Hell from Pastor Jenkins's sermons, hidden at the edge of Gracetown while people drove their cars and played with their children and ate ice cream cones on Main Street. Every sight around Robert amazed him: the woods speeding past them so fast, the empty road ahead, the crows in the treetops. So normal and everyday, with Hell so close by.

"Where are we going?" Robert said.

"To take a train to Papa in Chicago," Gloria said. She kicked away the tarp beside them to reveal a hidden suitcase. "We're going home, Robbie." Home was wherever Papa was.

"Y'all git down now," Miz Lottie said. "Duck so nobody sees you!"

Robert and Gloria hid beneath the warm tarp and held hands, nestled in their dark hiding place while Miz Lottie's truck rocked and swayed. They closed their eyes and felt their bones rattle as the old truck sped on the road to the train station, like astronauts taking off for the moon.

43

For the rest of their lives, the swamp and the truck ride would reside only in flashes of memory waking them when they tried to sleep, or in foggy dreams. They would remember the surreal relief when the woods opened up to paved roads, stoplights, and concrete. And peeling off blood and muddy swamp water for pressed collars and stiff, clean fabrics under the truck's tarp. And the tearful goodbye with Miz Lottie, clinging and sobbing before she practically cussed them out and sent Gloria to the ticket counter. Mercifully, perhaps in the way Mama had said she didn't remember all of the pain of birthing, over time they would willfully forget their time at the churning creek—although they would forever flinch at the sound of barking dogs.

"Go on to your future, girl," Miz Lottie whispered to Gloria, the last words she would hear from her godmother when she could feel her breath against her ear.

They arrived after dark at the Tallahassee train depot, which looked like the Colosseum to her. She and Robbie were still steeped in each horrific moment, bones still ringing from their ordeal even as Gloria counted out their fares and carefully pocketed the rest, afraid to loosen her fingers from the bills. Robert huddled close to her, pushing his face under her arm, both hands gripping so she could not pull away even if she wanted to—and they both knew she never would. Their clothes were cheerful and alive, but inside of them they were living ghosts.

Until the train began moving, they thought it never would. Every white person they saw on the train platform seemed to be looking at them even when they weren't. Every sound was a gunshot. *Please just let us get to Papa,* Gloria thought, and the train car lurched forward at last.

It was perhaps an hour later, when Robbie was sleeping against her, still holding tight, that Gloria noticed how filthy the Negro train car was. The smell broke through her fugue state first: the car smelled like a spittoon. None of the other half dozen Negro passengers were chewing tobacco or looked like they would, but a quick glance at the empty seats across from theirs revealed horrible stains. *It's not from the passengers; it's from spiteful white train workers,* her mind whispered to her. She was afraid to look at her own seat, which she was sure had stained the back of Miz Lottie's pretty pink dress and Robbie's new suit by now. The train was Jim Crow on wheels.

But in the morning the windows unveiled a wonderland passing at terrific speed, the trees and landscape a revelation. The red soil she had known her whole life was gone. The route map at the depot said this train's two-day journey would hurtle them through Georgia, Alabama, and Tennessee, then up to Missouri and Illinois. As excited as she was to find Papa, Gloria felt like she was being swallowed inside the endless world.

Robbie reluctantly had agreed to allow Gloria to take hold of the satchel he'd carried with him through the swamp, which he had miraculously kept dry. *But you can't look inside,* he'd told her. As much as Gloria's fingers itched to unwrap the string and open the large envelope he had stolen from the warden, the look in Robbie's eyes had convinced her that whatever was inside might prevent her from ever sleeping again. Once she gave it to Papa, he would give it to the NAACP—perhaps John Dorsey himself—and maybe no other child in Florida would have to suffer as Robbie had. But she also knew the way of things: everyone would try to say that only the warden left mauled in the creek had created the unholy suffering at that place, when the whole town had had a hand.

Robbie slept for most of the first day on the train. Gloria noticed that he was holding a tattered piece of paper and leaned over for a better look at the wrinkled sketch of a pleasant-looking boy's grinning face. Gloria did not recognize the boy.

A giggle from Robbie surprised her, but he was still asleep. Somewhere in his dreams, he was at play. She didn't know how she knew that he was visiting his dead friend.

But she did.

The sandwiches and pound cake Miz Lottie had packed for them lasted the first day, but their stomachs were growling as suppertime approached on the second. Liberation and hope were the only joys of the journey; everything else was hateful, from the stench to the heat to the poor bathroom facilities. At every stop, white passengers glared as they passed their windows like Negroes were a zoo display. Gloria did not dare try to leave the train at any of the stops. What would be the point? They would not have time to find food that would be served to Negroes, and she did not want to be left behind. Not when they were so close.

NOW ENTERING ILLINOIS, a sign beside the train tracks proclaimed, and her heart sang with a revelation. She thought about Papa's story of seeing Mama eating ice cream on Main Street in Gracetown. But they weren't in Gracetown anymore. They weren't even in the South.

Gloria patted down her hair and tried to straighten the creases in her dress. She spit on her palm and dabbed at dried flecks of mud on Robbie's face. They both must still look a fright, but she couldn't fix that now. She clutched the oversized pocketbook Miz Lottie had given her, which held both her money and the warden's envelope.

"You hungry?" she said.

Robbie nodded. He had barely said a word since the Reformatory, seeming younger than he had been before, not as old as his haunted eyes. He needed more time, that was all.

Gloria stood up and held out her hand for him. "Come on, then."

They swayed with the train cars as Gloria led Robbie away from the stench of the Negro car to the gangway outside. The air was already so different, cooler and lighter across their faces. Robbie's hand tightened around hers when they entered the train car with white passengers.

"Don't pay them any mind," Gloria said, and they kept their eyes fixed ahead.

Gloria had never ridden on a train before now, but she'd seen plenty in picture shows. This one looked exactly as she'd imagined, with white passengers sleeping or hidden behind their newspaper pages, riding free from bad smells.

"Are we gonna get in trouble?" Robbie whispered as they walked.

Gloria couldn't be sure, in truth, but she promised him they would be fine.

Finally, they reached a car unlike the rest—with crowded tables instead of just seats. They met a din of clinking silverware and conversations that dipped only slightly when they appeared through the doors, eyes rising to look at them. Gloria took her own advice and ignored the staring eyes, instead slipping into the first empty booth she saw. Instead of sitting across from her in the waiting space, Robbie squeezed in beside her.

The table had a white linen cloth over it like a church picnic and a basket of bread rolls. Plates, silverware, and glasses were already arranged. Robbie's hand hovered over the basket of bread, waiting for her permission. Gloria nodded, and Robbie stuffed a roll into his cheeks practically whole, glancing around nervously, expecting someone to object.

A stout Negro man in a white uniform and chef's cap came to their table and put down a menu. Robbie looked up at him with wide-eyed trepidation, as if he reminded him of someone he wanted to forget. "Y'all can afford these prices?" the man said gently, and Robbie relaxed at the kindness in his voice.

Gloria glanced at the menu's dinner offerings of pot roast,

swordfish, and stewed chicken. She had never heard of spending so much for a meal, but she counted out five dollars and laid it on the table. The man smiled at her, impressed and bemused.

"Where y'all from?" the man said.

"Florida," Gloria said.

"Me too. Marianna." He tipped his chef's hat. "Welcome home."

Union Station in Chicago was a city unto itself. As soon as Gloria and Robbie climbed down the steps, they were lost in waves of people rushing with casual urgency so different than in Gracetown: a sea of men in stylish hats and women wrapped in long, thin coats—even in summer! The night air nipped at their earlobes and fingertips. Whites and Negroes blended, matching each other's strides, crossing each other's paths without threats and epithets. Someone was playing a saxophone whose sultry song flew up across the ceiling nearly as high as the sky.

Gloria had memorized the address where Papa's letters were mailed, so they only needed to discover how to get to him. Would it be by taxi? A city train? Miz Lottie had had no knowledge of Chicago, so she had told them to find the information desk. Miz Lottie had also promised to try to find someone to meet them at the station, but she told Gloria that she might have to navigate Chicago on her own, at least at first.

For a bare instant, Gloria wanted to turn back and return to the train. At least the train was something she *knew*, and every new sight in Chicago paralyzed her with the realization that she alone was responsible for Robbie now. She felt sick to her stomach at the thought of heaping yet more suffering and uncertainty on her brother. Robbie was pulling close to her again, clinging as he had as soon as they climbed out of hiding in Miz Lottie's truck.

Gloria spotted the bright block letters at a booth in the center of the giant station: INFORMATION. White men and women in company uniforms waited at the counter, cheerfully answering questions and pointing out the way in the maze. Gloria hated the part of herself that hesitated to go to them, bracing for sneers or curses even if they were not in the South. Papa had told them that most white people in Chicago didn't like Negroes either; they were just more quiet about it and didn't post it on signs. Even after her first meal on an integrated train car, the memory of Mama eating ice cream without a care could not move her forward.

"What now?" Robbie whispered to her.

A knot of soldiers parted in front of the information desk, and Gloria was relieved to see the dark brown skin on the nape of a well-dressed man's neck standing a few feet in front of them. His back was facing them, but Gloria could see how self-assured he was as he scanned the crowd, standing at his full height with his hat canted to one side, his coat folded across his arm; a city Negro who might have been John Dorsey if he had been taller. He did not cast his eyes down from passing white men, and white women passing close to him did not shy away in fear.

"I'll ask that man there," Gloria said, pointing, and Robbie nodded with relief.

The man whirled around as if they had called his name.

Before he had fully turned, they recognized his chin. His profile. Gloria was afraid to trust her eyes, which were mirrored in the eyes of the man who turned to face them. His mouth fell open with the same surprise and wonder.

Robbie pulled his hand free from hers. "Papa!"

Robbie's shriek turned heads. But even strangers smiled at the reunion of this father and his children, how he lifted the boy up from the ground and swung him with deep laughter. And how he and his daughter hugged and swayed, openly weeping like a photograph from *Life* magazine of a soldier returning from war.

"You did it," he said to Gloria. "I don't know how, but you did it, girl."

"*We* did it," Gloria corrected him, hugging Robbie close. "Robbie got his own self free. Miz Lottie and I were just there to drive him away."

That wasn't the whole story. At the train station, Robbie didn't tell his father about the living friend he had lost and the dead friends he had made. Those would be stories for another day. Gloria did not yet tell him about the evidence of atrocities she had hidden away. But just as she had once seen the ribbon into Ruby McCollum's future, for once she saw her own.

They would be a family in Chicago. It would not be easy, but it would be easier.

One day she would walk on a college campus just like Mama had wanted for her. In years to come, she, Papa, and Robbie would sing freedom songs like the one that had come to her lips when she was afraid for their lives in the swamp.

When Robbie stared across the expanse of the train station with his father holding one hand and Gloria holding the other, a woman in a white dress shimmered in a bright shaft of light that shone from the ceiling like the roadway to heaven itself. Mama.

He didn't see her anymore after he blinked, but no sadness dampened this reunion day. He had learned that the dead walked beside the living.

Sometimes the dead could help you fly.

AUTHOR'S NOTE

Although I had a true-life relative named Robert Stephens who died at the Dozier School for Boys in Marianna, Florida, in the 1930s, *The Reformatory* is a work of fiction. None of the characters, even young Robert Stephens himself, depict the lives and histories of real people. Gracetown is fictitious.

I wrote this novel to honor the memory of Robert Stephens, so I depicted Redbone's stabbing as an homage to Robert's purported stabbing death in 1937 while he was imprisoned at Dozier. Robert's earache reflects what University of South Florida forensic anthropologist Erin Kimmerle revealed to me about his remains, which were unearthed in 2015: he had an ear infection so severe that she could see evidence of it nearly eighty years later.

I interviewed family members and survivors of the Dozier School, but no one I interviewed actually knew Robert Stephens or his parents because he died so long ago. His story in this novel is entirely fiction, including the persecution of his father, Robert Stephens, Sr.

But I wanted to give Robert Stephens a happier ending.

This character of Warden Fenton J. Haddock is also entirely fictitious. I created Haddock as an amalgam of a system of violence in children's incarceration—but the truth is that no one person can explain away the reported events at the Dozier School, or the Alabama Industrial School for Negro Children, or the Indigenous "schools" in Canada where so many children were buried. No one person can be blamed for our nation's current nightmare of mass incarceration.

The Reformatory has a central villain, but the actual villain is a *system* of dehumanization. As my character Gloria herself notes in the final chapter, "everyone would try to say that only the warden left mauled in the creek had created the unholy suffering at that place, when the whole town had had a hand."

I named Gloria after my late mother, civil rights activist Patricia Stephens Due. Whenever I wondered what Gloria should do next to try to free her brother, I asked myself, "What would Mom have done?"

Likewise, Attorney John Dorsey is modeled loosely after my father, "Freedom Lawyer" John Dorsey Due, Jr., who is eighty-eight years old at this writing. Dad told me about his experiences negotiating with Jim Crow judges in the 1960s, and he helped me craft the scene at the Gracetown Courthouse with the judge. He also accompanied me on several meetings and research trips to the grounds of the former Dozier School in Marianna, Florida. This novel honors my parents, too.

Too many children are still behind bars. Too many families have been torn asunder. To learn more about the true-life horrors in juvenile incarceration, read the book *Burning Down the House: The End of Juvenile Prison* by Nell Bernstein. To learn more about how the Jim Crow depicted in this novel in the 1950s still lingers in our prison system today, read *The New Jim Crow: Mass Incarceration in the Age of Colorblindness* by Michelle Alexander and watch the Netflix documentary *13th* by Ava DuVernay.

ACKNOWLEDGMENTS

More than ten years have passed since I first heard about the Dozier School for Boys and my unfortunate family connection there. I will attempt to thank all of the people who helped me create this novel.

As always, my first thanks must go to my family: in particular my husband, Steven Barnes, who accompanied me to the start of the excavation at Boot Hill and pushed me to keep writing this very difficult book year after year; our son, Jason (now nineteen), who was so intrigued by the history that he helped researchers at the start of the dig in Marianna; my stepdaughter, Nicki Barnes, for her eternal glow and joy; my sisters Johnita Due and Lydia Greisz, for their perpetual love and friendship; my father, John Due, whose company and wisdom on this project helped both of us ease our grief after the 2012 death of my mother, Patricia Stephens Due; and Priscilla Stephens Kruize, my aunt, for her civil rights activism and for attending the official burial of Robert Stephens, who was her uncle.

Thanks to University of South Florida forensic anthropologist Erin Kimmerle for her tireless work to bring the story of the buried and the missing boys from the Dozier School to light. As mothers, we talked about our passion for this story and the desire to try to find justice for the families who lost children at Dozier. (You can read about Kimmerle's involvement in her book *We Carry Their Bones: The Search for Justice at the Dozier School for Boys*.)

I first heard about Robert Stephens—and that he might be buried at Boot Hill at the Dozier School—from Nick Cox, a prosecutor in the Florida State Attorney's office. He spoke to me and my father, John Due, at length in March of 2013 to explain Robert's connection to the Dozier School and to let us know that his office had filed a petition with the state circuit court to allow the excavation project to unearth remains under Kimmerle's guidance. I still remember his sensitivity and thoroughness in that call, and for that I am grateful.

I do not have words to thank the survivors and their family members who spoke to me as I researched this book, including my aunt, civil rights activist Priscilla Stephens Kruize (proprietor of the Black Heritage Museum), who attended the funeral service for Robert Stephens in 2015 after his remains were found and properly buried.

I also celebrate my late uncle, Horace Walter Stephens, Jr., who carried the spirit of our family's history of community activism to his Boy Scout troop in Atlanta, the "Buffalo Soldiers."

I also would like to thank my relative Robert Stephens, who learned about the existence of his namesake the same way I did. As with me, no one in his immediate family had mentioned the death of Robert Stephens at the Dozier School in the 1930s. His story was buried too.

A special thanks to the survivors who spoke to me while I was researching this novel, including Charles Stephens (no relation), Cocomo Rock, and the late Robert Straley.

Special thanks to Elmore Bryant, the first Black mayor of Marianna, Florida (1985), who walked me and my father through Marianna and Dozier School history on our research trips together. (His interviews were purely informational and did not focus on accusations of abuse detailed by survivors.)

Thanks to the journalists who helped bring this story to public awareness: Carol Marbin Miller, Ben Montgomery, Lizette Alvarez, Ed Lavandera, and so many others.

I also want to acknowledge the Florida Memory project of the State Library and Archives of Florida for its extensive photo library on the Dozier School, which was tremendously helpful in writing this novel. See the collection online at www.floridamemory.com.

To my editor, Joe Monti, who believed in this book long before it was finished and gave it a home.

Thanks to the team at SK Global and the Mazur Kaplan Company, who optioned this book long before it was published, which gave me tremendous confidence as we dreamed of how Robert's story might look as a television series: Mitchell Kaplan (my former high school English teacher), Marcy Ross, Paula Mazur, and Kimesia Hartz.

And thanks to my literary agent, Donald Maass, who encouraged me to keep writing.

For further nonfiction reading on the Dozier School (not a complete list), read:

We Carry Their Bones: The Search for Justice at the Dozier School for Boys by Erin Kimmerle
The Boys of the Dark: A Story of Betrayal and Redemption in the Deep South by Robin Gaby Fisher
The Bones of Marianna: A Reform School, a Terrible Secret, and a Hundred-Year Fight for Justice by David Kushner
I Survived Dozier: The Deadliest Reform School in America by Richard Huntly
The White House Boys: An American Tragedy by Roger Dean Kiser
The Dozier School for Boys: Forensics, Survivors, and a Painful Past by Elizabeth A. Murray, PhD
The Boys of Dozier by Daryl McKenzie
Lies Uncovered: The Long Journey Home—The Truth About the Arthur G. Dozier School for Boys by Duane C. Fernandez, Sr.
It Still Hurts: My Father's Painful Account of Survival at the Florida Industrial School for Boys by Marshelle Smith Berry and Salih Izzaldin, edited by Joseph Carroll